Atlantis Afire

By

Gene Rowe

MINISTRY OF LIES

To request permissions, contact the publisher at
ministryofliespublishing@gmail.com

ISBN: 978-1-7390872-7-2

First paperback edition November 2025
Cover design by Getcovers

Ministry of Lies
12 Wellington Road
Norwich
NR2 3HT
UK

ministryoflies.co.uk

To X-Master and the future Architect of Mars

Cast of Characters (Roughly by Order of Appearance)

Arriving on the *Leviathan*

Dr Marie Lockard – marine biologist
Kate Lockard – Marie's daughter
Eddard Mitsos – businessman
Rennie Heiko – ex-military
Georges Hollande – New Socialist
Jacques Danté – New Socialist
Babatunde Odile – New Socialist

Hibernians

Colonel Eric Nesvorny – Head of the Internal Security Unit (ISU)
Colonel Tania Joseph – Head of the External Security Unit (ESU)
Marissa O'Neill – Premier of *Hibernia* and one of ruling triumvirate
Kerrie Sullivan – one of ruling triumvirate
Manfred Traore – one of ruling triumvirate
Major Fukuda – Nesvorny's deputy
General Domitus Kelly – nominal head of the *Hibernia* security forces
Dr Moses Killan – scientist
Dr Francesca Brown – scientist
Dr Ravindra Singh – scientist
Kai Dures – leader of the Stokers, husband of Karyn
Karyn Dures – leader of the Stokers, wife of Kai
Magdalen O' Hare – Stoker leader
Magdi – a Stoker
Annie – a Stoker
Seumus – a Stoker
Frida – a Stoker
Victor – a Stoker
Captain Kennedy – ESU soldier
Captain Bellamy – ESU patrol boat captain
Captain Rahul Singh – ESU patrol boat captain
Sergeant Taylor – member of ISU
Lieutenant Worsley – member of ISU

Lisboetas

Professor Miguel Figueroa – chief scientist
Dr Katerina Kalmik – scientist
Dr Luisa Teixeira – scientist
Dr Marco Grande – scientist
Raul Garcia – part of science team
Mike Resnos – part of science team
Victoria Soares – part of science team
Arantxa Perez – captain/ pilot of the *Fortunata*
Benny Zico – boat pilot
Tonio Janeiro – friend of Kate Lockard
Sara Velasquez – friend of Kate Lockard
Vita Fernandez – popular teenager
Joao Nascimento – Captain-Governor
Ernesto Blanco – chief engineer
Hector Bellarriva – systems analyst

Marseillais

Sebastian Deux – First Citizen
Marcel Louvain – captain of the *Marseilles*
Asher Jons – Ambassador of the *Marseilles* in *Hibernia*
Noma Obuya – Dieppe crew
Pierre – Dieppe crew
Abdul – Dieppe crew
Marc – Dieppe crew
Pascal – Dieppe crew
Captain Helene Boursis – head of the Apparatus (security division)
Lavie – reporter
Dr Youssef Bennani – scientist
Dr Sandrine Werner – scientist
Abaye – member of People's Committee
Mahroof – member of People's Committee
Li – member of People's Committee
Captain Luc Falcome – leader of fleet of converted gunboats
Matthieu – engineer
Bernard Gascaux – captain of the *St. Malo*

Stavangerans

Makka Frost – Head of Material Resources
Melissa de Voe – Makka's deputy
Magnus Solbakken – Ambassador of *Stavanger* in *Hibernia*
Frida Solbakken – Solbakken's wife
Cass Remillard – ex-head of security
Margarethe Olson – Premier of *Stavanger*
Hanna Bulow – Second of State
Anders Pedersen – deputy head of security
Nila Moroni – politician and fixer
Sven Ibsen – Foreman
Ana Ibsen – wife of Sven
Irina Vlassic – mistress of Sven
Claude Vardem – security
Judd Stallings – security
Monique McGregor – security
Martins Larsen – engineer and possible thief
Famke Holt – engineer and possible thief
Avi Leben – engineer and possible thief
Kamlash Patel – engineer and possible thief

Chapter 1

They were on the only shuttle to leave the *Leviathan.*

"Everyone strap in," came a voice over the intercom. "We have to leave *now.*"

There was a sharp hiss of pneumatic doors closing, followed by a jolt as the shuttle disconnected from its docking mechanism.

Marie Lockard fussed over her fifteen-year-old daughter's straps, her hands twisting nervously. "Is that secure? Are you in tight?"

"Yes, Mum. Don't panic."

"How can you be so calm?" To Marie, Kate seemed the most composed person in the cabin, the hubbub from which rose and fell in waves.

The shuttle jolted again, then there was a surge of acceleration that pushed Marie back into her seat and led to yelps of surprise and disquiet from other passengers.

"What was that noise in the ship?" asked Kate. "It sounded like gunfire. Was it?"

"I don't know."

"Mum! You do know. It was, wasn't it? Who was shooting who?"

Kate had a seat by the window, Marie beside her. In the aisle seat next to Marie, a firm-jawed, middle-aged man with close-cropped hair overheard the exchange and chuckled. "Seems like everyone at everyone else."

Marie turned slightly; the man was looking ahead rather than at them, appraising the enclosed space. The cabin had twenty-four rows of six seats, with an aisle down the middle, and they were near the back. The interior was white and padded, with porthole windows presently covered; at the head of the cabin, the broad door to the cockpit was closed, winking with an array of red lights suggesting that it was locked. A wide screen above the cockpit door – which would normally display flight information and instructions – was currently dark. Then Marie noticed that the man was bleeding slightly at the temple.

"You're cut. Were you hit?"

The man at last turned, and Marie saw that he had a small tattoo at the side of one eye, and she realised that he wasn't just a civilian.

"It's nothing. Clash of heads. But thanks for your concern… if it was concern?"

"Mum –"

"Wait a minute, Kate. Yes, it was."

The man smiled at Marie and then almost instantly his mouth returned to its firm disposition. "It was quite exciting, wasn't it? You did well to squeeze through and keep hold of your daughter. Not many innocents seem to have made it aboard."

Marie glanced in the direction of the other's head-twitch and realised that most of those in the cabin were male and relatively young. "Yes, well, it was down to Kate really. She saw a gap between two men who seemed to want to rip each other's heads off and pulled me through it."

"She might have saved your life. I'm Rennie Heiko. Your daughter is Kate, and you are?"

"Marie. Marie Lockard. What do you mean, saved my life? You don't think…?"

"The world has gone mad, Marie. On Earth, the main blocs seem determined to destroy themselves over trivial differences in beliefs, and it's exporting that intolerance everywhere. The *Leviathan* was full of fanatics – or didn't you notice?"

Marie nodded. The *Leviathan* had left from the privately owned Freelander Station, so its passengers were any that could afford its fares, no matter where they came from. In retrospect, allowing population mixing in these febrile times seemed like a bad idea. "But we're not all fanatics and refugees. Some of us are just moving on to a new life. Or at least, a new job."

"Outside the asylum?"

Marie matched the other's wry grin. "Well, that is a fringe benefit, true."

The shuttle juddered again causing someone nearby to swear, someone else to emit a shriek, and Marie to put out a hand to stop herself slamming into the seatback in front.

"Ah… QED."

"What?" asked Marie, as the shuttle bucked some more. "What was that?"

"Not turbulence," asserted Heiko, grimly. "It felt like a shockwave. Probably from –"

"A shock? You don't mean…?"

"What is it, Mum?" asked Kate, leaning forwards to look at the two adults.

"Mr Heiko thinks the ship… the *Leviathan*…"

"There's nothing to worry about now, girl," said the man, smiling quickly at Kate. "We're well away from it. Sit back and enjoy the flight."

Others had come to a similar conclusion to Heiko, judging from the hissed voices around them, from which Marie was able to pick out single words or short expressions: *madness*, *gone-up*, *reactor*, *fighting*, *idiots*…

But the tension slowly dissipated as the shuttle steadied, aided by an absence of disaster-confirming news from the cockpit – with the information screen remaining dark and the hidden pilots and crew remaining silent. After Marie parried attempts to talk by her daughter, the latter became quiet and broody. Marie occasionally stole glances at the man to her side, but Heiko soon closed his eyes – though not to sleep: he remained upright in his seat, seemingly meditating.

At last, a voice came over the intercom at about the same time the shuttle ceased its continuous trembling – as though emerging from rapids to calm water. "We're in the lower atmosphere, people. Unlocking windows. Welcome to Tethys." And at that, the white shutters over the porthole windows rose throughout the cabin, allowing natural light to spill in and supplement the artificial.

"Wow!" said Kate, who had the best view. "Look at the colours!"

Marie craned her head to see: the world racing by below was not the uniform blue many might expect of a water world – instead, it was a mosaic of colours, ranging from deep blues to greens, in some places gently transitioning from one shading to the next, in others changing abruptly, with mottled patches and swirls. And then she noticed a vein of black cutting across the ocean.

"See that black line," she said.

"Uh-huh. What is it? An abyss?"

Marie gave her head a small shake. "They're still not sure, even after ninety-five years. They call them *black cenotes*, as they reminded one of the very first surveyors of sinkholes in the sea – like the Great Blue Hole off Belize. But they're not cenotes, which are pools of water formed after collapsing rock – usually limestone. Wrong geology. And these are usually veinous, whereas cenotes tend to be rounded."

"So…" mused Kate, "the only thing they got right was the colour?"

Marie smiled. "Just about."

Kate turned to look at her mother. "But what are they, then?"

"Well, as I said, they're still not sure. There's often a steep temperature gradient between them and the surrounding waters. They're often very cold. They also tend to be richer in some minerals and compounds. What is known, is that they seem to be resistant to scanning, and probes that go in often don't come out again."

"That's creepy!"

"Yes, well, in the early years they couldn't afford the losses, so after a while, they just left them alone and built their city ships away from them. Researchers are about to start exploring them again, but with these latest problems I'm not sure how far they'll go. They might feel a need to start conserving resources if they can't restock from Earth so easily."

Kate had turned back to the view, speaking over her shoulder. "Is this what you're meant to be researching?"

"Well, partly, I guess."

"Geology? Chemistry?" A deep voice was suddenly at Marie's ear.

She shuddered and turned. Heiko was awake and trying to look past her to the porthole. "Uh… neither. I'm a marine biologist. I'm interested in the sea life."

"But I thought the… black cenotes? I have heard another term for them." Heiko didn't elaborate, but Marie knew the term he meant: *Dead zones.* "I heard they have no life. They are biologically uninteresting."

"That's not quite true. They *do* have some unusual microfauna. And in the depths, well, nobody knows."

Heiko nodded slowly. "And you've got a job trying to find out?"

"Not exclusively, no. But it's one of several projects I'm meant to be working on."

"Do you mind me asking where?"

"The *Lisboa*."

"I wish you luck getting there."

Marie now turned fully in her seat to face the man. Their destination was *Hibernia*, the largest of the city ships on the planet. "Luck? Do you think there's going to be a problem?"

Heiko's mouth scrunched into a frown. "For you? Maybe not."

"But for you, *maybe*? I couldn't help noticing your tattoo." She gestured to the small marking besides the man's left eye, which depicted five small gold dots linked in a zigzag. "Military?"

"It's not really a tattoo – but it's a bit of a giveaway, isn't it. Can't be helped. The standard systems interface is in the same place in most of the Earth militaries."

"I thought it was only for the elites, not regular forces."

Heiko's frown twitched into a gentle smile. "They do say that, true."

"So, I guess you're also moving on from *Hibernia*?"

"Not far, but far enough. After the news from Earth, and what I suspect has happened to the *Leviathan*, I expect our welcoming committee will be full of nervous people with many questions. I have resigned myself to being delayed. But as I said, you should be fine – unless they decide they're going to hoard every material and human resource that comes their way. The Hibernians do have form in this regards, and that's partly why the *Stavanger* has sought my services."

"In that case, Mr Heiko, it seems that it's *I* who need to wish *you* good luck."

* * *

Two rows behind, near the very back of the cabin, Eddard Mitsos leant against the padded wall, staring out the window at the shifting colours below, absently toying with a small silver device, oblong in shape and half the size of his little finger. Given the presumed loss of his luggage in the hold of the interstellar craft, it was certainly the most valuable possession he had left – in this system or in any. Or, at least, the terabyte of data on it was.

Mitsos was a well-preserved forty-three, with a tanned complexion and short, neatly cut hair. He wore a single-lapel navy jacket that was the fashion in certain parts of the western hemisphere, and he had a single gold stud in his right ear. Though seemingly innocent, the stud was connected to a fine filament that travelled from his ear to his cortex and held an array of infinitesimal detectors that could alert him to anything from radiation to pressure changes and motion, working best when he closed his eyes to prevent interference from his natural senses. And it was not the only modification his body hid. He looked at the man to his side and gave a wry smile: if only he knew!

Next to Mitsos, a man with long blond hair nervously twitched and muttered, as he had done for almost the entire flight. His allegiance was far more obvious given the New Socialist tattoo on the side of his neck and the antiquated hammer-and-sickle ring he bore on a finger of his left hand. His clothing was also notably rugged – an old-style denim, as opposed to Mitsos' non-stain, fully insulated nu-fabric jacket – although his fine accent and vocabulary confirmed that this dressing-down was a stylistic choice rather than a financial necessity.

They'd exchanged few words on the descent so far, partly because Mitsos was wary about how the other might react should he realise the enhancements he harboured – an elitist conceit that the NS particularly abhorred. At last, he ventured: "It seems we have escaped, and all is now plain sailing – as they say."

The man twitched as though prodded with a stun stick, then turned a confused look on Mitsos. Another man occupied the aisle seat beyond him, and Mitsos could now see that he, too, bore an NS tattoo on the neck. "Sailing? Ah, yes."

"But it was tense, eh?"

"Tense?" The other frowned. "Yes. I didn't know that… they didn't say…" He shook his head.

"You have an idea about what went on? In the *Leviathan*?"

The frown returned, and the other's eyes became suspicious. "No. It was nothing to do with us. And it's important that's clear to… those below."

Mitsos took the hint and chose to respond with an easy smile. "Of course. Probably a reactor problem. Captain pressed the wrong button in a panic. Anyway, where are you ultimately headed? The *Vladivostok*?"

"Eh? Oh, the ring?" The other noticed Mitsos' gaze. "No. The *Marseilles. The community*."

"Ah, yes, of course. And your friend, too?" Mitsos nodded at the man in the aisle seat, who had his eyes closed and might have been asleep.

"Sure. And a few others." The man twitched his head towards the seats in front.

Mitsos nodded again, but inwardly wondered how so many who professed egalitarian principles could afford the high expense of interstellar travel. Even he needed to make this trip a success to recoup his outlay. The thought made him clasp the memory stick firmly in the palm of his hand. "That's… interesting. How does it work – I mean, to get to the *Marseilles*? Do you need a special visa?"

"Yes. We – the NS – have ties with the state. My comrades and I were invited."

"Ah, that explains it," Mitsos muttered. Then louder: "I mean, that explains why there are so many of you. Or *were*…" In the end, he couldn't help himself.

"What?" The other tensed.

"Sorry. I was just thinking, you must have lost quite a few comrades on the ship. Such a shame. A shame about *all* the people." Mitsos shook his head as if in sorrow but struggled to stop a smirk from forming on his lips.

But the other was clearly not convinced. "Yes, it was. For us. And you? Did you have anyone on the ship, Mr…?"

"Me? No, I'm travelling alone. Just a small businessman, doing the bidding of my Earthly masters. Anyway, we seem to be descending quite quickly now. This is my first time off Earth, and yours too, I guess? So bloody expensive, eh?" He gave the other a brief flash of smile, then turned to look out the window, terminating the discussion.

Soon after, the shuttle swept down upon the runway of the great floating city of *Hibernia*.

Chapter 2

Near the summit of Mount Ardol, Makka Frost slid onto his bottom and propped himself against a slanting rock wall. The climb from the small, makeshift harbour had been arduous, and his brow was damp with sweat, as were his clothes – russet trousers and matching jacket with gold trim. He pulled off his work gloves and allowed himself a moment to rest and to appraise his surroundings.

Though the third tallest peak on the entire planet, the summit was a mere six-hundred metres above sea level. From here, most of what Frost saw was ocean – light blue around the fringes of the extinct volcano, darker beyond, and almost black when in shadow beneath the intermittent clouds that were scattered across the sky in clumps. He knew that the City Class ship *Stavanger* was anchored to the south behind the curve of the barren, grey-brown slope, and that the giant Nation Class *Hibernia* was perhaps sixty kilometres further away, at the farthest point of the small volcanic chain, in its permanent mooring by Mount Athol – the world's second-highest peak, which rose a scant few metres above his current elevation.

At the foot of the slope was the harbour – which was little more than a length of decking against the inclined rock, with a couple of prefab buildings and an open area that held a dozen metal containers and a couple of cranes. The whole structure was temporary: after they had collected their fill of volcanic rock, a barge would be sent to pick up the whole ensemble – to either return to the *Stavanger* or to shift further around the volcano to another spot for further harvesting. And close to the harbour, a dozen people on a shelf in the slope worked at machinery that broke up the rock, which would later be collected and transferred to the containers. A couple of boats were moored up: one small, one bulbous.

Another shadow appeared near Frost, elongating towards him.

"There's a drone above us," said a voice from out of the shadow.

"No surprise," said Frost. "They like to keep an eye on us. Make sure we're not taking more than we've been allotted."

"There's a whole fucking mountain, and they let us take pebbles." Melissa De Voe came to a halt beside the seated man, standing awkwardly, with one leg locked at the knee and the other flexed as she steadied herself against the slope. She was dressed in russet work clothes like Frost, with her hair cropped short in an identical manner to him. But whereas Frost's face was adorned with a short beard, hers bore a number of tattoos, most notably a silver trident diagonally above her left eyebrow. "As if they've any real right to the Range anyway."

"Oh, they have the right – by way of size, proximity, and power. And precedence. Much as we might hate it, they were here first. You're not against private ownership of goods, are you, Melissa?"

The woman scowled and ran a hand over the blonde bristles on her scalp. "You mean, *all property is theft*? Ha! If I believed that bullshit I'd emigrate to the *Marseilles*. No, but there's no sense in them hogging all this…" she waved a hand. "It'll take them millennia just to dig out Athol. This is just petty. *Mine mine mine*! Like fucking children."

Frost broke into a grin. "Sure. And it's not as if there's anything valuable here anyway. It's just gravel. Silicon, aluminium, sodium, potassium… bit of iron. Some magnesium. We've never found significant quantities of heavy metals or rare earths, and they haven't either, in spite of all their geological surveys and permanent drill sites. I suspect they're paranoid we might find something they don't."

"Fat chance." De Voe shifted her weight and looked about. "Found the next site, then?"

Frost had the decency to look guilty. He'd claimed their trek was necessary to scope out the next target – a place with the right geography for them to create their next harbour with relative ease – but that could have been done just as easily at sea level. He'd just wanted an excuse to extend his walk on real land. De Voe knew this, but as she'd clearly felt the same she'd not objected. "Not yet. And you?"

The woman looked down and smiled. "Oh, yeah. Somewhere… over there…" she waved a hand vaguely off to one side.

Frost laughed. "We're a couple of reprobates."

"Prerogatives of power."

"I'm pretty sure that's what the Hibernians say."

De Voe wrinkled her face at him in a mock sneer. When she allowed herself to express emotion, Frost thought, she *could* be good company. It was just a shame that she rarely strayed from her hard-arsed persona.

"Anyway, I guess we should at least fulfil our official brief," he continued. "So let's –"

A sonic boom interrupted him. They both turned to look into the sky in the rough direction from which the sound had come. After a moment, De Voe said: "Shuttle's early. I thought the first one wasn't due until this evening, assuming the *Leviathan's* in proper orbit."

Frost frowned. "You're right. Either *Leviathan* has parked in the wrong spot, or the shuttle's running on fumes. Someone's either cocked up or left in a hurry."

"Knowing Earthers, probably both. We expecting much cargo?"

"Oh, you betcha. Couple of containers of rare earths – everything from copper to lanthanum – and some precision machinery."

"Let's hope it all arrives then, eh, and the bastards don't take a sneaky cut again."

Ships from Earth were infrequent, and rarely more than twice a year. With the rumoured geopolitical problems 'back home', the time between arrivals had been lengthening. It had been nine months since the *Resolve* had come and gone, with the *Leviathan's* previous visit eight months before that. And last time, one of their cargo crates had mysteriously disappeared at *Hibernia's* port. While recycling had always been taken seriously aboard the *Stavanger* – as in every ship – the shortages in materials for electrical and computer components had led to a new statute that made careless wastage a criminal offence.

"I'd hoped to be present for the transfer, just to be sure. Maybe we should cut this excursion short?"

"Sure thing. And as your deputy, I should be there too."

* * *

They took the fast skiff from the harbour, leaving the rest of their team to continue its mining. The craft skimmed over the calm water: Tethys had no moon, and hence, no appreciable tides, which was a boon for the planet's vast ships. Not that the globe-circling ocean was an entirely peaceful place, Frost mused, as the skiff suddenly bobbled: the winds could create significant swells, while the occasional underwater eruption from still-active deep-water volcanos could put a crimp in anyone's day.

The water around the short volcanic chain was a shade of aquamarine, allowing clear viewing into the relatively shallow depths. For Frost, this had its good and bad points: the good was that you could see if there was anything sizeable below the surface that might cause a problem; the bad was that you could see if there was anything sizeable below the surface that could cause a problem. Though attacks on boats were infrequent, they weren't exactly rare, and being able to observe constant close calls was unnerving. The skiff mainly relied on speed for defence alongside an armoured hull (which nothing that was quick enough to catch them would likely be able to puncture): the main problem was being knocked from the boat by a strike, which was why Frost now tugged on his seat harness just to make sure.

De Voe noticed Frost's movements and couldn't help a small chuckle. "Don't trust Serge's driving, boss?" The pair sat side-by-side behind their pilot. There were two unoccupied rows of seats behind them and a powerful outboard motor at the stern.

"Serge? Sure. I just don't trust…" Frost twitched a thumb to indicate the open water.

De Voe smirked. "It's been ten years, hasn't it? And you're still spooked?"

"Twelve, actually." Frost had emigrated from New Zealand, whereas De Voe was a genuine native of Tethys, born and bred. She never seemed concerned about the wildlife, or at the very least, she was good at hiding it. "I just don't get how you can be so blasé," he continued. "We should have taken the launch."

"That'd take twice as long. Anyway, we've got plenty of protection, so relax."

"Relax? Yeah, great." Frost knew that Serge had a number of countermeasures at his fingertips, ranging from a bow-mounted harpoon and a mechanism on the keel for sending an electric pulse into the water, to a tank of red dye that was able to confuse the underwater denizens. But the knowledge didn't help settle his nerves.

He was therefore relieved when the *Stavanger* came into view – on rounding the volcanic edge – rapidly growing to fill the near horizon.

The *Stavanger* was one of seventeen City Class ships, most of which had been constructed over a forty year period by the shipwrights of *Hibernia*. Several more had been built by a rival consortium at the shipyard of the *Taiwan*, the world's other Nation Class ship, situated about six thousand kilometres away over the Xian Great Banks – where the seafloor rose up so that the water was only twenty metres deep in places, allowing (admittedly less-easy) access to other building material. The *Stavanger* itself was a giant craft with a population of close to thirty thousand: it was more than twice the length and perhaps three-times the width of the largest ancient aircraft carriers from Earth.

The skiff approached from the relatively low stern, beneath which a dozen monstrous propellors were linked to the craft's fusion engine, providing the power to shunt it along at up to ten knots when in motion. From this direction, they could see the ringed layers of the main habitation levels, with light glinting from a thousand windows, though they couldn't see the bridge at the upper level of the bow, the main arena in the middle of the ship, nor the manufactories and food processing vats in the lower levels. A long gash appeared in the starboard side of the ship at water level, where the *Stavanger's* fishing fleet and other craft were docked in a shallow, sheltered recess in the hull, which would be closed and drained when the city ship got underway.

The huge bulk of the *Stavanger* rose before them, cutting in front of Tethys' star, casting them into shadow, and sharpening the glare of the multitude of winking lights in the cavernous dock. Fair-haired Serge slowed the skiff and manoeuvred towards an empty bay in the interior between a couple of broad fishing boats, one of which swarmed with crew and seemed about to set sail. As they crossed the threshold, Frost heard the fishermen shouting out to each other and laughing. Serge slid effortlessly into the vacant slot, cutting power to the engine so that they coasted the last few metres. Decking appeared to their right. De Voe unstrapped quickly and leapt onto the landing; Frost waited for the thump and click of a locking mechanism – a sensor-driven adjustable cradle that lined up and captured the front of the skiff between metallic jaws – before he undid his own harness and followed his deputy.

From the dock, there were various doors to the interior of the ship: some were broad and placed to give easy access to freezer chambers or storehouses for collected biological or physical materials; others were smaller and designed for crew. Frost followed De Voe through one of the smaller doors, set beside the main control room for the dock, where half-a-dozen people in white uniforms used holographic displays to check the health of craft and their equipment, summon and direct crew, allocate bays, detail catches, direct cargo to appropriate stations, and many other feats of organisation.

The door hissed closed behind the pair, leaving them in an annexe with a lift and an emergency stairwell. Without awaiting instruction, De Voe entered the lift and chose level five. "Quick visit to the office, yes?" she said. "We can arrange our transfer to *Hibernia* from there."

Frost nodded assent.

The padded lift rose smoothly and within seconds delivered them to the level that held many of the city's administrative offices, including those of Natural Resources. Frost followed De Voe along a broad corridor with a dull laminate floor and pale blue walls. There were surprisingly few people about, and these seemed rushed and distracted. At one junction, they turned left, and a short way further came to their own offices, entering through a half-glassed double door.

Frost knew something was amiss as soon as they entered the room, which had a dozen terminals displaying inventories and projections. All of those within looked up, anxious.

"Right. We need a shuttle to the *Hib*," stated De Voe, without ceremony. "Famke can you… what?"

The blonde-haired woman at the nearest desk wore a similar russet-coloured uniform to the newcomers, although her shirt was untidily open at the neck. "Are you going to find out what happened?"

"Happened?" De Voe frowned. "What do you mean?"

Frost placed a hand on his deputy's arm. "The shuttle! It was early. What have we missed, Famke?"

The woman looked between the two in confusion, then across at a couple of her seated colleagues, then back again. "Don't you know? I thought… ah, maybe not. It's the *Leviathan*. It's… *gone*."

* * *

Miguel Figueroa looked over the railing at the water. His craft – the *Lisboa's* twelve-metre-long research vessel, the *Fortunata* – floated a short distance from a colour boundary. It presently bobbed over pale blue ocean; a short distance beyond this, the water appeared to turn green. But the green wasn't water, but rather, it was part of a three-hundred and forty square kilometre patch of native vegetation that was one of the reasons Tethys had an atmosphere comprising nearly twenty-three percent oxygen.

"Well, it doesn't *look* different," said Katerina Kalmik, coming to rest on the railing next to the man. "Are you sure?"

Figueroa continue to gaze at the water as if looking for something beneath the surface – and indeed, he quickly spotted shadows. "Yes, I'm sure. Or rather, Luisa is. It's not surprising, as the stuff has similar morphology to the common kelp analogue, but she says it's richer in nutrients. *Much* richer. And that's why there's so much frisky sea life at the fringes."

Kalmik laughed. "*Frisky?* Where did you pick up that expression?" She beamed at the short, grey-haired man, regarded by her team as a father figure as much as their research leader. Indeed, *Lisboa's* chief scientist had a soft voice and had only once been known to lose his temper.

Figueroa gently returned the smile of the blonde-haired woman, whose heart-shaped face bore a long, aquiline nose. "I think it's something I read from one of our new recruit's research papers – the one due on the *Leviathan*. She seems to have some nice turns of phrase." He turned his attention back to the water and nodded towards the patch. "*Why* the plants are different, though, that is what I'd like to find out."

"Hmmm. You say it has more nutrients for the native life forms? What about for *us*?"

"Yes, I suspect our food technicians will be able to wring more out of it in their vats. So *we* get another interesting puzzle to solve, and *they* get a richer crop. Everybody wins."

"As long as the *pelagics* aren't too *frisky*?"

Figueroa's expression turned more serious. "Yes, there is that."

"So," said Kalmik, "we're going to do a full audit of this ecosystem, yes?"

"Naturally."

"That'll be a pleasant surprise for our new recruit. I just hope she doesn't scare easily."

"I have little fear of that. She's apparently done free swimming with Great Whites off South Africa."

"Great Whites?" Kalmik scoffed. "Those little things? Ha! They're dumb, too. Not like the skrylars. Or the hive pikes. Or the –"

"Okay, okay!" Figueroa raised his hands and laughed. "I concede! She will need someone to watch over her to begin with. A big sister, perhaps?"

Kalmik frowned. "Sure. Okay. But as I've said before, I'm not sure what she really adds to the team. Her experiences are literally alien to ours."

"Her perspectives are different, that's true." Figueroa once more turned serious, his eyes wrinkling as they often did when he was talking shop. "And that is never a bad thing. She's also worked with cetaceans, including dolphins, so she's not unfamiliar with intelligent sea creatures. Besides, there is still very much that we don't know. In a century, we've explored only a fraction of the oceans. We've barely scratched the surface… or the sub-surface. And we're discovering new species all the time – just like now," he waved again at the patch of green. "You don't need to fear, Katerina, she is not taking anyone else's place, least of all your own. In fact, I would have hired more if I could have, but I guess we should be grateful that our masters have allowed us even this much."

Kalmik matched her superior's sombre expression. "Sure. I understand... I guess." Then she shrugged, smiled, leant in, and lowered her voice. "I just hope she doesn't turn out to be as big a pain in the ass as the last one."

Figueroa flicked a glance beyond the woman, and noted Marco Grande further along the decks, stomping about and muttering to himself. He didn't know whether to smile or frown. "Amen to that."

They didn't learn about the *Leviathan* until they returned to the mother ship four hours later.

* * *

The rotas had been agreed and the *Marseilles* was on the move.

Sebastian Deux lounged in the captain's chair on the bridge, legs splayed before him, long black hair spilling over the seat back. From here, he could see the endless ocean through the windows – far below and beyond the ship's broad and mighty prow – black under ominous clouds. The ship's controls around him were lit with innumerable lights, like a mini galaxy, while to either side sat officers in nests of curved stations that were rich with computer displays. The ship's actual captain, Marcel Louvain, stood behind him, no doubt anxious in case he decided to touch some button or flick some switch.

Let him stand and wait!

Deux was currently First Citizen, and would be for at least the next two years and then… who knew? In spite of the rules, the People's Committee was malleable. But even so, he didn't need his present title to direct their course: people listened to him, regardless of his position *or* theirs, and they always had. It was his gift. And what was *position* anyway, in a society of equals? Indeed, high office could even be made to appear somehow shameful – as the captain behind him was now finding.

Deux swivelled the chair to look back, piercing the tall, grey-haired man with his sharp green eyes. "Thank you for sharing, Citizen Louvain. I find it useful to experience everyone's vantage point, from the supposed low, to the supposed high, especially those who – for one reason or another – are exempted from the rotas."

Louvain did well to keep his expression neutral, Deux thought.

"There are only so many trained to run a ship like this, First Citizen," said the captain. "I am honoured to be among these. If this means I am held from the rotas – *like you* – then I regret it. I would of course be happy to work wherever the lottery placed me."

Like me? So he did have some steel under that respectful façade. Deux smiled. "Well said! You know, I was just thinking that we ought to train up more in the specialist skills of captaincy. Maybe half-a-dozen. What do you think of that? With such redundancy, we could then allow even you to join the lists for the regular rotation. What would you think of a spell in the fishing fleet? Or serving in one of the refectories?"

Louvain's expression was difficult to interpret. "Such as you did last year? It would be an honour to follow in your shoes."

Deux laughed. "You really *are* good, Citizen Louvain!" He rose to his feet. "And with that, I'll return the special chair to you. It's not as comfortable as I imagined it would be."

Louvain nodded, but remained standing. "Command isn't always comfortable, is it, Citizen?"

Now Deux frowned. What was the captain implying? Did he know of the difficulties he'd had in persuading the Committee of the necessity of their current perilous course? And if so, how? He would have to investigate the possibility of leaks. But not now. He nodded at the captain, and headed for one of the exits from the wide, low room.

The *Leviathan* was due: on it were important elements for his plan.

Chapter 3

The *Hibernia* was officially classed as a ship, but the only similarity it had with such craft was that it floated: it was far too big to actually move, and the fusion-powered propellors had been taken up and recycled without ever having been used. Indeed, further sections had been added beyond the ship's original stern, meaning there was little prospect of returning the floating behemoth to a mobile state.

The shuttle passengers saw little of the floating metropolis, however. Their craft glided the last few kilometres directly over the low volcanic stumps of the Northern Range, with stark Mount Athol only visible to those sitting to the right of the craft, much to Kate Lockard's frustration: those on her side could see little but the ocean stretching away to the horizon. Shortly after, the shuttle settled with scarcely a bump on the runway of the Nation Class ship and decelerated rapidly – throwing the passengers forwards into their restraining harnesses.

"Runway's along the northern edge," explained Heiko to Marie. "Apparently, it's the main one for shuttles on Tethys, although the *Taiwan* also has one."

"What about the City Class ships?" asked Marie. "They must have airports, too, surely?"

"Small ones for VTOL aircraft only. I don't think there's a lot of travel between the different ships that would necessitate more. But we'll soon see, eh?"

The passengers had to wait on the shuttle for some minutes to allow the external heat shields to cool, and then they exited near the rear.

Heiko rose and took a place in the aisle, making room for the others, but Marie waved him on. "Don't wait for us. I'd rather not get trampled in the exodus."

Heiko smiled and nodded. "It's been good to meet you, Marie, and you, Kate. Good luck on the *Lisboa*."

* * *

"Visa!" demanded the stern-faced man, holding out one hand. A gold ring around the sleeve of his black uniform suggested that he was more than a mere functionary, as did his silver hair.

Eddard Mitsos produced a slim plastic card and handed it over to the seated official. The capsule they occupied was small, low, and transparent from waist-height. Tethys' star shone through the Perspex ceiling, while tall buildings rose to one side and the flat runway lay to the other. The rest of the unprocessed shuttle passengers formed a line outside, queuing under a long Perspex shelter.

"*Mitsos?* Why are you here?"

"Well, I thought I'd have a bit of a look around your charming planet, starting here. Then I plan to go and see a few of the other ships. The *Bremen*. *Lisboa*. See what delights they have to offer."

"Offer?" The man scowled. Mitsos noticed his name stencilled on an enamel badge above the left breast: *Col. Eric Nesvorny*. "So, you're a tourist. Tourism is an expensive business – at least, it is coming all the way from Earth."

Mitsos pouted and smiled. "Not just tourism. I thought I'd scope out business opportunities, too. See who has what. Who needs what. See whether I might be able to help. Make some contacts. I'm sure you know how it is."

"Opportunities? So, what is your business?"

"Manufacturing."

The colonel of security waited for Mitsos to continue, but when he didn't, he prompted: "Manufacturing *what* exactly?" It was clear he didn't like his flippant attitude, which merely made Mitsos smile.

"Well, just about anything. You see, I have access to a factory of printers that'll churn out just about any product known to man. Material goes into a 3D template, energy is applied, and out pops whatever you want, within reason."

"Your factory is on Earth? It seems you may have some problem accessing it from now on, given recent events."

Mitsos merely shrugged. "*Might*. Have to see."

"You don't seem too concerned. Any reason for this?"

"Me? Nah. I'm a philosophical guy. I wasn't planning on taking the *Leviathan* back anyway – at least, not on this cycle. We'll just have to see if the next liner turns up on schedule. If yes, *great*, if not…" he shrugged again. "No point worrying, eh? Just have to make the best of things."

Nesvorny's frown deepened. "And that's the issue we have. Where are you planning on doing all this hopeful waiting? How much money do you have – and what will you do if you can't get more? We've enough deadbeats in *Hibernia*. We won't take any more."

"Don't worry, *Sergeant*, or whatever you are." Mitsos smiled. "I've already got an account at a bank here. Five figures. Trust me, I'm not going to be on the streets. But I'm not giving you any more info on my finances unless you've got a warrant or something." His expression suddenly firmed and he held the other's glare. "And don't mistake my easy nature for weakness. I'm above board here, and I don't appreciate being harried like this."

"Like this? Mr Mitsos, if I was going to harry you, it wouldn't be in view of the other arrivals, trust me." Nesvorny leant forwards. "And you shouldn't mistake my seniority here, or over-estimate how much clout you have. *Or* insult me." He settled back in his chair and tapped on the desk in thought, and then he smiled, although his expression lacked humour. "Very well. I'll grant you access for now – to *Hibernia* only, until we've time for further checks." He placed the other's card against an electronic tablet and tapped a command of authorisation and limitation. "You're lucky there's a long queue that needs sifting, or this discussion would continue somewhere less comfortable." He handed the card back to the other. "Leave now. The card will allow you to collect your luggage and exit immigration. Keep it with you at all times. It will alert you as to where and when you need to report."

Mitsos frowned as he took the card. "Luggage? Hah! That'll either be orbiting the planet or burning up on re-entry. Still – you have a nice day."

* * *

Rennie Heiko was next in line, ushered in by a black-uniformed guard armed with a stun baton. He watched the previous passenger head for a barrier at the end of the covered walkway, whistling unconcernedly. Heiko had seen the interviewer's expression through the walls, so the other's carefree attitude came as a surprise.

He entered the room through the transparent door. "Rennie Heiko," he announced – before being asked – and handed over his visa. "I'm just passing through. Got a contract with the *Stavanger*."

Nesvorny took the palm-sized card, and as he did so his eyes alighted on the newcomer's tattooed interface. He frowned, applied the visa to his terminal, then nodded at what it revealed. "Your details and authorisations scan. Normally, you'd be on your way quickly, or else you'd be having this interview with one of my staff instead of me, but circumstances are different today."

"Understood." Heiko stood up straight and looked ahead, as though on parade.

"I'm glad you understand. Now, your visa says you're a security expert. I can see that you're ex-military. In my book, that makes you a potential risk." He thought some more, trying to formulate his next question. At last, he said: "Tell me about the *Leviathan*. Convince me that you had nothing to do with what happened to it."

Heiko looked down at the other. The security officer had sharp blue eyes, a haircut more severe than his own, a large jaw, and nose that looked like it had once been broken and then left uncorrected. The man wanted to appear hard: the question arose, was he really as tough as he seemed? "I honestly can't say what happened at the end. But on the flight, there were tensions. It started with the usual name-calling. Then ambushes. Then one death, followed by another. And then the crew and passengers seemed to split along national and belief lines."

"And what was the source of these tensions?"

Heiko frowned. "Don't you… a*h*…" There was no way to communicate between the Earth and the other eleven inhabited systems aside from messages carried aboard the few ships that possessed the phenomenally expensive Wormhole Drive technology that was used to traverse between stars. Tethys' news would be as up to date as the last ship to arrive, which Heiko supposed would have been some time ago.

Nesvorny nodded at his apparent understanding. "Our last update was nine months ago. I got a little from some of the passengers before you, but only a little. So – humour me."

"Okay. Nine months? So, you're probably aware that there have been big advances in personal enhancement tech over the last couple of years, but I think a tipping point has recently been reached, with tech and bio enhancements affordable for just enough people to now be a problem. Some countries have allowed the practice, but others haven't – for philosophical, religious, or economic reasons. But it's not just East Asia and the Anglosphere against the rest of the world. There's a lot of strife *within* the tech-tolerant nations. For everyone who want enhancements and can afford them – or who think they'll be able to afford them in the future – there are ten that can't and fear becoming a subspecies. *Untermensch*."

"And on the ship?"

Heiko gave a grim smile. "There were lot of New Socialists heading for the *Marseilles*, and religious types heading for *Jeddah*. And a lot of wealthy people trying to escape with their new capabilities, maybe hoping to let the storm die down back home."

"Is it really that bad?"

Heiko nodded curtly. "The issue has touched a deep nerve. There's real hatred on both sides. On Earth, there's full economic war between the *pro-* and *anti*-blocs, and that's spilled over into a number of skirmishes. Two days before we departed, a tactical nuke was let off in California. It wasn't clear whether it came from Europe via Mexico, or was the work of a home-grown fundamentalist Christian sect."

Nesvorny's eyes widened. "A nuke? None of the others –"

"All of the passengers were on the station by then. There was an information shutdown. The cover story was that there'd been a major industrial accident. Of course, some of us are better connected. I'm sure I'm not the only one aboard to know the truth."

"So what exactly happened on the *Leviathan*?"

Heiko shrugged. "I kept myself to myself. As I said, the atmosphere was tense. The bars on the ship seemed to attract rabble-rousers. The New Socialists soon coalesced."

"Did you have any problems? After all, you're one of the originally enhanced. The tech was first developed for the military." Nesvorny waved a hand in the general direction of Heiko's left eye.

Heiko smiled gently. "Sure. But, like you, they were aware of what my tattoo meant, so they found easier prey. Apparently, the first guy to have an 'accident' was stupid enough to flaunt his new powers in the bar being used by the NS as an HQ. He won a drinking contest thanks to his nu-liver, then used the electro-pad in his index finger to shock the drunk who wouldn't pay up."

"Nu-liver? Electro-pad?" Nesvorny sat back in his chair and shook his head. "Clearly the tech has moved on. But what of the end? What happened? How did you and the others get aboard the shuttle?"

"I don't fully know. Some of us had gone to the loading bay early – not only those allocated to the first shuttle. Then the power began to glitch. Rumours were that some of the crew had let some NS onto the bridge to 'see' the captain, who, of course, had all sorts of artificial advantages, no doubt courtesy of his latest bonus. Then there were gunshots. Explosions. Fighting spilled over into the passenger dock. And everyone there decided that the best place to be was somewhere else. Fortunately, so did the shuttle pilot. I'm not sure how they managed to stop the surge at the doors, but they weren't stopping to check who had priority space on their ship. You want to know more, see if any of those who made it down are NS and interrogate them."

"I don't know what's worse – that we might be accepting people with hidden extra capabilities, like you, or taking in revolutionaries."

Heiko shrugged again. "As you don't have this tech on Tethys, I wouldn't be too concerned."

"That's right, we don't. We're a backwater. The problem is, we don't have much of anything apart from water. It's the loss of the *Leviathan's* cargo I fear most. Okay, Heiko…" he handed back the other's card. "Off you go. *Stavanger's* a short hop – don't let me detain you further."

* * *

In contrast to Rennie Heiko, Marie and Kate Lockard flew through formalities. The stern interrogator was happy with Marie's explanation and rapidly authorised the pair's entry into *Hibernia* as well as their onward transfer. They passed through an electronic gate that took them outside the boundary of the spaceport and found themselves in a plaza surrounded by a semi-circle of six-storey buildings with green-blue glass windows and balconies. The centre of the plaza had a stencilled motif that was initially difficult to interpret. Kate ran ahead, her backpack bulging like Marie's, containing the only possessions they'd managed to bring from the *Leviathan.*

"It's a big green thing. And there's a flag." Kate moved this way and that. "Ah, I see. It's the stars and stripes. But what's *this*?"

Marie caught up to her daughter. She'd also been looking down, trying to decipher the grand picture on which they'd been walking. "I think it's a shamrock. Clover."

"Right, I see. An American flag… two American flags… with a shamrock in between."

"That's right. The city… or ship… or whatever it is… was mainly laid down by East Coast Americans of Irish ancestry."

"*City*, Mum. I just can't see this as a ship. It's not moving, or rocking, and we're surrounded by mini skyscrapers. So, what do we do now? We've got no clothes or anything, and nowhere to sleep. When do we fly to the *Lisboa*?"

Marie dropped her rucksack on the ground atop a white star, and pulled out her datapad. "I should have read this on the flight down. Here's my file. There's meant to be a couple of hotels by the port, and a transfer office, too. We need to go back and follow the fence… *that way*. Come on."

Marie led them from the plaza, with datapad in one hand, calling out directions and details as they progressed. "See the tallest building there…" she waved towards a bulky tower that rose several stories above the buildings that ringed the plaza. "The Command Centre. That was intended to be the control centre of the ship, but it's now the seat of government. It's the tallest part of the city." They were in the Boston Quarter. Further on, she indicated the Tipperary Quarter, where residential complexes gave way to retail. The buildings were partly made of volcanic stone, and partly of a toughened glass, with small, crammed units that comprised shops, bars and restaurants, hosting apartments above. The narrow streets were given over to automated electric delivery carts following a one-way system, with pedestrian walkways to either side. There were few people on the streets, most of whom wore utilitarian clothing in shades of green, with sporadic security personnel in black.

Then the buildings on the north side gave way to windowless warehouses that abutted the runway hidden beyond. Occasionally, doors would slide open, and covered carts would emerge and join the road; they also saw several open-topped vehicles carrying security personnel or workers in rugged, brown one-piece uniforms.

They walked through the canyon of buildings towards open sky, and after ten minutes emerged onto a promenade, with the seemingly endless ocean before them. "The East Dock," declared Marie. "This is for the fishing fleet and leisure craft. Apparently, the West Dock on the other side is for military vessels."

"Military?" wondered Kate. "Why do they need military vessels? Are they at war with the fish?"

Marie smiled. "Or maybe it's mermaid raiders."

"Or kraken. Gotta be kraken."

Marie laughed. They'd been awake for nearly twenty hours, and for all the anxiety they'd faced getting from their quarters to the shuttle, the descent, the appalling news about the *Leviathan*, and their brief interrogation, her daughter seemed unconcerned, even in her element. She wondered whether there would be a price to pay later, when they had a chance to rest and think about what they'd been through and the fate of the few decent people they'd met aboard who'd not made it onto the shuttle – a price for both Kate *and* her. But now her daughter had skipped ahead to railings that curved across their view.

"Wow, we're high! I thought we'd just be able to touch the water."

Marie stepped up beside Kate and found that she spoke the truth: the floating harbour was some ten metres below the city's metallic edge. A variety of craft extended mostly to their right. Nearby, the craft were mainly working vessels with fishing or mining rigs; further off, there were some sailing craft – yachts with tall masts. The docking platform itself was sectioned into bays, each marked by a column topped with an electronic display that was protected from the elements by a transparent hemisphere. There were also electronic symbols set in the floor of the dock (some form of carbon composite?), that winked and flashed instructions – such as arrows and crosses – mostly in red and green.

Leaning out to peer along the edge of the platform to where it flexibly adjoined the great city ship proper, Marie noted a number of closed bay doors, like spacecraft airlocks, which she presumed allowed crew and cargo access to the interior beneath her feet. From the promenade, there initially seemed no way down onto the dock, until she spotted a box-like structure some metres away that looked like the housing of a lift.

"Look… that one's about to set off," said Kate, pointing.

Marie returned her attention below. One of the fishing craft nudged slowly from the dock: it was about fifteen metres long, and looked robust, with a curved roof over the cabin, and mechanisms to port and starboard that appeared to be automated net dispensers, like giant rollers on crane-like structures. The ship seemed to be made of some sort of polycarbon, and was powered by an unseen motor that churned the water into foam behind it. Half-a-dozen crew were on deck, dressed in shimmering, blue one-piece costumes, resting on railings or talking with each other.

"That looks fun," said Kate. "Shouldn't they be running about and doing things with ropes? And swearing a lot?"

"And drinking rum?" Marie smiled at her daughter. "Hmmm, yes, well I suspect they have fishing down to an art form here. Lots of automation. I guess the crew is mainly around to oversee the robotics and fix anything that goes wrong."

"Well, I love their suits. Coolest fishermen I've ever seen."

"They're probably made of some high-tech synthetic fabric, water proof, fully insulated, and Kevlar-like to resist the spikes of kraken."

"Really?" Kate turned, then noticed her mother smiling. "Oh, Mum!"

"Actually, I'm only half joking. We humans are an adaptive lot, so it's likely people forced to live on an ocean planet full of gnarly creatures will quickly develop means to survive and prosper."

"So, you're saying the fishermen are wearing evolved super-sowesters?"

Marie arched an eyebrow. "That's nicely put. I think I'll nick that expression."

"You're welcome!" Kate looked smug. "But the fee for using my copyright is something to eat. I'm starving!"

Not far away, they found a small eatery in the three-storey buildings facing the promenade. The narrow outlet – which seemed to have no name – had eight tables, two of which were occupied by pairs of diners. The menus shone electronically through the table top; the back of the room clearly led to the kitchen, but was unprotected and there were no staff in sight.

"I guess we just choose and tap to order," said Marie. "It seems fairly standard stuff."

"In that case, I'll have a burger and fries," said Kate, using her finger to scroll the menu in front of her up and down. "But I guess the food's all the same synthetic stuff really."

"Yes, it'll all be flavoured and shaped protein from food vats. But… hello. What's this – *havelik*? It's under the seafood section."

"Call yourself a marine biologist!" smiled Kate. "Well, if you don't know what it is, no one else will."

"I wonder if it's Tethyan, but there's no one to ask."

"Oh, Mum!" Kate leant towards the couple dining a short distance away. "Excuse me. Sir?"

The two men, dressed in brown coveralls, paused in their determined consumption and looked up. "Yes?" asked one, stocky and of rough appearance, yet with a surprisingly light voice.

"What is havelik? Is it local?"

The second man choked out a laugh; the first merely smiled. "Local? Oh, yeah. But it's no delicacy. You from Earth? I'd stick to the vat stuff."

"So, is it a fish?" asked Marie. "Something we can actually digest?"

"Well, it's a fish-like thing, sure. Edible?" The man exchanged looks with his thin-faced partner, who continued to smile and gently shake his head. "That depends on your tastebuds. It's the cheapest thing on the menu for a reason."

Marie smiled. "Sure. But I meant, it's a foreign organism, but is it okay for us, for humans, to eat? Is it processed in any way?"

The man shrugged. "Well, yeah, but minimally. Soaked in some concoction to remove something. Don't ask me details. But it's not poisonous, and your gut can work with it. *Usually*. If you're a new arrival maybe less so."

"Just don't get too far from the john," growled the other man, and then he laughed some more.

"Ah, right, thanks," said Marie. She firmed her expression and tapped on the menu.

"Mum! Well, don't expect me to clean up after you!"

Their orders were electronically sent. Around five minutes later, a door at the back opened and a hidden member of staff emerged with their food. She placed a plate with a long, pale and glistening filet of something – with new potatoes and carrots – before Marie, and a more recognisable plate of food before Kate, then she winked at Marie and headed off.

Marie noted the two men at the nearby table watching her with barely contained amusement.

She managed three mouthfuls before she lay down her fork. With a sheepish smile at her grinning daughter, she addressed the menu again and placed another order – a burger for herself, and a glass of something strong to take away the taste in her mouth.

After leaving the restaurant, they found the transfer office a short distance away, at the end of a row of buildings near the line of warehouses that formed a barrier to the spaceport. The office was wide and low ceilinged, with three staff, two of whom were in discussion with customers. The third – a red-haired woman – sat in a cubicle facing the door. She smiled at Marie and Kate as they approached, waving at the two seats on the other side of the desk to her, which mother and daughter duly occupied.

"How can I help?" The woman tapped on an electronic display on the desktop, not too dissimilar to the arrangement at the restaurant, but this changed the details displayed on a two-way screen that separated her from her clientele. "Where are you headed?"

"The *Lisboa*," said Marie.

"Nice and easy. No special visas or documents required." She swiped away at the desktop and a schedule appeared on the screen facing Marie and Kate which – Marie presumed – was mirrored on the reverse side facing the woman. "The next one is in about three weeks."

"Three weeks! I didn't think they'd be so infrequent."

"First time on Tethys?" The woman smiled gently. "Ah, of course you are. We don't get many 'repeats', given the lack of service with Earth nowadays. Just so's you know, there's not a lot of movement between the ships. There's not much need to, really. And we've pretty much got an all-roads-lead-to-Rome scenario here."

"So everything goes via *Hibernia*?"

"Pretty much." The woman maintained a soft smile that was already beginning to grate with Marie. "And services are often less frequent than they are today, when the cities send transports to collect their booty from the.... ah...." Now the woman's smile did slip.

Marie pressed on. "But three weeks? It doesn't sound like the *Lisboa* is that concerned with collecting their... *booty*."

"Uh, no. I guess they weren't expecting much this time, unlike some of the others. We've got shuttles from most of the other ships arriving and departing over the next couple of days."

"That puts things in perspective, Mum," said Kate, with a smirk. "Looks like you're not that significant after all."

"Thanks, Kate," said Marie, with some irritation. "That's a nice check to the ego." Looking back over the top of the screen, she asked: "Is there really no other way? How far is the *Lisboa*? Can we get there by boat?"

The woman looked down and tapped and slid her fingers across the table. "I'm afraid it's about thirteen-hundred kilometres away, south-south-west." Then she looked up and her smile reappeared. "But if you're expected, why not give your contact a call? If you're important..." her infuriating smile seemed to suggest that she thought this was unlikely, "they might arrange a pick-up. Worth a try?"

"Well... yes... I suppose so. How can I...?" Suddenly, the desktop in front of Marie came to life.

"There you go. Call's on the house."

Marie retrieved her comms tablet, found the necessary details, and tapped a number on the glowing numeric keypad on the tabletop. The screen in front of her darkened to black, then a red perimeter flashed several times. When the screen cleared, it showed a broad, brown face with a lumpen nose and age lines across its forehead and at the corner of its eyes.

"Marie Lockard? Oh, thank Deus! We heard about the *Leviathan* and feared the worst."

"Oh, Professor, hi! Ah, yes, we made it, Kate and I, though many others didn't. And now we're stranded here in *Hibernia*. I wonder if – ?"

"Of course, of course! A terrible affair. You must be traumatised! I'll arrange a shuttle to pick you up. Just give me an hour or so and I'll call you back. Ah… terrible!"

Marie noticed that on the other side of the screen the red-haired woman's annoying smile had soured.

Chapter 4

Colonel Eric Nesvorny took a seat at a table facing three others. The table was small compared to the one in the centre of the room that was used by *Hibernia's* ruling council when in session; he supposed it would have hosted advisers in normal times. Still, both tables were made of wood – expensively imported from Earth – as opposed to the typical synthetic furniture that was made from Mount Athol-mined material in the sub-level manufactories. For a moment, he stared at the clean, grained surface and wondered when they'd next receive more like it.

"Nesvorny," began the scowling woman in the middle of those opposite, "thanks for coming. We've important matters to discuss." Marissa O'Neill was effectively the premier of *Hibernia*, although she ruled in conjunction with Manfred Traore and Kerrie Sullivan, a triumvirate with the power to make exceptional decisions in times of crisis.

Nesvorny nodded curtly. "I am at your service."

"Of course you are," snapped O'Neill, running one hand through thick black hair that was tinged with grey. "Right, we need an update on what you know about the *Leviathan*. What did you learn from the survivors?"

Nesvorny frowned. "I haven't reported to my superior yet. Shouldn't General –?"

Traore stifled a laugh; O'Neill made a cutting gesture with one hand, and continued: "General Kelly has nothing to contribute."

"Probably still in bed," muttered Sullivan, a thickset woman with short red hair.

"But who with?" smirked Traore; lithe, smartly dressed, dark-skinned.

Nesvorny couldn't stop his mouth twitching at this. "Very well. In that case, it seems Earth politics was behind it. There was some conflict between factions for and against personal enhancement technology. But what exactly happened…?" he shrugged.

"How serious are things on Earth? Do you think the next ship –"

"The *Resolve*," muttered Sullivan.

"… yes, the *Resolve*. Do you think that's likely to come? Will there be a replacement for the *Leviathan*? Or are we on our own?"

Nesvorny sat back in his faux-leather seat. "There won't be a replacement – how could there be? No one on Earth will know about the *Leviathan* until it fails to return. It was due to remain for a month, and then would have taken six weeks to gain a safe distance in the outer system before activating its wormhole drive." He leant forwards and grasped his hands together. "I suspect they'll initially think there's some minor technical issue. At what point the Brightstar company begins to think it's not coming at all, I don't know. A week beyond schedule? A month? And even then, what could they do? The *Leviathan* was its only ship on this route. The company has three more *interstellars* servicing other systems, but how eager will they be to disrupt profitable trade and redirect one of those ships here?"

O'Neill stared at the security officer with her grey eyes. "So, you're saying we should effectively forget that option and look to the *Resolve*, due in… nine months?"

"Yes. I suspect Brightstar will ask the owners of the *Resolve* for a report when it returns."

"*If* it comes," muttered Sullivan. She looked aside to O'Neill. "Can we be sure it will?"

O'Neill continued to focus on Nesvorny. "Which brings us back to the question – how bad are things on Earth?"

"You're asking the wrong person."

"No, Colonel, I'm asking the person who has been asking the right people, which makes *you* the right person. Or have you been delinquent in your interrogations?"

Nesvorny managed to bite down on his annoyance: he'd not normally have conducted the immigration interviews, but he'd chosen to do so because of the unique circumstance, though his initiative meant nothing to O'Neill, who was famously blunt. And ambitious. And *vengeful*. "I have asked, of course. But I had to assess all of the arrivals quickly, so I couldn't *chat*. Still, I've identified a number of people I'll follow up, although I'm not sure how much they'll be able to add. None of the arrivals are top-level diplomats or people with special insight into what's going on back there."

"Yes, Colonel, but what is your top-line impression? How close is Earth to war?"

"The passengers were nervous." Nesvorny briefly closed his eyes as though this might help him recall their faces, their body language, the timbres of their voices, and the words they'd used. "There was even talk of use of a tactical nuclear weapon."

"Fuck!" said Traore, suddenly less sure of himself.

"A nuke!" exclaimed Sullivan. "That's… that's…"

O'Neill again made a cutting motion with her hand. "Conduct further interviews, then, Colonel. I want a full report by the end of the week. From what you are saying, we should perhaps assume that the next ship will not arrive. Start planning for self-sufficiency."

"That would make sense." Nesvorny opened his hands and rested them flat on the table.

"Indeed. And we need a second report on what supplies were lost on the *Leviathan*, on where we have critical deficiencies, and on how we might mitigate these."

"That is not –"

"I wasn't suggesting that *you* write the report, Colonel!" O'Neill turned to Sullivan. "You're the Minister for Resources, Kerrie."

"Uh, yes. I'll –"

"And there's the people issue, too," said Traore. "I've been saying this for some time. We've let people breed as much as they like. And they're still at it, especially the Stokers." He was referring to the community that lived in the poorest part of the city, around where the old engine room used to be. "We have several thousand more than we can sustain."

Nesvorny knew that he wasn't talking about deficiencies in food or energy, which was plentiful, but rather about the things that used elements that were in short supply; elements that were needed to run the machinery that kept the health service working, the manufactories functioning, and essentially support everything else necessary for civilisation.

"Look into it, Manfred," said O'Neill. "Liaise with Kerrie. I want to know the scale of problems and possible solutions. *All* solutions. From the mild to the extreme." She turned back to Nesvorny. "And that makes me think we *do* need a second report from you after all –

on military options. Assuming worst case, what might and can we do?"

"And the General?"

O'Neill shook her head abruptly. "Forget that moron. I'm instructing you personally. Understand? Good. Now, get out of here."

* * *

Hibernia's military, though the largest of all the city states on Tethys, was still modest in size: from a population approaching one hundred thousand, around seven hundred served in the black-uniformed organisation. Yet, the military was not so much an army as a souped-up police force with extra responsibilities. And though the head of this was accorded the military title of General, Domitus Kelly acted more like a politician than a soldier, rarely being seen beyond ceremonial duties. This left Kelly's deputies – Colonels Eric Nesvorny and Tania Joseph – to do most of the day-to-day work. Of these, Nesvorny had the greater power as Head of Internal Security, while Joseph, as Head of External Security, controlled eight gunboats (moored at the West Dock), a fleet of drones, and was responsible for agents in the nearest City Class ships. Thus, while Nesvorny's focus was on the people of *Hibernia*, Joseph's was on everyone else: as such, Nesvorny's latest assignment seemed to cross their unspoken boundary, requiring him to indulge in intel gathering from newcomers from Earth, many of whom intended to go elsewhere.

"Come in," Nesvorny called, in response to a knock on his office door. He was currently in what used to be the ship's command centre, on its bottom floor, with the very top floor (where he'd been summoned earlier) having been given over to the state's government.

The door opened, and in came a bald-headed man with a tell-tale oblong mark beside his left eye – a port through which he could receive updates to various enhancements he'd received in the Japanese Special Boarding Unit some years previously. But this was only the most visible of the man's adaptations. "Major Fukuda."

"Sir! I have an update on the NS passengers."

"Good. Take a seat."

Fukuda pulled out a chair and sat, placing his peaked cap neatly on the desk in front of him. "As you suspected, they knew each other." There had been a total of twenty-two NS members spread among the shuttle passengers, but they'd tried their best in the immigration queue to ignore each other as though they were strangers. But yesterday's interviews had revealed that their visas to the *Marseilles* had been issued within the space of one week, albeit to people from all over Earth. "They are staying at the Crown Hostel," continued Fukuda, "which was meant to be closed for refurbishment, but suddenly opened at their arrival. At least a dozen spent yesterday evening at O'Brien's bar next door. *Together.*"

"I assume the *Marseilles* representative was waiting for them and had their accommodation arranged?"

"Yes, sir. Oh, and he seems to have organised their transport, too. It's due to arrive in two days."

Nesvorny tapped his desk in thought. "I wonder what they're up to? The *Marseilles* is hardly in need of extra population, and I'm not sure I buy the arrivals' claims that they're on some kind of pilgrimage. Also, there's their profile. Did you notice anything unusual about them?"

Fukuda smiled, aware he was being tested. "They are all young and fit, and most are male."

"That's right." Nesvorny tapped his desk some more. "Remind me, what's the *Marseilles'* position now?"

"About six hundred kilometres south east, by the Koriev Shallows. So, yes, they are close." Fukuda's smile broadened. "They have the mining license after the *Stavanger.*"

Perhaps Nesvorny was becoming paranoid, expecting trouble everywhere. But the destruction of the *Leviathan* had shocked everyone. "I see."

"Maybe they have mining expertise?" said Fukuda.

"That is one explanation. But maybe we didn't dig deeply enough into their histories and motives yesterday." Maybe *I* didn't…

"There was little time, sir. They all had to be processed. It is understandable."

Nesvorny nodded. Fukuda was good. Very good. And as ambitious as he had once been. "I suppose we could invite one or two to return to respond to unanswered questions. But they will be gone in two days. They can cause us no trouble on the *Marseilles*."

Fukuda nodded. "Yes, sir. And if they did, that would then be Colonel Joseph's responsibility, not ours."

"True. Nevertheless, perhaps we need to find out more. Humans are creatures of habit. They will almost certainly regroup at O'Brien's this evening. Go plant some surveillance devices. I'm sure they'll speak freely after a few drinks. I want to know why they are really here, and what they know of events on the *Leviathan*, which I am sure is more than they let on yesterday."

"Of course, sir." Fukuda rose from his seat and replaced his cap. "Anything else?"

Nesvorny shook his head and twitched one hand to dismiss the other.

* * *

Nesvorny had one further important meeting that day. Around six o'clock Tethys Adjusted Time, just as he was thinking of heading home to the Boston District, he received a summons.

The command centre of the *Hibernia* was the tallest structure in the city – long and thin, it had originally been placed in the middle of the giant craft, but it was now somewhat forward of the midline after sixty years of slowly extending the stern. In some places, all of the communications and control systems had been completely ripped out and replaced, but in others, the old circuits and pipes had simply been hidden behind false walls or ceilings. Occasionally, he wondered whether there might be useable resources closer to hand than Earth, although ripping apart the now well-appointed interior of the administrative zone was clearly considered a step too far by those who'd grown accustomed to comfort.

On the sixth floor, two below what used to be the cockpit and was now the council meeting chamber, large offices lay to either side of a narrow corridor. Nesvorny strode along a thick, pale blue carpet to an office at the far end. For a moment, he peered through the window at the head of the corridor, which provided a view over the rooftops of the Charlestown building, a large crescent that curved around the city's main plaza and was home to *Hibernia's* most important people, including himself. Tethys' setting star caused the roofline to sparkle. Originally, the crescent had been lower, allowing a clear view of the ocean, but extra floors had been added over the years, and the spaceport had been repositioned to the bow area, which had also been extended and slanted at thirty degrees so that the city no longer had the profile of a proper ship.

Nesvorny turned away from the view. At the door, he peered into a small screen, and touched a pad to open a comm channel. "Nesvorny, as requested."

No answer came, but a *click* indicated that the door was unlocked, so he entered.

Manfred Traore lounged on a small sofa against a wall that was mostly glass and faced out over Charlestown. He nursed a tumbler containing a clear spirit. As Nesvorny entered, Traore rose, sauntered across to a large desk, placed his drink upon it, then perched on the edge. He smiled at his guest. "I'm glad I caught you before you bunked off. Grab a chair." He folded his arms as he waited for the other to do as instructed.

Nesvorny sat. "Okay. I'm here. What is it?"

"I thought we should talk about the situation – *mano-a-mano*."

"Without the rest of the triumvirate?"

Traore smiled. "At least for now. Best to scope out possibilities, I think, without other distractions. *Too many cooks* and all that."

Nesvorny nodded. He had been half expecting this. Traore's obsession was well-known, and evidently an irritation to his peers. But the man was well versed in the political arts; this was clearly an attempt to divide and conquer. "Go on."

Traore slid from the desk and took a couple of paces to the window-wall to look outside. "You live in the complex, don't you? We all do, we rulers of *Hibernia*." He turned to face the other. "It's nice, isn't it?"

Nesvorny shrugged. "Sure. But I thought you wanted to talk about something important, not homemaking."

Traore's smile broadened and he wagged a finger at the seated man. "Very good, Colonel. Homemaking! But I am making a point. Charlestown is where we live – rulers of the most important state on this world, and therefore, arguably, rulers *of* this world. We have the only functioning spaceport. We control the only readily minable resource on the planet. And yet, we have to do with 'nice'. The elevator to my block stopped working a week ago and hasn't been repaired. The electronics are constantly glitching. My neighbour – who runs the East Dock – got locked in her own apartment a few days ago, and she's decided she's had enough. She's had a handle and manual lock fitted to her front door." He leant back against the window and folded his arms. "In short, rather than advancing, we are going backwards. And why is that?"

"Too few resources," said Nesvorny. "We all know that. We can't get the elements for the electronics."

"Too few resources? Sure. Or too many people for the existing resources to go round."

Nesvorny smiled to himself. This was it. "You've made this argument before. Quite a few times, in fact."

"And I'll keep making it until you and our colleagues eventually get it."

"Oh, I understand. We all do. This is all part of one equation." Nesvorny folded his arms across his chest. "What isn't clear is what you want to do about it. Fewer people, yes. But that is why we're building a Town Class ship on the opposite side of Mount Athol. To take away those of our excess population who'd rather sail off by themselves."

"A ship that has merely drained our resources further – and will likely never be finished. Not now. I don't need to see Sullivan's report to know that the *Leviathan's* cargo was critical for the completion of the ship as well as our own renewal."

"I suspect you are right. But I still don't see where you are going. Fewer people? Do you wish to transport the Stokers to the middle of the Ulster Black and throw them in?"

Traore took a split second too long to answer. "No. That would be absurd."

"Are you sure that's what you truly believe? They are our people."

"Are they?" Traore pushed away from the window and slid closer, regaining his perch on his desk. "Most are first or second generation immigrants. Their allegiance is not clear."

"And that's a problem for you?"

Traore held up his hands and managed to control his smile. "Of course not. Not necessarily. After all, we allowed them to come and settle when we thought we could keep growing forever. More city ships. An endless ocean of opportunities. An outlet for the adventurous from Earth… and for the disaffected. But now we know there are limits. We expanded far too quickly. And is that the fault of the founders of *Hibernia* or their descendants?"

"So you *do* have a problem."

"As do *you*, Eric." Traore's smile returned, and his voice softened: it wasn't for nothing that he'd gained the nickname 'The Charmer'. "Where is most of the trouble in the city? Where do you have to expend most of *your* resources? The Engine Quarter."

"That's well known." Nesvorny shrugged. "But this is true of every city, here, on Earth, or anywhere else. There is always one area that's the source of more trouble than others. If the Engines were cleared, then Cork would take the mantle before long, and trouble would move there."

"So, we should do nothing? Is that your solution?"

"Far from it. I keep order. *Successfully*."

Traore raised his arms again. "Of course you do, Eric. Your effectiveness is well known. And that is why you are here. You heard O'Neill ask me for a report outlining our difficulties. I will provide it. I will also discuss options – options that will need to be enacted by Internal Security. By *you*, Eric. So, I need to get a sense of your loyalties."

Nesvorny scowled. "My loyalties are well known. What are you implying? And you still haven't told me the exact nature of your options."

"I'm implying nothing, Eric, nothing at all. Just testing the water. But let's assume, for example, that O'Neill comes around to my way of thinking."

"And Sullivan?"

Traore waved this away: she was unimportant. "Let's stick with O'Neill. She is a pragmatist. When half-a-dozen options are laid before her, all of which are bad, she will be able to bite the bullet. Suck it up. Do what needs to be done."

"And what is it that you think needs to be done, and that you think you can charm from our Premier? The Ulster Black option?"

Traore knew his nickname, and it amused him. "Oh, come on, Eric. I'm not a monster. But we are too many and have to reduce our population. You know it. O'Neill knows it. Even Sullivan knows it. The *how* is still something I'm considering. And, of course, I'd welcome any thoughts from you. Do you have any thoughts?"

Did he? Nesvorny stood. "We're going around in circles. If you don't mind, I am going to the theatre this evening. I have heard your concerns. I will give the matter some thought."

As Nesvorny moved towards the door, Traore said: "Wait! Before you go, Eric, you still haven't answered my question. About loyalty."

Nesvorny turned, anger in his eyes. "To the council? To the city? Yes. Don't question it ever again."

Chapter 5

Makka Frost and Melissa De Voe arrived at the Stavanger building on Consul Street in *Hibernia's* Derry Quarter at around midday, with Tethys' yellow star almost directly overhead. The buildings here were three-storeys high and made of white-painted volcanic stone, with wide, black doors sheltered beneath porches that were held up by pairs of Doric columns. Stavanger House stood at one end of the short street that housed the 'embassies' of all the planet's city states.

Magnus Solbakken – the *Stavanger* representative – answered the door and let them in. He was tall, with an angular face, blue eyes, light brown collar-length hair, and could have been any age between mid-thirties to mid-fifties. "Makka, Melissa, good to see you. Come in." He led them to a wide lounge off the main hallway and waved a hand to indicate that they should sit. The room had a bare stone floor, small meeting table at one end, and a number of chairs – upholstered in a light-blue fabric – loosely arranged around a smaller coffee table. Solbakken went straight to a sideboard on which sat a precious coffee machine, which he programmed with several taps on an electronic display. The machine began to gurgle. Over his shoulder, he announced: "You'll join me, yes?"

"Of course," said Frost. "Though you seem confident of our orders."

Solbakken laughed and turned to face the pair, who'd taken seats. "I'm afraid there is only one order available – generic coffee – though you may have it with or without milk. My machine is temperamental, and I don't have the funds to get it fixed. And I *definitely* don't have enough to get a new one."

"At least you've got something," muttered De Voe. "Us provincials have to make do with grinds and hot water. I think we're regressing."

"And things certainly aren't going to improve any time soon after, ah, yesterday's events. Not even in *Hibernia*. Excuse me, the beast has cleared its throat…" Solbakken turned back to the coffeemaker.

Frost sat back in the chair and observed the room. A large, framed picture of the *Stavanger* adorned one wall opposite a broad window that looked onto the street. Another picture on the end wall showed the old city in Norway after which the city ship had been named: the view was at night, the port illuminated by hundreds of lights. There was also a small bookcase against one wall with a score of books printed on real paper, but there was not a single electronic device in the room bar the one their host currently attended. After a moment, Frost wondered: "Is it just you here, Magnus?"

"Hang on…" Solbakken turned. Somehow he had acquired a tray, on which he loaded three stoneware cups and a small jug of milk. He walked over, placed the tray on the table, and then took the last of the blue-fabric chairs. "Right, please help yourselves. Now – alone? Well, yes. Did you expect I'd have staff?"

Frost let De Voe sort out her drink first. "No, but I wondered whether your wife…?"

"Frida? Sometimes. But she has work back home. Frankly, there's little enough for me to do around here."

"Big house, though," noted De Voe, cup raised to her lips.

"Sure. Too big. It – and the others on the street – were built when we all had greater… ambitions? Pretensions? Half the embassies are empty at the moment. And I've only been hanging on for the *Leviathan*. Now, I'm not sure whether I'll be needed here at all. But maybe I'll be needed *more*. I think that depends on you."

Frost had claimed his own cup by now. "More? Ah, you mean, to source our material needs?"

"Precisely. But if that's the case, you're going to have to find me something serious to trade with. Electronic goods in the official markets doubled in price overnight – in Tethyn Crypto, US Dollars, and Renminbi. And then there's the unofficial sources, if you don't mind gear *borrowed* from the unwary, by which I of course mean, stripped out of buildings and utilities by gangs from the Engine District."

"So, nothing got down from the *Leviathan*?" asked Frost. "At the port, the authorities kept mum. They wouldn't speak to us at all."

"They're all in shock. Although *we* had a couple of big containers aboard, I reckon at least half of the hold was full of *their* Earthly purchases. Rare earths. Wood. Medicines. Everything we can't get hold of."

"Fuck," said De Voe.

"So, we really have wasted the trip," said Frost.

Solbakken smiled. "Well, yes and no. It's not as if you've had far to come – unlike some of the other poor bastards flying in. And you've also got a decent-ish cup of coffee out of it. Plus, on the one shuttle that did make it, there was a passenger who needs a lift. In fact, I wasn't quite telling the truth earlier when I said I was alone." He suddenly stood. "If you'll excuse me, I won't be a moment." Solbakken strode to the door and exited the room.

"Fuck!" said De Voe again, once they were alone.

"We're going to have to tighten our belts even more," said Frost. "Worn electronics aren't going to get replaced. And as for batteries – *shit*!"

"I just hope our shuttles don't degrade, or we'll be rowing everywhere."

"When we get back, we need to do a thorough audit," said Frost. "Produce a list of essentials for Magnus."

"Aye."

The door opened, and Solbakken entered, followed by a stiff-backed man with close-cropped hair tinged with silver and a tattoo of sorts by his left eye.

"Makka, Melissa, can I introduce you to Rennie Heiko – he's our new Head of Security."

The man gave a faint smile and bowed his head slightly. "I'm pleased to meet you."

Frost and De Voe rose from their seats, the latter reluctantly.

"I'm Makka Frost, Head of Material Resources, and this is Melissa De Voe, my deputy." Frost edged around the table and approached with his hand out.

Heiko took the hand and shook it firmly. "I'm sorry I'm not what you expected. And hello, Ms De Voe."

"Call me *Melissa*." De Voe also shook hands, then forced a smile. "Are you sure you're not carrying anything of value? We could particularly use rare earths."

"Nothing but a comms tablet, I'm afraid, unless there's trace elements in me that I don't know about."

De Voe laughed. "Fortunately for you, there's little of use in your body, but if there were, I assure you it wouldn't be a laughing matter. We may soon get to the point where some people begin eyeing others up for spare parts."

Frost winced. "Anyway, if you want a lift, Rennie, you got it. There's not much reason for us to hang around here. Magnus..." he turned. "We'd appreciate it if you could stay on. Maybe we'll be in touch in few days with a wish list?"

Solbakken nodded. "Of course. But I advise you to get that list to me sooner rather than later. Prices are only going to go one way."

* * *

An hour later, Rennie Heiko and Melissa De Voe sat across from each other in the passenger section of *Stavanger's* shuttle on Landing Pad 4 of *Hibernia's* spaceport. Each of the ten rows had two single seats separated by a wide aisle. Fold-out tables were recessed under every porthole-style window and could be deployed into the ample legroom before the seats. They were alone in the middle of the cabin; at present, Makka Frost was at the front of the craft, visible beyond a transparent door, leaning over to talk to the pilot and co-pilot.

Heiko realised he could unlock his seat and swivel to face De Voe. "Plush. Like the interior of an executive jet."

"Sure, we've got plenty of room up here," said De Voe, turning her own seat to face the other. "As you probably noticed, most of the shuttle is cargo space beneath our feet. Frankly, there's not a lot of reason to use the shuttle apart from pick-ups from *Hibernia*. We only have two in our fleet – the second is essentially mothballed, only for use in an emergency. But the way things are going, we might have to cannibalise it for parts."

Heiko frowned. "Sounds desperate. Redundancy is always a good idea."

"Agreed, but what else can we do? Every machine in *Stavanger* has minute amounts of critical elements with special magnetic, electrical, or luminescent properties. But there are thousands, maybe even millions, of such parts in these machines, and these elements naturally degrade over time and get lost in recycling. The Tethyn system doesn't have a significant ring of asteroids like Sol, and we don't have any space-mining craft anyway. The oceans don't contain the elements we need, and nor do the few landmasses we can access, so…" She shrugged.

"And sorting this out is your responsibility?"

"Our section, yes."

Heiko nodded in thought. "I can see how this could make you unpopular in times of scarcity. The people who say 'no'. Wearing my new hat… have you had any problems?"

De Voe gave a wry smile, which had the effect of making the small anchor tattoo above her brow twitch. "Security matters? Hoarding? Theft? You'll have to talk to Cass about that. Your predecessor. For us? Nothing significant. People can become demanding. We cope. We try to be understanding… or at least, Makka does."

"The diplomat?"

"Sure. That's his modus."

"And yours?"

"Oh, I'm a shouter. When Makka gets too exasperated, I come in and say 'no' in a slightly different way. Between us, things get sorted."

"So, good cop, bad cop?"

"You could put it that way. What about you? I see you're ex-military. You must have a PhD in shouting."

Heiko's eyes sparkled. "Me? No. I hope I don't need to. I hope my demeanour shouts for me."

"I wish I had that presence." It was a credit to De Voe that she seemed to know exactly what he meant.

* * *

When they got underway, the shuttle lifted off vertically, then sped in the direction of the volcanic chain that Heiko had overflown in the *Leviathan's* shuttle the previous day. They never rose more than a couple of thousand metres above sea level.

Frost sat in the seat in front of De Voe, turning this one-eighty to face his deputy. After an apology to Heiko, he proceeded to talk shop with the woman, freeing the security man to focus on the view outside his window. Heiko marvelled at the subtle changes in colour in the ocean as the sun intermittently dappled the water from around intervening clouds.

Twenty minutes later, Heiko caught sight of the *Stavanger*. It reminded him of a cross between a cruise ship and an aircraft carrier, although it was far larger than anything he'd seen on Earth. As they descended towards the stern of the ship, he was momentarily reminded of coming in to land at Hong Kong's old airport – which still operated for private planes – with tall buildings suddenly rising towards him. The shuttle made a last-second course correction so that it circled around the ship and came in to a landing pad from over the sea. It gently settled on the landing strip, which had just two circular bullseyes for rotary-wing aircraft, the second being vacant.

"Welcome to the *Stavanger*," said Frost. "Do you know where you're meant to go?"

"Magnus kindly alerted the relevant parties," said Heiko. "Security HQ. Level six, zone three, apparently."

"We'll show you," said De Voe. "All the government services are spread over levels five and six, so you're not far from us."

The shuttle's engines had realigned for a vertical landing; they quickly shut down. Heiko followed Frost and De Voe down steps that slid from the craft's sole exit hatch. Outside, a cool wind had picked up, and they made the short walk to a wide entrance in the superstructure under cloud shadow.

"Weather's about to turn," muttered De Voe to Frost's back. "Might need to recall the mining party before evening."

"Sure thing. Check the forecast and action if necessary."

The door was apparently meant to open automatically, given the way Frost stopped and waited. After a couple of seconds, he muttered under his breath, thumped a faintly glowing pad to the right, and pushed.

De Voe shook her head and glanced over her shoulder at Heiko: "See? We're falling apart."

Heiko was led along one featureless corridor after another, apparently tracing the edge of the city ship. Then, after a couple of minutes, they turned inwards and emerged into a plaza. The ceiling here was double height, with a dozen businesses presenting faces to the concourse, some with plastic seating outside. Some were retail and services, but most were bars and eateries.

As they crossed, De Voe looked wistful. "Nearly lunchtime, Makka."

"Sure. But let's see to our guest first, and visit Meteo." Frost turned to face Heiko. "Behold, Geilo. Couple of decent bars here. We brew our own, of course, in the Agri-Deck, level U2. I recommend Bjorn's Castle, right over there. When you get done, come find us. If we're not there, Melissa usually holds court there most evenings."

De Voe nodded serenely. "Less pretentious here. But there are grander plazas elsewhere if that's your style."

"No, basic is fine by me," said Heiko. "Perhaps this evening then. I want to get properly settled first."

"Of course," said Frost. "On then."

They traversed the concourse, took a wide corridor, and found a bank of elevators. They got out on the sixth floor. From here, it was a short distance to the Security section at the end of a corridor, with an untenanted security desk acting as an island in a small area before broad, frosted doors.

"And here we part," said Frost. "Announce yourself at the desk, and I'm sure someone will pick up and come and let you in."

"Thanks for your help. Later?"

* * *

Heiko's hosts must have been alerted to the landing of the shuttle, for he was quickly met by a nervous young man in a blue uniform, who paced him through the Security section to an annex, where he was presented to another office with double doors. The man opened the door manually and waved for Heiko to enter, then bowed and stepped away, letting the door close between them.

Inside, there were five people, sat around a mid-sized conference table. They broke off their discussion on Heiko's entry, and all turned to face him. The nearest person – a tall, fair-haired man in a blue uniform with a silver badge on his breast pocket – stood up.

"Mr Heiko, sir. Pleased to meet you. I am Anders Pedersen, your number two. Would you please take a seat."

Heiko gave the man a quick smile and nod, and took the vacant chair indicated by the other, while Pedersen reclaimed his seat. As he did so, a white-haired woman directly opposite gave him a gentle smile, her eyes crinkling. She somehow dominated the room, with notably more elbow space than the two pairs sat to either side of her.

"Hello, Mr Heiko," she began. "I am delighted that you are here and survived the tragedy of the starship. I am Margarethe Olson, Premier of *Stavanger*. Given that we get few arrivals, and given your seniority, I thought I'd come to greet you personally."

"Thank you, ma'am. I'm honoured."

"Yes, well…" she turned to wave one frail hand. "This is Cass Remillard, your predecessor." She indicated the man sat between her and Pedersen – thinning grey hair, bushy brows and large eyes, also dressed in a blue uniform with pocket badge. "And to this side is Hanna Bulow, Second of State, and Nila Moroni, my chief secretary, gatekeeper, and fixer..." she smiled at the olive-skinned woman, continuing: "and someone who will undoubtedly occupy my current position in future – a case of *when*, not *if*."

Moroni didn't smile, but she did nod acknowledgement before turning a sharp eye upon the newcomer.

Heiko mouthed quiet greetings as he swept his gaze across the others, lingering a split-second on Moroni before returning attention to the Premier. "I didn't expect such a stately welcome. Thank you again."

"We're a small society here, on the *Stavanger*. I suppose it is similar elsewhere on Tethys. A new Head of Security counts as a big event, and certainly as big as anything else I've got on at the moment. So, it's really no problem." She gently rubbed her thin hands together, blue veins shining through paper-thin skin. "But I suddenly realise that this has the feel of an interview. Not my intention at all. We only just got here ourselves. Where's our hospitality? *Anders…*"

"Ah, yes, ma'am. Something to drink?" The man leapt to his feet once more, quickly departing through the door at Heiko's back.

"Now, while we're waiting, let's get to know each other. I'm afraid I wasn't part of your selection process – none of us were. We had to rely upon our trusted emissaries on Earth for that."

"Let's hope they chose well," said Moroni, speaking softly.

"Indeed!" Olson seemed amused by the assertion. "So, please, tell us a bit about yourself."

Heiko puckered his lips into a frown. He was surprised at Olson's admission and not a little disturbed at the implications. None of the people here had endorsed him; at present, he had no allies. "Where would you like me to begin? My service in the Finnish military?"

"Oh, no," said Olson. "Not that. We've seen the files. Finnish special forces. A period as a soldier of fortune with combat in several of the world's hot spots. Then security specialist and bodyguard in a couple of prestigious organisations. We can read! No, Mr Heiko, we'd like to find out who you *really* are. What *lies* behind the printed record."

"Like why you decided to leave Earth and come all the way out here," said Moroni, speaking the moment the old woman paused.

Heiko looked between the two women. "I assure you, I am not fleeing anything." He gave a gentle smile. Well, *not much*. "In truth, I can't honestly say one hundred percent why I came. I guess I just reached a point in my life where I either tried something new and different, or I decided to row back and settle into a steady, comfortable job, and to slowly slide into retirement. My children –"

"You have two," broke in Moroni, matter-of-factly.

"Yes, two. Matti and Annikki. They are well set in their careers, at opposite ends of the planet with their families. We're not un-close, but physical distance and circumstance mean we rarely meet more than once or twice a year anyway. And I have no other significant ties." He gave a gentle smile again, and shrugged. "There is nothing more salacious than that…" he turned slightly, "in spite of what your intel might suggest, Ms Moroni."

Remillard had been silent, but now he chuckled. "Well, at least he knows how to read the room."

Olson barked a laugh, and even Moroni's mouth twitched upwards. The aide said: "So, you think I am the chief inquisitor here?"

Bulow – who'd also been silent until now – muttered: "Certainly the one with the most to say." The comment from the handsome woman, who was perhaps only a couple of years younger than the Premier, with white hair that still retained hints of its original blonde, was meant to convey humour, but Heiko detected something more behind it.

Heiko's eyes sparkled. "I obviously meant no disrespect, but… this *is* an interview, isn't it? Otherwise, you would have been standing at my arrival. But I understand your concerns. I am a stranger come into your close family: you want to know if you can trust me not to steal the silverware or murder you in your beds. So, please, interrogate some more. It would be nice to take Mr Pedersen's hospitality – when he eventually gets back – at ease."

Olson laughed lightly again. "I think I like you, Mr Heiko. Your record says that you are good at security. I think you're not too bad at politics, either. In a small world like ours, diplomacy is very important."

"That's right," smirked Remillard. "With the resources you're going to get, you'll have to ask nicely more often than you'll want, because stomping about and making demands will get you nowhere."

"Except for grey hairs and an ulcer," said Olson. "As you can see from Cass' demeanour, he is more than happy at your arrival and his chance to step away from the plate."

Remillard chuckled. "Got me some fish-analogues to catch from my new boat. But I'll be happy to advise for a few months anyway."

The conversation lightened considerably after that. When Pedersen returned pushing a trolley covered with a wide selection of drinks, they all rose and clustered around it. But Heiko knew the form: he nursed a single glass of wine, and was especially attentive to the expressions and words of Nila Moroni.

Chapter 6

Eddard Mitsos had been in *Hibernia* for six days now, and was already monumentally bored. Though huge as a 'ship', as a sovereign nation the place was minute. It was bigger than the Vatican City, but… Monte Carlo? San Marino? Regardless of size, in Mitsos' view it had nowhere near the charm or history of those places. There were no real sights or landmarks beyond the cluster of tall buildings that had once been the control complex, which formed a raised spine down the centre of the domain. And the retail and dining units were generally small, narrow, and largely utilitarian. After all, the place manufactured little of interest to tourists, and no matter what colourful banner or name a bar or restaurant sported, its food came from the same raw materials as all the others, converted into shaped and textured protein in hidden vats and then soaked with appropriate flavourings. As far as Mitsos could tell, the only difference between standard worker cafés and the best restaurants in the Boston district was internal décor and price.

For the umpteenth time, Mitsos paused at a railing to look over the vast ocean – now at the south-east part of the city, from where the bulk of Mount Athol was invisible behind him, eclipsed by the central tower wall. The water was ten metres below, gently lapping against the hard metallic shore of the craft, a deep blue, its multitude of denizens hidden. He wondered what was down there, and whether even now there might be some creature just below the surface looking up at him. Though the two docks were away around the curve of the ship, Mitsos noted that there were a couple of floating platforms below, off to one side, separated from each other by a few metres. There was a flight of steps zigzagging down to the nearer one; following this up, he saw a gate-protected access to the stairway. Ambling over, he perused the gate, then reached for it and pushed. The gate moved easily. If he wished, he could step onto the top landing and descend to the platform. He smiled to himself, shook his head, and let the gate swing shut.

Turning to rest his back on the railing, Mitsos realised that he was close to the one area of real diversity in this magnolia city: rising four storeys high was a cluster of buildings set around a hundred metres back, peering over the two-storey structures that lined the 'coastal road' (as he had christened it). These edifices were darker in colour than those in front, and had a shabby and somewhat dissolute air. *The Engine Quarter.* The buildings, he knew – having browsed the relevant databases – had been slowly built without planning permission over the last forty years, surreptitiously and cheaply, incorporating and extending the part of the ship superstructure than connected to the engines in the ship's guts. Beneath them was the beating heart of the city ship: the fusion reactor and all the machinery that turned that power into electricity for homes and industry. And while the reactor itself would be well-maintained and guarded, the areas to its stern that held machinery for directing power to the ship's drive system and immense screws and shafts had been abandoned and left to decay. And it was there that the lowest of Hibernian society resided, untaxed and uncounted. Mitsos had wandered in the shadow of the grimy blocks just yesterday, but he'd been deterred from going far by unfriendly eyes. In any case, there was no entertainment – or profit – to be had there.

Profit? Mitsos again shook his head. *If not here, then where?*

* * *

A short time after, Mitsos found himself in the Cork District a little further around the coastal way, just far enough for the Engine Quarter tenements to be eclipsed from view by buildings constructed of the more common pale-brown stone. He pulled up in surprise at the sight of a familiar face crossing in front of him, and watched as the man pressed open the green-painted door of a bar and disappear inside. A small sign on a metal bracket perpendicular to the wall above the door showed a picture of a Leprechaun dressed in green, over which was written the name: O'Brien's.

After a moment's thought, Mitsos stepped up to the door and pushed through. Inside, the lighting was low and yellow; small tables lined the left-hand wall opposite a long bar, with a narrow passage between. The décor on the walls – mirrors and old Guinness posters – was typical of a multitude of Irish-themed bars on Earth. The near tables were unoccupied. As Mitsos carried on into the space, he noticed that the area beyond the end of the bar widened into a lounge with further tables, like islands. The man he'd followed raised a hand to someone in the deep interior and then turned to face the sole barman, whom he spoke to in a low voice.

Mitsos continued until he reached the man, then turned to also lean on the synthetic counter-top, which was lined with rubber mats and colourful bar towels. "So… what would you recommend?"

The man startled, then glanced at Mitsos. His serious face, framed by long blond hair, turned into a frown, but then his eyes widened in recognition. "The shuttle, right?"

"A coincidence, sure, but perhaps a happy one. Order me something, and I'll buy the round – deal?"

"Sure."

The barman returned from a beer pump and set a fizzy, straw-coloured drink in a straight glass on the counter.

"Same again, comrade. For my colleague."

The barman – square-shouldered and sharp-eyed – nodded, and returned to the beer pump without a word.

"I don't think we ever exchanged names, did we? I'm Eddard Mitsos."

"No, we didn't," said the other. "I'm Georges Hollande. You're the businessman, yeah?"

"Yes – and now a frustrated one, wondering what he is doing here."

"You've come to the wrong place for sympathy," said Hollande. "Private enterprise? Who suffers when you get rich, eh?"

Mitsos smiled wryly. "Sure, succeed and I do well, but fail and a lot of brothers and sisters back in my factory on Earth lose their jobs. It's not black and white. Though it might not be ideologically perfect, you wouldn't want my employees to starve, would you?"

The barman returned with a second glass of beer, which he placed on the counter. Mitsos flicked a payment card from an inside pocket of his jacket. "My round." He held his card to the scanner that materialised in the barman's hand.

Hollande nodded thanks. "Yeah, workers need to work. But it would be good if they were able to rely upon a compassionate state, not an indifferent individual looking out for himself."

"We're not all evil fat cats, you know."

Hollande turned sideways to face him, leaning one elbow on the bar. "You're not?" The small smile suggested he was unconvinced. "Somewhere your servants sweat, but you're here, swanning about a long way away, drinking beer."

Mitsos matched the smile. "As are you. The difference, though, is that *I* earned the beer we're *both* drinking."

"Yeah, but I'm now wondering what this one is actually going to cost me."

Mitsos momentarily tensed, but managed a chuckle and a small shake of the head. "Am I that obvious? Don't worry, Georges, I have no ulterior motive. I just saw you and fancied some company, since I've had no success getting anyone else to talk to me. These Hibernians are a dull and unresponsive lot."

Hollande's sharp smile gentled slightly. "Okay, then. You might as well join me. Got a couple of comrades waiting." He straightened, plucked his glass from the bar, and set off towards the back. After a pause, Mitsos collected his drink and followed.

Two men sat at a table by the back wall, one Black, one white. They looked up at Mitsos with unfriendly eyes.

"This is Babatunde and Jacques," said Hollande. "From the *Leviathan*. Comrades, this is Mr Mitsos – also from the ship."

Babatunde scowled. "He's not one of us. Is this wise?"

"What are we going to talk about that we haven't already? Until we get instructions, we've said all we can. Mitsos is bored and so am I."

Mitsos waited for Hollande to take one of the two vacant chairs at the table, then with an ingratiating smile at the seated men, he claimed the last. "Please, call me Eddard. And don't worry, I'm just here for a diversion. I'm also waiting."

"Waiting for what?" asked Jacques, who was in his late twenties, with close-cropped hair, a lumpen nose, and an NS tattoo on the back of the hand that clasped his beer glass.

"Insight? An invitation? Opportunity? Or absent any of this, the next ship back to Earth."

"Long wait then," said Jacques.

"So, what exactly is your business, Mitsos?" asked Hollande. "You've not said."

Mitsos instinctively reached a hand for the inner jacket pocket where the pen drive resided on which all his hopes depended. He managed to halt his hand's movement and redirect it to his glass, which he gently twirled. "I… make things. To order. Just about anything. I thought the people here might be open to business, but…" he shrugged and gave a pained smile, "there are only around half-a-dozen manufacturers in the city, and they seem completely uninterested. Four said *no thanks* before I got in the door. The two I got a chance to meet seemed to think I was crazy."

"If you make things on Earth, you are crazy," said Babatunde, who was a large man with a soft voice. "How are you going to get anything here?"

"Well, true, if I was planning on importing. But I was rather thinking of setting up a new branch here."

"So much for the workers sweating at your factories back home," muttered Hollande. "How are they going to benefit?"

"Life's complicated, but success here would mean more profit."

"For you."

"For my company," corrected Mitsos, carefully. "And that translates as better prospects for everyone."

Hollande grunted but chose not to respond.

"I don't get it," said Jacques. "Why would anyone let you set up a new factory here? They got nothing for you to build with. Where would the machines come from? And whatever you want to make, why can't they make it themselves?"

"All good questions, Jacques. What I have is a template. A *design*." How much did he dare say? His secret was one he didn't have any right to know and even less to sell. Industrial espionage was a serious crime: any attempt at patenting the illicitly hacked process back on Earth would quickly illuminate his guilt as brightly as a supernova – given his firm's small size and lack of research labs, and thus inability to prove provenance of the idea. In truth, he didn't know whether the promising experimental results would work to scale, particularly in Tethys' environment, but it had seemed one last chance to revive his fortunes…

"Design?" said Jacques.

Mitsos noticed the three staring at him intently, and realised that he'd faltered. He gave a wry smile and suddenly thought: *why the hell not?* "Yes, design. It's for a machine that can extract some of the key elements this world is missing from seawater."

Hollande laughed. "Philosopher's stone? If something sounds too good to be true, it almost certainly is. No wonder nobody wanted to meet you."

Babatunde also laughed. "Yeah, if this existed, we would have heard of it before on Earth. *Crazy.*"

Mitsos was irked; he had to take a deep breath to keep himself calm. "It's a prototype, so that's why no one's heard of it. And on Earth, it's not necessary or even economic. There's no shortage of the elements it can extract, either underground or in the asteroid belt. But here it might just be worth it."

"Prototype?" smirked Hollande. "I know what that means. It means something that looks good on paper, but after billions in R-and-D leads nowhere. I started a PhD in materials science in Zurich, so I've seen how universities and businesses throw money away on flights of fancy while the poor still suffer and the homeless freeze on winter streets."

Mitsos steeled his eyes, but managed to control his voice. "I understand what you are saying. But let me assure you, this is more than a piece of theory. The blueprints I have are for a machine that has been shown to work, and not just in a laboratory. *Proven* to work. There are patents pending…" *Just not for him.*

Jacques hadn't laughed. "So… what would it take to build this machine of yours? It would have to be big to sieve a lot of water."

"Another materials science drop-out?" Mitsos couldn't help himself, casting a glance at Hollande and winking.

"No. Physics. Doctorate actually. Spent time at CERN, then decided there was more to life than trying to make sense of numbers on screens. We're not as dumb as you think, Mitsos. Babatunde's an engineer, so if he's laughing, I'm not impressed."

"Forgive my cynicism. My mood has been coloured by the people I've been talking to the last few days."

"Managers?" sneered Jacques. "Accountants?"

Mitsos tilted his head and furrowed his brow. "Yeah. Probably. Businessmen. People with an eye on easy profit." He threw a glance at Hollande, and noted the other twitch. "Certainly not people with *vision*. Maybe not the *right* people?"

"So – how big?" repeated Jacques.

"Ah? Oh… big, sure, yet at the same time, surprisingly small. It would need a major power source, but power generation is not the problem on Tethys. Their cities' fusion reactors give more than enough for the peoples' needs. The control system could probably just about fit in this bar. And it's less a sieve than a molecular-sized net. It would be huge in area but –"

"Not in volume." Jacques sat back and nodded to himself.

"You sound like you are taking him seriously," said Hollande, suddenly intent.

"No. I'm just curious. But if what he has *does* work, it would be a game changer, no?"

"I still think he is crazy," said Babatunde, but with less confidence than before. "But, yeah, it would give an edge. And whoever controlled it could dictate terms. The world wouldn't be in hock to the Hibernian capitalists. Perhaps it wouldn't harm to look into this a little further?"

Mitsos shook his head slowly. "Well, I never expected to find fellow visionaries in a bar rather than a boardroom. I'm happy to talk to anyone, whether from *Hibernia*… or *Marseilles*?"

Jacques turned to Hollande. "Maybe we should introduce him to Jons? At least it'll give us something new to talk about while we wait for our pick-up."

Mitsos noticed the beer in front of him – as yet untouched – and lifted it to his lips to hide his smile.

* * *

Mitsos had been invited to a second round of drinks at O'Brien's, but not a third, as a number of others had begun to trickle into the bar –

some of whom he'd recognised from the *Leviathan's* shuttle – Hollande had decided that he was hindering the group's discussion of important matters, and quietly but firmly suggested it was time for him to leave. Mitsos had been more than happy to go, finding the political discussions a drag. But he'd left his contact details, and been assured that Hollande would get in touch in the near future to discuss business matters.

A day had passed, and then a second. By the third day, Mitsos had just about given up on the *Marseilles* connection, and was considering booking a flight to the *Bremen*, when his personal communicator signalled that he had a message. His first thought was that the gruff official he'd met on arrival had at last made good on his threat to bring him in for further interrogation, but he was relieved to find a flashing avatar of the old Soviet hammer and sickle. It was Hollande with a time and place.

The venue was an elegant building in the Derry Quarter, part of a small terrace with porches held up by somewhat innocuous columns, which reminded him of a time when he'd walked through parts of London while on a business trip. In keeping with the old-world theme, there was no electronic panel on the door and he had to use a heavy door knocker to thump out news of his arrival. After some seconds, the door was opened by Jacques. The other's expression was firm: "Come in," he said, brusquely.

He was led to a lounge off the main corridor, the furnishing sparse but neat. Inside, he found three others, scattered about the room on sofas and chairs that were upholstered in red. He recognised Hollande and Babatunde, but not the third – a man of medium height with a sharp black Van Dyke and hair that seemed to shine in the soft light of the room's small chandelier.

Hollande rose from his seat. "Mitsos. I'd like to introduce you to the ambassador from the *Marseilles*, Asher Jons. This is his embassy. I have told him everything you told us about your supposed wonder machine."

Jons sat in a plush chair, his elbows resting on its arms, his hands steepled before him. He made no move to rise and greet the newcomer. "Welcome, Mr Mitsos. Please find a seat."

Mitsos smiled quickly at the other, then allowed himself to be shown to a spare chair next to Hollande: Jacques stood at the doorway, leaning against the frame with arms folded. "Nice place," he said, once seated. "Regency? Neo-classical? I was never much good with architecture."

Jons didn't immediately respond, but continued to appraise Mitsos with sharp eyes. At last he said: "On Tethys, our news is always behind. But in *Marseilles*, we make a point of keeping as fully informed as possible. Geopolitical events. Social trends. Scientific advances. We always ensure that our invited guests bring with them full updates. Gigabytes. Terabytes. Knowledge is power, eh?"

Mitsos frowned. "I am pleased to hear it. But what –"

"What am I trying to say?" Jons clasped and unclasped his steepled fingers, then slowly lowered them into his lap. "I am saying that between Messrs Hollande, Danté and Odile, plus our other new comrades, we have a full imprint of the Official Global Wikipedia from the day the *Leviathan* left, plus copies of all sorts of other commercial and technical databases. And I have spent much of the last two days trying to find out *exactly* who you are."

"Very thorough." Mitsos locked eyes with the other. "And did you find anything?"

"Oh, yes. I found out that you have a single factory in South East Europe with about forty employees. I found out that your company is leveraged to the hilt and that you have had difficulty paying your debts. And I found no evidence of you having any research capacity whatsoever. Interesting, eh?"

Mitsos maintained eye contact. "Intriguing."

"Indeed. So, I thought, how on earth might you come upon this miracle machine that you claim to possess? And so I looked further. And I found out that you have family in the US, including a brother who works in a far more substantial enterprise with a research budget that exceeds your company's nominal value manyfold."

"You found my brother, Raki? That's great news. I don't suppose you have his number?"

Jons' lips curled into a lopsided grin. "Indeed, I do! But so do you. In any case, it's not hard to fill in the blanks from here."

Mitsos at last broke eye contact with the other, and sat back in his chair. He looked down, then up again, and smiled. "I guess you got me. So… did you invite me along just to *out* me? That seems somewhat gratuitous, and frankly a waste of both our time."

Jons paused again and ran his eyes over his guest's face. "You're right. I don't like wasting time. Fortunately for you, what my research into the activities of this major company did reveal was something else of interest. One of its research programme's is indeed on the topic of concern. One of my associates was able to find some research presentations, shareholder reports, and patent applications, which together suggest that they *do* have something of the nature you describe. And they also suggest that the program was on the verge of being cancelled for lack of clear financial benefits."

"As I said to your minions the other day: on Earth, the economics don't work. But maybe here?"

Jons nodded. "Yes, maybe here. *Maybe.* But it would be a risk. Resources are scant, and you would need a lot of what we have, and probably some of what we don't, just to build your prototype device."

Mitsos' smile was now genuine. "Life is risk, Mr Jons. How far are you willing to go for what could be a… what was it you said in the bar?" Mitsos looked at Babatunde. "A game changer?"

Babatunde nodded, but didn't speak. Jons chewed on his bottom lip, causing his Van Dyke beard to oscillate, as if attempting to point at Mitsos. Then Jons announced: "Mr Mitsos, you are a thief, but perhaps not a fraud. I don't care about that. Desperate people sometimes do desperate things. But this is beyond my authority. Something so large could only be approved by the First Citizen and the People's Committee. Do you fancy a trip to the *Marseilles*?"

Mitsos had stiffened at being called a thief, even though he knew it was true. But the offer more than made up for the insult. "You know what, Mr Jons? I'd love nothing more than to leave this tedious place. But…" he now raised one finger in warning. "You need to remember that I am a businessman, first and foremost. I am happy to come to your ship… city… I still don't know what to call it. But if we are ultimately to deal, you must accept that I will need to be appropriately compensated."

Jons laughed. "A true capitalist! Do not worry, Mr Mitsos, *if* you can persuade the First Citizen, and *if* your machine can be made to work, then we will be suitably grateful. Let us leave these negotiations to a more appropriate time, eh? Jacques… break out the vodka!"

Chapter 7

Kate Lockard had forgotten about school during their voyage from Earth. Or at least, she had buried it so deep in her mind that when the topic was raised on arrival at the *Lisboa* it had completely thrown her, like opening the curtains of her old home in Durban and expecting to see sunshine, but instead finding some foul monster leering at her through the nu-glass window. It wasn't that she was afraid of learning – far from it – but rather that she hated the ludicrous constraint of formal education. She wanted to read *what* she wanted *when* she wanted, and tread whatever path her inquisitive mind directed her, rather than be forced along a well-worn, arrow-straight highway, marching in step with many uninterested and limping peers.

"It'll be a chance for you to meet others of your cohort," her mother had claimed, ushering her out of the front door of their cosy new apartment aboard the *Lisboa* on her first day, a week-and-a-half ago. "Absorb the culture. Make some friends."

And she had.

Lessons were over for the day: Sara Velasquez and Tonio Janeiro settled to either side of Kate like a pair of bodyguards.

"What now?" asked Sara, a tall, thin girl with dark eyes and black hair. "The Bowl?"

"Not again," said Tonio, with something of a groan, peering around Kate at the other girl. He was a short, dark boy with chestnut-coloured hair, a round face, and full lips. "You're obsessed."

"Well, Kate likes it too."

"She liked it yesterday, and the day before yesterday, and the day before that. She'll get tired before long. Stop using her as an excuse."

Kate laughed and held out her hands as though to separate her new friends. "Okay. Enough! It's true – the Bowl is great. We've nothing like it on Earth. But variety is the spice of life. Where do you want to go, Tonio?"

"Me? Ah…"

"As I thought," said Sara, her wide mouth curving into a mischievous smile. "He doesn't know. He doesn't have an alternative. He's just trying to be awkward."

"That's not true. We could go to, ah, the Terrace…"

"Where all the losers go?"

"Isn't that what they all call *us*?" asked Kate.

Sara and Tonio were outliers: though the bulk of the class weren't actually unfriendly towards them – and none had been unkind to Kate since her introduction – they were seen as somewhat odd. Kate's addition to their club of two had come about more by chance than design, as she'd been seated on the back row of the classroom next to the pair on her very first day, then compelled to do a couple of group assignments with them.

"They're just jealous," said Sara. "They're afraid of our unconventional brilliance. It scares them. I feel sorry for them more than anything. But I don't really want to hang around with them. And nor do you, Tonio. Or is it because Vita?"

"No! Just… don't go there."

Kate winced slightly: Sara had previously alerted her that Tonio had something of a crush on Vita Fernandez. Unfortunately, so did most of the boys in the class. It wasn't that Vita was especially pretty (though she was far from unattractive), but rather that she had this astonishing confidence and an almost saintly demeanour: she never said a bad word about anyone, and had a tendency to greet everyone, no matter how unprepossessing, with a wide smile and cheerful words, as though they were a long-lost and much-loved friend. She was going to be a real man-killer, and certain of high office in politics one day. "Our future queen", Sara had admitted to Kate a couple of days ago.

"Exactly," said Sara. "Let's not *go there*. So, *not* the Terrace. And if not The Bowl, then where?"

Tonio shook his head gently, and then sighed. "Alright. But tomorrow, something different, or else I'm going to the Arcade alone."

"Fair enough." Sara linked arms with Kate, who was of a similar height – both being a head taller than the boy. "Let's go."

The school occupied a small arc of buildings on the sixth floor off the central well of the *Lisboa*, which from above looked like a giant coliseum around an arena floor of a communal park, with an inlet down the middle that led beneath the stern section and acted as a small harbour for pleasure craft. Forward of the ship's circular body was a smaller bulbous control section that in Kate's view looked like the head of a sea creature, and indeed, the impression of a giant sea turtle was confirmed by two long arms that curved out from the nexus of 'head' and 'body' and looked like flippers.

The little group headed downwards, their destination in the lowest part of the ship beneath the control hub. An elevator took them to sea level, disgorging them into a wide atrium that was busy with children heading home after school and workers knocking off after their day's toil. Sara skipped ahead, wending through the denizens and their shadows.

Kate had to hustle to keep up. She heard Tonio behind her mutter the word 'addiction', and nodded to herself. "Sara… slow down!" She quickly lost sight of the other, although she knew where she was headed.

The door to the service corridor was situated between a hairdressers and an electronic repair shop. It was painted green and unlabelled. Sara waited outside. On seeing the others, she smirked, turned, and opened the door, which had swung closed by the time Kate reached it. There was more cursing from Tonio. Kate entered, and found herself in a dimly lit corridor, with piping along one wall and various electronic junction boxes evenly spaced along the other. "I'm not going to run!" she yelled.

"Let her go," said Tonio. "I've already done my exercise for the day. Bloody circuits."

Kate winced at the word. The gym was more vertical than horizontal, taking advantage of the elevation of the school, set in a narrow space that fell all the way to the first level, with ramps, ropes, ledges, and all sorts of obstructions and trials to raise the heart rate and stretch the muscles. Like Tonio, she was beginning to feel the consequences of their earlier session. But there was little scope for Sara to evade them: the corridor wasn't especially long and ended in a circular stairwell. Kate took this, heading down below sea level.

After a few turns she came to the bottom of the well, and was met with another green-painted door, this one with flaking paint and a bowed indentation above the handle. It wasn't locked and swung back easily.

The chamber was low and ill-lit – with just a single strip of white light along the left edge of the ceiling. Around the walls, racks held indistinct boxes and bits of machinery. The door they'd used was clearly not the main entrance: Kate could just make out a set of double doors in the opposite wall, fifteen metres away, which she knew were locked. She felt Tonio at her side, and the pair linked arms and edged towards the centre of the room, from the floor of which sparkles of light flickered in a range of colours. Just four steps forwards the floor dropped, and with the change of viewing angle, the number of lights increased. A long blue light processed across the far side of the hemispherical floor recess, then dimmed and elided into black.

At the foot of the eight-metre-wide bowl, Sara was splayed, face down as was her custom. Kate and Tonio slipped onto their bottoms next to each other, their legs dangling over the curving edge. For a moment, there was silence, and then Sara exclaimed: "Ooooh!"

Kate noticed a greenish cloud ascend from somewhere beneath them: it oscillated and grew, leaving Sara's silhouette like a dark cut out in the green.

"Sea cloud," muttered Tonio. "Small one. Bit of a surprise."

"Why?" asked Kate.

"We're on the move and they prefer still waters. The fishing booms must be up, as they can't cope with that degree of turbulence."

Kate nodded gently at this: she'd leant that on the forward edge of the *Lisboa's* sea-turtle arms, thin nets were sometimes spooled out from booms to catch the ship's food as the craft moved through the ocean, while at other times, great rotating threshers were deployed that churned up sea foliage for similar purposes. On the rear aspect of the arms, slipways held other working craft: fishing vessels and research and exploration ships.

The glowing cloud slid along the bottom of the transparent bowl and then under the pair's feet and away from view. Sara pushed up slightly and adjusted her head to follow the shape, but once it was gone, she settled back into her original pose.

"You've got to admit, that was cool," said Kate.

"Sure," said Tonio, reluctantly. "I'm not saying it's not. And, yeah, I like it here too. It's just, you know, a change –"

"…is as good as a rest?" completed Kate.

A sliver of white light picked out the tip of Tonio's nose and a cheekbone as he turned to Kate. "Yeah, that's right. You've been here less than two weeks. Give it another month or two and then you'll know how I feel."

"I'm not sure I could ever get tired of this…" Kate waved a hand, and on cue, a glittering nebula of small, red-and-orange creatures swirled beneath them, then condensed and dissolved into the depths below. "It's like the night sky, but it *moves*. I'm just surprised this place is so hidden. Does no one else know about it?"

"Well, it's not the only place like this. You know there's a big public bowl, don't you?"

"Yeah, Mum told me, but we've not had time to see it. She says it's got rings of seats and table service and… well, it doesn't sound as *intimate* as this. We have this all to ourselves."

Tonio paused a moment then ventured: "Your mum? You've not told her about –?"

"God, no! Don't worry. It's our secret."

Tonio nodded in the dark, but said nothing.

They sat in silence for another twenty minutes, Sara so engrossed she ignored her friends completely. The sea life continued to roll across the great lens of their underwater observatory, but only sporadically, with whole minutes passing with nothing but black emptiness. It had been like this on their four previous visits since Kate had been inducted into Sara and Tonio's club, and apparently this was nothing compared to what they might see when the ship was at rest.

At last Kate said: "So… do you know when we're going to stop? When it's going to get *really* interesting?"

"No idea," said Tonio. "I think we're heading for a particular patch of sea forest between here and the Range. Dad said it's somewhere the scientists have identified as potentially interesting. Maybe your mum will know what it's all about. You should ask –"

"Whoa!" said Sara, suddenly jerking upwards. "That's… that's…"

Kate looked towards her unsettled friend, then did a double take, and found herself lifting her legs instinctively. Something moved beneath them – something that was somehow darker than the water itself, and large. Then, just beyond Sara, a giant white orb rose from the gloom, as big as the girl herself. The giant eye hovered for several seconds, unblinking, as whatever creature it belonged to matched the speed of the *Lisboa*, and then something long and tentacular rasped across the bottom of the bowl, apparently questing for the girl above. But after the desultory and unsuccessful inspection, the limb sank along with the eye until it was lost in the void.

"What the hell was that?" said Kate.

Tonio exhaled, while Sara recovered her composure and let out a nervous laugh.

"I've not seen anything *that* big," said Sara, "since…"

"Since *ever*," finished Tonio.

Sara sat back on her haunches in the foot of the bowl a moment longer, then she rose to her feet and scrambled up the sloping dip of the hemisphere.

"Well, that's the stuff of nightmares," said Kate. "You okay, Sara?"

The girl smiled, putting on a brave face. But when Tonio suggested they leave five minutes later, she didn't object.

* * *

Marie Lockard had had a busy two weeks since arriving on the *Lisboa*. For much of that time, she'd been locked in a desperate struggle with bureaucrats who'd wanted to clarify who she was, what she was doing, and why they should support her and her daughter. But after two days, they'd been found a home and were able to move out of temporary accommodation to apartment number 157.4 (representing its degrees around the coliseum from the stern centre line) on the fourth floor, alas with an internal-facing aspect. And a day after that, she'd seen Kate enrolled in the ship's only school. Aside from this, she'd been led on various tours around the giant craft and been introduced to dozens of new people, including every member of staff at the Lisboa Research Centre, as well as quite a few senior administrators, politicians, and even celebrities.

The one thing that had rapidly become clear to Marie was that Professor Miguel Figueroa was not just a quietly spoken academic but a figure of real significance. Unfortunately, her new boss' status meant that he was much in demand and difficult to pin down. After showing Marie to her office space and leaving her under the wing of his deputy, Dr Katerina Kalmik, Figueroa had disappeared for several days. With Kalmik also busy, Marie had been introduced to the main research database and essentially told to update herself on the team's various projects – which was precisely what she had done. Most of her time had been spent with Luisa Teixeira, with whom she shared the office, who'd kindly acceded to being remorselessly battered with questions.

The next time she met Figueroa, it had been that morning, when he'd suddenly appeared at the door to Marie's shared office.

"Luisa, and dear Marie, I have escaped. Time for some fun. I'll see you on the *Fortunata* in an hour."

And so here she was, seated in one rather worn cabin on a bench at a polycarbonate table that was affixed to the floor. Light speared into the small space through portholes in the wall behind her, illuminating Miguel Figueroa and Katerina Kalmik sitting across from her. There were currently eight others aboard, but these were engaged with piloting and running the ship, taking inventories, checking dive equipment, calibrating scientific instruments, and so on.

"At last! I am truly sorry, Marie, that this has taken so long. But you arrived just as we made some exciting discoveries, and we have been dealing with the consequences of this."

"I read about the new kelp analogue you discovered. Is that it?"

"Yes, indeed. It seems to have some useful properties, but more exciting is the prospect of a new ecosystem to study. Life begets life, so new life begets new life. I'd much rather have spent the last few days out at the forest, but instead we've been requesting access to Tethys' small suite of satellites to try to map out the extent of this new submarine flora."

"Map out?" Marie frowned. "How?"

"We discovered that it has a slightly different signature to the more familiar species when observed from space through infrared. Some good work by Luisa there. And as we are currently on the move, we wanted to see if there were any similar patches between here and the

Hibernia's demesne that we can take in *en route*… and I'm pleased to say there is. So, though we can't hang about here – we'll log the location and do what research we can over the next two-or-three weeks – I am happy to report that we're heading for another prime prospect, which happens to fringe another of the black cenotes."

"So, you've been negotiating our route with the captain?"

"With Joao Nascimento, the Captain-Governor, yes."

Marie gave her head a slight shake. "I am still trying to get used to the hierarchy here. Captain-Governor? The little man I met – he's captain *and* governor?"

"That's right," said Kalmik, joining the discussion. "At least, that's his title. He doesn't physically captain the ship, but he holds that nominal title. It's certainly up to him where we head, and he has a ceremonial seat in the bridge beside the operational captain."

"Okay. And… Professor, you were able to influence where we are heading next? I'm surprised the ship's master indulges you so much. I mean, indulges the scientists."

Figueroa looked momentarily startled, then his wizened face twisted into a gentle smile. "Ah, of course, you are from Earth. You must remember, things work differently here. You need to think, what is the purpose of this place; of the *Lisboa*; of all the great ships?"

"I don't get you. What do you mean by *purpose*?"

"I mean purpose. Reason. The existential question. Why are we here? What are we doing on Tethys?"

"Ah, I see. I can't really answer. I guess the ships are just places where people live – people who have come here for various reasons because they prefer it to anywhere else. I don't know if that answers your question."

Figueroa nodded slowly. "In its vagueness – it does. Marie, these ships are simply places for people to live, to have a life. A good life. As good a life as they can get. And the ships can pretty much go wherever they please on this world. We are not tied down – it is material resources we lack on Tethys, not energy ones. Our fusion engines use heavy water in minute quantities to create huge power. Our only restriction is to be close to the Range when *Hibernia* allows us to take our periodic turn at mining some extra resources. Beyond that, where do we go? Sitting still seems a shame. So who better to direct where we go than people who *do* have a purpose?"

"The ship's scientists? You?"

"Of course."

"But it's more than just that," said Kalmik, leaning in and resting a hand on Figueroa's arm. "We're more significant than it appears – even if Miguel is too modest to say. We are the premier resource of the *Lisboa*."

"Premier?" responded Figueroa, shyly.

"Yes, premier. We're a point of difference between the *Lisboa* and most of the other ships. We are a critical resource on this ship, or at least, the knowledge we provide and the findings we uncover are. I mean, look at our discovery of this new species of kelp. It's got nutritional advantages over other types. If we can identify where it is most likely to be found, we can trade this knowledge to others. What else is there to barter? Fish? *Water?*" She laughed. "No. When we speak… when Miguel speaks… and says: *Captain-Governor, I'd quite like to go to this spot eight hundred kilometres away…* the Captain just nods and changes course. If nothing comes of the diversion, so what? We've 'wasted' a little time that would have been 'wasted' anyway."

Marie smiled and shook her head. "It's like a research funder issuing you with a blank cheque."

"Not quite." Figueroa wagged a cautionary finger. "While we may have unlimited travel expenses, what we don't have is a blank cheque for *consumables* or *staff*. We haven't the resources to build a fleet of research vessels, or equip a dozen more laboratories, or recruit a hundred top scientists from Earth. We must still husband what we have – and that is why we are delighted that you decided to join us."

"Yes, especially after last time," Kalmik muttered, peering at one wall as if looking towards someone beyond.

"Now, Katrina, not so harsh. Marco has his uses."

Marie looked between the two and spoke quietly. "I know Marco is from Earth. You recruited him a couple of years ago, right? I have sensed some tensions. Is there anything I should know?"

"Yes," replied Kalmik. "He's a useless prick."

Figueroa frowned. "Katerina…"

"Well, not entirely then. He's just about able to swab the deck – if you can get him to come onto it."

"He is also a good data analyst."

"Sure, Miguel, but he wasn't hired to stay in a lab back on the mothership and play with numbers. We've got plenty of others who can do that just as well as he can, including some of the students. We wanted a field researcher who could help us gather material and observations – not someone who gets seasick and is so afraid of shadows in the water that if we go down in a storm, he'll probably choose to sink with the *Fortunata* than swim for safety."

"I'm surprised you recruited him," said Marie.

"Ah, yes," said Figueroa, "we perhaps should have interrogated him more thoroughly."

Kalmik snorted. "You make it sound as though it's our fault. No. His CV was highly embellished."

Figueroa shook his head. "No, Katerina, not *highly*. He had an impressive publication record, though it is true that he was not the first author on many of the papers. And he *does* have field experience of sorts."

"In the Mediterranean and North Sea? Yeah, very testing environments!"

"We asked the wrong questions and then misinterpreted the answers, because the latest ship was about to leave Earth and we wanted to make sure we had someone aboard it before the Captain-Governor changed his mind."

Kalmik folded her arms and shook her head, clearly having decided to say no more on the matter.

"These things happen," ventured Marie, her eyes flicking between the others. "I could also tell tales of past failings in recruitment. Though I see why in your case it's more significant. I just hope that *I* don't let you down."

"I'm sure you won't!" said Figueroa, although Kalmik – still clearly disgruntled – chose to reserve judgment.

* * *

"We'll go in here," said Kalmik. She smiled at Marie with her mouth, though not with her eyes. "Time for you to prove your worth."

Marie had already suited up: her drysuit was turquoise in colour, with bright orange bands to aid her visibility to others. She had a small but heavy tank on her back holding compressed air, which supplied its content via a hose to a full helmet that contained communication equipment. Aside from this, she wore a belt that held a small knife and collection bag.

As Marie wriggled the helmet to ensure a comfortable fit, Kalmik's voice came to her ears: "All good? As they say, *one-two*, *one-two*…"

Marie looked back up, noticing that Kalmik had acquired an earpiece. "Yes, I can hear you."

"Ditto. Okay – remember your briefing. Raul, Mike and Victoria are already in. They're doing the real work. Nothing fancy for you today – we just want you to get used to the equipment and the environment. Don't go too far into the forest, or too deep. But you do have a sample bag, so if you want to take a cutting, or spot anything else interesting, collect it and bring it back up."

"Got it."

"You've enough air for a couple of hours, but I want you up after half-an-hour. I've programmed a warning to pop up on the HUD inside your faceplate: don't ignore it. You can come back before then if you get spooked, but I'll be severely disappointed if you do."

"Not going to happen," said Marie. Then she looked down into the water a couple of metres below her dangling legs between her flippers. They were positioned right by the edge of the sea forest, with pale blue water directly underneath the boat, and a dark green-black line a couple of strokes ahead of her. She took a deep breath and slid into the water.

The suit was well insulated, so Marie didn't get the shock she sometimes experienced when wearing a wetsuit and dropping into cold water. Indeed, the water temperature was difficult to gauge, given that she wore gloves and her face was entirely encased. She immediately bent forwards so that she was looking down: the water about was clear for some metres, and initially seemed empty… until she realised that a small shadow down and to her right was actually a school of 'fish', about ten centimetres long, pale blue in colour and beautifully camouflaged against the water. The realisation made her wince and instinctively draw into something of a ball: *what else is there that I can't see?*

The motion spooked the school, which became clearer as the score of fish within jerked aside and then jetted off in formation. She didn't get a clear view of their physical form, but had the vague impression of dorsal and pectoral fins, two eyes, and a narrow mouth beneath. *Parallel evolution indeed!*

"Still okay down there?" It was Kalmik.

"Yes. Just getting my bearings."

"Okay, but don't stay in the open too long. The forest is much safer."

Marie quickly looked about to ensure that there was nothing else close by, then she straightened and kicked towards the wall of foliage ahead. From above, this had seemed dark, but from below the waves, with sunlight spearing into the water, the colour was much brighter, a golden-green hue. The long stalks, which reached from the surface to some unseen depth, were regularly spaced, perhaps a metre from thin trunk to thin trunk. Leaves were thickly clustered along the trunks, and reached out to fill the space between the separate kelp analogues. Marie instantly noticed that there seemed to be two types of leaf along each trunk – wider, oval-shaped leaves, which spread out as if basking in the intruding sunlight, and then narrower leaves, like writhing green tentacles. She suddenly became aware that there was other motile life among the stalks besides herself – noticing a number of small, needle-like creatures, which darted in and out of the leaves, clearly trying to peck at the trunks. These had got through in one place close by, rupturing the surface of a plant, which exuded a thick green goo that was clearly the prize on offer: other creatures then dove into the breach, fed, and backed out again with a circling motion of pectoral fins. But then one of the creatures got too close to a knot of the writhing leaves – which snapped out. The tiny fish was caught, wrapped up like a mummy, and squeezed until it ceased to move.

"Not defenceless after all," muttered Marie to herself. She paused a moment, then drew the small knife at her belt. It would be difficult to catch one of the small fish without a net, but the plant had helped: she carefully sliced, and brought away the small package of leaf-encased fish. As she did so, several of the defenders tried to wrap around her hand and wrist, but they didn't have the strength to defeat a bigger foe. She opened the sampling bag tied to her belt and inserted her trophy.

Marie soon lost all sense of time. She loved being in the water; it was the field work that she treasured most in her job. And the environment wasn't completely unfamiliar to her: she'd done dives in the past in the Great African Sea Forest, a stretch of giant bamboo kelp that spread north from Cape Town to the Namibian coastline. And the lifeforms here, though unusual, weren't so different from Terrestrial creatures: they seemed to have roughly similar morphologies; they filled similar predator-prey niches. Still, she ensured she followed the instructions she had been given: she didn't venture so far into the forest that she couldn't see its edge, nor did she descend very far, and certainly not to the base of the forest however deep that might be. And when she saw something that seemed slightly unusual – a growth on a stem; a small creature living between fronds – she carefully collected it and transferred it to her pouch.

When a red light began to wink a time warning to the right of her faceplate, she grimaced with disappointment. "*Damn*. Already?" She made her way back to the surface.

"How was your first dive in an alien ocean?" asked Figueroa, greeting Marie from near the top of the ladder. Kalmik was also there: she took Marie's extended arm and helped hoist her aboard.

"Fantastic. A real buzz."

"So nothing *scary*?" Kalmik spoke in a rising voice; as she did so, her eyes suddenly shifted elsewhere. Marie followed the other's gaze and saw Marco Grande loitering a few metres further along the deck. "Or maybe," continued Kalmik, "it's just that you've actually got a bit of *backbone*?" At this, Marco turned abruptly and headed for a door to the interior.

Marie frowned at the man's retreating back. "I… suppose it's just experience. I admit, I wet myself during my first free swim with Great Whites. But the unknown can be unsettling for anyone, especially first time."

"That it can," said Figueroa, looking between the women and then off to where Marco had gone. "Nevertheless, well done. Now – let's see what you've collected."

"Sure thing."

As Marie handed her sample bag to the professor, Kalmik clapped a hand on her shoulder and leant in to whisper. "Well, you've passed the first test. But sterner ones will come."

Marie's expression firmed. "Bring them on," she hissed in return. Then she started after Figueroa, who was eagerly ferrying her samples towards the main cabin.

Chapter 8

"*Here*," said Anders Pedersen. "Do you see?"

Rennie Heiko leant forwards to inspect the knot of cables. They were in a narrow service corridor in one of the sub-surface levels of the *Stavanger*. "It's been stripped," he said. "*Selectively*. But surely this should have been noticed before? Why aren't maintenance staff dealing with it already?"

"They probably don't know about it. The thieves aren't idiots – they know as much about the ship's circuitry as the state electricians. These wires could be linked to some back-up system, or something not well used. Maybe fire alarms? It might not be discovered until something that desperately needs to work *doesn't*, and then the shit hits the fan."

"So they know the circuits as well as the experts? Occam's razor implies that they may be one and the same. Inside job?"

Pedersen ran a hand through his short, fair hair. "Possibly. Or retired electricians, supplementing their state pensions."

"You talk in the plural. So, it's not a single prolific thief. How many are we looking at – and are they organised? Does *Stavanger* have crime gangs?"

Pedersen absently brushed some dust off his blue uniform; Heiko wore a similar one, which had been made for him a week ago. "That is unclear. We've never had a significant crime problem: we've even got a reputation among the ships for being strait-laced and law-abiding. Apart from some cannabis production in sub-level two – which we've always known about, and allowed, because it's contained and never led to any other issues – we've had nothing systematic since the hull was laid down. We've just had random, one-off events – the occasional drunken fight or crime of passion. That was until about four years ago, when theft of metals and electronic components became more obvious. It's getting troubling now, especially given recent events, but…" He shrugged.

"But you've not come across a *name*?"

"Huh?"

"Organisations have names. People need to know how to identify themselves as part of one clique and different from another. And with a name comes a hierarchy, rules, sometimes a uniform of sorts. If you can't give me a name, even from a rumour, that suggests we're not looking at an actual gang. *Yet.*"

"Yes, that makes sense. But… why 'yet'? You don't think…?"

"I do. If there are a number of people doing this, sooner or later they are going to come into contact with each other. Compete. *Coalesce.* Maybe then become greater than the sum of their parts. And at that point, they could threaten the security of this place, just as much as any external threat." Heiko looked towards the far end of the dingy corridor. *Oppressive.* "Let's get out of here and find somewhere we can talk tactics."

"With coffee?"

"Of course."

They retraced the way to the door they'd used to enter the corridor, then took some stairs to the sea level floor. Following Heiko's instruction to take him somewhere new, Pedersen led the way to a bank of lifts and selected the uppermost button in the first that arrived. After a short ride up, they disembarked into an annexe, then turned down one broad corridor lined with small retail outlets. At the end was a glass double door, which Pedersen pushed through, bringing them onto an open deck, sprinkled with small round tables sheltering under red-and-white striped parasols. A railing marked the edge of the platform, with an open-fronted café off to one side.

"Nice," said Heiko. "Shall we take a table by the edge?"

They were soon seated and attended by a waiter. Then, while Pedersen went inside to access a terminal from which he could report the theft to the appropriate maintenance department, Heiko studied his surroundings. It was a bright, warm day, and an intermittent breeze occasionally caused the parasols to shift and tip. From his chair, Heiko was able to see Mount Ardol in the mid distance; and some metres below, beyond various out-jutting levels, including a wider platform three floors down which hosted a couple more café-restaurants, was the wide, pale-blue sea.

The waiter was the first to return, with two cups of coffee: strong black for Heiko, foamy for his colleague. Heiko didn't realise Pedersen was back until his deputy declared: "It's done."

"Thanks."

As Pedersen sat, he declared: "This place is called the Aviary. No local birds, of course, but it's got a couple of cages of parrots inside."

"I expect the prices are as elevated as the aspect."

"Of course." Pedersen flicked a brief smile. "But we're on expenses, eh? You wanted somewhere new."

"Oh, I wasn't posting any judgment. Just a hypothesis. Is this where the masters of the ship come for a drink?"

"Yes. And food. The restaurant inside is reckoned one of the best in the city."

"City?" Heiko looked momentarily surprised. "I am still having trouble parsing what this place really is. From this table, looking around and down, it's clear we're on a ship, even though there is no sense of movement. Same in the service corridor. But I have occasionally found myself uncertain. And this place is clearly different from the *Hibernia*: I was only there for a couple of days, but within half-an-hour of landing I was happy to define *that* as a city."

"Don't worry. It's difficult for us too sometimes. People often use the words 'city' and 'ship' interchangeably – except on the *Hibernia*, where they tend to be quite dogmatic about the difference. Worse, they see themselves as a nation, and the rest of us as vagabonds. It helps them feel special."

Heiko took his first sip of coffee, then a second. "I don't know how much this is costing our expenses pot, but it's worth it. Best I've had on Tethys."

"Told you."

Heiko took another sip before reluctantly lowering his cup. "It probably won't look good if we're seen relaxing here in work hours, but I needed to see this place. And pretty much everywhere else on board, from the high to the low. I've got a lot to catch up on here. You're *Stavanger* born and bred, right? Ever been anywhere else?"

Pedersen lowered his own cup. "Not off-planet. Done a couple of sabbaticals, that's all. So the ship is pretty much my entire world. And it's not a big one. We've a population of around thirty thousand and a footprint – when you take into account that we live across decks, unlike Terrestrial cities – of somewhere like Monaco. I think you'll learn what you need to know soon enough." He took another taste of coffee and looked over the cup's rim. "By the end of the year, you might find yourself yearning for wider horizons."

"Maybe. But maybe I'll fit in. Become like you."

Pedersen didn't answer, and merely returned an enigmatic smile.

After a moment, Heiko realised he would get no more. "Okay. Let's talk shop. First, how did you know the wiring had been stripped in that corridor? It was the first one you took me to. Is it a frequent target for thieves?"

"No. I just got lucky. The second, third and fourth sub-levels are a maze of corridors, junctions, and small control rooms. There are literally miles of corridor, but there's no point in visiting most of it. The Service Department keep schematics, but even its staff are unfamiliar with some areas. And before you ask, no, we don't have camera coverage: we'd need too many, which would take valuable resources to make, and as I said, pilfering has not been a problem until relatively recently."

"Okay. Have you caught anyone yet? I'm assuming you must have had some success."

Pedersen's expression soured; he shook his head.

"No one? What about the thieves' networks? Fences? Buyers? They've got to exchange their loot to profit from it."

Pedersen shifted in his seat and looked away. "No. I think… I think that may be part of the reason why Cass decided to *retire.* As I said, we're not talking huge losses, but Moroni… I mean, *the Premier…* I know she hasn't been happy."

"You're suggesting he was asked to go? I've only spoken to him twice now – he seems confident. Competent. I guess first impressions can be deceiving."

Pedersen shrugged. "He's not incompetent. Great at community policing and seen as having safe hands. The random crimes I mentioned – they've all been dealt with professionally. I don't want to diss the boss. But these thefts have been frustrating for all of us. We're a small force, underequipped precisely because we're seldom needed. In *Hibernia*, they have real crime and they're actually needed, but even there they moan about under-resourcing."

Heiko toyed with his coffee cup. He wanted another sip, but that would hasten its end, and then he might have to propose further denuding limited police resources in order to get another. "So you decided to try a fresh approach? To recruit from outside?" He peered at his deputy. "How do you feel about my arrival, Anders? Were you expecting to slip into Cass' shoes?"

Pedersen pretended indifference; to Heiko, his body language told a different story to his words. "Nah. I'm content with my role."

Heiko nodded slowly. "Okay. But I'm still somewhat confused as to why *I* was hired. I'm not a policeman or a detective. My past roles have been more to do with personal and national security. But external threats to the *Stavanger* don't appear high on the agenda, unless there's more going on than people are telling me. Had I been you, I think I would have looked at someone used to running a big city police department."

"Your choice was a bit of a surprise to some of us." Pedersen smiled with his mouth only. "As you say, you're not a detective. You're something else. Something *more.*"

Heiko frowned and invited the other to continue with a look.

"Maybe your unusual past excited the recruiters, who were looking for something *different.*" Pedersen touched the side of his own eye. "You have this. I still don't understand what it is and what it allows you to do."

Heiko touched the copper-coloured implant at the side of his left eye and smiled wryly. "Here? Possibly not much. It's an interface between certain implanted systems and external aids." And it was only the most visible of his augmentations, although he had no desire to elaborate on the fulness of these. It was always good to have an edge. "More specifically, I've a processor in my brain linked to my visual and cognitive systems. The interface allows me to upload information from specialised battle systems. When linked – if I close my eyes to reduce interference from visual stimuli – I can see battle maps and simulations, updating in real-time. It's useful for a squad or platoon commander... or even, I suppose, a company commander." He raised both hands. "But outside the dedicated force?"

"That's all?" Pedersen seemed surprised. "Are you saying it's useless here?"

"Perhaps not entirely. But some adaptations would be needed to enable me to interface with whatever information systems you have, and these would also need to be adapted to produce output that my implant could make sense of. I'm sure you have the personnel to do this, but it's hardly a priority at the moment, is it?"

Pedersen frowned in thought, and eventually shook his head.

Heiko nodded to himself. There was no need to mention his adrenal gland stimulator and the fast-twitch muscle fibre adaptations he'd acquired from his time in the Finnish Special Forces. He'd given the other sufficient to think about for now; still, it would be best if he wasn't allowed to dwell on these matters. "Anyway, Anders, it's time to be concrete. These thefts: let's think about how we can thwart them and run down the perpetrators…"

* * *

Heiko's one-bed studio apartment lay off a small courtyard on the eighth level. This shared communal space had a trio of fine coniferous trees beneath a transparent ceiling, which was sufficiently high up the ship's superstructure to be retractable. For around two hours of the day, when Tethys' star was at its zenith, the roof opened allowing sunlight to directly play off the leaves of the trees. Rain was also allowed to breach the structure – to be absorbed by the trees and gravelled floor – as long as it wasn't too heavy; when it was, a sensor ordered the roof to close.

The problem for Heiko was that this relative luxury was invariably wasted on him: he was at his office for ten hours a day, so missed the chance to sit at one of the benches beneath the trees and bathe in the sun's natural warmth. Other than that, he was content with his accommodation – reputedly spacious and well-positioned for the ship, befitting his high status. And though he'd not formally met any of his neighbours from the square, he had received cheerful greetings on a number of occasions from the smart people who lived there as they hurried past to unseen destinations, which left him hopeful that he might ultimately find a social partner or two.

In the meantime, Heiko had been left to make his own entertainment in the evenings. Not being especially taken by the limited fare on the ship's 3D network, with its years'-old re-runs of Earth shows – plus the occasional soap opera recorded in the planet's only studios on *Hibernia* – he'd systematically started at the top of the ship and moved down, sampling every bar and eatery he could, though eschewing the nightclubs, gaming parlours, and handful of small theatres until he had exhausted all the easy options. The one trend he had noticed so far was that prices dropped significantly from one level to the next, while the ambient noise in the bars and cafés increased conversely.

This evening he found himself in Geilo – a wide plaza he'd passed through on his first day on the *Stavanger* en route to his new office. There was a 'steak' restaurant here – serving vat-grown protein, appropriately shaped and flavoured – and a pasta restaurant. There was also a small gaming parlour, a couple of retail outlets, a food stall selling kebab-like wraps, and several bars. The place was modestly busy, with competing music spilling from several of the venues, which – like most places on the ship – were open-fronted, with retractable glass walls. Then he spotted Bjorn's Castle – announced by a luminous sign showing a bear with a beer glass in one paw, with its other wrapped around a stone tower – and he recalled that this was meant to be a regular venue of the Material Resources team. He passed between a couple of tables, and at the faux-wood bar ordered himself a small beer, then he sat on a barstool to observe the clientele. A lot of the people around were dressed in uniforms and jumpsuits of various colours and styles, clearly having come straight from work, and some were already loud and boisterous.

He'd finished half his beer by the time he swivelled on his stool to check out the deep, low-lit interior of the bar, and was then surprised to see a familiar face. He picked up his drink and wended through tables to one that was set against the wall. A woman was there, dressed in a russet, one-piece uniform that was covered in wide pockets. She had short-cropped hair and a small tattoo in the shape of a trident diagonally above one eyebrow. On the table before her were two plates – one empty, the other with a few bread crusts –

along with a near-full glass of beer, and a tablet on which she was intently focused.

"So, this *is* your regular haunt," said Heiko. "Mind if I join you?"

Melissa De Voe looked up in surprise. "Mr Heiko. Well, it's taken you a couple of weeks, but you've made it at last. Sure. Grab a seat. Makka was here earlier – maybe his seat will still be warm."

Heiko settled at the table. They were in a pool of shadow, mid-way between two bright-yellow wall lanterns. "Thanks. But I'm not disturbing you, am I? Still working?"

"Always working. Makka is such a tyrant." She smiled, pushed away the tablet, and grasped her beer. "Only joking. The tyrant is really his wife. We were in the middle of discussing a drilling program when he got the call to come home. His son was being difficult or something, and she wanted to land the pain on him since we're back to Ardol tomorrow."

"A family man? But not you?"

"Not now. Too much to do. You the same? You came from Earth alone."

"Ah… yes and no. I had a family when I was young. They now have their own lives."

"So work is your mistress now?"

"Well, I've got to do something with my time."

"And wasn't there enough for you to do on Earth?" De Voe seemed amused. "I find that hard to believe."

"Earth has a lot of everything – good and bad. And sometimes the bad outweighs the good."

"That's pessimistic. How bad is it there? We know nothing down here, but the *Leviathan* going up clearly wasn't a good sign."

"It's just one of the Earth's periodic phases of mass psychosis. Everyone fearful and envious of everyone else. Politicians trying to exploit matters and making things worse. Too many people pushing too hard, meaning something has to give. A few years out of the madhouse seemed a nice remedy."

"Still, I do kind of envy you. The home world. Different oceans. More geology." She tipped her glass. "Wider variety of beer."

"You're pure *Stavanger*, right?"

"Sure. Never been anywhere else. Ever."

"Still, you have a strong community here, I guess. I admit, it's the one aspect of all this that has worried me – about entering a closed society. About what your people might think of newcomers like me taking over."

"Well, we do have a small gene pool *and* skills pool. So we've no choice at times. Long live diversity, I say. Problem?"

"Not really. But a couple of days ago I was talking to Anders, my deputy, and couldn't help but detect a degree of resentment. I suspect he wanted Cass' leather chair."

"I understand. I've been there. I've been Anders."

"What do you mean? You're a deputy too, aren't you? To Frost. Are you saying…?"

"Yep. He's also an import. New Zealand. Can't you tell from the accent? Listen to him talking about the *fush* in the ocean. It still cracks me up."

Heiko shrugged. The *Stavanger* had been bankrolled by the immense Norwegian Sovereign Wealth Fund and populated by Nordic types, so he generally felt comfortable given his origins, and perhaps that was why the accents of the people had not really registered with him. "Are you saying you harboured resentment when Frost arrived?"

"Perhaps a bit. But that was some time ago and I had no expectations then of being supremo, so in the end it wasn't a big issue. It also helped that Makka is a personable guy who didn't throw his weight around. It was also obvious that he knew his business."

Heiko's face crinkled into a smile. "Are you implicitly accusing me of being heavy-handed and inept?"

De Voe threw back her head and laughed, a surprisingly deep-throated sound. "Oh, no. Haven't you heard – I don't do subtlety. If I think you're a moron, I'm going to say it straight. In your case, the jury's still out. I'm not aware of any fuck ups you've made yet, which is a decent start. But let's see, eh?"

"I do wonder how much time I have. It seems that things have been slipping over the last couple of years. I'm not sure how long I'll be given before I'm judged inadequate."

De Voe arched an eyebrow. "You're concerned? You don't seem the type to be fazed by circumstance."

"Thank you. In my own mind, I agree. But I do like to do a good job. It's a core construct for me."

"Well, I'm happy to help in any way I can, though I'm not sure how."

"I think you can help me out right now." Heiko's smile returned. "You see, I'm not here solely for pleasure."

"Really?" De Voe smirked and gestured towards his beer.

"Really. I have set myself the task of *knowing* this place, it's every nook and cranny, from every angle. I'm officially off the clock, so I'll drink as much as I please… but I am moving through this level systematically. My plans are to finish this drink and move on. And that's where you can help."

"A pub crawl?" De Voe laughed again. "You want me to lead you on a pub crawl?"

"Yes. I want you to show me as many places as you can, and tell me as much about them as you can. Who drinks there. What are their quirks. Whether they're sources of trouble. And so on."

"And you're buying, eh?"

"Yes. Me personally. I've decided to keep off the expense account from now on. What do you say?"

"I say, I hope you've got a good liver and a decent supply of alcohol flushes to hand, or I'm going to be carrying you back to your apartment later, and you're going to look very unprofessional when you stagger into your office tomorrow morning."

Heiko smiled broadly now. "I don't think you need to worry about these things. I have a surprisingly robust liver. Drink up, then. Where are we heading next?"

* * *

"Good morning, Melissa." Frost smiled broadly at De Voe as she threw her holdall on the skiff's deck and then slumped into a seat next to him. "Bad morning, good night, or maybe a bit of both?"

"Smartarse." De Voe leant forwards and addressed their pilot. "Let's go, Serge." Then she turned back to Frost. "A *but* of both." She parodied her superior's accent, although in truth his pronunciation had never been so harsh, and it was barely detectable after years away from his homeland. "I met Rennie Heiko. Helped show him around. He can certainly hold his drink. I suspect he's had some weird Earth bioengineering done to his liver."

"*Thut's* clearly the only *pussible* answer if he *busted* you." This time Frost exaggerated his own Kiwi pronunciation.

De Voe laughed in appreciation, but the conversation on the short ride to Mount Ardol quickly subsided as the woman attempted to come to terms with her hangover.

On dry land, the two split: De Voe went to her small cabin to drop off her bag before finding the site foreman to discuss progress, while Frost headed to a larger hut that served as his office and the control centre of the mining operation.

In truth, Frost's presence wasn't critical. The site could be run just as well by De Voe, or even by Sven Ibsen, the foreman. After all, ninety percent of what they did was simply scraping, crushing, and loading. But Frost liked to be on solid ground; on countless times past, he'd wondered how he'd gotten to be where he was now – a geologist in about the only place in the known universe with no geology. Or at least, no *accessible* geology. And that meant he had to make the most of any chance to indulge his primary passion whenever *Stavanger* had the license to stock up on material supplies, which was once every two years.

On Frost's field desk in his hut was material related to the ten percent of their activities where he *could* make a contribution: a stratigraphic survey of Mount Ardol and the rest of the Range. The table held rock samples and printouts of findings from experimental drilling, as well as his portable computer – which he now switched on – which cast a three-dimensional projection of the subsurface geology, with its various strata picked out in different colours. What this showed was a complex structure of bands of varying widths with a number of fault-lines, with the strata tilted and curved in places as a consequence of past geological processes.

"What now… what now…" he murmured softly to himself. He reviewed the projection, then turned to look at various printouts, pondering where to strike next.

* * *

Eight days later, Frost stood in a small bowl of land several hundred metres away from the main mining operation and about ten metres above sea level. "All systems go?"

A short distance away, Sven Ibsen, the main site foreman, stood beside a control panel on the side of the *Stavanger's* only working drilling rig – a slim machine about four metres tall. Two more team members – in hard hats and russet work clothes – busied themselves by a portable generator that fed power to the drill.

Ibsen turned and gave the thumbs up. He then pressed a large red button and the noise of grinding rock and rotating machinery split the quiet.

"This might have to be the last one," said De Voe, leaning in to Frost to be heard. "We're running out of drill bits, and the rig needs some serious maintenance – new bearings and a ton of grease."

"I hear you," said Frost. "The lack of a second rig is killing us."

"Sure – it's a fatal lack of redundancy. Rennie made the same point about our shuttles. Maybe we shouldn't have broken the spare last time we were here."

"You make it sound like we were culpable," Frost shouted, "but it was age that took it."

"Try explaining that to Moroni."

"I did. I have. Countless times." Moroni had taken the financial reins of *Stavanger* a year ago, and she'd proven to be a tough negotiator. "But she's a sceptic about what we're doing here."

"And what are we doing here, boss?" De Voe's smile was wicked. "Looking for resources? Or solving a puzzle for personal gratification?"

"Why can't it be for both?" His deputy knew him too well – and perhaps so did Moroni. Maybe De Voe would be better at making a convincing case than him, bereft of the guilt he undoubtedly oozed during these occasions?

De Voe patted him on the shoulder. "Well, I've other things to do. *Productive* things."

Frost shook his head as he watched her go, swinging a hard hat from its chin strap.

After a moment's thought, he turned to head back to the main site. It would take a while for the drill to produce the new samples that'd enable him to update his models.

In fact, Frost became so engrossed in examining palaeontological samples in his hut, that he lost track of time altogether and forgot about the latest drill. Decrypting traces of long-dead Tethyn creatures was another of his interests, and so he'd been overjoyed when, on a previous cycle, they'd found a sixty-three million year old sandstone stratum containing an abundance of fossils, both marine and terrestrial. Ever since, he'd used every new visit to Ardol to expand the small dig – a short distance from their present location – to gain new samples. What he really yearned to discover was evidence of something land-dwelling that was *dinosauresque*, yet to date the best he'd found was a couple of small bones hinting at a creature the size of a cat. It could be that large terrestrial lifeforms had never formed on Tethys, given the relatively short time that evolution had been given to work on air-breathers during the occasional periods when planetary water levels had fallen enough to uncover significant land masses, but then again, there *could* still be evidence of real leviathans out there. He just needed the opportunity to do a proper excavation, rather than relying on his own efforts, occasionally abetted by De Voe's. But he knew that Moroni, and most of his team, would baulk at expending more resources on this sideshow.

It was late afternoon when he was brought out of his trance by the sounds of a motorised cart pulling up outside his hut. Frost paused a moment, with a fossil in one hand and a magnifying glass in the other, then he gently set these down atop the sheet of paper on which he had been drawing. He rose, paced to the door, and opened it. Outside, the tall foreman and one of his team were wriggling a heavy tray off the back of the cart. Within this were half-a-dozen cylindrical core samples, about a metre long, stacked side-by-side. Frost took a step forwards to help, then paused, turned, and hurried back inside. After rapidly clearing space on his sturdy camp table, he reached the door in time to allow the pair to sidle in and gently lower the tray onto the table.

"One more," said Ibsen.

Frost held the door open until the pair retrieved a second loaded tray, which they manhandled inside and set on the table next to the first.

"Thanks, Sven," said Frost.

"No problem. We dismantling the rig now?"

Frost looked at the samples and chewed his bottom lip. Had De Voe been here he might have been swayed, but… "No, not yet. There's no rush. You can do it tomorrow."

Ibsen frowned. "Right. Your call." He followed his colleague out of the door.

Frost turned his attention to the two trays. Ibsen had written numbers on the sides of the these with arrows, showing the relative depths of the different samples. He had a proper lab back on the *Stavanger* with an MRI scanner, where he could do a full characterisation of the different grains and pore fluids. Right now, he was mainly interested in what the different layers said about the stratigraphy of this part of Ardol, and for that, the microscope here would do.

He soon classified the upper layers from the first tray and added data to his overall topographical model. Then he turned to the second tray, containing materials from deeper in the earth. Here, he came across evidence of new strata, where the land had been tilted around forty degrees, making new beds accessible to their drilling. And then he spotted something in the last core to the far right of the box. He brushed this down and peered more closely. After a moment's thought, he found his small hammer and tapped away, removing a small sample. As he picked this up and examined it close to his eye, his excitement began to grow.

"Fuck me," he muttered.

He strode to the door, flung it open, and continued outside. A suntanned woman in a hard hat was nearby, holding a piece of piping in one hand. "Karin?" He rushed up to her. "Can you do me a favour? Can you go get Melissa. Sven, too. Ask them to come here pronto."

"Sure boss."

"Thanks."

Frost stood watching the woman as she headed towards the main mining site. As he did so, he muttered to himself once more: "*Fuck me.*"

* * *

"The geology of the Range is a mixed bag," said Frost. "The mountains superficially look volcanic, but they're not. No craters, you see. But much of the upper parts *are* igneous – the rock formed from cooling lava from volcanic eruptions in the past."

Heiko had been strolling on the main concourse of Level Six when he'd been accosted by an excited Makka Frost, who'd suggested that they head for a nearby refectory, which was where they now sat, nursing coffees. "So, where are the volcanoes then?"

"The ones that spewed the lava? We think there was a chain about forty miles to the south-west, now under a couple hundred metres of water. Anyway, geological processes have over many years tilted and scoured the landscape, so we've been left with what you see now. But the thing is, there are sedimentary strata beneath the igneous rock layers."

Heiko saw Frost's expectant look; he was sorry to disappoint. "Okay. And that's significant, is it?"

Frost smiled gently. "Well, it is in the sense that it implies Tethys once had major land masses, and that its igneous and metamorphic rocks were subjected to weathering processes by wind, water, and so on. Over time, sea levels have risen considerably and buried these strata – probably as a result of global warming. After all, there are no ice sheets on the planet, and we suspect that once there were."

"I am sure you are going somewhere with this, but I never did study geography or geology at school, so your teasers are lost on me."

"Sorry, Rennie. All I'm saying is that Mount Ardol has a range of rock types and so there's always been a possibility of finding something useful. Sedimentary rocks are important, because the metals we are desperately seeking are often found in what are called placer deposits. This is where you get an accumulation of minerals formed by gravity separation from a specific source rock during sedimentary processes. In short, denser sediments get left behind after some flow process – like a stream running – and they become concentrated."

"Right. And by 'denser' I'm guessing you mean things like metals?"

"Yes. Heavy metals. Rare earths." Frost clasped his hands together. "Now, most of our mining efforts just involve scraping away and pummelling the surface rock for building material. But we also drill down to sample the different strata layers just to see what's there. And so we've found different sedimentary layers in the past, but until now, nothing especially interesting. Sandstones mostly." He hunched forwards. "But guess what? Yesterday, we drilled into something a little bit different. Here, let me show you." He turned around and swung the satchel that had been hanging off the back of his chair around into his lap. Opening this, he rummaged about and produced a transparent bag, which he tossed onto the table.

Heiko picked up the bag. It contained several small rocks that were dark in colour but speckled with a lighter material. He'd fleetingly felt excitement, wondering whether Frost was going to uncover a nugget of gold, but this was… "Just rock? Am I missing something?"

"Well, yes and no, my friend. It's not just rock. It's black sand – and black sand can be suggestive of a placer formation."

"The type of deposit you've been looking for?" Heiko undid the seal of the bag and removed one lump. He tapped it on the table: it was hard. "So – you said 'indicates'? Is it, or isn't it? And if it is from one of these deposits, does this rock contain anything of use?"

Now Frost leant back and clasped his hands behind his head. "As to that, I'll know more in a couple of days. Melissa is overseeing the prospect, digging deeper and bring out more samples, and I've come back to use the lab to analyse the composition of this." He nodded at the sample on the table.

Heiko's mouth twitched into a smile – then almost instantly transformed into a frown. He hunched forwards, slid the piece of rock back into the bag, and then steepled his fingers over it, masking it from general view. He quickly glanced around the refectory, and was relieved to find that they hadn't attracted any particular attention. "Makka – why did you come to *me* with this news?"

"You... ah!" Frost unclasped his hands and leant forwards – unsettled by Heiko's frown. "I was... you were... just the first person I saw. I wanted to tell someone, and by luck it was you. Why?"

"You have something here that is potentially of great importance. I think maybe you should keep this news to yourself for now – and then let me know what you find. Can you do your analysis without alerting anyone else in your team or on the ship?"

"I can, yes." Frost began to look about as well, and then stole his hands forwards on the table so they could receive the package cupped by the security chief. "I guess there's no need to raise false hopes, eh?"

Heiko nodded, then forced a smile and pushed over the sample.

False hopes.

It was only later that he understood how that phrase reflected Frost's misunderstanding of the situation. But that was not the worst of his own errors – for it wasn't only Frost he should have spoken to about the need for caution.

Chapter 9

"Your wonder device has attracted interest," said Asher Jons, gently stroking his severe Van Dyke beard. His eyes twinkled with humour. "Our shuttle will come in six days' time to collect you and others from the *Leviathan*. Please be ready to depart then."

"I am ready to depart now!" said Mitsos. He currently sat on the bed of his tiny hotel room; Jons' face filled the screen of a terminal resting on a side table. "In fact, I was ready some time ago. Another week? Is the ship that far away?"

"Distance is not the issue, Mr Mitsos. Indeed, the *Marseilles* is relatively near, since we are due to take station off Mount Ardol in a few months' time to scrape away some meagre rock…" – Jons' face had darkened into a sneer – "…a *generous* allowance by the would-be masters of Tethys. No, the issue is our unreliable shuttle."

"I'm not sure I like the sounds of that. Is it held together with glue? Am I to risk a fiery or watery death en-route?"

"No. The unreliability is not quite as it seems."

"A deception?"

Jons frowned and appeared to look somewhere just off screen. When he looked back he said quietly: "This is a secure connection. Communications technology is something at which we surprisingly excel – or at least, it would be surprising to the Hibernians if they knew. Their own surveillance methods are lumpen and clumsy, but I do not wish to put them to the test. They might have bugged your room, but their tech is so ancient that this is unlikely. Indeed, the chambermaid swept your room for bugs this morning, when you went out for breakfast."

"Chambermaid?"

"There are many underprivileged people in this metropolis who sympathise with our politics. But as I was saying, we do not want to be too brazen in our discussions. The authorities are watching my associates ever-more closely, and I do not want to risk drawing further attention to our relationship by having you come to the embassy again."

"I hadn't realised Tethys was such a hotbed of activity. I thought I'd left all that shit behind on Earth."

Jons smiled. "Wherever there are humans, Mr Mitsos, there is competition. Inequality. *Strife*. If there is a heaven, I am sure God is tearing his platinum hair out having to separate the factions of the 'saved' from each other, and probably from the angels, too. There may be nectar for all – but who gets it first? Who is most favoured by the Lord's presence at dinner? Whose harps have the purest notes?"

"You're a philosopher, Ambassador."

"No. Merely a realist."

Mitsos gently shook his head. "Didn't Milton write a poem about it? *Paradise Fucked Up?* Is there anything I need to do before the pick-up?"

"Pay your bills. Keep a low profile. Do not approach any other manufacturer in the city. Do not discuss your project. And do not go again to O'Brien's or seek out the company of my comrades. You can access the shuttle schedule on your room's system. Arrive at the spaceport a couple of hours before the shuttle is due to give Security sufficient time to annoy and distract you. And provided your visa is in order, follow directions to the craft – your name will be on the passenger list."

"That sounds straightforward enough."

Jons nodded and cut the connection.

It was only later, when he looked at his electronic visa, that Mitsos remembered he'd had a temporary bar put on it, preventing him from leaving *Hibernia*. He'd not had any communication with the authorities since his meeting with the officer he'd been rude to. "Idiot!" he hissed to himself.

Should he contact Jons again to warn him and get further advice? In the end, he decided to settle the matter himself, and put in a call to the appropriate government department.

* * *

A bank of cloud obscured the sun, while a cool wind rippled the Hibernian flag – comprising two large, white stars on a green field – that flew from a flagpole above Nesvorny. The Head of Internal

Security was alone on the small platform atop the command and control centre of the old ship – one of the tallest points on *Hibernia* – with just a thin rail separating him from a sheer fall into a street several hundred metres below. From this point, he looked out towards the old stern, in which direction the ship's superstructure had been completely reshaped: parts had been repurposed and extended, and others dismantled and rebuilt in stone rather than metal. That zone was more clearly city than ship, but *in toto* it reflected the schizophrenic nature of the state. And by moving around the rim – circling the stairwell in the centre of the platform – he gained a full three-sixty view of his domain. He was able to see the two main docks, the governmental edifice on which the platform was perched, the gleaming glass of Charlestown, and the elegant neo-classical architecture of the diplomatic quarter. It was a grand reminder of his responsibility, and it was a perfect place to come and think. Sometimes he'd bring up a camp chair and a bottle of triple-distilled 'Irish' whisky – produced in the deeply buried comestibles deck that spread beneath his feet towards the port side of the old ship. But that was when he had more time to plan; today, he'd recently left an awkward meeting with the ruling triumvirate and had desperately needed to get some air.

But he'd not been present long, when his peace was interrupted.

"Sir – I was told you were here."

"Major Fukuda – you are invading my meditational space. Either you have so much spare time on your hands, you can afford to waste it coming up here, or you have something important to tell." Nesvorny smiled, leant back against the railing, and folded his arms across his chest. "I'll wager the latter."

Fukuda grimaced: the positioning of his superior meant he had to stand in the centre of the small platform; he seemed not to know what to do with his arms. "Not very important, but maybe interesting enough. We've had communication from a man called Eddard Mitsos, who was on the *Leviathan*. Apparently, you put a restriction on his visa. He wants this lifted so that he can leave." Fukuda edged over to the railing so that he, too, could lean. Nesvorny was forced to turn slightly to keep him in focus. "Given that you assigned me to watch the incomers, I was wondering why you did this, and whether there is anything I should know."

Nesvorny was momentarily surprised. "Mitsos? Ah, I remember. He is some sort of businessman. In truth, it was because he annoyed me. I put a sanction on about a dozen arrivals who had no clear plans for their stay in *Hibernia*, or no set idea about when they would move on. I did look into a few of them, but found nothing suspicious, and frankly didn't expect to. If this Mitsos wants to leave our realm, all the better. I have no particular desire to fence with him again. He can go."

Fukuda nodded. "So… not a major issue, then? Very well: I'll authorise the removal of the visa restriction."

But as Fukuda gently pushed away from the railing to leave, Nesvorny raised a hand to stall him. "Wait. As a matter of interest, do you know where he plans to go?"

"Ah, this is why it seemed to me the matter might be significant. I thought maybe you had linked him to the New Socialists. He plans to go to the *Marseilles*."

"The *Marseilles*?" Nesvorny's face scrunched into a frown. "I recall he claimed to be a cross between a tourist and a businessman. Now, neither of those creatures have anything to gain by going to the *Marseilles*. He'll have a miserable time on a ship full of people who are likely to scorn him and his ilk. *Interesting*." *Maybe I terminated my research prematurely?* "And that reminds me – what of the NS cabal? They would have left a couple of weeks ago if it weren't for the state of the *Marseilles'* decrepit shuttle. I asked you to watch them, but you've said nothing for days."

Fukuda stiffened. "I've said nothing, sir, as there is no news. I installed a listening device in O'Briens – their HQ – as you commanded. The first one glitched. I thought the second had, too, but then it started working, though it's recorded nothing so far except bar talk, mostly from locals. It's not a great environment for making sensitive recordings."

"I hope you didn't leave matters there."

"Of course not, sir. I had the entrance watched by one officer, but there were too many targets to follow and it wasn't clear who is important."

"Then you should have allocated more officers."

Fukuda's face twisted into a dangerous smile. "I did. I now have cameras installed and watched by officers emplaced in cafés to either side of the street near that bar, so that they can follow separate groups or individuals who leave in different directions."

Nesvorny nodded. Fukuda *was* good, though he hated to say this aloud. "As I would have done. And you're saying that you still haven't uncovered any suspicious activities?"

"Oh, they look suspicious – all of them, all of the time. They seem aware that they may be under observation. And so they go nowhere interesting and say nothing of interest. Their conversations, when my officers have been able to capture them, are anodyne. Mundane. Often involving juvenile politics."

"Do you think we need to continue surveillance?"

"Continue… and enhance. The *Marseilles* has now logged a flight plan for their shuttle to arrive in five days – hence Mitsos' request. That still gives them time to slip up."

Nesvorny looked down, troubled. What could they be up to that might threaten *Hibernia*? He looked up quickly. "Have they been to the Engine Quarter?"

Fukuda expression turned sly. "They have assiduously avoided it. Perhaps our only way to truly find out what they are doing is to pull some in for interrogation. Or – if you think that will alert them, and they'll have well-rehearsed stories – take down one of them without warning for, ah, *rigorous and informal* questioning."

Nesvorny's expression soured. On Earth, he'd been involved in the rendition of terrorist suspects. He wasn't a squeamish man, though some of the activities he'd been involved in had seemed unnecessarily brutal to him. "No, not yet. Not until we have actual evidence that something is going on."

"Like disappearing into the Engine Quarter for some hours without due cause?"

"Yes. That would be sufficient."

"And what about Mitsos? Have you changed your mind?"

Nesvorny still couldn't see Mitsos as a revolutionary. "No. Go ahead and authorise his visa change. But between now and then, I want you to pay more attention to him and his association with the others."

"I will."

* * *

"That door," said the manager of the Crown Hostel, pointing to the end of a corridor on the ground floor. "The stairs go down to Level Minus One. Take them, then follow the directions on your tablet." He about turned and headed back to the reception area.

Georges Hollande did as instructed, emerging from a cramped stairwell into a narrow corridor with dim strip lighting along the ceiling that cast a yellowish glow. The walls and floor were metal, unlike the stone of the hostel, a reminder that this had originally been a gigantic ship that had been altered above the waterline with materials mined from the Range, but which retained its true identity underneath. He considered the tablet in his hands: this showed a schematic of the level, with a blinking arrow indicating the direction he was meant to take. He turned left and set off.

Hollande had learned much about *Hibernia* since he'd arrived – his research directed by the hostel manager and the ambassador, Asher Jons. He knew, for example, that the network of corridors was vast and infested the city ship. On this level, they connected to the hidden industrial and agricultural zones – that spread from beneath the main docks – to the fusion plant towards the ship's stern; they also led to the hidden ghetto beneath the Engine Quarter – which was like an iceberg, its dirty and ill-kept manifestation above ground being but a part of its entirety, with most of its hidden population living in converted space down to Level Minus Four many metres below the waterline. The first subsurface level corridors also led to storage and function rooms in other basements – such as that of the building Hollande had been instructed to find, which lay in the Cork Quarter at the very edge of the Engine Quarter.

The corridors still hosted utilities for the city, with pipework and cables running along walls, as well as occasional junction boxes with winking lights. There were plenty of doors, too, though a fair number were grimy and clearly out of use. Some doors had the traditional wheel mechanism found in ships, while others had been replaced with more conventional handles, and some even had camera pads to allow those inside to look at visitors to decide whether they might be admitted or not. It was the latter type that tended to be named and numbered, sometimes in softly glowing neon lights: Consort Hotel; Baltimore Foods; Vanities (a personal grooming place?); Trattoria Rustica. As for the floors, these were flat and straight, without the step-overs Hollande associated with bulkhead doors, although every junction he came across seemed to have recessed portals, set within wide grooves, which he supposed could be activated to seal off an area in case of an exterior breach.

At first, Hollande imagined he was completely alone, but then he started to hear noises – the odd voice or banging of metal. Then he reached the end of a corridor, and found a wider junction. As he turned right, following his electronic instructions, he startled at the sight of a pair of men heading towards him – indistinct at first, then rapidly resolving. They walked abreast – for this corridor was wide enough to allow it – and each pushed a cart holding several plastic boxes with angular logos. The men looked at him with unfriendly eyes as he squeezed back against the wall to let them pass. And soon after, he came across a woman in an all-black jumpsuit, with a bulky electronic device tucked under one elbow, marching purposefully; she didn't even look at him.

From the wide corridor, Hollande took a left at a crossroads and soon after, another right into a narrower corridor, the lighting of which was glitching and inconsistent. He hadn't gone far down this, when a figure appeared out of the shadows. "Make way!"

Hollande had nowhere to go, so he again flattened himself against the wall. But it wasn't just one person this time: an unshaven man in a green jumpsuit with a torn front pocket was merely the vanguard: behind him were a dozen others, all in similar garb, and some only children. The man muttered an expletive as he squeezed past, as did one or two others, while someone grabbed at his groin and laughed, and then he felt a hand tug at his tablet, which he only just retained by tightening his grip. Then they were past. *Stokers?*

Twenty metres along the corridor, in the right wall, he found his target. The door here had no handle, but it did have a camera pad.

On the lintel was the number 115 in glowing blue. He pressed a call button below the camera, but nothing happened. After some seconds, he pressed it twice more. At last a voice came through. "Name?"

"Georges Hollande. I'm here –" But before he could finish, he heard a click, and the door started to swing back.

"Close the door behind you," demanded the voice from the speaker. "Then take the stairs."

He was in a dingy annexe, small yet wider than that in the sublevel of the Crown. The stairs were metal and zig-zagged through an opening in the ceiling. Ascending, he found a landing and another door, which he paused at. It had no handle, but when he pushed, it swung back easily enough, and he emerged into a corridor with a bare metal floor. At the end, waiting, was Asher Jons – smartly dressed in a suit, looking elegant with his neatly trimmed beard.

"Hollande – this way." Jons turned and led him further down the corridor into an open antechamber. The lighting here was warm and yellow, though not especially bright. In the room there was one other, seated on a small sofa set against a wall with closed doors to either side. The man slowly rose to his feet.

"We may as well talk here – there is space enough," said Jons. "Hollande – this is Kai Dures. He is one of the leaders of the people the Hibernians insultingly refer to as 'Stokers'."

The other man laughed: "I don't bite. Come in!" He was tall and broad-shouldered, with intense green eyes and hair that was as long as Hollande's, though his was black and flowed freely rather than blond and tied in a ponytail. Like those in the corridor, Dures wore a green jumpsuit, this one old and ill-fitting, strained at the chest and shoulders. He held out a hand, which Hollande noticed was covered in tattoos – though before he could analyse them he found them eclipsed by his own hand.

"It's good to meet you," said Hollande.

"Sit!" commanded Dures, with the flourish of a hand, and then he slouched back onto a worn grey sofa he'd previously occupied.

There were two armchairs in the small square space, one of which Jons had already taken; Hollande settled into the other, and felt himself sink into the well-used upholstery. He glanced between the two men and waited.

Jons spoke first – turning to Dures. "Monsieur Hollande, as I was telling you, is one of the few to survive the *Leviathan*. His past marks him out as having leadership potential. Alas, none of those we'd originally marked for senior roles made it."

"And you said… just twenty four?"

"In total, yes. Still, that's nearly a third of our recruited complement, so we fared rather better than any other party on the starliner. Our issue now is how to move our pieces."

"Pieces?" Hollande tried to sit forwards, although the chair made this difficult. He was excited: he'd sensed from his previous discussions with the ambassador that he was being considered for higher duties, and this now confirmed it. "You mean us and… our friends?"

Dures smiled with his mouth, but his eyes were piercing and seemed to suggest an emotion other than amusement. "*Stokers*. You can say it. The label doesn't offend me."

Hollande nodded slowly, unclear of the sincerity of the invitation. "Okay. *Stokers*. But I'm not familiar with the plans – we were to gain instruction here, and we've so far had to be careful in what we say in case we are overheard."

Jons pursed his lips. "That's so. But here we can speak freely. Ask what you want."

Hollande accepted defeat by the chair and fell back into its embrace. "Okay. I was never clear on our relationship with the Stokers." He thought of the dingy aspect of the Engine Quarters, and the dishevelled people he saw in the corridor. "Are we… to help them get away? Are they coming to the *Marseilles*?"

Jons laughed at this. "Do you know how many of them there are? No. We would welcome them, of course, but our city is full, and we scarcely have the means to support our own. Kai and his people belong here. Rather than they come to the *Marseilles*, let's just say that the *Marseilles* will come to them. Or at least, we will come to *Hibernia*."

Dures looked stern and simply nodded. "This is our place as much as any of those rich who live in Charlestown and deprive us of our rights."

"And we from Earth?" asked Hollande. "We are to facilitate this *coming*, yes?"

"Of course, Georges," said Jons. "We are all brothers and sisters here, striving for a common cause. *Égalité.* And this means that those *who have* need to share with those *who have not.* The rich of *Hibernia* need to share with the poor. And the wealthy state of *Hibernia* itself needs to share with impoverished states such as *Marseilles.*"

"The intent is there," growled Dures. "But the means are still unclear to me. We had hoped that your party would act as a bridge, a catalyst, Hollande. But there are few of you, and you are already in the eye of the security apparatus. With the full complement from the *Leviathan* arriving without drama, it is likely that no one would have looked at you and wondered at your continued presence on *Hibernia.* But now?"

"It's true that the destruction of the *Leviathan* and loss of many of your colleagues is a setback," said Jons. "And that has meant that we've had to rethink our plans. As Kai says, you have become of interest to the authorities, and that is why I have waited so long to introduce you to him – to be sure that our watchers are distracted and we could come here unobserved. And this is also why most of your party will have to take the shuttle to the *Marseilles* when it arrives in a few days' time – or as many of you as will fit in its passenger compartment. But that won't be all, giving us an excuse for some of you to remain and await the next shuttle… one that will be delayed, and then delayed some more."

"So, I will stay here?"

"You will," said Dures.

"And Danté and Odile," said Jons. "You three have particular skills that the Stokers can use to prepare for the fight back. And when the time is right, your other colleagues will surreptitiously return, perhaps with some Marseillais… but that is a plan not yet well formed."

Hollande nodded. He knew precisely what skills the others meant – ones honed within radical organisations throughout Europe and elsewhere. Still, he smiled gently and asked with faux innocence: "Skills? I'm not sure which ones you mean."

Dures' eyes flashed. "Bomb-making will do… for starters."

* * *

The rain had come with a vengeance.

For most of his three-and-a-half weeks in *Hibernia*, Mitsos had been fortunate with the weather: not always warm, but always dry. This morning things had changed.

"Can the shuttle still fly in this?" he asked the spaceport officer. He currently waited in one of the port's two small departure lounges set aside for passengers. The officer looked up from her array of screens and frowned. "Of course. This is nothing. It will be here."

"Nothing? You're joking!"

The uniformed woman observed him coolly. She clearly wished he would go away. But after a moment, she sighed. "You're new. From the *Leviathan*? We're a world of water. Warm water evaporates into the atmosphere. It has to come down sometimes." She waved a hand towards the runway beyond the Perspex window-wall. "Today is one of those sometimes. This is a Grade Four. Once you've seen a Grade Five storm, then you can say you've seen some serious weather." As if on cue, a monumental crack of lighting split the sky, visible through the transparent roof and pounding water. A roar of thunder a moment later indicated that the storm was close. The woman smiled insincerely. "Is there anything else I can do for you?"

Mitsos was left dumbstruck: he shook his head. When the woman returned attention to her screens, he turned and walked to a seat in the nearest untenanted row in the lounge.

The weather, however, was clearly affecting the other passengers too. These clustered together at the farther side of the lounge, talking excitedly and gesturing at the drama outside. There were around a score of them, also bound for the *Marseilles*: his fellow passengers. Mitsos vaguely recognised a couple from O'Brien's bar, from a week ago, but he felt no great desire to talk to them. They were not really his type. And frankly, had they appreciated his capitalistic philosophy and hidden augmentations they would likely have thrown him outside into the deluge rather than engage with him. He wondered if they had been informed about his potential importance?

In spite of the officer's blasé assurance, the shuttle was delayed – by almost an Earth hour. It came down vertically onto the nearest landing pad, perhaps thirty metres from the edge of the terminal. By this time the storm had eased to a Grade Three, and the mere deluge lacked lightning.

The officer stood by the wide exit door, peering outside. Mitsos joined the other passengers in forming a semicircle around her. He noted that the shuttle appeared to have four main engines, which rotated on axles to direct its thrust, all presently pointed towards the ground. Aside from this, the craft seemed to comprise a bulbous lower section with a slim section above, along which was a line of porthole windows. As he watched, a ramp lowered from the rear of the craft, meeting the partially flooded runway between giant rear wheels. As soon as it touched, a small vehicle raced from some hidden warehouse in a cloud of spray and slid into the shuttle's hold. After a couple of minutes, the vehicle backed out more slowly – presumably having directly delivered its cargo (including his luggage?) – then did a one-eighty turn and accelerated from view. Over the next ten minutes, three more vehicles followed the same procedure. After the last, the cargo door slowly rose up to form a seal with the body of the craft.

"Your turn now," announced the officer, loudly.

"What, in that?" said someone.

"Fuck that!" declared another.

"Either go now, or miss your flight – it's all the same to me. But I'd run if I were you – unless you want to get a little damp."

"Very funny," snarled the first man – tall and broad, with a shaven head and an NS tattoo clearly visible to Mitsos on the nape of his neck. "Let's get this over with."

Mitsos was the last to the door. He waited for the final person to complete their race to the flight of steps that led up to the passenger section of the shuttle. "Do you get a kick out of this?"

"A kick, sir?" The officer's smile was answer enough. "We provide various services to arriving shuttles, which need to be paid for. The other departure terminal has a telescoping tunnel and refreshments, amongst other things. The *Marseilles* chooses a minimum level of service. If you have an issue with the hurried process and lack of amenities, I suggest you take it up with them. Now – are you going or not?"

Mitsos was sodden by the time he ascended into the shuttle, and his head stung from the heavy impact of the rain. He was met in the entrance space by a middle-aged man with long dark hair holding a towel.

"You might need this," said the man, who was dressed in a grey utilitarian jumpsuit. He seemed amused.

Mitsos snatched the towel. "Yeah, very funny. I'm starting to hate this place."

"Oh, what place is that? Tethys in general?"

Mitsos turned to look into the cabin, and scowled. "Where do I sit… with the other drowned rats?"

The other's expression hardened. "Do you think you're too good to share with the comrades?"

Mitsos snapped his mouth shut to pre-empt an instinctive response. He tried again: "No. I merely meant it looks full. I can't see a spare seat."

The man – who was slim, and taller than Mitsos, but not by much – paused and ran his eyes over him. At last he said: "That's because it is full, *Mr Mitsos.* I thought you'd join me in the pilot's cabin, just behind the cockpit. After all, she and the reserve won't need it as they'll be flying." He opened out a hand to indicate a closed door in the direction of the front of the craft. "Yes?"

Mitsos paused, towel in hand. "I get the impression you aren't quite what you seem. Not merely an attendant."

"*Merely?* Oh, Mr Mitsos, I *am* merely an attendant – on this trip. At other times, I have *merely* been a fisherman, and *merely* a canteen worker, and *merely* an agronomist tending our hydroponics. But as well as an attendant, I happen to at present be First Citizen of the *Marseilles.* My name is Sebastian Deux."

Mitsos felt his face burning, and not only from the scouring of the rain. *Idiot!* He brought the towel to his face to give himself a chance to regain his composure. When he brought it away, he somehow found a smile. "Please forgive me my temper and insulting words, First Citizen. I've had a trying morning. I'd love to join you for the journey back… a chance to perhaps discuss my proposal? Oh – and thank you for the towel."

* * *

It was the day after the departure of the shuttle to the *Marseilles* that Nesvorny received an updated report on Mitsos. Fukuda had come to deliver it, standing to attention in his office, looking sharp in a crisp black uniform with a Hibernian major's golden, four-leaf clover insignia on the shoulders.

At his desk, Nesvorny's colonel status was indicated by a pair of clovers on each shoulder. "Tell me," he demanded.

Fukuda looked uneasy; a bead of sweat was evident on his bald brow, and this threatened to run down past the implant port by his left eye. "I have discovered his secret. The thing he has to sell."

Nesvorny pushed himself back from the desk and frowned. "Why am I getting the feeling this is something you should have discovered when we had Mitsos in arms' reach when we could have done something about it? Go on."

"He claims to have a template for machinery that will extract rare metals from ocean water."

"What!" Nesvorny was at first shocked… and then he began to laugh. "Extract? Is he planning on sieving the entire ocean?"

Some of the tension eased in Fukuda's shoulders, although his expression remained severe. "Yes, your reaction is similar to that of the manufacturers he approached."

"Manufacturers… *plural*?"

"He attempted to gain an audience with all six of our industrial companies. Some were uninterested. Those he talked to were astonished, sceptical, amused –"

Nesvorny held up a finger to stall the other. "Before you go on, I'd like to know, Fukuda, how the hell you only found out about this now?" It was rare to get a chance to put his deputy in his place; Nesvorny couldn't resist this one. "You've had several weeks. This could have been… *could be*… critical."

"Sir! My original focus was on the NS members. You recall, I only became aware that Mitsos was an issue a week ago. Since then, I have been focusing on his relationship with the NS. He'd already made his industrial approaches by then, so –"

"So you didn't think to look into his past activities?" Nesvorny shook his head, though he thought: was that *my* fault? "Okay. I am disappointed. Continue."

"There is little more to say." Fukuda had tensed up again: he looked at a point a metre over his superior's head. "They all rejected the idea. Some doubted he actually possessed any such template; others doubted whether any such device would work; and a couple suggested that, even if such a machine did work, it would be expensive to set up and lead to only minimal returns. In short, they thought Mitsos was either a charlatan or a moron."

Nesvorny leant forwards and placed his elbows on his desk. For a moment he looked down, as if searching for patterns in the mottled plasticised surface, but then he gave his head a small shake and looked up. "Maybe… maybe this is no bad thing. Perhaps Mitsos and the *Marseilles* are meant for each other – desperate fantasists. If they want to waste what little they have searching for unicorns, let them."

"But what if it works?"

"I trust the judgment of our experts. But if it does somehow work, and doesn't bankrupt the *Marseilles*, and produces usable amounts of key elements, then perhaps that would be no bad thing. We need to reduce our reliance on Earth, even if the gatekeepers end up being those fanatics." Nesvorny shrugged. "And if the concept works once, any machinery can be duplicated. I am sure if it came to it, we could outbid the miserabilists for Mitsos' services."

Fukuda grinned and at last looked down into Nesvorny's eyes. "Yes, sir. And if the worst came to the worst and he or they said 'no', we could always confiscate the mechanism from them. Only *Hibernia* has what it takes to up-scale production. It would be for the good of all of Tethys for it to be under our control."

"Indeed. So, Mitsos might be of use to us, one way or another. I think I need to talk to Colonel Joseph to ensure that she keeps an eye on him through her source on the *Marseilles*. In fact, see if she is around and set up a meeting. Now get out of here. Dismissed."

Chapter 10

Marie Lockard sat on the deck of the *Fortunata*, legs dangling over the side, checking her underwater dive tablet to remind herself of today's mission.

Over the last couple of weeks – with Marie now fully trusted to follow similar dive protocols and durations to the rest of the team – they had systematically mapped out this edge of the sea forest. They'd explored a volume three kilometres long, one-hundred metres 'wide' (from the edge inwards), and forty metres deep. If they'd had time they would have done more, but the *Lisboa* was shifting position to get closer to the *Hibernia* for their biennial rock harvest – even though that was not due to start for almost six months. According to Miguel Figueroa, this was on account of the Captain-Governor being twitchy following a previous cycle, when they'd planned their arrival with too little room for error, only to be delayed by a monstrous Grade Five storm and subsequent engine issues, resulting in them missing nearly a month of mining. So, now the tendency was to be over-cautious and arrive in the environs far too early. But in return for prematurely leaving their new find, the Captain had allowed himself to be directed by his scientists to a small, unexplored forest to the north-east of the *Hibernia*, fringing the Great Northern Cenote where it made its closest approach to the Range, just eighty kilometres away from the great ship's anchorage.

"But hasn't that already been surveyed?" Marie remembered asking the old professor a few days ago.

"No, my dear. That cenote acts as a barrier to the whole north polar region. It's never been an attractive prospect for the Hibernians, or for any of the city ships it built, which always saw more alluring possibilities to the south and west. Also, the Northern Fringe Forest is narrow, no more than half-a-kilometre wide, so its potential exploration would have brought people uncomfortably close to that cenote." He'd shrugged. "Plus, no one at the time had our degree of interest in the science of our world – they just wanted freedom and headed for what was seen as the best areas."

Half-a-kilometre wide? Marie was intrigued by the great dark lines that carved the ocean of Tethys, essentially acting like mountain ranges did on land in channelling human travel and settlement, and she was keen to take a closer look. But the forest here was six or seven kilometres wide along this side of the cenote – with nothing at all on the other side of the chasm – and so she'd not had the chance to get close as yet.

"Patience!" Figueroa had told her, just yesterday, his weathered brown face split into a smile. "We have decided that we will at last conduct a proper study of these beasts, and for that you will definitely be needed!"

But certainly not today.

Marie found herself looking out over the dark-green matting, lost in reminiscence. With a shake of the head, she returned her attention to the dive tablet. Today, she was due to map grid 28D, which was the inside edge of this section, one hundred metres into the forest. The ship would dump her over her designated spot after Kalmik had been dropped… which a *splash* from somewhere on the other side of the boat confirmed had just happened. Almost immediately, the *Fortunata* began to move, sliding ever-so-slowly over the top of the forest to ensure its propellor blades didn't snag. On Marie's tablet, she touched the screen and selected an option which showed the relative position of the team in the water – Kalmik's red dot was closest to the boat, but slowly diverging. It didn't take long to reach her own drop point.

"Good luck," said a voice from somewhere behind.

Marie turned to look over her shoulder. "Thanks, Marco. And you watch out for me – I'm relying on you, eh?"

Marco Grande rested his back against the cabin wall, two days' worth of dark stubble under slightly bloodshot eyes. He gave a nervous smile and a thumbs-up.

Marie turned, set down her tablet, and put on her helmet. Once this was secure, she reclaimed the tablet, clipped it to her dive belt, and slid into the water.

She'd felt mild trepidation on her first dive – but nothing more – and the lack of any marine incident since then had given her no reason to revise her attitude towards the alien ocean. Her crewmates had interpreted her unflustered manner in one of two ways: one set exalted her for having nerves of steel (unlike the derided Marco); the other was more reserved in judgment, and joked that she'd not yet faced any real test to prove her worth. Katerina Kalmik was chief of the sceptics, often stating, with a knowing smile: "We'll see…"

As she swam down one of the long, kelp-like plants, using it like a rope, Marie thought about what she'd experienced so far and how benign it had all been – nothing like the horror stories she'd heard, which were sometimes hyped up in Earth-produced documentaries about the extra-solar planet. But then again, the sea forest was a unique environment: its thickness was a deterrence to large creatures that might be dangerous, and it was instead home to a range of small, nimble lifeforms, that wove in and out of the stalks, or lived on the surface of the strands, and though there were plenty of predators, these knew their own limitations and focused on smaller prey. Indeed, as she descended Marie startled a weaverfish, which darted out from its home of woven strands and then hovered – protectively, but also cautiously – a short distance away. This fish analogue (*hell, just say fish*, she thought, *the locals do*) was about the size of a forearm, with flexible fins that it used like hands to twist leaves into bowers, but also to grasp prey which it then flensed with razor-like lips. Certainly, if the creature were her size, it would be a horror to encounter.

Marie carried on past the fish, taking care not to crumple its bower under her hand. Her intent was to start at the lowest point and then move across the face of her designated section. By now, the automated light in her helmet had activated, with sunlight struggling to penetrate this far down. The Lisboeta diving kit was a wonder to her, and so much more advanced than anything she'd worn on Earth – a result of evolution in a more challenging environment. Her drysuit, for example, was not just waterproof and warm, but tough, too, and full of all sorts of sensors. Apparently, it was stronger than Kevlar, would deflect a penetrating attack, and would certainly withstand the bite of any Terrestrial shark. More than that, it would respond to a bite with an explosive inflation that would not only startle the predator, but save the wearer from crush injuries – as well as from dissection. As for the helmet, this was a wonder of communication, with inbuilt microphone and continual, real-time connection with onboard systems – manned by Marco – that could project information across the interior of the faceplate.

Green numbers within Marie's faceplate now ticked over to '40m' – her target. The forest continued further down to unknown depths: had they the time, they would have explored deeper, but greater depth brought enhanced danger and was deemed an unnecessary risk, given that there was plenty of low-hanging fruit still available for collection. Nevertheless, Marie paused for a moment to consider the depths. Apparently, some kelp analogues (*no, you've got to stop this: just think 'kelp'!*) were free floating, with bulbous 'roots' that held their own peculiar ecosystems, while others were rooted in the seabed – these being particularly common in places where the sea was relatively shallow, such as the Xian Great Banks, where the *Taiwan* was permanently anchored. It had been assumed that this particular forest was free floating, though the roots might be hundreds of metres down. She suspected that they would gain far more scientific information by trying to go deep rather than wide – but she was still too early in her role to try to challenge her team's well-established routines.

Marie turned attention to her task. Over the next hour, slowly and systematically, she quartered her allotted sector. Her job mainly required identifying new lifeforms and taking notes on their habitats and behaviours. The tablet was critical for this, particularly for the free-swimming creatures, given that her knowledge of the native fauna was limited: all she needed to do was centre the creature in the tablet's camera, and its AI would flash a name if it had been recorded before, or a question mark if it hadn't. In the latter cases, she would attempt to follow the creature and get different and better angles on it. Sometimes, after a bit, the AI would decide it could identify the target after all, but on a few occasions it remained ignorant. Marie would then attempt to collect a sample of the creature if it was small enough to fit in her collection bag, or otherwise record her observations via the microphone in her helmet.

Aside from the free-swimming creatures, Marie carefully observed the kelp and its denizens. At one place, she found a peculiar blemish on a broad stalk. Was it disease? She cut a sample and put it into the collection bag at her waist.

Her dive time was coming to an end, and she'd identified three new creatures – two inhabitants of the kelp foliage and one free swimmer – when she got a strange sensation, an impression that something of significant size was near. She jerked her head around to look behind… but there was nothing. The ocean could do that to you – to anyone. She'd felt similar sensations before in the seas on Earth: usually it was no more than a shadow, or perhaps a result of the sun coming from behind a cloud and spearing sunlight into the water, illuminating small things that had been hidden. But once or twice it had been more. She remembered a giant grouper once gliding into view – right behind her, mere metres away, and seemingly unconcerned as to her presence. And on one occasion, she'd suddenly noticed a tiger shark, languidly swimming at the far reach of her vision, *stalking* her. That last memory caused Marie to tense and shudder. She slowly rotated three-sixty, just to make sure all was okay. There was noth–

There was something.

It was deeper into the forest, beyond her designated range. She caught sight of something black, slowly sliding in front of a clutch of kelp strands. She froze, one hand grasping a trunk. It was difficult to see with all the intervening greenery, but then she noticed several strands five metres away bow outwards, as though something was pressing into them. She tensed further, but whatever it was that had caused the disturbance was clearly heading away from her, *not* towards. The strands settled, the water now full of particulates from the plant, dancing in the beam of her helmet light. And then she realised she'd been holding her breath, and she exhaled and gave a half cough.

Seconds passed, but there was no further disturbance. Her courage returned slowly. After a moment's pause, she edged away from the trunk she'd been grasping, kicked her flippered feet, and pushed between several more strands that had been between her and the shadow. She reached the jostled patch and peered at the closest trunk – but saw nothing. No, *not* nothing: a one metre length of foliage was missing, as though stripped away. But she could see no bite marks or grooves within the trunk itself.

And then she got the sensation again – and pulled up her knees. Below? Was something *below* her? The helmet cast light into the deeper shadow… and the trunk Marie grasped *moved.*

Tugged.

"Marie?" came the voice of Marco. "Are you okay? Your heart rate leapt. And you've gone beyond your zone."

"Uh… Marco… yeah." She moved her head forwards and down, as though that might somehow aid her sight. But again, there was nothing. "*Nothing*," she muttered softly.

"What was that, Marie?"

"Uh, sorry. I said it's nothing."

"Okay. Well, your time is up, so come on back."

Gladly, she thought.

* * *

"We shouldn't be here," said Tonio, ducking a head to avoid a low steel beam.

"That's what you always say," said Sara from beyond the obstruction, flicking her long dark hair. "But if you didn't follow me, we'd have never found the Bowl."

"Yeah, I'm *really* glad of that," said Tonio, dripping with sarcasm. "What would we do without it?"

Sara smiled and arched an eyebrow at Kate beside her. As with most of the sub-surface levels, the strip lighting was set to a default 'low', leaving them in a perpetual twilight. "He loves it really. He just can't face admitting it."

"Bah! The Bowl is okay – that's all. But I still don't understand what you're looking for now. What is this place?"

"It's a back-up control room from the very early days of the construction."

The trio had been following Sara through a maze of dark corridors, accessed by another of the nondescript and forgotten doorways on the sea-level floor – this one at the end of a cul-de-sac beyond the entrance to a public gym. The corridor they'd just squeezed down had clearly not been intended for regular human access: they'd had to remove an already-loosened grill in a wall, which had revealed a narrow space full of pipework that, after a few metres of crawling on hands and knees and via another grill, popped out into their present location. Before them was a wide, curving console covered in keypads and other controls, with numerous dark monitors, while around them there were a couple of smaller console islands of similar design. The bulkhead in front of the main console held a wide display screen that was also dark.

"Control room? Sounds important – so why is it closed up and shut down?" asked Kate. "And how did you know where to look?"

"My dad's in Maintenance. He's very easy to grill for information. He loves telling stories about the hidden deck in particular – and showing me his maps. "

"Hidden deck?" wondered Kate.

"Yes. Where we are now. It's not really a whole deck. It's sub-level two, the lowest, but only parts of it are like this. It's where a lot of the original service facilities were put. And then newer systems were put in, and then even newer ones. A lot of the services were simply rerouted from the lost zones, as it was easier to start anew than repair and upgrade, and these places were just abandoned."

"I'm surprised," said Kate. "Don't you need every inch of space on the ship? I mean, it seems full. Look at our flat – it's kinda nice, but it's very compact."

"I sense a euphemism," said Tonio, who'd wandered over to a black leather chair, and was now seated and swivelling to-and-fro.

"How does it compare to your last place on Earth?" asked Sara.

"Well, in Durban we had a big, detached house on a hill, overlooking the bay. It was probably ten times as big as what we've got now."

"Ten!" gasped Tonio. "That's more than the Captain-Governor has. *Much* more. Does everyone on Earth live like a king?"

Kate laughed. "No. And it never seemed like we were living like royalty. We didn't have servants or anything. We just had, well, lots of space. Now I think about it, a lot of *wasted* space. We had a couple of rooms that were just filled with junk. A spare bedroom that was rarely used. A kitchen-diner that was too big for the two of us. And we had a decent garden outside, too, with space for a braai."

"What the hell is a braai?" asked Tonio.

"A barbeque. You know, a sort of open oven outside used to overcook meat."

"Right," said Tonio, looking at Kate as though she were mad.

"Anyway," Kate continued, "everything here is so tidy and efficient. My bed folds into the wall and then a desk slides out. That sort of thing."

"And you've left all that space for *here*," Tonio's voice was filled with disbelief.

"Not everything is about material possessions, you know."

"You sound like one of the Marseillais," said Sara.

Kate had learned about the socialists. She shook her head: "No way. I *like* material things. But…" she shrugged. "Mum wanted to come here. Her work is more important than *stuff*. This was too good an opportunity for her. I still have lots of nice things though, but they're all in storage back in South Africa. One day I'll get it all back – I hope."

"No way," said Sara. "You're here for good. Tonio and me, we won't let you go, eh?"

Tonio smiled at Kate and made a pistol shape with one hand, cocking his imaginary weapon.

"Thanks guys," Kate reached to wipe away a pretend tear. "I'm truly touched."

"I think I'm going to barf," laughed Tonio. "Enough! But – Sara – I still don't get why we're here."

"Isn't exploring enough of a reward in itself?" By now Sara had also slouched into a swivel chair. "You want *more*? Okay. Try this. My dad mentioned this place. The thing is, it's just been powered down – not completely disconnected from every system. Oh, some things have been stripped out and repurposed, and some of the functions have been disabled – like everything connected to the fusion plant – but in theory, some parts can be restarted."

"Right," said Tonio, cautiously. "And?"

"And you're an electronics buff. It's going to be your major, yeah? So, I've brought you a huge toy box. You can thank me now."

"What? You're mad!"

Kate was still standing – resting her back against a bulkhead. "You're not suggesting Tonio try to activate this…" she waved a hand to indicate the contents of the room. "I mean, for a start, won't someone know if the room suddenly comes to life again? Won't there be a power drain or something?"

Sara looked at Tonio and gave a mischievous smile. "Oh, I don't know. Tonio?"

The dark-skinned boy frowned, then swivelled his chair – which was one of five at the console, at the other end to that occupied by Sara – and considered the keypads before him. After a moment, he responded slowly: "Nooo... not necessarily." He swivelled back to face Sara. "Is it isolated from the main control centre?"

"Apparently it is, according to my dad."

"But... maybe not from peripheral systems?"

"As I said, from some, not all. The only way to tell is to start her up and have a look."

"And the power?" added Kate.

Tonio shook his head slowly. "Not a problem, I think. Actually running the electronics in this room won't take a lot of electricity, and with our fusion plant we have loads of capacity. I mean, we've so much we even keep the lighting on in all these abandoned sections – very low maybe, but still. Hmmm. I wonder: if we *can* start this up, what might we be able to access?"

"What about security cameras?" asked Sara.

Kate saw her gist. "You mean, spy on the ship?"

"Yeah. Watch the losers at the Terrace. See who Vita is infatuating next. Maybe access external locks to, well, places with fun stuff."

"Sara!" said Kate, in shock. "You're not suggesting breaking into–"

"The ice cream parlour on deck four?" she smiled innocently. "What a terrible thought!"

Tonio now laughed, and after a moment, so did Kate.

* * *

By the time she'd risen to the surface, Marie's intent to relate her experience had already been tempered. What, after all, had she seen? A shadow? A denuded stretch of kelp that could have been caused by almost anything? And then the first person she saw after climbing up a ladder onto deck was Katerina Kalmik. *Grinning*. And that was that.

"Anything exciting, Marie? Marco said you got the jitters."

"No. Nothing at all. It was a regulation dive." She pulled off her flippers, then walked past Kalmik, heading to the rear cabin to change. After that, she went to the main cabin to hand her sample bag and tablet to an eager Figueroa, and then she professed tiredness and headed to the sleeping cabin – with its bunk beds – to close her eyes and rest.

Back at the *Lisboa*, the *Fortunata* slid into a bay on the reverse side of the starboard wing of the great, turtle-shaped ship. Once secured in an adjustable cradle, a mechanism rose behind the research ship, closing access to the ocean, and the water drained from the dock leaving the craft sitting in its supporting frame. The crew began to depart along automated gangplanks onto the dock. On leaving the sleeping cabin, Marie spotted Figueroa and Kalmik standing on the deck in deep conversation. She paused a moment, and then quietly moved to the opposite side of the boat and took a gangplank there. She retraced past the secured bow of the *Fortunata*, with the mighty bulk of the *Lisboa* rising up before her – the bulbous 'head' of the command deck to her right, the edge of the body – with sun glinting off rows of windows – to the left.

As Marie hurried down the wide central walkway, past more drydocks, raised mechanisms holding vast nets or threshers, and the occasional small cabin – holding equipment or acting as control centres – she spotted Marco Grande's slouch-shouldered form. After a moment's thought, she increased her pace to catch him up.

"Marco – wait."

The other startled, then turned. "Oh. Marie. What do you want?"

"Where are you off to? The office? It's a bit late."

"No. I'm going for a drink."

"You know, I could use one too. Mind if I join you?"

Grande looked uncertain. He was perhaps in his late thirties, medium height, slim, and not unhandsome – though his eyebrows were rather bushy and his deep-set eyes always seemed to be dark ringed, making him appear perpetually exhausted. "Well…"

"Oh, come on. I don't bite."

"Okay then." He gave a weak smile. "But I don't go anywhere interesting."

"That's fine. Anywhere will do. I just thought it would be good if we had a chat – us Earthers."

"Fine."

Grande led the way to the end of the walkway, through large double doors that gave onto a small plaza surrounded by services and offices related to the running of the *Lisboa's* fleet, and then bore off into a corridor that had small eateries and bars to either side. They passed a number of places that would have done – each with its own style and theme, none overcrowded – until they reached the very end of the corridor, almost on the other side of the ship. The last couple of places here were quiet, with few customers. Marco led them into a bar called The Rigger, with small dark tables, yellow lanterns on the wall, and arrangements of twisted rope as a dominant motif.

"*Nice*," said Marie, unable to fully mask her feelings.

But Grande somehow missed the irony. "Yes. It's quiet. It means I don't get disturbed." He seemed unsure about what to do next. "Er… drink? Beer?"

"Sure." Marie took a table while Grande shuffled to the bar and spoke to the barman. Soon after, he returned holding two small glasses of a fizzy, pale yellow beverage. He placed the glasses on the table and took the chair opposite his partner.

Marie smiled thanks and took a quick drink. The beer was sharp, but not unpleasant. She then settled her glass, and watched the man, who gulped half of his beer in one go and then clasped the glass on the table with both hands, looking down.

The silence stretched. At last, Marie sighed. "So, Marco, I hear you've been here for a couple of years. From Italy?"

"Yes. Brindisi. And Malta."

When he didn't elaborate, Marie continued: "Why did you decide to come to Tethys? Not running away, I hope?" She smiled broadly to ensure the man understood she was teasing.

Grande looked up quickly, gave a pained smile, then looked down again. "No. No scandal. I just… I am a marine biologist. And statistician. This is what I do. I saw an advertisement and so… I came."

"But there must have been other jobs on Earth. Why this one?"

"It was the best for me. I like diving… I did like diving. Other jobs… I would mostly have been in an office."

"Right. Diving."

"I'm not a coward." Grande suddenly looked up. "That is what they say. That is what they have told you. I'm *not*."

Marie raised her hands. "I… I'm sure you're not. That's not why–"

"It's just… the water. Here. You go in, and there's that moment after you submerge when you're confused. You don't know where to look. Up. Down. Left. Right. You can only look one way, and you never know what's the other. And then there's the event horizon."

"The event…?"

"Sorry. It's a term I use. From astronomy. It's what I call the edge of sight, that area beyond which you can't see. *You* can't see. But there are plenty of things that can see beyond your range on Earth, and even more here. And… it's the not knowing. You're surrounded by a whole ocean… a whole *fucking* planet of water…" He had come alive. He shook his head, then repeated firmly: "I'm not a coward. But this… it's too much."

Marie nodded in sympathy. She absolutely understood. After a moment, she slowly reached out a hand and rested it on the other's arm. "I've been there too, Marco, I really have." How much did she dare say – about today? "In fact, I… had a moment. Earlier."

"I know. I saw your stats. I mentioned it to Kalmik. I am sorry about that. As soon as I said it, I regretted it. Maybe… maybe I just wanted to let her know that I'm not the only one. But I didn't mean to embarrass you."

"Don't worry about it. I can look after myself." At least she had now got him talking.

Grande twitched a smile; looked at her hand on his arm. "So… what caused your moment? Anything specific, or just…" he waved a hand in the rough direction of the ocean, "the blue."

"I don't know. I thought there was something in the forest, bigger and darker than anything I've seen or heard about. But it might have been nothing. Tired eyes. An overactive imagination. And I've got no actual evidence – my tablet was out of hand at the time. Has no one else reported anything similar?"

"Here? No. But this is an unusual forest, not just in terms of its biology."

"Yeah, I don't understand that. There's lots of sea forests across Tethys."

"Sure, but it's a *fringe* forest." Marco appeared to have calmed now. The tension in his shoulders had gone, and his grip on his glass had lessened. His smile was now more genuine. "It hugs up to a black cenote. Because of where it is, it's not been well explored, and nor have similar ones elsewhere. People have stuck to harvesting and exploring the open-ocean forests, or those anchored over shallows. People have generally been too afraid to get too close the to the cenotes, especially since the *Bridgeton*."

"The *Bridgeton*?" Marie frowned. "The ship that disappeared? But wasn't that some time ago?"

"Yes. Nearly twenty years. Big ship, too. Town Class – third generation. Smaller than the *Lisboa*, but still big. Self-sufficient. About five thousand residents. It was the first of its class, and almost the last. The *Hibernia* ran out of resources to build more, but a few years ago they got a number of shipments of key materials from Earth and started to build another one. But that's stalled again."

"I heard about the incident back on Earth – I mean, vaguely." Marie slowly slid her hand from the other's arm and settled it around her own glass. "It wasn't a big story. But I did see a documentary on it a few years back. It was meant to be crossing a cenote, wasn't it? But what I watched was a sensationalist account. The production company that made it had a bad reputation. They also did documentaries claiming Martians were real and were kidnapping colonists, and that vampires had been discovered on some other planet and were sucking people dry of blood on full moons. No one took their films seriously – except weirdo conspiracy theorists."

Grande actually chuckled at this. "Well, let me tell you what we actually know – which is little. The ship was built at *Hibernia*, and sailed for the Checkerboard. That's an area between a concentration of cenotes, with a large sea forest in the middle. Very rich fishing grounds. The weather is also usually calm – like the doldrums on

Earth – so fewer great storms. But it never arrived. It was there, then gone. No radio transmissions. Nothing."

"What about satellite images?"

"No. Tethys has few satellites, and the one that might have seen what happened to it was on the opposite side of the planet."

"So, what do people think happened?"

Grande paused to consider. "They think… the main hypothesis… is that rather than going around one of the cenotes, the *Bridgeton* took a short cut and attempted to cross one. Its last recorded position was very close to one. And then… who knows? It sank, and no one has ever been keen to search for the wreck, especially if it went into the black. It could be kilometres deep."

"Yes, but I still don't understand what happened at the cenote? Is it like a whirlpool – sucking down the ship?"

Grande shrugged. "That is a real mystery. Whirlpool? No. But the environment is strange: the water is very cold and visually almost impenetrable. In the past, some research ships have gone close to sample the waters, and found that they have an odd mix of chemicals and nutrients. They are called lifeless, because we can't see what life is in there, but they are not. A few fishing vessels have trawled them, and have caught fish. Odd fish. But then a fishing vessel disappeared – about a year before the *Bridgeton* – and that acted as a disincentive to further efforts. After all, there is no need – the oceans are full of catch."

"That *is* a mystery." Marie felt a sudden excitement. Truly new environments were scarce on Earth – so this, this was exactly the kind of thing that got her out of bed in the mornings.

Grande clearly saw her change of mood. "I know. It is fascinating. I, too, would like to know more. But… *Marie*," he said the name cautiously, as if trying it out for the first time, "be careful. I have seen your CV. Your experience is good, but this is not something to be taken lightly. To dive into a cenote?"

"Sure. I'm always careful. But this is why I am here." She looked down at her glass, at the bubbles rising from the depths of the beer. Carbon dioxide. It reminded her of something… there was something pertinent here, pertinent to the mystery. She shook her head. Maybe the answer would come to her subconscious as she slept.

She gave her head another small shake, then looked up at Grande. "Anyway, that's me. But what of you, Marco? What are your plans? To eventually return to– "

"No!" Grande didn't let her finish, his voice rising. Then he took a deep breath, and smiled sheepishly at Marie, whom he'd startled. "No, Marie. I am not going back to Earth. It would be like giving in. I'm *not* a coward. And I'm *not* a quitter. I know what people think. But I do valuable work here. And maybe one day… one day I'll show them. I'll face that demon. I want to do that. I *need* to do that. For myself most of all."

Marie smiled. "A hero is a scared person who faces fear and overcomes it." She raised a glass in salute. "I believe in you, Marco. And I'll drink to that."

Chapter 11

Makka Frost and Melissa De Voe hurried up to Rennie Heiko, who was standing just outside the entrance to the offices of the Security section.

"Rennie!" called Frost, excitedly. "We need to talk. It's important."

Heiko held up a warning finger. "Okay. Follow me." He led the way into Security, past a blue-uniformed officer at a reception desk, and continued to the end of the corridor where his own office was situated. As the office door closed behind the last to enter, he invited his visitors to sit. But the others were too energised to comply: Frost rested against one wall and De Voe leant down with both hands on the room's small conference table.

Frost declared: "We've had a hit. Made a find. Something significant."

"Really?" Heiko hitched up onto his desk, just beyond the table. "So – your analysis of the black sand was positive?"

"Yes! You remember I told you about placer deposits a couple of days ago? It seems we drilled into one. The sample I showed you, it's… well, I won't go into the details now, but it's something we've never come across before. A first for Tethys."

"And how big is this deposit?"

Frost and De Voe exchanged glances, then Frost continued: "We're not sure. Probably not huge. And given low mineral concentrations in the deposit, it's not going to fundamentally change the world. At least, we don't think so. But it is *something*."

"Great news then, but…" A thought occurred to Heiko, and he frowned, "…what exactly is the status of this find? Does *Stavanger* own it?"

"That's the problem," said Frost. "We're not sure. There's no precedent. *Hibernia* lays claim to the whole Range, though they only mine Mount Athol – not because they think it has any special properties, just because it's near to where they are berthed. They essentially lease out Mount Ardol to other cities to mine – for free because, well, they just think it's rubble and want to give the impression that they're not hogging everything, even though they actually are. But they set the rules to ensure everyone appreciates that they are in control."

"They only let one ship mine at a time," explained De Voe. "Four month stints only. We've got another two left before we have to make way for the next ship."

"Four months total?" Heiko mentally tried to do the maths. "But there are over twenty ships, so that means–"

Frost waved a hand to interrupt the calculation. "Yes, true, but there are only about half-a-dozen ships that take advantage of the offer. Ships that generally sail in this part of the globe. Others group around the *Taiwan*, or are truly peripatetic and simply trade for building material when they need it – leaving us to waste our time prospecting."

"Okay. But even so, half-a-dozen ships taking four month sequential residencies means… two years. Are you saying that once our stint is over, we won't be given access for another two years?"

"Yes," said Frost, "that's about right."

"And I'm guessing that two months isn't going to be long enough to mine appreciable quantities of whatever is in this deposit?"

"Right," said Frost. "If we go all-in, we're still not liable to extract much of what's there, and the yield of useful metals once the ore is cracked will be tiny."

"And when you stop, what then? Will the next ship take over your dig?"

Frost and De Voe exchanged glances again, then Frost looked back at Heiko and continued: "We're not sure. Certainly, we don't hold title over the area we mine, so a new arrival can start an entirely new dig, or they can just continue where we left off. And obviously, if they become aware of what we've found, they'll come back to ours."

"And when you return in two years' time, it could all be mined out?"

"Precisely!"

"*If* they know," asserted De Voe, giving her superior a meaningful look.

Heiko glanced between the two, trying to parse the sub-vocal communication going on between them. "So, given our own needs," he said, "this suggests we should disguise the dig and hope that no one else comes across the deposit… assuming you've got no plans to be altruistic."

De Voe started to shake her head, but Frost looked troubled. "I know it appears selfish," he said, "and maybe we *should* reveal our find so that everyone on Tethys can ultimately benefit, but– "

"But that's assuming the others are willing to be equally altruistic," said De Voe. "Makka – do you really believe that will happen? Our resources are low, and so are everyone else's, especially after what happened to the *Leviathan*. Whoever gets hold of this find will need most if not all of it. If we speak up, we might end up with *nothing*, or at least, nothing for some time, and then only at inflated prices we can't afford."

"Okay," said Heiko, "but what if you only tell the next arrival? *Surreptitiously*. Can you strike a deal? Maybe they'll reward you? Who's up next to the plate?"

"It's the *Marseilles*," said De Voe, face wrinkled in distaste.

"Fuck!" exclaimed Frost.

De Voe turned to fully face Heiko. "The people on the *Marseilles* are an antisocial lot – which is kind of an irony given their utilitarian philosophy. They'll look after their own first, no doubt about it. But I'm not sure they are ultimately the problem."

"*Hibernia*," said Frost, now nodding.

"You think they'll renege on the deal?" asked Heiko.

"Absolutely," said Frost. "*Hibernia* suffers the rest of us to pick at their mountain, but if they discover it actually holds something of value, they might not just shut off the discovery site, but the whole mountain. The whole Range. We could end up worse off than we are now. And their needs – as the planet's biggest polity – require some filling. We're not likely to see anything from the find."

"So, we can't let anyone else know," asserted De Voe. "This is ours. Finders keepers. I'm happy to show largesse to friends, but we have to put ourselves first. Altruism begins at home."

"I'm still not sure," said Frost. "I think… I think this is something beyond our pay grade. We need to alert the council. Let them decide."

"I agree," said Heiko. "It's not for us to set policy: we need to do our best to implement what our masters decide."

"So speaks the company man," muttered De Voe.

"Yes, Melissa. I'm Head of Security now. That's my role. It's not for me, or you, to decide the fate of the *Stavanger*. Don't you agree?"

De Voe stood up fully, crossed her arms, and scowled. "I suppose so, yes. *No.* Oh… I don't know. You're probably both right. But I fear loose lips. There's profit in treachery. Whether we get any say in this matter depends on everyone in the know keeping quiet and *Hibernia's* spies not finding out."

"Spies?" Heiko's eyes widened. "I've not heard anything about this. When was anyone going to tell me?"

Frost glanced at De Voe, then held up his hands. "Rennie, calm! It's just a rumour. An urban legend. *Probably.* It's an assumption that we all have, true on the other ships, too, that *Hibernia* has agents keeping them informed of our doings. But no one has ever caught an actual spy."

"Because there's never been anything major to report," said De Voe. "No one's been bothered to look, because no one's had any secrets worth protecting. But it might be different now. Rennie – maybe you should have a word with Cass. See what he has to say."

"Yes, I think I will."

Frost pushed himself from the wall on which he had been leaning. "Okay. You speak to Cass, and I'll have a quiet word with the Premier and arrange a confidential meeting with the council."

"But that still leaves the digging crew," said De Voe.

"Where are they now?" asked Heiko.

"Still on site. We thought it best to come and see you alone before we did anything."

"Right, I suggest the first thing we do – you and I, Melissa – is return to the site to have some firm words with those that remain. I hope you haven't left any of them with their communication devices?" Judging by the way the others looked at each other, they had. Heiko's heart sank. *False hopes?* Frost hadn't fully appreciated the reason for radio silence on their last meeting – but neither had *he*, or else he would have instructed Frost better. "*Damn!* Okay, let's move *now.* One of you, please call your team and emphasize their need for immediate silence. Oh, and get the foreman to collect everyone's communicators."

Heiko was already moving for the door.

* * *

Heiko was unbuckling his harness as Serge, at the wheel, slowed the skiff on approach to the temporary dock. He leapt onto the platform with De Voe right behind. Waiting for them, where the dock met firm land, was a tall, broad-shouldered man in a russet uniform with cropped blond hair.

"You're Ibsen, right?" said Heiko, on approach.

"Yessir." The man scowled at Heiko, then switched his gaze to the woman behind. "Melissa? What is this?"

"Sven – this is Rennie Heiko, Cass' replacement. Our new Head of Security."

Heiko already had a hand out: "Good to meet you, Sven. Sorry for the drama, but we have to move quickly here. You got Melissa's call – right?"

Ibsen cautiously took the other's hand. "Ya. And acted on it. Confiscated three comms pads. Got them secure in my hut."

"*Three?* But you have, what, thirty people on site?"

"This isn't Earth, Rennie," said De Voe. "Batteries are like gold dust. Not everyone has a comms pad, and those that do use them sparingly."

"That's right," said Ibsen. "And people with them don't like having them taken away. I've got three very unhappy workers at the moment."

"It's a shame I'm probably going to make them even more unhappy shortly. And you. As foreman, you have a pad too, right? I'll need that as well."

"The fuck you will!"

Heiko still had hold of the other's hand: now his grip tightened. Ibsen was the taller of the two, and younger, but he gasped, and when he tried to withdraw his hand, he found himself unable to do so. Heiko leant in: "Sven – I don't have time for games. Melissa told you why we need operational silence. You're smart. You understand. So work with me, please, not against me." And then he released the other's hand.

De Voe was suddenly beside the pair. "Do as he says, Sven, or you'll have me on your back too, and you definitely don't want that."

Ibsen took half a step back and raised his hands. "Right! Fine! It was just a–"

"Instinctive reaction," said Heiko. "I understand." He slapped the other on the arm and smiled. "I'd have reacted the same. So – your pad, and the others, please. Oh, and maybe we should continue this conversation out of public view. We seem to be attracting attention."

There were a couple of men some metres along the shelf, each hefting a tool of some sort and watching them with interest.

"Sven – take Rennie to your hut. I'll go have a word with the crew. Give me five minutes, eh?" Without awaiting a reply, De Voe headed towards the two men – raising an arm and hailing them.

Ibsen frowned, but he said nothing and did as asked. He led Heiko to a prefab hut off to one side of the shelf of land; half-a-dozen more huts of similar size ranged up the shallow, barren slope behind. Within the hut, there was a small table – on which were scattered a map and several printed diagrams – and four plastic chairs. There was also a sleeping cot along one wall.

"My office and bedroom. Please sit."

As Heiko pulled out a chair, Ibsen continued to the cot. There was a personal locker beneath this. He bent and rummaged within, then straightened and returned to the table, throwing a canvas bag onto it. Then, after a moment's pause, he reached into a wide pocket on his right thigh and pulled out a thin, rectangular device with a darkened screen.

"You'll get it back shortly," said Heiko. "I promise."

Ibsen nodded, leant forwards, and carefully placed the device next to the bag.

"Thanks. And while waiting for Melissa, perhaps we can chat. I'd like to get a sense of the timeline. I've heard from Makka and Melissa, but sometimes it's best to triangulate. Are you going to sit?"

"I think I'll stand for now."

Heiko frowned and looked the other over. Ibsen was still smarting – but there was something more. He feared it might be guilt. "Okay. So, I bumped into Makka a couple of days ago, or rather, he bumped into me. He had an interesting rock sample with him – dug out that morning?"

"Ya. Took a core sample – trying to further map out the geology of this part of the mountain. Didn't expect anything new, but the strata are inclined in such a way here that we managed to access an older layer. The black sand was five metres down below sea level."

"Difficult to get at?"

Ibsen shrugged. "Maybe. But at least it's not high up the slope, so we won't need to lug lots of gear uphill, and we might be able to mask what we're doing from watchers."

"Interesting. But what I want to know is, who was there when this – core? – was brought up? Who saw it? Who appreciated what it might imply?"

"Well, it was Makka, Melissa, me, and Karin Husa initially. The boss spotted it first and guessed what it was."

"Excited?"

"Makka? Fuck, yes. Most of us are just diggers, but he's a true geologist – him and Melissa."

"What about you and Karin?"

"I am, yeah. Got a bit of knowledge. Karin? No."

"So how did *you* react to this? And the crew?"

Ibsen smiled gently. "I thought it was interesting. Everyone else just thought... well... that's the boss, excited as ever over a little rock."

"No rushing off to phone friends and relatives back on the ship?"

"And say what? The boss has gone loco again? Waste of batteries."

Heiko observed the other's face intently. After a moment, he nodded. "Fine. So, what did you and the rest of the crew do next? Back to mining?"

"We've got a job to do, and not much time to do it. Most returned to excavating. Melissa identified a few more sites to drill core samples to try to get a sense of the size of the anomaly. Then she grabbed a couple of others and set about it."

"And what about today?"

"Not much to tell. A few hours ago, Melissa got a call from the boss on the big ship. Said he wanted her to come back, and she left. And now she's back... with you."

Heiko watched the other man avert his eyes, apparently finding something of interest on the floor. His own eyes hardened and he slowly shook his head. "I don't think that's quite all, is it? I think she said something more to you. She'll be back shortly. Shall we wait and then I can ask her directly?"

Ibsen crossed his arms and looked up, clearly now irate. "She didn't say much… not that I remember. She was also excited. Said… it might be something. Geological term."

"But you're also something of a geologist. You'd understand. What did she say?"

"Monazite," he scowled. "She said the sample contained monazite."

"A potentially valuable ore, eh? And what did you do next? Who did you tell?"

Ibsen briefly looked away again, then up, and spoke from under a furrowed brow. "No one here. They were at work and wouldn't have understood anyway."

Heiko slowly reached across the table and picked up the comms pad resting beside the canvas bag. "Look, Sven. You're not in trouble. You got some news and wanted to share. Most of us would have done the same. And no one told you not to. I blame myself for that – I should have been more awake when Makka came to me two days ago." He looked at the darkened face of the device. "Fingerprint? Optical scan?"

Ibsen sighed, and the tension seemed to leave him. "Optical." He held out a hand. "I'll unlock it. You'll find two calls. One to my wife, and one to Irina Vlassic."

The door opened, and De Voe entered, looking stern. "Holding pattern," she declared. Then she looked between the two men. "So what–?"

"Sven was just unlocking his pad for me," said Heiko. "I'm going to have a look at his history, and then I'll be placing an urgent call to Pedersen. After that, we can discuss what we do here."

* * *

"The black sand samples are largely composed of a mix of iron oxides," said Frost. "But the crucial thing is, we also found crystals of monazite within them."

"Monazite?" enunciated Nila Moroni, testing the unfamiliar word in her mouth.

"Yes. It's an ore that contains lanthanides. Cerium and lanthanum. Smaller traces of things like yttrium. And it's got a decent thorium oxide content too – about ten percent – which would make it a viable mining prospect back on Earth."

"Can I see?" Moroni held a hand across the conference table towards Frost.

To Heiko, the woman's expression was difficult to gauge, given the low lighting in the long, low-ceilinged control suite where they were having this emergency meeting. The same went for the expressions of the others arrayed around Moroni: Margarethe Olson, Hanna Bulow, and Cass Remillard. Heiko sat opposite this quartet next to Frost, with De Voe on the chief geologist's other side. The only other person present in the room was Anders Pedersen, who stood in shadow by the solid metal door behind him, hand resting surreptitiously on a loaded pistol.

Frost slid the piece of rock across the table into the questing hand. Moroni brought it up close to her eyes to inspect it. As she did so, Olson gently cleared her throat. "This is significant news indeed, Makka. Our own supply of rare earths. Or is it?"

"That is what we need to discuss," said Frost. "Our claim is uncertain."

"You mean *problematic*," said Moroni, turning the rock over in her hands. "But before considering what shit this might land us in… is this actually a viable mining operation for us, given our resources?"

Frost paused and quickly glanced at De Voe, then back to the woman opposite. "We believe so. Of course, with the machinery we've currently got, it would initially be a small scale operation, and it would take some time to dig down to the placer deposit and extract enough material to make refining worthwhile. Ideally, we could do with more and better mining equipment, though we could manufacture this, as we have the printer templates for our tool shop. And Melissa and I could certainly put together an appropriate refinery. Cracking monazite just needs heat and sulphuric acid, then washing out the residue and using various treatments to get the rare earths from the resulting sulphates."

Moroni finished her inspection and tossed the rock back onto the table. The thud caused Frost to falter. "So, realistically, that's a 'no' then," she said. "We don't have the equipment or the time to do this before our window of operation closes. Be honest, Makka – and set aside this thought of magicking up more equipment, which we haven't got the materials to produce anyway: what could you achieve in the two months we have left with what we currently have, even working flat-out, and assuming we let you have as many willing miners as you can fit on the site?"

"Well, yes, it would be a challenge."

"And this is assuming you could blithely hammer away, day and night, without considering the subterfuge that would be required." Moroni redirected her gaze. "Isn't that right, Mr Heiko? This is clearly the reason you are here with Makka and Melissa. You are obviously in the know already. Tell me what you think the real problems are."

Heiko nodded solemnly. "There are certainly security issues. I'm still trying to get my head around the politics of this place, but from what I understand, *Hibernia* is likely to be very interested in the find and might well claim it for itself."

"Legitimately so," said Bulow, whose face was almost entirely in shadow, though photons from the ceiling strip lights sparkled off her white hair. She turned slightly to address Olson at her side, her aquiline nose emerging into the light. "You know we mine under sufferance."

"That's true," said Olson. "But… let's run with this scenario a bit longer, shall we. Rennie, you were answering Nila's pertinent question. Please continue."

Heiko nodded curtly. "Yes. There are essentially two fault lines if you somehow wish to keep this matter from the Hibernians or anyone else. External and internal. I understand the Hibernians use a drone to keep an eye on proceedings – something I only learned about earlier today." He paused a moment: in fact, he'd only learnt about it on the journey back to the *Stavanger*. *Thanks for nothing, Melissa!* "Clearly, this could complicate things. We'd need a compelling cover story – which at the moment, no one seems to have. Short of this, any activity involving more staff or a sudden change of MO would be suspicious. Cover stories require significant planning and associated ground work over a lengthy period of time. Saying nothing would court disaster, but so would saying something with the wrong tone, to the wrong people, in the wrong way." He turned to face Frost. "I'm sorry, Makka: I just don't see how we achieve this in two months, or indeed, less, as it needs to be sorted *before* you act."

"Well, maybe–"

Moroni held up a hand. "Makka – please. Mr Heiko, I assume that this is the *external* risk you are referring to. Please explain the *internal*?"

"That is the risk of a leak from within the community of the *Stavanger*. Melissa and I earlier locked down the mining site, so no one from there is going to be speaking to anyone here for at least a week. But then the current rotation ends, and we need to think about how we handle the returning workers."

"*If* they are allowed to return," said Remillard, speaking for the first time.

"I'm not sure it would be feasible to keep them there," responded De Voe. "I guess this is part of the cover story Rennie is talking about."

"Thanks, Melissa, it is." Heiko paused a moment to collect his thoughts. "But we may not have even a week. Aside from us here, there are at least two more onboard who have been alerted to the find: Ana Ibsen and Irina Vlassic, respectively the wife and the *special friend* of Sven Ibsen, the foreman of the dig."

Remillard chortled. "This was never meant to be a poisoned chalice, son."

Heiko gave his predecessor a lop-sided grin. "Nevertheless, I thank you for making my first few weeks interesting."

"What have you done about these two?" asked Moroni brusquely.

"Anders has managed to isolate them. When we're done here, I'll immediately go and talk to them to see what has got out, and just how far this has spread. We may be in luck and it has gone nowhere to no one of significance." Now he glanced quickly at Remillard. "If Cass is not busy, I'd like to pick his brains on certain matters afterwards." *Melissa also mentioned spies.*

"Well, I was busy, but this takes precedence. Sure."

"Thank you." Heiko flashed a quick smile at Moroni, but then deliberately shifted his focus to Olson. "Premier, I appreciate this is a complex issue. But from a security perspective, can I request that the subject of our current discussion goes no further than those in this room – at least, until you make a strategic decision on what you plan to do?"

"Ah, thank you for the consideration." Olson returned a kindly smile, then looked askance. "Nila – all good?"

"Yes, Margarethe, I concur. But we should resolve this matter quickly while we are still able to shape the narrative. And this is what I see. We have a find that could enrich our society – one we discovered, and hence one we have a certain *moral* stake in. While Hanna is right that the find isn't legally ours, *Hibernia's* own claim is hardly beyond reproach."

"They don't see it that way," said Bulow.

"Exactly. And their tunnel vision is why they will certainly take over the find and leave us with nothing."

"Unless we go to them willingly," said Bulow. "Offer them the information freely. Agree to partner them in the dig."

De Voe laughed. "And stiff the *Marseilles*, which is due in two months? If I thought the Hibernians would agree, I'd almost be happy to go along with that."

"*You*, Melissa?" Moroni was suddenly taut. For a moment there was silence. Then Moroni continued: "You and Makka have done a good job, but the decision lies with the executive here."

De Voe tensed. "I understand. It was just a manner of speech."

"Yes, it was – but maybe a useful one." Moroni turned to her right. "Margarethe – perhaps we should continue this discussion alone… and with Hanna, of course. This is our task, our responsibility."

Olson frowned and looked uncertain. "Well, Nila, yes you are right. But… before we ask the others to leave, I think it is important that we gain all pertinent facts from them, no?"

"Of course, but I think–"

"No!" De Voe spoke louder than intended. "I'm sorry, but I don't think we've explored every option."

Moroni looked non-plussed. "What exactly have we missed?"

"I sense that people around this table have doubts about whether we can properly exploit this find practically. And I take your points. But we know the Hibernians aren't going to give us shit. Nor will the Marseillaise. But maybe… maybe those following might. The *Lisboa*? The *Alexandria*? They're run by decent people. If we don't act now, maybe we can act in concert with one of them? Develop Rennie's cover story in the meantime? And if our overtures to one of them goes nowhere, then by our next turn on Athol, in two years' time, we can have everything ready to go – machinery, excuses, everything."

Frost was nodding now. "Yes. I agree with Melissa. There are other options than just giving in to the Hibernians immediately."

Moroni raised a hand, causing all to turn and look at her. And then she smiled. "These are interesting options, and ones I hope we would have come up with ourselves in conclave. But *maybe* we wouldn't have, so thank you, Melissa, for your boldness. Nevertheless, my original point holds – you need to allow us to do our duty. So, quickly now, does anyone else have any other significant observation or fact that might aid our decision making? No?" She turned to Olson and smiled an invitation.

"Oh! In this case, thank you Makka, Melissa, Cass, and Rennie," said Olson. "Let us not detain you any longer. Or you, Anders… apart from getting us a round of coffees?"

Heiko rose with the others and caught Remillard's eye. He gave a twitch of the head and received a nod in reply.

* * *

"I should be speaking to our detainees, Cass, but while I've got you, Melissa said something to me earlier that caused me some concern."

They were in Heiko's office – which not long before had been Remillard's. The other quickly glanced at the leather-bound chair behind the large desk, gave a wistful smile, and pulled out a chair at the small conference table. Heiko had had the decency to eschew the master's chair, and was already seated at the table. "Melissa enjoys causing concern. What has she said this time?"

"She mentioned spies."

"*Spies!*" Remillard laughed. "I think Melissa has been watching too many Earth thrillers on the 3D. No, Rennie, I do not think there are any spies onboard, but…" He held up a warning hand. "That is not to say there aren't Hibernian eyes on the *Stavanger.*"

"Meaning?"

"Meaning that there are people aboard who have no especial affinity with us, our society, our culture. Do these actively spy for *Hibernia*, hacking into databases and stealing secrets? No. But might they occasionally offer reports and impressions? *Perhaps.* Now, we have a formal representative on *Hibernia* – I believe you've met Magnus."

"I have."

"Right. That's because *Hibernia* is the centre of our universe. But *they* have no official representative *here.* Why would they? It would be a waste of their time and resources. But they are unlikely to have zero interest in us."

"Okay. No spies. No ambassador or envoy. Informers?"

"Probably *informer*, singular."

Heiko scrunched his brow. "It sounds like you have thought about this before. Do you have a name?"

Remillard laughed. "No, I don't! It's not been a priority. Resource pilfering, as you've seen, is a priority; searching for an inoffensive ghost – no."

"It might be an issue now, though."

"I see that."

"So… no ideas at all? Is there anyone you know who shows ambivalence to the *Stavanger* and its people, or who has expressed admiration for *Hibernia*? And I assume we must be talking about someone at a modest level of seniority, as presumably a fisherman or teacher would have little access to information that might be of interest."

Remillard closed his eyes and leant backwards. After a moment he shook his head and opened his eyes again. "In truth, nobody leaps to mind. Look, I've delayed a fishing trip for this. Let me go and cogitate. It's amazing how a bit of solitary time holding a rod and looking over the wide ocean can aid contemplation."

"Thanks, Cass. I appreciate it. Enjoy your trip."

* * *

Heiko's last meeting of a busy day was with Irina Vlassic.

He'd already seen Ana Ibsen – a meeting that had been brief but tense. Mrs Ibsen worked as a retail manager in the Eastside Mall; she'd been dumbfounded and embarrassed at having been detained by Pedersen and then kept waiting in an office in the Security section for several hours – unmollified by endless coffee and pastries. When Heiko met her and revealed that the interview was because of a phone call from her husband, she had become angry – at Ibsen more than anyone else. In her own words, she was not a geologist and had no interest at all in 'rocks', and she'd not understood what he'd told her. In fact, her take-home message from the call had been that some event at the mine meant that Sven would probably have his sojourn on the island extended – which was just another excuse for him to be elsewhere. She said she'd not spoken to anyone else about the call, and Heiko believed her, letting her go with profuse apologies.

But that interview had left him cursing. Had he turned an inconsequential event that would have led nowhere into something else? Ana Ibsen would now have to explain herself to her colleagues and friends – and what story would she tell? His own explanation to her had been that Ibsen was causing mischief and they were trying to find out what rumours he was trying to circulate – an explanation that seemed somewhat lame, even to him. He'd embellished the tale by implying that his deputy had misunderstood instructions and that he was simply meant to invite her along at the end of her shift for a quick chat. It wasn't that he'd been trying to absolve himself of blame, but he'd simply seen this as the most believable scenario. So, the best case was that Ana Ibsen focused on police incompetence, which would likely piss Pederson off; the next best was that she raged at her husband for dropping her in the situation in the first place, causing ructions for the foreman; and the worst case was that she believed there actually *was* something suspicious going on at the mine.

And now here was Vlassic – who was a different creature altogether. She worked in the Material Resources section, like Ibsen, and knew more than a little about chemistry and geology. Once she got over her outrage at her treatment, her first words were: "Exciting, isn't it?"

Heiko momentarily closed his eyes and winced. Then he looked at the woman opposite with a serious expression: "Exciting, Ms Vlassic? It might be if it were true… but I'm afraid it isn't."

"What? What do you mean?"

"Mr Ibsen has been playing a little joke on his colleagues. Unfortunately, it has gotten out of hand, and while Mr Frost has seen the funny side of things, Ms De Voe is unhappy at being a victim of a planted sample and wants this nipped in the bud." He smiled inwardly at that invention: from what he knew of his colleagues' personalities, at least that angle was credible.

But Vlassic wasn't having it. "That doesn't sound like Sven. Practical jokes? And even if true, I don't see why I should be arrested for it and thrown in a cell for the afternoon."

Heiko could see why Ibsen had strayed: Vlassic was an attractive woman in her thirties, with long black hair and dark eyes, who shared similar interests to the man, and who had sought to defend him when his wife had not. "First, Ms Vlassic, you are not under arrest. I am sorry for how this has played out. I blame myself: my instructions to my deputy weren't sufficiently precise. I only wanted to have a quick talk at the end of the day, not for you to be brought here to await my convenience." At least this time he had attempted to shift the blame from Pedersen to himself. "And second, Mr Ibsen was simply a party to the joke, not its instigator. And as I said, it was well received for the most part, but Ms De Voe…" and now he was dropping Melissa in it! "…seems thinner skinned. But she also has a point that the nature of the rumour, if spread widely, could be destructive. Raising false hopes…" Heiko smiled at getting in *that* expression… "and also raising questions about the competence of the top team."

Vlassic's face seemed to flash through a number of emotions: anger, surprise, disbelief… and then relief. "So… I am free to go? And Sven isn't in trouble?"

Heiko softened his expression. "Yes… *Irina.* I think the touchy Ms De Voe may have something of a downer on Mr Ibsen for a while, but as long as she doesn't return to the *Stavanger* and find the place rife with misinformation and herself a source of mockery, then there is no problem. *As long as.*"

Vlassic now smiled uncertainly. "I understand. I'd only told a couple of people anyway… Perhaps I should call them to clarify matters?"

"Yes, please, Irina. Neither of us want harm to come to Mr Ibsen from his angry superior, eh?"

"Sure. Melissa can be a hard arse."

Heiko rose from his seat, startling the other, but then inducing the woman to rise, too. "Thank you, Irina, and once more, I am very sorry about your inconvenience. My deputy and I clearly have to work on our communication."

After the woman left, Heiko returned to his office and slumped at his desk. *A couple of people?* And how many more had *they* told? *Damn!* He would now have to hope that the new lie washed away whatever infection was at large in the ship, certainly before this mythical informer – *if* they truly existed – heard it and thought of including something on it within their latest treacherous update. He would have to talk to Pedersen about how they might track communications between the *Stavanger* and *Hibernia.*

Pedersen? His one confidante – *he hoped.* But what had Pedersen said to the other officers in the unit about today's events, and what did *they* make of matters? That was the problem with cover stories: they weren't as easy to set up as most people thought… *or* to maintain.

Chapter 12

"An interesting report, Colonel," said Manfred Traore. The two men were sitting in Traore's office, facing each other across a large wooden desk. To one side, a glass wall provided views over Charlestown.

"That was meant for O'Neill," said Nesvorny.

"She received it – and passed it to me to include in my own report to her. I thought I should discuss matters with you first, before giving her my overall thoughts."

"Discuss? Discuss what, exactly?"

Traore looked away and toyed with a glass of whisky, gently pushing it this way and that on his desk. Beside the glass was the tablet on which he had been reading Nesvorny's report. "I must admit, I am disappointed." He looked up at the other, who sat stiff-backed before him, dressed in his black uniform. "You were asked to provide a full report on security issues related to our current resource crisis – on problems and solutions. But here…" he pushed at the tablet, "there is nothing of substance. It's as though there are no problems."

"As you already know, there is theft of material by Stoker gangs – which is detailed."

"But surprisingly little of this."

Nesvorny locked eyes with the other. "The report lists confirmed losses. But stolen material is often not noticed until some system or device fails. Until reported, I cannot investigate. I provide the facts, not speculation."

"Oh, come on, Colonel! You know the situation is far worse than this," Traore pushed at the tablet again. "We are relying on your expert opinion as to how bad things might be – but you refuse to give it. And you provide no analysis of recent changes in thefts, which I understand are increasing."

"You understand? Who told you that?"

"So, it isn't true?"

"There has been a small uptick since the *Leviathan* disaster, yes. *Small.* Statistically uncertain. It is prudent to wait for more data."

"Then gather it, Colonel!"

"How – and with what?" Nesvorny leant forwards and angrily tapped a finger on the desk to emphasize his points. "First, I cannot send my force to check and test the state's equipment to see whether it is whole and works – my staff are not electricians or engineers. Second, even if they were, I lack the personnel to do this and keep the state secure at the same time."

"I'm not asking you to delve into the electronic heart of the city, Colonel. Rather, I suggest you approach the problem from the opposite direction. Raid the Engine Quarter. Find out who is really living there and what loot they are sitting on."

Nesvorny shook his head and scowled. "I need just cause to start breaking down doors – and there's presently no justification for it. If I did do a raid, there would be a riot. My responsibility is to maintain the peace, not breach it."

"You seem to be turning a blind eye. Ignoring a problem that all can see. By the time you act, it is liable to be too late. Don't you see the existential risk here?"

Nesvorny leant back and crossed his arms. "The only existential risk I see is if we provoke a revolt amongst a segment of our population for little reason."

"*Our* population?"

"The Stokers are Hibernians, just like you and I. They didn't emerge from the ocean."

"No, more like the sewers."

Nesvorny bit down on what he was going to say. Then he pushed back his chair and stood abruptly. "This discussion is going nowhere. I will not amend the report to invent a crisis so that you can justify your…social engineering? *Ethnic cleansing?* I will be clear about this when I next see O'Neill. Now I have work to do." He turned and headed for the door.

Traore waited for the main door to close, and then another thirty seconds to be sure. Then he called out: "Major Fukuda… come in."

Fukuda entered from a side door. He came to attention before the lounging Traore, who had rocked back in his chair and was now resting his legs on his desk.

"Sir!"

"You heard that?"

"I was listening, as instructed."

"So, you see what we have to deal with. Your superior isn't very accommodating."

"He works in his own way."

Traore smiled and tilted his head. "He has a reputation, sure. He was once feared. But has he gotten too long in the tooth? Developed too many scruples? Do we need new blood, perhaps? *Your* new blood?"

Fukuda maintained a severe expression, looking straight ahead rather than at Traore. "That is not for me to say."

"You are a man of ambition, no?"

Fukuda's mouth twisted into a gentle smile, but he didn't respond.

"We need to have a Head of Security who thinks of the state, first and foremost. Someone who is loyal. Someone who will do what needs to be done for the benefit of true Hibernians. Are you the one?"

Fukuda's brief smile disappeared. He at last looked down at Traore. "I am subordinate to Colonel Nesvorny. I must follow his orders."

"Subordinate for now. Prove yourself to me, and I will suggest your promotion above him. O'Neill will accept my recommendation."

Fukuda nodded once. "Tell me what you want me to do."

"Nesvorny refuses to act, insisting he will only *react*. Give him something to react against. I don't care what you do, or how you do it. All and any sins will be forgiven. Do you understand?"

"Yes, sir!"

* * *

Colonel Tania Joseph liked to hold court at the small West Dock that was home to her fleet of eight patrol craft. "Welcome to my domain, Eric. It's been a while."

Nesvorny removed his black beret – decorated with a pair of golden shamrocks – and stepped further into what Joseph referred to as her 'command centre', but which still had a feel of the repurposed storage shed it once had been. "It's a pleasure."

The black-uniformed woman extended one calloused hand, which Nesvorny grasped, shook once, and released. Joseph had a strong grip: she was of similar size and bulk to him, and prided herself on keeping fit. Her broad cheeks were smooth, though heavy lines at the corners of her eyes confirmed that age was catching up with her, while her short, brown hair had been bleached by the sun and was now close to blonde. "Let's talk in the bunker."

Nesvorny followed the woman through the narrow building, the walls of which were lined with desks at which sat six uniformed men and women, three facing monitors on each side of the aisle. There was a door in a partition at the back wall, which he entered behind his host.

The 'bunker' was a small space, perhaps four metres by three, with just a single window on the wall facing the door. There was a small desk under the window – demonstrating how rarely Joseph used the space for formal meetings – and three armchairs in a ring around a coffee table in front. To one side was a small fridge, atop of which were a couple of bottles of whisky and a decanter of some mysterious fluid.

"Sit," said Joseph. "You don't drink on duty, do you? What a waste. But my domain, my prerogative." She poured herself a glass from the decanter, gestured at a bottle that Nesvorny assumed held water, and shrugged when he shook his head. Then she took another chair and sat opposite him. "So… what gives?"

"Oh, nothing in particular. I just thought we should keep in touch."

"But a personal visit? I'm honoured." Joseph's mouth twitched into a half smile. They usually communicated electronically, the last time just a few days ago when Nesvorny had told her about Mitsos and asked if she might keep an eye on him through her contact on the *Marseilles*.

"In truth, I wanted to get away from HQ," said Nesvorny. "I have my own private space there – which used to be private until invaded by my deputy."

"Sanctum sanctorum breached? Ha, I get it! You should be safe from unwanted guests here."

"Thank you." Nesvorny found himself relaxing. Joseph hated formality; it was impossible to sit straight while she lounged, legs splayed, drink resting on her stomach. "But I'm not just fleeing others. I genuinely think we should liaise more often. Especially after the *Leviathan.* Matters have been getting tense for some time now. People are starting to realise that the minor issues we've been having are perhaps not so minor after all. And I'll wager it's not just here."

"Sure. *Entiendo.* Trans-world problems. We're all in just a little bit more shit than we were before the big ship went up. But I'm not sure how that impinges on us as a *couple.*" She leered slightly at the last. They'd had a brief fling some thirteen years ago – nothing serious. Since then, Nesvorny had married, had a child, and divorced, while Joseph had embarked on a long series of relationships, with both men and women.

"I'm not entirely sure, either. But we, here, are the centre of Tethys. Because we *have* the most, we also have the most to lose, and losses to the people of *Hibernia* are likely to impact on others elsewhere. I have been worrying recently about overlaps of interest."

"Now you've lost me."

Nesvorny frowned, noticed some lint on his trouser leg, and absently picked it off. "I mean, there are people in this city with a foot in both camps, Hibernian and *Other.* People who might come under *my* remit of interest, as head of Internal Security, but also under *yours* as chief of External Security."

"Like this businessman you wanted me to watch – Mitsos?"

"Yes, Mitsos. But not just him. Were you aware that a lot of the survivors from the *Leviathan* actually know each other, although they've been pretending they don't?"

"The largest party were heading for the *Marseilles*, so I guess you mean them."

"I do."

"You must have been checking up on them, yeah?"

"Sure. But we have no records from Earth, so their stories can't be validated. I don't believe them. And their profile concerns me, too. So, I've had them watched. And their behaviour has been odd. Secretive. *Knowing.* They have been acting as though they were being watched, and behaving accordingly, and not without a little tradecraft."

"But the *Marseilles* contingent have gone now. A few days ago. I don't see your problem."

"Most are gone – not all."

Joseph sighed. "Okay, maybe there are a handful left. And maybe they are malcontents from Earth. But even they will be gone on the next shuttle. They're nobodies. And what harm have they caused, for all their furtive behaviour? None – otherwise you would have said so. As I said, I don't see what your problem is. In fact, I don't see what the problem is for either of us. Are you sure you're not just bored, Eric, and inventing problems to keep yourself entertained? Or is this a distraction from the Stoker issue?" She smiled. "I hear Traore is still bleating."

Nesvorny scowled. "Maybe you're right. Anyway, I *have* been looking for an 'in' to the Stokers. They are insular and loyal. It's difficult to break into their society. And they are clever, too. Since our crackdown last year, they've been a lot more subtle in terms of what they steal, and got better at covering their tracks. They are organised, and I don't like it. And getting pressure from Traore doesn't help, either. I'll be damned if I let a politician tell me how to run my force."

"So, it's resentment that's stopping you from playing ball? I didn't realise you were so petty."

Nevsorny looked up sharply, but Joseph's smile suggested she was teasing him, rather than deliberately challenging. He still didn't like it. "I'm not. But I am the face and arm of the law here. *The law.* Traore doesn't give a shit about the law, and his motives are unsavoury."

"What are you going to do?"

"Redirect my attention to the locals. I've got nothing from the *Leviathan* people – they have come and mostly gone and left little mark. So, I *will* try to break into the Stokers – I just need to work out how." He paused and looked down. After several seconds he shrugged and re-focused on Joseph. "But that is my problem. What about you? Is there anything interesting happening in the wide world? And what about Mitsos?"

"It's too early to say anything about the man with the fantasy machine. Otherwise, what do you think? My days are peaceful. I have heard grumblings from my contacts on various ships, rueing the *Leviathan* loss. Some are considering rationing, others are stepping up patrolling areas around critical infrastructure, and some are even looking at the confiscation of superfluous gadgets. And that's all."

"What about our nearest neighbour? The *Stavanger*. You've got extra intel on them, haven't you?"

"You mean from the drones?" She shrugged. "What can I say. The drones show what they always show: people scraping and digging and pounding. It all looks the same to me. Frankly, we fly one just to remind our tenants who is in control. And after the *Leviathan*, I've cut back flights to twice a week: I'd hate to lose one of my babies."

"You've got plenty of others, no?"

Joseph frowned. "Half-a-dozen, sure. But that's half the number I had when I took over nine years ago. Wear and tear and no replacements."

"Still – we're entering parlous times. Probably not the moment to be cutting back on intel. Might be worth keeping on top of our neighbours even at the risk to your fleet."

Joseph's brow furrowed. "Not crossing jurisdictional boundaries are you, Eric?"

Nesvorny's raised his hands. "Not at all. It's completely your call. Just a suggestion."

"Fine. As a *suggestion* I'll consider it."

"And your source on the *Marseilles*? It might be worth putting them on alert, too."

"Right, Eric, now you're fucking pushing it!"

Nesvorny chuckled.

* * *

Fukuda's augments were seven years old and would undoubtedly be considered obsolete on Earth, but on Tethys they still gave him advantages.

In the third sub-level corridor, the lighting had been glitched deliberately – but he could still see in the infrared, unlike the two troopers who waited quietly in the dark twenty metres behind him, their flashlights turned off so as not to give their presence away.

Momentarily, the image somewhere in his visual cortex trembled and faded: all went black, and then the spooky red-on-black image returned. Fukuda touched the small port by his left ear into which he had earlier inserted the activation processor responsible for his enhanced sight – among other things. He wondered how long it would continue to function, not having been upgraded since his arrival on Tethys all those years ago. He dreaded the prospect of returning to *mere* humanity – a thought of being ordinary that had never sat well with him, even back in Japan, where he'd aspired to be fitter, faster, stronger than his peers. Then, he'd qualified for the Special Boarding Unit and received his first military-grade implants, which had left him on such a high he'd never really come down. But on Earth, he'd had little chance to make use of his new talents: Japan had been a waning power, it's population having fallen almost every year for a century, and when cuts had been mooted, he'd desperately sought an alternative – leaping at the prospect of heading off-world. And while action had been scant since his arrival in *Hibernia*, he'd always had the feeling that he was a lion amongst antelopes, albeit one on a leash. But now, at last, Traore had taken off that leash…

He focused on the movement at the end of the corridor and the two shapes working on the junction box there. One held a torch while the other cursed and pried. He spoke softly, his voice transmitted via the mic in his earpiece. "Hold position. Two targets. I will deal with them. Advance at the sound of conflict."

"Roger, sir."

That was McDonald. Perez was with him. They were two of his inner circle – nine loyal troopers who had fixed their colours to his mast. They were good people: skilled, discrete, but not corrupt – not as such. They weren't on the take; they were simply soldiers wanting to fight a war they believed needed to be fought who'd found a leader who thought as they did. They would report seeing what he told them to see; do what he told them to do.

Fukuda stole forwards, his excitement growing. This was their fourth night of patrolling since his meeting with Traore. They'd found nothing until now – the sub-levels around the Engine Quarter being extensive. But it had been the absence of light this evening that had given the game away: it either signified a recent theft (of cabling, electronics, super-conductors, circuits), or an ongoing attempt – and fortunately for him, it was the latter.

He continued to move, one careful, bent-kneed step after another. Ten metres. Then eight. The prey were still unaware of him, whispering softly and fiercely to each other. In the spectrum he now viewed, he could see they wore rough jumpsuits, and though the colour burned red in his altered sight he was certain that their true colour was green. He paused a moment to consider their belts, but noticed no weapons hanging there – which wasn't a surprise. The thieves wouldn't be expecting anyone to challenge them, and even so, would expect to have enough time to run should any member of Security turn a corner. But while they weren't equipped for a fight, Fukuda was. He slowly drew a heavy metal truncheon from his belt and smiled at the feel and balance of it. In the Unit, he had learnt how to use many weapons, from the advanced to the traditional.

Now closer – four metres. The voices of the others were clearer. One said: "Not that one. Cooling units, you twat. They'll notice."

"Fuck! I hate leaving this behind."

"Don't be greedy. You know the rules."

"Fuck Kai!" But the man withdrew slightly from the innards of the electronic cornucopia.

At this, Fukuda moved. Three quick paces, and suddenly he was at the shoulder of the unsuspecting thieves. Without word of warning, he raised his truncheon and brought it down on the nearer one's head – hard. He heard a crack, and felt a splash of blood upon his cheek. The assault was so swift and brutal that the man fell without a sound.

"What… *fuck*!" The second man stumbled back, dropping his torch and raising his arms as though that might protect him. It didn't.

Fukuda struck down on the other's arm and heard another crack, and then a scream. It was a break. Forearm. Fukuda barely paused: he struck the arm again, and when it was jerked away, exposing the other's head, the following blow connected with an ear. The man stumbled into the pipes on the wall, choking, flailing – but blind now, aside from a narrow cone of light from the dropped torch that revealed little more than the fallen man and Fukuda's black boots.

"No…" the other managed, but then a further blow to the top of the head sent him to the ground, where he quivered and lay still.

Fukuda had his breathing under control by the time his men arrived, their torches swaying wildly and interfering with his vision. He lifted one hand and clicked a tiny switch on the processor at the side of his eye, which cancelled his infrared vision, allowing him to see more natural colours in the gloomy torchlight.

"You've made a mess of them, sir," said McDonald, casting the light of his torch over the fallen men.

"Did they see you?" asked Perez.

Fukuda looked at his handiwork. He'd been quick. Maybe too quick? "Perhaps."

"Won't that be a problem?"

"Not at all." Fukuda smiled grimly at Perez. "I want them to know. Otherwise they might think this is from some other gang."

"It might make things difficult for us, sir," continued Perez.

"That is precisely what our sponsor wants."

"Well, this one might be able to say something," said McDonald, who'd been examining the pair more closely, "but not *that* one. I think you were too… *energetic* with him."

"All the better." Fukuda feigned indifference, but inwardly felt a strange sensation of guilt paired with exhilaration. "We only need one to report back. The message is now so much stronger."

McDonald stood and then, almost as an afterthought, kicked the still living man in the side.

Perez laughed.

Chapter 13

It had been a fraught introduction to the *Marseilles* for Eddard Mitsos, starting with the two-hour flight from *Hibernia*. During this, for the whole journey, he'd been sharply interrogated by Sebastian Deux – the actual leader of the city ship. He would normally have prepared intensely for an upcoming business meeting, but on this occasion, he'd come to the unexpected event flustered, drenched, and disorganised – factors that had clearly amused his adversary. By the time the shuttle landed, he had barely dried out, though he'd certainly been wrung out – not just of information he would have freely given, but of some he would not normally have divulged. Deux was clearly a clever operator.

Mitsos' first view of the *Marseilles* had been of the landing pad, high up on the stern, and then – during a forced dash through another squall – fleeting glimpses of a massive grey bulk with towers, wires, gantries. And once inside a low entrance suite with a chill interior, matters had not improved. He'd been held aside while the *Leviathan* immigrants were led away, and then been told to accompany a guard to a barren side room, where he'd been left for half-an-hour without refreshments or information, shivering in damp clothes.

At last, the guard returned: his uniform was grey and unadorned, with no sign of rank, though his belt and boots were gleaming black, as was the truncheon hanging from his belt. "Your baggage has been inspected and is clean. It will be delivered to your allocated quarters, two floors down."

"Allocated quarters? Is that where I have to go now?"

The guard seemed bored. "No. I am to take you now to a meeting with the People's Committee. Follow me."

"Another meeting? But I'm not–"

"These are my instructions. Come."

So here he was, tramping through nondescript passageways, past closed doors, through the occasional hushed atrium, down two flights of steps (*no elevator?*), and then they arrived at a broad double door, outside of which was another truncheon-bearing guard, this one a stern woman.

"The businessman," said the first guard.

"Right. I'll take him," said the second.

The first simply nodded and about-turned; the second appraised Mitsos coolly for a moment, running her eyes up and down – looking for weapons? At last, she said: "Okay. Let's go." She turned, knocked on the door loudly twice, then led the way in.

Mitsos found himself ushered before a long oblong table around which sat a dozen men and women – physically diverse, though of uniform attire in grey – all facing him, with Deux in the middle. There was a small chair, high-backed but without armrests, set a little back from the nearer edge of the table. A sickly yellow light illuminated the space; the floor was of some sort of rubberised material; and the only decoration in the room was in the form of two banners on the wall ahead, showing red scales of justice upon a white backdrop.

"Citizen Mitsos," began Deux, "welcome. Please sit. We have important matters to discuss."

Mitsos gave a pained smile and scanned the faces of those opposite, gently nodding greetings. "Hello. Thank you."

"I have already briefed the People's Committee, and they've also seen the analysis of our ambassador from *Hibernia*. But before we begin – where is it?"

"Where is what?"

"The template." Deux had a sardonic expression. "The design. Of this machine of yours. It wasn't in your baggage, so I assume it is on you. We'd like to see it, please."

"Uh – of course." Normally Mitsos would have baulked at the request, but his resistance was already low, and he was unable to resist either the command or the dozen pairs of eyes that were boring into him. He reached into an inner pocket of his brown jacket and retrieved the pen drive, hesitated a moment as he looked at it, and then jerked upright. He took a pace to the edge of the table, then reached across to place the drive in Deux's out-stretched hand.

"Excellent! Thank you." Deux looked smug. "I will pass this on to our engineering team, who will give it due consideration. And then we will see."

"See?" Mitsos croaked. He cleared his throat, then repeated: "See what?"

"See what they make of it. See whether they think it will work, and if so, what resources will be needed to make it work. And then we can do a cost-benefit analysis. At that point, Citizen Mitsos, we will know whether we have a deal or not."

"But we haven't discussed my… price." As he said the word, he saw movement across the table: one woman leant across to whisper to another; one man looked across at Deux; another woman shook her head slightly. But Deux seemed unaffected.

"Your price? Of course. We will give that due consideration, but at the moment it's somewhat premature, don't you think? If the engineering team are unimpressed, then haggling now would be a waste of time." He twitched a smile. "And if all is well, then at that time, we – the People's Committee – will deliberate, and come to a fair and equitable offer." He chuckled. "I can make no bargains myself, Citizen Mitsos. I am but the mouthpiece and instrument of this Committee. Together, we represent our people, and we will do what is best for them."

Mitsos noticed one or two at the table smile and nod, and couldn't help thinking: *are you really buying this?* "And… for me?"

"That goes without saying. We won't lack gratitude." Deux looked past Mitsos to the guard who stood behind him, whom he addressed: "I think you can lead our guest to his new quarters now. Thank you, Abaye."

Mitsos frowned, looked over his right shoulder at the approaching guard, and then back at Deux. "I am… being dismissed."

"Yes. Thank you for attending. I wanted the Committee to see you – and now they have. We have serious internal matters to discuss now. Someone will be in touch – in the meantime, please enjoy our beautiful city."

Mitsos felt himself reddening in embarrassment. His tongue tied, he rose, nodded, and allowed himself to be led away.

* * *

Mitsos' apartment was rudimentary and cramped – even worse than his small hotel in *Hibernia.* About the only electronic item in the place was a panel on one wall, which showed a limited number of old, Earth-produced programmes and some education and discussion shows that were apparently filmed in a local studio; the panel also acted as a comms device for internal calls only. Even the kitchen area – which was tiny, and comprised a single storage cupboard and a narrow counter-top for food preparation – had only a small microwave oven and no fridge-freezer. It seemed that people here were discouraged from eating at home instead of at communal diners that sat at key junctions on every level of the city ship.

He'd only just dragged himself from bed – where he'd been since yesterday afternoon, having been too exhausted by recent events, both physically and mentally, to explore – when the panel started to flash notice of an incoming message. The dull political discussion he'd been watching with half an eye then blinked off, and the face of a stern-looking woman dressed in a grey shirt appeared. Mitsos – who currently wore only his underpants – rapidly reached for the remote control to try to block the call, but to no effect.

"Citizen Mitsos. Good morning."

"How do you–"

The woman's hard face broke into a small smile. "You cannot. Citizens are not expected to keep secrets from the state, or to hide from instruction."

"What! You mean you can–"

"Yes, Citizen Mitsos. I can see that you have very colourful pants. But this is a digression. You are required to come to the Labour Share Office, Level 3, Section 4, Room 43, for an interview. This will take place in fifty-one minutes' time – so I suggest you prepare yourself."

"Labour… *what?*" Mitsos was flustered. He hunched forwards on his two-seat sofa in order to hide his scarcely clad groin from the inbuilt camera of the panel. "I don't understand. What–"

"All will be explained at the interview. The appointment details will be stored in your unit. You can recall them by pressing the button showing an envelope. Fifty minutes now. I will see you *in the flesh* shortly." Now she looked amused. The picture blinked off and the discussion programme returned.

"Fuck!" said Mitsos. He hurried to change and take a quick shower.

He duly discovered the Labour Share Office – though he was six minutes late. He found himself in an antechamber with half-a-dozen seats occupied by four others. There was nothing else in the room but a comms panel, which periodically changed to show a name. When it did so, one of the others – all of whom were dressed alike, in grey shirt and trousers – would stand up and go to the only door in the back wall, wait, and then enter after that room's previous occupant exited. As he waited, others came and went, but he was not called, and there was no one to talk to about this. At one point, in increasing annoyance, he stood and paced to the entrance door – on the verge of walking out. *Wasting my fucking time!* But discretion got the better of him, and he returned to sit with the other occupants. The space was silent throughout his wait, but while the others had personal comms devices to entertain them, he'd left his own in the apartment, having failed to connect it to the local wireless network.

At last, after an hour and a half, his name appeared on the screen. "*At fucking last*," he muttered. He brusquely pushed past the man emerging from the back-wall door, and found himself in a three-metre-square room with a single desk and the woman from the earlier call sitting opposite. The desk held a screen, raised at a forty-five degree angle, which symmetrically matched that on the side of his interviewer.

The woman looked like someone had pissed in her coffee: she had short grey hair, a wizened face, a small scar in her top lip, and a mouth that seemed to be set in a permanent frown. She wagged a finger indicating that Mitsos should sit. As he did so, he scowled: "I don't know what this is about or why I've been made to wait for so long. You said fifty minutes, not two-fu…, not two hours and fifty."

"You were late. As you're new, I've decided to see you anyway. Otherwise you would have been sanctioned. Do not be late for any future meeting."

Mitsos felt his hands clench into fists. It took immense effort to calm himself and cajole an insincere smile. "I am *sorry*, Ms. As you note, I am new here. So *please* can you humour me and tell me what the *hell* is going on? *Labour Share?*"

"Yes. On the *Marseilles* we have a labour share policy. As some jobs are more pleasant than others, we ensure equity in employment through job rotation, meaning that all have a chance to contribute in as many ways as they are able. So, Citizen Mitsos, what can you do? What skills do you have? Please look at the screen and touch those entries that match your abilities."

The screen showed three lists: manual skills, cognitive skills, and trained specialisms. "I don't understand."

"It's simple enough – or is reading Interplanetary English not one of your talents? I can display in Old French if you like?"

"No, I mean, why do *I* have to choose?"

The woman looked at him as though he were dumb. After a couple of seconds, she said: "You have chosen to come here. You have to contribute."

"I am contributing. Haven't you heard? I'm a businessman. I brought a template for a machine. Yesterday I met with your rulers to discuss it. When they go ahead and develop it, as I'm sure they will, it might just save this…" he waved a hand, but managed to tamp down on the word 'shithole', "this place. You're lucky to have me."

"I have heard of your history. It makes no difference. What are you doing today? *Nothing*. But you occupy an apartment. Use our electricity. Consume our food. Enjoy our entertainments. Until you are absolved of duties, you *must* contribute. Indicate what you can do, and a random allocation programme will interpret your entries and give you a role."

"I am not–"

"If you refuse, you will be arrested and held in a cell until a tribunal decides your punishment. If that is what you wish, take a seat out–"

"Wait! Oh, *fuck*! Okay. I'll do it!"

For five minutes, a fuming Mitsos tapped and swiped away at several screens. The allocation programme worked rapidly after that.

"It appears that you have very few useful skills," concluded the woman. "Why am I not surprised? Ah, here is your allocation: *fisherman*. Oh, you are in luck."

"Fisherman? Luck? What the hell do you mean?"

"Normally, you'd be expected to start promptly – perhaps in an hour or two. But the fleet has left for the day. So, you have an afternoon of leisure. Details will be sent to your apartment comms about where and when to assemble tomorrow morning – *early*." At last she smiled, and it was the most unpleasant expression Mitsos thought he'd ever seen. "I am happy to have facilitated your usefulness. Be productive in your new role. You may go."

* * *

Mitsos spent the rest of the day on the hunt. He wasn't sure how accessible Sebastian Deux truly was, in spite of his egalitarian speech the previous day, and so he wasn't surprised when he was unable to simply ask the comms unit in his apartment to place a call to him. But eventually he found the man in the early evening after hanging around an area a city map described as the governmental section. He noticed that there was one refectory that seemed slightly nicer than the others – the décor less faded; the meal range wider – and sure enough, that was where he spotted him.

"Deux! First Citizen!"

"Citizen Mitsos? What a surprise."

"Can we talk?"

Deux frowned. "I was about to eat, and then I have a meeting. There is little more to be said about your machine until the engineering group concludes its analysis."

"It's not about that. It's… can we sit?"

Deux ran a hand through his long hair and appeared non-plussed. "Very well – but quickly." He took two steps and slouched onto a chair at the end of the nearest long table, situated at the edge of the open refectory beside the concourse.

As Mitsos roughly dropped into the chair opposite, its legs squealed against the floor. "I had an interview earlier. An employment office or something."

"Yes?"

"That's right. And now I'm told I have to become a fisherman. *A fucking* fisherman! Aside from the fact that I get seasick, that isn't why I'm here."

"Seasick?" Deux smiled broadly. "Really? And yet you've come to Tethys?"

Mitsos waved this observation away in irritation. "It doesn't matter. What is important is: what are you going to do about it?"

"Me? Oh, absolutely nothing. Remember, Citizen Mitsos, you came to us. While you're here you obey our rules and traditions."

"But I'm a businessman. I didn't come for this. I came to engage in a mutually beneficial venture. Something important to both of us."

"So, you want special privileges? That is not how we function. You know this. You have seen it. Didn't I myself serve as an attendant on your flight here?"

Mitsos suspected that the other had actually done very little work on the outward flight to *Hibernia*, and he knew for a fact that Deux did little during the return save drink spirits and interrogate him, but he decided it wouldn't be wise to state this. "You… did. But I am not here as a settler or adherent to your cult, I–"

"Cult?" Deux's face darkened.

"I'm sorry, that was a poor choice of words. What I meant is–"

"You want to leave, Citizen Mitsos? To return to *Hibernia*?"

Mitsos opened his mouth to answer, then closed it. *Did he?* The answer was 'yes', but if he did so, that would likely be the end of any prospects of salvaging his business, either here or back on Earth, should he ever get the chance to return there. And it now occurred to him that he no longer had the template on which his salvation relied, with his backup copy having been destroyed on the *Leviathan.* If he left, would Deux give it back to him? Looking at the man opposite, he thought he knew the answer to that question. "No… No, I don't think so."

Deux steepled his fingers. "Are you sure? You are not a prisoner here. You can leave whenever you want." His face twisted into a wicked smile. "Well, when I say 'whenever', I of course mean, when the next shuttle leaves for *Hibernia.* Alas, I fear that might not be for quite some time, but just say so, and your name will be first on the passenger list."

Mitsos realised that he was trapped: he bowed his head. But he decided to have one last try. "I… respect your society. I really do. You know, I have some revolutionary forebears – fought against the fascists in Greece in World War Two. I had a grandfather who was a minister in Syriza. And cousins who are New Socialists. My workers… they are like family to me, not employees. But this… it's just unexpected. I'm not cut out for fishing or… other things. Isn't it best for me to focus on what I can do? What I'm good at?"

"Of course it is. I am in total agreement." Deux leant forwards and tapped him on the arm. His smile broadened further. "And that is why, if the allocation programme identified fishing as a match for your skills, then that is something I insist you do. Clearly it's a hidden talent! Ah… and now the person I must meet has arrived." He slapped the other's arm, laughed, and stood up. "Good luck tomorrow – I am sure you will catch plenty of fish."

Mitsos watched the other leave – hailing an attractive young blonde woman as she strode across the concourse.

* * *

The next morning, at six o'clock local time, when he would normally still be abed, Mitsos found himself standing on a wet, windswept dock. This abutted the starboard side of the great ship and held a rank of fishing craft on parallel slipways set at roughly forty-five degrees to it. As he huddled with the others assigned to the *Dieppe*, the whole dock began to judder and then slowly move, dropping two metres down to sea level to enable the fleet of trawlers to slide easily into the rain-lashed ocean.

"Board up, comrades," shouted the first mate. "Quick now!"

Mitsos followed the small crew to a number of ladders along the side of the trawler, which they ascended onto the deck. All were dressed in bright orange waterproofs, life vests, and sturdy boots, which they'd changed into earlier.

"What now?" he bellowed, above the sound of rain, wind and clanking mechanisms.

"Cabin for now," said the woman to whom he'd attached himself – a dark-skinned, shaven-headed woman called Noma, who looked fierce, but was kind enough. "Just keep close to me."

The rest of the day proved a nauseous, aching, miserable experience, which Mitsos doubted he would have survived without Noma's patient instruction, aided by the odd shout of warning from the first mate or other members of the crew.

"You've just been unlucky," said Noma, at one point in the afternoon, as they took a brief break inside. "A long Grade Three. Might be with us a couple more days. When the weather's better it can even be fun."

"Fun? You're fucking joking, right? Pulling and pushing, dodgy massive fucking hooks, nearly being decapitated by… well, I don't know what the hell that fucking kraken-like mother was. Fun?" And then – as a gust forced the *Dieppe* off the vertical – he leaned over to vomit on the cabin floor for the fourth (and not last) time in the day. At least the floor was a couple of centimetres deep in water and his stomach contents were almost entirely liquid, so it made little difference to their environment.

"Right – back to it, comrades," cried the first mate, poking his head through the cabin door. "Except you," he pointed at Mitsos. "You swab that up first! Come on – there's still time for another sweep!"

By the time the *Dieppe* returned to the *Marseilles* and settled into its berth – after ten hours at sea – Mitsos was utterly exhausted. But he had to carry on working, hefting boxes of their catch onto the dockside, the containers full of various fish-like creatures, mostly the size of his forearm. He didn't know what they were called, and didn't care. In fact, he'd picked up very little knowledge during the day – stubbornly resisting the imperative to learn, which to him would in some way have been tantamount to conceding defeat. He wasn't a fisherman, or trawlerman, or whatever the fuck they called themselves – not now, not ever. If they wanted to put him to forced labour he wasn't going to help them by displaying initiative. He'd do what they told him, when they told him, but no more than that and with as little effort as possible. Unfortunately, putting out and pulling in heavy nets could not be done without expending energy. And standing on the deck with a great spear to fend off fearsome creatures that wanted to steal their catch could not be done lackadaisically – not unless you wished to risk being snared by some tentacular limb and dragged overboard, or be impaled on the horn of some sort of jumping eel. *What the fuck were they?*

With their duty done, most of the crew headed off to bars in the Level Zero deck, near the dock. Noma briefly looked at him, but didn't issue an invite, while others scowled and cursed him under their breaths. And so he found his locker in the changing room and regained his absurd Earth clothing – his tailored jacket and expensive pleated trousers – and stumbled back to his apartment, where he collapsed and slept for twelve hours.

And then he was woken by his alarm.

"Oh, *fuck off!*"

The routine continued for another five days.

* * *

Mitsos was surprised by a knock on the door of his apartment. He slowly levered himself from the two-person sofa and made his stiff-backed way to the source of the sound. The lack of a bell or other alert mechanism was another instance of electronic deficit he'd noticed on the ship, along with the non-functioning elevators and lack of gadgetry in his new home.

A bigger surprise was who was waiting outside.

"Deux!"

The other smiled. "I'm not one for titles, but *First Citizen* would be more polite, no? I bring exciting news."

Mitsos shuffled back to allow the other to enter his living space, which had only enough room for the sofa, plus a single armchair that he tended to ignore as it sat at an acute angle to the comms panel – which was currently playing (at minimal volume) a sixty-year-old action adventure set in the USA.

Deux took the armchair; Mitsos stood a moment, wondering whether he ought to offer refreshments, before realising that he had nothing to give, and so he slouched down on the sofa instead.

"I guess it's no surprise you know where I live," muttered Mitsos.

"Not only do I know that, but I knew you were in." Deux smiled. "But don't take it personally – I know where everyone lives."

"So, we're all being bugged?"

"No, nothing so sinister. But our facial recognition security system is top notch for Tethys, and in my position I can call upon it for relevant facts. One thing I learned on my way here was that you've hardly been out. You go to work, and later, you go to the nearest communal refectory and then come straight home. You clearly like the accommodation we've given you."

Mitsos barked a laugh. "It's more that I don't like what's outside. I can't do anything – I don't have the local scrip."

"Oh, but surely a successful businessman like you has other funds? You can swap it at the Exchange Office. Somewhere on Level Five, I believe."

"Ha! Thanks but no thanks. I've seen your exchange rates. I'd rather keep my funds for when I can get fair value. There's nothing to spend it on anyway."

Deux's smile had already dissolved. "We have a different system here, true. But consider this: you currently reside in this apartment at no cost – what were you paying for your hotel in *Hibernia*? You eat at the refectory, where you receive basic meals for free. And though I see you continue to wear your Earth clothes – that pink is really something – you can also collect basic clothing for no cost. Entertainment and comms? Free. Likewise all services – from health to education. Unlike *Hibernia* or anywhere else on this world, Citizen Mitsos, we have no homeless, no hungry underclass."

"A real paradise," muttered Mitsos, unable to keep the sarcasm from his voice. "But don't you think the people should be allowed more than *basics*? A little luxury?"

"There is luxury, Mitsos. Tomorrow is pay day across the ship. Everyone, of every profession, will receive the same bonus – even you. Then you can get drunk at a bar, or choose a more delicious meal, get some new clothing, go see a show. Choice. Luxury. And no one lording it over anyone else."

"Not even you?" Mitsos was too tired to care. "So, your apartment is the same as this?"

A dangerous look entered the other's eyes. "My apartment? Yes, it is slightly bigger. I have affairs of state to deal with at all times. I need room to work, to meet. But it is not full of over-flowing chests of gold."

Mitsos closed his eyes and rubbed a temple. He knew he had over-stepped. He sighed. "I am sorry, First Citizen. I am just tired. I have never worked so hard. You said you had exciting news?"

"Yes. Let's move on, shall we." It was clear to Mitsos that Deux had definitely not psychologically moved on at all. "Our engineers have agreed to go ahead and build your machine."

"Have they?" Mitsos stared vacantly for a second, then realisation set in. "They think it will work?"

"Ah, no, that's not what they have concluded." Deux's wicked smile was back. "They have rather taken that for granted – going on the intelligence gained by Ambassador Jons. What they have decided is that they can at least make it, and they have identified the resources needed to do so. And the People's Committee has just decided to approve the scheme."

"They have?"

"You seem surprised, but I put my neck on the line for you and your ludicrous machine. If it works, the upfront cost might be repaid manyfold in the future. I managed to convince the other august members of my viewpoint."

"Ah… *thank you*. So… does that mean I am now in the clear?"

"I'm not sure what you mean."

"I mean, no more fishing. You're going to build the machine, so *that's* my contribution."

"That is your main concern?" Deux seemed surprised, but then he sat back to consider the statement a moment. His sly smile quickly returned. "So, you're an engineer, are you? You can help construct the machine?"

"You know I'm not," Mitsos replied, uneasily.

"In that case, what other aspect of the device's construction do you believe you can aid?"

"No, dammit!" Mitsos couldn't hold back his anger now. "If you want this, there are conditions. It's my machine. It's my patent–"

"Except that it's not, is it? It's not your patent at all."

"On Tethys, it is. I brought it to you."

"Yes, you did. And now *we* have it. Why shouldn't we do to you what you did to the true holder of the patent back on Earth, the one who really spent all the money and did all the research to develop it?"

"You wouldn't! Deux, I… I came to you in good faith. You wouldn't…"

Deux allowed several seconds to pass to allow Mitsos' anger to drain away and be replaced by appreciation of the reality of the situation. He had looked momentarily angry at Mitsos' outburst, but he was back in control once more, and his look was serious. *Calculating.*

"Citizen Mitsos, you did indeed bring this to us." He paused, letting the other wriggle. "And… we *are* grateful. I *think*. But the point is, we still do not know if the machine will truly work in our environment, or whether the economics stack up. What we do know is that to build it, our whole society is going to have to make sacrifices to supply the components and materials needed for it. In this sense, you and your machine are very much still on probation. Yet now you are here, *demanding* exceptional treatment."

"Hardly exceptional! I just… I want to be involved in my project, not–"

Deux raised one hand to stall him. "Let me offer you this. You must fulfil your current rotation. That is fair. Afterwards, request a review at the Labour Office. Think carefully about what the project requires and what skills you have that might contribute towards it, and be more careful in revising your answers to the skills survey. Then we shall see."

"My… rotation?"

"That's right. It's a process we all go through, even I."

"So, you mean…"

Now Deux's smile broadened, and the devil was back. "Yes, Citizen Mitsos. It's back to the boats for you."

Chapter 14

"I wish I'd never shown you," said Sara in exasperation.

"Well, you did," replied Tonio, "so it's all your fault."

They were in the abandoned, partially lit control suite – as they had been on each of the last three evenings after school, as well as twice the week before. Tonio had just emerged from within the guts of a console, the face panel of which was unscrewed and set upon a cleared space on the floor. He was holding a screwdriver. Sara and Kate sat in swivel chairs to either side of him, watching his efforts with varying degrees of boredom.

"I really need to go soon," said Kate. "I haven't done the biology assignment yet. Mum will be mad if I do badly on that one."

"That's fine," said Tonio. "Go if you want. Both of you."

"And leave you here alone," said Sara, "with the ghosts?"

"Ha-ha! But seriously, I'm fine. Go to The Bowl. Or go do your homework."

Kate shook her head. "No, we're staying." She noticed Sara's shoulders slump. "But it'd make it easier to bear if you explained what you're doing. Do you really think you can get it to work?"

Tonio pushed further back from the console and looked at Kate. "I'm just following the circuits, fixing wiring, stuff like that. I *know* the room is connected to the ship's power, because we have light, so it's a case of finding out why the power isn't getting to the main controls – because if it were, I'd be able to switch on the various systems. But the first time I tried, nothing happened – remember?" He tapped the side of his mouth with the screwdriver. "I found the main junction box last week, but I had to fix or replace a few things there. Fuses. Relays. And because I don't have replacement parts, I've had to scavenge them from other places in here – places I think are related to peripheral systems that might not be important."

"So are you any closer to, um, booting this up?" asked Kate.

"Yes, but I just wanted to do a few more checks first."

"Oh, Dios mio, Tonio," blurted Sara. "Just flick the master switch – or whatever you have to do. Give us some *hope*!"

"Well, I suppose I could try."

Kate smiled sweetly. "Go on, then. What's the worst that could happen?"

"*Nothing*. Or maybe some blown fuses. Oh, all right." He put the screwdriver down on the console, rose, and headed to a place in the corner of the room that was deep in shadow. Kate could only see his back as he leant over and spent some seconds shuffling and pushing and twisting. Then, at last, he said: "Okay. Ready?"

"Drum roll!" said Kate, at which Sara started to beat a rhythm on the console.

Suddenly, the main deck lit up in front of them, as did three of the monitors and the big screen at the front of the room, suffusing the space in pearlescent light.

"It's alive!" said Kate – somewhat manically – raising her arms.

"Fuck!" said Sara. "You did it!"

But Kate quickly had second thoughts. "Um… this isn't going to trip any alarms, is it?"

Tonio turned, his white teeth shining brightly in his dark face. "Alarms? Why would there be 'alarms'? No, I think we're safe."

Kate exhaled a long breath. "Whew! So… what now?"

"I need to play about with the controls and see what's working and what isn't." Tonio hurried back to his chair at the centre of the console, in front of which was one of the lit monitors. As he reached it, an image winked on the screen – one of a turtle and the words *Lisboa System Control*. "Yes!"

To Kate, Tonio looked slightly deranged in the light from the monitor, the very image of a mad scientist. Beyond, she noticed Sara's face turn sullen: "Great," said the girl. "But we're not going to be spying on the clique at the Terrace any time soon, are we?"

"Eh?" said Tonio. "Of course not. I don't know what we've got yet, or even if I can get into the main camera system. It might be password protected. Anything." He frowned, pushed back, then turned to look at Sara, presenting Kate with the back of his head. "You said your dad is in Maintenance and knows about this place. Do you think you can, well, see if he knows if there are any old systems operations manuals anywhere?"

"Ask Dad?" Sara frowned, then a smile slowly spread across her face. "No problem. I've got him wrapped around my little finger."

"Surreptitiously, of course," interjected Kate.

"Of course! I'm not an idiot. But there is a price."

"A price?" said Tonio. "But *you* want this as much as we do."

"Don't care. Still a price."

Kate laughed. She got up from her chair and took a couple of paces to Tonio, resting a hand on his shoulder. "I think you'd better put that panel back on and shut this down. I think we're heading to The Bowl. And that means I'm going to have put in an all-nighter to get my assignment done for tomorrow."

Tonio groaned, while Sara smirked and clenched a fist in triumph.

* * *

Marie was staring at a spreadsheet on a computer screen when the door to her shared office opened somewhere behind her. She heard Luisa Teixeira exclaim: "Professor!"

"Luisa… Marie… do you fancy a field trip?"

Marie swivelled to see Miguel Figueroa, whose wrinkled, walnut-coloured face bore a wide grin.

"Where to?" asked Teixeira. She was in her forties, although she looked younger, with a smooth complexion and soft brown hair that was always immaculately coiffed.

"We're in range of the Meridian Cenote. If we're going to conduct a proper analysis of these mysterious phenomena after all these years, now is as good a time to start as any."

"The cenote that curves to the north-west and becomes the Ulster Black?" asked Marie. "Where the fringe forest is? Our destination?"

"Correct, Marie, my dear."

"I thought we were going to pass it eighty kilometres to the west," said Teixeira.

"*Were* is correct. But Joao was happy to plot a route further east. We'll now parallel the Meridian from a distance of ten-to-twenty kilometres as we head north. It's less direct than our originally planned course, and will add a couple of days to our journey, but that's neither here nor there. And this means we're very much in range for the *Fortunata*."

Marie laughed and shook her head. "You've got the Captain-Governor eating out of the palm of your hand. How long have you kept this up your sleeve, Professor?"

Figueroa's smile broadened even further. "Ah, well, yes, I have known for a day or so, but I was keeping it as a little surprise."

Teixeira gently shook her head: she was not a woman who liked surprises. "Well, I wish you'd told us then. Sudden changes make it difficult to plan my lab work. I wanted to complete my profiling of the sea slugs today."

"Oh, Luisa, you are far too sensible. Marie?"

"Hell, yeah! Three weeks staring down microscopes at samples is making me bug-eyed."

"Then I'll see you on the docks. We push off in about an hour."

* * *

The *Fortunata* moved slowly and serenely over the calm ocean as it approached the edge of the misnamed 'cenote'. From Marie's position on deck, this appeared as a long, black line in the water, reminding her of a giant oil slick she had once seen. But it was the silence that was unnerving. On Earth, there might have been seabirds' cries, but Tethys had no bird life at all. And the gentle swell and lack of waves meant there was no slap of choppy water on the bows, with the boat easing across the surface as if on ice. Even the crew were quiet, holding their breaths and voices, mesmerised by the somewhat ominous aspect.

Marco Grande ghosted up to Marie's shoulder. "Be careful," he said, almost in a whisper. "Nobody knows what's down there."

"Sure," Marie hissed in return. "But that's why we're here: to find out."

Grande didn't respond: he gently squeezed past her shoulder and crept away, heading for the main cabin.

Katerina Kalmik stole along the deck towards Marie – her eyes also on Grande, only switching to Marie once the man was through the cabin door. "I see the coward has slunk off," she said in a low voice. "Good riddance. We don't need him jinxing us."

Marie pursed her lips, but refrained from comment. Instead, after a moment, she asked quietly: "So… what's the plan?"

"Victoria isn't going in. She's had second thoughts." Kalmik shrugged. "It's no matter. She's going to collect water samples from the boat. Finding out the chemical composition of the water and why it's black is one of our goals. Her samples will also reveal the nature of microbial life down there. We'll set out some fishing lines, too, to see what we can catch."

"And the rest of us?"

"You, me, Mike and Raul will go in after we illuminate the area. Miguel has set up a string of lights to attach to a buoy. We'll drop that in first."

"Well, that's a relief."

"Sure. *If* it works."

Marie frowned. Still in a low voice, she asked: "Why wouldn't it work? Lights… *light*. By definition."

"Yes, but how far they light depends upon the medium. Cenote waters have odd properties – they almost seem to absorb light. Drop in a low-powered torch and it's unlikely to illuminate an area more than a few cubic centimetres, and your helmet light's the same. I tried it once before, the one time we got close to a cenote."

Marie gave a half smile. "Was this from within the water, or above?"

Kalmik looked stern. "Above."

"Okay. So how much vision will we have with the professor's lights?"

"Does it matter? You're here for this – fearless Marie Lockard, the woman who free swims with Great Whites."

"Sure, I may have done that a few times in the past, but *only* when I could see them, and even then *only* after I'd had a chance to watch their behaviour and ensure they were indolent and unlikely to come and take an experimental bite out of me. This isn't quite the same thing."

"So, are you coming in or not? It sounds like you're having second thoughts, too." Kalmik smiled, but there was an edge to her challenge.

And something more: she appeared nervous and sought to avoid eye contact. It was clear to Marie that she was afraid.

"I'm in. Probably stupidly, but yes, don't worry about me. Just give me the signal."

Kalmik nodded. "Don't disappoint." She wormed past and continued to the stern, where Mike Resnos and Raul Garcia were waiting – already dressed in blue drysuits with bright orange flashes.

Marie returned her attention to the water. The *Fortunata* was now at the very edge of the cenote, having approached at a shallow angle – as though reluctant to actually take that final step over the boundary; but now it did. The bow slid across the line effortlessly, and then the outboard motors – so well baffled they were difficult to hear at the best of times – cut out completely, and the ship coasted forwards. The black edge came closer to Marie in the mid-section of the boat, then closer, and then she was over it… and felt suddenly cold, as though there were a steep temperature gradient at the boundary. Marie felt an icy breeze over her face, and shivered in spite of the warmth of her drysuit. And then she realised that the boat had completed its transition: all around was black, as though they were sitting in a dark pool, or drifting in the depths of space.

She was mesmerised for some seconds – until the door of the main cabin slammed opened, making her heart miss several beats. A curse from the stern revealed that she hadn't been the only one startled by the sudden noise.

"Sorry!" said Figueroa, a pained look on his face. He wrestled with a bundle of small bulbs that reminded Marie of the string of fairy lights she adorned her Christmas tree with every yuletide. "Ah, Marie, did I make you jump?"

She somehow found a smile. "Just a little. Are those the…" She petered off. It was clear they were the lights for the water.

"Yes. Follow me."

Marie let the professor pass, and then followed him to the small congregation at the stern.

Kalmik waited there, a small buoy clasped to her chest; she was flanked by Resnos and Garcia, both experienced divers.

Figueroa handed over one end of the light string, which Kalmik took and clipped onto the buoy. "We should set up spotlights on the hull to shine into the water," he said. "Task number one when we get back. But this will have to do for now." He took the opposite end of the line and inserted its plug into a socket set in the top of the gunwale, before closing a protective clasp over it. The lights spooled on the deck between the pair of them.

"Now… how do we get this out *there*?" Kalmik nodded towards the water. "I can't throw it far."

Figueroa frowned. "Just slip it in and I'll…" He dug around in a pocket for a small communicator. "Arantxa? Ahead please: dead slow."

Kalmik took this as her cue, and slowly lowered the buoy over the side, pausing for a moment with its base a centimetre above the surface, as though anxious not to disturb the water. Then she leant further out and finished the job, jerking backwards at the last second. But the buoy floated un-assailed, and the line of bulbs began to click over the gunwale and into the water. She quickly plucked up the strand and let it slide through her hands instead, pre-empting the somehow unsettling noise. The line disappeared into the dark, the individual bulbs currently unpowered.

"Good," muttered Figueroa. Then, as the spool came to an end after twenty metres or so, he addressed his communicator once more: "That's it, Arantxa. All stop." He smiled at the others. "I think it best if we leave a loop rather than pull the line taut to merely illuminate the surface. It'll allow us to see further down."

"Let's get ready," said Garcia, who had his helmet in one hand.

"What's the hurry?" said Marie, suddenly concerned. "Let's see what we're facing first, eh?"

Kalmik looked at her – but the expected challenge didn't come. "Marie is right. Miguel?"

"Of course, of course!"

As the quartet of divers lined the stern, Figueroa opened the transparent casing of a circuit box. He reached for a switch. "Here goes…"

As lights briefly flashed underwater along the line, several things happened at once. Water jetted up several metres into the air along the course of the lights, the buoy disappeared underwater, the line came taut, and the *Fortunata* jerked, as though being pulled to starboard. There was a scream from somewhere in the cabin; the group at the stern staggered; and Garcia overbalanced and fell backwards into the water.

Marie felt ice in her heart and a prickling all over her scalp. But she managed to stay upright, whereas Kalmik and Resnos fell forwards and then, over-correcting, backwards. Figueroa also stumbled and crashed into the rear wall of the cabin. Marie saw a spray of blood, but her attention was drawn to a cry from the water. She grasped the gunwale and pulled herself in the direction of the sound. The *Fortunata* stopped moving and rocked back upright, seemingly undamaged, save for the lights' cable which had been ripped from the power socket. Marie saw Garcia about three metres from the boat, his face pale; he splashed about like a non-swimmer dropped into the deep end of a swimming pool, making no forwards progress, using all his energy just to stay afloat. *Three metres.*

"Raul… take my hand."

Garcia was now gasping and seemed not to see her, but then his eyes began to focus, he looked around, and he struck out towards her. One frantic stroke, then a second, then… "Christ! What the…" he hunched up, as though trying to pull his legs away from something.

Marie reached further out, and suddenly Resnos was beside her, his arm reaching out too.

Garcia slapped at the water, spasmed, looked around wildly, then turned and launched himself the remaining distance to the boat, shouting: "Fuck… fuck…"

Marie and Resnos grabbed a hold of the man, and pulled. He came up quick – and whole. But Marie swore she saw, as his left leg came out of the water, a long, black shape, like a webbed hand, slide from his calf.

* * *

"Something grabbed me," said Garcia, as they clustered around him in the main cabin. They were now over blue water, with Arantxa having reacted quickly on her own initiative.

"Grabbed?" asked Figueroa, holding a compress to a cut on the back of his scalp – which was shallow but had bled prodigiously.

"Yes. It felt like a hand. It wasn't jaws." He splayed out on a bench seat, and turned his drysuit-encased leg this way and that. "See. No damage."

"I thought I saw something," said Marie. "Though I'm not sure. It could have just been water lapping up your calf. But it was hand-like. Long fingers. Webbed."

"*Christo!* What is down there?" asked Victoria Soares.

Kalmik and Resnos completed the cabin's immediate complement, with Grande standing apart, leaning on a wall at the far end.

"Did you see anything, Mike?" asked Kalmik. When the other slowly shook his head, she looked between Marie and Garcia. "I don't believe it. *Hands?* We've seen nothing like that on Tethys in over a hundred years. But there are plenty of creatures with tentacle-like limbs. Maybe it was just your imagination?"

Garcia was still pale; he chose not to answer. Marie shrugged: "Sure. I couldn't really say. Maybe it was a shadow, or a splayed tentacle. There's only really one way to find out."

"You're crazy!" said Soares. "You want to go back?"

"Today? No chance. But if something did grab Raul, it didn't actually harm him. Or us. Maybe we just need to be more cautious."

Figueroa cleared his throat to attract attention. "Yes, Marie. Maybe the light was too sudden. A shock. It likely caused whatever was down there to react. To bolt. I can make a light string with a dimmer function. We can drop it in the water like today, but increase the light level gradually so it's not a shock." He started to nod to himself. "Yes. We can see what level the marine life will tolerate. Even experiment with different spectra. Maybe some are less *irritating* than others?"

"Back to the workshop then, eh, Professor?" said Marie.

"Yes, I think so."

"But what about now?" asked Soares.

"We can still collect water samples while we're here," mused Kalmik. "So the entire day isn't wasted."

"Collect?" said Soares. "Well, you can collect the samples yourself! I'm not dangling myself over the side again today!"

Figueroa raised both hands – one holding a bloody bandage. "My dears, please. I think we have had a little bit of a shock today. Maybe we should return home. But after some quiet contemplation, I am sure we will realise how exciting today's events are. It seems these cenotes are indeed places of mystery. I for one can't wait to explore them further!"

Marie couldn't help grinning at the professor's enthusiasm – though she noticed that the others didn't seem quite so happy at future prospects. By the far wall, she noticed Grande turn and exit through a door onto the deck.

* * *

Sara had been good to her word, and within the week she'd delivered the appropriate link to Tonio to enable him to access an archive of stored documents related to the design and running of the *Lisboa*. But this proved to be only the start of the process. Tonio became immersed in the files and within a couple of days started to withdraw from his friends.

"He's been going to the control centre by himself," Sara confided to Kate early one evening. They were at the Chilly Cow Ice Cream Parlour on the fourth level, set in a small retail and entertainment complex that was especially popular with the ship's youth. The place – with its white walls and table tops, brown faux-leather seats, and wide glass counter protecting an assortment of widely coloured products – was a favourite haunt of Sara's. Tonio had cried off, as he had the last two post-school days. "I'm sure he's there now."

"That's a certainty. Do you think he's making progress? He's not saying very much. Is this normal for him?"

"Yeah – he gets like this. Trust me, I've known him since we were four. When he's got a problem, he's like a skrylar with a blimpfish. He just won't let go."

Kate frowned at the pale yellow gloop on her spoon. "Well, if he wants to solve an important problem, I'd like him to tell me what on Earth it is we're eating. You don't have cows, so it isn't frozen milk."

Sara smirked. "It's nothing *on* Earth, that's why. It may be artificial to you, but it's *goooood*. I could eat a bucketful."

"Good?" Kate grimaced. "You should try the real thing."

"Better than this? No way. You're just a snob. A food snob. Typical Earther." She put on an affected voice. "*Oh, back home we have the best of everything.*"

"Yeah, that's right. I have a deep yearning for *real* food–"

"Made of dead animals and stuff squeezed out of live ones? Ugh! And you think *you're* civilised?"

Kate considered the 'ice cream' a moment longer, then her mouth twisted into a devilish grin. "If you like it so much… have it!" She flicked the contents at her friend.

The impostor ice cream struck Sara mid-chest on her green school shirt.

"You… I'll…"

Kate laughed. "You'll what? Return fire and waste your fix? Go on then, give me your best shot!"

As Sara contemplated the cost of vengeance, her tablet started to vibrate across the white table.

Kate held up her hands. "Okay, I'm sorry. I surrender! Are you going to answer that?"

Sara scowled, then stuck the heaped spoon into her mouth and moved it with her lips so that it poked off to one side, then she pulled the tablet towards her with both hands. She tapped on a message icon and Tonio's face appeared, suffused in shadow, and upside down to Kate. It was clear where he was.

In spite of the poor light, they could see he was grinning. "Well, I'm in at last. Come and see."

Sara spoke around the spoon. "Really? Good for you. Give us half-an-hour. I want another bowl."

Kate struck her forehead with the palm of her hand.

* * *

"Now, don't you dare say anything negative. You won't believe how much hassle it's been to get this far. I had to find an emergency password, and do a system reboot, then work around various bugs, and I had to actually go to the hardware, too. Not the processors themselves – that's beyond me – but the various electronic connections." They had assembled in the old control centre, which was now well lit, with several monitor screens glowing gently and red and green lights winking from various places along the main console.

"Oh, you love it really," said Sara, standing a short way from the boy, her arms folded across her chest. "You should be thanking me for finding this place and giving you a puzzle to solve."

"Why are you worried, Tonio?" asked Kate, who stood beside Sara.

"I guess it's about expectations. I know what you hope to get, but…"

"I really hate that word," said Sara. "Go on – disappoint me."

"The thing to remember is that this control room was set up as a redundant, emergency one, in case of problems with the main one. It was also only in operation during the early phases of ship construction before most of the habitation decks were laid down."

"I think he means before the Chilly Cow," said Kate, looking at Sara anxiously, "and before the Terrace. Which means–"

"It's not plugged in to the newer systems," finished Tonio.

"So, it's useless," sighed Sara. "All that effort for nothing."

"That's exactly what I thought you'd say," said Tonio, struggling to keep annoyance from his voice. "But it's not useless at all. There are still a lot of interesting things I can do. *Look*." He turned in his seat and hit a key on the pad in front of him. The image on the large screen at the front of the room changed to show a schematic. "This is the sub-level of The Bowl. You can see that *here*." He clicked another key, and an area on the schematic began to glow in red. Then Tonio typed another command, and the screen split: the schematic now occupied the left-hand side, while on the right was a live shot of the interior of The Bowl. "See. There's a camera there, and it still works. And more. Watch this." He tapped yet again, and the image to the right suddenly brightened. "Ta-da!"

"What did you do?" asked Kate.

"I simply reconnected the room to the power supply and turned on the main lights from here – so we won't have to skulk around under the residual lighting anymore." He swivelled to face the girls.

"Well, that's better," said Kate, looking worriedly at Sara, who still seemed to be working out what this meant.

"Yes – and before you say something sarcastic like, 'whoopie, we'll have a bit of light', I reckon most of the electronics in there still work – including spotlights under the bowl itself."

"Spotlights?" said Sara, her expression vacillating between confusion and hope. "You mean… like the ones under the public bowl?"

Tonio was now smiling broadly. "Oh, yeah!"

"Wow! You're a genius!" Sara took a quick step forwards, put her hands to either side of the boy's face, and delivered a kiss to his forehead. "Let's go! Let's go *now*!"

"Wait," laughed Tonio, extricating himself. "There's more."

"Like what?" said Kate, relieved at Sara's transformation.

"Well, there are quite a few abandoned rooms around here – I don't know what's in them yet, but there must be other interesting things. Oh, and here's something cool." He swivelled his chair so he was facing the keyboard again, and worked at it. The schematic to the left of the screen changed and began to flash in a number of different places. "Here. Did you know there are a number of air locks at the bottom of the ship? I counted eight."

"Airlocks?" said Kate.

"Well, you know what I mean. Where you can get out, under the ship. To do repairs. Stuff like that. Most have been deactivated. I think only two are currently in use, but I can reactivate the others."

"That's great," said Sara. "We can now go diving without anyone knowing – if we wanted to, which I don't. Well done anyway. But… The Bowl? Yes?"

Tonio turned back a final time: he looked first at Sara, then over to Kate. "What do you think?"

"I think if we don't go soon," said Kate, "Sara is probably going to explode. It might be safest if we give in."

Tonio adopted a serious expression. "In that case… I concur."

Sara whooped.

* * *

"Oh, Kate… you're here. Nice to see you. I wondered if you'd been kidnapped." The two almost collided as Marie entered the apartment just as Kate was about to leave.

"Is that sarcasm, Mum?"

"Well, you've not been around much. I guess it's because you've been having fun with your new friends. But since you've not told me much about what you've been getting up to, I don't really know."

"Yeah, well, I'm a teenager, aren't I? I'm not *meant* to talk to you. It's against the inter-generational rules. And I probably won't say much for the next four or five years either, so you should get used to it."

Marie correctly read the mischievous smile, and returned it. "I should probably count myself lucky then, eh? All the gossip about boys and the bitching about other girls? Blech, who needs it!"

Kate poked out her tongue. "Boys? Yeah, right." She stepped back, looking for a way past, but Marie solidly occupied the doorway. "Anyway, you've not been around much yourself," Kate continued. "I've been regularly coming back to an empty home, *Mother*. Making myself dinner. Doing my homework like a good girl. Very parental. I'm surprised you remember who I am. It's just been work-work-work… or is it drink-drink-drink?"

"I admit, I've been forced to imbibe occasionally." Marie winked, and then sighed. "But I'm afraid it's mostly been work." She frowned: she *had* been rather absent. Not that she was worried about her daughter: Kate had always been highly independent and responsible. She should have taken a greater interest, but after Kate had survived her first day at school, then mentioned that she had made some friends, Marie had essentially assumed that all was well and turned the majority of her focus back to her professional issues. It was a wonder Kate had chosen to stay with her, not Dirk, after their split. But maybe it was *because* she was so hands-off that her daughter had favoured her?

"That's nice," said Kate. "Well, it's what you wanted, so excuse me, I need to go out."

"Out where?" Marie realised she ought to at least make some effort. "Why don't we sit down and have some tea first? I'll tell you about my day if you tell me about yours?"

"And that's supposed to be an offer I can't refuse?" But Kate did pause, try to look beyond Marie's shoulder, then sighed and stepped back. "Well, I suppose they can wait a few minutes. But you've got to put the kettle on, and supply the biscuits – I know you have a pack hidden at the back of the drawer."

"Ah – that explains where they've been going."

They retreated to the tiny kitchen area that led off the lounge. There was a small table there, only big enough to seat two. As Kate slouched down, Marie retrieved some green tea capsules from a tin, boiled some water, then poured two cups. During this, she was mute, her thoughts on events of the last week.

When Marie at last sat, Kate peered at her from the side of her face. "Soooo… here we are. Well, here I am. You seem to be elsewhere."

"Sorry. I've had an intense few days."

"You might as well get it off your chest then, now that you've *forced* me to stay behind and disrupted my social life. It's about the cenote, right?"

Marie flashed a quick smile. "That's right. What have I told you?"

"Absolutely nothing. Last Friday you muttered something incomprehensible about your boat trip out to it, and that's about it. The last couple of days you were gone from the flat before I even got up. *Child neglect.*"

"Ah, yes." Though Kate was smiling, Marie couldn't help feeling a degree of guilt. "It's just been a bit hectic. Thing will settle down soon, I'm sure. The cenote? Right. I think I told you we'd had problems. When we dropped some lights over the side, the… *water…* didn't like it." She hadn't mentioned Raul's close encounter: with the passing of time, consensus had been growing that it had been nothing; a fish brushing past, or maybe even his leg catching the string of lights torn from the gunwale. "So, the Prof has been experimenting with light strings. Three days ago, we tried again and got a similar result. We dropped in the lights unlit, then Miguel started to turn them up, but they were barely visible when…" Marie raised both hands into the air. "Up went the water and out went the lights. We'd rigged up the connection on the gunwale so it would disconnect more easily with pressure, and the boat wasn't buffeted by whatever attacked the lights."

"Attacked?"

"Just an expression. I don't mean by a creature. It could be some sort of natural phenomenon. But it was less violent, and we managed to fish out the end of the strand with a billhook and retrieve the buoy. Yesterday and today it's been much the same, trying different coloured lights in case it's something to do with the spectra."

"That sounds spooky. So, you still don't know what's down there?"

"Not in terms of sea life. Or rather, *major* sea life. We've now got plenty of samples of water, collected from various depths. The mineral content is definitely unusual, and we've been finding a lot of micro-organisms that haven't been seen before."

"Haven't you tried a bit of fishing?"

"Yes, we have. But nothing is biting. Maybe there is nothing sizeable down there? We'll only really be able to tell once we go down and have a look. But without light, it's difficult."

"Well, rather you than me. I'm not sure how sensible it is poking about in an alien Bermuda Triangle."

"Yes, I suppose it is a bit similar. Ships disappearing, or at least, one big ship some years ago, and perhaps some fishing vessels too."

"And nearly you! Do you think it's the same aliens on Earth coming here and continuing their evil kidnap regime?"

Marie smiled. Kate had a great imagination. "There have been other explanations for the missing ships and planes in the Triangle, you know. Not everything comes down to aliens."

Kate took a sip of tea, and peered over the cup's rim. "Oh, yeah? Like what?"

"Like… oh my!" Marie suddenly jerked upright. "Could it be?"

"Be what?"

"*Natural.* Yes…" she stood. "Kate, I'm sorry, but I think I need to put in a call to the professor."

"You knock yourself out. Does that mean I'm free to go?"

"Uh, yes. I'll see you later. Have fun."

It was only after the door closed behind her daughter, that Marie realised she'd not asked Kate about her own recent activities. As she sat in the lounge, tapping a call on her tablet's keypad, she muttered to herself: "*Some mother you are.*"

* * *

"The Bermuda Triangle?" said Miguel Figueroa, sat at a small conference table in an anteroom where the team usually met to strategise. Katerina Kalmik was next to him.

"Yes, that's right," said Marie, seated on a sofa in her own lounge. She had propped her tablet up on a coffee table so she didn't have to hold it. "Haven't you heard of it?"

"I'm afraid not, my dear. Katerina – no?" The woman pouted and shook her head.

"Ah, well, I guess it's not something that's travelled out to the stars. You have your own mysteries and fables. Well, it's an area in the Atlantic Ocean where there have been a lot of mysterious disappearances, not only of ships, but planes, too. There have been a lot of myths around it; a lot of fantastical explanations. One is that aliens have been kidnapping people. Another is that it's down to waterspouts. But the most credible explanation is methane gas."

"Methane?" Figueroa looked puzzled. "You mean, from the ocean?"

"Yes. It's been proven that sizeable amounts of methane gas exist in some spots on the ocean floor on Earth. Some experts believe that if methane leaks into the water from the sea bed, it can rise as giant bubbles which are able to sink ships and even cause planes to crash. And it can potentially happen rapidly, in just seconds, denying those onboard the time to radio for help or abandon ship."

"Sounds like a fairy story," said Kalmik, crossing her arms.

"No, it's more than that. Although I don't think a sinking has ever been witnessed, the theory has a lot of credibility. But you see where I'm going with this?"

"I do, Marie," said Figueroa. "You're suggesting a similar mechanism might be responsible for the loss of the *Bridgeton*. And maybe even recent events with us. But I'm not sure how light could react with gas in the water to produce the effects we've seen. We're not talking about a lot of heat, although given the coldness of the water… *hmmm*."

"Well, I'm not buying it," said Kalmik.

In her lounge, Marie grimaced. "Katerina, you're also not buying sea life as an explanation, so unless you're going to put your chips behind extra-terrestrials, I'm not sure what you think is the cause of what we've experienced."

Kalmik scowled, but then closed her eyes and rocked back. After a couple of seconds, she opened her eyes, and sighed. "Okay. Of those two explanations… maybe there's something to your new one."

"I'm not saying it *is* methane. In fact, we'd smell it if it were. But maybe it's something like it."

"Yes, Marie," said Figueroa. "This *is* an interesting hypothesis. We need to at least test it out. We can start by collecting samples of the air above the cenote, perhaps before and after we have a light-reaction episode. We can discuss it more tomorrow. Thank you!" He turned to Kalmik: "You see? Marie brings a different perspective. I told you she'd be a valuable addition to the team."

"Sure. I'm glad she's bringing something to the party… *at last*."

Back in her lounge, Marie's bright mood suddenly dissipated.

Chapter 15

It had been two weeks since Frost's announcement of the discovery of monazite. During that time, he had overseen several more drills attempting to chart the location, depth, and breadth of the placer deposit containing the ore. While the emerging news was good, in that the volume of minable material was potentially significant, there was commensurate bad news.

"We can't do it," Frost declared to De Voe. They were sitting on the bare rock of Mount Ardol a short distance above the latest drill site, knees drawn up to stop themselves from sliding down. "We'd have to excavate a huge area, and there's no way we could hide that from drones, or the next ship to arrive, or even make a realistic start laying the groundwork before we're moved on."

De Voe tossed a rock down the slope. "Yeah, that's my reading, too. What a pisser. So, where does that leave us?"

"Still in limbo." Frost watched the small party below – Ibsen and a couple of crew tending the drill, about to extract another core sample to enhance their knowledge further. "No change there."

"Nothing from the big bosses?"

"You know as much as I do."

"Do I?" De Voe squinted at her superior, holding a hand up to shield her eyes from the lowering sun. "Have you really heard nothing from them? I got the impression I pissed off Her Majesty at that meeting. I'm off her Christmas card list, and out of the loop."

"Her Majesty? Oh…" Frost realised she wasn't talking about Olson. "I'm not so sure. Nila likes good people, even if they're difficult. You're in that camp. Anyway," he smiled, "I'm hurt that you think I'd keep something from you."

"Ha! I see your pain is deep!" She tossed a pebble at him, which bounced off the thigh of his russet work trousers. Then she turned thoughtful. "But what about Rennie? Do you think they've spoken to him? Maybe we're both on the outside now – literally, being exiled out here."

"Maybe. It'd certainly be a surprise if they hadn't come to a decision by now. Nila is usually very decisive."

"Trouble in the boardroom?"

"Could be. But that would imply someone is standing up to Nila and what she thinks is best. Could Margarethe do it?" He slowly shook his head.

"Maybe she could if Hanna supported her. Ah – politics!" De Voe scrounged up a handful of loose scree and tossed another small rock down the hillside. "The simple fact is, we've no good options. We either bend over for the Hibernians and hope they're sufficiently appreciative to at least use lube, or… I don't know. Wait for Nila to come up with some Machiavellian plan, or for Rennie to come up with some sort of cracking cover story for all this. I wonder what *he* is thinking?"

"Haven't you asked him?" Frost looked at De Voe with a sly smile. "I thought you two were close."

"Makka – please fuck off! We've had a couple of drinks together, that's all. And I haven't seen him for a week, as I've been stuck out here with you. And no, I haven't been secretly speaking to him on my tablet at night." She grinned back. "Besides, he's older than he looks."

"So you *have* looked!" Frost braced himself to deflect a stone as De Voe raised an arm in mock threat. "Hold! Hold!" he laughed. "But seriously, it would be good to have a word with him. Touch base. See if he does have any news. Fancy a trip back to HQ?"

"Are you suggesting I prostitute myself for information?"

"Not at all. Well… *yes*, actually. Not in a carnal sense, though, unless you really want to."

De Voe shook her head, but her smile was broad. "Okay, enough of the innuendo. I'm getting depressed out here anyway. I'll summon Serge. And what about you? Staying here?"

"Naturally. I want to map out the full extent of this beautiful prospect that we're never likely to get to play with."

* * *

"So, that means we're totally secure?" Heiko asked his deputy – from askance – as they proceeded side-by-side down the corridor.

"Seems so," said Pedersen. "More or less."

Heiko shook his head gently. "I'm still getting used to the differences between Earth and Tethys. Sometimes they seem to work in our favour, sometimes against." They'd just visited the Communications Centre at the very top of the *Stavanger*, where various clever people had bombarded them with information about the workings of the ship's network. Heiko still found the physics difficult to comprehend at a fundamental level, relying on others to translate talk of electromagnetic waves, transmitters, receivers, frequencies, and the like, into simpler language. "In this case, our infrastructure only supports wireless connection between our citizens' specific mobile data devices and the cell tower here, yes? The lack of optical fibre cables between ships means that no one can call to another ship, right?"

Pedersen smiled graciously. "As I told you before, it *is* possible to communicate with other ships, but that's done via satellite in the Centre, and all such calls need to be authorised and are recorded – as you saw."

"And you're sure no one has an individual satellite phone?"

"Ninety-nine percent sure. More than that. Add a point nine nine. There's just no justification for such devices, and there's no manufacturer of them on the planet. We city ships live in our own bubbles, with minimal communication between us, and only then on important matters, such as when a shuttle is due."

They reached the end of the corridor, where there was an elevator and a flight of stairs – which the civic-minded tended to use to reduce wear on circuitry. There was also a door to the outside, which Heiko decided to take. They emerged onto a small, sheltered terrace with a couple of telescopes fixed onto railings, although he doubted the spot was used much, save by Comms Centre workers when fancying a bit of fresh air or sunshine. There was a chill wind at present. Heiko reached the edge, turned, and rested his back against a railing so that he could look directly at his deputy.

"That still leaves point zero zero one unaccounted for. Or have I missed a zero? I appreciate you don't want to be definite; I don't either. Let's assume there is a way. What is it? How would an informer normally communicate? A physical message on a shuttle run?"

"That makes sense, yes. But shuttles are rare. If there's an informer, they would have sent their last update on the one that picked you up from *Hibernia... somehow*. There've been no shuttles since, and there isn't likely to be another for some time, unless Ambassador Solbakken manages a large purchase of materials and we have to pick them up."

"And you're sure our comms devices can't be tweaked to transmit to the orbiting communication satellites?"

"I'm not an expert, but I think not. There are very few people aboard with the skills and resources to do this."

Heiko momentarily closed his eyes to remove distractions and allow himself to think. "So… any extraordinary communication would have to go via the Centre behind us?"

"Yes. And as you saw, transmissions to *Hibernia* via the satellite are rare. The last one recorded was three weeks ago to Solbakken from the Premier, and then a response was recorded from him a day later and relayed back to her via the wifi network."

"I didn't like to ask when we were in there, but what if one of the specialists is an informer? Could they send a message and not record it?"

"Ah… now I understand why you asked about their shift patterns. They said there were always two on duty, which would mean two informers."

"Or the informer waiting for their partner to take a comfort break?" Heiko folded his arms. "It seems to me that we need to keep an eye on the Centre. It's the choke point. How do we do so in a non-suspicious, non-offensive manner? Hmmm. I think I need a coffee. On me. Let's strategize out of this wind."

* * *

"Here I am," said Heiko, wandering up to the table in Bjorn's Castle at which De Voe was seated. "I must admit, I was surprised by your call. But delighted, of course."

"Yeah, well, don't let it go to your head. This isn't a date. I'm not *that* desperate." De Voe smiled, and then winked for good measure to emphasize that she was only joking. "Take a seat. I got you a beer."

Heiko was still in uniform, albeit he'd undone his shirt's top bottom to symbolise being off duty. As he sat, he returned De Voe's smile. "Okay, so, you're not after my flesh. I can live with that. In that case, what do you want? A chance to even the score?"

"Ha! I know you've had liver work. From what I've read, you mercenaries do it so you can filter toxins as well as alcohol. You wouldn't have bested me otherwise. Well, maybe you would, but not so easily. By the way, this is my second – try to keep up." She waited for Heiko to embrace his own glass before continuing. "But seriously, I've been chatting with Makka, and we're confused about what the fuck is going on. Two weeks? Moroni is not that inefficient. So…?"

"You wonder whether you've been sidelined, and you think I might know something? That's interesting."

"What is? Moroni, or our paranoia?"

"Moroni. I'm also in the dark, Melissa. But I'm not completely surprised by the delay. It's an intractable problem. Still, the window for a variety of options is closing. I'm concerned that more and more people on the *Stavanger* are being exposed to the situation ashore and may work out what is going on."

"Yeah, well, we couldn't think of a legitimate reason to alter shift patterns to prevent that, but Ibsen is now fully on board. And as far as the others in the mining team are concerned, we are still *looking* but not *finding*."

"Still, a leaky vessel has a tendency to… leak."

De Voe laughed. "Head of Security and master of words and metaphor."

"Now, that is definitely untrue. The problem is, I'm currently failing as a master of strategy, too. I admit, I can't see an easy cover story for you digging up half of Mount Ardol."

De Voe looked sour. "Yeah, well, if it's any consolation, nor can we. Makka has come to the conclusion that there's no way we can extract what we want without giving the game away, and I feel the same."

Heiko lowered his glass after another pull. "Well, that takes one option off the table. Have you updated our superiors about your conclusion?"

"Ah, no. Not yet. Do you think we should?"

"It's information pertinent to the decision, so, sure. Though they're not fools. I think Moroni, at least, will have already reached this conclusion."

"Okay. I'll think about it. But there's the question of how."

Heiko smiled wryly. "You're not feeling bruised about your last encounter with the heir apparent, are you?"

"Never! But the message really needs to come from Makka. And I fear drawing attention to this matter will undermine the option of keeping the find to ourselves."

"Yes, it will. It seems to reduce our choices to *who* to tell about our find, and *when*."

They discussed the matter further, but events soon threatened to overtake them.

De Voe had just returned from the bar with another round, when Heiko's palm-sized comms unit began to buzz. He picked it up, and his expression turned stony.

"I see. Thanks, Anders. I'll meet you there."

"A problem?"

"Could be. I have to go. But… I'll call you later, okay?"

Heiko stood and stalked from the bar. As he moved, he reached up to address the top button of his blue uniform shirt.

* * *

"What did you send?" asked Heiko, firmly.

"That is none of your business, Mr Heiko." Hanna Bulow wore a haughty expression on her patrician face. "I think you overstep your authority."

There were five people in total in the Communications Centre. One of the technicians – as arranged – had alerted Pedersen that the satellite link was being accessed, and Pedersen had in turn alerted Heiko. The two security officers had arrived at about the same time and managed to intercept the *Stavanger's* Deputy Premier as she was leaving, escorting her back through the doors. The technicians now stood around in the background, clearly wishing they were somewhere else. Heiko turned to the nearest tech. "I was told you record what is sent, yes?"

"Er, yes and no. We record when the uplink is used, but not the content." He waved to a side suite with a thick, glass-panelled door. "Users send from there, privately. Visual and audio."

"Who did she call?"

"Magnus Solbakken," declared Bulow, interrupting. "Our ambassador on *Hibernia*. Do you have a problem with that?"

Heiko flicked a glance at the woman, whose white-blonde hair shimmered in the low light like a halo, but he continued speaking to the technician. "Is that true?"

"Well, yes, I guess so. The call went through to the embassy."

"Okay. Then a quick call back should confirm–"

"If it'll save you time," Bulow announced, "I didn't manage to speak to him. He wasn't available. So I spoke to someone else. A simple-minded woman. One of his staff, I guess."

"Staff?" Heiko turned to fully consider the woman. "I stayed at the embassy a short time before I was picked up, and spoke to Magnus. He said he didn't have any staff."

Bulow smiled and shook her head slowly. "Really? Do you think our ambassador cleans and tidies his official residence himself? He obviously meant permanent staff from the *Stavanger*."

"So, you spent some minutes speaking to a Hibernian cleaner?"

Bulow looked non-plussed. "I've no idea what her role was. She seemed confused. I'm not sure she knew him well. I did think it was maybe a wrong number."

"And what did you speak about?"

Bulow decided enough was enough. "That is of no concern to you. Affairs of state above your pay grade. Step aside and let me leave."

But Heiko held out an arm to prevent her passage, and she was too dignified to try to push past him. "Affairs of state discussed with a home-help in the evening? Really, Ms Bulow? You–"

Pedersen had been on his comms unit, speaking softly. He now leant in: "Sir, they're on their way. Five minutes."

"Thanks. Ms Bulow, let's pause a moment." Heiko turned back to the main tech. "Is there somewhere we can speak privately in here?"

The technician pointed at the door to the uplink room. "There's a small conference table in there, for when the council hold live meetings with Mr Solbakken."

"Thank you. Could you please set up a call to the embassy, but don't connect until we're all assembled and I say so. Ms Bulow, please follow our friend in."

After an uncomfortable few minutes in silence, with Bulow seething at one end of the table and the technician setting up the required connection – both under the eye of Heiko, who leant against one wall – the door to the suite opened. Pedersen ushered in Margarethe Olson and Nila Moroni, both in stylish dresses, having apparently been called from some evening's entertainment.

"Hanna?" said Olson, uncertainly. "What is this?"

"Premier!" said Heiko. "Please take a seat… and you too, Ms Moroni. Sorry to drag you away, but an issue has occurred that we must resolve."

The women sat, with Moroni casting evil glances at both Bulow and Heiko. "Okay. What the fuck is going on?" she said.

"I have been concerned about certain matters – that we should perhaps refrain from discussing at the moment…" he looked meaningfully towards the technician, "and how they might be communicated with our competitors on *Hibernia*. Apart from physically during a shuttle transfer, the satellite link is the only clear means of communication. Ms Bulow is the first to use this medium since the matter came to our attention. Hold." Heiko took two paces to stand behind the technician. "I think we need to discuss matters in private. What should I…?"

"Er, it's all set. Just tap this key here, and the call will be made." He rose, looked around the room uncertainly, and then departed.

Heiko waited for the door to close fully, then took care to alternate his gaze between Olson and Moroni. "Ms Bulow made a late call to our ambassador and apparently spoke to someone else in the residence instead. I thought you should know, and I would appreciate your backing in this interrogation."

"Of course," said Moroni. "Hanna – what the fuck are you up to?"

Bulow returned the other's glare, her face a mask of distaste and even contempt. "I have been attempting to help resolve our problem on my own initiative. As Deputy Premier, and *second* of state behind Margarethe, that's within my remit. I don't have to get your approval for everything… or *anything*, actually."

"At the moment, no, but–"

Heiko stepped in. "Ms Bulow, it might help your cause if you explain your actions fully."

Bulow broke the stare with Moroni, looked to Heiko, then focused on Olson. "Margarethe, we have been going around in circles. *She* has cast the Hibernians as tyrants, not to be trusted, but the truth is we just don't know how they will react. I simply thought it wise to seek advice from someone who knows them better than any of us; someone who regularly meets their leaders and will have better insight than we do. It's something we probably should have done before now, but I feared that *she* – fearing the answers Magnus might give, and under some absurd pretence of security – would veto it, and convince you to do the same."

Moroni scowled, but Olson held up a hand: "That… *does* make sense. To talk to Magnus. But… this subterfuge?"

"I know it doesn't look good," said Bulow, "but what choice did I have? We are on the verge of making a monumental mistake. With Magnus' support, I am sure we could break the deadlock. The Hibernians will appreciate us, and they will share. I am sure of it. What they won't tolerate is treachery." She folded her arms and looked defiant.

"I do see…" began Olson.

"Very well," said Moroni. "We are here, and Magnus is on the end of the line." She smiled now, without an ounce of humour. "It seems I have been outmanoeuvred. Heiko – press the damned button. Place the call."

"Yes, Rennie," said Olson. "Please go ahead."

Heiko turned in the seat before the console and hit the call button. The monitor before him displayed the call number and flashed a dozen times. At last, the screen cleared to show a middle-aged man with blue eyes and light brown hair dressed in a dark blue buttonless shirt.

The man showed a moment of confusion, then scrunched his face. "Ah… is that you, Mr Heiko? I am sorry, we only met briefly. Head of Security? Ah, of course."

"Good evening, Mr Solbakken. I am sorry to disturb you, but I am here with the ruling council – Premier Olson, Ms Moroni, and Ms

Bulow." Heiko pushed back his chair, so that the camera above the monitor was able to show those sitting at the conference table behind. Heiko glanced quickly at Bulow, and continued: "And I am glad you are in residence this time."

"Ah, hello all. But… this time?"

"Ms Bulow placed a call less than half-an-hour ago. Apparently you weren't in."

"I said, 'available'," said Bulow, quickly. "Not that he was necessarily 'out'."

Solbakken ran a hand through his hair. "Ah, well, I have been in all evening, and most definitely available. What is going on?"

As all eyes in the room fixed upon Bulow; the woman's brow furrowed and various emotions seemed to cross her face. "When I called, the call was answered rapidly. By a woman. She said she didn't know–"

"Alas, there is no woman here," said Solbakken. "Please ensure my wife is aware of this!"

Moroni was first to the attack. "Hanna – what the fuck did you say to this woman?"

"Nothing incriminating," Bulow raised her hands defensively, "I swear!"

Innocent.

Duped.

But Heiko wasn't entirely sure he believed it. *Any* of it.

Olson quickly cut the call, leaving broader matters undiscussed so as not to worry Solbakken.

* * *

An hour later, in the more comfortable surroundings of Olson's official apartment – on the same floor as the government offices, and about five times the size of Heiko's designated rooms – three people sat in comfortable seats around a low coffee table. Heiko nursed a glass of flavoured water, while Olson and Moroni each held something stronger. Bulow had not been invited: she'd been barred from using the satellite link in any capacity, although she was currently at large and unconstrained.

"So, what do we make of that?" began Olson.

"You mean, is Hanna an incompetent fool, or is she a traitor?" said Moroni. "I'd like to hear what our Head of Security thinks."

Heiko took his time to compose a response. "The thing that disturbs me most is the *time*. Her call lasted six minutes and twenty-three seconds. That is the recorded length of her conversation with this mysterious woman. Ms Bulow claims she only spoke to ask about Magnus, and then had a confused discussion trying to establish who the woman was. She said she did not mention the mineral find at all. Six minutes."

"She's lying," stated Moroni.

Heiko smiled gently, but did not respond.

"But why?" asked Olson, waving an arm and sloshing the amber fluid in her glass.

Heiko looked from Olson to Moroni – pointedly.

Olson took the hint. "A problem with Nila?"

"I'm new here," said Heiko. "I don't know your personal histories. But even at our first meeting I detected some antipathy. Has Ms Bulow been in her position long?"

"She's been my deputy for eight years," said Olson.

"And is she ambitious?"

"She's never come across as such."

Moroni snorted. "Sometimes ambition grows in shadows. I see what you're saying, Heiko. She felt threatened by me."

Heiko nodded slowly. "On our first meeting, you were identified to me as the future by the Premier herself. I suspect that hurt."

"But this is no recent event," said Moroni. "She can't have decided to turn traitor after that meeting."

"I suspect not. Your star must have been rising from well before then. Years? How long since she began to be sidelined? Also, there are two explanations for this mysterious woman: the first is that she is a contact Ms Bulow knew would answer her call; the second is that the Hibernians are actively monitoring satellite calls and this interception proved opportune – at just the moment someone from here decided to reveal something important. From what I have learned from Cass and Anders, it's unlikely the Hibernians have the resources or motivation to do this. And further… ah…" Heiko's communicator buzzed. He put his glass of water on the floor and attended to the device. "This might prove instructive."

He took the call under the intent eyes of the two women, responding with a series of monosyllables. Then he closed the communicator and slipped it into the pocket of his uniform jacket. "And there we have it. That was the chief technician we spoke to earlier. It seems that there are two numbers to the embassy, the old and the new, with *both* being listed in the database as 'embassy'. Ms Bulow requested to be linked to the old number, which she presumably knew would not go to Magnus, but to this other person."

"So it would simply be recorded in the logs as 'embassy'," said Moroni, "and if caught, she would have a good excuse for making a mistake."

Heiko no longer smiled; he nodded once.

"The treacherous bitch," hissed Moroni. "That means she must have told them everything."

"Yes," said Heiko. "I think we must work under that assumption."

Olson shook her head sadly. "Oh, Hanna, what have you done?"

***

De Voe wasn't surprised to receive a call from Heiko – he had, after all, said he'd get back in touch. But she was surprised at the subsequent invitation.

"Melissa – events are afoot. If you're still sober, can you join us? With Makka away, and being in the know, I think you should come. The Premier's private apartment – government quarters. You should be able to do a quick database search for the location. Ten minutes?"

"Uh... yes. I'll just... make it fifteen."

That gave her just enough time to freshen up and take a quick-acting liver flush – and then use a public toilet close to her destination as the pill began its work.

She was greeted at the broad front door to the apartment by Anders Pedersen, who led her inside to the dining room before he stepped back against a wall. There, she found a table messily scattered with trays of food, half-empty bottles, comms devices, and even some print-outs. The situation must have been bad, as she noticed even

Heiko holding a glass of something golden and clearly alcoholic. Olson and Moroni were present, and they also held glasses.

The three around the table turned to look at her. Olson said: "Melissa – you've made it. Please sit if you want. We've already started."

De Voe noted that all the others stood, so she decided to do likewise. "Thank you, Premier. Started what?"

Moroni suddenly laughed. "Trying to work out how to get out of this shitstorm." She placed her glass heavily on the table. "Heiko – fill her in. I need the washroom."

De Voe watched Moroni leave the room, and turned to Heiko: "The call you got, right?"

"Yes, Melissa. Long story short, it appears that deputy Bulow has – either deliberately or inadvertently – alerted the Hibernians to our situation."

"Fuck! Er… excuse me, Premier."

Olson gave a strained smile. "I might not have used that expression, Melissa, but I've certainly thought it a number of times this evening."

"We need to tell Makka."

"Yes, we do," said Olson. "But you are his right hand, and he is away and probably asleep, and even if not, I find these conferences where most are in one room and one or more are linked remotely to be a complete bother. You can communicate with him once we're done – either tonight or tomorrow, that's up to you."

"Okay. So, how can I help? What are we debating?"

"MLCOAs, MDCOAs…" Olson looked askance at Heiko. "Our security chief has a wide variety of acronyms. In short, we are discussing – to use your expression – what the *fuck* we do now."

"Ah…" She looked between the Premier and Heiko. "And where are you at with this?"

"Rennie?" Olson threw the floor open to the other.

"I'm afraid we've not got very far, Melissa. We do not think the Hibernians will react immediately. They have no need to. They can take their time to act whenever they want and in whatever way they want. They could even wait to see if we actually start trying to mine our find, saving them effort and allowing us to pinpoint the deposit for them. But if they play hardball, there is little we can do militarily. They have far superior forces to us, and we could never fortify and hold the mine. We would have to concede. So, any solution would need to be political, unless you have a play."

"I'm not sure what you mean."

Heiko paused to sip from his glass. "What I mean is that Ms Bulow isn't a geologist. We don't know what exactly she has reported, but it might not be precise, or even convincing. Is there something you could do to misdirect? Salt the earth, as it were. Prepare a fake site that might yield something a bit like this black sand ore, but which is worthless."

"I see." As she paused to think, she fixed on the half-empty bottles on the table. She'd not been offered a drink and didn't want to ask, but she could have really used a shot of something. "I'll discuss this with Makka, but… I'm not hopeful. We've drilled a lot of holes, and most of these aren't far from the shelf we're mining for raw stock. The Hibernians know where we are mining – we have been overflown by their drones a number of times, most recently three days ago. And to somehow disguise the find itself, so they come up with nothing, or something else when drilling in the same place… no. Sorry. Won't work."

Moroni ghosted back into the room, drawing the eyes of everyone else. "What have I missed?"

Olson summarised. "It seems the geologists' answer is 'no'."

"Worth checking anyway," said Moroni. She went back to her original position at the table and collected her glass, immediately taking a sip.

"This seems to mean we are left with a political decision," said Olson. "Do we confess immediately? Do we wait for an opportune moment to reveal matters later? Or do we continue to stay mum? To my mind, if we respond immediately, there may still be a chance of negotiating some benefits."

"Really?" said Moroni. "Hanna will make it clear that our response is solely because she's outed us."

"Maybe, maybe not. After all, we hadn't come to a firm conclusion to keep the find from them. Telling them *was* still on the table. A quick response now could cause confusion. The Hibernians might wish to appear magnanimous, to let it appear that we voluntarily announced the find to avoid having to draw attention to their own subterfuge."

"I might buy that if Hanna wasn't still around, actively briefing against us." Moroni lowered her voice and turned to Heiko. "To me, this is a security issue. Heiko – could you remove her from the board to pre-empt these problems?"

"Nila!" Olson seemed genuinely shocked. "You don't mean that?"

Moroni chose not to respond.

"Whether she does or doesn't," said Heiko, "I don't think that option would likely work in our favour. It would be clear to all that we'd deliberately extinguished a Hibernian asset. That cat is already out of the bag."

Olson's frown deepened. "I notice you didn't say you *wouldn't*, Rennie, only that you think it unwise."

Heiko raised an eyebrow, but also chose not to respond. Moroni looked away and casually noted: "Frankly, Margarethe, I'd do it myself. Treason is a heinous crime. But we should accept our expert's advice. We can't exterminate the rat, but on *Stavanger* she is finished. If they take our ore, they'll have to take her with it."

Olson sighed. "I have known her for so long. She has served our state well. But you are right. Yet, I am still to be convinced that there is any other option aside from our immediate–"

"Abject surrender?" finished Moroni.

"Quite."

Heiko cleared his throat. "If we are fully exploring alternatives, here is one. We believe Ms Bulow has betrayed us. What if she hasn't? To reveal all now would definitely give the game away." He folded his arms. "Also, we have not formally accused her. If we *appear* to believe her, then you three can resume your political discussions. But maybe you two could secretly talk to Magnus first. Brief him. And then you can all four have a conference on the subject, with Magnus quietly instructed to advocate revealing our find. And then – Ms Moroni – perhaps you could *grudgingly* come around. This might cause Ms Bulow some uncertainty, so that when you inform the Hibernians in a few days' time this might allow us to receive the benefit of the doubt." He shrugged: "But whether they will share still seems a matter of contention to me."

"You're sneaky, Heiko," said Moroni, nodding slowly. "I knew you were more than just a thug in a uniform. I agree. We can use these as delaying tactics. Frankly, I don't want to give the bastards anything now. But also, if we delay, we can cast this as an attempt to fully verify our find so as to avoid raising expectations..."

The conversation continued for another hour.

Various options were considered, some dismissed, some retained for further analysis. At one point, Heiko noticed De Voe's longing stare at the bottles on the table and he poured her a drink. And then he pushed one of the bottles across to her. The Premier's private stash! De Voe knew she'd regret it tomorrow, but by this stage didn't care.

"Thanks for an interesting evening, Rennie," she slurred later, as they stood by the opening doors to an elevator. When he flashed a quick smile, she momentarily thought of inviting him to join her. But then Heiko guided her into the lift, mouthed a silent 'good night', and – like a good citizen – headed to a nearby stairwell.

Chapter 16

Kai Dures and Georges Hollande reached the site within ten minutes of receiving an alert. They found a woman flat on her back, a piece of fabric draped over her face, and a man propped against a wall, his face bloodied, his nose crushed, his arm being carefully immobilised by a medic wearing a green jumpsuit similar to that of both the victims and the newcomers. The overhead strip light occasionally flickered as another man worked at a junction box a little distance away, trying to stabilise the current flow. There were three others in the party, armed with cudgels, who waited further down the corridor, watching out for Security personnel.

Dures squatted down beside the medic and spoke directly to the injured man. "Who did this?"

The man appeared woozy, his eyes having trouble focusing. But at last he recognised his questioner and struggled to speak. "Secure… security. Black shirts." He panted with the effort, then turned to look towards the prone woman. "Callie?"

"Gone," said Dures, his face hard. "But not forgotten. Not forgiven."

He rose and turned away from the scene, fists clenched.

"Another?" asked Hollande, quietly.

Dures looked down at the man from Earth: they were both tall, but Dures had the edge. "The fourth attack in three weeks. Another death."

"Is it always this way?"

Dures barked a laugh. "This? Oh, no. This is something new. Something different. Black shirts coming out of the dark, breaking bones, and not even stopping to make an arrest?"

"Rogues?" wondered Hollande. "Vigilantes?"

Dures shook his head but didn't answer. Instead, he headed towards the three guards who'd watched him arrive and who now turned to face him. Hollande followed a step behind.

"Did you make the call?" asked Dures.

"Yes, Chief," said one – face dark, scarred. "Came on them by chance. The attack happened maybe an hour ago." They were presently under the Tipperary district, second sub-level, mid-way between the Engine Quarter and the Command Quarter. Most of the rooms along the corridor were locked and dark, but several had faintly glowing signs and stronger locks, suggesting they were used as storage basements. It wasn't an area where respectable citizens tended to roam. "Bit of luck really – being this far out. Called in a clean-up team first, then you."

Dures nodded. "You did right, Madgi. And you've seen no one else?"

"There was a scared local ten minutes ago. He saw us, shat himself, and left. We can't wait long. If he did call it in, we'll have Security here very soon."

Dures looked past the man, down the corridor: the light there was consistent, but low, yellow. "Okay. I've seen enough. Fall back. Get your men to carry Callie."

Magdi paused a moment, then muttered: "How much longer, Chief? They've always treated us like dirt. Now this."

Dures' expression firmed, and his eyes widened. "*No longer.*" He turned. "Hollande – come. It is time we put your teachings into practice."

"*For the citizens,*" muttered Hollande.

* * *

The launch pulled up to the dock on Mount Athol, nosing between another security launch and a broad, currently empty, barge. Colonel Eric Nesvorny was moving before it came to rest, leaping onto the stone quay past a worker who was in the process of tying up the craft. He strode along the quay towards a cluster of small buildings on the shore, where a black-uniformed woman waited, sitting in the driving seat of a small, open-top buggy. As he approached, he noticed double golden shamrocks on the woman's shoulders, which matched his own.

"Eric," she called, "welcome to dry land."

"Tania. We going far?"

"Far enough to make walking a chore. Get in."

Nesvorny climbed into the front passenger seat, at which Colonel Tania Joseph set the electric vehicle in motion. As they drove, Nesvorny noted how their presence on Athol had grown. For many years it had been just a mining station with the temporary rotation of staff. But over the last ten years it had developed into a more permanent settlement. The site offices had been the first to be constructed of stone, followed by a number of service and retail outlets, and then individual worker lodgings had sprung up to replace the large, dormitory-like structure in which the workforce had previously been housed. Apparently, a couple of manufactories had also been set up within the last year, and they'd even managed to constitute soil in places, binding it with low trees and shrubs, giving the place a town-like feel. Indeed, it had become known colloquially as Stonetown, and now boasted a permanent population of a couple of hundred to go along with the transient workforce of maybe four times that number.

The road ran along the waterline. The open cast mine lay away to the right, the noise of drilling and crushing carrying on the light breeze, although the mine itself was currently invisible around a low outcrop of the gently shelving mountain. But Joseph turned left at the next junction, heading in the opposite direction. After another minute, on a road devoid of other traffic or pedestrians, they curved inland and uphill. Their destination was clear: a wide, single-storey stone building with four windows and a small parking lot that currently hosted two buggies of the same make as their own. Joseph pulled in next to them.

"I know this isn't technically *Hibernia*, Tania, but remind me how this became part of your empire and not mine."

Joseph gave a low chuckle, turning to face Nesvorny. "Not jealous, are you? I didn't think it mattered, but this is where the drones are controlled from, so I've always had a presence. But you're welcome to share jurisdiction if you want. Frankly, it's a waste of my resources having to divert officers to separate drunken miners in the bars downtown."

"The miners – any of them Stokers?"

"Probably. It's difficult to tell. When they leave their ghetto and change out of their green, they look just like you and I. Why?"

Nesvorny gave his head a brusque shake. "I don't want problems in the city exported here."

"No problems here – at the moment, anyway."

"If the situation changes, we might have to rethink how we police Stonetown."

"Sure: *if.* And honestly, you'd be welcome to it. You coming in or not?"

"Lead on. I'm dying to hear your news and why you think it's important enough to drag me out here."

Joseph smirked. "Oh, you'll see. Come." She disembarked and headed through the front door to the building. The antechamber had a number of black-uniformed personnel, standing about, talking and laughing. As they saw Joseph, they halted their conversations, turned, and stood to attention. The woman simply nodded and carried on past. At the end of a short corridor was the control room, comprising some seating against the back wall and half-a-dozen stations with monitors. Only two of the stations were currently in use, the monitors of which showed complex images in a number of windows – diagnostics, as well as moving visuals from two drones, one giving a view over open water, the other showing ant-like figures scurrying around mining works.

Joseph took a seat at the back.

"Two drones at once?" said Nesvorny, sitting beside the woman. "Given how precious you are about their usage, something must be afoot."

"Oh, it is. I'm going to have a permanent presence now over the site that's being mined by the *Stavanger.*"

"With two drones? I didn't realise the site was that large."

"It isn't. I'm using the second to buzz the *Stavanger.* I'll leave it up where they can see it. I haven't decided whether to make this a daily event, or more random – in order to keep them on their toes."

"Provocative. Any reason why?"

Joseph grasped the arms of her chair and scooted it around so that she could face her guest properly. She smiled broadly: "I got a bite.

My informer on the *Stavanger* sent a message a couple of days ago. Guess what?"

"Must be something to do with their mining, given your interest. They haven't found something useful, have they?"

"Possibly so. A deposit bearing an ore called monazite that's rich in rare earths. Well, when I say 'rich', I mean it may indicate a minable source – according to the experts I've been consulting here – which isn't exactly the same thing."

"Well, that is definitely *something.*" Nesvorny ran a hand through the silver bristles on his head. "It seems too good to be true. After all these years?"

"The experts think it's perfectly feasible. But there are a lot of unknowns before we get too excited – mainly, the size of the deposit. Still, the prospect seems good enough for the Stavangerans to be considering hiding it from us."

"You mean, there's been no official notification?"

"Not yet. And my source didn't think there would be."

"What are the legal issues here? Would the claim be ours or theirs?"

Joseph gave a wry grin. "What do you mean by 'legal issues'? Each city ship has its own laws – there is no Tethyn statute book. But the entire Range is ours – by possession and might. None have ever questioned this. Which makes the find ours unless we say otherwise. In short, the Stavangerans are attempting theft. *Major* theft. And that, Eric, is a crime."

"Clearly. I guess they might be within their moral rights to ask for a finder's fee, but nothing more. How are you going to deal with this? Have you informed the triumvirate?"

"Not yet. That's why I asked you here. I wanted to get your opinion first. You know them better than I."

"Yeah, unfortunately. Traore is your immediate superior, as he is mine, having overall responsibility for defence and foreign affairs." Nesvorny looked sour. "That means *technically* you should inform him. And that means he will present it to O'Neill and Sullivan as his own achievement, and gain extra kudos."

"A problem?"

"Traore is not a man who should be encouraged in any way. I guarantee, if you tell him, he will sit on the information while he formulates a plan for his own benefit. He sees everyone in his own image, and will assume the Stavangerans have been treacherous – as he would be – and will demand a stern response. To kick down the door – even if it is unlocked and already half open."

"Sounds like we may get some action at last."

"Yes, but be careful what you wish for."

Joseph's expression turned serious. "I understand. Action brings the risk of casualties. But it's why we exist. You wouldn't have been so circumspect in the past."

Nesvorny sighed. "Maybe you're right. Maybe age has mellowed me. But order doesn't necessarily need to be kept at the end of a gun barrel."

"Not *necessarily*, no. But unless you've got an alternative, I'll update Traore… though not just yet. I want to compile a dossier on the Stavangerans and what they're up to, and give my informer time to clarify matters."

"Sure. There's no rush. If there is a find, it's not going anywhere. Let me think about possible alternatives to the aggrandisement of Traore."

"Fine. I'll give you advance warning before I say anything, in case you have any last thoughts. Oh, and I'm trusting you, Eric. No stealing my thunder."

"I wouldn't dream of it." He stood. "Much as I'd like to see your drones in action, you've given me a lot to think about."

"I was going to offer you lunch."

"Rain check?"

"You're no fun, Eric. Definitely getting old. Let's go then."

They returned to the buggy, and Joseph drove her guest back to the dock. From the parking lot, they sauntered over to the quay, but before reaching the waiting launch, Nesvorny slowed. "Ah – and while I've got you, and talking of informers, what of my other matter? What news from the *Marseilles*?"

"You mean about the businessman, Mitsos? Absolutely nothing."

Nesvorny frowned. "*Still* nothing?"

"Nope. He's not been mentioned in any report – but we only get a few a year, generally following some key event."

"And isn't this a key event? The shuttle did arrive, didn't it? And he was aboard?"

"I presume so. Maybe he's proven unimportant. Perhaps the Marseillais have had second thoughts about this machine you claimed he wanted to build. It never sounded credible to me."

"Or to the manufacturers here. Still, I'm surprised there's no news of him. Even if they saw through his fantasy, I'd expect his presence to arouse some interest among the populace. I can't see him being noiselessly absorbed into the proletariat. It's more likely he'd be strung up as a deceitful capitalist."

Joseph laughed. "I wouldn't put that past them. But remember, my informant isn't likely to have access to every piece of news or executive decision. Maybe Mitsos was quietly dropped overboard – no fuss; no mess."

Nesvorny wasn't convinced. "Are you sure your informer is sound?"

"Sure? Of course not. They're just someone we pay a little extra in order to send us the occasional surreptitious report on their ship's state of play. They're not superspies. And the *Marseilles* has always been the most challenging place to recruit from, so… *no*."

Nesvorny halted, causing Joseph to pull up and face him. "Have you asked your informer specifically to look into him?"

"No. I could pretend that's because we don't want to unduly influence their report to bias what they're looking for, but the truth is that my informers have a very simple brief to report major news about ship movements, morale, and activities. We don't actively handle them. As I said, they're not superspies."

"Right. But you *could* ask, couldn't you?"

Joseph frowned. "Stepping mighty close to a boundary there, Eric."

"Look, Tania, don't give me that bullshit. You're not so precious – and nor am I. This could be important for *Hibernia*."

Joseph scowled. "Okay, okay. Just for you then. Old time's sake." She smiled and winked. "I'll do it. But don't make a habit of trespassing into my manor – and you owe me. You've stood me up for lunch, so how about a drink at The Ivy?"

"I'm not sure the favour is worth *that* much," Nesvorny sighed. "Okay – send your message."

* * *

Magdi had volunteered for the task with two others – Callie's siblings, Annie and Seamus. They were on the move now, having earlier received instruction from Kai and the Earthers… or were they *Marseillais* now? Well, wherever the foreigners were from, they were allies to the cause – ones with special skills that had been absent in the community. In his backpack was a bomb they'd made using chemicals from the sub-level hydroponics farm, a detonator smuggled back from the mining operation on Mount Athol, and a remote device built from stolen electrical components.

They were on the first sub-level, just over the boundary in the Cork Quarter. It was an area that used to have some life a decade ago, when it had hosted a casino, a few bars, some cheap pop-up restaurants that served heavily spiced havelik (tolerable even to non-Stokers when the belly was full of alcohol), and the belowground entrances to several flop houses. *Used to have.* The spread of the Stokers had gradually infringed on the boundary, lowering the class of the area further – according to the locals – leading to urban flight. The casino still did some business, and two bars remained – now often full of Stokers – but the flop house doors had been sealed and the eateries had retreated along the corridor beyond the nearest cross junction. But while there were fewer locals now, there were more Security patrols to keep the peace. *Their* peace.

They reached their destination – what used to be Henry's Hop House, a bar that had closed last year. The neon sign was still evident, though unlit, and the steel compartment was closed and welded shut to prevent access – for above, there might be a small shop, café, or even home; a different world altogether, of light versus dark, and no one wanted to risk intrusion from the devils who now ruled much of the underworld hereabouts.

"Here – yeah?" said Annie. She wore the green, as they all did, though her uniform was baggy and seemed too large for her.

Seamus was also slim, with gaunt cheeks and a bad haircut. "Yeah, Magdi. Time to roll."

They'd chosen this spot as it was on a well-worn Security beat, though a safe fifty metres from the nearest open enterprise. Security had become lazy and predictable: they knew a patrol would be along in ten minutes or so. As Magdi dropped the rucksack and fussed at the device within, his comrades stood around him, providing some shielding in the dim light. He carefully inserted the detonator, retrieved the control, then checked there was a good signal. And that was it. Nothing subtle: they didn't need to be. There were no cameras or passers-by, and those further down the corridor who spotted them would never tell the authorities what they'd seen.

Magdi pushed the rucksack hard against the wall and zipped it up. "Done. Let's move."

They retreated back the way they had come until they were opposite Bar Pastis. The interior had faint red lighting and four patrons, all Stokers. Seumus entered, as planned, and ordered an absinthe; Magdi and Annie stayed outside, pretending to be a couple, watching the location of the bomb. Their biggest threat now was if someone passing saw the rucksack and decided to take it.

But they had timed things well.

Only a couple of minutes had passed, when Magdi saw the expected patrol emerge from shadow, moving slowly towards them: two officers of uncertain sex in black uniforms.

Magdi looked over Annie's shoulder to where Seamus was at the door: he nodded.

At that moment, one of the patrons rose to leave, but when they reached the door, Seamus blocked it and whispered: "A moment, comrade."

The patrol moved closer and closer – and then one of the officers saw the rucksack.

Magdi smiled. "Go on," he hissed, "take a look." The remote was in his hand.

The officer was now on their haunches. They reached for the rucksack, pulled it towards them… and Magdi pressed the trigger.

The explosion was meant to be small: they had few resources to waste, plus the enclosed architecture of the tunnels was certain to magnify and channel any blast. Even so, the noise was loud, and Magdi was buffeted and had to cling hold of Annie to stop them both from falling.

And then there was silence.

Magdi straightened and shook his head to try to clear the ringing in his ears. He looked back down the corridor and saw two broken shapes upon the floor. Then Seumus was at his side, a wide smile on his face. "For Callie!" he hissed.

He heard a sob from Annie, but when he looked down into her tear-streaked face, he saw that she was beaming.

* * *

Nesvorny was commanded to present himself to the ruling triumvirate the following morning. As he waited outside the boardroom in the old command centre, he was surprised when his deputy, Major Fukuda, arrived, uniform pristine, cap held to his side under one arm.

"Fukuda? What the hell are you doing here? I thought I left you in charge at the scene."

Fukuda's face was expressionless. "Yes, sir. But I received instruction shortly after you left to report here."

"Instruction? From whom?"

"From Mr Traore. He insisted."

Before he could delve into the matter further, the door opened, and a woman in an expensive suit emerged. Secretary? Advisor? She made no introductions: "Please go in." She shut the door behind the two men, remaining outside.

Marissa O'Neill, Kerrie Sullivan and Manfred Traore looked up from behind a conference table: the Terror, the Shadow, and the Charmer. There was nowhere to sit on the near side of the table, so the men were compelled to remain standing next to each other – like naughty children before their headmaster, thought Nesvorny, remembering school days from long ago.

"What the fuck is going on, Nesvorny?" began O'Neill. Her face was pale, green eyes intense, black hair in the shape of a helmet, thick on top and over the ears and then cut short beneath.

"That's what I've been trying to find out – ma'am. Unfortunately, I was called here while–"

"Don't you *fucking* talk back to me!" O'Neill slammed the table. This made red-haired Sullivan quiver, although Traore simply grinned. Nesvorny had never heard O'Neill swear before – and now she'd done it twice. "I don't want excuses. I don't want silence. A shrug. Nothing like your last report. What… is… going… on?"

Nesvorny clenched his teeth and held the woman's glare. "Ma'am – I can only give answers I know. I cannot and will not invent convenient responses. The facts are this: last night, in the Cork District, there was an explosion. Two of my officers were killed. Given the location and the result, it appears to have been some sort of bomb, deliberately targeting my people. I can't tell you who did it yet, and that investigation is likely to take some time."

"Why?" asked Sullivan.

"Why?" Nesvorny was thrown by the sheer stupidity of the question. "Because there are no witnesses, no suspects, and no history of any event like this before. There is nowhere to start."

"Oh, come on, Eric," said Traore, insouciantly. "Nowhere? You said Cork District, but I suspect it was rather near the Engine Quarter. And that is where you must start. That is where you must look. Or do you disagree?"

"I agree, in principle. It's probable that the perpetrators were Stokers, but there's no motive for this act. It's not their MO. It may be that the bomb discovered and upset by my officers was intended for others. A grudge?"

"Really, Nesvorny?" scowled O'Neill. "That is desperate."

"Not at all. The Stokers' crimes have always been low level. Non-violent. And I have ensured my policing gives them no cause to complain. We play a game of cat and mouse. Sometimes we catch them at their theft, sometimes they get away–"

"*Sometimes*?" laughed Sullivan.

Nesvorny struggled to hold his temper in check. He paused a moment and took a couple of deep breaths. "I play the hand I am dealt, ma'am. Faced with a large and cohesive community, I would be a fool to push too hard. In short, this attack makes no sense to me."

"To you?" said Traore. "What about to you, Major Fukuda? Does it make sense to *you*?"

"Sir? I… yes. I think so."

Nesvorny turned to look at Fukuda, then back to Traore, whose hand hid a subtle smile.

"The Stokers are angry," Fukuda continued. "I have heard rumours. Of attacks that they blame on us."

"*What?*" Nesvorny turned fully now. "What rumours are these? This is new to–"

"Colonel!" O'Neill was almost out of her seat. "Let him finish!"

"Ma'am – that is all. I have said little because…. Colonel Nesvorny deals in facts. I have had my sources try to establish where these rumours came from. I would have updated him, once I had more to say."

"It seems that we were right to invite Major Fukuda," said Traore. His eyes were now laughing. "I suggest you empower him to find out the truth about these matters. He, at least, seems to know where to look to solve this problem."

"Yes, you clearly have a valuable resource, Nesvorny," stated O'Neill. "One you need to use more. I suggest you employ all means at your disposal to find whoever killed those officers and bring them down. No more excuses. Understand?"

"Yes, ma'am," said Nesvorny, slowly. "I understand very well." On turning to leave, his gaze lingered on the man on the other side of the table.

Chapter 17

It had taken Eddard Mitsos two weeks to succumb to Noma's invitations to join the crew of the *Dieppe* at their usual bar – The Matelot – after their return from a fishing expedition. He'd resisted until then for various reasons. In the first place, the exhaustion he'd felt after each trip had been so debilitating he'd scarcely been able to do more than drag himself back to his apartment to collapse into lengthy sleep. In the second, he wasn't a big drinker anyway: in fact, that was part of the reason he'd had a liver augment back on Earth, to enable him to keep up in boozy business negotiations and take advantage of potential rivals. Indeed, his second augment – enabling him to switch off pain receptors in his brain – had been inspired after one of his victims had taken exception to this and hired some thugs to teach him a painful lesson. And third, he'd just somehow felt that joining the others would finalise acceptance of his current position and mark a kind of defeat. But in the end, and with two weeks' of worker credits in his pocket, slightly greater energy, and afflicted with immense boredom, he'd given in.

And it had been okay. Surprisingly. The suspicious crew had – by the end of the first evening, perhaps impressed by his drinking capacity – started to cut him some slack. They tolerated him, grudgingly nodding greetings. And though they bored Mitsos, at least they weren't as earnest as the *Leviathan* socialists with whom he'd had the occasional drink in *Hibernia.* They talked of fishing; of the *Marseilles* football league; of entertainment shows; and of personal triumphs and traumas. It wasn't that they were apolitical – they all fully bought in to their society's cultural dogma – it was just that their beliefs were so confidently ingrained that none felt any need to speak of them. Until one day, at the end of the third week, Noma had.

"Are you going to sign up?" she said to Mitsos, while the others were heatedly discussing whether Red Banner were likely to retain their title this year or be supplanted by the Ghetto Warriors.

"For what?"

"Training. Arms. Urban warfare. With the NS?"

"The NS? The arrivals from the *Leviathan*?"

Noma gave him a peculiar look. "Of course. You were on the ship with them – how can you not know?"

"Sorry, Noma, but I don't know what the fuck you're talking about. I met a few of them in *Hibernia*, but we weren't close friends. In fact, they were dull and suspicious and I had no interest in their plots."

The woman thought a moment, then picked up her glass of beer and drained it. "Come on. I'll show you."

"But I've still got… okay. What the hell. Let's go."

Noma led him from the level zero bar along corridors, through atriums, up some stairs, down others, and after ten minutes or so they emerged onto a terrace overlooking a sunken arena of sorts. "This is where they train. Look."

Mitsos couldn't work out where in the city ship they were, but it was a significant space: although he'd limited his explorations, he was still surprised he hadn't come across this before. The space they were in seemed to be three decks deep; there was another level of terraces above them, visible circling the cavernous space, and this was dotted with observers who had a better view than he did. And below…

"What the hell are they doing?"

"I told you – training."

The arena had been sectioned with movable screens and low, roofless buildings, like a city block in a war zone. Throughout were various people, mostly crouching and moving slowly, and it appeared that they were armed.

"Do they have *guns*?"

"Yeah – of sorts. Pneumatic. They fire rubber bullets. Bad shit if they're fired on maximum power – and can be lethal. But they're practising on a low setting. Apparently still stings like fuck if you're hit."

Mitsos was intrigued. He couldn't see the whole of the drama from this height and angle, but he could see enough to get a flavour of events. He saw one group of half-a-dozen with blue armbands on their standard grey clothing, making slow progress along one faux wall, lined up behind a shaven-headed man who looked vaguely familiar. *O'Brien's bar?* They appeared to be stalking. He didn't really need to see more; he could fill in the blanks.

"Team Bravo in red armbands, are they?"

Noma shrugged. "I guess so."

"And why are they doing this? What *exactly* are they training for?"

Noma seemed unsure. "Self-defence. In case we have a… disagreement… with the Hibernians."

"Why would that happen? I don't think you've got anything they're likely to want. Not unless my machine proves a roaring success – then they might want *that*." He laughed unconvincingly.

"Maybe yes, maybe no. But the revolution is coming."

"Revolution?"

"The people of Tethys against the imperialists. Our rulers. They've got it coming."

"Shit! I'm surrounded by fuckwits. Earth is full of them, and then there's *you* lot."

Noma bridled. "That's okay for you to say. You're a businessman. Part of the elite. One of *them*."

"Hey – anything I *have* I worked for. Okay, not always honestly, but I never inherited it, if that's what you mean."

There was a sudden shout from below, and a blizzard of projectiles started to ping off walls and ricochet into the air. Mitsos instinctively ducked, though they were likely out of range. "Fucking stupid," he muttered. "You're not really thinking of joining this band of wargamers, are you?"

"Well, there's extra credit."

"Great. But there's only so much beer you can drink and so many grey clothes you can buy. So what's the point of that?"

"It's also supporting the people – joining a militia battalion. There's kudos. You're contributing to something important."

"Contributing? There's that word again. I'm really starting to hate it. Well, I don't know where this lunacy is heading, but I definitely want no part of it. And look, Noma, I'd stay clear too if I were you. If all this turns out to be just play, you're going to at least end up badly bruised. If this is something more, then your prospects are worse than that. I know. I'm from Earth. It's happening all over the globe there, all the time. Even if things aren't all wonderful on Tethys, you live in peace and should be thankful for that."

Noma flashed a quick smile, but to Mitsos it seemed – as she returned her eager attention to the mock battle below – that her mind was already made up.

* * *

Opening the door to an urgent knocking, Mitsos found a pair of men outside, their work uniforms the standard grey, though they had lightning bolt insignia above their breast pockets. One thrust a tablet forwards for his inspection: "By the order of the People's Committee, we have come to harvest materials for the good of society."

"Harvest? Good of society? What…?"

"Please let us in, comrade. We have a duty to perform."

Mitsos stepped back and allowed the pair to enter. They each wore work belts that were laden with tools, and the second pushed a cart holding transparent containers that were full of circuit boards, electronic components, and wires. Had he been less tired, he might have put up more resistance. "So – what exactly do you want?"

"This unit has a microwave oven according to records."

"Yeah," Mitsos waved a hand. "Kitchen." He followed the second man and his cart. When the first man set about the built-in oven, taking a screwdriver to its front door, he choked out a laugh of disbelief. "You're kidding, right?"

The second man turned. "You're not the only one. An admin program ran a lottery. This block was selected, along with several others. The components are badly needed for an important new initiative."

And then it struck Mitsos what he meant. "You mean – the Rare Element Extraction Net? The new machine being built in Engineering?"

"You know about that, comrade?"

Mitsos' laugh was more genuine now. "Know about it? It's *my* fucking machine. Hell… go for it. Take what you want. But apart from the microwave, there's fuck all else unless you want the comms panel."

"No, comrade. Information is indispensable to the people. We never take that."

"Sure, you wouldn't then be able to issue commands to the sheep or spy on them through their cameras, eh?" He held up his hands to stall any answer. "Well, go for it, and then let yourselves out when you're done. I'm off to drink away my workers' bonus. I would say *don't steal anything*, but there's fuck all to steal."

He didn't even bother to shut the front door on his way out.

* * *

Nothing good ever seemed to come through the comms panel. The shows from Earth were dated, while the home-produced programmes were tedious and proselytising. But worst of all was the occasional programme interruption from a state representative with some announcement or instruction. The ones aimed at the general population were bad enough – usually an exhortation to do or not do something, such as cast waste overboard – but the ones personally directed to him were chilling. His first one had been from the woman at the Labour Share Office. His second had been from the Fishing Fleet Manager, berating him for oversleeping and giving him his first and only official warning, with some unnamed sanction threatened if he missed his boat again. And his third was from a severe individual in a grey-black uniform, wearing the sort of peaked cap that spoke of authority, threat, and probably a god complex.

"Citizen Mitsos, I am Captain Helene Boursis of the ISA. You are commanded to come to the Security Office, level five, immediately."

"Fuck! What have I done?"

"That remains to be seen. You have ten minutes."

"Look, I'm exhausted. I just got back from work. Can't I at least take a shower?"

The woman's eyes widened, perhaps unused to having someone try to negotiate with her. "Ten minutes, or I will send officers to escort you. Your behaviour will then be deemed anti-social and there will be consequences."

Mitsos inwardly cursed. Authority had always nettled him; he just could not resist trying to tweak its metaphorical nose. "Okay – but I stink. You've been warned. Where on level five?"

The woman acquired a harsh smile. "Don't worry. You can't miss us." The connection was cut, and on the 2D panel, the classic film he'd been watching came back on, just as some alien creature began to burst through the chest of an unfortunate spaceship crewmember.

"I know how you feel, my friend."

By the time he reached the Security Office – which took up the whole 'southern' segment of level five – his heart was racing. *What have I done?*

The Office was accessed via a wide corridor, with manned desks on either side of the entrance to a wide plaza dominated by a sculpture of something brutalist and heroic in grey stone – some sort of human effigy with arm raised and fist clenched. At the left-hand desk, another officer of the Internal Security Apparatus raised their head to look at him, then turned to consider a screen to their side.

"Eddard Mitsos," the woman said. She also wore a grey-black uniform, with her cap neatly resting on the desk. "Room 18." She twitched her head, indicating that he should pass. As he did so, he noticed a photo capture of his sweaty face and wild, uncombed hair, beneath which the face recognition software displayed his name and various numbers.

In the plaza, he turned left and followed the circular, glass-fronted wall of offices, which started at '1' and progressed in order. Office 18 was different: it had a solid, metal door rather than a transparent glass one. As he stood in front of this, it began to open slowly and automatically. *More face recognition tech?*

"Sit down!" Captain Boursis pointed to a chair to her right in the small… cell? She sat at a desk to the left. "Do not speak."

"What?"

"I said, do not speak! If you disobey any more commands you will be sanctioned!"

He clamped his jaw, just about cutting off a response.

And there he sat, completely ignored. The Captain had a keyboard and screen, which she tapped and swiped away at. Then, after about five minutes, the door opened and another officer came in, bearing a chair. This was set near the woman at a slight angle, pointing towards him.

So – we're expecting company…

At last, after about twenty minutes, the door opened once more – and in came Sebastian Deux.

"First Citizen!" declared the woman.

"Captain Boursis. Apologies for the delay."

"Your time is valuable."

"It is." He took the spare seat and swivelled to look at Mitsos. "Citizen Mitsos – good to see you looking so *worked.* I approve."

Mitsos smiled, then pointedly looked at Captain Boursis, his mouth still clamped shut.

Without humour, she announced: "You can speak now."

"Thank you, Captain. First Citizen – I didn't wish to risk a beating by saying 'hello'. I suppose it is also good to see you, although I don't know why I'm here, and I would have happily met you without the implicit threat of violence."

"You've been threatened with violence? Really?" Deux shook his head. "Please don't exaggerate. You're here because something has come up that needs to be addressed in a more formal manner."

"About the REEN? Don't tell me a message has somehow got through from Earth, and you're holding me for extradition because of patent theft?"

"No. That would be less of a concern. Captain – perhaps you can take this?"

Boursis nodded brusquely. "The Hibernians have a contact on board – someone who sends them reports about us."

"A spy?"

She shrugged. "Spy? Informant? Sympathiser? The label doesn't matter. Of course, we discovered them some years ago. After *persuasion*, they now work through the ISA. Usually, they submit reports every six months – cleared though this office. They have never been asked to do anything directly against the city, and they've never been directed in their analysis in any way."

"Okay." Mitsos looked between the two opposite: Deux was hard to read; Boursis spoke succinctly without emotion.

"However," Boursis continued, "earlier today, the contact received an actual request: they were specifically asked about *you*. The question is, why?"

"Ah. Didn't they elaborate?"

Boursis looked askance at her screen. "The actual message was: *Eddard Mitsos arrived from Hibernia on the last shuttle. Please look into his status and activities, and report.*"

Deux shuffled in his seat. "We are currently at a delicate juncture, Citizen Mitsos. You may or may not have become aware of activities related to the other survivors of the *Leviathan*. What we need to protect against is information on our true activities getting out. So, one possibility is that you are, in fact, some sort of plant. A *real* spy, sent here with a tempting cover story. And now the Hibernians are wondering why you haven't reported back and are worried that you have been uncovered."

"What? No!" The blood drained from Mitsos' face. "I promise you, I'm genuine."

"What do you mean by 'genuine'?" asked Boursis. "A *real* liar and thief, as opposed to a *pretend* one?"

"Oh, come on! You know I'm from Earth, not *Hibernia*. I was on the *Leviathan*. You have people here who can vouch for me."

Boursis quickly looked at Deux, who was now rubbing a hand thoughtfully across his thin mouth. He nodded for her to continue. "No one is denying that," she said, carefully. "But you were in *Hibernia* for weeks. Here is one scenario: you tried to sell your machine, but without success. Maybe you were told for certain it wouldn't work. And then, stranded and lacking funds, you were approached and an offer was made."

"That's… ridiculous." Although he said it, even he wasn't convinced. "I'm not a spy. I wouldn't even know how to–"

"Oh, but you *are*," said Deux, suddenly. "*Industrial espionage*. You have form."

"No, I don't. That wasn't me. That was my brother. He stole the patent and passed it to me. I'm straight. Look, the REEN will prove it. When it works, you'll see. That will prove my innocence."

Deux held up one finger to stall Boursis' next question. "So… you expect us to continue with your machine – continue pumping resources into it – in the hope that it isn't a white elephant? Or perhaps, a Trojan Horse? A device intended to fool us?"

"Yes!" Mitsos tried to remain calm, but his heart was now hammering in his chest and he felt vaguely unwell. "I mean – your man in *Hibernia*, the Ambassador, he looked into my story and said it was sound. Do you really think the Hibernians could plant that information? Are they that desperate to find out what you're doing that they'd construct such an elaborate ruse? And that would also mean they don't trust their contact here, either. Are you sure this isn't just paranoia?"

Boursis leant across to Deux. "Maybe it doesn't matter if this machine is real or not. If they don't believe it will work and he…" she nodded at Mitsos, "was desperate, then…"

"Yes, I see." Deux nodded. "Whether it works or not might be incidental." He fixed a calculating look upon Mitsos. "In that case, perhaps we should continue with this REEN. Much of the resources have been collected anyway. And if it doesn't work–"

"It'll work," blurted Mitsos. "I swear!"

"If it doesn't, Citizen Mitsos, I will be very unhappy with you. We all will."

Mitsos chuckled unconvincingly. "I guess my reputation depends on this. Until then – back to the boats, eh?"

"Oh, no. You misunderstand. If it doesn't work, then you are *definitely* in trouble. But as the Captain pointed out, even if it does work that doesn't necessarily clear you of potential complicity."

"He can't be allowed any opportunity to communicate externally," said Boursis. "He clearly hasn't managed to do so yet, or they wouldn't have sent that message. We need to interrogate him more fully."

Deux's wicked smile returned. "We do, Captain. Detain him, then, and find out all you can, using whatever methods you see fit."

"And what about Hervé?"

"Interrogate her again. But logically, the worst case is that the Hibernians now suspect she has been compromised, rather than that she is a traitor. Regardless, produce a report for her to send back. In it, announce that Citizen Mitsos has had a terrible accident and is no longer with us. It might, after all, prove to be an eventuality that does come to pass."

For once, Mitsos was entirely lost for words.

At that moment, the door opened – perhaps in response to a silent alarm from Boursis – and two hefty officers entered and advanced on him.

Chapter 18

For the past two weeks, the *Lisboa* had continued northwards, running parallel to the Meridian Cenote at a safe distance. And roughly every other day during that period, Marie had journeyed out on the *Fortunata* to continue studying that mysterious region of black water.

Though Marie's Bermuda Triangle hypothesis (or was it Kate's?) had not been proven as such, assessing the composition of the air over the cenote had revealed some oddities.

"Composition again elevated in carbon dioxide and methane," said Figueroa, rasping the grey stubble on his somewhat flaccid jowls. "It is a consistent feature. Most peculiar."

Marie sat with Figueroa, Kalmik, and Teixeira around a table in the main cabin of the *Fortunata*. They were currently floating a good hundred metres from the edge of the anomaly, having earlier crossed the dark boundary to collect yet more water and air samples. "So, what's causing it?" she asked. "Geological processes, or biological?"

"A conundrum, for sure," said Figueroa. "It wouldn't surprise me if the cenotes follow continental plate boundaries and subduction zones, with perhaps the strange chemical composition coming from deep water vents. That's always been my thought. But as the waters here are very deep, we've never got to the seabed to find out, and we can't see anything anyway. There's so much to map below, so little equipment to do so, and until now, no desire by anyone to explore these fascinating regions."

"I agree," said Kalmik. "*Geological.* Biologics don't make sense. Our fishing lines haven't caught anything in days, and if there's little significant life in the upper region, then I'm not sure why there would be in lower regions – which our water samples show have similar chemical, nutrient, and micro-organism content."

But Marie wasn't entirely convinced. She couldn't get out of her head the dark shadow on Raul's calf when he'd been pulled from the water, or the strange nature of the erupting sea – their analysis having yet to demonstrate how the lights they'd used could react with anything chemical in the cold, strange water to produce an effect of that kind. "Hmmm, maybe. But maybe there *is* life below, we're just using the wrong bait to tempt it?"

"You're welcome to use yourself for that purpose if you want," said Kalmik, with a mischievous smile. Then she leant in and spoke more quietly: "Or we could toss Marco overboard and get some use out of him." Marco Grande was aboard, but currently in the galley helping to prepare a light meal for the rest of the crew.

"Katrina!" chided Figueroa. "Please!"

Kalmik raised her hands. "I'm only joking, Miguel!"

But everyone around the table knew she wasn't.

"We've only used the lines," said Marie, ignoring Kalmik's gambit. "Perhaps we should try to trawl with a net? Can we borrow a fishing boat?"

Figueroa nodded gently. "Yes, Marie, that did occur to me. Between us, I have already approached one of the skippers I know, but she was far from keen. It wasn't just a case of not wanting to allow us aboard while she set her nets for us, it was that she didn't want to allow her boat anywhere near the cenote. I'm afraid the ghost of the *Bridgetown* still haunts."

"Not just the *Bridgetown*," noted Kalmik. "At least three fishing boats disappeared before and after that event while trawling close to cenotes. Fishermen are a suspicious lot on Tethys. There's plenty of fish in the open ocean, so they see absolutely no reason to risk life and livelihood trying somewhere else."

"In that case," persisted Marie, "can't we jerry-rig a net from the *Fortunata*? Professor – with your resources, couldn't we borrow or even buy a net?"

"*Resources* is the key word, my dear. We don't manufacture the specific synthetic polymeric fibres the nets are made of. These are a regular stock item on the ships from Earth, which is why people are so nervous since the, ah, *Leviathan*." His face scrunched into a devious smile. "But I suppose we could try to *steal* something. For the sake of the advancement of knowledge, it might be worth it, eh?"

This time, everyone knew that the speaker *was* joking. But Marie wished he wasn't.

* * *

"Okay," said Marie, entering the cabin in her drysuit, "I'm ready."

"For what?" asked Kalmik.

This time – two days after the previous excursion – the central cabin was occupied by Kalmik, Figueroa, Garcia, and Grande.

"Last trip, you suggested I use myself as bait. Well, I'm ready. You have the equivalent of a shark cage, yes? Set it up. I'm going in."

"Marie, my dear, are you sure?" Figueroa was concerned.

"Look, Professor, I'm a marine biologist, not a geologist or a chemist. I came here to help explore the underwater world of Tethys – not sit on a boat collecting water and air samples, then staring at spreadsheets. I'm not sure we're making any progress; I want to help. I'm also not convinced the effects we've seen are down to natural chemical processes. They just don't look or feel right. If there's anything down there, the only way we're going to find out is to go and look."

"But *you* suggested the natural explanation," said Kalmik, perhaps taken aback that her bluff had actually been called. "The Bermuda Triangle hypothesis? That was your idea."

"To be fair, my daughter put it into my head. But it's not something I necessarily believe in. It was just a hypothesis. But as good scientists, we need to consider several hypotheses – disconfirming one after another until we are left with what is likely to be the truth."

Figueroa seemed confused, as though uncertain as to whether he was happy or sad at this turn of events. Garcia rested against the cabin's main table, arms folded, staring at her, while Grande stood quietly by the rear bulkhead, keeping his thoughts to himself. This left Kalmik as the main interrogator. "Wow. Really? When did you decide on this?"

Marie frowned. "I… well, to be honest, just now. I guess it's been in my subconscious since you mentioned it, Katerina, but having failed to get a net, a bite, or anything different in our sampling just now…" she shrugged. "Anyway, look, if the hypothesis is that the waters are dead, then there's nothing to worry about. If I'm in a cage I'll be protected. Plus, I'll be wearing one of your wonder suits. We've nothing like these on Earth. It's like body armour with an explosive reactive mechanism. I'll be safe."

"Put like that, it's a convincing argument," said Kalmik. "Still–"

"You're crazy," said Garcia, who perhaps unsurprisingly was the only one aboard certain the phenomena they'd observed had a biological basis. "But if you're up for it… so am I." His handsome face broke into a smile, though there was worry behind his eyes. "It's time to prove I'm not a fantasist."

"Miguel," said Kalmik, turning to face their leader. "If you're okay, so am I. Say the word."

Figueroa stared off into space for a moment, then gave a curt shake of the head. "Very well. I admit I am excited to see what you find… if anything."

* * *

They only had one cage, but it was heavy, made of aluminium with titanium reinforcement – a sure sign of the potential perils of the oceans of Tethys. Both Marie and Garcia were in their drysuits, though Marie had the honour of going first, with Garcia as back-up. The winch at the stern of the boat had already hoisted the assembled cage off the deck and over the starboard side, where it swung gently from momentum a metre or so over the black water.

"Your headlamp is set at the maximum illumination tolerated by the water," said Kalmik, squatting beside her. "So, you're barely going to have enough light to see your hand at arm's length. I guess you're just going to have to wait and see if anything comes to you. We've also fixed lamps to bars in all four walls of the cage – you can switch them on in turn when you feel comfortable." Then she paused and looked almost sheepish. "I… think I misjudged you. And frankly, rather you than me, so good luck." She stood, tapped Marie on the top of her head, and sauntered over to the winch mechanism, which was being controlled by Mike Resnos and Luisa Teixera.

Marie watched the cage as it was slowly lowered into the water, like a pen being dipped in a well of ink. She tensed as it initially touched the surface, but it continued without resistance and slid all the way in, until the only part visible was the pair of flotation tanks and the top half metre of metal. She scooted away as Resnos came over to secure the cage to the side of the boat with one rope; Garcia helped by doing the same with a second further along.

As Marie was fixing her mask and snorkel, she sensed someone behind her.

"Maybe one day."

"Marco?"

Grande flashed a shy smile. "I thought I'd check up on you. A snorkel?"

"Yes. Scuba gear produces noise and bubbles, which are likely to scare away anything below. That'd be a bit pointless with the low visibility."

"Well, stay safe. I'll have a coffee waiting for you when you come back up."

"Thanks."

As Grande moved off, Marie rose to her flippered feet and flapped the two metres to the edge of the now-secured cage, with Resnos retreating before her and returning to the winch. She realised that everyone on deck was watching her intently. She put thoughts of them aside and moved to the gunwale and swung her legs over the side, adjusting her belt, on which she had a knife and a metre-long baton attached. Finally, she pulled a headlight – on a strap – down around her forehead.

Now or never, she thought, then wriggled the snorkel into her mouth, bit down, and slid over the side.

The water was *cold*: though her drysuit was insulated and she wore gloves, her face was exposed, and the sudden change in temperature made her gasp. Combined with her world suddenly turning dark, she felt a moment of disorientation and panic, slapping an arm rather too vigorously, propelling her head above the waterline. Sounds of muffled human voices carried to her, but she sought to ignore the distraction. She tread water a moment, adjusted her mask and snorkel, and then rapidly sank back down again.

The dim light from the torch on her forehead revealed very little. The water seemed clear to a distance up to her wrist, with her hands fading into non-existence beyond. Still breathing somewhat heavily, she turned around three-sixty. She couldn't even see the bars of the cage until she gave a gentle kick towards one of the sides, which she grasped with both hands as it resolved from the murk. Pulling herself down, she saw a lamp, strapped against the bars and reached for its 'on' switch…

This time, she saw a flicker of movement, and instinctively pulled away from the cage bars. The light had very briefly illuminated – startled? – something. She calmed her breathing again: it hadn't seemed large. And as she allowed her eyes to get used to the gloom, she did now see *something*: small organisms with dark scales, bobbing in-and-out of view, mere smudges of life without any discernible features.

Marie slowly rose to the surface and took a breath or two, still feeling tense but slightly more focused. Sinking again, she felt her way around the cage to each of the other three sides, finding the secured lamps, and flicking them on. There were no more immediate signs of movement, and even the microscopic lifeforms dissipated, as though gently pushed from the cage by a breeze.

By now, Marie floated in the middle of a gloomy cave, with brighter patches eliding into pitch black before then brightening again. But after the initial easing of nerves from the increase in light, she began to feel a growing disquiet again. At the corner of her eye, she thought she saw something. But when she turned to look, there was just the gloom… and then another spasm in the dark, another turn… more nothing. Her eyes – or rather, mind – seemed to be playing tricks on her. She drew the baton to give her reassurance.

Marie rose for more air without breaking the surface, and this time slowly sank to the bottom of the cage. She approached too quickly, getting her flippers intertwined, and drifted to the side of the cage backwards.

And that was when she *felt* something. Between her shoulder blades. It was just a caress, but it startled her. She pushed off the bars behind her with her hands, and frantically turned to see… what? The grey-lit water rippled. Was there…?

She drifted backwards again until her back touched the opposite side of the cage.

And again felt a nudge at the small of her back, just above the waist. And then the belt moved, as though tugged.

Marie shot to the surface.

* * *

Garcia and Kalmik helped her out; Figueroa was close behind, his face etched with concern.

"Marie?" said Kalmik.

"Fuck!" Marie twisted to sit on the gunwale, raising her legs fully from the water, and tore off her mask, dislodging the headlamp too.

"Marie…" Kalmik continued, "what did you see? What happened?"

For a moment Marie looked down at the water with wide eyes, but then she deliberately shut them and took a couple of deep breaths. *It was nothing.* "Nothing," she repeated out loud. "Whew. Really. I'm okay. Just a bit twitchy." She turned slightly to look at the concerned and intrigued faces around her. "I just got into a bit of state. It's *spooky* down there."

"Too damned right," muttered Garcia.

"Nothing?" echoed Kalmik.

Marie blew out another deep breath. "Okay, maybe not absolutely nothing. I mean, I didn't see anything bigger than a fingernail but I felt something prod me a couple of times. It was almost as if there was something *playing* with me. Coming up from behind. Getting me to jump." She shook her head. "Give me a few minutes to get myself together, then I'll go in again."

Suddenly Grande was there, steaming drink in a cup. "This'll help," he said.

Kalmik scowled, but made way for him to ease through.

* * *

Garcia went in while Marie recovered with her coffee – towel wrapped around her shoulders, sitting on a storage box close to the winch. He lasted six minutes before his own hurried exit.

"I see what you mean," he huffed. "That is *intense.*"

"Did you see or feel anything?" asked Marie, from her seated position.

"No. Not consciously anyway. But sub-consciously, I swear there is something down there. Maybe a lot of somethings, lurking just beyond the limit of the light."

"Are you two deliberately trying to scare us?" asked Kalmik, who stood next to Garcia. "Because if you are, it's working."

"Too right," said Resnos, leaning against the winch. "I'll go in if you want. But only if you really, *really* want."

"I'm not sure anyone else should go in today," said Figueroa. "We should take gentle steps. Science is usually an incremental process, rather than a *eureka* one. Marie and Raul have established that we can dive safely here… at least in the cage. But what would improve our chances of detecting the mysterious lurkers – if they do indeed exist? More lights?"

"Maybe," said Marie. "But we need to be careful. I wouldn't like to be down there and switch on a lamp that increases the lumens beyond the threshold that makes the water – or what's in it – feisty."

"Feisty?" Kalmik grinned. "Another technical Lockardian expression?" She glanced at Figueroa, who twitched a smile back.

Marie was puzzled. "I'm sorry… have I missed something?"

"Miguel said you used some interesting turns of phrase in your published work," said Kalmik. "Don't worry. I'm not having a go at you."

"Uh, right. Anyway, I'm happy to experiment further. But as the professor says, maybe not today."

* * *

"So this is the Terrace," said Kate. "At last!"

They were on an upper level of the circular arena that comprised the body of the 'sea turtle', seated around a small, circular table on an out-jutting terrace with a transparent floor. Looking between her feet, Kate could see the main sports pitch, pool, and park. A football team, all in red, appeared to be having a practice session on the pitch; the pool was busy; while in the park, the occasional stroller could be seen emerging from between clusters of trees and then disappearing again.

"Yeah, cool, isn't it," said Tonio, smugly. Sara had at last conceded a reward to Tonio for his efforts in the abandoned control room and in reinvigorating the Bowl.

"I don't see why you've got an issue with this place," said Kate, turning to Sara. "It's great."

"It's not the place," said Sara, clearly uncomfortable. She leaned in between the other two, pushing aside her glass of blue fruit juice. "It's the clientele."

They were at the edge of the terrace, close to the waist-high Perspex barrier separating them from the well. The three nearest tables, spaced evenly about, were occupied by fellow students also fresh from school. Two of the tables were populated by their classmates.

"Social phobia," said Tonio, nodding. "Why do you think she insists we always sit at the back or in a corner, or arrive first and leave last? And why do you think she likes hanging around deserted places and empty tunnels?"

"I don't have a problem with people," Sara scowled, "just *these* people."

Kate decided not to challenge her. Apart from one small group that occasionally whispered about them and made snide comments when any of them got too close, their classmates seemed mostly oblivious to Kate and her friends, and none had been actively unkind to Kate since she had arrived. Their main focus seemed to be on other things, namely, football, swimming, and each other. And there, on one of the nearby tables, was the class's centre of gravity: Vita Fernandez, with her court of admirers. In fact, the handsome girl with long chestnut hair had so many supplicants, they'd dragged chairs over from several other tables and spread well beyond their due orbit.

"See!" said Sara, clearly noticing Kate's gaze. "*Them.*"

"But why? Vita hasn't done anything wrong."

"Hasn't she? Maybe not that you've seen, but she will."

Kate noticed Sara glance at Tonio quickly, and realised that the boy was sat at an angle that made it seem as if he was looking at them, although he merely had to stretch his neck gently to the right to observe the other table.

"It's not envy, is it?" said Tonio.

"It's not lust, is it?" retorted Sara.

Tonio winced. "That's not fair."

"Hormones rarely are," said Sara.

"Ha! What about *yours*?"

"Tonio – just don't go–"

"Jo-lene, Jo-lene, Jo-leeeen–"

Sara stood up. "Oh… *fuck you.*" And suddenly she was gone.

Kate stared open mouthed at her friend's back, and then at Tonio, who seemed equally shocked. "Tonio… what just happened?"

"Uh… I was an idiot. But she started it. You saw it."

"Started what? And who or what is 'Jolene'?"

Tonio continued to stare at where Sara had gone – into the interior of the Terrace café, under red-and-green awnings. When it was clear she wasn't coming back, he winced a smile at Kate. "Jolene? It's an ancient song from Earth. I would have thought you'd know it. By a woman. Dolly something. About a woman who steals another's man."

Kate nodded. The tune came back to her, and she began to hum it. It was from the twentieth century, which was still seen as the premier era for popular music. Then she understood. "Ah, right. So did Vita steal Sara's *boyfriend*?"

"Well, no, not really. I mean, they weren't actually boyfriend-girlfriend. I don't think Diego knew, or knows, that Sara likes him. Or liked him. She now sees him as just another worthless acolyte. And Vita didn't steal him anyway. She's been with Franz for the last few months, but I guess Diego still, you know…"

"Ah, right. And you too?"

Now Tonio looked flustered. "Oh, come on, Kate! I'm not…" He paused as laughter rippled from the other table. To Kate, it looked as if the demure Vita had just said something moderately amusing, and those clustered around her – mostly boys, but a few girls also – had made certain to show their appreciation.

Kate smiled gently and shook her head. "Maybe *this* is what she's afraid of."

"What?"

"You! Admit it, Tonio, you're hooked. Maybe she's afraid you'll gravitate to Vita as well, leaving her by herself in the corner of the room."

"Well, she's got you now," he replied. "And anyway, she's a friend. My *best* friend. So I *wouldn't*."

"Hmm, well, it might not be a bad idea to try to convince her of that."

The boy sighed. "I suppose you're right. Let's go find her. I've got a good idea where she's gone."

"Me too."

The pair rose and left their unfinished drinks on the table. But they had to pass by the congregation. As they drew level, the girl at the centre of everything spotted them, lifted her head, smiled, and said: "Hey! Hello, Kate! Hi, Tonio!"

Kate raised a hand in acknowledgement, then she gently shoved the boy – who'd juddered to a tongue-tied halt in front of her – towards the exit.

* * *

The science team had considered various alternatives in their experimentation over the last few days. One idea had been to turn on the lights *before* dropping the cage overboard, but like their very first attempt with a string of lights and a buoy, this seemed too much for 'the below': even with just the four dim lights – one on each side – the cage had creaked and buckled as it entered the water, as though being shaken by an invisible hand. It had been enough to startle the *Fortunata's* crew into abandoning that ploy. Next, they'd rigged up a remote device, allowing them to switch on the lights from above – thus avoiding the risk of reaching the light intolerance level with anyone exposed. This time, they'd managed to turn on six without getting a response, though at the seventh, the cage had juddered with sufficient force to rock the boat. They hadn't risked an eighth.

Figueroa had insisted that they confirm the reliability of this outcome, and so they'd moved along the edge of the cenote, periodically dropping the cage overboard and validating their previous findings. At last, today, he was content: "Six, but no more. Are you happy, Marie?"

"Sure." And she slid into the water.

This time, however, with the lights already on, the experience was different to before. The zone of light was a little broader, with fewer completely unlit areas, and she sensed nothing.

"No good," she said, clambering out ten minutes later. "I think having the full six on is sufficient to drive away any life but not enough to provoke a violent response. I suggest we go back to Plan A: I'll drop in the dark, then switch on the lights one at a time, until I've got all six on. If anything's there, it should stick about until then. There might be a tipping point where I get a chance to look at it before it swims off."

"Yeah, makes sense," said Kalmik. "But maybe you should let someone else have a go now?" She had suited up along with Garcia, but was yet to take to the water.

"Well… if you're sure," said Marie.

"I am. I've got this."

Marie smiled quickly and shuffled aside, but inwardly thought: *pulling rank*! Then she sensed a presence at her shoulder, and found a gently steaming cup appear from behind. Grande hissed in her ear: "Let's hope she has… *fun*."

Marie took the cup without looking back, but whispered: "*Bitch*."

Then Marie, Grande, Garcia, and Figueroa lined the gunwale and watched Kalmik's first foray into the black.

It didn't last long.

Shortly after the third pale light came on, seen from above as little more than a sparkle, like a star in the depths of space, a figure surged upwards and erupted from the water.

All four jerked back instinctively, but Marie was the first to recover, and managed to take Kalmik's scrabbling hand, then Grande leant over and grabbed the snorkeller by an upper arm.

Kalmik slithered onto the deck and ripped off her mask and snorkel; somehow, her headlamp was gone. Her eyes were wide, and she panted several breaths, before shouting: "Fuck! That is… *fuck*!"

They helped her to her feet and between them ferried her to the main cabin, Marie with a last backwards look at the unperturbed black water. Somewhere on route, Kalmik lost a flipper. But by the time they eased her down onto the bench seating by the wall, she had managed to calm herself. She looked directly at Marie, ignoring the others.

"You're right. *Biological.* There is something there and it's clever. It deliberately kept from my sight. Kept out of the light. Then it decided to toy with me."

Marie nodded. "Yes. That what I've sensed. So, what exactly happened?"

"I settled at the bottom of the cage to switch on the lights. I thought I felt something touch my flipper. But when I looked down, there was nothing. So I carried on. After the third light, something reached for me from behind."

"Reached?" said Figueroa.

"Yes, reached. It wasn't something darting in and prodding me, like a curious fish."

"What do you mean?" said Figueroa. "How do you know?"

"Because it took hold of the back of my headband and flipped it off."

Marie nodded. The shape she'd seen on Garcia's leg had seemed like a long-fingered, webbed hand. And she'd felt something pluck at her belt. "We need eyes in the back of our heads. An underwater camera, pointing backwards. Next time…"

Kalmik choked out a humourless laugh. "Next time, Marie, it's all yours." She stood, found herself facing a faintly smiling Grande, muttered a quiet curse, and brushed past him, heading for the door to the inner cabins.

But there wasn't a next time.

As they drew close to the *Lisboa* under a rapidly darkening sky, the first drops of rain from what would prove to be a Class Four storm started to fall heavily onto the deck. The storm would keep all of the smaller boats in dock for some days, by which time they were on approach to their immediate destination – the fringe forest around the Ulster Black.

Chapter 19

"What are we doing here, Makka?" asked Melissa De Voe, lounging in a camp chair in Frost's hut on the lower slope of Mount Ardol. "I mean, *really* doing? The game's up – it's just a question of when the owner of the board decides he's had enough and wants us to stop playing."

Frost had gotten the news about their apparent betrayal a few days ago – delivered in person by De Voe after her early morning transfer from the *Stavanger.* He'd vacillated about whether to take the skiff straight back to talk to Heiko, the Premier, anyone, but De Voe had dissuaded him. The politics were beyond his influence. He sighed. "We're doing our job, Melissa. That's all we can do."

"Mining our quota, yes. But further mapping out the deposit? For the Hibernians?"

"It costs us little and may still put us in good stead. They may appreciate a portfolio of data that'll save them time. They may let us participate. They may give us a cut."

De Voe scoffed; she rocked her chair upright and stood. "Sorry, Makka, I just don't see it. I want no further part in this. Helping those bastards steal our find."

"Ours?"

De Voe frowned down at him: he was sitting upright in his chair, arms resting on a cluttered table. "Okay. Mainly ours," she conceded. "Or at least, *partly* ours."

Frost gave a pained smile. They were never going to agree on this. He'd thought long and hard about matters, and couldn't help but conclude that the Hibernians were within their rights, both to be annoyed at them, and to assert their claim. He was now of the view that they should confess immediately and do their best to cooperate. Part of him hoped that, as one of the key geologists on the planet, the Hibernians would at least allow him to stay involved and see the mining through to completion. "I understand. We've only three weeks left anyway. If you want to stick with the harvesting, I'm fine with–"

"I want to go back to the *Stavanger.* Ibsen can see the harvest to completion and sort out the striking of the camp."

"Ah, yes, of course."

The woman nodded, and headed for the door.

As she pulled it open, Frost suddenly called: "Melissa? Are we… still good?"

De Voe turned and looked back at him. She twitched a weary smile. "Don't worry, boss. We're good. I'll keep you updated on the decisions from the ship. I think I'm sufficiently 'in' now, that if the big bosses don't let me know, Rennie will."

Frost returned a pained smile, and when the door closed, went immediately back to his charts.

* * *

It was the spare shuttle that gave the game away.

Heiko had been told on his initial journey to the *Stavanger* that the ship had only one functional shuttle, and that its second had been essentially put into reserve storage. Being an asset of potential security value, Heiko had felt it within his rights to ask that the policy be rethought; that the shuttle – if not actively used – should at least be kept in a state of readiness. But when there'd been an attempt to 'turn the engine over', as the chief maintenance engineer had put it, they'd encountered a nasty surprise. Opening up the engine compartment and pulling off panels had revealed that much of the wiring had been stripped, and whole banks of circuitry were missing. In short, the shuttle was going nowhere – possibly ever again.

It had clearly been an inside job. The question was, who? The chief engineer was in the clear: he'd not objected to the plan, and been puzzled and then outraged at what he'd found. But there were several of his staff who'd been less eager to attend to their work, and one had even called in sick on the day of the restart.

"Famke Holt, Avi Leben and Kamlash Patel," said Pedersen, scrolling through the profiles on his tablet.

"That's right," said Heiko, who'd just sent the files across. "Do any of them have form?"

As soon as the theft had been discovered, Heiko had led Martins Larsen aside for a surreptitious debrief in order not to alert the main suspects, and these were the names he'd come up with. Heiko had kept them close to his chest, just in case anyone in the security department was playing both sides. He'd felt slightly guilty at not trusting his new team, but there were nearly forty in total, and he'd not had a chance to thoroughly review all of their credentials, while he'd left Pedersen to concentrate on the issue of Bulow and whether or not she was acting alone.

Pedersen pursed his lips and gently shook his head. "No. None of them ring a bell. What do you suspect them of?"

"Major theft. One or more may be responsible for turning the second shuttle into a loosely held together pile of garbage. I found out that a couple have storage units here."

They were presently at the entrance to the Uberwald, an area towards the rear of the *Stavanger*, first sub-level, to the port side of the sealed fusion complex – a zone so tightly locked down that even Heiko would have struggled to get through the front door. Being on the periphery of a sealed, secure zone, and leading nowhere, the Uberwald had been left to decay from wider view. Its compartments still shouted 'ship' rather than 'city', and most were small lock ups and workshops, with a couple of convenience shops to service the denizens, plus a micro-distillery with adjacent unnamed bar. The word 'Uberwald' had been sprayed in green paint over one wall of the narrow entrance corridor; the walls and floor were unclad metal. Aside from Heiko and Pedersen, there were two other officers present, also dressed in blue uniforms.

"So – we're going in?" said Pedersen.

"Not a problem, is it?"

Pedersen looked circumspect. "No. I guess not. We don't have any no-go zones on the *Stavanger*. Nothing like the Engine Quarter on *Hibernia*. But..."

"But what, Anders? You seem reticent."

Pedersen lowered his tablet and briefly glanced at the two officers standing behind Heiko: Judd Stallings and Monique McGregor – a pair who'd already become trusted favourites. He grimaced. "But if we don't have trouble here, it's also because we don't push too hard.

I agree, if anything illicit is going on, it'll probably be here. But it's small scale. Maybe more effort than it's worth."

"It might have been small scale once, but not any longer." Heiko fixed his stare on the other. "Do you want to lead, or take up the rear?"

"Oh… yes. I'll lead."

"The profiles I sent you identify our target locations."

Pedersen pursed his lips again, and nodded. After quickly referring to the information on the tablet, he turned and crossed the threshold into the Uberwald. There was a long corridor with a plain metal wall to the left – beyond which was the fusion centre – and a succession of closed rooms to the right, numbered above their doorways, and sometimes marked with a name or arcane symbol, usually in fluorescent paint. They didn't see anyone until they came to a small junction, which opened out to the right into a small plaza, the ceiling just two metres high. A sound of hammer on metal and hiss of soldering came to Heiko's ears: around the plaza were various rooms, some closed, a couple open, with people inside at work over synth-stone benches, bent over partly disassembled machinery. One man with a beard looked up and his eyes widened. But Pedersen didn't stop, and led them to the right through the plaza and into another, slightly wider corridor, this one with doors and rooms off both sides.

"What were they working on?" asked Heiko, from behind Pedersen's shoulder.

Pedersen didn't look back. In a muffled voice, he said: "Who knows. Maybe repairing some domestic machinery? Cheaper here than further up."

The corridor was now wide enough for perhaps three to link arms and walk abreast. It was well lit, though austere and without decoration. They began to pass people coming from the opposite direction. To Heiko, most seemed surprised and uncomfortable, failing to meet his gaze. He even heard one man utter a curse under his breath.

A second, wider plaza occupied a crossroads, with corridors heading off all of the cardinal compass points. There were six or seven workshops here, plus the distillery/bar, where several people in dirty overalls sat on stools along wall counters, obscuring the view of the interior. This time, Heiko noticed all eyes turn towards them, and several of those at work ceased and looked up. Pedersen paused to consider the tablet, then turned left again, heading stern-wards. "Red South 14," he muttered. "Just along…"

Ten metres ahead, three people clustered in the corridor outside one unit, the shutters to which were raised up. Heiko recognised Famke Holt and Kamlish Patel, two of the suspect engineers, although he didn't know the third – a short, ugly man with large ears, but well-cut hair and a clean red jumpsuit that seemed to have a number of electronic accessories poking from pockets on thighs and arms. The trio turned to look at them uncertainly, and then Holt leant down and spoke rapidly to her shorter colleague, Patel.

Heiko knew what was going to happen: he quickly stepped around Pedersen and started to move. "Holt… Patel…" he called. "Stay, please."

The man in red quickly looked at the others, scowled… and then turned to run. Eyes wide, Kamlish started to raise his arms, but then had second thoughts, perhaps triggered by his departing colleague. He turned to follow him. Famke Holt, however, stepped into the storage space and out of sight.

"Secure the unit," yelled Heiko, moving into a lope. "Judd – after me."

The others only had a small head start. In a dozen strides, Heiko was behind Patel, who suddenly turned, starting to raise an arm… and Heiko slammed into his chest, forcing him back against the wall.

"I… What… Sorry…" gasped the engineer, but Heiko was already looking past him, where the man in red was coming to another junction. He turned right – port-wards.

"I've got him, sir," said Stallings.

Heiko withdrew his arm from the detained man's chest, and set off after the other, without looking back. Half-a-dozen more strides and he was at the junction, turned, and found the corridor ahead blocked by four people heading in his direction, spread out. And most of the doorways here were open, too, with curious workers and residents looking out of their little work spaces, voices raised in query.

A few more long steps and Heiko was in front of the quartet, who seemed less than keen to move.

"What's up, man?" asked one, edging into his path.

"Step aside, sir," commanded Heiko.

The man moved away, slowly, but then two women behind slid across to block his path. Heiko peered over the tops of their heads… and saw more people moving into the corridor, stepping out from their holes to have a look at what was going on.

He knew it was pointless, but Heiko wove through the obstructions and spent several minutes peering into the small units that were open, occasionally tugging at the doors to closed units to check that they were locked, but then he came to another crossroads, and when the three people he spoke to there all shrugged or smirked and said they'd seen no one in red, he gave up and returned to his colleagues.

Pedersen, Stallings, and McGregor waited outside the storage unit, with Holt and Patel each held firmly by one of the junior officers. Pedersen's expression was severe. "No luck?"

"No. But I'd recognise him again – assuming our friends here refuse to identify him." Heiko came to a halt before Famke Holt – tall, fair-haired, early fifties, a small tattoo of something smudged onto her neck. "Who was he?"

"The man who ran off?" She smiled. Whereas Patel shifted nervously, she seemed controlled. "I didn't ask his name. I guess he wanted something, but you scared him off, so we won't know what, eh?"

There was little point pushing the matter. He turned to look into the unit. It was just three metres wide, the same deep, and had walls lined with shelves. Two large metal boxes sat on the floor at the back. "If we turn those out," said Heiko, "are we going to find things that shouldn't be there?"

She shrugged. "I don't know. It's Kamlish's unit anyway."

"What?" gasped the other detainee. "You…" But he ran out of words.

Heiko sighed. "I don't want to have this discussion here. We are already attracting attention. Anders – while we take these two for interrogation, call in some help. I want the contents of this place listed and checked. The chief engineer should be able to identify anything from the shuttle. I suspect there will be items from other jobs, too. Check the databases."

"Sir! And… what are your plans now?"

"After having a word with these two, I plan to see how our programming team are getting on with my augment program. Though I *think* I will be able to identify our fleeing friend from memory, I should have been able to get water-tight evidence on him through my modified visual system. Meantime, I'm just going to have to look at a load of mugshots. I am assuming he will be there."

But as he subsequently found out, the Security Department had surprisingly few photos of criminal types, and his search proved fruitless.

* * *

"Why are we *here*?" asked De Voe.

"You mean here as opposed to Bjorn's Castle?" Heiko smiled absently and looked around. They were in a bar in the Trollmarkt – a small area on level zero, towards the stern of the ship, almost directly over the fusion drive and the Uberwald. The bar itself – low-ceilinged, wide, dark, with scarred synthetic furniture and walls covered in fluorescent graffiti – was one of three that clustered around an open plaza that also held a tattoo parlour, a shop selling trawler sweepings disguised with spice, and a basic 3D printer's den – where you could get any of a multitude of (smallish) items manufactured, as long as the proprietor had a template for it.

"Well, Bjorn's is a fair enough bar. Prices good. The range of drinks is the same as everywhere else. And it's close to my flat – which you've never seen." De Voe gave a mischievous smile.

But Heiko was distracted and missed the hint. "I've not been here before – but it's definitely been on my 'to do' list. It's the regular haunt of some people I've recently encountered."

De Voe sighed. "You mean villains?"

"Yes. Scavengers. They seem to be at the heart of all of the crime aboard."

"Heart?"

"Yes. On Earth, it's different. Drugs are the heart there. Solve the drugs problem and you pretty much break the crime spiral. It's not just the drugs themselves that are illegal, it's all the activity that goes with them. Addicts stealing to afford their fix; gangs in turf wars; dealers with lots of spare cash expanding into other areas of criminality. Here, it's scavengers. Spare parts are the drugs of Tethys. In fact, you don't have a drugs problem. Your society is too close, too small. Addicts would be obvious and could be identified and dealt with easily. Dealers too. And any attempt at growing or producing drugs in a sizeable enough quantity to be a problem would be difficult to hide for long."

De Voe lowered her glass of lager. "Sure. It's true for the *Stavanger* - for *hard* drugs. But *Hibernia* has some problems. *Taiwan* too. And the *Amsterdam* grows cannabis in state facilities, so it's legal and controlled. But we're not a junkie world."

"Right. Here, it's the scavengers who either use the resources they steal to enhance their own lot, or sell what they steal to increase their ready cash for…" he waved his hands "Beer? Fine dining? Better apartments? I'm not sure you have much else."

"Boats," said De Voe, nodding sagely. "That's the big ticket item around here. Like fast cars on Earth? They're a sign of status. It takes a lot to build a new one. On the *Stavanger*, we don't have a shipyard as such, though the repair shops along the docks cobble together one or two new ones a year. Otherwise you've got to import them from *Hibernia.* So most new owners buy and renovate existing craft from others who are forced to sell for one reason or another. So, if you want to know who is really profiting, that's where you should look. Get a list of private boats and see whether their owners have the right status. And it's not a big list. There are only about twenty or thirty pleasure craft in total."

Heiko frowned and looked intently at the woman. "Now why haven't I heard this before? Why did I have to learn this from you, and not from my team? No one has said a thing about boats – not even Pedersen."

De Voe took a drink. As she lowered her glass, she casually wondered: "Maybe Pedersen has a boat himself? Cass Remillard certainly has one. He talks about it often enough."

Heiko's frown deepened. "You're not suggesting…?"

"Me?" De Voe flashed a quick smile. "Oh, no. It's not worth my while, health, or wealth, to speculate on the matter."

"That is… something to think about. Melissa, you've already made this evening worthwhile."

De Voe's mischievous smile returned. "Let's see if we can't make it even more profitable, eh? But in the meantime, why *exactly* are we here?"

"Eh? Oh, I'm just looking, really. And I'm trying something out."

"Now you're being mysterious. What? Ah…" De Voe focused on the metallic glint by the side of Heiko's left eye. "Your bionics?"

"Yes."

"X-ray vision? Are you scanning the regulars for hidden weapons?" She smiled and nodded in the general direction of the bar.

Heiko returned the smile. "I wish. No, but a couple of my team are decent programmers and electrical engineers. They were able to take an old augment program and revive it."

"So, what is this superpower of yours?"

"Related to my eyes? Actually, there are several. In theory, I can view tactical data – essentially like a HUD, scrolling over my eye – but we've yet to establish the software for this. When we do, I'll be able to wirelessly access ship data from things like security cameras. Today, I'm testing the function we *have* sorted out: visual recording and playback. I want to check how well this works, and tomorrow I hope to go through the patrons I've photographed to identify them. See if any are known troublemakers or their associates."

"Recording what you see?" De Voe frowned. "Well, I hope you edit it first, or you'll end up with a lot of clips of me."

"No, I'm not currently using video. I'm taking snapshots only."

"But you *could* video?"

"I could."

De Voe leered. "Well, that could lead to all sorts of illicit pornographic possibilities."

Heiko looked uncomfortable. "Pornographic?"

"Well, sure. Let's say for some reason we both end up drunk at the end of the evening. You come back to see my apartment, and one thing leads to another. How do I know I won't end up as the star of a skin flick?"

"Ah, I assure you, I wouldn't…"

"Wouldn't what? Come back to mine? Fool around? Or record it?"

This time Heiko got the woman's hint. He was somewhat out of practice after his divorce from Elsa. Working too hard? Starting to feel old? De Voe wasn't especially attractive… but nor was she *unattractive*. And her look was predatory. He gave a barely perceptible shake of the head. It didn't seem like a good idea to him, though he somehow felt he wasn't going to get much of a say in the matter.

"While you're thinking about what level of depravity is acceptable," De Voe said, standing, "I'll get another round in."

What did they say about mixing business with pleasure? Heiko watched the woman heading for the bar. It was only then that he realised she'd put on something casual, rather than her regular russet-coloured work clothes. Pale blue. Figure-hugging. "You're screwed," he muttered to himself, "or soon will be."

* * *

The satellite link to *Hibernia* closed down.

Heiko noticed a smile steal across Hanna Bulow's face as she announced: "It's as I suggested – the Hibernians are likely to be reasonable."

Margarethe Olson sat at the centre of the table facing the now-dark screen. "Magnus certainly seems to agree with you." She turned to Nila Moroni, who'd been strangely reserved during their conference call with the ambassador. "Nila – I'm afraid I am coming around to Hanna's point of view."

A faint look of disgust crossed Moroni's face. Heiko knew how hard this was for her: in spite of being an expert in the political arts, she truly despised Bulow. "I am not unreasonable. I think you were always more aligned with Hanna's view than mine anyway. I thought Magnus would be more negative. Perhaps I have misjudged our adversaries – though it pains me to say so."

Olson turned to Heiko next. "Rennie – I value your judgment, too. You have become an important part of our little team. What do you think?"

Heiko noticed Bulow's gaze turn towards him: unfriendly; calculating. He ignored her. "It's my job to maintain order and ensure that the laws of the *Stavanger* are respected, and that is all. I am relatively new in any case – I have no insight into what the Hibernians are likely to think or do. No, you are the elected representatives of the people of this place – whatever you decide, I will support."

"Thank you."

"However…" Heiko raised one warning finger. It was time for him to play his role. They knew Bulow wasn't a complete fool: if they rolled over too easily it would look suspect, and so he – rather than Moroni – had been directed to challenge the woman. "However," he repeated, "I must still register my disapproval of Ms Bulow's activities. They were reckless and could have proven disastrous. We still do not know who the woman was she spoke to, this wrong number. From here on, for the sake of security, I need to be assured that matters potentially threatening the ship are run past me; that there is no more wildcard behaviour."

"Noted," said Olson, severely. "Hanna – your methods were unconventional–"

"*Stupid*," muttered Moroni.

Olson faltered slightly, grimaced at Moroni, then continued. "*Unconventional.* I understand your motives, but next time, you need to place your faith in us. In *me*."

Bulow looked between the other three. To Heiko, it seemed she was struggling with whether to accept the rebuke. But after a moment, she manufactured a contrite expression: "Yes. I agree. It was unwise. I'm sorry, Margarethe…" she looked past Moroni to Heiko, "and to you, Mr Heiko. I will try to keep myself under better control. Perhaps we need to work on our communications, eh?"

Heiko nodded, but felt vaguely unsettled. As the political dance continued around him, he replayed Bulow's words in his mind. *Work on our communications.* Where had he heard that phrase before? And then he realised it was from himself. He'd used the expression to… whom? One of Ibsen's contacts? *Yes.* He'd been referring to his communication with Pedersen, to excuse the women's heavy-handed detention. And hadn't he repeated it to Pedersen later, when explaining the affair and why he had appeared to lay at least some of the blame on him? So… had Bulow used the phrase deliberately? And if so, how had she learned it? And from whom? Pedersen himself?

"So," said Moroni, her voice rising and cutting through Heiko's musings, "when are we going to fall on our sword?"

"Not immediately," said Olson. "I would like to get a full report from Dr Frost first. A substantial and useful document may provide an excuse for our tardiness in alerting them to our find."

"Agreed," said Moroni, brusquely. "That will make it seem as though we are simply being cautious. *Thorough.* And if the Hibernians are indeed reasonable, they may be more inclined to reward us for the substantial work we've already put in."

"Yes. *Reciprocity.* Will you contact Makka for me, Nila, and ask him for a timeframe?"

And that was that.

Heiko was updated by De Voe later, when they met up at her favourite bar: Frost had asked for four days to do a professional job.

As it turned out, they didn't have that long.

Chapter 20

When they broke his finger, Eddard Mitsos screamed, even though he didn't need to. But he definitely felt nauseous, so when he threw up after they broke his second, that was genuine.

"Enough," said Captain Boursis, recoiling at the stench.

The guard with the pliers stepped back, a scowl of disgust on his face.

Mitsos lolled in the chair to which he had been strapped, his wrists secured to its armrests, his right hand bloodied and twisted. He kept his eyes closed – partly to avoid looking at his hand, but also to avoid catching the eye of his interrogator, who sat directly opposite. He didn't know how someone tormented as he had been was meant to look, and didn't want to rouse suspicions. He already doubted whether his initial screams had been sufficiently loud or of the right pitch.

"Look at me!" demanded Boursis. "Open your eyes and look!"

Mitsos felt the other's boot contact his calf. It was not meant to be an instrument of pain, he guessed, but rather just an effort to get him to focus. All he felt on his calf – as on his hand – was a numbness, a residual sense of pressure applied and then released. The twenty three thousand bitdollars he'd spent on the pain-capping procedure on his dorsal posterior insula – three months after an angry competitor had hired some thugs to put him in intensive care – was the best money he'd ever spent.

"I said," continued Boursis, delivering another kick, "look at me!"

"Yeah, yeah," Mitsos slurred, lolling his head from the left, where he'd vomited, to vaguely face the source of the voice. "I'm looking." He opened his eyes in a squint. He still felt somewhat queasy.

"Do you want us to continue? Do you?"

"No... please... no. Just... tell me what you want me to say. I'll say it."

The woman – who had grey hair shaved close to her scalp, and a square, dimpled jaw – shook her head slowly. "This isn't the

Inquisition. I'm not seeking a confession for a show trial. I simply want the truth."

Mitsos felt a sudden lance of pain in his right hand, and twitched. Wearing off? He pressed his tongue firmly into the back molar that triggered the cap, and the pain subsided. But in doing so, he managed to bite his tongue – something that would normally have him banging the wall, but which now led to nothing but a low throb. That was going to sting, too, when he eased back to sensory normality. "I… I've told you everything. If you don't believe me now, when will you?"

Boursis scanned his face with her blue eyes, trying to read him. She sighed. "Not yet." She turned to the guard. "Again."

"No!" Mitsos shouted, rousing himself. Too much? Too little? "No. Okay. I'll tell. In *Hibernia*, I agreed to… to… I don't know… kill Deux. That's right. And then… then to sink the ship. Yeah. That's right…" He struggled in the chair. "I'm meant to… I don't… I'm meant…" And he slumped back again and turned away.

Boursis held up a hand to stay the guard with the pliers. Mitsos could feel her eyes on him. And then, after some seconds, she sighed again. "Take him to the cells."

A second guard, who'd been standing at the back of the room, joined the torturer, and they roughly released the straps and dragged him to his feet. Mitsos remembered to yell when his right hand came into contact with one of the guard's legs.

A couple of hours later, a medic came and tended to his broken fingers, setting them in splints and bandaging his hand. She even gave him some painkillers. He smiled wryly at that. "Thanks for nothing," he muttered.

The next day, he was 'invited' to attend another interview. But this one was different to those of the first two days, in which he had been battered with questions after spending time in a tiny cell – in which he'd been denied the chance to sleep by random recorded screams – and the third, in which he'd been waterboarded, and the fourth, in which he'd been maimed. This time, Boursis greeted him politely and had a guard fetch him coffee.

"Citizen Mitsos, I am sorry for the last few days, but we had to be sure."

Mitsos had a substantial beard by now, and his stained grey shirt and trousers stank. "I understand." He gave a weak smile and looked at the other coyly, holding his natural brio in check. "So… do you believe me? Or is this still part of the process?"

"I believe you *enough*. I suspect the Hibernians genuinely doubt your machine, let you leave, and are simply curious as to whether we have taken it up. I do not think you are colluding with them for any deeper purpose, but…" here she raised one warning finger, "that does not mean you are beyond suspicion, or that we won't be keeping an eye on you. I suggest you think very carefully about where you go and what you do while you are with us."

Mitsos gave a wry smile. "So… no lurking around the Comms Centre or buying fusion engineers a drink?"

"You get the picture."

"And what now?"

"Now I am busy. Finish your coffee quick, if you want it. Then you can go."

"Go where?"

"Home for a shower, perhaps. You have missed your shift for the fleet." She gave a grim smile. "Perhaps contact the Labour Share Office and ask for an interview. Explain your disability. Then it's up to them."

Mitsos left the coffee.

* * *

"Don't you see my hand?" Mitsos waved the bandaged appendage under the woman's eyes the next day. "Have you ever been on a trawler? How much do you think I'll be able to do with this?"

"The breaks are stable? Pinned? You have painkillers, don't you?"

Mitsos was aghast. "You're joking, right?"

He noticed the woman's seemingly permanent frown dissolve into a smile – and not an evil one, either. Her eyes crinkled at the edges in genuine amusement.

"You are!" said Mitsos. "Thank fuck!" At that moment, he could have leapt over the sloping monitor set into the table between them and kissed the Labour Share Office bureaucrat – in spite of her age and plain appearance.

"We're not tyrants, Mr Mitsos. We only expect people to do what they can, to the best of their ability. On the screen, you will see a tab labelled 'Exceptions'. Touch that, and enter details of your temporary disability. The system will take it into account and reassign you to a more suitable job."

"Right. Every cloud and all that."

Mitsos followed instructions and updated the Labour Allocation Program. After a moment's electronic thought, the screen changed and his new fate was revealed.

"Ah," said the woman, her smile evaporating. "How ironic."

"Labour Share Administrator? But isn't that here? This office? This… job?"

"It is. But it's not… *oh*." The woman's brow furrowed, and then realisation appeared to dawn, for her face suddenly flickered through a kaleidoscope of emotions – concern, anger, and then defeat. Her eyes roved about the monitor on her side of the desk, and the fingers of her right hand tapped the screen. Finally, she shook her head and sat back, her eyes unfocused.

Mitsos observed this with growing humour. "Something wrong, miss? You seem consternated."

The woman focused on Mitsos and her mouth firmed. "I thought I had more time. It appears not. My next rotation is in three days. It seems you will be my replacement. Before I go, I will need to train you."

Mitsos threw back his head and laughed – long and loud.

* * *

Though the training proved awkward, given the frostiness of his tutor, the job itself was simple. Mitsos even had scripts to read and decision trees to follow in cases where a new interviewee protested their assignment. He thought he might have to use this for his own first customer, when the LAP decided his predecessor should go to the fish reprocessing factory in the bowels of the ship. But, in the end, she didn't give him that satisfaction, and at the close of the third day, she stalked from the office without even a 'goodbye'.

* * *

Mitsos hadn't seen Noma for a couple of weeks. After his release, he'd limited his movements to his tiny apartment, his new office, and the refectory on the most direct route between these two places. This evening was the first time he dared venture from that circuit, heading to the Bar Pastis, which was the usual haunt of the *Dieppe's* crew after its daily duty.

"Where've you been?" Noma had noticed Mitsos standing uncertainly near the double-doored entrance to the bar and had come over to greet him. "We heard rumours that you were taken for non-communal activities."

Mitsos considered the woman: her dark skin was bruised yellow on her forehead and on one cheek, while one eye seemed somewhat swollen. "Non-communal? Is that the euphemism you use?"

"So, you were?"

"I'm here, aren't I? If my *non-communality* had been proven, would I be?" Mitsos noticed the old crew sat around two pushed-together tables some metres into the bar, picked out by one sharp wall light. They were looking towards them, and didn't appear especially happy to see him.

"Still not an answer," said Noma. She started to turn away, then glimpsed his bandaged hand and paused. "They go for the fingers. And yet you're here." She looked back up. "You must have talked… and been found innocent."

"You know about what they do?"

"Yeah. And not just rumours. Everyone knows someone who's been interviewed. Usually for saying the wrong thing in the wrong way at the wrong time." She looked over to her crewmates, then gave a signal with one hand and turned back to face Mitsos. "Want a drink? Maybe not here. What about the Sickle? The crew of the *Boulogne* go there. Not a bad lot. They won't object to just the two of us."

"Sure. And from the looks of you, you could do with a drink as much as me." He gestured at her face.

"What? Oh, *this*." Noma touched her cheek. "Nothing really. Took a rubber bullet in the face. The one I got yesterday on the tit hurt much more."

Mitsos barked a laugh, and Noma smiled too. She took his elbow – the one above his injured hand – and guided him across the echoing plaza to the bar opposite. They passed under a sign with the bar's name illuminated in gold and wove through the dingy interior, settling at a table by the back wall underneath an old and frayed, red-and-gold flag of the Soviet Union. Noma went to the bar to collect some drinks, which she ferried back to the table. Mitsos noticed she'd developed a limp; she spilled the top half-centimetre of beer when she plunked down the glasses.

"Thigh too?" asked Mitsos.

"Knee. And before you say anything, I twisted it on deck earlier today."

"Fishing is a risky enough business," said Mitsos. "All the more reason not to endanger your health playing soldiers with a bunch of student revolutionaries."

"I thought you'd bring this up. It's why we're here not the Pastis. All the crew have signed up for militia training. Some are serious. You might have got some kudos for your hand, but you'd have lost that and more for mocking their patriotism."

"Patriotism? Is that what it is?" Mitsos slowly shook his head. "Look, Noma, I'm just concerned about you. You're the only person in this floating circle of hell who's shown me any kindness."

"Maybe if you didn't insult our ship, our people, our principles, you'd find a few more who'd be willing to be kind."

"Yeah, well, I grew up amongst people like…" He was going to say 'you', but managed to save himself, "like the fanatics from the *Leviathan*. My credentials are solid. I started working class, then set up a business to improve my lot and that of my family. That doesn't make me a bad person. And from what I've seen, people like those teaching you urban warfare tactics, or whatever the hell it is they're teaching, they almost always make matters worse for those they claim to be representing, not better."

Noma scowled. "Your experience is on Earth. It's different here. Fewer resources. More needy."

Mitsos sighed. Noma was hardly a friend, but she was all he had. He held up his hands. "Okay. I've had my say. Whatever you do is your choice. Just be careful. I don't know where all this is heading, but don't go volunteering for some sort of suicide mission, eh?"

"Sure. I'm not an idiot."

"Great." He smiled. "And I really do appreciate you for taking pity on me. You don't have to."

"No, I don't. But you were made my responsibility on the *Dieppe*, and I take that seriously. On the ship and off. So… are you going to tell me what's been going on, or not?"

"You mean about my little… *accident*?" He raised his hand and twisted it about. "Well…" How much could he say? And then it occurred to him that there might be another reason for Noma's interest in him, beyond his charm and personality. His smile began to fade. Even so… he'd told the truth before; if he told it again, perhaps that would reinforce his message. "It was just a misunderstanding. You know I brought a design to the ship for a device to extract rare elements from ocean water, yeah? Well, to be honest, I only came after everyone on *Hibernia* had rejected it. But now it seems someone from there has been in contact with someone from here asking about me. I suppose it naturally aroused suspicions. Led to questions about my *bona fides*. Made it seem as if I might have been some sort of plant, or spy, or something."

"Yeah, that would cause some concern."

"Concern? Too fucking right!" The anger he felt was very real. But as he looked at the woman, he nodded to himself, and added. "Fucking *Hibernians*."

Noma looked surprised. "Hibernians?"

"Yeah. The bastards wouldn't do business with me, and then this. Setting me up. Maybe they had second thoughts and they've decided to try to undermine me. Don't want the *Marseilles* to get my device. Hope you'll abandon it. Maybe you'll let me go. Then they can pick me up when I get back."

Noma looked wary. "It seems you managed to convince the Apparatus you are legit."

Mitsos' broken hand rested on the table by his beer glass. He tipped it up. "Eventually. But as you see, it wasn't easy."

"Sounds like maybe you owe the Hibernians some payback."

"Payback?" He laughed. Then he plucked up his beer with his good hand, deciding he needed to hide his treacherous mouth with its uncontrollable smile. This was too easy. With his glass in front of his face, he said: "You know, maybe when my hand is better, I'll join up with your little militia after all, eh? I don't know what you're planning, but the target has got to be them. *Bastards!*"

He was proud of the venom he managed to instil into his last hiss. And even more at Noma's relieved expression. She'd bought it.

* * *

"It *works?*"

"You sound surprised, Citizen Mitsos. *Interesting.*" Deux's look was inscrutable. Or was that *bemusement?*

Mitsos stood on an external terrace of the *Marseilles* beside Sebastian Deux. They were half way up the structure on the starboard side, leaning on a railing, looking over the pale blue ocean towards two adapted fishing trawlers, which kept pace with the giant city ship and each other. The furthest boat was indistinct, just a smudge in the distance, while the fine net of filament Mitsos knew was being dragged between the two craft was not visible in any way, not even as a line of disturbance on the water's surface.

Mitsos exhaled deeply. *It worked?* When he'd been collected from his office by a member of the Apparatus, dressed in their grey-black two-tone uniform with a red stripe on the arm, he'd feared the worst, especially as the man had refused to explain himself beyond the brusque command 'come'. Was he to be 'interviewed' further? Emerging through the doorway to the outside and seeing the First Citizen had brought no immediate relief – merely changed his fear from that of torture to one of imminent defenestration. He now attempted insouciance. "*No.* Of course not." He saw a sly grin curve the other's face, and straightened his shoulders. "I *knew* it would work. The data from Earth was unambiguous. The issue was only of how well. Of the economics."

"Ah, yes. *Economics.* And that, Citizen Mitsos, is still the issue." Deux turned ninety degrees to face him. "The filament net does indeed attract a number of heavier elements from the water. *Trace* elements. And the amounts from the first trial were tiny. *Microscopic.*"

"How much?"

"After running the filament through your *Disassociator*? Enough to maybe replace all the key working parts of a *single* comms tablet."

The remnants of Mitsos' euphoria drained. "But the trial was small, wasn't it? That's usually the way of trials. Start small, then expand, extend."

"Indeed. The current run has been going since dawn and will continue to dusk. Six times as long as the first. So, maybe we'll harvest enough critical resources for… half-a-dozen tablets? We are truly rich." The sarcasm in Deux's voice was terrifying.

"That's a start," said Mitsos. "But things can be tweaked. Made more efficient. More filament nets. More trawlers. Small amounts over time add up."

"Citizen Mitsos, if we made ten times more of your nets – which we can't because, ironically, we lack the resources to do so – and trawled the oceans constantly for a century, then we might successfully accumulate the same amount of resources that were in the cargo bay of the *Leviathan* when it was destroyed. But even that excludes any account of the output costs of manufacturing the components of your device, or subsequent wear and tear on machinery. I would be long dead before we likely made any net gain. *Long* dead – largely because some of our enraged citizens would cast me to the creatures of the deep." His smile now – which Mitsos caught from the corner of his eye – was utterly without humour. "But as you say, it's just a case of scale. In an ideal world of perfectly functioning machines, utopia awaits. Hallelujah!"

Mitsos found himself gripping the railing so tightly it made his injured hand throb. He refused to turn to face the other fully, instead focusing on the two trawlers. "It sounds like you are giving up. But it's too soon. I am convinced improvements can be made, that it can be made to– "

"You're convinced? Really? *Look at me!*"

Mitsos reluctantly pulled one hand from the rail and turned square-on to the long-haired man. For once, no rebellious counter slipped from his lips, his mind appreciating the peril of his situation. "So… so what…?"

"What are we going to do? We are going to carry on. The concept is proven, and the trials will be gradually expanded. But slowly. Because we *both* know that those you approached in *Hibernia* were correct. We have a saying that the Hibernians know the price of everything and the value of nothing. And they do seem to be right here about the price, but I can still extract *value*. You see, your device provides hope. And therefore, *I* have given our people hope. For now."

Mitsos nodded gently. "I see that. But even if you are right about the machine, you must appreciate that I've been straight with you. I delivered the template for a machine that works the way I said it would. I always said there were uncertainties. I never misrepresented what I brought to you… which I still haven't been paid for, by the way. I have been honest."

Deux didn't respond immediately; he ran his eyes over Mitsos' face. *Letting me sweat*, thought Mitsos, who was now well acquainted with the other's calculating MO. Even had he brought him the wealth of Croesus, the other would likely have paused, sighed, and ultimately given no more than grudging acknowledgement. So how would he react now?

At last, Deux nodded slowly, and actually smiled. "Honest Citizen Mitsos? Well, why not? And you want a reward? Very well. Here is the first part of your payment. I realise that I have been a bit selfish, casting this machine as somehow my own. But now the citizens will be fully informed of its true originator. And given that a special new role has emerged, I am within my powers to override the computer in your own office to reassign you. You didn't like that job anyway, eh? Two weeks are surely enough. So you are going to get your wish. You will become the new head of Project Cornucopia, and more importantly, its new *face*. What do you think of *that*?"

Mitsos' relief lasted for less than a second before the other's intent became apparent. "Scapegoat? You're setting me up as a scapegoat!"

"Of course I am, Citizen Mitsos. When the trials ultimately end in failure, I'd rather the good citizens tore someone else limb-from-limb. But don't take offence. All is but a game – a game I am rather good at playing. And *nil desperandum*. I took a chance on your machine as a reserve stratagem. Had it worked, then my premier plan could have been put on hold – one that has also suffered from the fiery demise of the *Leviathan*."

"Stratagem?" Mitsos understood. "The training. The militia. The New Socialists from Earth."

"Precisely! You see, Citizen Mitsos, we are in need. We were in dire need before the destruction of the liner, and that has multiplied since. In truth, I do not think the *Marseilles* is viable any more. Our healthcare system is collapsing as machinery fails – our sole MRI scanner packed up before you arrived – and our fishing fleet is slowly dwindling, as our ships and their machinery break and cannot be repaired. Should critical systems in the fusion plant fail, we will be truly fucked. And it's not just us. In ten years, I see the number of city ships on Tethys halving – maybe in only five, if contact with Earth is not rapidly re-established. The weaker ships will be abandoned and ultimately pillaged. I do not know what will then happen to the people on them, for who has the capacity, or desire, to take them? As First Citizen, it is my responsibility to look after our people, and if your device cannot satisfy our needs, then I must find another way, another source, to do so."

"*Hibernia?*" Mitsos thought of Noma; serious, dutiful, patriotic Noma. A woman who'd looked out for him… and quite possibly informed on him, too. But in spite of that, he didn't think she deserved to be thrown into some pointless battle, just to help aggrandise Deux. "You… don't need to do that."

"That?" Deux's smile became lop-sided. "What exactly do you mean by *that*?"

"You're going to attack *Hibernia*. I mean, you have people practising with guns in a mock-up of an urban landscape. It doesn't take a genius to work out what that means."

"Maybe it does, Citizen Mitsos. You really don't understand the half of this alternative stratagem. We are simply preparing for the worst. For the end of days. I have no specific evil intent. Trust me. But this is not your concern. Now, let us discuss your new role."

Mitsos was going to get what he wanted all along – so why did he suddenly feel that he might be better off back on the *Dieppe*?

Chapter 21

The *Lisboa's* giant fusion-powered propellors had ceased to turn. Off the starboard side, not a hundred metres distant, the Northern Fringe Forest of the Ulster Black was evident as a dark region beyond the pale blue ocean, stretching all the way to the horizon. From here, under intermittent cloud shadows, it appeared black, but Marie knew that the vegetation was mainly a deep green colour.

"Will this do, Miguel?" asked Joao Nascimento, Captain-Governor of the *Lisboa*, standing next to a transparent, waist-high barrier. He was a short, dark man with greying kinky hair – inherited from his mother – and wore a slightly crumpled white uniform decorated with various golden badges.

"Yes – perfect!" said Miguel Figueroa, who was slightly taller than the other, though both had lumpen faces and shared a similar slouch. "From here, we can easily explore the forest. And once we have given the all clear, as it were, it will be easy to deploy the harvester nets from the front wings and allow our giant turtle to eat its fill."

Marie looked between the two men: both calm, soft-spoken, and generous, they could have been brothers, or even twins. It was little wonder they were held in high regard – Nascimento by the populace, which had kept him in power for thirteen years, and Figueroa by his staff. She stood next to Kalmik, along with the rest of the senior scientific staff, having been graciously invited to the Captain-Governor's 'crow's nest' – an open deck directly over the main control room.

Nascimento pursed his lips. "I am not sure I desire to move any closer to the cenote, but certainly, our trawlers will have quick access from here. We are well-stocked for now, so there is no rush to plunder this new, especially nutritious bounty. But, Miguel…" he carefully took the other by an elbow in a gesture of familiarity, "two weeks, eh? Well-stocked doesn't mean *infinitely* stocked."

"Of course, my friend. In truth, we could both play at once – we could conduct our research in an area to the stern of your harvesting, and be unaffected by it. But I'd still like to make sure we aren't committing some ecological travesty first, by doing a more fulsome mapping of the flora and fauna of this ecosystem."

Nascimento smiled broadly. "Always concerned about life, and the careful application of the scientific method. It will be as you wish."

Kalmik leant across and whispered to Marie: "Wrapped around little finger." But Marie wasn't so sure. Nascimento might seem benign, but no one achieved power in politics by being naïve, or a pushover.

"Now, I should return to the trials of governance. You and your team…" Nascimento turned to smile at the milling group, "are welcome to stay and enjoy the view as long as you like." He winked at Marie, and then headed for the double doors at the back of the platform.

Naturally, Figueroa allowed his team a short time only. "My dears, I am sure you are as keen as I am to explore this new ecosystem. Shall we get to it?"

* * *

The Northern Fringe Forest was a fairly uniform half kilometre wide, stretching along a thirty-five kilometres length of the Ulster Black – a north-western branch of the great Meridian cenote that curved to within twenty-two kilometres of *Hibernia* and Mount Athol.

"And the Hibernians have never explored this area?" asked Marie, sitting at the table in the main cabin of the *Fortunata* following Figueroa's briefing on their targets for the day.

"No, my dear. Their eyes have always looked in other directions."

"There's another sea forest about forty klicks further north of the Range, which they harvest instead," said Kalmik. "Sure, it's a bit further, but it keeps them away from the Black. And frankly, I'm surprised our revered Captain-Governor has come as close to this one as he has. We barely need the *Fortunata*: we could swim to the forest edge from the *Lisboa*."

"Joao is a practical man," said Figueroa. "He is less inclined to jump at superstition than most." He stood, a gleam entering his eyes. "In short, Marie, we are truly pioneers here. The book of knowledge is currently blank, waiting for us to fill its pages with data and sketches. *Vamos!*'

Marie was soon in the water, conducting a rudimentary survey of lifeforms in a set volume of forest, up to thirty metres down. She immediately felt more comfortable than during her previous forest dives, which *had* been nervy affairs, but because of the contrast with the most recent dives in pitch black water, today's expedition now seemed tame. And familiarity with the ecosystem also helped: she was soon recording the same species of small, fish-like creatures as before. And being less twitchy, she now found herself able to metaphorically sit back, scan, and take a wider perspective on the environment. It was thus forty minutes into the dive that, holding the stem of one giant kelp analogue, she drifted into the space between it and the next, and looked directly along a furrow in the forest, a clear line between rows of plants that was only populated by outstretched leaves from the stems to either side. Intrigued, she tapped the side of her helmet faceplate, which caused it to take a number of pictures from an inbuilt camera.

It was all a matter of perspective. Of alignment.

On her previous dives, she'd entered the water at an angle to the neat rows, which had given her the impression of a jumbled forest, with stems here and there. The foliage was also quite thick for the most part, which limited vision at any one point, preventing a good, clear view of the relationship of the stems to one another. But now that she had seen the pattern once, she knew what she was looking for.

She drifted across to the stem in the opposite 'row', then rounded it to the further side, attempting to keep a parallel orientation. And there, once beyond, she placed herself in the centre of the next 'furrow' – perhaps only a metre wide – and used her arms to peel back the obscuring leaves. It was difficult, because the foliage beyond continued to roll and churn, as if the plants themselves were waving, but after a few minutes, a gap randomly appeared – and Marie was able to see a good twenty metres in a straight line between stems.

It appeared that Tethys' nature was very well behaved. Either that, or…

Marie suddenly felt cold, as though someone had run an ice cube across the back of her neck. She moved her head around; looked three-sixty; then looked down. She remembered the shadow from her last fringe forest dive, and the mischievous prodding in the cage in the cenote. For the next twenty minutes she forgot all about the mapping task she had been given, and did nothing but float and stare…

* * *

"Luisa, do you have any recording of dives in normal sea forests?" said Marie.

Luisa Teixeira sat at a terminal in the main cabin from which she had access to much of their cumulated research data. "What do you mean by 'normal'?"

"I mean, *not* fringe forest. The free-floating stuff away from the cenotes."

"Of course. Hours of it. Many hours of it. The professor likes to be thorough. Why?"

Marie held up a hand. She'd completed her dive, passed her notes and samples to Figueroa in his little onboard office, and then sought out her *Lisboa* office mate. "Actually, forget that. Well, no. I want to have a look later, but… have you got any shots of sea forests from overhead?"

"You mean, like from orbiting observation satellites? Well, maybe. But I'd have to check. I doubt we have much."

"But you *have* been viewing the oceans from space, yes? I remember someone identified this forest as having a similar infrared pattern to the first nutrient-rich forest you studied."

Teixeira winced. She was clearly reluctant to help, likely having more than enough work to do already. "Well, I suppose. But it'd help if I knew exactly what you were looking for. It might narrow my search."

"That's difficult to say. I've… seen something. Here. And I just wondered whether the *architecture* of the fringe forest is the same as the more common type."

Teixeira turned to look up at Marie. "What have you seen?"

Marie smiled awkwardly. "It's probably nothing. I don't want to say anything now and embarrass myself."

"Okay. I won't press. But later, I'm going to ply you with drinks. You'll slip up sometime."

"Maybe after a few drinks, and I'll laugh it off too. But it's also that I don't want to put an idea into anyone's head. Let me try to marshal evidence and show it to you all, and then see if you notice the same thing I've noticed. Does that make sense?"

"Perfectly. Like a blinded research process. Okay. But you'll have to wait. I've got to file and categorise a load of data first. I'll have a look when I get back to the office on the big ship. Okay?"

* * *

But Teixeira remained busy for the next couple of days, during which Marie did two more dives. On the first, she'd been completely disorientated, and then distracted by the discovery of a new eel-like creature that seemed to occupy the deeper sections of the kelp forest. She'd spent much of her time chasing it between stalks, trying to capture it without success. But on the second, she had again found herself at just the right angle, and in a sparser area of foliage, to detect the pattern of ranks in the forest. But no one else had yet volunteered any insights about the holistic nature of the forest back on the surface, and so she'd continued to bite her tongue. Back in her office, tired of waiting, she'd prodded Teixeira to at least point to the electronic folders that might hold satellite imagery, as well as video data from past sea forest dives, so that she could start searching them herself.

She was working on this data now, accessed from her tablet at home, when Kate returned after an evening out.

"Hi, Mum. You seem busy. Online dating site, maybe?"

Marie looked up and gave her daughter a mock scowl. "Me? You're the one disappearing for hours without a word and coming home late. Where have you been? Boyfriend?"

"Touché, Mum. I think us Lockards are too strong-willed for the men around here. No. Just been out with Sara and Tonio. Usual things. Drinking. Drugs. Bit of vandalism. You know how it is with us feckless teenagers."

Marie smiled. "Well, as long as no assault or murder is involved, I think I'm okay with that. Have you eaten?"

"Yep. Had reconstituted fish-gruel from a packet before I went out. And then ice-cream-that-isn't from the Chilly Cow. These Lisboetas have weird tastes."

"Says the girl who likes crocodile steaks."

"Ha – you like them too."

Marie smiled, but in spite of having seen little of her daughter recently, she couldn't keep her eyes from straying back to the tablet screen. She paused for slightly too long: when she looked back, she noticed Kate standing with arms folded and an arch look on her face.

"Am I interrupting something critical, Mother? Should I just go back out?"

Marie sighed. "No. I'm sorry, Kate. It's just, well, work. As usual."

"Either your prof is a real slave driver or you're angling for promotion."

"Neither of those things. It's just another conundrum."

"Like the Bermuda Triangle thing? Cool. Can I see?" Kate swerved around the table that separated them and squeezed onto the banquette seating beside Marie. "What's *that*?"

Marie edged over slightly, leaving the tablet on its stand propped on the table between them. "On the left is the fringe forest. Pictures taken earlier today. On the right is an archive shot of one of the other sea forests."

"So you're comparing them? Right, what am I meant to be seeing?"

"Ah, now that would be telling." Marie frowned and looked askance at her daughter. Perhaps this was the acid test? The satellite imagery had been a waste of time: the subsurface patterns of the different forests were obscured by distance, shadow, and the general spread of surface foliage, and so forests of every type just appeared blurred from above – whatever wavelength she viewed it through. And that left her going through videos of the fringe and non-fringe forests. She'd decided the most scientific approach was to take one hundred random snaps of the two types and to compare and contrast them, taking whatever measurements on screen she could – such as foliage density and distance between stalks. She'd only just begun her analysis, but here was a completely uninformed observer.

"Colour… looks the same. Greeny-black and the odd bit of gold when the sunlight strikes the upper part."

"Very good."

"Right. What next?" Kate moved her head closer to the screen. She had always been good at puzzles, at pattern recognition. IQ tests confirmed she had great visual-spatial skills. "The leaves… kind of look the same. Maybe… a bit broader in the fringe ones?"

Marie smiled and nodded. "Yes. That's something we've observed. They have a slightly different composition, and the fringe ones have higher concentrations of certain nutrients."

Kate looked smug. "Right. Good. What else? Hmmm…"

After some minutes, Marie squeezed out from behind the table and went to the kitchen alcove. By this time, Kate was flicking between different images, utterly intent on her task. Marie decided to make herself a coffee. She would have offered her daughter one, too, had it not been for the time of the evening. She'd probably be awake half the night now, lying in bed, her mind churning.

She returned to find Kate with scrunched brows, in deep thought.

"Anything else, oh precocious daughter of mine?"

"Maybe. Are these all random pictures, or have you deliberately selected certain ones?"

"They're random. The fringe forest pictures were taken by others. I deliberately excluded certain shots I took."

Kate nodded. "Okay. Then I have an answer. No – a *hypothesis*."

Marie set her cup down and felt an odd tension. "You do? Go on."

"Well, there's a clear difference between the two forest types in terms of, well, *tidiness*. The normal forests are just really unkempt. Like your bedroom."

"Thanks!"

Kate looked askance and smiled. "No problem."

"And the fringe forest?"

Kate paused a moment, her mouth twitching, as if searching for appropriate words. "Well, the fringe forests are… *cultivated*."

Marie nearly knocked over her coffee.

* * *

"So you see, the two forest types have a number of consistent differences." Marie concluded her small presentation – or at least, *nearly* did. She had a few more pictures she planned to display, but only when the moment was right.

"Thank you, Marie," said Miguel Figueroa. "That is very interesting. We have been so focused on the minutiae of the ecosystem, the individual creatures, that we have literally not been able to see the wood for the trees. I am glad that *someone* has been looking."

The senior science team currently occupied their main meeting room, some sat at the big oval table, chairs pushed out at an angle to aid forward viewing, others sat at chairs around the walls, and one standing up at the back. Some had glasses of water, others nursed cups of tea or coffee. Marie looked first to Figueroa, who sat closest to her at the head of the table, then slowly scanned the others searching for a hint of recognition. Katerina Kalmik looked vaguely non-plussed; Teixeira nodded gently. Marco Grande – at the back of the room – appeared to be gazing at some invisible object on the ceiling. As ever, the main dive team – Mike Resnos, Raul Garcia, Victoria Soares – sat together, looking among each other, smiling, winking. *If only Kate were here!*

Marie sighed. It was amazing how often the most informed could miss the most obvious, their minds already focused on their own particular interests, and cluttered with learned theories. "Does no one see the implication of this?"

"Implication?" asked Figueroa, surprised. "Aha! You are leading us somewhere. Scattering breadcrumbs. But where?"

Marie smiled. At least the professor had got *that.* Could he make the final leap? "Sort of."

"This is your mystery, isn't it?" said Teixeira. "Okay. But I don't see what you're getting at."

"So, the strands in the kelp forest are more regularly spaced," said Kalmik. "I get that. I buy your analysis. Why? Simple. They have evolved to achieve a more optimal spacing to take advantage of the sunlight on the surface and the concentration of micro-organisms in the water."

Figueroa nodded. "Indeed. Kelp strands that grow too closely together will compete for similar resources. Become entangled. Natural selection will ensure over time an optimal… or rather, *more* optimal… arrangement. Or do you have another suggestion?"

"I do. Professor, there is 'more regular', and then there is… *this*." She tapped on her tablet, and the image projected large on the back wall changed. She looked up quickly, scanning the faces in front of her again.

Teixeira gasped: "I *see*."

"There is another way to attain regularity," Marie jumped in, continuing before her office mate could elaborate. She waved a hand at the picture behind, which she'd taken two days ago, and which showed a clear gap between two rows of kelp with the leaves serendipitously arranged to minimise obscuration, lined up with almost military precision. "Especially regularity like this. And it's got nothing to do with *natural* processes."

Figueroa saw it too. "Surely not! Marie, you're not suggesting…"

Kalmik laughed; the trio of dive scientists started to whisper sharply at each other.

"I am," concluded Marie. "This is *artificial*. The higher nutrition content added to the efficient planting of the kelp speaks to me of something planned. Something directed by *purpose*. This didn't emerge naturally: someone, or something, *nurtured* this. And if you don't believe me, here is the same shot with the foliage digitally removed to just show the strands." The picture changed, and the pattern became crystal clear. "And to show it's not a fluke, here is another picture from the day before, in an area a kilometre away, also remastered…" The picture changed. "And here is another one, from a shot I took on the first day from yet another area…"

The room fell silent.

After some seconds, Kalmik declared: "Preposterous!" But she lacked conviction.

"Marie, that is… *remarkable*," declared Figueroa. "But if you're right, then the question is, who are the farmers and where are they?"

Marie's smile faded. "I think *where* they are is obvious. The fringe forests are so-called because they line certain areas that we haven't been able to successfully explore yet."

"And now you're really freaking me out," said Kalmik.

"My dear Katerina," said Figueroa, "I think our splendid new recruit is freaking us *all* out."

* * *

After the argument three weeks ago, Tonio had been remarkably diplomatic in dealing with his friend, and though Sara had been somewhat sniffy at first, after a while she'd realised that she couldn't continue playing hard-done-by.

"Stop being *nice*!" she'd exclaimed. "I know I over-reacted, but you're just trying to make me feel guilty now!"

Sara had even allowed them to go to the Terrace on a couple of occasions as penance, though Kate and Tonio had let her choose the table they sat at (in some far corner, out of the way), and Tonio had done his best to restrict his wistful glances at the sublime Vita Fernandez to moments when Sara was highly distracted or else had gone inside the café to use its facilities.

But that still meant the Bowl was their regular destination, perhaps two days in every three. Now that Tonio had fixed the lighting – and linked a dormant computer to the ship's main servers – they'd do their homework here first, before lowering the lights and watching the submarine world through the concave reinforced glass of the observation blister... or at least, watch Sara while *she* watched, mesmerised, resting in the bottom of the bowl.

"So, are you going to follow your mum?" asked Tonio. "Be a marine biologist, or whatever it is she is?"

"I guess so," said Kate, swivelling in her chair at the small console from which the lights could be turned on to illuminate the water beneath. She switched her gaze as she turned, from Sara lying prostrate in the hollow, to Tonio, swivelling in another chair by the main door. "I've not really thought about it. It would be logical, and Mum would like it. But it depends on where we end up. If we stay here, I have no choice really. If we go back to Earth, I'll have more options. I'm interested in philosophy, but I don't know what I'd do with a degree in it."

"Maybe work in one of those fast food restaurants I hear about?" said Tonio, with a smirk.

"Ha-ha! But that's the problem. I just don't know what I want to do. What about you?"

"Oh, that's easy," said Tonio. "Footballer. Or rock star."

"Now I know you're joking. I've seen you in PE. You wouldn't get in the *girl's* team! And I've heard you sing – or *try* to."

"Rock stars don't need to be able to sing well. They just shout a bit with a gravelly voice. And anyway, I'd be a goalkeeper, not an outfield player."

"So let me get this straight," said Kate, ceasing her turning and leaning forwards, a wry smile playing across her face. "Your aim in life is to either be a singer who can't actually sing, or a footballer who can't actually control a ball with his feet? I'd have thought with your skill in electronics, that's where you'd go."

"You are a girl with no soul or vision," sighed Tonio. "So much for dreams."

"Sometimes dreams turn out to be nightmares." Kate frowned. "I should know."

"Eh? What's this? Some deep personal trauma?" Tonio beamed at her, then seemed to do a mental double-take, and frowned. "Ah... I'm not, like, mocking you. Is there anything...?"

Kate pouted. "No, not really. I don't suppose I can claim to be some sort of martyr. I'm not Job. It's just... Mum and Dad were *good. We* were good. And then Mum got her dream job, back in South Africa. I don't know. Dad had a good position at a university in Australia, and we liked the lifestyle there. And then he couldn't get anything as good in Durban, and ended up in Cape Town. And it all sort of went downhill from there."

"Right." Tonio looked uncomfortable. "Is that why you, er..."

"Came here? I guess. South Africa was no longer the dream we'd hoped for, so Mum decided to get out, and this place seemed perfect."

"For you too? Don't you miss your home? Your dad?"

"Yes and no. South Africa was actually quite dangerous outside the compounds. It wasn't like Australia or other places we lived. And

Dad just sort of withdrew. I could have stayed with him, but…" she shrugged. "I didn't want to let Mum down. She needs someone to look after her."

"Whoa!" said Sara, suddenly. She got to her hands and knees, and then sat back onto her calves. "What was *that*?"

"What was what?" asked Tonio. He almost seemed relieved at the distraction. "We can't see anything except for your fat butt."

Sara ignored the slight, and moved into a crouch and then backed up the slope, all the while swinging her head one way and then the other.

"What did you see, Sara?" asked Kate, rising from her seat and taking a hesitant step towards the other girl. Then she held out an arm, which Sara glimpsed from the corner of her eye: she reached up to take it, allowing Kate to pull her over the lip.

"I'm not sure. I think maybe we've been discovered."

"Who by?" said Tonio, joining the others and peering downwards.

"I think it was a diver. Just over there. They came towards the glass, and made me jump. Then they turned and were off."

"Well, I don't see anyone," said Tonio. "And it wouldn't really matter anyway. We're hardly doing anything illegal. We didn't break in, and we haven't stolen anything."

"Hang on," said Kate. She retraced to the console, and there turned off the lights for the entire room, including the residual lighting in the ceiling that had been on ever since they'd found the place. As soon as she did so, she heard a slight yelp.

"Tell us what you're doing first!" said Tonio. "That gave me a scare."

Kate stayed by the various switches rather than blunder back to her friends. The room was utterly dark now, and to her, Tonio and Sara were merely smudges within a greater night. The ocean under the inverted dome was also pitch black. "Ah… that didn't work."

"What, trying to hide us?" asked Tonio.

"No. I thought if it was a diver, we'd see their dive lights. I see nothing from here. What about you two?"

"I'm going back down," said Sara.

Kate heard a rustling as Sara returned to her usual position, undeterred by a hiss from Tonio.

Seconds passed, and the darkness remained. Often, bioluminescent creatures would come to investigate the bottom of the bowl, perhaps drawn by the strip light from the ceiling shining through, and so maybe the absence of light removed that attraction.

The three teens remained silent, almost holding their breaths.

And then there was a soft, low sound, a thud, and Sara gasped: "Oh!"

"What was that?" asked Tonio.

Again, Kate heard Sara shuffling about. Then the girl said: "Something butted the glass. Not hard. I didn't see it. I can't see anything. Shit!" This time she jumped, and Kate heard the *thud* more clearly.

"Yeah, I heard that!" said Tonio.

"I don't like this," said Sara. "I'm getting off… oh!"

This time, they almost *felt* the blow, the contact. And then, immediately after the blow, there was a second strike, and then a third. And a split second after, Kate sensed her friends, arm-in-arm, stumble towards her. She put out a hand, and felt Tonio, who squawked and then gave a nervous laugh.

"Go away!" cried the boy into the darkness. "There's no one home."

Sara was breathing hard. Now she muttered: "That diver has some *serious* issues. Trying to…" there was another thump, "scare us."

"Well, two can play that game," said Kate. "Let's see how he likes *this*…" she reached back with one hand towards the lever that Tonio had reconnected to the main electricity circuit when in the hidden control room. "Full throttle!" Kate yanked the lever down all the way, blazing the submarine lights to full illumination.

Before the lever had even got half-way, the sight revealed was both shocking and confusing. They didn't see a single diver. What they saw instead was a dark whorl, an indistinct motion, not in one place, but seemingly everywhere, accompanied by a churn of bubbles, that rose and burst against the bottom of the glass with such force that it seemed to thrum like a mighty cello played by a giant.

And then the bubbles dissipated, and the lights revealed nothing but empty ocean.

"What the *hell* was that?" said Tonio.

"I don't know," said Kate. "But I think maybe I've had enough of this place for one evening. Sara?"

The other's face was now spookily visible, up-lit by photons escaping from the beams pointing into the ocean. She smiled unconvincingly. "Maybe… maybe the Terrace won't be so bad at this time. After you, Tonio."

Chapter 22

"Boats," announced a voice over the comms speaker. "Eight of them. Moving fast."

Rennie Heiko leaned away from the mic and looked at Anders Pedersen, whose eyes had widened. "What exactly does that mean?" he asked.

"I don't know. We've never had anything like this happen before. Eight boats rounding Mount Ardol? It's *Hibernia.* There's no one else with that hardware."

Heiko leant back towards the mic set into the monitor in the small comms office in the security section. The screen had been black, but now lit up, initially showing pale blue sky, then the top of someone's head, and then the face of Sven Ibsen. "Sven? Can you clarify? What is the nature of these boats? Where are they going?"

"Hang on, Heiko. I'm here with the boss. He's got binocs." The view changed as Ibsen's handheld device was momentarily lowered, and then Ibsen's voice dropped in volume. Heiko heard: "Makka? What the fuck is going on?"

There was a pause, as Makka Frost presumably relayed an update to his foreman. After some seconds, the picture refocused on Ibsen's face. "They're big boats, and armed. Machine gun or cannon on the front. It looks like the entire Hibernian navy."

"Destination?"

"Can't say at the moment, but judging by the direction they've come from and… oh, wait. What?" The last word was shouted to someone out of shot. "Fuck!" Ibsen refocused again. "It looks like two are peeling off and heading straight for us. The other six are heading west. They're coming to you."

Heiko quickly exchanged glances with Pedersen, then looked into the inbuilt camera on the monitor. "Okay, Sven – tell Makka not to do anything to antagonise them. Play ball. But if you've anything of value – material or information – now's the time to hide it. Just in case. Things tend to go missing at times like this."

"Roger that."

"What's the ETA for the *Stavanger* rendezvous?"

"For the six? Can't be certain. Skiff takes fifteen-twenty minutes. These are moving faster. Say fifteen, but plan for ten."

"Thanks, Sven. Any further intel, let us know. I'll probably be off this line, but someone will update me. Over and out."

Heiko pushed away from the screen and turned to face his deputy.

Pedersen was frowning and slowly shaking his head. "Well, this is a first," he said. "A visit from the Hibernian navy."

"Six boats? What's their complement?"

"Crew would probably be half-a-dozen each, but I suspect they'll be loaded with members of their External Security Unit. Could be twenty on each. Hundred and twenty in total. And properly armed, too, not with the sort of crowd-control stuff we have."

"And we've got just forty active officers, some of whom are off duty and probably in bed." Heiko shook his head. "I wasn't going to suggest trying to hold them off, but the numbers make that decision for us. We're going to have to go along with whatever the Hibernians want for now. Assemble everyone who's available, but leave one comms officer here. The Hibernians will have to use our docks unless they're planning on firing grapples over our sides, so we'll meet them there."

"Weapons, sir?"

Heiko thought a moment. "No. Batons only. We don't want to give anyone an excuse to start a shooting match on either side, especially if they have the more lethal guns. But send a couple of officers to the armoury. Get them to collect every other gun and ammo, and hide them somewhere."

"Every other?"

"We don't want to make it obvious. Let's let the Hibernians think we're low on weapons – if they decide to look. It's not inconceivable we'd be short of gear."

"Right." Pedersen stood to go. "And you, sir?"

"I'm heading to the docks. But first, I need to inform the Premier."

* * *

Colonel Eric Nesvorny was alerted by his opposite number in the External Security Unit just ten minutes before she left with her fleet.

"Sorry, Eric," Joseph had said. "Got orders from Traore this morning, and been organising since then. Also, he instructed an embargo on comms, just in case. But I thought you should know as a courtesy. Don't spread it though."

And shortly after that, he'd gotten his own orders to move.

Fukuda reported as commanded, cap held to his side by one elbow. "Sir!"

Nesvorny rose to his feet and straightened his own uniform. "The world has gone mad, Major Fukuda. We've been instructed to kick the hornet's nest."

"Sir?" Fukuda's expression was unreadable. "Hornet's nest?"

"Old Earth expression. Concerns doing something you really, *really* don't want to do unless you want to get seriously stung."

"Understood. How big a team?"

Nesvorny laughed. "*Everyone.* Everyone available in the barracks. Get them into full body armour and hand out the pneumatic rifles, then assemble in the parade hall. Oh-thirty. Got that?"

"Sir!" Fukuda turned to leave, but then something struck Nesvorny.

"Fukuda – hold." He waited for his deputy to turn. "You never asked what we're going to do."

"Engine Quarter, sir. It's obvious." But Fukuda's mouth trembled, as though fighting a smile.

"This *is* news to you, isn't it? Or were you already informed?"

"I suspected we would move soon, sir, especially after the second bomb yesterday. Difficult times demand difficult decisions, and sometimes bold action."

"That's not exactly what I asked." Nesvorny appraised his deputy. Fukuda gave little away – but Nesvorny suspected him, ever since the other's invite to the meeting with the triumvirate and the way Traore had looked at him during that affair. He had not commented before, but maybe it was time to put the squeeze on. He moved around his desk, hitched one thigh onto it, and held his cap between both hands. "So, Fukuda, what the fuck is going on?"

"Sir? I don't know."

"Don't play innocent with me. Traore has approached you. Off record. Behind my back. Offered you something? Don't take me for a fool."

Fukuda at last looked uncomfortable, nudged from his serene centre. "Minister Traore and I met… socially."

Nesvorny barked a laugh. "You don't get paid enough to go to the sort of events he goes to. You'd only meet 'socially' if you were moonlighting as a waiter. As your commanding officer, I am ordering you to tell me what the fuck is going on. He may be nominally head of security in *Hibernia* – the man Kelly reports to when he's sober – but there is a chain of command."

"Have I disobeyed orders, sir?"

"You're still avoiding answering."

Fukuda continued to stare into the mid distance, avoiding Nesvorny's eyes. He had no easy escape route. At last, he said: "Minister Traore stopped by my office a couple of times, wanting advice – informally. He is clearly concerned about the Stoker situation."

"Still minimal info, Fukuda. I want to know how entwined you two are. We can stay here all day. Best make the assembly oh-forty. Or will we need even more time?"

"He… thinks that we are not doing enough to counter the threat. He thought the new patrols you put on after the first bombing, and the extra searches, weren't working. He asked my view."

"Really? And what response did you give?"

"I noted that you were my superior, and I followed your orders."

"For now?"

"For as long as you are my superior, sir."

"Hmmm." Nesvorny slipped off the desk. He'd get no more from the man. The implicit threat was clear. "Very well. Assemble the troops. Oh-thirty."

"It will be done."

Nesvorny had to discuss the action with a small strategy team, with whom he'd coordinate the raid. Fukuda would lead it. He didn't really need to see or address his force, but he felt it part of his responsibility to do so. He arrived at the giant parade hall – the largest assembly space in his domain – at oh-twenty, and wasn't surprised to find the two hundred and twenty assembled troopers already in ranks and fully equipped. It was almost as if they'd been tipped off early.

"Everyone but me," Nesvorny murmured to himself.

* * *

The raid started to go wrong almost immediately. Nesvorny watched it unfold in the strategy room, where his team of eight passed orders from him to Fukuda – and his various squad leaders – and then reported back progress. The new data was constantly fed into their battle system, updating on different monitors as well as on the 3D holographic campaign map that floated above the central table.

"Squad Bravo is taking fire," declared that squad's dedicated controller. On the 3D display, the icon representing that particular squad – which was attempting to enter the Engine Quarter on the second sub-level from the direction of the Command District in the centre of the ship – started to blink red.

"Bravo too?" muttered Nesvorny, who paced the floor, too nervous to sit.

"Now Delta," said a different controller, and another light started to blink, this one in a similar region to Bravo, but on sub-level one.

"That's now four," said Nesvorny. Only Alpha and Foxtrot, at the edges, had made any real progress. He looked at the icon for Golf – the reserve squad – and wondered whether to deploy it. Instead, he asked: "Casualties? All report."

The controllers took it in turn to relay the numbers of injured, until Echo's liaison cursed. "One KIA. Another critical, being evacuated. Three light wounded."

Now a death? "Get me Fukuda. Personal comms." He dropped into his chair – the biggest and most central in the room – and found a headset.

After a few moments, Fukuda's voice came to him. "Sir!"

"Fukuda – what the fuck is going on? Where the fuck did they get projectile weapons?"

"No idea, sir. But they don't have many. The rate of fire at the breach points is slight. Might only be one at each. It's nothing."

"Nothing? You are aware that several squads have stalled completely, and you are taking casualties, including at least one KIA."

"Acceptable attrition, sir."

"Acceptable? For what gain?"

"We're flushing out the troublemakers. Hitting them before they've got a chance to arm further."

Nesvorny paused in sudden doubt. *Guns?* They'd not known about those until today. They couldn't have come on the *Leviathan*, so they must have been made in the Engine Quarter. And whoever had the knowledge to make four, or eight, or however many they had, would clearly be able to manufacture more. And he wouldn't have known about it without the raid. Was Traore right? Was he losing it? But… would they ever have used the guns without this heavy-handed assault?

He shook his head and realised that Fukuda had been speaking.

"Say again, Fukuda. I lost that."

"I said, we got a high-profile target. Kai Dures' wife. Echo got her. She was with three others, including a guy with a gun. Two of them now deceased, including the gunman. There's no further fire in that zone."

"You got Karyn Dures? How–"

"Only concussed. We're bringing her in. She's got a lot of questions to answer."

"Dures? *Fuck!* Okay, Traore has his prize. That's enough. Pull out."

"But the other gunmen, sir?"

"I said, pull out. We've got enough casualties. And God only knows how many Stokers we've harmed – innocent as well as guilty. If you think this will stop the bombings, you've got a lot to learn."

"But we now have a hostage, sir."

"Pull out!" Nesvorny ripped off the headset and threw it onto the floor.

They'd entered the Engine Quarter in different locations in order to begin a thorough search for stolen items, and to look for evidence on who had made the two bombs that had been detonated in the ship, two weeks apart. He'd not expected actual resistance, more sullen non-compliance. But the Stokers had seen them coming and been willing to actually fight. *Why?* And as for Karyn Dures? Her husband was nominally the leader of the Stokers and the suspected mastermind of their pillaging gangs. He was wanted for theft, but that was all. And given Dures' level of protection – as well as the relatively low-level charges – Nesvorny had been content to allow him his freedom. But having taken his formidable wife – who some claimed was more than *just* the power behind the throne – they'd stepped over some invisible but widely accepted boundary. "The Rubicon," he muttered. He suspected that there was no going back from here.

Traore had wanted a war. It now looked like he was going to get one.

* * *

They had been corralled into the council chamber at the top of the ship – Olsen, Moroni, Bulow, Heiko, and Pedersen. The rest of the elected council of twelve, with whom Heiko had had only fleeting interactions, had been dismissed – a sign that the Hibernians were well informed on where true power in the *Stavanger* resided. He'd not been armed on the first encounter with the raiders at the docks, though Pedersen had had a baton, which had been immediately confiscated.

Currently, they sat under the eyes of two Hibernian troopers in black uniforms, who guarded the exit. A third trooper continued to set up a special comms device to allow a satellite connection, while the group's leader, Colonel Tania Joseph, lounged on the table, perched on one buttock and swinging a leg insolently. She'd asked for silence, and Heiko – recognising where the power currently lay – had gestured to the others to accede.

At last, the third trooper finished, made a connection, then stepped back as a holographic projection sprung to life in the middle of the chamber. This showed three people – two women and a man, sat in a line at a table.

"Premier Olsen," began the woman in the middle. "I don't think we've ever met in person. It's a shame we should do so like this, under these circumstances." The woman had a stern face, framed by thick black hair that only seemed to reach the top of her ears.

Olson had remained calm throughout the affair so far – after her initial shock – and appeared to be coping better than Moroni, who Heiko could see was seething, while Bulow was difficult to read. "Premier O'Neill," Olson nodded, "I would like to say I'm pleased to meet you, but that would not be truthful. What is the meaning of this assault on our sovereignty?"

O'Neill frowned. "Sovereignty? This isn't an invasion, Olson." She'd already dropped the respectful title. "We have no wish to take over your little ship. No, this is a merely a visit. A random check. *Customs control.*" The dark man besides her chuckled, but she ignored him. "Only in this case, we are not concerned with items being smuggled into our territory, but of things illicitly being taken out."

Olson smiled serenely. "I think there is some confusion here, and you have acted prematurely. To continue your analogy, we haven't left your territory yet. You have effectively arrested us while we were in the process of completing our customs declaration."

"Well said," muttered Moroni.

"Thank you, Nila. Premier O'Neill, we won't play games. We know what this is about. We found a potentially useful deposit of rare earths in our latest dig – something you seem to have become aware of, although I do not know how." Olson looked straight at the screen, conspicuously ignoring Bulow, who sat beside her. "But we have not attempted to exploit this, or to hide it. In fact, we have been compiling a comprehensive dossier for you on the find, which we'd planned to submit within a couple of days."

The man in the holograph laughed again, while the red-haired woman to O'Neill's other side simply smiled and raised a hand to her mouth. "Really, Olson?" O'Neill's frown never wavered. "That is not what we heard."

"Oh? And what have you heard? Maybe your *spy* didn't have the whole story? Or maybe they misunderstood?"

O'Neill made an irritated, dismissive gesture with one hand. "I am not interested in vague or fickle intentions, only reality. Do you deny that you've known about this find in our territory for weeks? You've had plenty of time to tell us, and plenty more time to strategize. If you had indeed decided to tell us – perhaps grudgingly – that does not mean you might not have changed your mind. But we are here now. This play is over."

"Really?" said Olson. "And what do you plan to do while you are here?"

This time, O'Neill's grim expression did flex into something of a smile. "Oh, collect all relevant information on the find, and then, perhaps, conduct a thorough search for contraband."

"Contraband!" Moroni could control herself no more. "There is no contraband..."

"Nila–" Olson turned to the woman and placed one hand on her forearm, but it had no effect.

"...there is nothing on the *Stavanger* except a few lumps of ore. *Unprocessed* ore. Its net value is probably less than the cost of one of your extravagant haircuts. You can take those rocks and leave. Half-an-hour should suffice."

The grinning man in the display leant across and whispered something into O'Neill's ear. The woman's expression had steeled at mention of her hair; whatever the man told her didn't enhance her mood. She nodded once, then continued: "Ms... Moroni? I was talking to the leader of this place. You're here on sufferance. Speak again, and I'll have the room cleared. Adults only."

Heiko briefly closed his eyes and thought, *this could get ugly.* But when he glanced across at Moroni he was surprised at what he saw: the rebuke seemed to have centred the woman. She was now smiling, although it was not the sort of smile he would ever wish directed at him.

Moroni arched an eyebrow and simply nodded.

"Olson," said O'Neill, looking directly ahead once more. "We have an issue of trust. *You* have broken the bond of trust, not us. Our security detachment will conduct the search I mentioned, and leave when they are satisfied that you have no hidden stash of ore, or anything else that belongs to *Hibernia.* I require you to provide them with accommodation and space to work, and not to interfere with their searches. Until they leave, your own security team are relieved of duties. Aside from you two..." she looked down, perhaps at some notes, "Heiko and Pedersen. You will accompany Colonel Joseph for debrief. Instruct your troops to return to their homes and remove their uniforms in the meantime."

Olson turned to Heiko, who now said to the holograph: "As you wish."

"And our site on Ardol?" asked Olson, looking back.

"You have broken the agreement in spirit if not in letter. Your term ends now. Your team will return here after they are checked for illicit material, and the mining site will be secured by us. And as for the future – and whether you will be allowed to return – that will depend upon your level of cooperation. We are done here."

Without the opportunity for any riposte, the picture winked out.

* * *

They met at Olson's state apartment – although this time, there were only three of them.

As he took a seat, having eschewed the offer of a drink, Heiko peered between the two women sat beyond a low coffee table on separate two-person sofas. "Just us, Premier? No Ms Bulow?"

"We thought – under the circumstances – it might be best to meet without her," said Olson, "although please do not inform Hanna of this fact."

"Of course."

"But you also seem to be missing someone," said Moroni. "We assumed you would bring Pedersen." Moroni took a quick sip of the spirit in her tumbler. "Should we wait?"

"Ah, now I have my own admission, which I hope you will also keep secret. I deliberately left him ignorant of this meeting."

Moroni sat forwards, eyes keen. "Interesting. Why?"

Heiko frowned and his brow furrowed. "Nothing tangible or definitive. Anders is probably sound. But certain recent events – that I don't wish to go into now – have raised a flag. I think things have become a bit too cosy between my department and... *others*. I don't know where the connections are, or how strong they are, so I thought it would be best to take no risk at present."

Moroni and Olson exchanged glances but not words, then Olson gave a brief headshake and looked back at Heiko. "I don't like this –

not at all. It seems the circle of trust is rapidly shrinking. Now we are just three."

"On the bright side," said Moroni, without humour, "we can't shrink much further from here."

"Quite," said Olson. "Okay. Let's start. Rennie – from your perspective, where do we stand?"

"Under military occupation, as simple as that. My team has been temporarily disbanded, and it was touch and go whether Anders and I were going to be detained. As it is, we have been allowed to remain free to act as liaison between the occupiers and the people of *Stavanger*, to maintain calm and be held responsible for any unrest."

"Can we resist?" asked Olson. "Should we?"

"I think that really depends upon the Hibernians and their true intentions. Their leaders said this wasn't an annexation, and I believe them. It's not feasible. They have far too few troops to hold us for any length of time. Give me a few days and I guarantee I'll be able to recruit enough hotheads to leave our unwanted guests cut off and surrounded in a small part of the ship with no choice but to evacuate or starve. So, we could resist. Should we? That depends upon how long they plan to stay."

"And what they truly want," added Moroni.

"Indeed," said Heiko. "They can't really believe we mined out the seam, or deposit, or whatever it is called, and that we've stashed half the mountain in our holds. So that suggests they're making some sort of political statement."

"I could almost live with that," said Olson. "What concerns me most is that this may be taken as an excuse to deny us even a finder's fee, or worse, to revoke our mining rights altogether."

"Yes, and this might explain their appearance *now*," said Moroni. "Had they waited any longer, we might have formally alerted them to the find and removed the possibility of this action. Now they will be able to claim the whole find for themselves. I'm sure they'll also be keen to transmit what they've done to all the ships visiting Ardol."

"*Pour encourager les autres*," muttered Heiko.

"Sorry, Rennie," said Olson. "What was that?"

"An old expression. Voltaire. From *Candide*. He suggested that the British hung their Admiral Byng for failure to defend Menorca against the French as a symbol – to 'encourage' the other admirals to show more skill and backbone or risk a similar fate."

Moroni laughed. "Definitely more than a brute in a uniform."

Heiko returned a lopsided smile. "Military college isn't just about weapons training."

Olson sighed. "So, you think we are being made an example of. A very public one. After this, no one will dare try to hide anything from the Hibernians or challenge them in any way. And there seems to be nothing we can do about it."

"From a military perspective – no. We *could* drive them off the *Stavanger*, but then what? We couldn't invade Ardol – and any resistance would, as you say, likely spell the end of your future mining prospects. But if you allow, I will at least prepare for action in case the Hibernians overstay their welcome. I have already had some weapons hidden. I can keep an eye on our guests – where they barrack, what they get up to, what their routines are."

"And you'll involve Pedersen in this?" asked Moroni.

"Of course. I'm not sure I could do this without him. But I will be careful in how I present this stratagem to him. It's not that I suspect him of being a traitor, but I wouldn't want to leave something in his hands that might be traded for a tempting reward. Just a precaution, you understand."

"I still find it hard to believe that Anders is guilty of anything significant," said Olson, but this time adding, after a quick side glance, "and yes, Nila, I know you had some doubts about Security before we appointed Rennie."

Moroni was content with that recognition. "Okay. That is the military angle," she said. "But we must now decide the political one – and also think about how we handle our own snake in the grass."

Olson was clearly uncomfortable with the topic. "I know things look bad for Hanna, but when you told us about the invasion, Rennie, Hanna seemed as shocked as we were. I am convinced she didn't know it was going to happen, and she never had the chance to send another message after that first one, *or* receive one."

"And you still haven't challenged her?" asked Heiko. "You have allowed her to think we believe her?"

"She believes Margarethe," said Moroni. "But it's clear she knows I don't trust her, and there's nothing I can do about that." She leant forwards and placed her now-empty glass on the coffee table, then turned to Olson. "And much as I hate to say this, we may need to enact a new play – one in which you, Margarethe, turn to her as confidante at my expense. Perhaps you can suggest I have become unstable." She smirked. "She'll believe that, because she *wants* to believe it."

Olson nodded. "I see. But what is the aim of this new game?"

"To convince Bulow to act as a bridge between us and the Hibernians. To get her to convince them that we are above board and that we were genuinely going to tell them everything. To suggest that we have no ill-feelings; that we're not angry, but confused. Maybe also to note that our prospecting expertise is high, and that it would be mutually beneficial to form a partnership to develop the deposit. I hate to say it, but she is probably the only weapon we've got. We need to make sure we point it in the right direction."

"And what's in it for her?" wondered Heiko.

"Well, assuming you're right and the Hibernians aren't here to stay, and so won't be installing her as their new regent, it'll cement her importance to them and perhaps convince her of her position as number two here, as heir apparent."

Heiko gave a wry grin. "I think I'll leave the *Machiavelli* to you, and stick to my *Sun Tzu*. But maybe we should break up now. I don't want to be seen leaving here after a meeting with you."

"Nor we with you, Rennie," said Olson. "Please find a way to keep us informed. Thank you."

* * *

"Let's fuck them up!" fumed Melissa De Voe. "I don't give a *fuck* about legalities, this is a piss take."

Heiko rested side-on to the balcony railings of the woman's apartment, which was on a mid-level of the ship towards the bow on the starboard side. Someone of her status would normally live in a pad higher up, but the exterior position and sea view compensated for this, while the apartment was at the edge of the Geilo district the woman considered her home turf. He lowered his hands in a calming motion. "Melissa – we need cool heads."

"That's all right for you to say. You're new. This is probably still just a job for you. Someone has taken over your office. For us, it's personal. Deeply personal. *Bastards!*"

Heiko refrained from comment, allowing the woman to blow herself out. De Voe thumped the railing with one palm, but then looked up at him and appeared to appreciate what she'd said. She blew out her cheeks and wrinkled her brow, causing the trident tattoo by her eyeline to flex. She somehow found a sheepish smile. "Sorry. Bit harsh maybe."

"Don't worry about me. And you're probably right. I have less history, less investment. But in this case, maybe it allows me to take a more objective view."

"Does nothing ruffle you? I've never seen you angry."

"Oh, plenty of things make me angry. I just hide it better."

De Voe's smile firmed. "That's meant to be bad for you, isn't it? Bottling up your emotions. Repressing them. Also makes it hard for others to work out what you really think… like what you think about me."

Heiko laughed. "Are you fishing for compliments? If so, I think you're all right, Melissa."

"All right? Is that one of Casanova's lines? Fuck, you can be hard work."

"The ex-Mrs Heiko would agree with you. But I'm getting on. I had some exciting times when I was younger in my line of work. I've found a way to cope. Getting this old dog to change is probably a lost cause."

De Voe reached a hand along the railing until it made contact with his resting arm. "Don't worry. I'm not that sort of girl. I think you're okay, too. What a pair of fucking romantics we are, eh?"

"At least we're now talking about love not war, which is an improvement."

De Voe's hand withdrew slightly. "Is it?"

"Trust me, it is. The Hibernians are going to lord it over us for a few days. Couple weeks, max. And then they're going to leave and we can sail away."

"And probably not come back." She shook her head. "That would be tough on Makka. He's a real rockhopper. Not good for me either, come to that."

"If the worst comes to the worst, maybe you could hire yourselves out to the Hibernians. I'm sure they could use your skills."

"I'm sure they could, but it'll be a cold day in hell before I ever work for them."

"What about one of the other ships?"

De Voe sighed and turned her back on the railing and the ocean. "Maybe. Makka's a Kiwi. He's been here some time, but it wouldn't be such a loss for him. But I'm *Stavanger*, born and bred. I don't know anywhere else. I've visited *Hibernia* a handful of times, and that's it." She turned to look at Heiko. "How do you do it? Hopping about on Earth, and then abandoning home altogether and coming to an alien world?"

"Military family. As a kid, we moved about with my parents' assignments. First couple of times, it was hard. And then you learn to make new friends. Enjoy new experiences. And eventually, you start to become restless when you're in the same place too long. I was excited to come here."

"Yeah, Rennie, but now you've got me worried. You're a gun for hire. How soon before you get bored here and decide to move on again, to somewhere more exciting?"

Heiko frowned. "I would be lying if I said that's not an issue. But believe me, while I'm here, I'm *Stavanger* all the way. And when I move on, I'll keep a part of *Stavanger* in my heart. I wouldn't – and never have – left one job to join a direct competitor or enemy."

De Voe forced a smile. "You're an honest man, Rennie. And an honourable one." She reached out a hand. "So come on, then. While I've got you, I want to make best use of you. Come and take my mind off our current woes."

Heiko took De Voe's hand and allowed her to lead him inside.

Chapter 23

Eddard Mitsos didn't know why he bothered attending meetings like the one currently taking place in the small, square, airless room on Zero Deck that had been assigned to the project. He didn't understand most of what his small team of engineers and scientists were talking about, and they knew it. After a modicum of politeness at the first meeting, they'd stopped bothering to consult (or even address) him at the subsequent ones. They now made all of the decisions on how to amend the design of the extractor machine to increase its yield, and then gave him an idiot sheet so that he could update the People's Committee and the 'Megaphone' – the highly censored electronic journal of the *Marseilles*.

His team.

Now *that* was a joke.

He was pretty sure that power and responsibility were meant to correlate – after all, that was how the aphorism went. And he was certain that the best autocrats somehow managed to tip the scales to accumulate power *without* responsibility. He must have been the only person in human history for whom the reverse was the case: he had no real power in spite of his title, but *all* of the responsibility.

Of course, on the *Marseilles*, there wasn't meant to be any power differential, or at least, *status* differential. *In theory*. Managing the team wasn't meant to make him better than them, and he got no extra monetary credits for it. But in practice, there were differentials all over the place. His team of six, for example, had such high expertise that they were excluded from the job rotation process: they were special, and bloody well knew it. And there were others like them – such as the small number of qualified ship captains. And then there were people like Deux, whose nominal power was actually very real: in his case, it was his centrality to the decision making and enforcement apparatus that formed his power base. On Earth, Mitsos had always felt that he had a chance; he was an operator; he could manoeuvre circumstances in various ways to get what he wanted. But here, he was very much the bait fish seeking to avoid a tank full of sharks. And he couldn't see how that situation was ever going to change. Or at least, how it was ever going to get better, for he saw an endless number of ways in which it could get worse.

"Citizen Mitsos," said Youssef Bennani, "we have finished, and are in agreement."

"Ah," said Mitsos, drawn from his daydreaming. "That's great. What are you planning to do?"

Bennani gave a sly smile and looked at his colleagues around the table. Several smiled back, and Werner choked back a laugh. "It is complicated. We will… remodulate the torsion conductor to allow elemental hyper-calibration."

Mitsos scanned the faces around the table. No one was prepared to look into his eyes, and Sandrine Werner appeared to be on the verge of a having a fit. "Oh… fuck you."

Bennani raised a hand. "I'm sorry, Citizen." But he clearly wasn't. "I could not resist. But what we are planning is technical. *Difficult.* I will send a user-friendly update later. Is that okay?"

Mitsos shook his head and sighed. "Whatever. Send it by six. I've got to attend the People's Committee. They want another update. Add it to the details on the latest yields." There was no point making a bigger fuss: he'd only make himself look even more foolish.

* * *

"Citizen Mitsos," said the assistant, "you can come in now."

Mitsos entered the conference chamber and found himself under the gaze of the twelve members of the People's Committee – all randomly selected by computer program – plus their elected head, First Citizen Sebastian Deux. He broadcast his best business smile – honed over countless meetings, conferences, and informal (often 'accidental') encounters – to convey that here was a sympathetic-yet-serious man. Usually, this induced a reciprocal smile, but this time it was met with expressions that ranged from the suspicious to the downright unfriendly. As he reached the single chair placed before the raised platform on which the table was set, he focused on Deux – sitting at the very centre – and wondered what briefing he'd already given his colleagues. *Bastard!*

"Please sit, Citizen Mitsos," said Deux, a mischievous smirk on his face.

Mitsos broadened his smile further. "First Citizen! Noble members of the Committee! I am at your service."

"Noble?" said Deux, manipulating his face to suggest an affront that Mitsos was sure he didn't feel. "That's an unfortunate choice of words."

"Oh..." *for fuck's sake*, thought Mitsos, though he managed to say instead, "I apologise. It's a common expression, but I see what you mean. Our language is infested with terms of dubious origin. I'm sure none of us here have blue blood in our veins – I certainly don't."

"Yes – it's a fact you seem keen to highlight at every possible opportunity," mocked Deux. "We understand. You are merely *nouveau* riche." Mitsos felt his face start to burn, but as he opened his mouth to respond, Deux dramatically raised a hand to cut him off. "But enough! We've asked you here for an update on the progress of your machine."

"*My* machine?" It had originally been referred to as the Rare Element Extraction Net, or REEN, in order to dissociate it from Mitsos when Deux had wanted to claim it as his own initiative, but now it seemed it had been returned to him. "Well, the *REEN* continues to function well. The mechanism is sturdy, and we have had no breakdowns or losses with the net."

"Surely that is to be expected," said Deux. "I'm not sure why it would experience significant wear and tear so soon after its manufacture."

"You're right. But prototypes are always susceptible to malfunction. It comes with the territory. The fact that it has suffered no failures so far is a testament to its robustness."

Deux waved a hand in irritation. "Fine. It works. But what we're interested in is how *well* it works. When we authorised this experiment, it was on the basis of your firm assurances that the initial yields would be dramatically increased. Have they been?"

"Well, my team continue to tweak the filament net in terms of its composition, and vary the current passing through it. In fact, I have a document detailing the different experiments done and–"

"Citizen Mitsos, we are not scientists here. If you must, you can send the technical report to Abaye, and he will make it available to any here who wish to read it. Let's cut to the chase, eh? *Yields*."

Mitsos knew how to garnish reports for partners and shareholders. "I am pleased to say, yields are increasing dramatically. Our latest trial produced a staggering one hundred and sixty percent increase from the first in terms of collecting key elements."

"Key?" said the woman sat to Deux's left. "So, not all? Which ones?"

"Er… lanthanum and cerium, I believe, although I'd have to check."

"And this trial," said the man directly to Deux's right, "it's the same length as the first, is it?"

Mitsos looked at the two people bracketing a smiling Deux, both dressed in standard grey. *What is going on?* "Ah, not quite. The latest was a bit longer."

"So, the increase is just due to running the sweep for longer?" continued the man, looking aghast.

"No! Or, rather, yes, but only in part–"

"So, Citizen Mitsos," interjected Deux, "if you adjust for the difference in running time, what is the yield improvement *per time unit*?"

"Adjusting for… excuse my maths. My team gave me unadjusted figures–"

"Did they?" smirked Deux. "Really? Perhaps we should ask them to join us. It seems only fair to give them the opportunity to explain their negligence."

"That won't be necessary. Now that I come to think of it, the adjusted figures were in a different column." Mitsos looked up as though calculating, or attempting to remember, but he knew the figures very well. Had the report already been sent to Deux? And had Deux shared it with his favoured supporters? *Fuck!* "Ah… I believe it is… around… forty percent."

"Rounding up?" asked Deux. "Can't you be more precise? Again, should we call–?"

"Ah, yes, it's thirty-six percent. I rounded to the nearest ten."

As Deux shook his head – while grinning ear-to-ear – the unsmiling woman to his side asked: "Thirty-six percent sounds a lot, but it's a lot of very little, isn't it? From one teaspoonful to… one-and-a-third?"

"You make a pertinent point, Citizen," said Mitsos, who could now feel the sweat beading his brow and the heat in his cheeks. "That is true. Nevertheless, the important thing to focus on is that we have a robust, functioning machine that we continue to successfully adapt to significantly increase its efficiency. I–"

"Okay, Citizen Mitsos," declared Deux, turning serious. "Comedy hour is over. Send your full report to Abaye. Citizens Mahroof and Li…" he turned to deliberately look at the man and woman who sat to either side of him, "will give it due consideration. Perhaps they can extract more from the report than you. Maybe another thirty-six percent?" At that, a couple of the committee broke into laughter. Deux smiled at his own joke. "We'll give you another couple of weeks to massage more from the ocean… and from the figures produced by your team. We'll be closing in on the *Hibernia* by then, and at that juncture may have to make some important decisions regarding the project. Which neatly leads to the next item on our agenda, which is not for your ears, Citizen Mitsos, so thank you: you may go."

Mitsos left on unsteady legs, and once outside, slumped against the wall of the corridor. He really, *really* needed a drink.

He returned to the Bar Pastis, which he'd not been to for a couple of weeks. But Noma wasn't there, and nor were any of the crew of the *Dieppe*. *Strange*. In the end, he got drunk alone.

* * *

The next morning, Mitsos got up early and headed out with a clear head, thanks to his enhanced liver function, which had rapidly processed and expelled the alcohol from his bender, allowing him a restful night's sleep. He took the broad central stairway onto Zero Deck, following the human flow along a wide corridor to the starboard side of the great ship. Most here were trawlermen, notable for the shabbiness of their grey-issue clothing, which would soon be covered by more colourful waterproofs. The noise level rose as more and more dropped into the corridor from other stairways, until the space was filled, movement slowed, and the crowd bunched up. The bulk of the fishing crews then began to syphon off to the right where the locker rooms were. Mitsos edged over to the left, from where he saw flashing orange lights set high in the wall above a broad opening: the internal dry dock.

Where the wall fell away, he edged onto a wide concourse: here, the ceiling height doubled, occupying space where the first level would otherwise have been. Looking directly ahead, he saw three trawlers, set bow to stern. Beyond this were parallel gangways – hosting all sorts of lifting and repair machinery – that ran between further rows of boats. He headed to the 'back' wall to his left and began to traverse the concourse at the rear of the boats, which sat in dry cradles that would be flooded when the bulkhead to the right was raised, allowing the craft to egress through the great 'front' wall. As he walked he drew curious glances, since he wore neither the orange or yellow waterproofs of the fishers, nor the dark blue overalls of the dockworkers, nor even the standard grey issue of administrators, having retained his Earth-bought brown jacket.

Weaving in and out of people in orange and blue, he passed successive gangways, looking up at glowing signage that identified the ships docked along them. He spotted the *Boulogne*, but not the *Dieppe*. The fishing fleet had ten rows allocated to it, although the last of these was empty of craft. A bulkhead then obscured his view, running from back wall to front. There was a second dock beyond – accessed through a wide doorway – the two chambers separated to enable one or the other to be opened to the ocean, but not necessarily both. A member of the security apparatus – in black and grey – sat on a fixed stool at a checkpoint podium.

Mitsos paused a moment, unsure of his next move. The front wall hadn't opened – and wouldn't do so until the great ship came to a halt – which meant the *Dieppe* couldn't have launched yet. For a moment, the thought occurred to him that it might have gone down at sea, but then he shook his head: there'd be no hiding *that* news, even if *The Megaphone* tended to accentuate positives. Logically, then, it was in the secondary dock, used for repairs, and home to an assortment of craft used for generic purposes – transport, patrol, research. He suspected the two trawlers dedicated to the REEN project must be within, although he didn't know for certain: after his experiences on the *Dieppe*, he'd had no desire to come to the docks ever again.

The guard didn't seem to be paying much attention to those wandering past in either direction, so Mitsos decided to take a look. But as he approached, the officer – a fair-haired man in a peaked cap – looked up, frowned, and raised a hand. "Citizen!"

Mitsos paused again: through the partition, he could see several more slipways and a smattering of craft – some beneath cranes that were set on rails in the floor. He stepped over to the officer. "Yes, Citizen?"

"What is your purpose here?" He eyed Mitsos up and down.

"I am the head of the REEN project. I have come to see my boats and discuss matters related to the, ah, calibration of the primary mechanism."

The guard frowned. "The secondary dock is currently restricted access only."

"But you're not checking the others walking through."

"That's because the face recognition system tells me they have clearance."

Mitsos looked up and noticed the cameras set in the ceiling above, then he quickly glanced at the guard's podium, catching the glow of a recessed terminal. "Ah, of course. I didn't know. But what's the big issue? Why the secrecy?"

The guard stiffened. "If you don't know, Citizen, then you have no right to know. What's your name?" he looked down at his terminal, which presumably was being updated by the recognition software at that very moment. "Ah… Citizen Mitsos."

"That's right. And I'm sure your data will confirm that I hold the position I just said. If I am not on your approved list, I should be, no? Or do you think the REEN project is unimportant?"

"I need to consult–"

"Mitsos? Citizen Mitsos?"

Mitsos and the guard turned towards the approaching voice. The newcomer was bearded and wore blue, although his uniform was clean, unlike that of the majority of the dock workers.

"Bennani," said Mitsos, nodding in recognition.

"What's going on? Have you come to lend a hand, Citizen?"

The guard looked between the two, but said nothing.

"I thought as project head I should be more involved, so that when the First Citizen questions me about progress, I am able to give him a more comprehensive update. That makes sense, no? Who left me off the list? You?"

Bennani scowled. "The list is of citizens who *work* on the project, not overseers."

"Well, your uniform doesn't suggest you have been getting your hands – or anything else – dirty." Mitsos smiled mischievously. "Perhaps later, eh, after your own bout of overseeing?"

"I need to be close to the crew to program adjustments to the REEN itself."

"On the boats? You can't do that remotely? Hmmm. Anyway, it seems to me that as project head, if anyone is providing lists – a tiresome administrative function, surely – it should be me."

"I was project head when the new policy was initiated, before you joined us."

"And I am head now, so surely responsibility should pass to me, no?"

Bennani glowered at him a moment, but then gave an exasperated sigh and turned to the guard. "Okay. You know I have authority. Your system will verify this. Please add Citizen Mitsos to the roster of approved personnel."

The guard peered at Mitsos, nodding slowly. "Very well. You can pass."

"Thank you," said Mitsos. "You're a credit to your profession, Citizen." He winked. "Right, Bennani, why don't you give me a tour and explain to me what you're updating for the next trial."

Muttering under his breath, Bennani led the way to the REEN vessels, set on opposite sides of one gangway towards the middle of the enclosed space. He began a desultory tour and briefing. But Mitsos barely listened. Instead, he scanned the interior of the dock, seeking his old ship.

It was when they boarded the second REEN boat that Mitsos got a look at what was happening on the far side of the dock. There, he noticed three trawlers in a line, all of which appeared to be undergoing significant refurbishment, judging by the cranes that loomed over them and the dockworkers on their decks, their activity accompanied by the sounds of hammering and the glare of blowtorches. The middle one was the *Dieppe*. And though he saw no sign of Noma, he did recognise a couple of the grey-clad people on its deck as old acquaintances from the *Leviathan*. And then he saw what they were fussing over: just forward of the wheelhouse, was the unmistakeable profile of a small cannon.

* * *

Mitsos didn't see Noma at the dock the next morning, but he did the one after that.

"Noma!" he called, hurrying along the concourse away from the gangway to the REEN vessels.

The woman was amid a clutch of colleagues moving towards the *Dieppe* at the far end of the dock. She turned, saw him, and spoke to the man next to her. The man quickly glanced at Mitsos, then gave a brusque nod, and set about ushering the rest of their curious crew onwards. Noma remained, waiting for him.

"Well, here you are," said Mitsos. "I was worried about you."

"About me?" said the woman. Her face broke into a smile. "Why?"

"You've not been at the Pastis. I thought either you'd been taken by a kraken, or succumbed to rubber bullet wounds while playing soldiers. But you're here and whole."

"Yes. And so are you." She glanced at his broken hand, which was still bandaged, albeit with less material and now in a pink wrapping rather than a white one. "I feared you might have further upset the Apparatus." She frowned and looked about. "But… why are you *here*?"

"Easy enough question to answer. They moved me from the Labour Share Office to head the REEN project." He half turned and gestured behind him: "Those are my boats over there."

Noma ignored the redirection and kept her eyes on him. "So, you got what you wanted."

"Ah, yes. Well, they do say you should be careful what you wish for. There's also an expression about poisoned chalices that is apt."

Noma's brow furrowed. "You're having second thoughts? Why?"

Mitsos opened his mouth to reply, then closed it and looked around. No one was paying them any attention, but he felt exposed. There were cameras everywhere. And then he realised that Noma's attire was different: she wore neither orange, blue, nor grey, but a pocketed overall that had a peculiar black-blue pattern. Camouflage? For night-time operations? "I suspect we're both busy. Why don't we meet up later for a beer. Old times' sake? I owe you."

"Okay. Why not."

"Great. Usual place?"

"You mean the Pastis? My militia group meets elsewhere."

"Militia? Ah. Rowdy lot, I suppose. Yeah, Pastis. Nine?"

She paused, as though having second thoughts, but then sighed, nodded once, and turned back towards her boat.

* * *

When Noma arrived twenty minutes late, Mitsos was waiting for her with a beer, having himself arrived half-an-hour early. He'd found a quiet table in a dark corner well away from the nearest camera – a hemispherical orb just above the bar, which was presumably intended to give a three-sixty coverage of the area, but due to the angles of the interior, didn't.

"I couldn't find you," said Noma, pulling out a chair and dropping onto it.

"That explains it!" said Mitsos with a smirk. "I thought I'd been stood up."

"Yeah, well, I did think about that." She suddenly sat upright as though prodded with a sharp stick, swivelling in her seat to look all around. After a moment, she nodded grimly, seeming to recognise that they occupied a strategic corner, and returned a quizzical expression. "And… maybe you did, too?"

"No. I was always coming. But I don't like being followed by invisible eyes, and I guess I'm not the best person to be seen with after my little chat with the Apparatus."

"You're *not*, so… thanks. For the beer, too."

"*De nada*." Mitsos raised his glass and took a drink, watching the woman do the same. He noted: "I see you're back in civvies now. Wearing your best grey party clothes. *Nice*."

"I didn't expect to be complemented on my… oh. I see. Civvies?"

"They have a uniform for you now. And I couldn't help noticing that the *Dieppe* has got some extra… *protection*. Fuck those kraken, eh? They'll not take another trawlerman to his watery grave."

"Very funny."

"But seriously, Noma, I do worry about you. This is getting beyond playing soldiers or keeping people busy and distracted in times of hardship. You're turning trawlers into gunboats. Three? And with the loss of two more boats for the REEN project, can the fleet still provide?"

"The ocean is full of things to eat. That's not our problem. We could send out half the fleet and still catch enough food, especially with the protein stores nearly always full."

"Right – that's my last point dealt with. Now – *gunboats*? Just who are you expecting to fight off, if not sea monsters?"

Noma looked uncomfortable. "Maybe I shouldn't have come. This is classified. Even I don't know. There's just rumours. You shouldn't be asking."

For a moment it looked as though the woman was going to rise up, but Mitsos quickly leant across and placed a hand on her forearm. "Wait, Noma. Please. I'm not just being nosy. You remember I talked about a poisoned chalice earlier?"

"Yeah."

"Well, these things are all tied up. What you're doing and what I'm doing. I'm just trying to get a feel for what my chances are."

"I don't understand. What do you mean?"

"You know I've talked with Deux, the First Citizen?" He saw her nod. "These two schemes are part of a general plan of his. A and B. He's relying on one of them succeeding. Now, if we accept that he is truly working for the good of the *Marseilles* and its people, then the logical conclusion is that this ship is fucked and he is gambling on two low-probability, high-risk but potentially high-pay out bets. If we're going to be less generous – and that's my inclination – it's that while the *Marseilles* is not in a great place, it is tenable, but Deux is desperate for glory. For power. And he doesn't give a fuck who gets hurt in achieving it."

"That's almost treasonous." Noma now did start to rise, but Mitsos kept hold of her arm.

"Please, Noma. Hear me out. Sit."

"Take your hand off me."

Mitsos paused, then let go. Noma straightened, vacillated, but slumped back onto her chair.

"Thank you," he said.

"You've got until I finish my drink."

"Fair enough. I'm nearly done anyway. And you realise I'm taking a huge personal risk talking to you? I suspect you were asked to keep an eye on me at the start, and maybe you're still reporting back, or maybe you've been released from that responsibility. Whoa – don't get up. We both know how things work, and I'm not having a dig at you." This time Noma had merely leant forwards and placed her hands on the table, barely rising from her seat. Again, she subsided.

"Go on."

"I just wanted to say… be careful. One, or possibly both, of us are likely to get seriously burned here. Probably both. My project isn't going well – that's why Deux passed it to me. When it fails, he plans for me to take the blame, not him. What happens to me then, I don't know. You may think I'm a tricky businessman, but I've always been upfront here, trying to make things better for all of us. I don't deserve *this*." He lifted his bandaged hand. "Or whatever else Deux has got in store for me. And you and the crew, Noma, you also don't deserve to be thrown into some sort of fight–"

"*For the people*," she blurted. "For the people, we'd give everything!"

"I know. I appreciate it. And I know I mocked your patriotism. It was a cheap shot from a cynical man. For the people… *yes*. But what I'm saying is, I'm not sure that you're doing this for the people. I suspect you're doing this for the ego of one man instead. And *that's* not right."

Noma stared at him for some moments, then said: "You're assuming the two don't overlap. What is good for the people may also be good for the First Citizen, and vice versa. And even if you're right, I don't know what you expect me to do about it. Resign from the militia? Desert my crew?" She picked up her glass and with three long gulps drained it. She placed the glass heavily on the table, and stood. But her glower suddenly softened, and she sighed. "Thanks for your concern, Mitsos. I won't report this conversation. But *you* be careful."

Mitsos watched her leave. It seemed he'd be drinking alone again.

Chapter 24

"We've put this off long enough," said Marie. "It's time."

"To find the kelp farmers?" said Kalmik, uncertainly. "I still don't know how I feel about this… *any* of this."

"We've done the analysis now on a week's worth of data, and confirmed the symmetry of the kelp rows. Something funny is going on."

"That's true, my dear," said Miguel Figueroa, hovering near the two women in the main cabin of the *Fortunata*. "The hypothesis has been confirmed."

"The *regularity* has been confirmed, yes," said Kalmik, eyeing Marie as she zipped up her drysuit and began to fuss at the rest of her diving gear. "But not the origin of it. There could still be a natural explanation. I mean, in the last week, has anyone encountered any of these farmers tending their crops?"

"Sure," said Marie. "But in that case, disproving the hypothesis that the fields are intelligently designed will promote the 'natural' hypothesis. We need to put this to bed. And we're agreed that the likely hiding place of the farmers is within the black."

"Well, I'm certainly not trying to deter you from the experiment," said Kalmik. "I just don't want to have to go in and fish you out when you encounter something unintelligent but with a lot of teeth."

"You won't have to. Mike and Raul have drawn that short straw."

Figueroa looked stern. "I still wish you'd consider going in with a buddy. Someone to cover your back."

Marie had affixed her sampling bag and knife to her belt; she now worried at her mask and goggles. They'd attached a small camera to the side of the goggles, facing forwards, and she had a waterproof earpiece, too. Without her helmet, she wouldn't have the inbuilt mic to report on what she saw, but at least she could take instruction. She paused to look at Figueroa's crinkled face. "Me too. But if the farmers are as intelligent and shy as we think, and have been approaching us from behind in the water, then I need to leave my back exposed, and hope the rear-facing camera catches my stalker. If there's two of us, from what we've seen so far, they may stay away."

She watched as Figueroa and Kalmik exchanged glances. She knew both were torn – fearing the dive, but eager at what it might reveal. The pair struggled to find further excuses, so Marie turned her attention to her final piece of gear – a headband with a light to the front, and a small camera to the rear. She gently folded this into one palm, then looked up. "Right. That's it. I'm ready. Are you coming to see me off?"

"I think I'll stay and keep an eye on the camera feed," said Kalmik.

"Professor?"

"Ah… me too. I admit, I am as excited as I have been for a good many years. Intelligent alien life? That would be remarkable. *Revolutionary*. We've settled on a dozen planets and come across nothing brighter than a Terran dog."

Marie couldn't help but smile. "Nobel Prize, Professor? I don't think you have to be Earth-based to receive it."

"I would never have dared such a dream. Let's do it! Good luck, my dear!"

Marie nodded at the man, then at Kalmik, who was already settled before a monitor that was receiving her two cameras' pictures, displayed split-screen. She stepped from the cabin onto the *Fortunata's* deck. The cage had already been lowered into the inky water, the boat having taken up a position just beyond the junction of fringe forest and cenote.

Mike Resnos stood by the cage winch, while Raul Garcia stood at the gunwale, holding up a pair of flippers.

"You'll need these," he said. Then he held up his other hand: "and maybe *this* – just in case."

"A speargun?" Marie frowned. "If there is intelligent life down there, I'd rather not conclude *first contact* by shooting it and committing xenocide."

"If something attacks you, it'll be self-defence," said Garcia. "We can't be sure they are friendly. Territoriality is a common trait in animals."

"Yeah… well said." Marie took the flippers, sat on the gunwale, and pulled them on. Then, hesitatingly, she took the proffered speargun and rested it beside her. Next, she pulled on the mask and snorkel. She wet the mask with spit and drew it over her eyes. Finally, she put on the headband and wriggled it to ensure the light sat at the centre of her forehead. "Katerina," she asked, "is the camera working?" – forgetting the absence of a mic. Fortunately, her colleagues understood: Resnos quickly stepped across to the door of the cabin and leant in to speak.

"Ah, Miguel here," said Figueroa, his voice coming through her earpiece. "I can see that Mr Grande has just joined you from somewhere towards the bow. Look out – he's behind you!"

Marie quickly glanced back, saw Grande resting on the bulkhead of the cabin, smiling sheepishly, and she laughed and gave him a thumbs-up. Then she bit down on the mouthpiece of the snorkel and draped her legs over the side of the boat. Immediately before her, the water was a fuzzy grey, diffusely lit by the maximum number of lights that their experiments had discovered the 'water' would tolerate. The lightest grey outlined the sides of the cage, where the lights were strung; the centre was somewhat darker; and about a metre beyond the edge of the cage the natural midnight black quickly resumed. She switched on the forehead light with a gloved hand, took hold of the speargun, then slipped over the side, plunging a metre or so into the water.

As ever, Marie felt a moment of disorientation, bubbles of displaced air playing around her, with a cold shock from where water touched the exposed skin on her face. She gently kicked her feet, steadied herself with stroking hands, and found a kind of equilibrium.

She stayed near the surface for a short time, addressing her mask and headband and ensuring the fits were snug. She surfaced for more air, then dove to the bottom of the cage a couple of metres down, letting her knees sink to the metal bars of the floor.

And there she waited.

She knew that the fringe forest was just a few metres behind her, but it might as well have been on the other side of the world for all that she could see. Still, she felt calm: she'd now done dozens of dives in the supposedly perilous ocean of Tethys – whether in different sea forests, or protected by a cage in the misnamed cenotes – without suffering any harm, with each dive bolstering her confidence and assuaging her nerves. And now she found the grey somewhat comforting rather than spooky, like a protecting blanket between her and whatever was beyond, the insipid light seeming to act as a repelling kryptonite. But was it *too* repelling?

Marie surfaced and dove, surfaced and dove, every couple of minutes. She settled in different positions, in different orientations. But sensed… *nothing.*

After perhaps twenty minutes, she surfaced once more and tread water. Extricating the snorkel mouthpiece, she shouted up to Garcia, who leant over the side, ready to reach down an arm and pluck her out if necessary. "Raul – there's nothing. Are you sure the light settings are right?"

"Positive. We know they're not too bright, as the water seems okay." He smiled. "It's not throwing a – what did you call it – hissy fit?"

"I think they must be at maximum deterrence. Can you turn them down a bit? Frankly, they don't help vision much anyway."

"Gotcha. But let me check with the Prof. first, eh?"

"Sure. I'll wait below."

Marie put in her mouthpiece, gave a good blow, then took a lungful of air and rolled over, pulling herself down to the floor of the cage again.

After perhaps thirty seconds, the lights began to dim. They were set at mid-height in the cage, so there had been less grey wash at the bottom anyway. Now Marie felt as though the night was somehow reaching for her. And then in her ears, for the first time in a while, she heard Figueroa's voice. "Marie," he hissed. "Please stay still."

She felt an itch between her shoulder blades. If she'd had her scuba gear she could have asked what was going on via its internal mic, but now she was helpless. She tried to keep her head still, so as not to undermine the camera on the back of her headband, and peered left and right through the sides of her mask. But it was difficult, and she found her neck twisting ever so slightly each way.

Figueroa's hushed voice came again – as though he was afraid that speaking too loud, even away in the boat's cabin, might scare off whatever might be around her. "It's… not clear, Marie. We thought there were shadows, ah! What's…" His voice cut off and Marie instinctively began to curl into a defensive ball, hunching her shoulders.

"Marie, stay calm. There is…"

The cage rocked.

Marie sensed something behind her… or was it below? She twisted her head suddenly, and the light on her headband caught *something*. Motion. A rippling shadow. And then the cage shunted again, from where she'd been looking. Her air running out, and disturbed, she straightened her legs on the bottom, pressed her flippers on the floor, and pushed.

But didn't rise far.

On her right calf, something snagged; she felt pressure; a squeeze; she jerked over to that side. She attempted to kick her legs, but only one functioned. She gagged for air, pulled the water with her left hand… and then – without further options – pointed the speargun in her right hand downwards, and fired.

The pressure on her leg released, the cage rocked violently around her, and she shot to the surface. As she broke water, gasping, coughing into her mouthpiece, she noticed two arms reaching for her: Garcia and Resnos. Dropping the speargun, she raised her arms and let the men haul her up. But as her belly flopped onto the gunwale, the whole boat quivered and tilted, and the cage seemed to twist in the water, as though pulled away from the boat. The men aboard swayed as though drunk, but kept a hold of her and pulled her the rest of the way out.

"Watch out!" she heard – from Grande?

There was a heavy creak, and the winch jerked, like a fishing rod bending at the pull of a giant fish. Over, over, the boat started to tip… and then she saw Grande at the winch. He struck a lever with the flat of one hand, releasing the cage, and suddenly the boat snapped back upright and then continued further beyond the vertical. The winch groaned; the water behind splashed; Garcia staggered backwards and fell; and the boat teetered and bobbed until it settled on an even keel.

Then there was a moment of stunned silence, which was terminated by the loud roar of the engine, as Arantxa Perez, the pilot, whether ordered to or on her own initiative, set the *Fortunata* in motion, towards the relative safety of the fringe forest.

* * *

"So, we've lost the cage," scowled Kalmik. "*Well done*, Grande."

Marie sat next to the accused man in the main cabin, which currently hosted everyone aboard, bar the pilot. Figueroa, Resnos, Soares, and Garcia were scattered about, some sitting, others standing. Marie sensed Grande slowly shake his head, but as he didn't seem inclined to speak, she spoke for him. "It was quick thinking. Whatever had hold of the cage seemed intent on pulling it away – and capsizing us in the process."

"Don't defend him, Marie," said Kalmik. "The *Fortunata* is robust. The winch would have broken before we got flipped. Or more likely, whatever was pulling the cage would have got tired and let go."

"You can't know that. You weren't on deck – you didn't see the *force* being exerted."

Kalmik smiled humourlessly. "So, you think he was right?"

Marie glanced quickly at the man, his face dark with stubble, his lips pursed tight, his angry eyes directed at the woman sat across the table. "I… don't know. Maybe."

As Kalmik scoff-laughed and crossed her arms, Figueroa – who stood by the cabin's door – raised his hands in placation. "Please, everyone, let us be calm. What has happened, has happened. I am sure Marco did what he felt was best." He flashed a sympathetic smile at Grande. "Thank you, Marco. But it is… *unfortunate*."

"You mean, we're fucked," said Kalmik. "We only had the one cage. How long till we fabricate another – assuming you can beg the materials for it, Miguel? Weeks? We'll be long gone by then. That only leaves free diving, which after today I don't think even Marie would dare."

"Perhaps not," said Figueroa. "There is no need for anyone to go in again. I have been thinking, maybe we can lower a series of poles into the water, with low lights and cameras, and see what comes to investigate them? After all, we were going to affix cameras to the cage once we got the chance – the human option was merely the quickest and easiest one."

"Yes, Professor, that makes sense," said Marie. "But I'm still not sure the lights will *attract* rather than *deter*. I think it's the human presence that provokes interest."

"Let's dangle Marco over the side and let them come and prod him, then."

"Katerina, please!" said Figueroa. "No more on this! It is unproductive. There are still things we can try, and we will."

Marie turned to face Kalmik. "You said 'let them'. So you agree there is something down there?"

"Something, yes. Intelligent? A farmer? For me, the jury is still out."

"What did my cameras show?" Marie alternated her gaze between the seated Kalmik and standing Figueroa. "You saw something. What about when the cage was attacked and I was grabbed?"

"Hah!" said Kalmik. "Mostly shadows and bubbles – and certainly not a big hand on your leg."

"I think we need to study the film carefully back on the *Lisboa*," said Figueroa. "Frame-by-frame. And maybe Luisa can work her magic and clean it up."

"Then what are we waiting for?" said Marie. "I'm keen to get a glimpse of whatever is in there."

"Indeed, my dear. I think we are certainly done here for the day."

* * *

"Marco – wait up!"

The man turned as Marie hurried up to him in the corridor leading to the science department. "Ah… Marie… hi."

"Ready for the show? I wonder what Luisa has found?"

"I just hope that if she has discovered something, it's significant. I mean… big? Fearsome?"

Marie reached the other's side, and the pair continued in step. "Why's that?"

"I know it's selfish, but it might save me from further embarrassment. Can you imagine Kalmik's response if whatever was down there turns out to be small and inoffensive, and I lost the cage to save us from *that*?"

"I see what you mean, but I don't think you need to worry. Whatever grabbed me wasn't weak, and nor was whatever took the cage. There *must* have been more than one of them – they managed to tip the boat. I'm pretty sure you're going to be vindicated."

They reached the double doors that opened into the department, then took a corridor to the left and followed it to its end. They caught sight of Victoria Soares entering the auditorium there, the door swinging closed just before they reached it.

Grande held the door open and bowed slightly, allowing Marie to enter first. The auditorium was small, just half-a-dozen rows descending to a presentation pit with a podium, with a gloomy and incomprehensible 3D projection hovering in the air above it. Luisa Teixeira stood at the podium, toying with a computer keyboard. Figueroa and Kalmik sat in the front row, while Perez, Garcia, Resnos, and Soares were scattered about.

Marie took a seat, noticed Grande wavering, then shuffled across and waved for him to sit in the now-vacant place beside her.

Teixeira looked up, scanned the room, then nodded. "All here, I think."

Figueroa looked around, and frowned. "Just us? None of the junior staff or students?"

Kalmik turned briefly too. "Yes, Miguel. I think we should keep this between us for now. No point scaring the children."

"Ah, right, in that case…" Figueroa turned back. "Luisa – please proceed."

"Right. So. I won't mess about. There was a lot of film – nearly half-an-hour in total. I'm going to concentrate on the last minute only. In fact, it's less than a minute. That doesn't mean the earlier shots showed absolutely nothing – in fact, there are all sorts of shadows and changes in shading. *Lots*. If I had to bet, I think Marie was under constant surveillance from a number of these… farmers? I don't know what to call them."

"Farmers will do," said Miguel.

"*For now*," said Kalmik, quickly.

"Right. Farmers. So – a lot. But they kept sufficiently far away that I couldn't get anything distinct at all. I've done my best but," she shrugged, "the data-cleaning software I have is thirty years old, and we've had no updates from Earth since, and might not get any more for some time."

"I am certain you have done your best, my dear," said Figueroa. "No need to apologise."

"Thanks. So, I'll run through the last few seconds from when Katerina and the Professor thought they saw something and warned Marie. I'll pause at interesting moments." She addressed the keyboard. The lights in the auditorium dimmed, and the faintly glowing cube that floated over the podium brightened by contrast. What it presently showed was grey with a darker smudge to one side and two cage bars clear in the foreground. Teixeira used a pointing stick she pulled from some slot in the podium. "This shape seems to be one. It must be what the guys saw. I'll roll forwards, quarter speed."

The dark pattern intensified, grew, then faded, and slid off to the left.

"Another now from the right, watch."

A second smudge slid in from the right. It seemed round, but then became ovoid, and then lengthened further vertically.

"I think what you are seeing," said Teixeira, "is something swimming towards Marie's back, front on, then pausing and flipping upright – like someone stopping and pulling up to tread water. That's the only way I can think of explaining the change in shape."

"That would suggest a strange anatomy or means of locomotion," said Figueroa. "Almost humanoid. Are you sure you're not anthropomorphising?"

"Most Tethyn creatures are like Earth ones," said Teixeira. "They're generally long and thin and streamlined for swimming, or cloudlike for floating in the currents, or globular with tentacles when on the ocean floor or in the kelp forests. Whatever this is, it seems of the long and thin type, but as you say, it moves like a human, as fish like sharks don't suddenly pull up and float perpendicular to the gradient. But I've more evidence that this is something more like us. Watch."

She tapped the keyboard. Marie saw the black shape hover, then slide away as had the first. In the water, she must have backed up at this stage, because the cage bars had separated and nearly disappeared off to either side, suggesting the camera was shooting right between them. And then a third shape darkened from the grey, towards the bottom of the holographic cube. It seemed to move quickly and… the picture canted to one side.

"Strike one," said Teixeira. "This was the first hit on the cage. Marie must have turned around, because the rear camera showed nothing for a couple of seconds, but the front camera…" she clicked on something and the image changed, showing grey smudges and various cage bars, moving as the camera-wearer's head moved. "Shows this…"

Marie found herself leaning forwards to get a better look. "Is that… a flipper?" she said. "The end of a flipper?"

Teixeira froze the shot, and expanded one part of it. "Yes and no. It's deep black, and long, but natural not synthetic. It's a glimpse through the bars at the bottom of the cage at whatever hit and then continued to swim past. It certainly looks like the end of a long webbed foot. But I'm not surprised you didn't recognise it first time, as you and it were moving too quickly." She played the scene on, which showed bubbles, bars, grey light, and then it seemed the diver's head moved to face back up towards the surface. "There's nothing more of interest from the front camera, so I'll switch to the reverse again. And *this* is the money shot."

Marie found herself holding her breath; she sensed Grande beside her also straining forwards to look. Then the picture on the screen clarified and… there was a shriek; a curse; and a nervous laugh. In the picture, in slow-motion, reaching towards the camera, was a long, black, six-fingered hand, webbed, with nails that looked like they could puncture steel. But then the picture moved on, the hand fell back amidst a sudden eruption of bubbles, and then it disappeared off the bottom of the shot.

"And that, I guess, is when you surged up, Marie," concluded Teixeira. "And it snagged you. I haven't got any more decent shots. I don't know if the spear you fired hit it. There is just grey and black and confusion, and then you are being pulled from the water."

Marie exhaled heavily, and noticed Grande looking at her with wide eyes. "I *was* grabbed," she said at last. "And so was Raul, that first time. I said I saw something similar."

All the others in the auditorium had turned and shuffled in their seats to look at Marie. Figueroa said: "Yes, I think we owe you both an apology for not entirely believing you that time. I don't know whether to feel disturbed or, well, *elated*."

"It's like nothing we've encountered on Tethys before," said Kalmik. "And that… that *was* like a hand. I don't know if this thing actually farms, but it might have the anatomical apparatus to do so."

"Yes, Katerina, it surely does." Figueroa's lumped face struggled to find an appropriate expression. "This is… the most important find since humanity landed on Tethys. *Remarkable*."

"But what I don't get," said Kalmik, "is if these creatures are planting and somehow farming the kelp, then why haven't we seen them before? They seem to be hiding out in the black. No one's actually seen them in a fringe forest."

"I had a thought about this," said Marie. Her heart was still racing somewhat, but the chance to address an intellectual question helped her shake the image of the grasping hand from her immediate consciousness. "Look, we know that they don't like the light. But when we study the forest, we keep to the upper region during the day to take advantage of the sunlight spearing through the water. Although we haven't measured it, it's clear the levels of illumination we work under are higher than those the creatures are prepared to tolerate – even at the lowest depths we go. Perhaps if we extend our search downwards, we may find them there."

"Oh, that's great," said Kalmik. "Very comforting. The thought that right below us we've had hordes of these things lurking all along, maybe watching us and hoping we stray a bit too far." She shook her head in disbelief. "And are you seriously suggesting going down there? We rarely go beyond thirty metres. You see the implications, right? Down there, if something grabs you, what are you going to do? Ask it to politely wait while you slowly ascend in order to stop nitrogen bubbles forming in your body? And when they do the alien equivalent of telling you to *fuck off*, race to the surface and accept a nice dose of *the bends*?"

"No, I'm not suggesting that. I was just pointing it out. The alternative is to dive the fringe forest at night."

Kalmik raised her hands as if to physically shove the other away. "Right, so, now you want to go in the forest in the black of night, with no cage, essentially surrounded by *ropes*? What could *possibly* go wrong? You're welcome to it. I'll sit it out with Grande, and you can call me a coward."

Marie felt Grande stiffen beside her, but she chuckled. "Well, me too. I wasn't volunteering – I was just trying to explain an anomaly."

"I do not think cowardice is an appropriate term," said Figueroa. "I have not dived in the open ocean for more than a decade, and I am in admiration of all of you that do so. Marie's point is well made, though, and makes a great deal of sense to me. I am sure it is so. The question is, then, how do we capture images of these farmers, given the natural difficulties and our limited equipment?"

"No infrared cameras, Professor?" asked Marie.

"Not in store, I'm afraid, and we have few enough high quality ones. But Luisa…?"

Teixeira smiled. "Yes, I've adapted a couple. One IR, and another for passive thermal imaging. They're ready to be tried out. Of course, we're assuming the creatures aren't annoyed by light in the IR spectrum too, and then there's the issue of whether the cameras will attract attention and be investigated by them. But if the creatures are active around their crops or in the black, we might be able to get some film of them."

"*Excellent*, Luisa," said Figueroa. "You see, Katarina, all is not lost. Let us now think on how to best deploy these new toys."

* * *

They had brought their dinner in cartons to watch the show.

"I still haven't gotten used to this," said Kate, holding up a grey-brown sliver of artificial meat on her fork. It was dripping in gravy. "I mean, although it does look like a slice of beef, and it tastes roughly like it should, at the end of the day, it's just fish, and that's pretty disgusting."

"It's *not* fish," said Tonio. "It's mostly moulded and flavoured protein."

"Yeah, and the raw ingredient comes from?"

"From whatever is caught in the nets. Okay, that might be fish-analogues but, well, if you're going to get picky, you might just as well say 'oh, I don't like eating stars', because ultimately, every atom in the fish and in your 'beef' was once part of a star."

Kate smirked and shook her head. "No way am I letting you get away with that. You could use that sophistry to justify anything. *Oh, no, I didn't kill Tonio, Mum, because he's really just star stuff, and even though he's lying in a pool of blood without his head he is still star stuff, so what's the problem?* There's billions of years between a star becoming a fish, but probably only a few weeks between the fish becoming a steak."

"But it *is* beef!" insisted Tonio. "The constituents of the fish have been transformed to have a similar chemical composition and structure to the flesh of *real* cows."

"Well, not entirely. If you compared this thing…" Kate flapped the object on her fork, flicking gravy onto the floor, "with the mooing thing with four legs, you will find lots of differences. So – it's not cow, nuh-uh!"

"Okay, but it's definitely not fish, either! If you–"

"Enough!" laughed Sara. "We're not here to debate the origins of food. And… 'sophistry', Kate? Really? That's just showing off."

"Not really," grinned Kate, in the dim light of the Bowl. "If I *really* wanted to show off, I'd have started going on about ontology. In fact, that's an appropriate subject when it comes to what makes food beef or not beef."

"Argh!" exclaimed Tonio. "I give up! Whatever you say! I always thought it was a mistake having an optional module on philosophy. This is what happens when you go to a separate class from us. It gives you no skills whatsoever except the ability to annoy your friends."

"Annoy? You mean crush you with the weight of logical argument."

"I said enough!" Sara raised her arms again, laughing. "And while you've been bickering, I've already finished my star-beef-fish supper. It's time for some action."

"Sure," said Kate, dropping her fork into her half-empty carton. "My appetite has been un-whetted."

"Well, I'm still eating," said Tonio, "but you carry on. You know how to control the lights now, Kate. The price is what's left of your dinner."

"Deal!"

Sara placed her empty carton on the console and swiftly took her position in the bowl itself, while Kate and Tonio swapped chairs, so Kate had command of the room's array of lights – both those within the room, and the spotlights outside the ship.

"Are we ready?" asked Kate. "Then I will begin…"

They'd been experimenting for the last couple of weeks, ever since their first sighting of the strange creature that had butted the bowl and startled Sara. It hadn't appeared the day after that, but it had on the following one, and every day since. No, not 'it'. *Them.* The previous day they had caught sight of at least four separate creatures, roiling around each other and then zooming from the dark to make Sara jump and laugh. What they had found was that the creatures didn't like much light, and so they'd had to carefully calibrate to find a fine line of tolerability – enough to alert the creatures to their presence without repelling them, yet bright enough so that Kate and her friends could just about see them. So, Kate now turned off all the lights, save the residual strip light in the ceiling, and then gently touched the spotlights so that they glowed faintly beneath the bowl.

It didn't take long.

"They're here," whispered Sara, her voice carrying easily in the large, mostly empty room.

Kate left her seat and went over to the great hemispherical bowl, laying on the floor with her head hanging over the edge. Sara lay in the very centre, a couple of metres down at the nadir, but there was plenty of uncovered glass on the sloping sides through which others could see. She heard the sound of Tonio behind her, chewing softly, still intent on his dinner.

As Sara hissed and cooed, a long shape glided past her and up the exterior of the bowl, allowing Kate a decent view. The creature was perhaps two-and-a-half metres in length – thin and streamlined, looking something like a cross between a stretched human and a shark, with a quartet of 'fins' that circled the centre of its body, below which it differentiated into a pair of 'legs' that ended in flipper-like appendages, which it generally kicked in tandem like a butterfly swimmer, though it could use them independently to alter its direction of travel. But it was the top half that was most intriguing, even horridly fascinating: above the 'torso' was a long, oval 'head' with large, black, glossy, lidless eyes that were shaped like lozenges, a hidden smudge of a mouth, and then, sprouting from what could only be called shoulders, two long, sinewy arms that ended in six-fingered hands with wicked-looking talons.

The creature disappeared, and then Kate glimpsed another ghosting along the glass to Sara's other side. This moved as the first: the creatures generally kept their arms straight and locked, and there even seemed some sort of hook on the wrist to keep the arms joined and pointed straight, like a dagger in the water, with propulsive force provided by the powerful legs only. But as they'd been shocked to find out, the creatures could unhook their arms, too, and then they became human-like, allowing them to 'stand' upright like divers treading water. The first time one had come up and placed a 'hand' directly over Sara's pressed-down face, it had caused the girl to shriek and scurry away, although Sara now seemed to relish the play, as if she could somehow communicate through the glass with the creature.

"I wonder what it is?" said Tonio, making Kate start. He scrunched down beside her. "I've definitely not seen anything like it before, and it's not in the textbooks."

"Uh-huh."

"I bet your mum would know."

"Sure," said Kate. "But you know I can't ask her. *Sara.*"

"Yeah, Sara's Number One Secret."

Kate had mentioned asking her mum a week ago, but that idea had been shot down by Sara instantly. She was right in that – in order to account for the strange sighting – they'd have to tell her mum about the bowl, but Kate hadn't initially been sure that would be a problem. *Why would Mum be bothered about us finding and using this place?* But then Sara had pointed out that if the creature was indeed new, every marine biologist on the ship would want to study it, and even if they didn't get into trouble, they would lose exclusive access to this place – and maybe access entirely. Given Sara's fixation, Kate wasn't prepared to risk her friendship just so her mum could get the data to write another article in a scientific journal.

But while familiarity had reduced the scare factor for their little group, it had clearly also emboldened the creatures. And this evening, they started to come thick and fast.

"Whoa!" gasped Tonio, as three creatures flashed past to one side, almost in a line.

"There… look!" said Kate, and to the other side, another group slid past the glass, almost rubbing it. "That's… three… six… Sara – are you communing?"

"Uh, yes. There are two here. Next to each other. They're… waving at me."

"Eight," declared Tonio. "Twice as many as yesterday."

"At least," said Kate. "A whole… pod? School? Pack?"

"We need to name them," said Tonio. "Then, if anyone finds out later, we can claim them first. I suggest… black… eel… men. Yeah. Black Eelmen. Copyright, Tonio Janeiro. Let the royalties commence!"

Kate chuckled, and waited for Sara's response – but the girl was so rapt she didn't even turn. After a few second, she said: "You might have won by default. No. What about… *Diver Fish*. Because they do look like scuba divers who have been tortured on the rack."

"That would make them *Tortured Diver Fish*," said Tonio, "which is also kind of cool. But I still prefer mine. Whoa!" One of the creatures now struck the glass almost directly beneath them, essentially performing a somersault turn and thumping the glass with its powerful flipper-feet. "Maybe make that *Psycho Black Eelmen*. Or better, *Black Psycho Eelmen*. What do you think, Sara?"

At last the girl stirred. She pushed herself up, turned, and then scrabbled up the slope to her friends. It was only as she came close that the strip light partially illuminated her face. From behind her, where she'd left, a creature thumped the glass – perhaps displeased at her departure.

"You okay?" asked Kate.

"Huh? Oh… yeah." Sara sat on the edge to the other side of Kate. "I'm fine. But… I'm not sure about these things now."

"What do you mean?" asked Tonio, pulling up into a seated position so he could look at Sara over Kate back. "I thought they were your new BFFs. You seem more interested in them than us."

Thump.

"Well, I was," said Sara, her expression thoughtful. "But… you know what I like about this place? It's seeing all the different creatures, the different shapes and colours. It's like art. *Beautiful.*"

"Yeah… so?" said Kate.

Thump.

"Well, I've just realised something. Since we saw the first of these things, about two weeks ago…" *Thump*, "we've not seen anything else." *Thump.* "And I mean *anything.*"

"They've painted your canvas completely black," said Kate, frowning.

Thump. Thump. Thump.

"You're right," said Tonio. "Okay, what about *Black Psycho Ocean-Emptying Eelmen.*"

"I think I'd like you to turn the lights on now," said Sara.

Thump. Thump. Thump. Thump. Thump.

* * *

"Hi, Mum," said Kate, coming through the door of the compact apartment. Marie was at the kitchen table, back to the wall, a tablet propped in front of her.

"Nice to see you, Kate." Marie arched an eyebrow. "And it's not even midnight."

"Ha-ha." Kate pulled out the small table's second chair and slumped onto it. "I could say the same about you."

"Have you eaten? I didn't see a dirty plate in the sink."

"That's cheek. I always wash up. I'm the responsible one in this relationship."

Marie smiled at her daughter. She wasn't wrong: if anyone was liable to leave a mess, it was Marie herself. And talk of food reminded her that she'd been so caught up in the events of the day that it was *she* who hadn't eaten. "What did you have?"

"Well, that's difficult to say. We had a debate earlier. I think the conclusion was a sort of hybrid of fish, beef, and star stuff."

"We? Did your friends come around?"

"What – *here*? I suppose Sara could squeeze in, but Tonio would probably have to stay in the corridor."

Marie's smile broadened. "It's not *that* small."

"Oh, come on, Mum, our *toilet* in Durban was bigger than this place. Anyway, no, I grabbed a ready meal from a vending machine on zero deck. What about you?"

"Ah, now I have to admit my own guilt. I've been a bit distracted. I've had an interesting day."

Kate rocked back on the chair, the space so narrow her back came to rest against the kitchen counter behind. "But I thought you stayed aboard today – after your little excitement yesterday, which you've still not explained to me."

"No, I haven't, have I?" Marie quickly glanced at her screen, which currently held incriminating evidence. It was true that she'd not told her daughter about the events in the cenote, but that wasn't a deliberate policy; she'd just been too focused on work, and their lives had been intersecting less and less over the last couple of weeks. But looking at the still shot of the grasping 'hand', she now wondered whether it would be a good idea after all. What had Kalmik said earlier about 'scaring the children'? She looked up from the screen and saw Kate twirling a strand of hair and watching her in amusement. "Sorry, Kate, did you say something?"

"Nothing at all. You zoned out again, Mum. I was waiting for you to elaborate on why your day was so interesting it's led you to the verge of starvation, as well as your customary child neglect. Is this something to do with the cultivators?"

"Ah… well, it's just general dive stuff. Boat repairs." She gently pulled the tablet towards her. "Things like that."

Kate suddenly frowned and tipped forward in her chair. "I wonder…"

"Wonder? About what?"

"Oh, nothing, just something about… school." Kate stood up. "Well, it's getting late, and I don't want to be nagged about having to get up for school tomorrow. So, I'll…" But she'd only taken two steps before suddenly turning. She looked back at Marie, then down at the tablet she was shielding. "You're hiding something, aren't you?"

Marie drew the tablet even closer to her chest. "I… suppose I am. But it's not something that should be widely shared."

"So it *is* about the cultivators."

Marie sighed. "We've gone with *farmers* for now, though Katerina isn't yet convinced."

"And you've got a picture of one there, haven't you? Come on, show me. Or don't you trust me?"

Marie frowned and tilted the tablet away a little, so she could better see the image. She didn't keep things from Kate – that was one of the unspoken rules. The honesty pact that had begun in Durban, when things had started going awry with Dirk, and precocious Kate had insisted on being treated like an adult. She hadn't deliberately broken that pact yet – and wouldn't now. She sighed heavily. "Okay. You know we had issues yesterday with the boat. I was diving in a cage in the cenote. We were trying to draw these farmers close. They're a bit shy, but they can be a bit… temperamental."

"Temperamental… or just *mental?*"

Marie nodded. "Perhaps. Anyway, we didn't get much except one clear shot." She flexed the tablet in her hands, undecided.

Kate moved closer, so that she was standing at the side of the table, looking down at the obliquely held tablet. "Let's see."

"It is a bit… scary. If I show you, Kate, honestly, I don't want you telling your friends or anyone else. Not yet. We want to learn more before breaking this news to the ship and the wider world."

"Promise. So…" Marie turned the tablet so that Kate could see – and didn't get the reaction she expected. "Yes! I knew it!"

"Kate?"

"Oh… *shit!*" Kate looked sheepish, and then she evolved a pained smile. "I've… got my own secret. But now *you* have to promise *me* that it stays between us. Really, Mum, Sara will hate me forever otherwise."

Chapter 25

Makka Frost was not entirely surprised at being singled out.

Captain Kennedy, who led the Hibernian unit, stood at his shoulder as he watched the last tranche of the *Stavanger* mining crew climb aboard the skiff. Sven Ibsen remained on the dock: he spoke heatedly to one gun-toting guard, who relented, stepped back, and allowed him to retrace his steps from the skiff to where Frost stood at the landward end of the temporary dock.

"Well… we're off, I guess."

"Looks like it, Sven."

"Any idea when you'll follow?"

Frost pursed his lips and shook his head. "I'm afraid you're asking the wrong man." He turned slightly: "Captain?"

Kennedy was a tall, red-haired man with a skew-whiff nose – broken and never set straight. "Unclear. My orders are to keep you here until we've got a full understanding of the site. The others can go. They're expendable."

"Put your gun down and tell me I'm expendable again, you bastard," said Ibsen, "and I'll show you what that means."

As Kennedy cursed, the guard who'd followed the foreman closed up, but Frost put out a hand to pre-empt violence. "Sven… please. This achieves nothing."

"It makes me feel better." But his hands remained at his sides. "It's not just you, though, boss. What about our gear? Who's going to pack that up and bring the transporter back?"

"Good question." Frost again turned and raised an eyebrow at the glaring officer in black.

"That's still to be decided," scowled Kennedy. "You hardly need it on your little ship, do you? So there's no rush."

"There might be no rush," said Ibsen, "but I don't trust you cunts not to steal it."

"Corporal – get this man out of my face. If he won't get into the boat, throw him into the water and he can take his chances with the sea life." The guard now laid a hand forcefully on Ibsen's arm – who stiffened and clenched a fist, but managed to restrain himself. "What you people don't realise," continued Kennedy, "is that this is our territory. You were guests – but now you're just trespassers. You can play the victim card all you like, but we're within our rights and you've brought this on yourselves. Now… piss off!"

The guard took the dismissal as a cue to start tugging the irate foreman, who muttered a curse, exchanged a final angry look with Frost, nodded, and then turned and stalked back to the skiff, shaking off the guard's hand.

Frost looked askance at Kennedy. "You've made a friend for life there."

"I'm not here to make friends, I'm here to follow orders. Now – come with me. I need some things explained."

Kennedy didn't wait; he started off towards the old camp behind the dock. Frost gave a final look at the skiff, holding the last half-dozen of his crew, and waited for Ibsen to step aboard. Only after that did he turn to follow the other – but slowly, at his own pace.

The new arrivals had brought a couple of large brown tents with them, which they'd set up to one side of the camp. To Frost, it looked like these would accommodate about a dozen in total: he suspected they'd brought more tents, but had taken a liking to the miners' prefab quarters and decided to occupy them instead. Indeed, as he ambled after the officer, he saw a pair of troopers emerge from the door to one of the dormitory huts, laughing and at ease.

He found Kennedy waiting impatiently outside Frost's own cabin, arms crossed.

"The sooner we log everything, the sooner your services become redundant, the sooner you can go."

"Maybe I'm in no rush to leave dry land."

Kennedy clicked his tongue, then turned and entered the hut. At least he held the door open for Frost.

Inside, there was a trooper, sat at the field table, with stacks of charts and documents put in several piles, and Frost's tablet set before him. Kennedy waved a hand towards the scene. "First things first – your password, please."

"Ah… I'm not sure about the legality of that. Maybe I need to consult with someone."

"Really, Dr Frost? Are you going to play that game? This is going to get opened and searched one way or another. We have the skill to hack it if we have to, but that will take time, and may mean it comes with us back to *Hibernia*. Do you want that?"

"I'd rather not." Frost sighed. "Okay, it's 'theodolite', with the second 'o' replaced by a zero."

The trooper entered the data, then turned the tablet around. "Now finger scan, please," he said.

Frost stepped forwards and touched his right index finger to the screen.

"Retinal too?" asked Kennedy.

"No, sir," said the trooper. "Only two-factor."

"Well, we hardly expected data theft," said Frost, edging over to the seated soldier and peering over his shoulder. "Please be careful. I don't want you wiping out important files."

"Record the whole drive," instructed Kennedy.

"But that is my whole life," said Frost, his equanimity starting to fray. "Personal files. Data on resources in the *Stavanger*. You have *no* right to those. Taking that is tantamount to espionage. You'd better be clear on the limits of your remit here, Captain, or you'll have to answer for it. Look, I'll point you towards all the files related to the current dig and you can just copy those – and I won't make a fuss. It's an organised system. It'll be obvious if I'm trying to deceive you."

"Sir?" queried the trooper.

Kennedy appeared undecided. "I… suppose you have a point."

"Yeah. I'm just keen not to have any erotic recordings suddenly appearing on your social net." Frost winced a smile. "I'm sure you understand."

For a moment Kennedy maintained his firm expression, but then his mouth twitched into a smile. "Very well. Martins – let him direct you. But if you think he is trying to hide something, let me know." Kennedy faced Frost. "You only get one strike with me, Dr Frost. Full disclosure immediately: any games and everything will come with us back to *Hibernia*. Understand?"

Frost nodded assent.

After Kennedy left, he took trooper Martins through his neatly organised folders. There was little point in hiding most of what they'd found – after all, he'd been summarising it in the report he'd been preparing on the matter, which had been intended for the invaders anyway. And as for the few gems of information he'd already considered keeping aside – well, that was safe: he'd taken Heiko's advice the previous day and used the interlude between spotting the approaching craft and their arrival on Ardol to move anything sensitive elsewhere. Martins felt no inclination to delve into the folder marked 'Personal', and even had he done so, Frost doubted he would have paid any attention to the sub(sub) folder entitled *Kiwi Dreams*.

* * *

"What about now?"

Heiko blinked his left eye shut and a confusion of images assaulted his mind. Through his right eye, he still saw officer Vardem, dressed in civvies, sitting in an island surrounded by ghostly glowing monitors, while somewhere else – someplace undefined by direction, and indeed, somehow superimposing the image from his right eye – he saw a wide plaza and people moving through it. He felt vaguely dizzy. But when he closed his right eye, the ill-lit operations room and the shaven-headed officer disappeared, while the image of the main plaza of Trollmarkt clarified and his dizziness faded. "Yes… that's it."

"What do you see?"

"The Trollmarkt. From one of the new cameras set in the ceiling. I recognise the shisha bar."

"And now?"

The image in his head changed. The people somehow *jumped*, and Heiko realised he was now seeing them from the other camera they'd installed in the plaza in the aftermath of their quest to find the stolen parts from the shuttle – installed in an attempt to identify the man in the red jumpsuit who'd escaped them. "I see… well, there's no need to describe. It's clearly from camera two. High resolution, but stationary. Ah, no, I've got a live feed. Can I change the views myself?"

"I don't know – can you?"

As Heiko concentrated, he noticed several icons along the bottom of the scene. He focused on a winking arrow and mentally dragged it over to one icon, which resolved as a compass. Moving the arrow over this caused the camera itself to move this way and that, and the focus changed. He looked directly into the open frontage of the shisha bar – *Sultan's*, according to the spray painted lettering on the wall to the left of the opening. Three workers were currently at a small table, sucking on water pipes and exhaling vapour. He reported: "Yes, I can. Excellent work, Claude. Can I access all of the cameras from here?"

"Wait a second." Heiko heard frantic tapping, then Vardem announced: "You should be able to now. Do you see a new icon? Upper left?"

"Yes, I've got it." Heiko mentally moved the arrow and clicked on the new icon, which consisted of three parallel lines, and suddenly he was looking at a screenshot of a page listing all of the security cameras in the *Stavanger* and their locations. There were fewer than twenty: the low level of crime on the ship meant there had been little need to expend limited resources building cameras to monitor behaviour. In fact, the two recently installed ones in the Uberwald Trollmarkt had been the first deployed in years – and the last two in their stores. He directed the arrow to one, and found an external shot over the retractable dock that abutted the starboard side of the great ship. It was currently full, the six launches from *Hibernia* taking up one guarded section.

Heiko nodded to himself, then opened his eyes. A ghost image of the dock floated in front of officer Bardem, who was looking at him expectantly. Heiko reached up to his left temple and located the small device plugged into the interface beside his left eye. As he slid this out, the interface cover closed, and the ghost vanished. He smiled at Vardem. "I think, Claude, we are now in business."

"Yes, sir. What now?"

"Will the system continue to run, even in your absence?"

"As long as I leave it on – the system, not the monitors. The cameras will continue to send their data to our server, and you can access it through the device and your implant. We've received no orders to shut things down – just not to show up. Unless you've heard different, sir?"

"No. I'm surprised they haven't taken control of this section, though, rather than just closing it off. It would be helpful to them for keeping an eye on the good citizens. I guess the lack of resistance has made them complacent."

Vardem ran a hand over his stubbled head. "Yes, sir. But also, having dismissed everyone in the section, they've got rid of anyone who could help them run this place."

"True. I'm taking this as an added sign that they don't intend on staying long. But if they do have second thoughts and take over… I'll still be fine?"

"Doubly so, as it should guarantee they keep things switched on and running. And unless they're very sophisticated, they won't know you have external access."

Heiko nodded. "Good. Now let's sneak out of here as quietly as we can, in case someone decides to investigate. And… thanks, Claude. You've taken a risk – above and beyond."

"No problem, sir. Anything to get back at the bastards. Just let me know when you need me again. I'm up for it. We all are."

Heiko saw steel in the other's eyes, and he was glad.

* * *

"Rennie? The arseholes are here. *Material Resources.* They're hacking into our systems. Turning it over. Hey!" De Voe's voice faded, and then Heiko heard: "Leave that alone, you bastards, or I'll…" Her voice strengthened again: "Sorry, Rennie. Can you get here? They're completely ransacking the–"

The call cut off.

It took Heiko five minutes to throw on his uniform jacket and get to the Material Resources section from his apartment. As he approached the entrance he saw a pair of black-clad Hibernians lounging by the double doors. They saw him stride towards them across the concourse, and must have noted the symbols of rank on his uniform, for they straightened and carefully brought their rifles around to point forwards and down.

One of the men sidled over to stand directly before the doors. "Yes?"

"I'm Rennie Heiko, Head of Security. I was summoned here."

"Summoned?" The man – short, brown haired, with a freckled face and corporal's insignia on his arms – frowned and looked Heiko up and down. "By whom? We've heard nothing."

"I just got the call. Maybe it's not made it to you yet."

"You still didn't say who from. The Colonel?"

"Yes, of course. There seems to be some tension here. I have come to moderate."

The men glanced at each other, clearly uncertain, then the second – darker and broader than his colleague – noted: "You're in uniform. I thought you were told to stand down."

"Not all of us. Are you going to let me through, or should we just wait for your colonel?"

At that point, sounds of commotion came from behind the doors. Heiko tensed – but so too did the troopers, and they were armed. The pair nervously looked about, trying to keep an eye on him, but also looking behind them. The doors swung open to reveal two more troopers – a man lending a shoulder to a woman whose chest was splashed with crimson, and who held a bloody rag to her nose. When the doors opened, the sounds from behind rose, and Heiko was sure he could hear De Voe, cursing like a hoary sailor from a bygone age. But then the doors swung shut, dampening the shouting, and the man growled: "Make way! Make way!"

"What's going on?" asked the corporal, stepping aside.

"One of them," he nodded towards Heiko, "has gone psycho. Taking Cooper to the doc."

Heiko smiled gently. "See, soldier. I said I'd come to moderate."

The noise from behind the doors rose again. As the man dragged off his injured colleague, and the two sentries exchanged more uncertain glances, the doors opened once more – this time, vigorously, causing the men to scurry out of the way, and Heiko to step back too.

The scrum that emerged contained four people: Melissa De Voe was cursing and thrashing about, while three more troopers in black – two men, one woman, all with close-cropped hair – attempted to restrain her, holding onto her arms while trying to avoid head-butts and knee strikes.

When De Voe saw Heiko, she momentarily ceased her resistance. "Rennie!"

Heiko eased into the path of the scrum and held up two arms. "Hold! Whoa! What's going on? Melissa?"

"She's interfering with our searches," gasped the female officer, pulling away slightly. "She assaulted Cooper. We're–"

"Cunt!" De Voe used the opportunity to twist and deliver a savage headbutt to the nose of one of the men, who stumbled and then let go, allowing her to twist and throw a punch at the second man, which he half ducked, allowing it to glance off the top of his head. The gasping woman then tried to get hold of De Voe's other arm, while one of the gun-toting sentries raised his weapon…

"Enough!" Heiko stepped in, knocked aside the weapon, and then chopped up beneath the soldier's chin, sending him crumpling to the ground. When the stunned corporal turned, he walked into a hammerfist to the nose, which felled him, too. Heiko then heard a shout from behind – the guard who'd been ferrying the injured woman. Without looking around, Heiko turned and executed a roundhouse kick, which caught the advancing newcomer flush in the face, knocking him cold. When he turned back, he saw that De Voe had managed to stick a thumb into the female officer's eye, eliciting a shriek as she fell away with hands to her face, leaving just the last male trooper hanging off one of her flailing arms. Finally, De Voe used her elbow to good effect, causing the last of those restraining her to let go and stumble back, holding a split lip.

"Stop! Stop now!"

The shout came from the concourse – a woman's voice, but deep. Heiko looked up, and saw Colonel Joseph with three others – all except her with weapons raised and pointing towards him. He took two quick steps back to be level with De Voe, raising his hands as he did so. He quickly glanced aside and smiled at the panting woman – bloodstained, though not with her own blood. "Hi!" he said softly.

"Hi back."

"What the fuck is going on?" said Joseph, stalking closer while glancing at the carnage around her. At least two of her troopers were out cold, and the rest sat or lolled on the floor, nursing wounds and groaning. "Mr Heiko?"

"Colonel Joseph. It seems there has been a little misunderstanding."

"A… *misunderstanding?*"

"Indeed. It seems your troopers misunderstood our resolve. While we are prepared to cooperate, we are not prepared to have our facilities trashed, or to be assaulted and abused. Miss De Voe protested and was treated disrespectfully. The perpetrators have hopefully learnt their lesson."

Joseph's face seemed to vacillate between a number of emotions, mainly disbelief and anger. At last she got herself under control. "If my troops went overboard, you could have come to me about it. This is unacceptable. I can't allow this challenge to our authority." She again looked at the carnage around them. In total, there were seven disabled personnel who'd need treatment, and maybe even evacuation. "I need to consult my superiors – and yours. Until I decide what to do with you, you will come with us. Both of you. That will happen, one way or another."

"Bitch!" hissed De Voe. "Why don't you–"

But Heiko reached out one calming hand. "Okay. We'll accompany you. But I'd advise you not to attempt to lay hands on either of us."

Joseph's eyes widened. She was about to speak, but then had a change of mind. She closed her mouth; looked around again; then nodded grimly. "Okay, Mr Heiko. But you must give me your word that you will come peacefully."

"I do. And Melissa also."

"Do I?"

Heiko gave a sideways glance. "You've had your fun for now. Will you throttle back – for me?"

De Voe sighed and gave an airy gesture with one arm. "Okay. I'll behave."

Joseph barked various orders to those around and on her communicator. More troops emerged from their pillaging of the Material Resources section, and then from the stairwells leading onto the concourse. There were a score of troopers around them before a squad of four was chosen to escort Heiko and De Voe to captivity – apparently to a storage room near the invaders' temporary headquarters on zero level near the docks. As they set off, two marched in front, two well behind.

"Impressive," muttered Heiko, as they started moving.

De Voe smiled and shrugged. "I had the advantage. I was trying to hurt them, while they were only trying to restrain me. If they'd been trying to cause me harm, they would have won."

"True. Still – if you want a job in Security after this, you're welcome."

"I might need it if they bar us from Ardol. But… ha, maybe it'll be fun."

"For you, perhaps, but maybe not for the criminal community."

De Voe laughed.

* * *

"Rennie, I'm surprised, and a little disappointed."

"I'm sorry, Premier. Instinct took over."

They were meeting in a small office normally used by dock staff, just along the corridor from the makeshift cell into which Heiko and De Voe had been placed. Colonel Joseph had grudgingly acceded to the *Stavanger* Premier's request for the meeting, but only after letting her prisoners stew overnight. Joseph had also wanted a guard to stay in the room with them, but Olson had refused this condition, and after a short stand-off the Hibernian had decided there was little to be gained by insisting. The guard now waited outside the closed door instead.

"I suppose I can understand that," said Olson. "I assume they were manhandling Melissa?"

Heiko grinned. "Well, they were *trying* to. When one decided to point a gun at her, I thought it was time to intervene. Still, I regret leaving you in this situation. Is there any news?"

"I… is it safe to talk?"

"I believe so, Premier. This isn't a sophisticated operation. Bugs? No. And letting us speak unobserved is a sign of confidence on their part. What can we do? We have played ball until now… barring yesterday's unfortunate events."

"Very well. Frankly, I just wanted to check you were alright, and it seems that you are. What happens from now on is uncertain. The Colonel has no idea what to do to with you. We're not at war, so you're not a POW. And your assault took place on *Stavanger*, over which they ultimately have no authority. So, who would try you, for what crime, and where? And a mitigation of self-defence seems strong. I get the impression she hasn't spoken to her superiors about the incident – perhaps to avoid embarrassment. I am guessing she'll leave you locked up until they leave, and probably drop the key into the ocean on their way out – just to increase the inconvenience."

Heiko nodded slowly. "Yes, that's my suspicion, too. And I'm guessing their departure won't be far off. They've established their base by the docks, ready for a quick exit, rather than occupying the Comms section or the Control Centre, as military doctrine for invaders would dictate. And as for the Security section, they simply confiscated all the weapons in the armoury and locked it up. They were going through the Resources section thoroughly, though, but I can't imagine there is much to take from there, bar electronic data. Melissa concurs. So, if they are done there, what else is left for them to do?"

"I really don't know. Anders has stepped into your shoes and is keeping an eye on them, but I'm afraid they are saying little to either him or me."

"Or to Ms Bulow?"

"Nothing – as far as I am aware."

Heiko leant back in his chair, looked down, and frowned. "So what *are* they doing now… *right* now?"

"I'm afraid we'll have to wait and see."

* * *

But Heiko had the tools to find out.

"So that's how it works," said De Voe, watching Heiko insert the adaptor into the augment socket by his left eye. "I dread to think where you hid that."

Heiko raised an eyebrow at the smirking woman. "Fortunately, no great subterfuge was required. It rested innocently in my wallet. They never even patted us down, did they?"

"Sloppy, eh?"

Heiko shrugged. "They'd no need to, and wouldn't have known what it was even if they'd found it. Besides, I sensed the guards weren't too keen to get that close to us."

"Hah! I wonder why?"

Heiko's smile returned. "Yes, I wonder. Now… let me look."

He closed his eyes and the general menu was suddenly in his mind. He began to systematically flick through the different cameras on the *Stavanger*. These were not especially well placed: some covered parts of the ship that weren't well frequented, having been installed soon after the ship was built (like the fusion reactor and food processing deck), while there were few in newer areas where they were needed. For example, there'd been none in Uberwald until Heiko had insisted on installing their last two cameras there, and the absence of coverage of the shuttle landing pad and hanger (a later upgrade) had undermined their search for those who'd pilfered the shuttle components. However, the entrances to both the Comms section and the Command Centre were covered, as was the bridge itself. Heiko noticed two black-uniformed guards milling at the back of the bridge – looking bored, as well they might, given that the *Stavanger* was at rest and activity there was minimal. The entrance to the Security section was also covered, and that showed nothing at all: the desk at the front was closed, the lights off, the doors locked – although Heiko had a key, which the Hibernians had not been interested in tracing once they'd emptied the armoury.

The other cameras seemed to show life on board proceeding as usual, with no sign of the thinly stretched occupiers, until he got to the storage bays on the first sub level. These were well connected with the docks, the food processing section, and the manufactory, which relied on programmable 3D printers in adjacent workshops to turn whatever raw materials they mined from Ardol into anything that was needed. The storage bays were connected to key facilities by rail systems that were used by battery-charged carts. Heiko noticed that some of these carts were in motion, accompanied by a couple of dozen Hibernians. The carts were loaded with closed crates that were slowly sliding along rails back towards the dock.

"Anything yet?" asked De Voe, growing impatient.

"Hang on, let me…" The storage area was relatively well covered by five different cameras – emphasising where the critical area of the ship had always been: materials and resources. Heiko switched between these, gaining shots from in front of several of the storage bays. The bulk of Hibernian activity seemed to be around the smallest of these – Bay E – the wide, low doors of which were open. "Bay E," he announced, reading the giant letter in red from above the portal. "What it is it used for?"

"E? That's critical components. Usually small items. Batteries. Transistors. Silicon chips. Everything we salvage from broken or outdated equipment. It's essentially our treasure store, our Central Bank our… what's that place on Earth with all the gold?"

"Fort Knox?"

"Yeah, that. Why do you ask?"

Heiko's expression turned grim. He removed the adaptor and opened his eyes. "Why? Because it seems that the Hibernians are now indulging in theft on a grand scale. They appear to be emptying it and transferring its contents to their boats at the dock."

De Voe's jaw dropped. "The fuckers!"

* * *

Less than twenty-four hours later, the door to the impromptu cell was opened by Anders Pedersen. This was about an hour after the last Hibernian boat left – observed by Heiko using his augments. Heiko and De Voe emerged to find an august welcoming committee: Margarethe Olson and Nila Moroni stood behind Pedersen.

"I know," said Heiko, before the others could speak. "I watched it all." He tapped the copper-coloured oblong beside his left eye. "How much did they take?"

"Almost everything," seethed Moroni. "That's our lifeblood. We'll be crippled without it."

"It could even raise questions about the viability of the *Stavanger* in the medium term," said Olson, shaking her head. Her face was pale, as though she were in shock.

"Have you had any explanation or demand?" asked Heiko.

"No, not yet," said Moroni. "Their leader – Joseph – seemed to think it was funny. Said she was only following orders, and to take it up with her superiors."

Pedersen shifted on his feet, uncomfortably. "There was nothing we could do, sir."

"Don't worry, Anders," said Heiko. "I know. We couldn't have anticipated they'd be so flagrant. But they're gone now and they won't catch us on the hop again."

De Voe muttered a variety of curses. "We can't let the bastards get away with it. We need to get it back. All of it."

"Yes, Marisa," said Heiko. "We do."

"Ah… and not only our material resources, Heiko," said Moroni. "I'm afraid you don't know everything. It's not just our stores they've taken to *Hibernia*: they've taken Makka Frost, too."

Chapter 26

"They came too soon," snarled Kai Dures. "We weren't ready." They were in a dingy basement at the edge of the Engine Quarter.

Asher Johns slowly nodded and reached across to sympathetically touch the other's corded forearm as it rested on the table. "I'm sorry about Karyn."

"Karyn will be fine," Dures moved his arm from the other's reach and his eyes gleamed. "She can look after herself. We'll get her out. I'm less worried about her than our schedule. We were unprepared. We need to drastically increase our rate of production. Guns. Bombs. Hollande?"

Georges Hollande sat on the opposite side of the table between Babatunde Odile and Jacques Danté. He quickly looked to either side, seeking support. No one had elected him leader of the New Socialist contingent, yet that was the role he had somehow acquired – and he wasn't sure he liked it. When the others made no response, he sighed. "Guns… yes. We have made more than were distributed, both ceramic and metal."

"How many?" Dures leant over the table menacingly.

"Thirty? Forty?"

"Then why the *fuck* haven't they been handed out?"

Hollande recoiled somewhat: Dures was an imposing man, with large, calloused hands that looked like they could crush a steel pipe. He didn't enjoy being on the end of his wrath, particularly given that blame for the delays lay elsewhere. "Because of lack of bullets. Making the gunpowder needed for these, and setting up a production line, has been slow. We've been looking at ways to synthesise the necessary ingredients in a safe and efficient manner. Perhaps… perhaps we haven't been as productive as we could have been."

"Can you step up production now?"

Hollande looked to his right. "Baba?"

"It's not a problem," said Odile, airily. "Our mini chemical plant is now on-line. It's just a matter of time and resources."

"And explosives?" asked Dures.

Danté spoke without Hollande having to prompt him. "TNT is easy to make. It's just been a question of priorities. We have enough for a dozen bombs already. More. We just need manpower."

"Then you'll have it!" declared Dures. "Whatever you want – materials, workers, just name it. From now on – whatever you want, you get, no arguments."

Hollande exchanged glances with his colleagues and smiled uncertainly. "That's… good."

"But this is only one part of the equation," continued Dures. "Johns – what of the *Marseilles*?"

Johns gently frisked his black goatee. "It approaches. It is due to take up position near Mount Ardol in three weeks. From its current position, it will swing close to *Hibernia* in just over two."

"Two weeks!" Dures sat back and smiled. "I pity the Hibernians. Another two weeks with my dear wife? And once she is out, there'll be hell to pay."

"Do you know where they are keeping her?" asked Johns.

"Yes. They have a small number of holding cells in the Security section. Plans are already being made to free her at the optimal time. Not before."

Hollande had met Dures' wife on a couple of occasions: they were a well matched couple. Indeed, he suspected that he would rather face an angry Kai than an angry Karyn. He wondered how the Hibernians would cope.

* * *

Colonel Eric Nesvorny stared across the table in the small interview room at a woman wearing a Stokers' green boilersuit – her tall height evident, even though she was seated. She had tawny hair that cascaded over her shoulders, though it was oddly shaved to the left around her ear, where a raised white scar was visible. Aside from that, her features were regular and her blue eyes sparkled with life: he suspected that one of the beauticians used by the elite would quickly be able to bring out a hidden gem, perhaps even one the libidinous Traore might appreciate.

"Like what you see?" said the woman.

Nesvorny frowned and gently shook his head. "In no way, Ms Dures."

"Are you sure?" Karyn Dures smiled, her expression suddenly transformed from venomous to enticing. "Why not come closer for a better look?"

"I'd rather not get in range of your teeth, Dures. I'm fine where I am." The woman's arms were cuffed to those of her chair. Nesvorny quickly looked at the dark patch on the chest of her clothing – a still-damp blood stain from where she had bitten one of his men who'd come in range, tearing off a part of his cheek. "And you… you're in enough trouble as it is."

"Am I really?"

"Aside from the guard you bit, and the one whose eye you put out on capture, I have two dead and a score more with other wounds. You will be charged as directly responsible for these, or at least complicit."

"I'm sorry we didn't get more of you bastards." She still smiled, almost sweetly. "You want to try again? Next time you won't be so lucky. In any case, my lawyer – I'm sure you have to give me one – will be pleading self-defence. *You* attacked *us*."

"We conducted a legitimate search for illicit materials after recent bomb attacks – well within our mandate. And the presence of guns showed we weren't wrong in our suspicions. So, you can play the victim card as much as you like, it'll get you nowhere."

"It wouldn't have anyway, would it? The laws of *Hibernia* don't apply to you, and the protections written in those laws don't apply to us." She gave a curt laugh. "And you wonder why we're not happy with the status quo?"

"I'm not going to get into a debate on social justice. If I told you I had some sympathy for you and your people, you wouldn't believe me anyway. But whatever sympathy I had is now being tested." He leant forwards slightly: "Where did you get the guns?"

She still smiled, but with a closed mouth.

After a pause of several seconds, Nesvorny growled: "You're not helping your cause."

"Maybe, maybe not. But I'm not helping *yours*, either. Isn't this the point where you try to make me an offer? Behave and tell you everything and you'll offer me reduced time? Ha! Fuck off!"

"You're not the only one in custody, Dures, or the only one we've talked to." He frowned at that. Fukuda had been working on some of the other detainees, and clearly not by the book. While he understood his deputy's frustration, and the anger among his own unit, he couldn't condone his interrogation technique – or risk him anywhere near Dures. If news got out that she'd been harmed, the Engine Quarter would likely explode.

"Talked to?" She smiled wryly. "Sure. Then you've no need to question me."

"You obviously know more than they do."

She shrugged. "I'm bored with this. Why don't you tell me what you know – or think you know – and we can go from there."

Now Nesvorny smiled. "And I thought *I* was conducting this interview. Okay. To save time, we know you didn't import them on the *Leviathan*, and we know they're new. That leads us to one conclusion."

"That we made them? Of course. We're poor, not stupid. The physics, the mechanics, it's not difficult."

"No, not technically. But you need the right information, and information in the common datasphere is restricted, unlike Earth. Did someone on the last ship bring that information with them?"

Dures scowled. "You continue to underestimate us. There is nothing about constructing weapons that is difficult. No skills that we haven't already got from our labour in the manufactories, or with the fishing fleet, or at the dockyard on Athol."

"True. But you know what, Dures? The guns are identical. And they're well-constructed – not handmade. Somewhere there is a production line using a template and 3D printers. I doubt you came up with these things from first principles and after a lengthy developmental process. You got external help."

She smiled again but refused to answer.

After another pause, Nesvorny went on. "I'm pretty certain of the *who*. I've been checking. There were a number of New Socialists aboard the *Leviathan* who were meant to transfer to the *Marseilles*, but never did. In fact, they've vanished. Did you get the information from them? Where are they? And where is your factory?"

Dures shrugged. "Fuck if I know."

"If?"

Again the smile. "Okay, the fuck if I tell you. Happy now?"

"Look, Dures, you need to give this up. If you don't, we're all going to suffer – and to what end? What do you really think you're going to achieve? Revolution? I know there are more of you than our records suggest, but you've not got enough to challenge the state. We're on to you now. Don't think we won't tear the Engine Quarter apart if we have to, and I promise you, there are some who want to do just that." He frowned and pushed back in his chair. How much should he say? He noticed the woman's face scrunch in concentration. "But *I* don't. You've made your point. Let heads cool. Why not give the politicians a chance to respond? I'm asking you – for your sake, and the sake of your people – stand down."

Dures' expression had turned serious. She slowly shook her head: "You've had your chance. There have been decades of petty discrimination, and you've done nothing. You can't change. You *won't*. And don't forget, it was *you* who started this – your vigilantes, your death squads. *You* drew first blood. *You* took the first lives. This interview is finished. Take me to my cage."

After Dures was collected by a quartet of heavily armed guards, Nesvorny continued to sit in his chair, staring vacantly at the opposite wall. *First blood? First lives? Death squads?* Had he missed something?

* * *

Nesvorny didn't manage to corner Major Fukuda until late in the afternoon as they'd both been busy dealing with the continuing aftermath of the raid three days ago. He'd just come from the St Mary Hospital in the Tipperary District, where one ward had been set aside for the injured troopers from the operation. That was *Hibernia's* second hospital, used by the common folk: St Columba's, on the third level of the Command Centre, was reserved for the elite, and had far better facilities, including the only functioning MRI scanner on the city ship after the one at St Mary's had ceased functioning a week ago and couldn't be repaired for want of parts. The injured were suffering unnecessarily as a result, but there was nothing he could do about it.

"We were premature, Major," said Nesvorny, striding towards the other in the level zero hangar that held the Internal Security Unit's few patrol vehicles. "We gave up on the *Marseilles* contingent too easily."

"Sir?" Fukuda waited by the door to one of their three armoured personnel carriers. "What do you mean?"

Nesvorny came to a halt. "I've been checking exit visas. Three names stand out – people who'd planned to go to the *Marseilles*, but didn't take the last transfer a couple of months ago. Keeping track of the New Socialist contingent was a task I assigned to you."

Fukuda stiffened. "Yes, sir. I... we... agreed that their possible threat dissipated when most took the shuttle. You redirected me to the businessman, Mitsos."

"True. I am not blaming you, Fukuda. We assumed the *Marseilles* would send another shuttle to pick up the remainder, but it never did. The issue is this: two days after the shuttle left, the remaining three checked out of their hostel – and have not checked into another."

"They've disappeared?"

"Yes, Fukuda. And that's difficult in *Hibernia.* In fact, there is only one place they can possibly hide and not be noticed or recorded, where we have no cameras, conduct no patrols, and where census takers fear to tread."

"The Engine Quarter."

Nesvorny folded his arms. "So, rabble from Earth planning on a visit to *Marseilles* are abandoned and taken in by a people with whom they have a natural affinity. People liable to have alternative skills and perhaps datafiles that we don't. The calculation is not difficult."

"The Stokers got the weapon designs from them? But I interrogated several of the captured Stokers and they said nothing about this."

"Low level rebels, maybe kept out of the loop? Karyn Dures wouldn't say either, but when I mentioned the New Socialists from the *Leviathan* to her, she didn't blink. It's them all right."

"Then we need to find them. Another raid–"

"Wait!" Nesvorny straightened and stood directly before the other, looking into his eyes. What was his game? How deep into this was he; how deep into Traore's pocket? And where could he send his deputy that would cause least harm? "No. Not a raid. Something more subtle. I want you to go over everything we know about these men. Records. Any and all past surveillance clips. Anyone they've talked to. Bring in your informants. Bugs. Cameras. Drones. Make this your number one priority, Major. And *before* you act, bring your findings to me and we'll discuss what to do about them. In the meantime, I will interrogate the prisoners further and take over the scheduling of patrols at the edges of the Engine Quarter."

Fukuda shifted on his feet uncomfortably. "If you're sure, sir. But it's mostly paperwork. I can still– "

"*No.* I want you focused. I'm aware that I've been too removed from the streets and our foot soldiers. I need to re-engage with them. *Talk* to them. It'll do me good to get my hands dirty."

Fukuda's expression firmed: he stood to attention, gave a small bow of assent, and then turned and strode off between the parked carriers. Nesvorny's eyes followed him all the way to the exit.

* * *

Manfred Traore loved power. It made him *hard.* He liked it so much he'd do almost anything to achieve and hold it: flattery, bullying, even obsequious submission – although he naturally preferred some plays to others. But in the end, he knew who he was, what he wanted, and what that required – good and bad. He'd been well taught, after all. His father, who'd come to *Hibernia* in the first wave of colonists, had been a wealthy man in the West African Union until he'd crossed swords with the wrong people, forcing him to flee with his immediate family and a couple of cases of Terran credits. And he'd done well during his time on *Hibernia*, too, before the accident that had killed him, laying the gold-paved path that his son had followed. *Laid.* But it was Traore who'd reached the path's end and then extended it with further gilt he'd acquired himself.

He'd done what was necessary. Among his sacrifices was a short affair with O'Neill – a woman as voracious as he, but admittedly cleverer. He appreciated that and could live with it. And Sullivan? He'd done her a number of financial favours. Both had helped him up the political ladder, having seen his value. He was a man prepared to act so that they didn't have to; he told lies to enable them to speak the truth; and he was their fall guy for when the time was ripe, the one who would be cast to the wolves. But that hadn't happened over the six years of the triumvirate, and now the equation had changed somewhat: though O'Neill was untouchable, he fancied he had risen above Sullivan in the power index: with what he knew of the latter's finances and sexual peccadillos, he could ruin her with a simple call to any of *Hibernia's* chief editors – which she had begun to realise.

"Is it wise to stir this pot?" Sullivan asked, eying him warily. They'd been speaking of the Engine Quarter raid. "Especially given the *Stavanger* operation?"

Traore smiled broadly. "The two provide cover for each other. They are two approaches to one problem. And if matters go awry in one, we can focus the media's eyes upon the other. The liberals are too shocked to know what to attack anyway."

"Liberals!" scoffed O'Neill. She slammed her heavy crystal glass onto the small coffee table around which they sat. "Short-sighted fools. Fuck them."

"Yes, Marissa," said Traore. "I agree. What can they do? What can they say?"

"I'm surprised they've said as much as they have," said Sullivan. She stared at Traore. "You have links with the *Times* and the *Shield*, but still they whine. Can't you bring them under control?"

"I can't control *all* opinion." He sipped on his glass of single malt Scotch, poured from one of the last bottles to make it from Earth around a year ago. "Okay, a couple of journalists have been less than enthusiastic – but that's all. Read the editorials: they're roughly supportive."

Sullivan didn't look convinced. "That hack from the *Times* had a story about my links to the mining company we're sending to appraise the Ardol find, implying favouritism in granting the mining rights. Why did they take that angle?"

"Relax, Kerrie," Traore struggled to keep the smile from his face. "They're just being mischievous. They don't dare make a formal accusation."

O'Neill shook her head slowly – the motion an instruction for the others to look at her. "No, they don't. It's not the *Times* or the *Shield* I'm worried about, but the *Morning Wave*. They have been genuinely critical. *Bastards*. Don't they understand how difficult things are? How close we are to the precipice?"

"Perhaps you need to say this more bluntly," mused Traore. "Give them some choice facts. Scare them. Scare their readers. Your first public announcement focused on the wrongdoing of the Stavangerans and the Stokers. Maybe in your next, you should focus on the consequences of their behaviour in these times of resource crisis."

O'Neill scowled at him. She didn't like receiving advice, but she was intelligent enough to follow it when it was good. "Sure. You can write it for me."

"As you wish." He grinned at Sullivan – who normally drafted O'Neill's speeches – unable to help himself. But then he thought: *pull it back*. He wasn't at war with Sullivan – not now, maybe not ever. "But… with Kerrie's aid, of course. She has a better way with words."

Sullivan's frown transformed into a weak smile and nod.

"Whatever," concluded O'Neill. "I'll issue a state address tomorrow at noon. Get it to me by nine so I can go over it. Now – updates. Manfred – tell me about the *Stavanger* scenario."

Traore took another sip of his Scotch, savouring the attention as much as his drink. His portfolio included both internal and external security, and so he knew more than his peers, and could choose what information to dispense and what to withhold. "Colonel Joseph has returned, bearing… *gifts*. She couldn't find any evidence of mined material, confirming that their find is recent. But she decided to empty a warehouse or two, just in case. Consider the seized material a bond for good behaviour, or maybe a fine for misdeeds."

O'Neill laughed. "Joseph? She didn't do that of her own accord, Manfred!"

"Ah, I may have made a polite suggestion."

"That will piss them off." O'Neill leant forwards and grasped her crystal tumbler, raising it in a toast to the other. "Bravo! We needed to teach them a lesson. This is a harsh one, but fair, I think."

Sullivan grimaced and looked between the others. "Is this really wise? Is it legal?"

Traore grinned broadly. "I'm surprised you want to talk of legalities, Kerrie, after your earlier criticism of media discussion of the mining company that you effectively own. Legality is a fuzzy concept here."

"Yes, might is right," grunted O'Neill. "You don't fuck with the big dog, unless you want to get bitten. How have they responded so far?"

"They've been trying to contact us. I thought it best to leave the response to you after this discussion, and let them stew in the meantime. I didn't want to overstep, ma'am. I simply present you with... *opportunities.*"

O'Neill slowly settled back into her seat, her expression turning thoughtful. "There are many issues to weigh up here. The deterrent effect on others. The power we now hold over the *Stavanger.* And what does the haul contain? Anything we desperately need? Like for the broken MRI?"

"I'll have a full inventory provided."

"Good. I'll frame this as a bond to begin with – to be returned after *full* cooperation. If something goes missing in the meantime, we can attribute that to accounting errors perhaps. But any excuse – *any* – and we will take it all." She took a sip of her own poison, then continued: "And what of the operation on Ardol?"

"Joseph has left a detachment of forty. We've retained the *Stavanger's* mining equipment, too, so further drilling can begin in a few days. I understand Kerrie's company – ah, I mean, the assigned contractor..." Traore winked at Sullivan, "is planning on shipping across their entire workforce and every rig and piece of machinery they have. It'll take a while to get established and up to full production though."

"Excellent."

"Oh... and one more thing," Traore continued. "Their chief geologist – a Dr Frost – has kindly *agreed* to join us on *Hibernia.* He's apparently well-regarded by our own geologists, so I thought it might be useful for them to talk to him."

"And maybe we can offer him an alternative contract – one he can't refuse?" O'Neill's smile was dangerous.

"Or *dare* not refuse?" This time, it was Traore who raised his glass in a toast to the Premier.

Now Sullivan couldn't help but laugh.

The news Traore had to provide about events in the Engine Quarter was less positive, but he had already won the encounter, and his framing of 'minor setbacks' did little to dim his star in the others' eyes. He didn't reveal how troubled he really was by events on *Hibernia* itself.

* * *

Nesvorny had spent a couple of days talking to the men and women of the Internal Security Unit – cautiously to some, insistently to others, depending upon their demeanour and his mood. *Vigilantes. Death squads.* He'd not used those words, and nor had any of those he'd spoken to. But something wasn't right. They'd mostly feigned ignorance, until pressed, when the odd trooper broke and revealed that there had been rumours that something *might* have been happening off the record. But none admitted that it was *them*, and nor would any name suspects – or even admit to being able to recall the names of those from whom they'd heard the rumours in the first place. But he'd been persistent, and at last been pointed in a particular direction – by a surreptitious nod from one, and a meaningful glance from another. *Squad Five.* Fukuda's loyalists. Hardly a surprise. They scared the others. And though they didn't scare him, their potential involvement and link to Fukuda – and therefore to Traore – caused him to hesitate. Accusation and interrogation would give the game away.

He needed to know more, so he'd come to interrogate Karyn Dures again. He faced her now – alone. As before, her arms were strapped to the chair for his safety.

Dures laughed at his question. "Don't pretend you didn't know about it. You're their leader, aren't you? Or has the legendary Colonel Nesvorny lost control of his own unit?"

Had he? Was he going soft? Nesvorny sighed. He looked down at the desk, noticing a groove that had been carved in the synthetic surface, meandering like a river over a floodplain. When he looked back up, the woman had an expression of curiosity on her face. "Ms Dures," he said wearily, "why don't we stop playing games, eh? Just for a few minutes. Pretend you don't hate me. Put aside your assumption that I wish you and your people harm, and that I'm trying to trick you. I'm asking a simple question – answering it truthfully cannot implicate you in anything. And if I do already know the answer, what will it cost you – apart from time you'd otherwise be spending in your cell? And if I really *don't* – you can assume I am losing control, if you want – then it'll help me see more clearly. That is all."

For a moment, Dures actually appeared stunned. Her brow wrinkled. She smiled; frowned; smiled again. At last she said: "You *don't* know, do you?"

And so she told him.

She related every one of the assaults that had been carried out in the dark, on the fringes of the Engine Quarter, over the period before the first bomb was planted. She related the names of those beaten to death, and those who'd merely been broken and left in bloody pools. She gave times and dates, and repeated these when he produced his tablet and decided to write them down.

At the end he sat back, stunned. "We started it."

"The violence, yes. But it was coming anyway. Nothing was going to stop it."

"Nothing?" Nesvorny stared into the woman's eyes. "No one? What about you?"

She smiled again, but wistfully, without her usual challenge. "Maybe not even if I wanted to. Something has got to change. If I don't do anything, or my husband doesn't, then before long we'll be replaced by someone who will."

Nesvorny called the guards to take her back to her cell. But as she was led past him, still sitting at the desk, she turned to face him.

"Colonel – keep your head down, eh? Perhaps you're not the worst of your kind."

Chapter 27

In Old Europe, Eddard Mitsos was able to function. He had friends, family, allies to watch his back and provide him with aid and advice. He understood the cultural rules and norms. He knew how to negotiate bureaucratic obstacles, how to influence people in power, how to bribe politicians. And not just in Old Europe: his brother had moved to the US to join another branch of his extended family, and, through them, he had discovered how to get on there too. Though they were new markets with different procedures, the same tricks largely worked.

But on the *Marseilles* it was different. He had no roots, no grounding, no knowledge. It was an alien culture. He did not belong here and didn't know how to operate. Nothing he did was right, and it seemed as though everyone around was eager to tell him so.

Youssef Bennani laughed. "You don't understand at all, do you?" They currently stood on the deck of one of the boats assigned to the REEN project, which was settled in a cradle in an internal bay of the dry dock.

Mitsos fumed. "No, I don't have a science PhD – or whatever Mickey Mouse qualification they give here for being a good socialist who knows what the periodic table looks like. I manage. I make decisions. I leave it to you play about with test tubes and report to me in a language the rest of the universe can understand. If I don't get it, then you're not explaining it right."

Bennani's eyes widened and his mouth firmed. At least Mitsos had managed to wipe the smile off his face. "Citizen Mitsos, our degrees are as rigorous as those from universities on Earth. My specialism is–"

"So, you've published papers in prestigious scientific journals, have you?" Mitsos smirked. Trust the academic to be side-tracked by a challenge to his credentials. Although he only had a modest economics degree from Thessaloniki University, he had learned about academic processes and sensibilities from an uncle who'd been a professor in Bologna. "No, I didn't think so." He held up a hand as

Bennani's mouth opened like a stranded fish on a riverbank gasping for air. "You didn't come up with the science for the REEN either. *Better* scientists on Earth did that. You're just following instructions like a child with a plastic construction kit. So wind your neck in, lose the jargon, and tell me again."

To his credit, Bennani didn't explode or storm off. He closed his mouth, glared for a couple of seconds, and exhaled one deep breath. "Okay. Try this. Your machine... *doesn't... fucking... work*!"

"But it does. Your own reports – which I've forwarded to the People's Committee – say it does."

Bennani smiled grimly. "Okay. Let me rephrase. We have not seen any increased collection of elements over the last thirteen days. We have changed the intensity of the current flowing through the filament and made subtle changes to the composition of the microfibres of the net. We cannot get anywhere near a viable return from ocean trawling to make up for predicted degradation of the materials used in the boats and in the net itself. Do you understand *that*? I cannot simplify any further."

Mitsos' own smile dissipated. It was clear that the REEN was an expensive white elephant. The issue now was how long he could delay someone with a massive *fucking* gun from putting it down – and most likely, him too. "You said 'predicted'. In my area of expertise, it's known that economic forecasts aren't worth shit. You've too little data to make any sensible predictions. We need to collect more data. So, I don't want any predictions in your next report, do you hear?" The one substantive managerial thing he had achieved in his new tenure was to ensure that all reports came to him first – and him alone – rather than being leaked to the Committee and to Deux. In the two previous weekly reports, he'd managed to massage certain figures and delete certain paragraphs. Bennani and his team may have suspected this, but Mitsos had been careful to keep the submitted reports from them and give the impression that he was simply passing them on unaltered.

"No predictions?"

"Or extrapolations. Simply record what each trawl has produced. Emphasise the cumulative output. In the end, that is all that matters.

The Committee are already aware of the start-up costs of the project, so there is no need to repeat this."

"But it is important to provide running costs, otherwise you only have half of the equation. I am not happy omitting this data. If you prevent us from noting this, I will have to approach my People's Representative to notify them of behaviour prejudicial to society."

Of course he was right. It was the difference between turnover and profits. Mitsos knew that, and Bennani knew that he knew. "Very well. But only actual documented costs. We'll consider projected wear and tear in another report."

Bennani had recovered his composure completely. He folded his arms. "So, what do you want us to do now… *master.*"

"Prepare the boats and head on out. Drive faster. Go around in bloody circles. I don't know – just try something different. Call it *Condition 32*, or whatever. Use your brains. Until the Committee tells us to halt, we will do our best to make this work. Do you understand?"

Bennani nodded slowly. "Oh, yes, Citizen Mitsos. I understand. I understand *very* well."

"Fine. And I see no reason to be chasing you every day, so continue the next series of studies and we'll touch base again in… three days?"

"You want another three days?"

Bennani's grin was now infuriating. The project's next report was due around then – one they both suspected would be its last.

He had until then to find a way out.

* * *

Three days. That was the figure that dominated Mitsos' thoughts as he lay in his small single bed in his drab apartment that night. Three days.

The *Marseilles* was on approach to *Hibernia*, around five hundred kilometres away, its route well known, its expected course detailed on newsfeeds. In three days of slow sailing it would be close, due to pass south of the greatest ship on Tethys on its way to its mining station off Mount Ardol. But it would make its *closest* approach on day four...

Mitsos would just have to delay the next report. Maybe lie. Say they had exciting new data that he wanted to include – buy them off with false promises and fantasies. He was sure they would go for it. In fact, given Deux's *other* plan was close to fruition, he suspected the First Citizen's eyes and focus would be elsewhere. Maybe he'd appreciate the removal of a distraction?

So, *maybe* four days. And perhaps more? He'd seen the preparations of the *Marseilles* shock force, and wasn't impressed. On his trip around the docks that morning he'd noted six trawlers set aside and armed with canon, and a final three in the frantic process of conversion. The trawlers had a crew of a dozen when used for their original purpose, but of course, could hold significantly more once all the fishing gear had been cleared out. So what force could the *Marseilles* field? Three hundred? Four hundred? To take over all of *Hibernia*? It was laughable, unless… unless they were expecting help from the state ship itself. *Hmmmmm.*

If the assault failed, he would be finished – used as something to distract from the disaster, to take the heat off of those who'd decided to waste resources and lives on a mini war. *Unless* the defeat was total and the Hibernians struck back. If they did, then he stood a chance of getting away before being rounded up, or at least, of laying low while the Apparatus and what remained of the ship's new force battled to retain control of their home.

If *Marseilles* won, however, there would be much else for Deux and his Committee to focus on, not least the administration of a new prize. In that context, he and his project would surely seem inconsequential. Could he offer his services to manage the conquered industry? Would Deux trust him with that after the REEN fiasco and their querulous relationship? He doubted it. It was more likely that he'd be imprisoned in some concentration camp with all the other enemies of the people, to be re-educated or somehow retired from existence.

Calculations, calculations…

He didn't want to take the chance, to remain in easy reach and sight of Captain Boursis and her sadists. If he could get to *Hibernia*, hiding would be easier. Then what? Make a deal with the Hibernians? Offer his services? They were a bunch of pricks, but at least they were capitalist pricks, and he understood them considerably better than he did his current hosts.

Four days, then.

He knew what he had to do.

* * *

"Noma! Wait up!"

It was the following evening, and Mitsos had been waiting in the entrance corridor to the docks for the woman's return. She was dressed in her military fatigues, surrounded by comrades from the *Dieppe*. The woman drew up, looking startled, while those around looked at him with expressions ranging from indifference to mild hostility.

"Pierre… Abdul… Marc… good to see you." Mitsos effected bonhomie, knowing that Noma might not be the only one he had to convince. "Sorry to delay you." He made a show of looking over their weapons, carried on straps over shoulders. "Warriors of the people! I wish I'd had the guts to join you at the start. Noma – can we talk?"

The woman looked at him as though he had gone mad. "I… suppose so."

A couple of the name-checked men muttered greetings, then as a group they moved off, leaving Noma behind. Mitsos stood close to her and leaned in. "Can I buy you a drink?"

They were soon ensconced in the Matelot – the old haunt of the *Dieppe's* crew, when the craft had been used for its original purpose. It was as shabby as before, reeking of sweat and fish oils, with several of its ceiling lights out, unable to be replaced for lack of spares, leaving spots of gloom between over-lit zones. Mitsos managed to snare a table in one of these areas of shadow, and bought the first round. He hadn't got far in explaining his change of heart, when Noma declared: "You haven't had the training."

"Noma – can I be straight with you? You know I'm heading the REEN project?"

"Of course. I hear it's doing well. The *Megaphone* says it's drawing key elements from the ocean in increasing amounts."

"Yeah, well, you shouldn't always believe what you read."

"So it's not?"

"Oh, yes, it is working in a way, and with every tweak it's collecting more and more. But it's not going to solve our resources problems. In fact – strictly between you and me – it's using more material than it's collecting. You're being strung along."

Noma stared. "What? That can't be true. Why would they tell us these things otherwise?"

"Sorry, Noma, it's true. Who should know better than me, eh? You remember I told you a couple of weeks ago about our First Citizen? No – please – don't get up. I'm not having a go at him. But remember I said I was being set up to fall if the project failed?" He chuckled softly. "I can't blame Deux really. I'm sure I'd do the same myself. Anyone politically astute would. But… my time is approaching. At some point there's going to be an announcement about the real state of affairs with the REEN. It'll probably state that I've misrepresented the success – but I promise you, Noma, it's not me doing this. There'll be a scandal. I'll be arrested, and – knowing the psychos in your security apparatus – probably tortured. You *know* that goes on." He moved his right hand to draw the woman's attention: it still had a light bandage on it. "And then I'll probably be put on a show trial, after which… well… I don't know your range of punishments, but whatever's the worst option, it'll be that."

Noma's eyes were wide. Mitsos could see her struggling to deny something she knew deep down was the truth. "It… You… What are you…?"

"So you see where I stand, don't you? I've *got* to get out. I've got to get away from here, from the *Marseilles*. And as far as I can see, there's only one route out – and that is on one of the assault boats."

Noma was clearly still struggling with how to react to his news. At last she said: "You do realise what we're going to do, don't you? We are not visiting for a conference. We're going to fight. To free the oppressed of *Hibernia*."

"I'd rather take my chances getting shot by Hibernians than stay here and face almost certain… *discomfiture*."

Noma looked puzzled, and then smiled at his understatement. But the smile quickly faded and she shook her head. "I'm sorry… Eddard. It's just not possible."

"It's always possible, Noma. There is *always* a way. If you can't convince the crew to let me join you as a soldier, what about as a crewman? Or… I know… what about as a guide? Have any of you been to the *Hibernia* before?"

"You weren't there for long…" But there was doubt in her voice.

"No, but longer than you or any of the others. So, I can crew. I can guide. Maybe tell them I am desperate to display my loyalty to the cause. Missing out is crushing my spirit. Or, if the worst comes to the worst, let's not tell them at all. Smuggle me aboard. There are dead spaces where fishing equipment was stored that won't be checked. In fact, if we do this, you can legitimately deny knowledge of it. If I'm caught, it'll just be on my head. You know I won't betray you."

She looked deeply unhappy. "Not voluntarily."

"Please, Noma. This is my *life*."

Mitsos knew how to bargain. To pander, to plead. To assail his opponent's vanity or compassion. He kept on at the woman.

Eventually, Noma stood. "I'll think about it."

"Thank you, Noma. But please, think quickly."

She looked down at him, gave a brusque nod, and headed for the exit of the bar.

* * *

The announcement was timed to coincide with people's regular lunch break – clearly for maximum impact.

Mitsos was sitting by himself in his nearest refectory, eating a bland meal comprising an oval-shaped piece of synthetic meat from the protein vats with three small carrots and a single potato from the hydroponics plant in the sub-level decks. The comms screens set near the ceiling in the four corners of the large, oblong space started to wink on-and-off, drawing the eyes of all around. Then the screens cleared to reveal the stern-faced image of Captain Boursis of the Apparatus, sat at a desk, looking neat in her black-and-grey uniform. A buzz of sound helped draw the attention of even the most distracted and unobservant.

"Attention, citizens," came a voice. "Attention. This is an important public announcement. Attention."

Mitsos put down his fork and pushed aside his plate. He was close to one corner and had to tip his neck back to look at the nearest screen. After a moment's pause, Boursis began to speak.

"Citizens of *Marseilles*, it is my duty to relate the result of an important judgment by the Judicial Panel of the People's Committee." The picture on the screen slowly split: to the left was Boursis, and to the right was a still picture of two men, one above the other. They were young, perhaps in their twenties or early thirties, one with fair hair, one dark, and both looking as though they had recently been in a fight, with blackened eyes and bruises all over their faces. Boursis continued: "Citizens Ty Columba and Ahmed Idrissa were accused of stealing weapons produced for the Citizen Militia in order to rend them down to component parts for sale on the black market. Two days ago they were apprehended by the Apparatus. Yesterday, they were tried by the Judicial Panel and found guilty without mitigations. In these straitened times, the Panel concluded that there could be only one punishment."

The low murmuring in the canteen had gradually subsided; Mitsos quickly glanced around and saw that all were now rapt. Back on the screen, the picture dissolved completely to be replaced by a live feed from a location towards the top of the ship, where two men were standing next to each other on a ledge, arms behind their backs, shot by a camera from just below. To the sides of the men were officers of the Apparatus, who edged around and placed something around their necks. When the officers pulled away, nooses were clearly visible. Boursis' voice continued to provide commentary. "In accordance with the Updated Penal Code, sanctioned by the First Citizen and the People's Committee in the wake of the destruction of the *Leviathan* – and in recognition of the severe implications for the resources of the *Marseilles* – the sentence will now be carried out. Citizens who steal from the community no longer deserve a place within it."

The figures were propelled forwards by some unseen force from behind, and dropped over the edge of the deck on which they stood. The camera didn't spare viewers from the brutality of the execution, indeed, the shot zoomed to show the tortured faces of the slowly strangling men. In the refectory, there were gasps of shock, the odd muttered expletive, and even a nervous laugh.

Mitsos turned away from the screen.

He'd hidden himself away from affairs ever since he'd arrived, interacting little, doing his job and returning to his tiny apartment, rarely watching the limited televisual offerings on his home screen. There could have been a dozen such executions in his months aboard and he'd not have noticed. But he certainly noticed now.

He *had* to get off the ship.

* * *

"Okay. There may be a way."

Noma had left it late. It was the evening of the third day since Mitsos had spoken to her – *pleaded* with her. He'd missed the deadline for submission of his latest damning report, but was unsurprised that he'd not been called up on this. The atmosphere on the *Marseilles* was tense. Everyone knew that something was going on, even if they didn't know the exact details, and the word *Hibernia* could be frequently heard in muttered exchanges in the refectories, state retail outlets, and corridors of the grand city ship. Patrols of the Apparatus seemed to be everywhere, and the nature of activity around the internal dock had changed dramatically: today, the fishing fleet had remained berthed, and while the two REEN trawlers had been allowed out, they'd been required to return in the early afternoon, with Mitsos being asked to leave – along with his team – soon after they docked.

Mitsos had been lurking around the exterior corridor to the dock for several hours, hoping to catch sight of Noma – and when he had at last done so, she had been trailing behind her crewmates, clearly deliberately. She'd glanced at him and silently mouthed the word 'Matelot', then continued on as though he didn't exist.

"Thank God," said Mitsos at the bar later, clenching a fist. "Noma – I could kiss you!"

The woman gave a wry smile and held up one hand. "Libby would object, so please don't."

"I could kiss her, too. So… what is it?"

Noma leant in, so her mouth was mere centimetres from his ear: Mitsos had gone straight to the old bar after seeing Noma, but the woman hadn't appeared for another eighty minutes, and when she had, she'd ignored him, got herself a drink, and then selected an upright counter near one corner so gloomy that even the grizzled patrons had forsaken it. They stood on opposite sides of the slim partition. "Don't get too excited. You don't know what I have to offer."

"At this point, anything will do. Did you see the executions yesterday? Tell me."

"The emergency equipment locker in the main cabin. It used to hold flares, spare life jackets, a medical kit. But over the years it's been mostly cleared out and the equipment hasn't been replaced. Do you remember where it is?"

Mitsos closed his eyes and thought back to his cursory induction to the *Dieppe*. He vaguely recalled… "It's that top-opening box in the cabin, around a metre long. Used as a bench."

"That's right. It's not locked. If you can get into it, the lid will drop shut, and someone will sit on top. It won't be checked, and you will be safe until we reached *Hibernia*."

Mitsos frowned. "It'll be a close fit. I hope it's not airtight or I'll suffocate."

Noma looked grim. "I cannot say for sure, but I think not. You know the state of the boat. No join is perfect or straight, not anymore. But that's all I've found. It's that or you take your chances here."

"Devil and the deep blue sea," muttered Mitsos. "No, I'll take it. But how do I get aboard?"

"That will be up to you." Noma surreptitiously looked around the bar, reassuring herself that they could not be heard. Then she leant even closer, so that Mitsos could feel her hot breath on his cheek. "We go tomorrow night – or rather, in the early hours. Three o'clock. Our closest approach to *Hibernia* is timed for then, and the enemy will be asleep and unsuspecting. But how you get there is up to you. I'm sorry I can't do more."

Mitsos pulled back slightly and looked into the other's deep brown eyes. Then he nodded. A door had been left ajar, almost literally. "Do you know when you'll be loading up?"

"About midnight. You'll need to be holed up by then. I don't know how well the ship will be watched. Not closely. No trouble is expected. But there will probably be activity all evening, testing systems, loading equipment."

Mitsos' eyes defocused as he shifted his vision internally. "I can get in to the REEN vessels tomorrow morning, even if they are not allowed out. *Probably*. Then..." he looked back up, refocused. "Then I need a maintenance jumpsuit and opportunity. But as you say, that is up to me."

Noma nodded once, then leant close one final time. "Citizen Mitsos. *Eddard*. This is it. Please... don't attempt to talk to me again. For both our sakes. Good luck." She pushed away from the counter, turned, and without looking back, made her way from the bar.

"And good luck to you, too, Noma," whispered Mitsos. "Stay safe."

Chapter 28

It had been too late the previous day for Kate to disclose the full nature of her secret to Marie, and she'd refused to provide any more detail, insisting that only *showing* would suffice. And so Marie had been forced to endure a bothersome day in the research unit, suspecting that the few photographs over which her team were raving would soon be eclipsed by something far more dramatic. Consequently, she exhibited less enthusiasm for Teixeira's analyses than she might otherwise have done.

"You don't seem that interested," said Kalmik at one point. "It looks like you were right about these farmers, but they're already yesterday's news to you. Wow!"

Marie simply winced and made a comment about feeling a little unwell.

By mid-afternoon, her listlessness was infecting everyone.

"Go, dear Marie!" said Figueroa at last. "Take the rest of the day off. Relax! Recuperate! I suspect that this is a delayed reaction to your encounter with our robust new friends in the forest."

But this proved to be a bad idea. She fretted at the apartment, awaiting Kate's return from school, and then grew increasingly frustrated as the afternoon ticked into evening, and still her daughter didn't show. It was nearly seven o' clock when she did at last come through the door.

Kate must have noticed the thunderous expression on Marie's face, for she held up her hands and gasped out: "Sorry, Mum! I had to play along with Sara to avoid suspicion. I cried off as soon as I could. The coast is now clear – we can go."

Marie followed Kate down to level zero, then through some long-forgotten doorway into a maintenance tunnel, and then down various short flights of steps.

"This isn't the most direct route," Kate said over her shoulder. "But it's the way we're used to using. The main door to the Bowl was locked, until Tonio found a way to open it from… well, from somewhere else. We still come this way, though, as there's less chance of us being seen or followed."

"The Bowl?"

"Yes, it's just through *here*." She swung open a green-painted metal door and led the way into a wide, low-ceilinged room, only faintly lit from a ceiling strip light. "Ta-dah!"

Marie followed her daughter into the space, at first unsure as to where she was. Gradually, her mind began to make sense of her surroundings: there were racks and shelves along the walls, a console deck, double doors opposite, and a dark well in the middle of the room. She edged forwards.

"Mind your step," said Kate, her hand gently clasping Marie's nearer arm. "It's a bit dark now. When we first found the place, there'd often be some light coming up through the bottom of the bowl – bioluminescent life. But that seems to have been scared away… or *eaten*."

"Eaten? What do you mean? By what?"

"Boy, are you in for a shock. Wait here." Kate disengaged her hand and then shuffled across to the console. As she took a seat and started flipping switches, she continued: "Sara likes to lay in the bottom of the bowl, but I wouldn't advise it unless you want to risk a coronary… not with these things. But why don't you lay down at the edge."

Marie did as instructed. She now realised that there was indeed a hemispherical bowl in the centre of the room, several metres across. It was a significantly smaller version of the public bowl that sat at the base of the coliseum in the centre of the ship, which was usually covered by a floor and used for sporting events or the occasional concert, but at other times was uncovered to allow the Lisboetas to admire the submarine world. At present, she could see nothing except a faint reflectance of the strip light along one of the curving sides. "Okay. What now?"

"Now hold onto your hat… or maybe your bowels. Just let me… I've got to be careful…"

Spotlights beneath the ship, along the edge of bowl, came to gentle, fuzzy life. The deep black of the water elided into a dark grey, but only so far, and then the level of illumination stabilised.

"Any more and they go a bit crazy. This should be enough to pique their interest."

Marie knew what her daughter was talking about. Somehow, the girl and her friends had found the same new lifeform that the research team had discovered in the cenote, and through their own careful experimentation uncovered the same facts as Marie's team had without even having to leave the *Lisboa*. "This is amazing, Kate. It's a perfect lab."

Kate laughed. "Oh, no. None of this is amazing, but *this* is. *Look!*"

Marie had been looking directly at her daughter; at Kate's command, she turned her head… and saw one of the creatures, darker than the ill-lit waters, floating just beyond the glass dip of the bowl. It drifted closer until it was able to press its two, long-fingered hands against the glass, its ellipsoid head, shiny like a beetle's carapace, somehow *looking* at her. Marie swore gently.

"I think it likes you," said Kate.

"It's… I'm… speechless."

"I don't get how it sees," Kate continued. "It's like a stretched person with claws and flippers, wearing a crushed motorcycle helmet."

The creature continued to drift next to the glass, intrigued. "I think it's head *is* its eyes," mused Marie. "Or *eye*. I suspect the whole surface is covered in light-sensitive cells. That would give it great all-round vision, and maybe explain why it's so sensitive to bright light."

"Yeah, I guess so." Kate had remained seated. "But where's its mouth? Under the chin?"

"Maybe…"

A second creature emerged slowly from the black, and took up position beside the first, wicked-looking hands also pressed against the bowl. And then a third emerged and took up a similar position to the other side. The three continued to 'stare' at Marie. *Directly* at her.

"Spooky, eh?" said Kate.

"Uh… yes. How long have you known about this?"

"The Bowl? Months. The creatures? A few days. A week. A bit longer?"

Marie gently shook her head. The research team had been risking their lives in the open water for nothing. But of course, how were the kids to know that? And then…

Thump.

Marie gasped and scuttled back. A fourth creature had shot from the black and struck the glass right under her chin. She swore again, this time more vigorously.

"Yeah, they do that after a while," said Kate. "It's like some try to hypnotise you, then they sneak up and attack. Sara has gone right off them. They're the reason I managed to bring us here this early." She raised her voice now: "Right, bug-eyed monsters. Attack Mum again and you know what you're going to get!"

Marie slowly got to her feet and moved across to stand beside her daughter. "You said 'attack'. Do they always become aggressive?"

"Yes. Every time. I certainly wouldn't want to get in the water with them… oh!" Kate turned to stare at Marie. "You have, haven't you?"

"I'm afraid so. But maybe… maybe no more. Not until we've studied them safely and got some idea of their behavioural triggers." As she spoke, there was another hollow thud from something striking the glass. Then another.

"Right, they've finished playing now. They'll keep this up until we turn off the lights, or until we turn them brighter, and then: *pow*! They go berserk, then disappear until next time."

"I know I promised I'd keep your secret, Kate, but I can't. This is *big*. Too big. I'm going to have to tell the Prof. and the team about this."

Kate returned a wry smile. "Yeah, I guessed that would be so. I'm not even going to get mad at you. But at least let us still come here when you're not using it. Please, Mum. I don't know how I'm going to square this with Sara as it is."

Marie touched her daughter on the arm. "I promise I'll try. Now… let's get out of here before we stir the creatures up any more. I'll contact the Prof. first and take it from there. He will be the most sympathetic."

"Fine. But you own me big time for this. And Sara. God knows how she's going to react. I think I'd rather go for a swim with the BEMs than tell her."

"BEMs? Oh, Bug-eyed..." Marie laughed. "Honestly, Kate, you wouldn't. You *really* wouldn't."

* * *

"You told your mum?" gasped Sara the next day, just after school was finished. "That's why you've been so twitchy all day."

"Oooooooh, shit!" said Tonio, looking between the two girls.

"I'm sorry, Sara, I really am. But the creatures – the BEMs – they've been causing some problems. My mum has actually been diving near them. She was attacked, and so were some of her crew."

Sara stood by the peeling green door between the hairdressers and the electronic repair shop on level zero, and gaped, her face going through various contortions.

"Breathe, Sara, *breathe*!" said Tonio, in concern.

"Apparently they've even been attacking their research boat," Kate hastily continued. "When I saw Mum looking at a picture of one of the creatures on her tablet, I had to tell her. It's *important*."

"So... so that means... what? She's there now? With all the science nerds? In *our* Bowl?"

"I guess so."

"Guess?" asked Tonio.

"Well, she called her boss yesterday evening when we got back home, and she was gone by the time I got up. She gets like that when she's into something. But she said she'd try to make it good for us so we can still go to the Bowl when they're not at work."

"*Try?*" echoed Sara, still confused; unsettled; angry?

Kate raised her hands defensively, as though expecting the other girl to launch at her. "She's good. And her boss is nice. I met him once. Professor Figueroa. I'm sure he won't–"

"Try?" repeated Sara. She backed against the door and slid down onto her backside.

Tonio knelt beside her, then Kate took a step closer and did the same.

"Sara – I'm really, really sorry."

Sara looked between her friends... and then her mouth twisted into a smile – albeit a weak one. "I understand. It's not your fault,

Kate. It's those monsters. They scared all the fish away. They scare me, too. I… don't want to watch them anymore."

Kate breathed a huge sigh of relief and Tonio chuckled: "Bloodshed averted!"

"So, what do we do now?" asked Sara.

"Well, I wouldn't go to the Bowl today. I'll check with Mum later when she's back from whatever planet she's on."

"That gives us two options then," said Tonio. "Either the control room – assuming *Kate The Snitch* hasn't told her mum about that too – or the Terrace."

Kate raised her hands again. "No, really, I didn't tell her about our other secret place. Honest! But I think Sara should decide today."

"Like every other," said Tonio, but with a smirk and a wink.

Sara nodded. "Okay. Fine. In that case, I choose neither. It's the Chilly Cow instead." Her smile was now more genuine. "And Kate has to eat a double portion of Lisboeta 'ice cream' as penance."

Kate groaned. "I think I'd rather you just hit me."

* * *

The research team had spent a week in the Bowl, having turned it into their new field lab, tidying it up, filling the empty shelves with files and cameras and assorted pieces of equipment. They'd also wrestled another desk and some additional chairs in through the main double doors to give them places to sit and work. Even so, space was cramped, given that the bowl itself took up perhaps a third of the diameter of the room, and Figueroa had decided to limit capacity to a maximum of five, with access granted to core team members only.

Currently, aside from Marie, who swivelled in the chair at the main control console, the room held Figueroa, Kalmik, Teixeira and Grande – the latter sat at the keyboard of a computer, facing a screen that projected from front and back, so that all could see what was on display.

"So, that's now eight confirmed," said Kalmik. The main room light was on, making viewing through the bowl itself almost impossible. Though the farmers might well be observing them from the other side, they assumed that the overall light level was bright enough to deter them approaching the glass too closely.

"Eight definites," said Grande. On the computer screen, pictures of eight of the farmers appeared in two rows of four, with annotations beside each indicating dimensions and relevant distinguishing features. "But undoubtedly there are more – ones we've only glimpsed."

"And Bent Finger is their leader," Kalmik asserted.

"I think so," said Marie. On the screen, Grande had highlighted one of the eight farmers, notable for having a twisted digit on its left hand. "Not only does BF show up most times, but the attitude of the others seem subservient. They flank it protectively, and get out of its way when it decides to move."

"A hierarchy," said Figueroa, seated on a chair at the edge of the bowl, facing the others. "Dextrous hands. Evidence of cultivation – though we haven't actually seen them at work in their fields. They are clearly intelligent. But *how* intelligent?"

"And what sort of society do they have?" wondered Kalmik. "Do they have underwater cities in the deep black? Or are they like most other sea life we have seen – free swimming."

"We haven't seen them using any tools," noted Marie. "And I'm not sure what material they could use to build homes or other civic structures, unless they somehow use the kelp to make shelter – like weaverbirds on Earth."

"Yes, maybe so," said Figueroa. "Perhaps lower down, away from the light, maybe on the stems or between them. How I wish we had a decent submersible."

"*Taiwan* has two," said Kalmik. "Or so I heard. And doesn't *Hibernia* have one as well? Unused? Couldn't we ask to borrow it?"

"We did once, dear Katerina, some years ago. Their response was to ask what we would pay to rent it. And that was back when we might have actually had something to trade. I am certainly happy to ask them again – we're virtually in their backyard at the moment – although I fear they have become *more* rather than *less* grasping. So, we should not hold out too great a hope there."

"Would you really like to go down *there* in a sub?" asked Marie, with a grin. "I mean, having seen what they can do to a boat of the surface?"

"Me? No fucking way!" said Kalmik. "I'm happy to leave that to you, Mike and Raul. Or we could perhaps pilot it remotely."

Marie saw a wry smile snake across Grande's face at the computer. It had been noticeable that over recent times, Kalmik had been less mocking of his lack of bravery; now she tended to simply ignore him. "True – but I'm not sure it would come back in one piece, if at all. Could we afford the Hibernian's indemnity?"

Figueroa frowned. "Another good point. So, let's set that idea aside for now. Let's focus on what we can do, here and now, and preferably, in the safety of this space."

Marie frowned and shifted uncomfortably. "I think *safety* is the operative word, Prof. Intelligence and aggression might not be entirely synonymous concepts, but there seems to be some sort of corelation. It's not just humans that can be cruel – we've seen it in other intelligent species, too, like chimpanzees. These farmers are likely to be territorial, and have the wits to defend what is theirs, and maybe even to act in concert. And we don't know how many farmers there are, or how organised they are, or how far they will go to defend themselves and deter us. I get the impression that they are studying us as much as we are them, and I don't like the way they follow observation with targeted attacks on the glass at different points and from different directions."

"And it's not just the bowl," said Teixeira, who sat beside Grande. "They also took their time before striking at the *Fortunata* and the dive cage."

"Perhaps," said Figueroa, "though I wouldn't call those *unprovoked* attacks. Remember, we are in their domain now. If the situation were reversed, I am sure we would also be robust."

"Ha! We'd probably wipe them out completely, just to be sure," said Kalmik. "We're one intelligent species that certainly does have form in the genocide arena."

"Indeed, Katerina," said Figueroa. "However, I think we are both presently safe from each other. I just wonder whether it might be possible to communicate with them. That's what I'd like to try next.

They do seem interested enough to concentrate on us. What sort of scheme could we try? Some sort of show and tell? Let's assemble tomorrow for a brainstorm in the main seminar room."

"Tomorrow?" Something had been nagging at the back of Marie's mind. *The date.* "Ah… *tomorrow.* I think we are going to be communicating with our new subjects quite loudly then regardless, and I'm not sure the message we'll be sending is all that positive. Professor, didn't you say that Captain-Governor Nacimiento plans to unleash the harvesters tomorrow?"

"Ah, Marie, I fear you are right."

"So, how do you think they'll feel about us trashing their crops?"

Kalmik swore and Figueroa started in his seat. "I think I shall call Joao immediately. Katerina… Marie… would you care to accompany me to a meeting? For moral support?"

* * *

Nacimiento listened to their evidence patiently. He already knew that the science team had found some unusual new life, but Figueroa had not elaborated on its likely intelligence.

"So, old friend," said the Captain-Governor, "are you suggesting that this new super-kelp, with which you have enticed us, is now out of bounds? That we must leave these environs hungry?"

"I appreciate how much we need to resupply. I am not saying entirely, *no*. Katerina? Marie?"

Marie had remained silent during Figueroa's presentation – held in Nacimiento's small private cabin just off the control room – as had Kalmik sat beside her. She now met Figueroa's pained glance, noticed Kalmik pout and exhale, and decided it was time. "Well, Professor, if we don't care about pillaging and destroying the crops and gardens of possibly the only other intelligent species that has been discovered outside Earth, then go ahead. I am sure future historians will be kind to us, and absolutely *won't* group us with all the other rapacious human colonisations in the past, and *nor* will they compare us to the ecosystem-fucking humans of the twentieth and twenty-first centuries." She folded her arms.

"Ouch!" said Figueroa.

Kalmik stirred and turned to look at her. "That's a bit of an exaggeration, Marie. I don't think anyone's suggesting we harvest the whole forest."

"Now? No. But this is how it starts. Remember the Amazon rain forest?"

"Again, *exaggeration.* We're one ship out of around twenty on a vast planet. We're not going to get out of control like we did on Earth. There are huge resource constraints – as we're experiencing now. Whatever we take isn't going to make a dent in the volume of sea forest here. A fraction of a fraction of a *fraction* of a percent. We're plucking a few apples from a single tree in a vast orchard. I think the farmers can spare it."

Marie shook her head slowly. "I can't believe you're suggesting this, Katerina. Or you, Professor. We don't know how many farmers there are, or how badly they need the kelp, or how close they are to subsistence levels."

As Figueroa continued to look troubled, and Nacimiento observed without comment, Kalmik shook her own head. "Oh, Marie, *come on.* Look at the size and health of the forest? Does this strike you as an environment on the edge? You've come here with a typically idealistic Earther perspective. Sometimes we have to make tough decisions. Don't we deserve to survive too?"

"I thought you agreed with the importance of our find?" said Marie. "Of doing careful research? Where did this come from?"

"I do agree, but I'm not dogmatic like you. The Captain-Governor didn't sail us all the way here just to do a research project. I wish the world revolved around us entirely, but it doesn't."

Nacimiento cleared his throat. "Yes, thank you, Dr Kalmik. I am pleased that you appreciate the bigger picture and my responsibilities."

"Professor?" said Marie.

"Ah, dear Marie, this is a dilemma. Of course you are right, but I hate to admit that Katerina also has a point."

"But if we start collecting… what about the farmers? We can't see where they are? We might kill some. Kill many. And again, we don't know how they will react."

"There is a risk, yes," agreed Figueroa. "But I think we can ameliorate it. Joao…" he turned to face the Captain-Governor. "Could we send out trawlers, rather than using the sweeps along the *Lisboa's* arms? I realise this is inefficient, but it would enable us to control the size and depth of out harvesting better. Take the top few metres, like a haircut. We have never seen the creatures in the upper areas of the forest during daytime – presumably because of the daylight penetrating these, and so–"

"Professor, that's not quite true," interrupted Marie. "They came near the surface when we went down in the cage."

"In the cenote, Marie," said Kalmik. "Not the fringe forest."

"Well, we can't be sure. Also… also, the boats will provide shadows, like the *Lisboa* does. We've seen the farmers under the bowl during daytime."

Kalmik gave a frustrated gasp and threw up her hands. "Really, Marie, you're getting absurd now. I agree with Miguel. We can give the forest a haircut as he says. It won't destroy the forest, and it's highly unlikely to kill any farmers. And the noise of the harvesters will probably drive them away, rather than attract them."

"You can't be sure–"

Nacimiento held up both hands, slowly, the light from the ceiling catching the gold emblems of status on his sleeves. "People! Please! Dr Lockard, you give an eloquent defence…" he smiled at her wistfully, his craggy face crinkling at the corners of the eyes and mouth, "but Miguel and Dr Kalmik have, I think, recognised certain necessities. Miguel, old friend…" he lowered his arms and looked at Figueroa. "I will delay the harvesting by a day. And it will proceed carefully, as you request. Please come up with a plan as to how we can do this with minimal likely harm to these farmers and their ecosystem, and I will consider it. By tomorrow?"

Figueroa nodded slowly. "Thank you, Joao. We'll get right on it."

When they left, Marie stalked ahead of the others and refused to look back.

* * *

They first realised that something was wrong during their lunch break.

Lisboa's sole school allowed pupils an hour for lunch. Younger children were required to eat at a small refectory within the school itself, but teens were allowed to go where they pleased, with many returning to their home apartments – nowhere being more than five minutes' walk away from the complex. But others chose to eat with friends at one of the three state refectories situated around the coliseum at the heart of the city ship, where basic but nutritious food was available to all.

Tonio noticed it first. "What's going on over there?" He pointed between Kate and Sara, who sat opposite. They were in the Refectory Almeida, on Level Three, which only had a small frontage onto the well of the coliseum, but was deep, with its walls covered in murals depicting a quaint old town and rolling hills and forests. "They seem wired."

Kate and Sara turned as one to look at where he was pointing. Kate saw a small group of people, a couple sitting, several standing, talking excitedly. One man was gesticulating; a couple held hands over mouths. Another man touched one of his colleagues on the arm, then turned and hurried towards an exit. Meanwhile, others seated nearby started to look around at the animated discussion. A woman from an adjacent table stood, jerkily, and paced over to join the debate; the level of noise started to rise. Someone emitted a partly restrained shriek; a couple more jumped to their feet and headed towards the main exit…

"Whatever it is," said Kate, "it's not good."

"Something's happened," agreed Sara. "Something *bad*."

"Everyone's looking now," said Tonio, waving his hand to indicate the rest of the diners.

Kate saw it was true. It was then that she noticed a small light winking on her tablet, which she'd placed on the table beside her plate of food. She tapped, and the screen came alive. "Uh-oh. Message from school." Sara turned to look down at the tablet too, but Tonio continued to scan the room, craning his neck this way and that, trying to catch words from those around. "It says: *In light of today's events, lessons this afternoon are cancelled*."

"As my dad would say, *fuck*!" said Tonio, now looking down and trying to read the tablet from upside down. "Does it explain why?"

Kate scanned the message, then summarised. "No. It just says that younger children will remain there, until collected by parents. Others can choose where to go. Uh… and it mentions pastoral services, available to whoever needs them."

"Pastoral!" said Sara. "You mean… the school shrink who talks to people when…" She couldn't finish.

By now, the exodus from the refectory had gathered pace. Kate looked about, as did her friends. But while Tonio and Sara gaped, she reached out a hand and managed to snare the arm of a woman in brown work overalls. "Sorry… miss… sorry. What is going–?"

"They're gone." The woman's face was pale, her hair – which had been tied up into some sort of bun – was unravelling around her face. "Sunk. Both of them."

"Both of…?"

"The harvesters. The two sent to… Oh, sorry, I must…" She disengaged her arm and hurried off.

"No!" said Sara. "Two ships? In these waters?"

"Shit!" said Tonio, eyes wide. "Some of the kids… Manuel. Maybe Sofia. They have parents on the boats."

"Maybe not these boats, though," said Sara, firmly. "It's only two."

"Two! We've never lost two before," said Tonio. "In fact, we haven't lost one since the *Aventura* six years ago. What could have caused it?"

Kate looked grim. She knew, and after a moment, her friends' expressions changed, suggesting they realised too.

"Monsters!" said Sara.

They decided that, for once, it might be most responsible to split and return to their respective homes. On the way, Kate came across a group of people clustered beneath an information monitor, showing the ship's main news presenter sitting at a desk, looking solemn, the border of the image in black. As Kate looked up at the screen, she caught the announcer's fateful words: "… all hands lost."

Chapter 29

The satellite link was cut.

In the Comms Centre, Heiko – who'd sat with De Voe to the side of the conference table out of camera shot – watched the rulers of *Stavanger* closely. Olson shook her head slowly, her expression grim; Moroni looked enraged, as though about to leap up to assault the monitor that had recently displayed the triumvirate from *Hibernia*; while Bulow… Bulow slumped in her seat, holding a hand before her eyes.

"*Bastards!*" hissed Moroni, at last. "A *good behaviour* bond?"

De Voe had managed to control herself throughout the short meeting. She now exhaled deeply, getting rid of all the air she'd held in while listening to the preposterous and patronising lecture from O'Neill. "And Makka… a *guest*? Fuck is he a guest. He's a fucking hostage!"

Olson turned to look at De Voe and Heiko. She wearily waved a hand. "Melissa, Rennie, why don't you join us."

Heiko and De Voe moved to sit to one side of Moroni, who was nearest to them. Heiko noticed that this made the balance of the table lopsided, with Bulow outnumbered by those facing her. *Aptly*, he thought. She'd been invited by Olson, with Moroni unable to contest the move, given that the ploy to enhance Bulow's status had been her own idea.

"Okay," began Olson, "let's try to think matters through–"

But before she got any further, Bulow groaned: "I'm *sorry*." She continued to shield her eyes, her head bowed even lower, her chin resting on her chest. "I didn't think… didn't think it would come to this." She took away her hand and looked up, her eyes teary.

Moroni looked as though she were about to turn her wrath from the screen to the other, her eyes wide, but Olson quickly reached one hand across and grasped her forearm. "Hanna?" Her firm expression gentled. She didn't need to say any more: the single word was an invitation to unburden.

"You were right. Margarethe... Nila... I'm so sorry. I didn't mean to put the ship at risk. Or Dr Frost. I was just meant to keep them updated on events here. It seemed innocent enough. I thought they were just interested in our general affairs for the sake of it."

"What did they offer you?" asked Moroni, speaking low.

"Little. Just a promise of good relations. Of influence. Some status in the future–"

"To replace me?" continued Moroni. "And Margarethe?"

"No! Not formally. Not a coup. Just... a chance in the future to present myself as their preferred candidate. As someone who could deal with them to our *mutual* benefit. I mean, it seemed a good strategic move. After all, I was achieving nothing here by myself."

Moroni scoffed a laugh and sat back in her chair, waving one hand dismissively.

Olson glanced at Moroni quickly, then looked back and asked: "How long, Hanna? When?"

"Two years. On our last visit to the area. We went to that reception on *Hibernia.* Us three and our partners at the time. Solbakken. Cass. We were kept late, and then it seemed to make sense to stay overnight. But the embassy isn't big, so some of us were put up elsewhere. It was Manfred Traore who approached me. I was... going through a rough patch."

"With Jorgen," nodded Olson. "I remember. You split as soon as you got back."

"Yes, that's right. Traore was so... *compelling.*"

Moroni laughed again, but this time with less venom. "They don't call him *The Charmer* for nothing."

"Even now I'm not sure what happened. He may have slipped something into my drink. But it was fun. He was interesting and persuasive, and he seemed to be asking for so little – just a bit of information now and then. Until a couple of weeks ago, I'd only sent three messages. The last was after we took position off Ardol. I spoke to Traore. He said they'd send an invitation for another reception, but nothing arrived. I guess the *Leviathan* took their minds off of it."

"And since you told them about our find?" asked Olson.

"Nothing – I swear. In fact, I didn't even get to speak to Traore – I got some bored functionary. Maybe that's why it took a few days for them to get organised?"

Heiko now leant in. "Ms Bulow, did no one contact you from the boarding party? Colonel Joseph, for example?"

"No. I think she knows about me, but… no."

"It must suck to be ignored after you've sold out yourself and your ship." But Moroni was calm now, her observation almost wry. "And no envelope of Tethyn credits, either?"

Bulow looked directly at Moroni. She seemed tired now, the tears at the corners of her eyes reabsorbed or surreptitiously wiped away. "We have had our difficulties, Nila. I don't deny this may have played a part in me doing what I did, and maybe I did hope to overshadow you once more. You have a right to be angry with me. But what the Hibernians have done puts the future of the ship at risk. With no access to materials from Earth, and our reserves confiscated, everything that breaks now is going to be hard to repair. They have decided to look out for themselves and fuck everyone else. It's understandable. But I am still a Stavangeran. I will do what I have to do to make this right."

"Really?" said Moroni. "And what might that be? What do you think we should do?"

Bulow's expression firmed. "Why, it's obvious. We have to get our stuff back. *All* of it."

Olson raised her eyebrows in surprise; Moroni laughed once more, then continued: "Sure. But how? Using *your* influence? Do you want us to leave while you use the satellite link to place a call?"

Bulow shook her head slowly. "No. I'm not going to beg. They've used me."

"Then what *are* you suggesting, Hanna?" asked Olson.

Bulow turned to look at Heiko. "*Him.* Use Heiko. Give him whatever he wants. Let him do whatever he wants to do." Anger now crossed her face. "And Mr Heiko, if you want to put a bullet between *that bastard's* eyes, please feel free to do so."

Moroni slapped the table with one palm. "That's more like it!"

But Olson was troubled. "Hanna… Nila… think about what you are saying. I share your passion for revenge, but Rennie is one man with few resources. I doubt whether he could even get aboard the *Hibernia*, let alone retrieve our resources and Makka. And then what? War with *Hibernia*?"

Heiko cleared his throat. He had been mulling over such matters for the last couple of days, ever since they'd become aware of the Hibernians' theft. "I have been thinking about what a military response might look like. I think a surgical strike, with minimal causalities, *might* be possible. Margarethe – you mentioned 'war', but I don't think it is likely to come to that."

"Please convince me, Rennie."

"For a start, as I noted before, they lack the resources to actually conquer and hold us. We *allowed* them to board last time. If they try to return, I'll have an armed force ready to respond. We'll sink most of their boats before they get close. I don't believe they are stupid. If we manage to get back with our goods, they are likely to suck it up and accept the stalemate. We have a moral right; if they try to attack us it will undermine them politically across the planet, won't it, especially when they fail?"

"I think he's got a point," said Moroni.

But Olson wasn't convinced. "I'll accept your analysis on the prospects of war. But if we do this, it will sever our link to them forever. We'll certainly not be invited back to Ardol. And worse, I think we can assume that when ships do start to visit again from Earth – whenever that might be – that anything shipped for us will be retained. They will cut us off from all Earth resources."

Moroni frowned. "I'm not sure that's true, Margarethe. They may make things difficult, but I doubt whether they'll break the diplomatic code. We will still have Solbakken at the embassy. Any orders he places on our behalf can come in a diplomatic bag. Perhaps the worst is that they would refuse entry of goods from a shuttle – but *Hibernia* isn't the only point of entry."

"*Taiwan*," said Bulow. "They have a runway and receive their own shipments separately."

"Yes, that's right." Moroni was nodding slowly to herself. "It might mean having to relocate to the southern hemisphere. Change our strategic orientation. But that is worst case." She looked directly at Olson. "But even that may not be necessary. As long as Heiko doesn't do too much damage, who would we be falling out with? *Hibernia?* The people of *Hibernia*? Or the current regime? History turns. They've been in power for some time. Their acts against us reek of desperation. They cannot last forever. Maybe whoever follows will be more conciliatory?"

Olson broke eye contact with Moroni. She looked down at the table top, then closed her eyes. Heiko watched the others around the table as they watched their leader. In the end, Olson was Premier and they would do what she said. At last, the silver-haired woman opened her eyes and turned to face Heiko. "Rennie – can you do it? A rescue mission, not an assault? Minimal casualties – and preferably none?"

Heiko took time to answer. "Is it possible? Maybe. But military endeavours almost never go as planned. You need to accept that there are likely to be difficulties. Still, if this is your command, then I am happy to try it."

Olson looked first at Moroni and then at Bulow. Both nodded without speaking. "Very well. Plan your raid, Rennie, and ensure our defences are prepared in case it fails."

"And *also* in case it succeeds," added Moroni.

Heiko nodded firmly, once, and stood to leave.

* * *

The Hibernian Institute of Science was a relatively new building, a two-storey structure made from local stone, part of a terrace situated within easy reach of the eastern docks. Makka Frost had been provided accommodation on the upper floor in a hastily converted storeroom, which now contained a single bed set among shelves and assorted filing cabinets. And being a storeroom, the place had a lock to keep out potential pilferers, or in this case, keep in 'guests'. When he was allowed out after his first night (having spent the two previous nights in the Security section in a purpose-built cell), he noticed a chair outside the door, which he guessed had been occupied all night by his military chaperone.

He now sat at a mid-sized conference table on the lower floor. This held a variety of breakfast items, including juices, coffee, and pastries. Opposite, with half-finished drinks and plates scattered with residual crumbs, sat three others: Drs Moses Killan, Francesca Brown, and Ravindra Singh. His guard presumably waited outside the room's closed door.

"I'm sorry, Makka, I didn't intend for this to happen," said Killan, the Head of the Institute, a man in his sixties with a good head of auburn hair that was untinged by grey. "When we were alerted to your discovery, we were asked how useful it would be to speak to you, and I naturally said that it would be great. I didn't realise that the ESU would translate my words in the way it has; I didn't intend for you to be kidnapped. Please believe me!"

Frost looked at the three sat opposite and recognised their anguish as sincere. He had met them all before – both physically and through video conferences – to talk shop: Brown many times, and Killan and Singh at least twice. Two years ago, during the *Stavanger's* previous residency at Ardol, he had spent three days on *Hibernia* as a true guest, and even been given a tour of the mining site on Athol. These were simply scientists who were dedicated to their profession and had little interest in matters of politics. He sighed and gave his head a gentle shake, then considered the spread before him. He poured himself a coffee, then added whitener from a pot, and stirred. "Don't worry, Moses," he said at last. "I do believe you. But that doesn't change my situation. I am still here against my will, watched by a guard, unable to leave."

"I will tell Security that we have talked. That you have cooperated. And that we don't need to keep you any longer."

"Thank you. But I'm not sure it'll make much difference. I think my presence here suits your masters. It gives them leverage over the *Stavanger.* And it's an insurance policy in case they experience any difficulties at the site."

"Difficulties?" wondered Brown. Like the others, she was neatly dressed, as though this were a formal interview. She was a thin woman in her late forties, with long straight hair and sharp cheekbones. "What do you mean?"

Frost gave a lopsided smile. "Oh, I don't know. Maybe something unexpected in one of the drill holes that might prove *challenging*? Coordinates that are subtly off?"

"You haven't sabotaged the pitch, have you?" Singh appeared shocked. He was bearded, neat, and had a slight paunch. "Makka – not you!"

Frost held up his hands. "Please, don't get me wrong. There's nothing that I or any of my team could do to hide, contaminate, or invalidate the deposit we found. But that doesn't mean we couldn't have a little fun. Work out our irritation. Between me and you, of course."

The three looked among themselves uncertainly. "Ah… I understand, Makka," said Killan. "I can't say as I approve, but under the circumstances, who's to say we wouldn't do the same. There's no danger…?"

Frost realised that he shouldn't have spoken. These people weren't his friends even if they weren't his enemies. "No, Moses, nothing harmful. And I've said too much. I assume you will be the ones taken to the dig to supervise it?"

They again exchanged glances. "That's right," said Killan. "Francesca and Ravindra will both be going. Tomorrow, in fact. I am less of a field operative nowadays."

"Okay. Well, guys, you have been warned. Consider the matter an intellectual challenge. A puzzle. I only wish I had weaker adversaries." He smiled and took a sip of his coffee. "I hope this heads-up will suffice. Of course, you could always tell the uniformed lot. Maybe they'd try to beat the information out of me."

Killan raised both hands. "No! Makka, please do not concern yourself about this. But…" he looked unsettled. "But… it *does* occur to me that it would be useful for you to join us. At the dig and… also here? We would love to work with you. I think my colleagues wouldn't disagree if I were to say that you are the premier geologist on Tethys." He looked to left and right, where the others looked serious, though each nodded gently. "I hate to say this, but *Hibernia* is going to be the place to be over the next few years, as we establish this mine and do more thorough surveys of the area around the pitch. We'd love to pick up your contract."

"Ah!" Frost slowly sat back in his seat. *The offer*. He'd half expected it. And maybe this was the real reason he was here. Perhaps Killan had said as much when asked about him, ensuring his kidnapping.

"That is very kind of you, Moses, but I do have a contract with *Stavanger*, and I am a man of some principle."

"You don't need to decide now," said Killan hurriedly. "Please take your time. There's no rush."

"Sure – there's no rush if they are going to keep me here. Is that going to happen, Moses? Do you know more than you're letting on?"

Again the other raised his hands. "No, really, this is not in my jurisdiction. I will make representation for your return, but in case I am unsuccessful, let us at least keep you here in some comfort. And maybe in the meantime we can talk some more about geology?"

Frost gave a noncommittal shrug. "I suppose it beats staring at the walls of a cell."

"Ah… yes. Is there anything else we can do for you? I mean, while we wait to hear about your–"

"Fate?" Frost smiled wryly. "I suppose more coffee would be a good start. And perhaps you could let my people know where I am. Magnus Solbakken at the embassy for one." He watched the others look among themselves once more, and concluded: "He really doesn't bite!"

"Okay," said Brown, at last. "I've spoken to Mr Solbakken once or twice. I suppose I could drop by and let him know. That's hardly a breach of instructions, is it?"

"No, I guess not," said Killan, though he sounded far from certain. "Very well. Francesca – you do that, and I will see to Makka's other request. More coffee shouldn't be a problem."

Oh well, thought Frost, *I might as well make myself comfortable*. The coffee in *Hibernia* was *so* much better than on the *Stavanger*. Perhaps captivity wasn't all bad?

* * *

Melissa De Voe watched Heiko conclude the presentation of his initial plan, four hours after the meeting with *Stavanger's* leaders.

"…but these are provisional thoughts only," said the man, gesturing at the 2D projection on the wall of the main meeting room in the Security section. "Comments? Questions?"

There were about a dozen security personnel scattered around the space, some sitting, others propped on tables, still others standing against the walls. Pedersen was close to the front: he shook his head and laughed. "I don't know why you've called this a 'planning meeting', sir. It looks like you've got everything sorted already."

"Not so, Anders. This is merely an outline. Who I want to take with me and what I want to do. The fine details are where the mission succeeds or fails, and there are still a lot of holes. The main one is how we get us…" he waved an arm to encompass the uniformed personnel currently in the room, "to here…" he pointed at a spot on the schematic of *Hibernia*, "and back home again, safely, and *with* our booty."

De Voe watched the discussion play out. It didn't take long to realise – even in the absence of military training – that Heiko was right: there were a lot of holes in the plan. One of these concerned the lack of intel on their various targets. Although they had a good idea where the stolen containers would be stored – given familiarity within the team of the geography of *Hibernia* – they had no idea where Makka Frost was being held, and they weren't likely to get that until they were in *Hibernia* itself, at which point they planned to let loose Claude Vardem, their electronics ace, to have at their enemy's systems. But while they were fairly confident that he would be able to do the hack, finding the relevant information was not guaranteed. In any case, without this information beforehand, they couldn't plan the rescue, and had no idea how long they would need to stay in enemy territory – for stay they must until all was done, as it was clear they'd only get one shot at this.

Consequently, the mission was expected to require at least one night holed up in *Hibernia*. And here the second major problem arose: as they'd have to sneak aboard, their only realistic base was the embassy building. Though Solbakken would be surprised at the team's arrival, he'd certainly be cooperative. But the size of his venue restricted their numbers, which was why Heiko had limited his raiding party to about a dozen.

The third issue was how to get to *Hibernia* in the first place. A shuttle landing was infeasible, given that they couldn't turn up out of the blue, for the Hibernians' air traffic system would alert their foe.

That meant they had to come by sea, where – Vardem assured them – there was no sophisticated ship tracking system. "But you won't be able to dock anonymously," Vardem concluded. He had supplanted Heiko at the tactical display, and loaded a variety of shots of the Hibernian docks onto the screen. "Whether West or East – the military or public docks – these will shut down at sunset, so we can't just creep in. And if we arrive before sunset, the dockmaster will record our presence when they allocate us a berth, and so there will go any secrecy. Maybe it would be best to draw close and then to swim?"

"In these waters?" said one of the men in the audience. "Are you mad?"

Vardem shrugged. "It doesn't have to be far, and only the once. As Commander Heiko says, we'll have to steal a cargo boat to get away with our prize anyway."

"It'll be once all right!" said another from the crowd – to some laughter.

Pedersen was perched on the opposite side of the room to Heiko. He'd said little during the discussion so far. Now he raised a hand to draw the room's attention. "I think you're dismissing the boat option too quickly. While a visit might draw some attention, it might not be *significant* attention."

To De Voe, Pedersen seemed uncomfortable. Heiko clearly noticed something too. "What are their procedures for visiting craft?" he said. "I'm assuming they're something like the immigration procedures at the spaceport, which weren't exactly friendly."

Pedersen slowly shook his head. "No, not at all. The Hibernians' concern is new visitors from Earth – not visitors from elsewhere on Tethys. There's no immigration control at the docks – why would there be? The only visitors they get from outside their state are usually pleasure craft from other city ships that are passing through en route to Ardol. There are too few of these to make a fuss. So, a visitor would go into the dockmaster's books, and probably no further."

Heiko smiled. "You have an advantage over us, Anders. I am new, and none of the troops seem to have experience of this matter. Did you acquire this knowledge from Cass Remillard? He has a boat. Perhaps we should invite him to join us?"

"Cass? Ah, no. Personal experience. I have my own boat. Didn't you know?"

De Voe coughed in surprise, drawing Heiko's attention. Once she locked eyes with him, she smiled and raised her eyebrows. She'd told Heiko before that he ought to check boat registry if he wanted to follow the trail of onboard corruption. Heiko clearly understood her non-vocal message, for he frowned and nodded once before turning back to Pedersen.

The discussion continued for another half-an-hour as the plan was refined further. Pedersen's revelation at least gave them a new option for getting to *Hibernia*, though Heiko's deputy was unhappy at the prospect of using his own pride and joy in the operation and pointed out that his boat would only accommodate half the strike team.

"Cass owns the biggest private boat," Pedersen concluded. "You might just squeeze the team below decks on that."

The mission was set to leave in the late afternoon on the following day, arriving at *Hibernia* just before sunset, enabling them to take advantage of darkness to creep off the boat from the East Dock.

"Right – that gives us about twenty hours to prepare," concluded Heiko. "Anders – I'll leave this with you. Meantime, I need to visit Cass and then, I suspect, the Premier to get an Executive Order after he says 'no'."

De Voe followed Heiko out of the room, then along the corridor and through the exit from the Security section. At the first opportunity, she pulled him up.

"Rennie – there's one more thing that's not been discussed."

Heiko looked at her, his face inscrutable. "No. Sorry, Melissa."

She smiled back as sweetly as she could – not a natural expression for her: she suspected it probably looked scary to an external observer. "I'm acting Head of Material Resources. I have a *lot* of skin in this game. I'm best placed to identify our plundered resources. I know Solbakken better than you or Pedersen or anyone else who's going, and, of course, I know Makka and might be able to guess what he's up to. You can call me the liaison officer if you like, but I *am* going."

Heiko's expression softened. After a moment, he sighed. "Of course you are, Melissa. But I had to try."

She nodded. "Thanks for not trying too hard. Now, shall we go and twist Cass' arm? You can sit on him while I apply the thumbscrews."

Heiko gave a small bow. "Whatever you say, Ms De Voe."

* * *

An Executive Order hadn't been required. When the issue was raised with Remillard, he'd agreed to the requested loan of his boat – though on the proviso that he captained it on the raid. With De Voe also added to the line up, and after a frank appraisal by Remillard of his craft's capacity, the mission team had been reduced by four. Aside from Heiko and Pedersen, there were now just seven other troopers from the Security unit, and several fewer cases of gear.

And that wasn't all.

"It's going to be at least a Grade Three," the meteorologist had said. "Quite possibly a Four. And… well… I don't want to speculate further."

They'd had reasonable weather over the last month – fine, warm, and with little more than the occasional shower. There was usually a price to be paid for these spells, though, with Tethys Nature balancing out over the long run. And that balancing was about to start.

"It's coming from the north-west, and will follow you to *Hibernia*," the meteorologist had continued. "Expect heavy rain by mid-afternoon."

And so the plan had changed again, and around eleven a.m. the next day – several hours earlier than scheduled – the *Cormorant* launched from its dry dock into the vast blue-green ocean, with Remillard at the wheel and the sparsely equipped raiding party squeezed aboard.

"At least the wind is in our favour," Remillard said, as the *Stavanger* fell away to their stern. In his hi-tech wheelhouse, he controlled all the sheets to the sail, as well as the battery operated motor. "It'll save us charge and speed us on our way."

De Voe and Heiko were with him in the enclosed cabin towards the front of the boat on an upper deck. "It's an odd design," said

Heiko. "Like a hybrid between a traditional sailing ship and a motor yacht."

"You noticed, eh?" said Remillard, raising his bushy brows. "It's a Tethys thing. The sail is just to give us the illusion that we are proper sailors: it would be foolish on these oceans to not have a powerful motor with a decent range. But with the materials for replacing and rejuvenating batteries in short supply, the sailing ship is likely to make a proper comeback soon."

"I don't like the look of those clouds," said De Voe. "How long will it take to get to *Hibernia*?"

"We're maybe eighty kilometres away since we moved away from Ardol." Remillard motioned towards the volcanic chain visible off to the port side, which was a jagged line of brown on the horizon. "I don't want to draw too close to the Range in case we come into contact with a patrol and are asked questions, and I want to minimise use of the batteries too, just in case. So, we could be there in four hours."

"Before the heavy rain is due?" asked Heiko.

"From what the met people say, yes. That's what you want, isn't it?"

Heiko frowned. "Not *quite*. I'd like to get close, then await the downpour. I assume any fishing boats and leisure craft will be harboured by then, and people will be in shelter rather than loitering along the docks with inquisitive eyes."

"Gotcha. Try to make the best from adversity. I approve. Sure. If we're in the environs and the rain hasn't arrived, I'll dawdle until it does."

"Thanks, Cass. I think I'll go see how the others are settling in. Melissa?"

De Voe gave a small shake of the head. "I don't want to get in your way. I'll stick here for a bit."

Heiko exited the cabin.

For several minutes, De Voe sat in a padded chair behind Remillard, watching as he gently coaxed the wheel and occasionally touched some illuminated button or fiddled with some other control. A small radar screen on a panel near the wheel remained blank, confirming the lack of sea traffic in their environs. After a while, Remillard began to hum.

On heading out from the recessed dock of the *Stavanger*, the water had appeared a light blue under the sun of Tethys, though it didn't take long for clouds to begin to accumulate, producing darker shadows over the water. And within twenty minutes, the sunlight disappeared completely and the water became almost black. Around this time, the wind began to strengthen and Remillard cut off his humming and began to mutter and pay more heed to his controls. The journey had been smooth, but now wind-driven waves made the going bumpier. On top of this, there was the occasional thump and groan, as though the ship had struck some underwater barrier. De Voe at first thought she was imagining things, but on the third occasion a low noise and creak was accompanied by a distinct jerking of the boat, causing her to pitch to one side and take an armrest in the kidneys.

"Fuck! What was *that*? Just a wave?"

Remillard flicked a quick glance over his shoulder, then faced forwards again, presenting the back of his head to her: grey hair, thinning towards the top. "Could be. But probably something below getting in the way."

"Something? It felt quite big."

"Well, sure. There's lot of big things down there. You know that."

"Hell, the only time I get to sea is when shuttling between Ardol and the *Stavanger*. Never had a major incident… well, not for some time." Then she remembered the last time she'd been on the skiff with Frost, and how he tended to sit in the centre of the boat, away from the sides, gripping his lifejacket in firm hands. It made her smile. "How big a problem is it to you?"

"I'd be lying if I said it was no problem. But the *Cormorant* is double-hulled polycarbonate – like most of our yachts and trawlers. She's tough, and big enough to deter most things."

"But what about that last bump?"

Remillard shrugged and didn't turn. "Maybe something too slow in getting out of the way. Or something coming up for an experimental nibble."

"So… deranged Hibernians, a Class Four storm, and sea monsters? Just a nice, relaxing jaunt."

Remillard chuckled, though he soon returned to his humming.

An hour or so later, De Voe made her excuses then made her rocky way to the main cabin. On entering, she found a small, fixed table, with bench seating around three sides. Heiko and Pedersen were here, along with the sharp-faced man called Claude Vardem. All were hunched over a tablet displaying a schematic.

"Ah… am I interrupting? Sorry."

The three men looked up. Heiko smiled. "Did you just apologise, Melissa?"

"Fuck! It must have slipped out. Anyway, I'll–"

"No, don't worry. Come in. We're about done. Frankly, we've got as far as we can without seeing the real lie of the land. Grab a seat."

Vardem began to rise. "I'll just…"

"Sure, Claude," said Heiko. "We'll revisit this later."

The man squeezed out from around the table and took the door outside, passing De Voe.

"Watch yourself out there," she said. "Rain's just started." She took the vacated seat next to Heiko, opposite Pedersen. "So… everything sorted? And where are the others?"

"Getting comfy in the hold, I hope," said Heiko. "Which reminds me, we need to sort out alibis. When we come in, us three and Cass will present as the full crew while the others hide up. In case we're asked, I suggest you become Remillard's niece."

"Does he have a niece?"

"Well, he does now. Mary Remillard, perhaps?"

"Fine. But are they going to ask? ID cards? Finger prints?"

Heiko turned to Pedersen. "Anders?"

"Well, I have less experience than Cass, but they tend to just log the name of the captain and maybe note crew numbers. They don't have any strict rules about what to do, as visits are rare."

De Voe looked sharply at Heiko, then back to Pedersen. "It's good we've got you. Another boat owner. What are the chances, eh? So, when did you join Cass on the waves?"

Pedersen turned away and looked uninterested. "Couple of years ago, I think. It's no big thing… and nor is the boat."

"But you have been to *Hibernia* in it?" she continued.

"Twice." He paused, then looked up and away quickly. "Or maybe three times."

"You're not sure?" De Voe noticed Heiko relax backwards on his bench and thought she detected a small smile forming. "It must be a significant event."

"Well, yes. I'd forgotten about my first time. It was on our last tour. I'd just picked her up and wanted a longer run."

"Hmmm, so, once last tour, and twice this? Did you know about this, Rennie?"

"The first time was before he arrived," said Pedersen, hastily. "The second not long after."

"So – before our find?" said De Voe.

Now Pedersen did look up, and he wasn't happy. "I'm not sure what you're implying, Ms De Voe. But the answer is 'yes, before'."

She smiled broadly, unperturbed. "Oh, I'm implying nothing. Just interested. Making small talk. I was wondering if things might have changed *since* the find, but of course, you have definitely been visible in the *Stavanger* since then. I wonder about Cass, though? What do you think?"

"Cass is his own man. You'd have to ask him."

"Hmm, Rennie, perhaps we should? Important intel, don't you think?"

"Oh, yes," he laughed, "I certainly do!"

Shortly after, De Voe returned to the wheelhouse where she continued her enquiries. But Remillard didn't appear put out by the question – when she found an excuse to ask it – and admitted that he hadn't paid a visit to *Hibernia* for a couple of months, when he'd gone to see a theatre show, get drunk, and spend a couple of nights.

About ten minutes after this, the rain really started to come down. Heiko – wearing a crewman's overalls – ducked into the cabin. He was drenched.

"Well, Cass," he said, using a handkerchief to wipe the water from his face, "I doubt that dawdling will be necessary. The deluge is early. How long now?"

"An hour. Bit less." The boat keeled over to one side, causing Heiko to grab at the wall and De Voe to further bruise her kidneys. "I think I'll drop the sail now. It might be for the best."

In fact, it took them nearly an hour and a quarter, during which Remillard's humming ceased, his temperament became less even, and his swearing became more colourful. At last, spotlights set in the bow of the *Cormorant*, and around the wheelhouse, picked out the bulk of *Hibernia*, approached from the north-west. He struggled the craft around the state ship's northern edge until the eastern docks became apparent, and then he started working at a short-range radio.

Light suddenly came on, outlining the berth they'd been allocated. Remillard became tense and focused, aligning as accurately as he could, and then, once the water calmed within the sheltering arms of the dock, nudging them forwards until they were close. He barked for Heiko and Pedersen to take to the deck to secure them at their berth with ropes.

They had made it to *Hibernia*.

Now all they needed to do was slink off of the boat without being seen and find their way to the Stavangeran embassy. And while prying eyes might not prove a problem, by the looks of Heiko when he returned to the wheelhouse, drowning en route might.

Chapter 30

"Nothing," said Fukuda.

"Nothing?" Nesvorny was sat at the desk in his office, his deputy standing to attention before it.

"No, sir. It's like they disappeared. As you discovered, Babatunde Odile, Jacques Danté, and Georges Hollande left the Crown hostel two days after the shuttle took their colleagues to the *Marseilles*. As they didn't go to *O'Brien's* on the evening of the departure, we decided to pull the observation team the next morning. There seemed no point in having them watch empty space for a few stragglers."

"And no other sightings?" Nesvorny hadn't expected Fukuda to make progress with his task; that wasn't why he had given it to him.

"We don't have the sort of face recognition system they apparently use on the *Marseilles*, so we've got no camera shots." Fukuda paused a moment, then continued in softer tones: "But I did show their photographs to a couple of the prisoners from the raid. When I *insisted*, one said they *had* seen them in the Engine Quarter."

"I told you to leave the interviewing to me." But had he actively forbidden Fukuda from talking to the prisoners? Nesvorny scowled. *Imprecision.*

"Sorry, sir. I hadn't realised I was excluded from the interrogation process. You did insist I solve this problem. I've gone as far as I can. Like I said last time, the answer lies in the Engine Quarter. We need to go back in force."

Nesvorny knew it was true. And how many more weapons had been fabricated in the week or so since the initial raid? If the ISU backed off, would the Stokers do the same? Were the weapons defensive – or *offensive*? His last interview with Karyn Dures had hinted at more than simple self-preservation, at planning for something more *revolutionary*. Was he simply a man standing between two sides determined to fight, trying to hold them at arm's length as they attempted to land blows on each other? Dures had already turned down his appeal for calm; Traore would also. As such, what were his options? To step aside and let them at it? To allow chaos in

Hibernia? And what if the Stokers won? They didn't represent the state's population: even if the most outrageous estimates of their hidden numbers was correct, they probably made up no more than a quarter of *Hibernia's* inhabitants. But where they might have an advantage in numbers was in those willing to fight: they were passionate and driven by a sense of grievance, whereas the majority were… what? Unconcerned? Unaware? Privileged? *Soft?*

"Sir?"

Nesvorny shook himself and looked up. Fukuda seemed mildly amused. "I was thinking, Major. About numbers."

"Of whom, sir?"

"Us. Them. Stokers. Citizens." Nesvorny tapped on his desk, distractedly. "During the raid… how many guns did they have?"

"We captured four, but they had more. At least a dozen."

"A dozen that we know of. But they almost certainly had more that weren't used." Twenty? Thirty? And how quickly could they manufacture even more? If they had one production line… half-a-dozen a day? He shook his head. "And what do we have? How many?"

"Guns or troops, sir?"

"Both."

Nesvorny dealt with the big issues; Fukuda and his subordinates dealt with day-to-day logistics. Fukuda paused to consider the question. "In terms of lethal weapons, we have maybe sixty in the armoury, plus larger calibre machine guns on our three personnel carriers. Additionally, we've maybe another hundred rifles that fire non-lethal rubber bullets. Our men are usually just armed with batons when on patrol."

"And troops?"

"About four hundred and thirty."

"That's ISU. What about the ESU? Do you know what Joseph has?"

Fukuda grimaced. "Not off the top of my head, sir. Around two hundred? Two fifty? They'll have some more rifles, but their main weapons are the machine guns on their eight patrol boats."

"So, if we combined, we could perhaps amass around seven hundred troops, and maybe a hundred guns?" Nesvorny tapped his desk some more. "How adequate do you think this will be, Major, if the Stokers decide they've really had enough?"

It was clear that Fukuda was starting to see the problem. "It... will be difficult, sir. But that is all the more reason to act now, before they are organised. Before they make more guns and bombs."

And that was it. That was the calculation. They were effectively in an arms race – but his side had been sleeping when the starting pistol had gone off, and now found its opponent already streaking towards the finish line. In the end, he was the state's head of security – given the irrelevance of General Domitus Kelly – and it was his job to deal with the matter.

"We need to prepare, Fukuda. I accept that. Very well. Start drawing up a plan for a decisive raid in a couple of days. Give me options. Issue body armour to as many troops as possible. Break open the arsenal. I will get in touch with Traore about restarting weapons production, though that may take a few days, and I'll speak to Colonel Joseph, too."

Fukuda smiled; to Nesvorny, it seemed an expression of victory.

* * *

"Back in one piece?" Nesvorny strode along the Eastern Dock, having descended stairs from the 'ground level' of the city state, which was actually two levels above the old sea line. Colonel Tania Joseph was ahead of him, standing next to one of her moored patrol boats, having just finished conversing with a crewman aboard.

The uniformed woman turned and smiled. "Eric! Of course. Did you think I might not make it?"

Nesvorny drew to a halt. "I think if you took one of your boats along the Styx and met Hades himself, you'd somehow work out a way to return."

"With the high-calibre beauty I've got," she laughed, twitching a thumb towards the ominous weapon over her shoulder, "I'd riddle the shithead full of holes and set the damned free." She crossed her arms and gave the other a wry smile. "But I don't think you're really here to ask about my health. What do you want?"

"Can we chat freely?"

"You mean, furtively?" She turned to the crewman who was still on deck near the boat's cabin. "Tanadice – out! Take a break. Half-an-hour should be fine."

The crewman mumbled acknowledgement and stepped onto the pier. Joseph climbed aboard and held out a hand to help up Nesvorny. The machine gun was at the front of the vessel; she ignored the doorway to the cabin and led to the stern, where broad gunwales allowed the pair to sit, facing each other. Overhead, the sun had disappeared behind dark clouds, and a chill breeze blew in from the ocean.

"Will this do?"

There were patrol boats moored to either side, but their decks were empty. Nesvorny nodded. "Yes. It's good."

Joseph folded her arms again. "Go on, then."

For a moment, Nesvorny paused, assembling his thoughts. "Your mission went well, I hear."

"Pretty much. We caught the Stavangerans by surprise. We now hold the mining site, and came away from the ship itself with some recompense for their misdeeds. No causalities – apart from bumps and bruises. Text book."

"You don't anticipate any retaliation?"

"From the Stavangerans? What can they do? Nah. We also have a couple of containers from their supplies as a… what was it that snake Traore called it? – a 'good behaviour bond'."

"Traore again?"

"Who else? O'Neill lets him do whatever he wants. To my mind, that's dangerous – like giving a naughty child a box of venomous spiders and hoping he doesn't cause mischief. But that's politics, eh? I just do what I'm told."

Nesvorny's smile had sunk at the mention of Traore's name. "So, now the Stavangerans hate us too? And what of the people on the other ships?"

Joseph shrugged. "They probably don't know what's been going on. But maybe their ambassadors have passed on the intel? Maybe O'Neill herself has sent them a message? No one's told me anything. You?"

"I didn't even know you'd stolen their treasure."

"Need-to-know, knowledge is power, etcetera. But again, I sense you're here for more than just a catch up. The city is tense, yet you've forsaken your command for a social visit? That's not the Eric I know."

"I'm starting to wonder whether the Eric you know still exists," he sighed. "Maybe I have been at this too long. I'm finding it more and more difficult to turn a blind eye to the injustices in our state – from the highest level to the lowest."

"A policeman starting to think for himself?" Joseph's amused smile was back. "Dangerous. *Very* dangerous. It's Traore, isn't it? I'm largely out of his sightlines, so I have it easier, but you? I guess he's at you all the time. No wonder you're jaded."

"Traore is just a symptom of something worse. And in our current circumstances?"

"You mean, the existential crisis?"

"Well put. Yes. It seems to me that there are two paths we can tread. One is cooperative, making the most of all the resources we have – people and material – not just in *Hibernia*, but across all Tethys. And the other is to double-down, to decide that 'we' must prevail, no matter what it costs."

"The strong survive, Eric."

"Does that mean you're with Traore and O'Neill?"

"Didn't say that." Joseph's smile at last dissipated. "As I said, I'm not a politician. I was just stating a fact. In times like this, it's best to be among the strong, not the weak."

"But what if by coming together we gain strength?"

Joseph slowly shook her head. "What is this, Eric? You found religion?"

"Far from it. Religion is unthinking cant. Maybe I've woken up and I'm only just starting to think?"

"Well, don't think too close to me. I don't want to end up as collateral damage."

Nesvorny looked away for a moment, peering at the seemingly endless ocean of Tethys. In spite of its calm, he knew that there was peril beneath its waves, though still, it held food and energy and a chance for life away from a home world that seemed to be undergoing another of its destructive spasms. People had come to Tethys to get away from that, but in the end, it was clear that they'd brought their demons with them. Perhaps it was naïve to expect otherwise. Yet, he continued to feel there might be a better way…

"Well, it's been nice talking philosophy with you, Eric, but again, I sense this isn't why you are here."

Nesvorny sighed and returned his eyes to Joseph. "Philosophy? No… but maybe, *yes*. The two paths, Tania. You've been sent down the dark path already, while I'm about to start along it myself. And I'm not really sure if I should go, though I don't see an off ramp."

"You're going to clear out the Engine Quarter, yes?"

"That's what Traore wants. That's what Fukuda wants. And the Stokers… I think that's what they want, too. At least, I think they want us to try. *Casus belli*. It'll be the spark that allows their leaders to mobilise their people. And I'm in the middle: damned if I do, damned if I don't."

"I sympathise, Eric. I really do. But this has been coming for some time. You… ah, I see." Joseph started to nod slowly. "The reason for your visit. You need me and mine."

"*Probably*. Did you know they have guns and bombs now? Some of the Earthers from the *Leviathan* have been helping the Stokers to make them."

"Maybe Traore was right all along? We should have moved quicker. *Earlier*."

"Or maybe we should have been talking to them? Building bridges? Bringing them into the open? Giving them less reason to want to fight us?"

"There you go again. Bring back the real Colonel Eric Nesvorny!"

He frowned. "Well, both approaches seem too late now. But I'm determined to minimise bloodshed. If I have to strike, I want to do it surgically. Maximum force at key points to strike off the head and isolate the real fighters. If Traore has his way, we'll seal all the corridors into the Engine Quarter and set the whole *fucking* lot ablaze. I'll not have that."

Joseph stared at him a moment. At last, she said: "Okay, Eric. Point taken. What do you want from me?"

Nesvorny exhaled deeply, letting the rage go. "I can't say for sure. I just want to know what forces you have available, to alert you to be ready in case I need you, and to be sure you will come if I call."

"Half my force is spread over Mounts Ardol and Athol. My main armament is with the boats, but they'll do you no good inland. You can have access to my drone fleet, but they won't be much use in the tunnels of the Engine Quarter. Still, I've maybe a hundred and twenty troops currently in barracks, with weapons for most."

"Strategic reserve?"

"Sure. But if you're going to put my lads and lasses at risk, I want to know your full plans. I need to be on the inside."

Nesvorny nodded, grim-faced. "Of course. Thank you, Tania. Perhaps between us we can try to contain this shitshow… though I fear otherwise."

"So, what are you plans now?"

"I need to talk to Traore. I've been avoiding him for a couple of days. I'm going to appear to concede. In the meantime, can you start readying your force?"

"Anything for a friend… no matter how deranged he has become."

* * *

Nesvorny always wondered what the people who'd inspired the Kennedy Club would have thought of having their name purloined by the elite of *Hibernia.* The clan from the old USA had been sharp political operators, true, but also Democrats (big 'd' and small), whereas those with membership in the club had only a passing interest in the democratic will of the people, and this seemed to have lessened with time. Elections had once taken place every four years, but now were every five; voting requirements had been gradually tightened, disenfranchising most of the residents of the Engine Quarter as well as poorer members of the Cork and Tipperary Districts; the limitation to two terms as leader had been repealed to allow up to four, and that would undoubtedly change further should O'Neill close in on that limit and decide she'd like to hold on; and there had been a slew of subtle legislative changes over the last ten years to increase the opacity of the state's workings, giving certain organisations special contractor rights, meaning they didn't have to bid for work at all, just indicate an interest. And as for the club itself, membership required appropriate sponsorship, and was in any case essentially closed, being limited to forty and requiring a death before new blood could be brought in.

"I'm here to see Manfred Traore," Nesvorny said to the doorman. The club was in the Boston Quarter in an elegant two-storey building of neo-classical design, surrounded by a small park, not far from the glass complex of Charlestown where most of the elite lived – including himself.

The man – dressed in a black suit – gave a sharp, humourless smile. "You are expected. Please follow me."

Nesvorny was led down a carpeted corridor, lit by small chandeliers, past a number of closed doors made of real wood. At the end was a further closed door, which the man opened, entered, and stepped aside. Nesvorny followed and found himself in a room dominated by red leather sofas, small coffee tables, and – to one side – a large billiard table. The elite of *Hibernia* had clearly seen images of the clubs of the wealthy back on Earth and had tried to recreate the template as closely as possible. *Billiards?* He wondered if any of the members even knew how to play.

At this time – early evening – the place was only sparsely attended. Aside from one elderly man who appeared to be snoozing in a chair by a window, there were just two others: Traore sat in one Chesterfield holding a glass of something alcoholic, speaking expansively to a short man with a ruddy face and lumped nose who wore a uniform similar to Nesvorny's – only his was crumpled and bore a gold star on the sleeves. Traore saw him and raised his glass: "Colonel! Come join us."

Nesvorny took a half-dozen slow paces to the pair. It was only as he got close that the second man looked up blearily. "*General*," said Nesvorny, nodding a greeting.

""Yes… yes, I am," said the other, almost as if surprised himself. "What are you doing here, Nesvorny? You're not a member."

"I invited him, Domitus," said Traore. "Or rather, he wanted to talk, and as it is outside office hours, I'm not prepared to let him interfere with my schedule." He looked at Nesvorny and winked: "Even I need a little playtime, eh? There's more to life than working." He switched attention back to General Domitus Kelly. "So, Domitus, your underling needs a seat. Perhaps you should move on, eh?"

"Move…?"

"Yes, *move*. To another room. The library, perhaps? I think the Colonel has sensitive matters to discuss for our ears only, and Mannheim over there seems dead to the world, and quite possibly *dead* dead, given his age. He won't tell."

Kelly still seemed confused. "Move? Sensitive? If it's a security matter, then maybe I should–"

"Domitus!" Traore spoke more harshly now. "Please go. You can take the bottle with you," he indicated the expensive-looking bottle of malt on the table. "The Colonel doesn't drink while on duty. You do. So… off!"

Kelly rose meekly, turned to head for the door – where the servant in black was still waiting – but then remembered something, turned back, snatched up the bottle, then exited without a backwards glance. The servant followed him and closed the door.

Nesvorny took the vacant seat and rested his cap in his lap. "Thank you for seeing me."

Traore waved his glass airily. "No problem. But it must be important if you're prepared to contest a 'wait until tomorrow' directive. Guns? Bombs? Ms Dures? Or all three?"

"All three, and more."

"Ah, then it *is* important. *Interesting*. Go on."

So Nesvorny did. He related the state of play with the Stokers, his suspicions about where they had got their weapons, the *Leviathan* connection, and the intransigence of Karyn Dures.

When he came to an end, Traore laughed. "At last you realise the problem, Colonel. It has taken some time, but I am glad you made it in the end. I thought we might have to look elsewhere for someone with the relevant analytical skills and drive. So, what are your intentions?"

"I'm assembling the ISU to conduct a full raid. We will enter the Engine Quarter and not leave until we have found the production line, the missing New Socialists from the *Leviathan*, and Kai Dures himself."

"Excellent!"

"But I must warn you: it's going to be bloody. This time, I don't think the Stokers are going to back down. But I can see no other way. This is the lesser of many evils."

Traore nodded. "Yes, and once the Stokers are defanged and leaderless, they will be easier to deal with en masse. Clear them out. Move them on… somewhere else."

He held his tongue. He knew what Traore saw as the end game; he also knew it would be far harder to enact than his superior expected. "I take it, then, that I have your permission to proceed? That you will support this with the triumvirate? And that I will be allowed to see it through and not be pulled up after the first casualty?"

"Certainly. We are not so squeamish. You know that. And the media can be handled."

Nesvorny held the other's eye, nodded, and abruptly stood. "Thank you."

He had just reached the door, when Traore called out: "Oh, Colonel." When he turned, he saw Traore leering. "Do a good job, and who knows, you might find sponsorship to this noble establishment. Whether in place of ancient Mr Mannheim in the corner, or the General, whose health, I fear, has been badly affected by his long affair with the demon drink."

Nesvorny managed a smile of sorts, nodded again, and headed through the door. As he strode along the soft carpet to the entrance, he wondered whether the air might actually be sweeter in the depths of the Engine Quarter than in the Kennedy Club.

* * *

The area under the Engine Quarter was a maze of false walls and hidden doors, most of which had been established over the last fifty years. Georges Hollande still didn't understand its geography, and he wouldn't be able to find his way out without a guide. They were currently on the very lowest level of the city ship: the surface was effectively at level two; the waterline was level zero; and they were four levels below that… or was it five? All he knew was that about four metres beneath his feet – through the metal floor and two thick polycarbon hulls that wouldn't corrode, was the ocean of Tethys. But he had long stopped thinking of *Hibernia* as a ship – and in that he had become one with the natives. Instead, it was an island; a city state; it was Atlantis, its people considering themselves the advanced and urbane masters of this world, surrounded by unsophisticated vagrants roaming the ocean in search of who-knew-what. Or at least, the 'true' Hibernians considered themselves this way: the Stokers were 'others', the descendants of a lower caste of people allowed to immigrate to *Hibernia* in order to take all the lowly jobs, but then shut away out of sight, allowed to live as they pleased as long as they didn't in any way impinge on the rest of society. But while those *above* controlled their breeding to concentrate their limited resources, those *below* – the Stokers – had multiplied. To Hollande's eye, this wasn't from some fecklessness or lack of discipline, but was cultural: the Stokers found pleasure in family rather than in physical resources – of which they had little anyway. And until recently, they had muddled along, if not happy, then quietly content. They lived in small cabins carved from larger ones; they ate and drank well enough; and they had plenty of jobs to keep themselves occupied. Indeed, Kai Dures had told him over beer some weeks ago that nearly half of those in Stonetown were Stokers, as were forty percent of those working in the sublevel manufactories and hydroponics plants, as well as thirty percent in the power sections and on the trawler fleets. It seemed likely that those in power had no real appreciation of how much they now relied upon the untouchables from the Engine Quarter.

His guide – an orange-haired woman called Frida – led him through an unmarked door in a dim corridor, sporadically lit (and intentionally so). As he stepped over a sill, he saw the production line laid out before him; it was somewhat unprepossessing. On a succession of benches, six 3D printers were at work, clicking away, manipulating raw resources into different parts of the short-barrelled rifle they had selected as their preferred design. At a space at the back of the room, a group of three workers collected the parts when finished, slotted them together, then placed the final assembled weapons in a rack, ready to be collected and dispensed. Hollande saw his colleagues – Danté and Odile – waiting for him.

"Georges!" said Odile, standing in greeting.

Danté looked around, but continued to lounge on a bench; he merely nodded.

"Comrades. Are we ready?"

"I am," said Odile. "They're being dispensed tonight. There'll be three grenades per assault cadre plus one bomb to breach more difficult barriers."

Hollande nodded. The explosives were being manufactured at the same level but on the opposite side of the city, to ensure that a raid or chance find wouldn't take out all of their resources. "And ammunition?"

Danté shrugged. "We are working at it. But we should have at least twenty rounds per gun when everything kicks off. And my team will continue to produce for as long as needed."

"Overnight?"

"The people are dedicated. They work in shifts."

Hollande turned to look for Frida, his liaison, who had taken over main responsibility for gun production once he'd ensured the printers were working and the process was sound. She had wandered over to the trio of assemblers and was talking to them. "Frida – how is it looking?"

The woman turned to consider the weapons in the racks. "With these, we now have one hundred and thirty two." She grinned, her white teeth shining through a grubby face. "The bastards are going to be fecking surprised."

"Good. I'll report to Kai." He turned back to his old comrades. "Where will you be when it kicks off?"

Odile and Danté quickly looked at each other. Odile spoke first: "With the cadres, of course. I am not missing out this time."

Hollande knew what he meant. Odile had been working to foment trouble in Nigeria when the Great Paris Banlieue revolt took off. Hollande and Danté had both been involved, managing to flee the country after the revolt was suppressed. It was part of the reason that they – and some of their companions on the *Leviathan* – had taken the offer from the *Marseilles* to come to Tethys; a chance to lay low for a while and practice their skills in a pristine environment. "Can you be spared?"

"I have taught them all I know," said Odile. "I am redundant in the factory."

"*Moi aussi*," said Danté, reverting to their native tongue as though to flaunt his revolutionary credentials. "Et tu, Georges?"

"This time? No. I will follow the uprising with Kai. He wants someone nearby who can talk to our comrades on the *Marseilles*. And that is where I must go now." He looked across. "Frida?"

"I'm needed here. Victor will guide you back."

* * *

"They are close… *very* close." Asher Jons had made it to their usual meeting place in a sub-level basement room in a building at the junction of the Cork and Engine Quarters.

Kai Dures leant forwards, excited. He clasped his tattooed hands together. "So – tonight?"

"Yes… *probably*. You know there is a storm coming. At least a Class Three. Maybe a Four."

Hollande looked between the two men, trying to interpret this news. Aside from them, there were just two others in the room – a man named Magdi, and a woman named Annie – who stood against the grey walls and merely listened.

"All the more reason to come now," said Dures, green eyes flashing. "If they don't come tonight, it'll be worse tomorrow, and they may be shut out for a week."

Jons was clearly unhappy. He stroked his Van Dyke. "I know our plan was for tonight. Or rather, for tomorrow in the early hours. But sometimes life tosses a caterpillar in the salad bowl. The First Citizen is as eager as you for this to take place, but I do not want to raise expectations too high. The assault force *will* take to its boats, but if the storm does turn into a Four by the time they launch, I see no way they will be able to cross the gap."

"The *Marseilles* must come nearer, then," said Dures. "Shorten the distance."

"If they do so, they will alert the Hibernians and draw attention to themselves. They have already informed the locals that they will approach to within ten kilometres, which is virtually hand-shaking distance. The Hibernians will think nothing of this – the *Marseilles* is following a logical course to complete their journey to Mount Ardol. But any closer?" He shrugged.

Dures slowly reclined in his grey, somewhat threadbare armchair. To Hollande, it seemed as though he was struggling to parse this data. At last he growled: "Okay. But I cannot start the revolt until it is confirmed that the attempt has been made – *and succeeded*. That means the *Marseilles* contingent might find there are more troops ready to counter them than otherwise."

"I understand," said Jons. "As will they. But on the bright side, there are unlikely to be many ISU about in the rain, nor any ESU in their patrol boats."

"With heightened peril comes heightened opportunity. I am a risk-taker. For me, the odds are too good to ignore. Return to the embassy and persuade them of my view on this."

"Very well."

"In the meantime, I will instruct my people to take their positions in readiness. Keep us informed through our secure comms."

Hollande realised it was going to be a long night.

Chapter 31

"The storm," asked Sebastian Deux, "how bad will it be?"

Captain Marcel Louvain stood before the First Citizen on the bridge of the *Marseilles*, having been evicted from his own command chair. He could feel the eyes of his team on his back, having noticed the noise drop off since the other's arrival. There was usually a hum of conversation, but now those attending the great ship's controls spoke in a whisper, if at all, keen to listen in on the conversation. "I am not a meteorologist, First Citizen. You should ask them."

"But you have already spoken to them." Deux flicked a strand of his long, black hair over his shoulder. "You have some understanding of their gibberish. Whenever I've asked for their advice in the past, they've given me *probabilities.* They seem scared to state anything definitive in case they are proven wrong."

"It's an inexact science," said Louvain, levelly. "There is nothing you or I can do about it."

"Maybe, maybe not. But you seem to have a skill in translating their vague forecasts. You hear what they say and then take decisions – not just for the *Marseilles*, but for the fishing fleet, too. Given that we have not yet sunk, nor had any major weather-related incidences since you took command, it seems you have a degree of competence."

"The fishing fleet is different to your little project."

Deux scowled. "It's far from *little*, or a *project.* We are going to help our repressed and exploited comrades in *Hibernia*, and in the process, help free all the oppressed people of Tethys from the Hibernian elite's tyranny."

"Tyranny?" Louvain could barely contain a smile. "I feel strangely un-oppressed." He knew he shouldn't toy with Deux, but sometimes the man was too preposterous. A gasp from somewhere behind suggested that at least one of his team thought he'd gone too far.

Deux hooded his eyes. "So, you are against what we are doing? Be very careful, Captain. Some might consider your tepid support – or is that cynicism? – anti-social."

Louvain sighed. He was too old to be terrorised by egomaniacs like Deux, but also too old to risk his hard-earned position – for he had little doubt that Deux would send him to the fishing fleet as a deckhand at the slightest perceived afront. And after all, he was Marseillaise. He *did* believe in socialist principles. But time had mellowed him, and whereas in the past he might have enthusiastically joined Deux's crusade, he now believed in a gentler, more consensual path to equality. "My support is not tepid, First Citizen. The Hibernians treat us all like medieval serfs, and I certainly have no love for them. So… what exactly do you want from me?"

"I want your recommendation. Can we set the fleet to sea? They plan to launch at three in the morning. Is this wise? Would you continue? Or would you defer?"

Louvain's mouth twitched, fighting another smile. It seemed that Deux was trying to diffuse responsibility, hence this public show rather than a private word in his cabin. The fleet sinks – *his fault.* The fleet delayed, the moment passing – *his fault.* "If the fleet were setting out to trawl, then I would say hold. Under no circumstances would I send it out."

"But it's not."

"No, but the boats are the same." Louvain paused, then sighed: he would not be able to dissemble. "But their task is different, I agree. They won't be setting or retrieving nets – merely travelling a dozen kilometres or so to the *Hibernia*, directly and quickly, yes?"

"That's right. So… will it be safe to launch?"

Louvain sighed again. "That really depends upon your risk profile. Launch into a Class Three and most will probably make it. In a Class Four? Maybe half. At three o'clock, the status of the storm is unclear. Earlier is better. Can you launch at two? You may still lose a boat or two, but I would expect most to reach their target."

Deux sat back. At last, he uncovered a smile. "Thank you, Captain. It's not the best of news, but not the worst. Our comrades are prepared for sacrifice, but I will do my best to preserve their lives. I will update the plans."

"I wish the fleet Godspeed," said Louvain. And he meant it. His only reservation was that a success in this enterprise would further aggrandise and embolden a dangerous man; but sometimes you couldn't have everything you wanted.

* * *

Mitsos never heard the news about the change of plans – although in the end he wasn't unhappy about it.

He'd spent the afternoon hanging around the internal dry docks by the two boats of the REEN project, which had returned early after their latest trawl of the ocean. Bennani had been there with some of the others, analysing data on the elements picked up by the ultra-fine net, which had been spooled and retracted into one of the vessels. After a while, Mitsos had retreated to the second vessel, once its crew had departed, and hunkered down there. The others had clearly been relieved when he left, and hadn't cared where he'd gone to. Mitsos knew they would have expected him to leave the docks altogether.

From his new position, he'd surreptitiously watched his team pack up and leave a couple of hours later. They'd left the net itself aboard the first boat: the quantities of rare elements it was accumulating was so small that they only took it for a 'wash' – to extract the molecules of metal collected – at the end of the week. After that, he'd been able to move a bit more freely: the remains of the fishing fleet had been left in port for the day in the primary dock, so the only other activity in the secondary one had been around the customised warcraft, and that had been minimal.

Activity only started to really ramp up around ten o'clock. The ships assigned to the *Hibernia* venture were lined along four parallel quays of the dock, three along each. For most of these, the refurbishments had been about removing things rather than adding them, with all fishing-related rigs and equipment taken off, and the craft given a coat of grey paint to enhance their anonymity. It was only the three in the final row that had been fitted with some sort of gun on their forward decks. It was clear to Mitsos that these were for insurance only: the overall mission involved getting the invading force safely ashore, not engaging in a sea battle with purpose-built patrol boats. He supposed the guns were largely meant to scare off approaching craft, and perhaps to send a few shells into *Hibernia* if necessary: he doubted their crew would be competent to hit anything moving towards them at speed, such as one of the enemy's vessels.

He spent the last hours nervously watching the dockworkers as they moved to-and-fro under harsh lights set in the cavernous ceiling. Watching… and waiting. He could see the *Dieppe* from within the main cabin of the REEN boat, which today had been allocated the furthest quay in the secondary dock – but though it was relatively close, he had no idea how to get there without being seen and challenged. He hadn't managed to acquire a dark blue overall of the sort worn by dockworkers, nor the military-style fatigues worn by the assault force: he currently wore his worn grey jumpsuit from his time as a trawlerman, which he'd brought with him in a small rucksack (and changed into after leaving the scientists) along with a bottle of water, a packet of protein paste for sustenance, and a small knife – *just in case.*

The time on his tablet showed 23.42 when he noticed a sudden change of activity. The sporadic maintenance people began to converge in small groups and then make their way to the main concourse that led to the exit to the primary dock with its checkpoint. As they merged, voices were raised in greeting and there was the occasional laugh. *Shift change?*

He had no time to lose.

He crept from the cabin onto the deck and stepped onto the quay, which had been deserted since his team had left. He headed to where it met the concourse, and watched the backs of the people in blue heading away, then he started towards the appropriate pier further down – which was now empty of life. His heart pounding, he turned onto the relevant quay and scampered towards the *Dieppe*, which occupied the middle berth between two other boats. He'd just come level, however, when he noticed a figure in blue emerge from the boat farthest along, hurrying and muttering, but looking down at something in his hands. Mitsos leapt onto the *Dieppe* and dropped to the floor, hoping he'd not been seen and that the raised gunwale would hide him from view.

Then he heard a voice. "Wait! Guy!"

There had been *two* on the furthest boat.

"What?" came the nearer voice.

"The bracket's not tight."

"It'll hold. They're not going to cruise around the fucking globe."

"But the storm–"

"Fuck the storm. If you're that concerned, leave a message at the gate. I'm off duty, comrade."

The first man stomped past, and Mitsos heard footsteps of the second a short time after. Once those receded, he crawled on his belly to the main cabin, found the old emergency locker mentioned by Noma, and squeezed in. It wasn't exactly empty – there was a pair of old lifejackets within – but these would at least act as pillows in the cramped space. It was dark when he closed the box, but not pitch black: a line of light along one edge of the lid showed where a seam had moved over time. It wasn't enough to see by, but he hoped it would allow sufficient air into his coffin-like space.

Still, he had light from his tablet to see by.

It was now 23.56.

The crew began to clamber aboard about twenty minutes later, after which there was constant noise – shouts, laughs, curses – some from directly over his head. The louder voices were male, but some were female, though he never detected Noma's low, lush tones.

He'd expected a tense three hour wait, so when the craft began to move at 01.54, he was pleasantly surprised… until the boat hit the water.

* * *

The crossing seemed to go on forever.

The boat rolled continuously in the turbulent sea, throwing Mitsos this way and that. The leftover life vests in his hidey-hole served as some sort of cushion, saving him from being battered against the chest's sides, but they could do nothing to counter his seasickness. It wasn't long before he was thanking the fact that he'd missed lunch and dinner while hiding out: once he started to retch, he produced little more than water, though the familiar pungent smell of vomit exacerbated his nausea. But he wasn't detected, as every pitch or drop that threw him about noisily did the same to those sitting on top of the chest, or arrayed about the cabin, and he caught frequent groans, howls, shrieks, and curses through the gap along the edge of the lid.

The worst moments came with the drops – which Mitsos supposed were due to the *Dieppe* falling from some wave crest – which caused him to levitate into the air, once with enough force to strike the lid and raise it a millimetre or two against a sudden lack of resistance, presumably as those sitting above were synchronously elevated.

In the end, he didn't know how long the transfer took, as he hadn't the stomach to look at the timer on his tablet, though he knew they'd made it when the motion of the boat began to change and twist, and it began to bob more languidly than before. The sense of forwards motion abated, and the voices above became louder, with one deep male voice especially prominent, shouting undecipherable commands.

At last, he heard a different set of sounds, including a loud scraping, which he imagined might be from the side of the boat coming into contact with something solid, and then there were higher pitched scrabblings and scrapings. The boat still rocked from side-to-side, but now movement seemed to be restricted to just one dimension. Then the rising voices began to drop again, before tailing off completely.

Mitsos could bear it no longer: in the dark, he reached to check his largely empty rucksack was still on his back, and his tablet was safe in the Velcro pocket of his rough work trousers, and then he pushed up on the lid with both hands. He didn't know if anyone would still be in the cabin – and by this point, he didn't care. An excited shout confirmed that he was not alone.

"What the fuck are you doing here?"

"Who is it?" said a second voice, also male.

"I don't... *Mitsos*?"

Mitsos' legs were boneless; he couldn't stand, and was happy to allow himself to be grabbed by the owners of the voices and held up. He closed his eyes against the sudden piercing light from the cabin. He still felt nauseous – a feeling not helped as a swell lifted the boat and threw it against whatever they were moored against, causing the two men holding his arms to stumble and curse.

"Fuck – what are we… going to do… with him…" said one, his speech marking time with the rhythm of waves.

"Let's get… off this… ship. Bring him…"

And so he was dragged through the cabin, onto the deck, and then somehow manhandled over the gunwales onto a slick platform, perhaps two-metres wide, which was like a narrow shore under a cliff face that extended to both sides as far as he could see in lights cast by a dozen or more swaying torches held by others from the assault party. But while Mitsos felt a moment of relief at the return of stability beneath his feet, he soon faced further torment, as rain pelted onto his crown with a ferocity like a physical assault, forcing him to bow his head. The sound of the rain and wind was such they overwhelmed all human voices. One of those at his side let go, perhaps slipping or seeking to gain their own equilibrium; but the other continued to drag at him, and Mitsos at last got his legs working and willingly aided his captor. As they passed the bow of the *Dieppe* – which rose and fell by the quay – they were pummelled into the 'cliff' by a wave. *Metal*, thought Mitsos. Not rock. Not a cliff. *The Hibernia*. His shoulder stung from the impact, but being closer to the edge provided some shelter from the worst of the rain. He looked up, and caught sight of a stairway that curled up the metal cliff, which he saw was already occupied by the invaders, slowly forcing their way upwards. And then he felt a tug on his arm, and within seconds he and his guard were at the foot of the stairwell – the other thrusting him forwards and shouting inchoately. But Mitsos understood; squeezed past; began to climb.

It was maybe four or five metres to the top, and he came directly behind another, keeping close, using them as a shield against the worst of the weather. He emerged at the top of the circular well, and found a gate fixed open, and saw that he had indeed reached *Hibernia* – with a looming wall of buildings forming a new horizon, yellow and orange lights winking from along the indistinct mass, and a clutch of people across the road fifty metres down – a road that separated the walkway on which he stood from a pavement running alongside the buildings. Looking up and down the street, Mitsos noticed the invaders from the other boats struggling towards the knot of people. Without waiting for his guard to catch up, he bowed his head and chased after the person who'd been above him on the stairwell. At one point, he slipped on the road and went down. The water on the road was an inch deep, and flowed with the camber to unseen drainage points. A squall then struck him with full fury, pushing him down again, and then sliding him a metre or so along the lubricated street. Gasping, Mitsos managed to use his hands to bring himself to a halt, and then he pushed up, and like an unsteady newborn colt, he staggered forwards, passing another dark figure rolling in the spray…

He converged on the destination group at the same time as three others, and together they were grasped and bundled through a doorway into a well-lit building that was full of moaning, cursing people, with someone further in – stood upon a table – shouting: "Keep moving. Go! Go!"

Buffeted from behind by more new arrivals, Mitsos carried on. At least his head was now spared the assault, but his face felt numb. He was able to at least look around, and thought: *restaurant.* The place seemed to be a diner of some sort, its tables pushed away from the door and the central area, with a serving counter at the back, on which stood a couple of people dressed in green jumpsuits – *dry* jumpsuits – directing traffic to an annex to one side. Mitsos followed the slowing stream into a side room, and then, at last, to another door in the back wall. He came to a halt at the back of a queue – behind a man who had a gun on a strap over one shoulder of sodden military fatigues, his hair battered flat onto his head, with blood oozing behind an ear that seemed to have been torn by the force of the deluge.

Those in the queue were strangely quiet – perhaps too exhausted to speak – and no one challenged him. Then he was at the door, and found himself in another stairwell, leading down. There was no chance of escape from here: he felt a hand on his back, and started down the stairs after the bloody-eared man. A few more winds, and then another antechamber; another door; and then he found himself in a tunnel – a corridor. A woman in green acted as a barrier to one side, ushering new arrivals in the opposite direction. He continued, gradually starting to feel more alive, his nausea gone, his legs regaining strength, but the abating numbness in his head was rapidly replaced by pain, especially at the back of his neck, which felt like it had been scoured by sandpaper. Those in front appeared to be recovering too, walking more upright – though silently. Every few metres they passed another green-clothed guide, and these accounted for the relative quiet: each one held a finger raised to their lips. Looking about, Mitsos was now able to make out – in the light from a single strip in the ceiling – closed doors and shuttered units. Some seemed to be cellars to dwellings above, marked with nothing but a street number, while others seemed to be business premises, closed for the night – small workshops, the occasional retail outlet, a tattoo parlour, a bar.

After a couple of hundred metres, there was a four-way junction, with another usher, who pointed them down a perpendicular corridor. And after perhaps another hundred, hundred-and-fifty metres, a final usher blocked the way and directed the flow into a single open doorway that led into a surprisingly large space, both wide and long, with an upper mezzanine. Voices came through the open door, and these amplified once within.

"Eddard!"

Mitsos' heart skipped a beat, and he couldn't restrain a smile. "Noma!"

The dark-skinned woman squeezed between a pair of colleagues and closed the gap between them. The expression on her face was difficult to interpret – somewhere between relief and surprise. "You got out."

"Yeah, I left the second the fat arses sitting over me got off the box."

She looked him up and down, and frowned. "No one has said anything?"

"You mean about my lack of disguise? It was a bit hectic, but yeah…" he looked around, and spotted the man who'd pushed him up the stairwell entering the door. The man saw him, dropped a hand onto his shouldered rifle, and strode over. "In fact, speak of the devil."

"Mitsos! What the fuck are you doing here?"

"Ah… Pierre. Well, you wouldn't believe me, would you, if I said I got drunk and fell asleep in the emergency supplies chest?" The other scowled. "I guess that's a *no*. What about amnesia? I banged my head, woke up, and found myself here."

The man glanced at Noma, then back at Mitsos, edging his weapon around so that its barrel was pointed at him. "This isn't funny. Are you a spy?"

"For the Hibernians? Those wankers? No way. In fact, I owe them big time. I would have joined up, comrade, but I left it too late."

Pierre shook his head and looked at the woman. "Noma? You know him best. Did you have anything to do with this?"

She raised her hands. "No, Pierre. But he's speaking the truth. I know he hates the Hibernians. He asked me before how he could join us, and I told him he couldn't."

"Yeah, citizen, it's got nothing to do with her. This is all down to me. Give me a weapon. Point me the way."

Pierre continued to shake his head. "I don't know what to believe. I don't trust you, Mitsos. Never have. But I've got more important things to deal with now. Noma – watch him. We'll sort this out later." He turned and stalked off towards a small cluster of senior figures who were currently in debate with several Hibernians wearing green.

"Take this," said Noma, handing him a red armband. "It might stop you getting shot."

Mitsos at last noticed that the *Marseilles* contingent all wore two armbands; Noma had offered him one of hers. He took it without speaking and rolled it onto his right arm. Then he looked up sheepishly. "Thanks, Noma. I really owe you."

"You do. Now stay by me, keep quiet, and don't cause trouble. I don't want to be punished for letting you escape. And I'm going to get sick very quickly of explaining why you are here with us."

"Sorry about that. I'd hate for you to get anywhere near as sick as I was." He smirked and held up his hands. "I promise, I'll behave."

For now, he added to himself.

* * *

Mitsos tried to keep a low profile. He joined Noma at one side of the hall, where those who'd come on the *Dieppe* assembled – the old crew members plus assorted others who'd been assigned to their squad. As he'd been the last off the boat – with Pierre and another man – Noma only had to explain his presence once. He scanned the faces of those assembled: a couple – Marc and Abdul – gave him nods of recognition; some old crewmates looked on him with suspicion; but most of the others seemed uninterested. Indeed, most appeared somewhat traumatised by their journey from the *Marseilles*, and looked haggard, sodden, and dismayed.

The conversation was whispered and low key, so Mitsos turned to assess the room. The purpose of the space was unclear – a general assembly point? It lacked furniture or other features, and appeared to have been constructed by removing walls between units, as well as the ceiling in order to double the room height, with the mezzanine being leftover flooring from above. The *Marseilles* contingent was distributed throughout the room in clumps of around twenty – presumably the squads from each boat sticking together. Over the course of fifteen minutes, more arrived, and several new clusters formed. Gradually, arrivals slowed and then eventually stopped. In the meantime, the squad leaders formed a separate group, which included several of the natives dressed in their standard green jumpsuits.

The first time Mitsos spoke, it was to lean across to Noma and hiss in her ear: "Pierre's coming."

Noma turned to face their squad leader, inducing others to turn to see what she was looking at.

Pierre – a somewhat grizzled man, with dark eyebrows, short hair, and a heavily lined face – drew to a halt. He stood, looking down at his team – sitting or squatting on the bare metal floor. "Listen up, citizens. The plan has evolved." He squatted to be on the same level as the others, who shuffled closer. Mitsos was already nearby, albeit at the edge of the group. "The original plan was to head for the West Docks, which has space for some of the fleet to moor, but instead we've been arrayed along the southern end of *Hibernia*. The whole city is ringed by a sea-level platform with mooring posts, but no facilities."

"Isn't the *Dieppe* at risk," asked Abdul. "There's no shelter. She might be smashed against the quay."

Pierre was clearly discomforted by the thought. "That can't be helped. The West Docks might be defended, and it's across the city from our allies *here*. We would have got nowhere in this weather, even if we'd managed to successfully enter the docks. The *Dieppe* and the other boats will have to ride it out. They can't risk a return to the *Marseilles* now – conditions are worse than when we set off."

Mitsos noticed unhappy faces, and several of the squad – all old crew – started to whisper to each other. Their loyalty to the stinking old trawler was as great as to anything else, and they were clearly perturbed about the prospects for it.

Pierre made a calming motion with his hands. "Remember the bigger picture, citizens! We are here to free the people of *Hibernia*. There will be losses. We know this."

"Did all the boats make it?" asked a woman Mitsos didn't know. She'd been looking around the hall, either counting or looking for someone.

"Nearly all," said Pierre. "The *St. Jean*… we don't know."

"If it's not here by now, it's not coming," said Abdul, bitterly. "You know that, Pierre."

The squad leader appeared unable to look his crewmate in the eye. "If you realise that, don't press me to say it. It's a miracle the rest of us made it."

"So, what now?" asked Noma.

"As I said, plans have evolved." Pierre seemed happier returning to his brief. "We couldn't get to the Docks, and our allies couldn't either. No one is doing anything outside until the storm dies down – and God knows when that will be. It could be a couple of days. So, we're keeping to the sub-levels. We're going to break into several units and head for the East Dock, the Internal Security Unit's HQ, and the Command Centre. Stokers are going to join and guide us, and at the same time they have other units that are going to strike at the Hibernian elite."

"Now?" asked a man squatting nearby. "I'm fucked, Citizen."

"At four-thirty. It's about ten-to-four. You've got a bit of time to rest. Our hosts are bringing hot soup and drinks shortly."

"And what about him?" This was from a man called Pascal, whom Mitsos had never got on with: tall, lean, and sharp-featured.

"He's unimportant. We'll discuss him with the *Marseilles* when we have time. He'll have to come with us for now." Pierre turned to face him. "Mitsos – make yourself useful. Medic. Porter. No gun. And don't run off. If you try, you're open season."

"So, I can shoot him?" said Pascal.

"Yeah – but *only* if he runs."

Mitsos smiled at Pascal and raised his eyebrows – an unnecessary provocation, but one he couldn't resist. Afterwards, seeing the way Pascal's eyes kept returning to him, Mitsos thought to himself: *You're a fucking idiot!*

He moved even closer to Noma.

Chapter 32

"They're gone – completely. No wreckage. No bodies." The shock in Captain-Governor Nacimiento's voice was palpable.

"Nothing?" repeated Figueroa.

Marie had been urgently summoned to attend a meeting with Nacimiento in his private suite, along with Figueroa and Kalmik. Their host had been so distracted, he'd not even offered his guests a drink.

"Yes. The rescue boat was on location fifteen minutes after it received a radio cry for help. It reported that the two harvesters had completely disappeared."

"How wide was its search?" asked Figueroa, in trembling voice. "How… *deep*?"

Nacimiento ran a hand across his forehead. "Ah, now there I suspect the answer to both your questions is 'not very'. The captain was somewhat evasive on return. I believe fear drove them away from their search after a very short time. They avoided passing over the fringe forest altogether and left as soon as their boat was attacked."

"Attacked?" said Kalmik.

"That is what the captain claimed. He said something struck the bottom of their boat several times. *Hard.* They withdrew a hundred metres, but soon after it happened again, and that is when they decided to leave the area altogether."

Figueroa sat back, his mouth open, but wordless. He looked between Marie and Kalmik. "I… don't know what to say. It's a tragedy."

"It seems these farmers have teeth," said Nacimiento.

"I suppose they do." Figueroa focused on Marie. "And you, Marie, my dear, you warned about this."

Marie was as shocked as the others. "I take no credit for the foresight. I didn't expect anything so *terminal.* We knew the farmers could get feisty, but… no warning shot? The full-on nuclear option?"

"So, what do we do now?" asked Nacimiento.

"Get the fuck out of here," said Kalmik. "I've had a bad feeling about this ever since our first encounter with the farmers, and especially after we developed the pictures from Marie's latest dive. I'm no Marco – you know that – but even I wouldn't go into the water with them around. What if they're wating for us, and they see us as easy to kill?"

"But that's all the more reason to stay," said Marie. "To study them. To try to work out a way to communicate with them."

"I think they've learned how to communicate with us very well," said Kalmik, dryly. "And there's no need for a Rosetta Stone to translate. They just said: *fuck off now, or die*."

"Although I am worried about these creatures," said Nacimiento, "I also have a responsibility to the families of those who died to attempt to retrieve their bodies."

"*If* they still exist," said Kalmik. "We know these farmers tend the kelp, presumably for food. But we haven't seen their teeth. I'll bet that somewhere under that black ellipsoid of a head, they have some pretty sharp incisors. Apex predators. They're probably omnivorous, like us. What if they decided they quite like the taste of human flesh?"

Marie looked among her colleagues, trying to divine the general feeling in the room. But all she got was fear and confusion. "I accept that, Katerina," she said. "But this is the find of the century. Or *every* century. We can't let fear drive us away. Professor…?"

"Marie," Figueroa held up both hands, "yes, you're right. But sometimes… sometimes discretion is the better policy. I agree we need to study these creatures more – but maybe not these *particular* ones, and maybe not *now*. Perhaps it would be wise to pause, and think, and plan. If there are farmers here, then it makes sense that there are more cultivating the other fringe forests by cenotes. Perhaps we can cautiously approach a different group where our reputation hasn't been, ah, *sullied*."

"*Our* reputation?" Kalmik was suddenly angry.

"We did try to steal and trash their crops," said Marie, quickly, as Figueroa blanched.

"A small section, sure," said Kalmik. "But I think their response was a little OTT."

"Maybe they had no choice but to be strident," said Marie. "The harvesters would have made a lot of noise. Caused a lot of damage. I'm not sure there was any other way they could have made their feelings known – not like emerging from the water and gently tapping the captain on the shoulder and saying 'please stop'."

Kalmik folded her arms. "Be that as it may, we can't let their actions go unpunished. There will be people onboard, too – people who lost loved ones – who might wonder what we're going to do about those who killed them. If you're attacked by an animal, it's important to slap it on the nose so it appreciates not to do it again."

"You're saying we should attack them?" Marie was appalled. "But they're not animals!"

"I also couldn't condone some sort of revenge mission," said Figueroa.

"The people onboard might be harder to dissuade… but this isn't our problem." Kalmik looked quickly at Nacimiento, and then she sighed and unfolded her arms. "Look, I'm not suggesting we violently respond for purposes of revenge. But what if our lack of response is interpreted as a communication from *us* to *them*. They are intelligent creatures. Maybe they will interpret our message as saying that we are soft touches. Toothless. Maybe no different from bait fish."

Marie swore under her breath. "That… is not a terrible observation."

"Marie!" exclaimed Figueroa. "I can't believe you're coming around to her view."

"I'm not! Well, not entirely. The point is, we're in this mess because we disrespected Nature. We know it's red in tooth and claw. We know these farmers are intelligent, and the only other intelligent species we know about – us – is territorial, vengeful, vindictive. It was always likely that they were going to respond in some way. I just think this amplifies why we need to study the farmers more *now*. *These* farmers. And *urgently*. We need to fully characterise them – find out what they eat, find out their psychology. Only this will tell us if we really need to fear them, and whether we need to make the sort of power demonstration Katerina is talking about."

Nacimiento raised one hand slowly to attract the attention of all. "This is an interesting discussion. But I need to remind you that we are running short of certain supplies. We came here to harvest, and now that seems unwise. We will need to move on very soon – perhaps to a more conventional forest."

"Oh, I think if we're desperate, Captain," we could still harvest here." Kalmik had acquired a dangerous smile. "We can lower the threshers from the *Lisboa's* wings and do a few sweeps over the fringe. There's no way these farmers are going to be able to sink *us* so easily! This way we would restock *and* demonstrate why we shouldn't be fucked with in one go."

"Katerina!" gasped Figueroa.

Nacimiento smiled sadly. "No, we are not that desperate for supplies, and although I agree that some aboard might wish revenge, I am not prepared to be recorded in history as the man who found a new race of intelligent beings and then attacked it. And I do not want to take the *Lisboa* anywhere near this cenote and its forest. So, where does this leave us? Miguel?"

Figueroa appeared tortured. He looked between Marie and Kalmik for advice.

Marie noticed the woman fold her arms again and slowly shake her head; she jumped in before the other could speak. "One more trip," she said. "Just one more. In the *Fortunata*. We can get to the site where the harvesters went down and at least have a look."

"How–?" began Nacimiento.

"Lights!" said Marie. "We know that light is like kryptonite to them. Let's put strong lights beneath the *Fortunata*, and then go to the site *slowly* in order to usher them away. You said, sir, that we owed it to the relatives of the missing to look for them. Well, we can do that, and at the same time give a non-lethal demonstration of power, as Katerina might put it. We remind the farmers that we know how to harm them – and by approaching their domain cautiously, maybe we also send the message that we have no ill-intent; that we could have cruised over the forest and *then* turned on the lights fully, but we chose not to."

Nacimiento nodded slowly: "Miguel – the *Fortunata* is your boat. It would be your risk. I am prepared to stay for this one foray – as Dr Lockard notes, for the sake of the missing and their families – but it's up to you."

"Well, you can go without me!" said Kalmik.

"Ah… yes, Katerina…" Figueroa appeared undecided. But at last he nodded. "I… think, for several reasons, we should perhaps make one last foray to this site, but with volunteer crew only. Marie makes a good point about our advantage here. And anything else we can learn about these creatures will be immensely valuable."

Marie let out the breath she had been holding.

"Very well," said Nacimiento. "One last expedition. But it must be tomorrow at the latest. We are not far from *Hibernia*, which lies around eighty kilometres to the south-west of here. We have had no communication with them for some time. I think it wise to pay our respects, update them on our find, and let them know of our tragedy. They will be able to transmit our story to the other ships and the rest of the world."

"Yeah," said Kalmik, "and it might be interesting to see how they react to the reality of having aggressive, intelligent aliens living a relatively short distance away from them."

"I'm sure they'll feel it further justifies their self-imposed exclusion from the area," said Nacimiento. "But I do hope they don't try to steal your thunder, Miguel."

Marie suddenly felt uneasy – and not from the prospect of the upcoming trip on the *Fortunata*.

* * *

"I'm in," said Grande. The whole senior science team was assembled in the main auditorium of the Research Centre.

"*You?*" said Kalmik, unable to mask her disbelief.

"Of course. I wouldn't want to be thought of as a coward."

Marie struggled to restrain a smile and had to cover her mouth with one hand.

"There's a difference between cowardice and rational behaviour. And with you volunteering, I now appreciate just how insane this expedition is." Kalmik turned to Figueroa. "Miguel: won't you reconsider? We can't risk losing the *Fortunata*."

"What about the people on it?" said Marie, with a mischievous smile.

"Of course. That is implicit." Kalmik was clearly annoyed, not least because, one after another, all of the team – bar Victoria Soares – had volunteered, making her an outlier.

"Do not fret, Katerina," said Figueroa. "We will be especially careful. The *Fortunata* is like a child to me – you all are. And now we are quorate, I believe." He turned to Marie. "Is the boat prepared?"

"Yup. Lights have been fixed below, as have a number of cameras. And we've also put two of Luisa's new infrared cameras on drop lines, so we'll be able to see beyond the light horizon once we get into position."

Teixeira smiled. "I'm glad my hard work wasn't in vain after all."

"Excellent!" declared Figueroa. "Then let's go, before sanity descends and we all start having second thoughts."

* * *

Marie was last to board – feeling an extra responsibility for the safety of the crew, and wanting to ensure that none had second thoughts and wanted to bail out. As usual, Arantxa Perez took the helm; Figueroa, Grande, and Teixeira set up in the main cabin, where they worked at the computers; and Resnos, Garcia, and Marie herself, took to the deck at the back – all three wearing their drysuits as a matter of habit, though none had any intention of entering the water that day.

It took twenty minutes to reach the fringe forest where the two harvesters had gone down, the *Fortunata* moving at no more than half-speed, the water beneath its keel aglow from a dozen lights. During the transit, they saw no sign of menace: the water was calm, and the world was silent except for the soft churn of the ship's motor. Overhead, the sky was overcast, with a wall of darkness away to the west.

"That doesn't look good," said Marie at one point. "Reminds me of the storm we had as we were leaving the last sea forest."

"Yeah, well, that's because it *is* similar." Resnos folded his arms, leant on the gunwale, and smiled. Garcia had gone off to the front of the boat where the second infrared camera had been placed, leaving the two alone. "Haven't you been paying attention to the forecasts?"

"Uh, no. So, when is it due?"

Resnos shook his head gently. "You need to keep up to date with the meteo, Marie. To be a true Tethyn, you roll out of bed and check the forecast, and only then get up for breakfast. In fact, many check before even getting out of bed. The weather can really ruin your day otherwise. Anyway, it's still a day or two away, coming from the north west."

"Is it going to rain?"

"Today? Probably not. Tomorrow? Very likely. The day after? Stay inside and *do not* open any windows."

"A Class Three?"

"Meteo expect it to be a Four."

"Ah..." Marie nodded to herself. "Maybe that helps explain our Captain-Governor's urge to get out of here this afternoon."

"He has an urge? You tell me. Seems you've moved into exalted company. I don't get personal audiences with Nacimiento... *Your Majesty.*"

Marie laughed. "Oh, stop tugging your forelock, peasant, and get back to work."

"Yes, ma'am!" Resnos bowed, then bent to consider the infrared camera and its kit on the deck at his feet.

It was shortly after this that Perez slowed the boat further, just as a dark line across the ocean indicated the submarine edge of the fringe forest. Marie and Resnos moved over to the starboard side to watch as the *Fortunata* coasted the last few metres: they crossed the shadow line and came to a gentle stop. The ocean was deathly still, with barely a swell or ripple from the light westerly breeze. To Marie, the silence was eerie – the absence of the cries of seabirds somehow unsettling.

Marie touched Resnos on the arm, and mouthed 'inside' – almost afraid to break the silence – then left for the cabin. There, she found that three screens had been set up next to each other, with Teixera sat on a chair at a keyboard before the middle one, while Grande sat off to one side, fussing with computer equipment. Figueroa stood just behind the woman. Marie came to the professor's side. "What are we looking at?"

"Ah, Marie. The central display shows the view below the boat. The left and right screens show the two infrared camera shots – or will do, once they are lowered into the water and switched on."

At that moment, the centre display showed the tops of the kelp forest tickling the bottom of the boat. Teixeira touched an intercom switch and said: "Arantxa – we're not quite there. Forward slow, please. I'm pretty sure you will know when we've arrived."

"Si," came a voice through speakers. "Forward slow."

For nearly a minute, Marie watched the kelp wave languidly in the turbulence from the research boat's movement, golden green in the lights on the hull – and then the view suddenly changed. The kelp fell away and there was clear water between the bottom of the hull and the foliage top – clear, and *empty*.

Teixeira addressed the intercom: "Arantxa – all stop."

"Yes, I see it."

"Like a haircut," muttered Marie.

Figueroa looked at her askance. "Yes, that's right. The harvesters will have taken the top few metres off of the forest. They clearly started here."

"Or *ended* here," said Marie. "But what I don't get is this: the kelp is buoyant, yes? So – where is the harvested material?"

"In the hold of the boats," said Teixeira, still staring at the screen.

"What – all of it? No debris at all?"

"I guess the farmers are a tidy lot," said Figueroa. "They have cleaned up the mess we made."

Marie frowned to herself and concentrated on the screen. Nothing swam in the three-to-four metre space above the cropped forest top, and she saw no significant movement in the kelp, which stood erect in the near-absent current. "It's as we've observed before," she said at last. "Our light – and the sunlight – seems to be keeping the farmers away."

"Or maybe they're sleeping," said Figueroa. "With their antipathy to light, perhaps they are nocturnal, unless, that is, they are rudely awaken by, *ah*…"

"By us? Sure. Makes sense. Is it time to look deeper, and *darker*?"

"I believe it is, my dear. Will you do the honours?"

Marie left the cabin. She first went forwards to see Garcia and ask him to lower his infrared camera, then circled to the rear where she repeated her request to Resnos. Then she returned to the cabin to find fuzzy images now upon the left and right screens. The central, brighter image from a camera attached to the middle of the hull, remained largely still, but the others wavered as the cameras were slowly lowered, reaching the canopy of the denuded forest, and then continuing on. The images cleared somewhat as the cameras went deeper and as light interference from the spotlights waned.

"They're now about seven metres deep," said Teixeira. "Eight... Ten..." The slim camera cables were thirty-five metres long. After a short while longer, she announced: "That's it."

"Well, they work," said Figueroa, "though in retrospect, I'm not sure what we expected to see. They are at depths not far beyond those at which we have dived, and the harvesters will be at the bottom of the ocean."

"True," said Marie. "But I thought we might pick up something caught in the kelp. Some residue– "

"Fuck!" said Teixera jerking backwards suddenly. "What is... oh!"

Marie saw it now, on the right screen, where the camera had settled in the space between kelp rows – unlike the one displaying to the left screen, which lay close to a long stalk and had a far more restricted view. On the right was one of the farmers – its long body a red smudge in the infrared. "What is it doing?"

"It appears to be treading water," said Figueroa.

"What – right next to the camera?" said Marie. "*Facing* the camera?"

"Ah, I see what you mean. It's examining it. Ah... and it's off."

The creature turned, using its arms and long hands to reposition itself, and then its powerful legs and flipper-like feet to propel itself into the depth.

"Well, that's the first confirmed sighting of a farmer in the forest rather than the open water," said Marie. "It suggests we may have been doing our surveys only just above their daytime pasture. And that's a pretty disturbing thought."

They didn't have long to wait for their next surprise.

"No!" said Teixeira, bring a hand to her mouth. She seemed to be better at interpreting the red-and-black images. On the screen was another farmer, but it wasn't alone. In its arms it held something that was difficult to make out at first, for it was cooler and obscured the heat from the creature's chest.

"Is that…?" began Figueroa.

Marie cursed, while Teixeira looked down and away. "Yes, Prof. I think it is."

The farmer had a body with it – a human body. Next to each other, the size and power of the creature was apparent – broader and longer, it manipulated the corpse easily, like a parent with a toddler. It nudged closer to the camera, filling the screen and then – as if realising what the camera was – it withdrew slightly and pushed the face of the corpse towards the lens. As Teixeira sobbed softly, Figueroa put a gentle hand upon her shoulder. The saving grace was that the body was long dead and held little residual heat, so the face was indistinct – a shape with a ridge where the nose should be, and a darker smudge for the mouth.

"What's it doing?" asked Teixera, glancing up and down again. "It's playing with him."

Him? Her? Marie couldn't tell the sex of the body – until the creature withdrew slightly and she gasped. "Naked! It's *stripped* him."

The creature loomed close again, it's head now next to that of the corpse. And this time its head somehow *opened.* It was difficult to tell how, but there was suddenly a space somewhere in its ellipsoid face, presumably where its dark mouth was, which appeared a brighter red from a greater heat. And then it moved its mouth over the corpse's neck, and the red disappeared as the mouth closed. "Oh, no!" exclaimed Figueroa.

On the screen, the dull shape of the corpse changed symmetry, as the head flopped to one side, the neck seemingly bitten through.

Teixeira pushed away from the console, rose, and staggered from the cabin.

Marie watched in horror as the creature pulled back slightly, then twisted the body to show its handiwork. And then it turned nonchalantly, and with its prize, dove beyond the sight of the camera.

Marie and Figueroa were silent, looking at each other aghast. But then Marie glimpsed something else on the screen and her eyes widened. "Christ! Look at *that*!" On the centre screen, displaying the feed from the camera attached to the bottom of the boat, there was another farmer, but this one was different from all of the others they had seen. "It's got something on its head. It's… green. Kelp?" She started a slightly hysterical laugh and declared: "Sunglasses! It's put on sunglasses!"

Figueroa was at first too shocked to speak, but then he seemed to appreciate what Marie meant. "It's protecting its eyes."

"Eyes? Yes. Or whatever it uses to sense the world around it. Light-sensitive cells across its whole head, I reckon." It was now maybe three metres beneath the boat, floating in light that would normally send its kind racing away in distress. But this one endured – albeit at a distance – and seemed to be assessing the bottom of the boat.

It was then that Marie heard a shriek from outside. She was first out of the cabin, with Figueroa just behind. Resnos and Texeira were at the stern, Teixera's head buried in the man's shoulder, his arms around her.

"What happened?" asked Marie.

"Something came from the water," said Resnos, his face pale. "It… shot from starboard, went over the cabin, and dropped over there." He used his chin to point off to the port side.

"What was it?" asked Marie.

"I don't…"

And then another shape shot from the water. Marie heard a light splash behind, but before she could turn, caught a glimpse of something high up, a dark, round shape; she tracked it as it disappeared somewhere towards the bow. There was a shout from that direction: Garcia.

"Raul…" Marie called to the unseen man, but then there was an explosion of water behind. She turned in time to see three, four more projectiles breach the ocean, and these had a lower trajectory. A couple missed, but one thumped on top of the cabin, and then rolled along its roof towards its rear edge, where it teetered for a moment, before dropping with a sickening thus onto an emergency box set against the cabin wall. And this time, all could see what it was.

Resnos turned away and pulled Teixera's head close so she wouldn't be able to see; Figueroa groaned; Marie gaped and staggered back.

It was a head.

A *human* head.

As Marie reeled at the sight, she heard a number of shouts from around the boat: from the cabin, where Grande had been watching the screens hitherto mutely; from the wheelhouse, where Perez must have at last recognised the nature of the shapes arcing through the air; but loudest of all, from the bow – a shout that turned into a scream, and was followed by a loud splash.

Resnos acted first: he disengaged Teixeira and headed towards where Garcia had been. Marie stared dumbly for a fraction of a second, then moved after the man. They circled to the front, and found an empty deck: Garcia was gone, as was the cable for the infrared camera, which had been torn from the adaptor on the deck. Resnos moved to the rail at the front, leaning on the gunwale. "Raul!" he shouted.

Marie watched his back; saw his shoulders tense, his hands gripping the rail hard, releasing, gripping again. She knew what he was thinking: it was the same thing she was. There was a man in the water. They should dive in. Find him. Save him. But to do so…

She stepped up to Resnos and reached an arm around him, just to be sure he didn't do something stupid. Then she looked around and up, gazing through the glass into the raised wheelhouse, where Perez stared at them in shock.

"Arantxa – get us out of here. Full speed."

But that wasn't the last of their shocks.

It took some seconds for the pilot to address the controls, turning the boat so that it was facing back towards the *Lisboa*, and applying power to the propellor. From somewhere astern, a final object was spat from the water, arcing high through the air with supreme accuracy. By this stage, Marie and Resnos had staggered back to the stern, where Figueroa now stood with an inconsolable Teixeira. They all looked, their eyes drawn automatically upwards, then tracing the projectile down, down… where it thudded onto the deck.

Raul Garcia's bloodied head skimmed and bounced across the surface then rolled in a spiral to end at Marie's feet – looking up with an expression of intense surprise.

* * *

"You've got to look at this," said Tonio.

"What?" asked Sara, grinning broadly. "Are you spying on dream-girl Vita? Have you managed to hack into the cameras at the Terrace?"

"Ha-ha!" said Tonio. "No. It's much more interesting than that, though maybe not so… *sexy.*"

Kate looked between her friends and smiled. They were always able to cheer her up, even at times like this. She watched Sara saunter over from a secondary console to the central one, where Tonio sat like an organist in a cathedral.

"Show me!" commanded Sara.

Tonio tapped away; the main screen in the dim control room lit up. "This is the Bowl. *Our* Bowl."

"I see that. So? You've had access to the cameras there for some time. What's new?"

"Well, before I only had access to *this* camera, showing the room itself. But the eggheads installed new cameras at the edge looking through the bowl into the water, and then linked these in to the current network. So, I found them, and I can now control them as well as the floodlights that point down." He smirked. "I can not only tune-in when they're there and see what they're seeing, but I can control everything remotely when they're away – like now."

"Yeah – where are they?" wondered Sara. "They've not been around all day. Kate – where's your mum?"

Kate lounged against the console to Tonio's other side. "I don't know. She tells me nothing. Well… that's not true, actually. She does talk to me when we get the chance, but recently, she's been out when I've been in, and vice versa. And since the news yesterday…" she shrugged. "I heard her come back late last night when I was in bed, but she was gone when I got up."

"So, she doesn't know us seniors have today off to *grieve*?" Sara smiled, and then her mouth quickly turned into a frown. Kate understood her dilemma. No one really knew how to react to the news of the loss of the harvesters. Over thirty people had disappeared… *drowned.* Although none of those were immediate family to anyone in their class, they'd still got the day off school, and it was clear that Sara, like Kate, was struggling to find the right balance in how happy to appear about this. *Damn guilt!*

"I suspect she knows, but what can she do? Stay home to 'console' me? Tcha! She trusts me. And anyway, this is a big thing for her. I guess she's a bit freaked out about whether these new aliens are responsible for the sinkings or not."

"Of course they are," said Sara, her frown deepening. "They're monsters. You've both seen that."

Tonio swivelled in his seat to face away from the console and looked between the girls.

"Well, I'm not sure that's been demonstrated yet," said Kate. "I know you blame them for the disappearance of the sea life, but I doubt they've actually *eaten* it all, rather than just scared it off."

"They scared me off, too," said Sara. "I don't like them. They ooze menace. Do you want to bet against them being responsible for the harvesters?"

"No. Definitely not. I think they did it. Two harvesters? In fine weather? I'm just saying, we haven't *actually* seen them do anything bad, and until yesterday, I don't think Mum and her team had either. It could have been some sort of accident."

"Oh, come on, Kate. How do you accidentally sink two boats so quickly they barely manage to get out a distress signal between them?"

Kate sighed. "Okay. Yeah. That's difficult to justify. It just sucks to think that if these things are actually intelligent, that our first encounter with them ends in a fight. According to Mum, this find is like the Holy Grail, but now it seems like the Grail is still full of blood."

"Whoa, Kate," said Tonio. "That's kind of poetic. You sure you don't want to major in the arts instead of a sensible subject?"

Kate flashed the boy a smile, but didn't respond. The image in her head disturbed her, as did Sara's somewhat horrified expression.

"Right, enough of this," continued Tonio. "Do you want to see what I can do, or not?" He swivelled in his seat and started to play at the keyboard again.

Kate flashed a cautious smile at Sara, then moved to the boy's shoulder, and a moment later felt Sara move beside her. "Go on, then."

Tonio's fingers blurred and then he slapped the 'return' key, and the image on the wide central screen turned black, or rather, a washed grey. "We're now looking through the bowl. The eggheads found that increasing and decreasing the light seems to act as a signal, so here goes." He played on a couple of keys, tapping one, then the other. On screen, the grey darkened, lightened, darkened, and then there it was, slowly emerging from the depths, a farmer.

"It's *him*," gasped Kate. "Bent Finger. Their boss. And what's he *wearing*?"

The farmer approached the glass, it's ellipsoid head swaddled in something that made it appear a different shade to rest of its body.

"Balaclava," said Sara.

"More like a ski mask," said Tonio. "It's whole face is covered… even its eyes."

"How do you two know the difference between Earth head gear from cold climes?" asked Kate. "I bet there's nothing like a balaclava or ski mask on the whole planet."

"Oh, come on, Kate," said Tonio, over his shoulder. "We're not complete dummies. We've got an archive with every movie made on Earth up to about the one-thirties."

Kate didn't respond. She was entranced by the vision of the creature staring through the bottom of the *Lisboa*, seemingly looking directly at her. Other shapes emerged from the gloom: two more farmers, which took position to either side of Bent Finger. The leader turned its head to consider the newcomers, then made jerking motions, first to one, then the other, clearly communicating instructions. The two turned and swam off, while Bent Finger returned to appraise the bowl. It reached its two long hands forwards and appeared to caress the glass, then started tapping at it with one taloned nail. Then it pushed back, as though to widen its field of vision to encompass the entire bowl. It treaded water for some seconds before another farmer appeared from one side – this carrying something close to its chest. Kate couldn't work out what the object was: it looked like a long, fat cigar, maybe one-to-two metres in length, and indeed, just like a cigar it was tightly wrapped. *Kelp leaves*, thought Kate.

Bent Finger turned to the new arrival and did more of the strange head-jerking. The other farmer paused a moment, then continued on with its cargo, heading in the direction of the centre of the ship. And suddenly there were more farmers – a *lot* more. They came from the same direction and swam past their leader, some carrying more of the fat cigars, others carrying smaller bundles, some carrying nothing at all.

"Ten… fifteen…"

Kate glanced to the side, where Sara was softly counting.

The procession lasted several minutes. Sara's counting became more approximate; around eighty, she stopped. And all the while, Bent Finger ignored the activity around it and kept staring at the bowl and the camera that was recording it.

At last the stream slowed, and then stopped, leaving Bent Finger alone. The creature drifted up and down, gave some sort of nod, then whisked around and headed in the direction of the swarm.

Kate and the others held their breaths for some seconds, but no more farmers appeared, and nor did Bent Finger return.

"Well," said Tonio, at last. "*That* was something new."

"Hundreds," whispered Sara. "There were *hundreds*."

"That's definitely more than anyone has seen before," said Tonio. "Anyone *but us*. And *I* recorded it."

"What… Tonio?" said Kate. "You did?"

Tonio half-turned and smirked. "Well, it's a default option really, so I can't take much credit. It records when the lights pass a certain threshold. But if I hadn't been operating them, then none of that would have been recorded."

"Will the scientists be able to see it?" said Kate.

"Ah, well, I was going to delete it in case they come back and wonder why their lights were going on-and-off by themselves, so…"

"Don't!" said Kate, sharply. "Tonio – I think this is important. Mum will want to see it."

"Er, right," said Tonio, turning completely around in his seat and looking between the standing girls, his expression now serious. "But I'm not sure I like this. The eggheads have already evicted us from the Bowl. Okay, I'm not obsessed with it like Sara was, but it was *our* secret pad. They don't know about this place, but if they find out, they'll probably try to kick us out from here, too."

"Well, I'm not saying we have to admit to everything… or anything, really," said Kate. "But can't you just leave the recording where it is? If they find it, they'll probably be less interested in how the camera started recording than the sight itself – especially if they're all like Mum, with her tunnel vision."

"Riiiiight," said Tonio, clearly still unconvinced. "And what if they don't find it? Why are they going to look into past recordings any time soon? And if they don't?"

"If they do, I'll find out pretty quickly from Mum. And if they don't, well, we'll have to work out a way to direct them to it. But the key thing is, the recording is still there."

Tonio turned. "Sara – what do you think?"

The girl nodded slowly. "I think Kate is right. If these *things* are up to something, we need to know what. Otherwise…" she paused, "we won't know where to go to destroy them."

* * *

"I told you it was insane," said Kalmik, shaking her head. "And now Raul is dead."

"I don't think that helps, Katerina," said Figueroa.

"Maybe not," the woman continued, "but it's important to state this for the record. I'm not saying this on the basis of hindsight."

Nacimiento stirred. He'd been sitting quietly, listening to the report from Figueroa and Kate, clearly stunned by the account, his old age suddenly apparent as his natural vivacity leached away. "Dr Kalmik, please. We erred in not listening to Dr Lockard in going ahead with the harvesting in the first place, and perhaps we have done so again in returning to the site of the disaster. Poor Raul. I know his parents. His mother… did you know we had a liaison once? Many years ago. The poor woman, and her husband. And his family. I believe he has two children?"

Figueroa leant across the table and patted the Captain-Governor on the pristine sleeve of his uniform with its gold symbols of rank. "Joao, it is terrible. But there are dozens more who are also bereft."

"I know. But I admit, I do not know any of their close relatives like I do Raul's. It makes everything so personal. It focuses the mind. What are we to do now to stop these tragedies?"

Figueroa looked lost too. He turned to Kate, appealing for help.

"Leave," she said. "We just need to leave. And we need to warn everyone else on the planet to stay away from the fringe forests – though it seems they do anyway."

"You mean, just brush this off?" said Kalmik. "Write the whole thing off as a loss? Admit defeat?"

"I'm not sure what you mean by 'defeat'," said Kate. "It's a word with implications. The opposite is victory. You're framing this as a competition. A *fight.* It's nothing like that. We've stumbled upon a… *wonderous*… thing. But we've blundered. And there's no one to blame for that: we're in a completely novel situation, and we are human. *Fallible.* We've been acting with incomplete knowledge." Kate paused, and realised the other three were staring at her – relying on her. Even Kalmik. "I'm not saying we should leave forever – just for now. And when we return – whether here, or another fringe forest – we need to do so with much more caution. Take things slowly, *very* slowly. Be meticulous. But we need cool heads now. Let's take ourselves out of the game, and away from the farmers, so there's no more opportunity for conflict. After all, we were meant to be leaving later today, so why change the plan?"

Figueroa nodded. "Indeed, my dear. *Cool heads.* Joao – I suggest we be careful in how we communicate about today's events. I have instructed my team not to spread details of the, ah, nature of what unfolded. The… *heads*…"

This time, it was Kate who reached across to squeeze the other's arm in sympathy.

Kalmik scowled. "Okay. That is a strategy. I just hope that these things… I'm not going to call them farmers any more. What about *reapers*? I just hope these reapers are also content to stand down and let us leave."

Nacimiento looked up at this. "Why would you say that, Dr Kalmik?"

"Why? Well, with the harvesters, we showed them that we are weak and easy to kill. Now they will see us fleeing from them like cowards. We have also discovered that they do indeed have teeth and, worse, *attitude.* I'll bet they're curious. And they're certainly not afraid of us. What if they decide they don't want to let us go? What if they decide to *chase* us?"

Kate nodded slowly. Nature was a cruel mistress; it didn't protect the weak. If they turned their backs now, were they signalling to the planet's apex predator that they were legitimate prey? She had an uncomfortable suspicion that Kalmik might be right.

Chapter 33

Getting to the embassy turned out to be considerably more difficult than getting to *Hibernia* – and this had nothing to do with any challenge from the security services.

The rain sluiced the street beyond the entrance to the Eastern Docks, flowing down the road in a torrent strong enough the make the incautious slip, while the downward pressure of rain was difficult to bear, and even painful.

Cass Remillard – who had greater familiarity with the geography of *Hibernia* than anyone else – took point, with the rest of the team strung out behind in a human chain, heads bowed, eyes down, rain drumming off jacket hoods, single hands stretched out to rest on the shoulders of those in front.

On the positive side, there was absolutely no one on the streets to see them. But as they trudged, Melissa De Voe wondered whether there might be eyes inside any of the sporadically lit windows of the buildings – eyes looking out at them in curiosity or concern. If so, would their owners contact the authorities to alert them? *Perhaps mental health experts*, she thought to herself, for no one sane would be out in this.

It would have been better to drop to a subsurface level, but Remillard had assured them that there would be plenty of activity below, even at this time – just gone midnight – and indeed, considerably more than usual as a result of all the displaced people who would otherwise have been travelling above ground. It was just as well they had Remillard to lead them, for De Voe realised she had exaggerated her own experience and would never have been able to find her way to the embassy under current conditions.

Keeping her hand on Heiko's shoulder – who was second in line behind Remillard – was difficult. Though she was tall for a woman, Heiko still had the advantage on her, and after a short while her shoulder began to ache from holding up her arm. She should have jumped in behind Remillard, who was perhaps twenty centimetres shorter than Heiko. Worse, she felt Pedersen's heavy hand pressing down upon her own shoulder – for he was of similar height to Heiko.

"*Fuck!*" she shouted, though she doubted anyone heard her above the violent drumming of the rain, which made it difficult for her to even hear her own thoughts.

After some minutes, they crossed an empty street and found themselves under awnings that jutted over the windows of a line of now-closed retail outlets and protected the pavement beneath. The intensity of the rain lessened, but didn't completely abate, as the gusting wind threw water horizontally too, and indeed, the noise increased further with the heavenly drummer having a larger, longer target on which to practise its music. Looking up quickly – now that she had the chance – De Voe saw the awning rippling and bowing under the weather's assault, and wondered whether the retractable shelter was intended to be deployed under such circumstances. Maybe it would suffice for a Class Two or Three; maybe someone had erred in leaving it unfurled? As she watched, a great updraft punched the awning upwards, making it strain mightily. "They've fucked up," she muttered. There was no way the canvas roof was going to last the night, or maybe even the hour.

But someone's error helped immensely. She felt Heiko raise up, and Pedersen's hand lift from her shoulder, then like the two men, she took the opportunity to straighten her back and flex her shoulder – but it was a momentary relief only. No one spoke – a pointless exercise. Then Heiko began to move again, a little more upright, and she was forced into action too. And though her sight improved, in that she could now see the buildings to her side up close and unobscured, it was difficult to make out anything behind the glass frontages, given the shadows and confusing reflections from streetlights, refracting from water on window panes.

At the next junction, the full horror of the external conditions returned as they curved down a perpendicular street where those responsible for building maintenance *hadn't* been so careless. A cross wind caused De Voe to stagger and momentarily lose her grip on Heiko. She frantically scrabbled and found it again. "Someone's going to die for this," she cursed. But again, no one heard her.

The journey seemed to last forever, but was probably no more than twenty minutes. They turned, and were suddenly on an elegant street, where porticoes of stone provided better protection from the elements. De Voe now recognised where they were: Consul Street, in the Derry Quarter. They slowed, as Remillard checked numbers, moved on, checked again.

At last, their guide found the right number – beside a wide, black door with a porch held up by Doric columns. There was room for De Voe to squeeze under the shelter with Heiko and Remillard, though Pedersen was left exposed behind her.

Remillard knocked, waited some seconds, knocked again harder. It wasn't until his fifth knock – now a hammering with a closed fist – that evidence of life greeted them: light shone from behind closed curtains from a room to one side of the door, and then through the transom window over the door itself. By now, De Voe was to the side of Heiko and looking directly over Remillard's shoulder. She saw the door open slightly, pause, then open more fully… and there was Magnus Solbakken, in a blue dressing gown, a look of astonishment on his face.

* * *

"I have found space for the rest of your team upstairs," said Solbakken, emerging through the door of the lounge. "I'm afraid you'll have to sleep here – either that, or in the cellars, which are considerably gloomier."

"I think here will do," said Heiko, who seemed to have been less affected by the pounding they'd received than the others – and certainly less than *her*, De Voe thought. "Thank you, Magnus. Some bedding would be appreciated, though."

"Sure. I'll see to that shortly. But now you seem to have recovered somewhat — I hope the coffee helped and, ah, I see Cass has been at my brandy – I would rather like to find out what on Tethys is going on."

They had all been given towels and stripped off to their underwear, the room looking like the coy beginning to some sort of orgy. De Voe looked at Remillard's somewhat flabby frame – drawn by his laughter, as he raised his tumbler of golden fluid – which was at odds to the toned physiques of Heiko and Pedersen, who seemed well-matched. She momentarily wondered who'd win in a fight, but then her mouth twitched into a smile as she remembered the ease with which Heiko had dealt with the Hibernian invaders during her tussle with them back on the *Stavanger.* In spite of his greater age – with grey tinging his hair – it was clear that Heiko was dangerous… and she *liked* that. She momentarily had lascivious thoughts, but then saw Heiko's mouth moving, and realised he had been speaking. Her hearing had not entirely recovered: she shook her head, and poked a finger in one ear, displacing water with a squelch, and then the volume rose.

"… well, it's certainly a shock," said Solbakken, responding to Heiko's unheard words.

"We couldn't risk alerting you through the satellite link," said Heiko. "Sorry."

"I understand. I just wish I could offer you better accommodation."

"Honestly, Magnus, this is fine. The help we really need is in tracking down Makka Frost and our purloined resources."

Solbakken came around to sit in a chair, facing his semi-clad, towel-wielding guests. "So, you've decided to take direct action? I am surprised… but *not* disappointed. I may have some information on Makka, but not on our stolen treasure."

"One out of two," said Heiko. "So, you've seen Makka?"

"Seen him? No. I have tried, but I've been palmed off so far. He's not a prisoner, apparently, and therefore he has no need of any sort of representation. Instead, he is a 'willing guest' at the Hibernian Institute of Science."

"And where is that?" asked Heiko.

"I've been there before," said De Voe. "It's on the edge of the Derry Quarter, I think."

"That's right," said Solbakken. "It's back the way you came, but further inland. It's part of the university complex."

"And is he sleeping there, too? Does it have accommodation?"

"Ah, now there you have me. I don't know. He could be there, or at a nearby hotel or…" Solbakken waved a hand airily. "Just about anywhere."

Heiko continued to rub himself lightly with his towel, while looking down in thought. De Voe watched him, and noticed that everyone else in the room was doing the same – waiting for him to speak. "Okay." Heiko looked up again at their host. "We can't be sure where he is at this time, but you expect him to be at this institute during office hours, no?"

"I guess so. I doubt they'll let him wander freely. It's the obvious place to keep him while they interrogate him about the find and other issues."

"Like how to best exploit the deposit," nodded De Voe.

"Okay," said Heiko. "Then we'll need to wait until daylight to extract him… *somehow*. But I think we're all tired and need to rest. And I need to think. We can firm up plans tomorrow morning."

De Voe was relieved at his decision – although she wasn't about to admit this was so.

* * *

When the lights came on in the lounge, Heiko blinked, then instinctively rolled away, bunching up the blanket that had been covering him.

"Sorry everyone – something's up."

He recognised Solbakken's voice after a dazed second, then heard a groan from a short distance away. He sat up, pushing off the blanket fully, and appraised the situation. Solbakken stood by the open door; next to Heiko – laying on the carpeted floor – were De Voe, Remillard, and Pedersen, in parallel. The room's furniture had been pushed against the wall to make space for the visitors' sleeping area. He leapt up – partially dressed – and moved to the nearest chair, in which he slumped.

"I don't know what's going on," continued Solbakken, casting an amused eye over the others, "but I just got an alert on my communicator. We're locked down. *Everyone*. There's a city-wide curfew in force, and no one is allowed out on the streets."

"Is this common?" asked Heiko. He reached beneath the chair, where he'd placed his boots, and began to put them on. De Voe passed between him and their rude awakener and sat in an adjacent chair.

"Not at all. It's part of a government warning system linked to everyone's communicator. It was set up some years ago to give advice after a Class Five hit, and people were caught unprepared. I can't remember the last time it was used, and I've never had anything like this happen."

Remillard had found a chair on the other side of the room, and was playing with his own communicator. "I got nothing."

"You don't have Hibernian kit. Have you logged into the local net yet?"

"Ah, no."

"Then that's why," said Solbakken.

"Is the warning because of the storm?" asked Heiko, sitting up straight. Where had he left his tablet?

Solbakken pouted his lips and considered a moment. "No. I don't think so. This is a full curfew – above *and* below ground. Normally, life retreats underground during storms, which don't have any impact in the sublevels, so why prevent people moving about? No one will be able to get to work or school."

"Is it something to do with us, then?" asked De Voe, rubbing one sleepy eye.

"It could be, but I'm not sure how. You arrived in the dead of night in the middle of a storm, and all you've done since is sleep."

"Sleep?" De Voe's arch expression suggested she'd not had much of that. "Ha-ha! What time is it?"

"If it were us," mused Heiko, ignoring the question, "and they suspected a *Stavanger* link, then why the curfew? This embassy would be a natural hideout, so why not surround it quietly rather than alerting us that there might be a problem?"

"Well, maybe they are outside right now?" said Remillard. He looked old under the harsh light. "Perhaps they're hoping to spook us into running." He turned to Solbakken. "I'm guessing they still respect diplomatic immunity. Maybe they'd rather take us in the open than cause a diplomatic incident?"

Solbakken smiled grimly. "You mean, *another* diplomatic incident. I think they well-and-truly trampled over our sovereign rights when they sent their soldiers to the *Stavanger*."

"That's an interesting thought," said Heiko. "But I don't think this lockdown can be because of us. If they did know about our arrival, it would be best to keep that intel to themselves, observe us from a distance, and be ready to strike when we incautiously leave. Still, it would be remiss not to rule this option out. We do have a portable drone in our kit, which we could launch from an upper storey window, but I doubt it'll fly in this weather." He looked down in thought, then smiled and looked up again. "We need another way to track our opponents – and that's why Claude Vardem is on the team."

Remillard coughed a laugh. "The Magic Man? Of course."

"Want me to go and wake him, sir?" asked Pedersen. He was already standing, fully dressed, and looked fresh and awake.

"Thanks, Anders."

They waited for the other to leave, then Heiko continued: "If it *is* to do with us, then it would have to be related to someone noting the arrival of Cass' boat and alerting authorities, and that would provide a clear *Stavanger* link. But then they would know we couldn't be great in number given the boat's size, so a full curfew seems excessive, does it not? So, if we're not the cause of this, Magnus, and nor is the storm, what else could it be?"

"Hmmm, there was recently a raid on the Engine Quarter. Turned out the Stokers have acquired some weapons, and a couple of the ISU were killed. That's a big thing around here – the first losses in the line of duty since I became ambassador. Perhaps there's another raid going on, or perhaps some of the gunmen who escaped are at large in the wider city? That would be my bet."

"So, what do we do?" asked De Voe. "We came to get Makka and our stolen gear. We can't do that skulking around here."

Heiko raised a hand, a thought occurring. "Cass – something you said. *Diplomatic immunity*. Magnus – is that still a prerogative here? If you got caught breaking curfew, could you flash your ID and escape arrest?"

Solbakken opened his eyes wide. "Ah… that is an interesting thought. I wouldn't like to say. I guess as a foreigner with some status… *maybe*. I'm not sure a normal grunt would want to risk causing an incident, although I doubt I would be allowed to wander the streets breaking an official order. Perhaps I'd be escorted back here?" He frowned. "I'm not sure I like the look in your eye, Mr Heiko."

"Oh, I do," said De Voe. "Come on, Rennie. Cough it up."

"There's nothing more to say. It's just the germ of an idea. I think, Magnus, what you say makes sense. But what would happen would likely depend upon a number of factors. How far we were from the embassy when caught; whether we had a valid story for why we were out and about; and as you say, the nature of whoever caught us, whether a ranker or an officer."

"I note you use the word 'we'," said Solbakken, "which at least eases my concern at being thrown into the firing line alone."

"Yes – although it couldn't be the whole team. Anyone with you would have to pretend to be fellow embassy staff, and I know you don't have many."

"Many?" Solbakken raised an amused eyebrow.

"Okay, *any*. But that's not likely to be widely known. I suspect two of us could risk it."

"You and me?" confirmed Solbakken.

"And *me*," said De Voe.

"Melissa – three might be pushing it," said Heiko.

"Nonsense. You're his personal escort and I'm his PA. Also, if we're going for Makka, I want to be there."

"You think he wouldn't trust Magnus and I enough to come with us?"

"I'm not saying that, Rennie. But I have relevant knowledge here. Who knows when it might come in handy, especially if we're going to the Science Institute. I've been there once before on a visit with Makka. Met some of the people. All that. I hope you're not trying to *protect* me for personal reasons?"

Heiko felt somewhat unsettled by the comment, and by the other's inscrutable expression. He raised both hands: "I can honestly say, Melissa, that is not the case. I know you can look after yourself."

"Good," said De Voe, brusquely. "Then it's settled. Us three. Cass can hold the fort with Anders and the rest."

At that moment, the door to the lounge opened, and Pedersen entered followed by Claude Vardem, both tall and blond and wearing light-coloured jackets. Vardem came to a loose attention and looked at Heiko. "Sir!"

"Claude – sorry for the early call, but we need you. There's something going on, and we need to access the Hibernians' secure systems to find out what it is. Are you familiar with their network?"

"Not intimately, but the Hibernians' sophistication isn't great." Vardem gave a lop-sided smile. "Frankly, there's no need for it to be. There's no real spying on the planet, and little to gain from computer theft – especially as most of the criminals in *Hibernia* are already in power. Their network security is a joke."

Remillard laughed at this; Solbakken grinned and shook his head slightly.

Heiko smiled in sympathy. "*Stavanger*… and *Hibernia* too? Is it like this on all Tethys?"

Vardem considered a moment. "I can't really say. It's said they're more savvy in Taiwan. And on the *Marseilles*, they apparently have good surveillance tech and capabilities – but that's been developed in order to keep an eye on their own population, not others."

"Is it a structural weakness then, or is it just you… *Magic Man*?" Heiko glanced at Remillard. He'd not heard Vardem's nickname before; it reminded him that there was still much he didn't know about this planet, his new home, and the people who lived here. "How did you get to be such a hotshot?"

"I'm not. To be honest, I'll bet there are thousands of teenagers on Earth who are more competent than I am. Maybe millions. It's really, as you say, *structural*. But in the land of the blind, the one-eyed man is king – and all that." Vardem shrugged. "I'd like to think I'm an ace hacker, but I'm a realist. It is what it is."

"So can you get into their systems?" asked Heiko. "Can you patch me in, like on the *Stavanger*?"

Vardem smiled. "Oh, yeah. Undoubtedly. It's just a question of exactly *what* I can give you access to, and how long it'll take."

"Okay, assuming you start right away, what could you give me in an hour – if we decide to leave then?"

Vardem turned to face Solbakken. "Ambassador – I assume you have a decent computer that's hard-wired into the Hibernian network?"

"Of course."

"Then show it to me, please, sir. And then I need three things," he said, turning back to his superior.

"Go on," said Heiko.

"First, my bag from upstairs. I've got some software I developed that I need to download. Second, peace and quiet. You can't keep bugging me while I work. And third, a litre of coffee: black; extra strong."

* * *

In the end, they left an hour and forty minutes later, through a door in the basement that opened into a corridor on Sublevel One. It had just gone eight o' clock in the morning. They'd delayed to allow Vardem more time, but also after last minute doubts.

"If no one's allowed out, then how do we know Makka's going to be at the Institute rather than in some hotel or detention centre?"

Heiko had cursed at that observation. Melissa was right – they couldn't know. But in the end, it had just seemed best to do *something* rather than *nothing*. Frost might be at the Institute, or the curfew might shortly end and he'd duly be delivered, *or* maybe they could at least get inside and then wait for him to arrive later in the day – presumably in a building presently devoid of employees. As such, the curfew might even work to their advantage.

The clincher had been when Vardem had announced: "Aha! Lazy, lazy guys…"

The sublevel *was* deserted.

Heiko led the way: in spite of his lack of knowledge of *Hibernia's* geography, he now had an advantage over Solbakken and De Voe, with Vardem having transferred a schematic of the city state straight into his augment via the adaptor Heiko always carried with him. Closing his eyes, he could bring up the map with the sublevel route marked in red. What's more, Vardem was intermittently transferring more information to him wirelessly, while relating what he was doing via an earpiece.

"Whoa! Something is going off under the Command Centre now. Looks like Sublevel Two… That's pretty close."

"Thanks, Claude," he spoke in a low voice into his mic. "Do we need to reroute?"

"No. But definitely keep to your level. Don't drop down."

"Roger that." Heiko had paused and crouched: he noticed Solbakken and De Voe looking at him curiously. Louder, he said: "No problem. Let's keep going."

He led them along the empty corridor, walking briskly. It was broad here, well-maintained and lit. To one side were the basement entrances to homes and businesses, while to the other was a line of small craft shops and eateries, with glass fronts, which were closed and dark.

At a junction, they turned right. They hadn't gone far when, five metres ahead, a darkened window lit up in the right wall. Heiko moved to the same wall, leaning against the window of a shop that declared itself to be a 'Flavor Emporium'. He crouched.

Behind him, Solbakken whispered: "The owner probably lives above. Checking stock perhaps?"

Heiko nodded, but didn't respond. He crept along the wall to a position where he could peer inside. He noticed some movement and quickly withdrew his head. Then he turned to address the others: "A woman, I think. I don't want to be seen and reported. Let's give it five."

But before a minute had passed, another window lit up – this time from a unit on the left wall, perhaps ten metres behind them.

"What the fuck?" said De Voe.

"Is the curfew over?" asked Solbakken, crouched beside the others. He pulled out his communicator to check for governmental messages.

Heiko raised a finger. "Claude? We're getting some activity here. Is lockdown still in force?"

"Most definitely. In fact, things are getting worse. I'm now tracking reports of action in half-a-dozen places. It seems to have started near the Engine Quarter, but now there's stuff going off under the Command Centre, by the ISU's HQ, and even towards the Western Docks. Coordinated and extensive. It's like an uprising."

"Okay. Keep looking for a central comms source in their security system to patch me into."

"Roger, sir."

"So?" asked De Voe.

"Claude thinks it's a full-on revolt. Lockdown still in effect."

"Then what the hell is going on… *shit*!" De Voe flinched. The premises on the other side of the Flavor Emporium suddenly lit up.

Solbakken chuckled nervously. "If there's a revolt, these folks haven't been told about it. Seems they're getting ready to open up as soon as the all clear is given."

"Are we far from the Institute?" asked De Voe.

Heiko closed his eyes and checked. "No. We're nearly at the edge of the Derry District." He straightened. "There's nothing for it. Walk purposefully in the centre of the corridor, as though we have the right. If we're reported, and things are as busy as Claude suggests, I doubt whether any of the security forces will get here anytime soon. Ready?"

"Go on, Magnus," said De Voe, also straightening. "You take the lead. We'll follow behind like the serfs we're meant to be."

Solbakken stood and strode off, looking straight ahead. Heiko fell in behind, with De Voe next to him. He couldn't help a quick sideways glance as they passed the next shop, and what he saw was the back of a woman, leaning over a counter and searching for something behind it. By the time they reached the next junction, a couple more lights had come on.

"Left here," said Heiko, "then right at the next junction. Then we're under the university and away from retail units."

Six minutes later, they turned down another corridor, passing under an arch with a Latin inscription. No one had shouted at them or otherwise shown any alarm. Solbakken slowed and turned. "Well, that was exciting. Heiko – you can take point now. I think we're close."

"Yes, we–"

"Stop!" The voice was that of a woman, slightly shrill.

Heiko tensed and instinctively raised his hands slowly. The voice was from further down the corridor. He saw one woman striding towards them, and she had some sort of gun in her hands. Several metres behind her, a cluster of others appeared from around a corner. There were perhaps a dozen of them.

"Stay calm everyone," said Heiko. "Especially you, Melissa. They're armed and twitchy."

De Voe hissed, but turned slowly and held up her hands in the universal sign of submission – as did Solbakken.

The woman was dressed in an old green jumpsuit. Her hair was unevenly shaved, and she had a tattoo on one cheek. Her eyes were wide with excitement. She gestured with her rifle for them to move aside. Once she was level, and their backs were against the corridor wall, she came to a halt.

"Who are you? You don't look like ISU?"

One of the others in her party hurried up – a man similarly dressed, but with long black hair and thick brows.

"They've seen us. Kill them, and let's move on."

"What the fuck? They're not ISU. Look at them. Curfew breakers. We're not killing civilians. It'd be a waste of bullets."

"We can't take them with us, Annie, and we can't let them go. Use your knife."

"Fuck you, Seumus."

The rest of the party turned up. To Heiko, they appeared something of a rabble. Unlike professionals, they clustered together for mutual support: an enemy would have been able to wipe them all out with a single burst of automatic fire.

"Wait," said Heiko, calmly. "Do you know who we are? This is Magnus Solbakken – Ambassador of Stavanger – and we're his staff. We're not Hibernians. You're Stokers? We're not your enemies. And frankly, under current circumstances, we could even turn out to be your friends. But kill the Stavangeran ambassador, and you'll automatically have another enemy."

The man and the woman looked at each other, clearly undecided. Then the man called Seumus started: "We can't–"

"Look," said Heiko, "we're trying to rescue one of our own who was kidnapped by Hibernian Security. We've no interest in what you're up to. Why don't you go your way, and we'll go ours?"

"I don't know who the fuck you are," said the woman called Annie. "You could be spies. *Plainclothes.*" She ran her eyes over them. "What's in your bags." Both Heiko and De Voe had rucksacks, which contained their tablets, and Heiko's had a baton – but no other weapons.

"We're wasting time," said another man in the group. "We can't be late."

"I'll tell you what," said Heiko. "You don't entirely trust us. I get that. Why don't we come along with you then? *Quietly*. We can stay at the rear. Place one of your team behind us with a gun, so we can't run. Then, when we get to where you're going, and your secret is no longer at risk of being leaked, you can let us go on our way."

"Annie…" warned Seumus.

The woman stepped back and smiled. "Okay then, Seumus. You want to knife them – go on. You do it. Or if you don't want to get sticky, shoot them. I'm sure the sound *won't* alert the Blackshirts. What are you waiting for?"

"Bah! Len's right. We haven't got time. Okay – we'll do it your way. You three – come with us. Len – walk behind. If they do move, shoot them – and this fucker first." He glowered at Heiko. "Let's move. You still point, Annie?"

The woman redirected her rifle so it was pointing at her comrade. "Me? Oh, yeah. Got some bullets need firing – but at the right people."

She turned and stalked off, heading away from the university sector and back down the corridor from which Heiko and his team had come. The rest of the party brushed past, leaving Heiko, De Voe, and Solbakken with the stern-faced Len. The man twitched his rifle, indicating that they should follow the rest of his party. "And no talking," he clarified.

They didn't backtrack too far – only to the end of the corridor they'd just come down, and then they turned in the opposite direction, avoiding the retail area with the lights. There was a stairwell in an annexe a little further along. They took the stairs down to the second sublevel, and emerged into a world with lighting about half the level of the one above, and walls that were solid, occasionally with wide doorways and glowing entry scanners. Heiko noticed one large unit labelled as 'Power Substation 12C', and another appeared to be a water storage unit. Most of the units had alphanumeric codes by their metal doors, but no other label.

Heiko continued to receive news from Vardem, and managed at one juncture to quietly update the other. "We've been waylaid, Claude. *Stokers.*" He'd then been unable to respond to the other's queries for a minute or so, until turning a corner allowed him to hiss – unobserved by Len – "Situation stable here, but can't respond. Continue to update."

And then he got the message he'd been waiting for. "Sir – I've cracked it. Hacked a link to their Strategy Room. You'll see new icons in your menu. I hope you can make use of the data."

And lo, Heiko found he was able to access various camera and computer systems at the very heart of the ISU's domain, and scroll through tactical maps and reports. His attention diverted, he stumbled and fell into De Voe, who wrapped an arm around him to keep him upright.

"Cut that out," snarled a voice from behind. "No touching."

And soon after, Heiko heard the first sound of gunfire.

* * *

They arrived at their destination about twenty minutes after being picked up. Still on Sublevel Two, they came to an open area – low ceilinged, circular, receiving four perpendicular corridors. To Heiko, this seemed to have been set up as a command hub: at the very centre of the space were a couple of portable tables with computing equipment, with a small group clustered around this, viewing monitors with flickering maps and displays.

The gunfire was louder here and more consistent, and seemed to be coming from the corridor to the left of the one from which they'd emerged. Len pointed to an area against one barren curving wall and commanded that they sit. After they'd done so, their guard's attention waned: he stood at an angle, gun roughly pointed in their direction, but looking towards the activity in the centre of the circular space and doing his best to hear what was going on. He gradually edged further away.

That was when Heiko noticed a familiar face.

"Uh-oh. *Trouble*," he whispered, leaning in to the others while raising a hand to surreptitiously cover the tell-tale copper port at the side of his eye.

"What is it?" asked De Voe.

"That one over there. In the leader conclave. He's from Earth. One of the New Socialists. I recognise him from the *Leviathan*."

"So?"

"You remember I told you about the trouble on Earth and the *Leviathan* itself? My little adaptation is a kind of heresy to the socialists. A toy for the elite to ingrain our superiority over the common people. If he recognises me, or sees I've got an augment, things could get tricky."

"Well, if he does create a fuss," hissed De Voe, "you could offer to use your toy to help them. You currently know things about the Hibernian forces they don't. Make a trade."

"It's possible. Nice idea. But I'd rather stay out of this fight – in spite of what I said to our captors earlier."

Solbakken leant in until his head was almost touching those of the others. "I agree. We should only do what we must to reclaim what's ours. As representative of our state, I couldn't condone us unilaterally deciding to go to war – whether directly or indirectly."

"You lot are so weak," muttered De Voe. "The Hibernians are the villains here. Anything that unsettles them is good for us. And what if this leads to a regime change? Rennie – isn't that what Olson is hoping for some day? A chance to reset relations? We're more likely to reset on favourable terms if we help these rebels in some way. Then they'll owe us, no?"

"*If* they win," said Heiko. "But we don't know the state of play. The range of forces. How the battle is going. If we attach ourselves to the losing side, who knows how the Hibernian elite might respond?"

De Voe waved a hand irritably and sat back. "Okay. Whatever. I've had my say."

Len turned around for a periodic glance. "Oi! I said no talking!"

The man's shout caused a pair of those in the central conclave – who'd been joined by the leaders of their captors – to turn and look in their direction. One of these was a man with long blond hair in a ponytail with a tattoo on the side of his neck wearing old-style denim that wasn't manufactured on Tethys. Annie and Seumus also turned to look, then turned back, and a frantic conversation ensued.

"Ah, I think we're about to be in the spotlight," said Heiko.

Sure enough, the conversation ended, and four of the group sauntered over – leaving three more still worrying over their displays. Among these four, one stood out – taller than the rest, and muscular, with long dark hair, a firm jaw, and deep-set eyes. Len nervously joined these as they passed him.

"Who are you?" asked the big man. "Why are you here?"

Heiko quickly glanced at Solbakken and gave a small nod.

"Ah, hello," said Solbakken. "We're Stavangerans. My name is Magnus Solbakken, ambassador to *Hibernia*, and these are my staff. As to why we're here… you'll have to ask your colleagues. They detained us while we were en route to the Institute of Science to try to negotiate the release of our chief geologist, who the Hibernians decided to kidnap a few days ago."

"They were breaking curfew," said Seumus. "We couldn't let them go in case they were plainclothes, or in case they rat on us."

The tall man raised a hand to pre-empt further discussion. He looked at Solbakken, then turned to look at De Voe – who returned his gaze firmly – then Heiko, who smiled and gave a small nod while gently rubbing at the side of his eye as though he had an itch. Then the big man broke into a smile. "Stavangerans? Can you prove this?"

Solbakken reached inside his jacket to an inner pocket. He had brought his appropriate diplomatic ID as insurance. He handed it over with a gracious bow – or as gracious as could be delivered when sitting uncomfortably on a bare metal floor.

"Ambassador?" The man scanned the laminated card before quickly returning it. "I'm sorry you've been delayed. I am Kai Dures. You may have heard of me."

"Of course. You have a certain reputation. You are feared by the authorities… but I'd never heard of any dislike of Stavangerans before, so this is a surprise."

"It wasn't I who detained you, but I understand why my comrades did. It's dangerous walking around the sublevels today. You are lucky you weren't shot." He considered Solbakken some more. As Heiko observed the exchange, he became aware that he himself was being scrutinised – feeling another's eyes on him like a physical weight. He deliberately avoided looking at the blond-haired man. "You said *kidnapped.* Interesting choice of words. They also *kidnapped* my wife."

"We perhaps have more in common than we have differences," said Solbakken. "I take it these gunshots and this... *activity*... is about you trying to rescue her?"

"That, yes, and more." Dures considered him a moment further, then declared. "I see no reason to detain you further, but I fear letting you go might jeopardise you from stray shots – and I would hate to see you harmed by the other side, or by mine. You are some way from the embassy, I think, and the Institute of Science... at the university? That is close to the action–" There was a shout of excitement from the command station at the centre of the room. Dures twitched and half-turned, then looked back. "Ambassador – I'm afraid I can't let you go yet. But I see no reason to keep you under the sights of a gun. Stay here for now, but keep out of the way. There are refreshments over there..." he twitched his head towards some spot behind him. "Now I must see to business."

As Dures walked off, and the other Stokers followed him, Heiko was aware of the blond man pausing a second longer, before he too turned and hurried after the others.

"Well," said De Voe. "We're not dead yet. But we're no closer to saving Makka."

"Maybe we're not," said Heiko, focusing on the back of the Earther, "but maybe we *are.*"

Chapter 34

"They caught us by surprise," said Nesvorny. "*Completely*. While we were preparing our own raid, they got in first."

Traore looked out of the monitor screen, unruffled as ever. "So, it seems my concerns weren't exaggerated, after all. I assume you have matters in hand? When will the curfew end? It's becoming tiresome: I don't appreciate being told I have to stay in my apartment."

"I don't think you realise how serious this is."

"So tell me. What does our leader think?"

"O'Neill? I don't know. I thought as my reporting head, I should update you first."

Traore smiled. "Wise not to disturb Marissa… or is it?"

Nesvorny could see the other's mind working, and easily guess what he was thinking. Bearers of bad news rarely did well, but Traore would be able to put whatever slant on proceedings he wanted. He'd undoubtedly emphasize how his oft-stated fears had been realised, while he, Nesvorny, had been lax and bore most of the responsibility for the troubles. "I am sure you will find a way to phrase matters to your advantage."

"*My* advantage?" Traore's smile broadened and he wagged a finger at Nesvorny from the screen. "Careful, Colonel. That's could almost be considered insubordination. Given your failures in the lead up to this, I ought to demand that Kelly dismiss you immediately, and replace you with someone more obedient." Nesvorny scowled, knowing who he meant. "But I think you need to clean up your own mess. Ah… wait." Traore's eyes shifted to look off to the side. "And speak of the devil. I think Marissa is awake and wants to talk to me. I assume she slept through your earlier alert… which you should have got permission for, by the way--"

"I had no choice," Nesvorny interrupted. "I couldn't contact you, either."

Traore's expression firmed. "Colonel, I don't need to justify myself to you. I do not exist shackled to a communicator in case you want to tell me something or make some demand. You answer to me, not vice versa. Enough of this! Marissa will be annoyed I'm not answering. Tell me quickly what I need to know."

Nesvorny seethed. It took some effort to calm himself; he stared at the screen, breathing deeply. "Okay," he said at last. "These are the facts. Three hours ago, one of our observation posts on Sublevel Two, at the Tipperary-Engine Quarter boundary, went offline. Ten minutes after that, a second, further along the boundary, reported being attacked, and it went offline seconds later. By the time I was woken and reached our command centre, a third had gone down, with their last post reporting that they were under attack. A relief squad also came under fire and had to retreat. Since then, I've called my entire force to arms and have sent squads to key junctions throughout the city. But I have nowhere enough troops, especially as my squads keep getting outflanked by Stokers dropping to lower or upper levels and emerging behind them."

"Ah… " Traore's confidence began to wane. "That's clearly not good. Losses?"

"I can't say. Whole squads have disappeared – killed, captured, I've no idea. Over one hundred are unaccounted for, and that's growing by the minute."

"A hundred!"

"What's more, the rebels now have free rein over eighty to ninety percent of the city. I have established pockets of resistance at critical points. My HQ. The Western Docks. The spaceport. The Command Centre."

"And here?"

"Charlestown? No. But you're in the Boston Quarter, not far from the Command Centre. Make your way there, and stay in Sublevel One. If it gets tricky, go above ground – we've no reports of rebels in the open."

"That's because of the *fucking* storm! I am not going into *that*, Colonel!" Traore's demeanour had changed completely, and Nesvorny couldn't help but smile inwardly at this. "But… Marissa will be here, too." Traore straightened and attempted to regain control. "Colonel, I demand that you send an escort to get us. A *strong* one."

"It will be difficult."

"I don't *fucking* care! Send them. Send Fukuda and his boys. They're real soldiers."

"I will see who I can spare."

"Colonel! I am about to talk to O'Neill. You *will* come get us. My apartment. No. She will make me go to hers. *Fuck!* Okay. Her apartment. Ten minutes."

"That's simply not possible." Nesvorny glared at the screen and took two deep breaths. "Half-an-hour. Be ready to move."

"Fuck you!" said Traore, and cut the connection.

* * *

Ten minutes later, the precarity of their situation became more evident.

Fukuda emerged into the bunker of the ISU command centre. This was on the level beneath the main Security HQ, which, while safe from the storm behind thick shuttered windows, was too noisy from the sound of wind and rain to be effectively used. With him were a couple of his notorious Squad Five, who dragged a prisoner between them.

Nesvorny received the other's salute. Fukuda's eyes were wide and alive, his normally pristine black uniform crumpled and dirty; there was a pistol in a holster at his waist. "What is it, Major?"

"News I thought I should deliver firsthand, sir." He looked over his shoulder: his troopers, both male, dragged their captive forwards and threw him roughly to the floor.

Nesvorny looked over the man. He was dressed in a grey uniform of sorts with red armbands. The man pushed himself up so he rested on his knees: his hair was cropped very short, and half his face was covered in blood from a deep gash above the eyebrow, which still oozed. "Who are you?" he asked. "You're not a Stoker."

The man look dazed, swaying slightly.

"Marseillaise," said Fukuda, when the other didn't respond. "We came across a small squad trying to creep towards the Command Centre. They ran when we started firing, and left him behind."

"From the *Marseilles*?" Nesvorny frowned. "Just him, or the whole squad?"

"All of them, from what we could make out. They were all dressed the same way. There were about a dozen, all armed."

"Where is the *Marseilles* now? It's next in line for the Ardol dig, isn't it?"

"Yes, sir. I haven't had time to check, but it must be close. *Very* close, if he came from it recently."

Nesvorny glanced at Fukuda, then back to the man. "I asked who you are. Why are you here?"

The man's eyes at last focused. He smiled, and blood stained his teeth. "*Fascists*," he muttered. "Your time is over."

Fukuda leant down and grabbed the man's cheek firmly, digging in his nails and causing the other to yelp. "When did you arrive? How many are you?"

"Fukuda…" But Nesvorny instantly felt a modicum of shame, for his rebuke was a whisper more than a shout. He needed answers, and he knew that his deputy would be able to get them – *if* he allowed it.

Fukuda maintained his grip, but flashed an annoyed look at Nesvorny. "Sir – we need this intel."

"We do."

"I will get it." He grabbed the other's ear and tugged viciously, partly ripping it from his head and causing the other to scream and grab for the torn flesh, crumpling to the ground when Fukuda released him.

Aside from the sobbing and moaning of the prostrate man, the room was silent: Nesvorny looked about, and noticed that all of those at their terminals had ceased the low murmurs into their mics and were looking at the scene. He firmed his expression. "Okay, that will do," he said to Fukuda, but without heat. Then he dropped to one knee so he could look at the man lying on his side, who stared back with wide, terrified eyes. "We asked you some questions. You *will* answer them. First – who are you?"

"Fabian Lafarge," he whimpered. "Of… of… the *La Rochelle*. Strike Unit Eight."

"When?"

"Last night. I mean… this morning. Early hours."

"In the storm?"

"Before… before it got bad."

Nesvorny gaped. This had taken some planning. The men from Earth who'd been left behind? The others who'd gone to the *Marseilles*? "How many came with you?"

"Two hundred… maybe three… I don't know. I'm just a… citizen soldier."

"All armed?"

"Yes."

Nesvorny stood back up; stepped away. "They had help," he muttered, to himself more than anyone. "From Earth. From the *Marseilles*."

"They must outnumber us, sir," said Fukuda, looking between Nesvorny and the squirming captive. "This lot plus the Stokers. But they're not professionals."

"And are we, Major?" said Nesvorny, quietly. "We have proper uniforms. Better discipline, maybe. Some extra training. But we're not soldiers – we've never had a war."

"Some of us have," said Fukuda. And Nesvorny realised it was true. His deputy had served in the Japanese special forces. He'd fought in North Korea and in various actions against the Chinese. And he'd recruited the best and hardest of the ISU to his own Squad Five.

"Okay, Major. We need to interrogate this man more fully and more… *sympathetically*. But we can assume this has been long planned. And that means they will be clear on what they are doing and where to strike. And that means one of their targets will be…" *The head.* "It's good you're here, Major. Take your squad and get over to Charlestown. O'Neill's apartment. We'll send you precise directions en route. Find O'Neill. Traore. Sullivan, if you can. Then get them to the West Docks. We'll retreat there if we have to. Colonel Joseph will be there, and we'll have a means of escape if needs be."

Fukuda's expression was enigmatic. He nodded, but didn't respond, and gestured to his two troopers as he passed: they turned to follow, leaving the prisoner on the floor at Nesvorny's feet.

* * *

Escape had proven impossible for Mitsos. It wasn't just that Noma stuck close to him, but that there was a rear guard, too, who prevented him from lagging behind and slipping away. Meanwhile, the environment had provided no suitable opportunity: after leaving the muster point with others from the *Marseilles*, they'd progressed through a series of empty corridors bordered by locked and dark units of various sorts that provided nothing to duck under or hide behind.

They were more numerous now, too. The *Dieppe* contingent had numbered over twenty, but to this had been added about a dozen Stokers, dressed in green, along with a dark-skinned man from Earth – called Odile – who'd apparently been on the *Leviathan*. As such, the party's attempt at noiselessness was largely in vain, with a constant rustle and clink accompanying its progress.

Mitsos had no idea where they were going. Even Noma had shrugged when he'd asked her during one brief pause. But he knew that it was towards danger: they hadn't been gone from the muster point more than ten minutes, when the first sounds of gunshots began to reach them, echoing down the corridors. But the sound was deceiving: he'd think the violence was far away, then they'd cross over a junction, and suddenly the volume would rise dramatically, and he'd jump and duck, expecting bullets to start flying over his head. And yet they'd seen nothing of note – not until about forty minutes after they left.

Their first action took place when they came across a small patrol of the black-uniformed 'ISU' (as they were called by the Stokers; his old crew simply called them 'fascists'). Their point man – moving some metres ahead of the main group – spotted them around a corner, then frantically hushed everyone behind and made them drop to the ground. Several of the group then crept up to join the man, and soon after, these stepped out and began firing down the corridor to their left. The encounter was quickly over: when the party moved on again – down that corridor – they passed three corpses on the floor, lying in bloody pools. Mitsos almost retched at the sight of the one in the middle: it was a woman, on her back, her face a gruesome mess where a bullet had passed through an eye.

Their second action was a messier affair. This time, they came across a temporary barrier erected across a corridor, with a handful of the enemy behind it. This firefight went on half an hour, initially inconclusive, the nature of the corridor ensuring that their group couldn't make use of its numerical advantage, with only a few able to peek around the corner to fire at any one time, and none suicidal enough to actually charge the enemy position. But then the firing from the others started to falter, then stop altogether: they had seemingly run out of bullets. After their foe retreated, the rebels took the position without bloodshed.

They moved on again, but not far, pausing at an open area with a couple of benches – like a lay-by for pedestrians. Here, Pierre – the leader of the *Dieppe* contingent – came together with the Stoker leader and the Earther. Mitsos watched the confab from a short distance away with Noma. After turning a wary eye on his companion, and noting her excited expression, he couldn't stop himself.

"Noma – this isn't a game. You're shooting people… *real* people. Do you even know who they are? Maybe they've got family. Young children. You're okay with this, are you?"

The woman at first tried to avoid his eyes. "Suddenly moral, Mitsos? I don't believe it."

"Look, I may not be the straightest guy on Earth, or Tethys, but this is a whole new level of villainy. I'm not shooting people in the *fucking* face!"

That clearly stung. He saw Noma twitch, but then her mouth firmed and she looked at him from under heavy brows. "No… but you're supporting a system that harms people just as much, even more, only it does so slowly. These people we're fighting are wearing the uniform of fascists. They're suppressing the people of *Hibernia.* They have chosen their side – and accepted their pieces of silver. They're not innocents. When they're gone, the people will be able to breathe." She turned and stalked away.

Mitsos shook his head. He had heard words like these before. There was no point in arguing. After all, he'd cynically played up his own family's revolutionary past to try to curry favour with Deux, the People's Committee, and the crew of the *Dieppe* – and he hadn't been exaggerating. His ancestors *had* been ardent socialists. *Communists.* And then they'd gotten into business, achieved some successes, and their ardour had miraculously cooled. They'd raised themselves – so why couldn't others? And it hadn't taken bullets to do so, just hard work and a modicum of sharp practice. But was he actually right? He supposed if he got a chance to explain himself to Noma and his old crew – without being strung up half way through – they'd probably say the same as he: *heard it all before*. Two intransigent positions? Was there any way people could resolve their differences peacefully? Maybe it was a fatal human flaw; maybe the answer was 'no'. All he did know was that *this* couldn't be right. Kill these people in black uniforms, and then what? Replace them with another lot, in black-and-grey? Captain Boursis? Sure, that would *really* make *Hibernia* a more heavenly place.

Noma had joined a small group now clustered around the leaders. The Stoker was showing his tablet, speaking low, and pointing at the screen. Some decision seemed to have been reached. Noma turned away, saw Mitsos, hesitated, then strode over – her rifle on a strap over her shoulder. "Come on. We're going."

"Have they decided who we're going to murder next?"

Noma's eyes widened in fury. "We're murdering no one! I've protected you since you were assigned to the *Dieppe*. I made a mistake. You've played at being one of us, but you're not. I should leave you."

"But you can't," said Mitsos. "You have your orders." He smiled at her, but inwardly was cursing. Why couldn't he control his tongue, just for once? *Murder?* He sighed. "Noma – I'm sorry. It's all a bit tense. I'm not cut out for this. I appreciate all you've done. Look – I'm zipping it!" He made the motion of pulling a couple of fingers across his mouth.

Noma shook her head, unmollified, and turned. "Keep up," she muttered over her shoulder.

After a moment, he started after her.

"West Docks," said Noma quietly, some minutes later, once she'd allowed Mitsos to take position beside her. "Just in case you're interested. It's where their military dock is."

"That sounds like the sort of place that might be well defended."

"Well, we're not going to be alone. We're sticking to this level. Another group will attack on Sublevel One, and a third will creep up from Sublevel Three, through the dock's deep storage area."

"Thanks for the update." He smiled as though he meant it.

"It's nothing." Noma turned away and started to speed up again, but Mitsos caught her arm.

"Be careful," he said. "I don't want to have to risk my life dragging you to safety if you're hit." He smiled uncertainly. "Also, I'm not really sure what to do with this medipack they've got me carrying – so spare me from the embarrassment of revealing my incompetence, eh."

This time, Noma broke. Her serious expression gentled and she gave a brief nod, though she didn't respond.

The next fight erupted suddenly.

As they came around a corner, the point man was hit with several bullets, and fell.

For the next hour, they moved nowhere. The party members took it in turns to approach the corner and let off a round or two, usually without even looking, while bullets continued to whistle down the perpendicular corridor and ricochet off the walls. At the back of the cluster, the leaders fussed around a tablet and spoke through mics, getting and providing updates. Once more, Mitsos was stuck in the middle, unable to go forward or retreat.

The stalemate was broken unexpectedly by a volley of shots from behind… and sudden panic. As Mitsos hit the ground, the others turned to point their guns back down the corridor. Almost instantly, a man – Amal from the *Dieppe* – fell heavily on top of him, gasping and bloody.

As those around him opened fire at the unseen attackers, the sound level in the confined space was almost painful. Mitsos held his hands over his ears, then realised that one was wet from Amal's blood. Then he heard a female shriek, and another body dropped beside him: Noma.

"Fuck!" He scrabbled from beneath the now-lifeless Amal towards Noma, a metre away. Her eyes were wide in shock; her rifle dropped; her hands holding her belly, red and black in the dim light.

"Stay still!" he hissed, and Noma's eyes turned on him. He wasn't a trained medic, though he did have some rudimentary knowledge. Most of those who had augments developed a kind of fascination with what their procedure would involve, and in his case, he'd had his liver replaced with one grown from his own stem cells, but altered and improved to enhance its efficiency in various ways. He'd wanted to know exactly what was going to be cut and plumbed, and so now he had an image in his head of what an abdomen *should* look like.

"Noma… calm… it's okay." He peeled her hands away slowly. "It's gone through the flesh. Do you hear? Through the flesh. It's missed your organs." He *hoped.* Might the bullet have nicked a kidney? But people had two, so they could survive without one, couldn't they? But they definitely couldn't survive loss of blood. He twisted onto his back and rummaged in the small medikit he'd been given, ripping out a bandage. Turning, he pressed the thick, white gauze tightly over Noma's wound, and heard her groan.

The firing intensified, and others around him fell, quivered, screamed. He saw Pierre shout a slogan and start to rush forwards – but then he jerked to a halt and pitched to the ground. The Earther threw something and there was a flash and explosion down the corridor, which momentarily caused all firing to cease, mainly because the pressure wave knocked over those still standing – on both sides. Then the firing from their opponents restarted… and wasn't returned. Those of the rebel group still alive pressed into the steel floor, but they weren't spared, with bullets walking along the ground to take them, although MItsos was further away and the angles saved him. He pulled himself towards Noma's head and said – as loud as he dared – "Quiet! Don't move. Play dead."

The firing ceased.

Ten seconds passed, then twenty. Then Mitsos heard voices approaching, but couldn't make out the words, in part due to a constant ringing in his ears. His face was now pressed down, between Noma's side and the floor. He didn't dare move or look up.

He heard people moving, getting closer. There were careful steps, then a grunt from a few metres away, and a shot. The movement continued, and he sensed a presence – someone nearby, hovering, looking, breathing heavily. He felt a boot prod him in the thigh, but it wasn't hard and he managed to remain still. Then the owner of the boot moved on, stepping over him and the silent Noma.

People continued moving past, and then clear words came to him. "Careful, ma'am. You don't want to trip."

"I don't intent to, Major." The voice was female, but harsh. "But I'm going to dock your wages for this. These shoes are tenth generation Blahniks, and the blood is ruining them."

There was a commotion a short way ahead, and another loud shot, which caused the woman to curse. *Coup de grace*, thought Mitsos. But it wasn't Noma.

And then the new party was past and around the corner, with loud voices alerting the defenders from that direction not to fire. The sounds of their movement and occasional words decreased, and then it was silent.

Mitsos waited for another minute. When he was sure he was alone, he pushed himself up and looked about. The whole party was down. *Dead.* All those he'd known on the *Dieppe*. There was Pierre, further down, having made a last charge. Closer were Marc and Abdul. Behind him, near the corner, was Pascal. The Stokers were scattered in between. The Earther called Odile, who'd had some sort of grenade, was chewed up by multiple rounds. And Noma… she now gasped a long-held breath, and began to tremble.

Mitsos got to his knees. "It's okay, Noma. They're gone. We're safe." He looked at her wound more closely; the blood had already stopped flowing and begun to congeal. It looked ugly under the bandage, but it was clear to him that nothing vital had been hit. "I'm no doctor," he said, "but I'm pretty sure you're going to live."

She sighed… and began to cry. Mitsos misunderstood. "Seriously – you're going to be okay."

"Not me," she said, slowly pushing herself up. "Them. The crew. They're all dead. My family."

"Uh… yeah… but… they gave their lives for a cause." He felt slightly dirty saying it. *Disingenuous.* But now was not the time for cynicism.

"Yes… they did. For the people."

"But you'll live," he repeated, "and maybe so will I." It was his chance. *Finally.* He got to his feet slowly. "Keep the pressure on that bandage and make your way back the way we came." He waved in the relevant direction. "Find the rest. They'll take care of you."

Noma pulled herself up into a sitting position, one hand still clutching the bandage to her side. Her eyes were still wide, and tears streaked her cheeks. "What about you?"

"You know why I came. I've got to get away from Deux. I'll probably be seen as a deserter for leaving the *Marseilles* without permission. I can't take the chance. I'm going another way. I'll hide out. Wait to see who wins. Then play it by ear."

"Okay. I understand. Thank you, Eddard."

He smiled in the faint light. "No problem. But now we're even. Maybe I'm even ahead?"

She somehow found a smile. "Maybe."

He helped Noma to her feet, and together they staggered away from the battlefield. After a short distance, Mitsos turned at the next junction, heading towards what he hoped was a neutral area – one from which no sounds of firing could be heard – leaving his last crewmate to limp onwards alone.

Ten minutes later, he blundered into a two-person patrol of the Hibernian ISU.

That was unlucky.

But as he and they had been moving quietly, and they unexpectedly came together at another junction, he had been instinctively slammed to the floor, rather than shot.

And as it turned out, that would prove very lucky indeed.

* * *

"He has augments," said Georges Hollande. "The man with the ambassador. I thought I recognised him. He was on the *Leviathan*."

"So?" Dures appeared distracted, looking about the plaza where they'd established their temporary HQ in the northern part of the city.

"It's a crime against the people."

"Is it?" Dures turned to Hollande, a look of surprise on his face.

"It is. He is setting himself above the masses, making himself more than them, buying himself advantages with his wealth. On Earth, it is the main fissure between the elite and the common people."

"He doesn't look especially wealthy to me," said Dures, turning to look towards the *Stavanger* contingent, which huddled in animated discussion. "In any case, this isn't Earth. This is Tethys. We have different concerns here."

"But–"

"Is he with the Stavangerans?"

Hollande recoiled slightly from the curt question. Dures could transition from calm to perilous at the snap of a finger – even in the middle of a sentence. "I… don't know. I didn't have much to do with him on the ship. I suppose he could be."

"Do you think the Hibernians are sophisticated and long-thinking enough to recruit him to come from Earth just to spy on this other, insignificant ship?" Now Dures appeared mocking.

"Ah… maybe not."

"So, what do you want us to do with him? Hold him? Tear out his implants – whatever they are? Hold a people's court? A show trial?"

"I just… think we need to be careful. To watch him. Not to assume he is with us."

"But he's not with us – he's with the Stavangerans. That is clear."

Hollande looked away from the other's amused expression. "Yes."

"Georges. *Comrade.*" Dures' tone changed again. "We value your aid. But in the end, this is *our* revolt – a Tethyn one. We have our own problems without importing more from Earth. And we've already seen that your problems are severe. The destruction of the *Leviathan* proved that." He reached down and placed a callused hand on Hollande's shoulder, giving it a vice-like squeeze. "Maybe playtime is over, and you should return to your factory. I have many more volunteers waiting for weapons." He released his grip, and stalked away to the command tables in the centre of the space.

Hollande felt embarrassed. But he had no intention of returning to safety behind the lines. And though the Stokers had other concerns, they weren't the only ones now present. He spotted a contingent of the Marseillaise, and with them were fellow brothers and sisters from the NS, who'd helped train them for this insurrection. His concerns would be taken more seriously there.

He turned a last look on the ambassador's supposed assistant, who was going nowhere at the moment. And when he was allowed to leave… well, Hollande would try to ensure that he kept eyes upon him. He had no intention of allowing this particular cancer from Earth to spread.

* * *

The evacuation pained Nesvorny, but he'd been left with no choice.

Everything on the strategic displays had been going red over the last couple of hours. The whole south of the city ship was a no-go area, and the rebels had got to the levels beneath the Command Centre and were moving their way up through it. The Comms Centre at the top – where the satellite relay was located – was now isolated: he'd been too late, and expected the enemy to soon start broadcasting the overthrow of the present regime. It was somewhat premature, of course, but people believed what they were told. He accepted that he couldn't relieve the Command Centre; the East Docks were hard pressed; and even his HQ was being squeezed from a number of different directions. The spaceport and the West Docks seemed to be the only viable exits – and the former was of little use, as there were few shuttles, and where would they fly to anyway? That left Joseph's stronghold at the West Docks.

"Eric? What the hell!"

"Tania!" He had made it through, escorted by Squad Three. They'd seen no action, but had come across corpses on the way – dressed in all manner of uniform, from those in the black of the ISU, to others wearing green or grey.

"You're being here means things are either going very well – and you can afford to leave your HQ – or very badly. I think I can guess which." They were in the ESU command suite, Sublevel One, which had direct access to the docks at sea level. The double-height suite – where half-a-dozen troopers in black sat at consoles – had broad, rain-sluiced windows to one side, where pearly grey light shone in. "I've been trying to keep on top of things, but I scarcely believe what we're being told from your end. Where did they get this army? The *Marseilles*?"

Nesvorny looked around. No one was paying them attention, but he still preferred a more discrete venue. "Can we talk in private?"

"Sure – and I promise, whatever news you've got, I've got something even more shocking. This way."

There was a small office through one wall. As soon as they entered and Nesvorny closed the door behind, Joseph turned, perched on a desk, and spoke without allowing him time to take a seat. "You go first. How bad?"

Nesvorny leant back against the door. "Very. I've placed small units between here and my HQ to leave the route of retreat open, but that's all. I sent Fukuda to collect our leadership and bring them here – have they arrived?"

"Not yet, but I had some comms a few minutes ago saying they are close."

Nesvorny nodded. That was good news… he supposed. "Okay, we're not defeated yet, especially with your troops. If we barricade ourselves here, we can hold out. Regroup. When the weather clears, we'll also have your boats and other units on Athol and Ardol. Control the sea. Strike them where they don't expect. They can't defend the whole sea line."

"You seem to be placing a lot of trust in the ESU. You know we are a fraction the size of the ISU."

"Sure, but I think I can preserve at least two hundred of my own, maybe more. And given the geography, here at the edge, it'll be difficult for the enemy to outflank us or force their way through the corridors. Of course, when the weather improves they can come at us from street level, but still, I think we can hold."

Joseph scrunched her face up, clearly unconvinced. "Well, I'm in. What else can I do? But I guess it'll depend on how O'Neill wants to play it."

"Thanks. So… what is this news you have?"

Joseph smiled and shook her head. "I can barely believe I'm saying this, but… about an hour ago we received a distress call from the *Lisboa*."

"*Lisboa?* By satellite?"

"No. They're close enough that we can pick up their electromagnetic communications. In fact, I got a direct call from Joao Nacimiento, their Captain-Governor."

"*You?*"

"Yes. Don't look surprised. All mayday signals get routed through my office."

"Right. *Lisboa?* What's the problem."

Joseph struggled for the right words. "Nacimiento said… they're under attack."

"Them too? The *Marseilles* again? In this weather? What the hell is going on? What are you going to do?"

"What can I do? They're about thirty kilometres away. Even if I wanted to send help, I can't in this weather, and I'm not sure what a boatload of my troops could do even if they survived the journey. Who's attacking them is also somewhat… *unusual.* It's not the *Marseilles.*"

"*Another* ship?" asked Nesvorny.

Joseph's mouth twitched. "I'm not sure I want to say. Either I'm an idiot, or they are. I first thought they were trying to play me for a fool, but… as I said, the message was from the Captain-Governor himself."

Nesvorny didn't respond: he crossed his arms and waited.

Joseph exhaled a breath. "Okay. But don't laugh. They said they're being attacked by *aliens.*"

"Aliens?"

"You're taking this calmly."

"How else should I take it? It's difficult to parse. Aliens? Little green men in flying saucers?"

"Ah, no. These are apparently big black ones from underwater. Nacimiento admitted it sounded incredible and he didn't want to say too much, just that they are intelligent and live in the cenotes."

Nesvorny nodded slowly. "We've avoided those places ever since we arrived on the planet. I take it this might explain the missing ships. Still… incredible. And untimely."

"With this storm–"

"Not just with the storm, but wider events – a rebellion on *Hibernia* and this occurring at the same time? It seems we are cursed. Or perhaps, we've cursed ourselves with our own stupidity. So, what are you going to do if you're not sending aid?"

Joseph shrugged. "Send good wishes and ask them to hold on until after the storm. I really don't know how big or serious this attack is. Surely nothing can sink a city class ship."

"They said the same about the Titanic."

"Sure. Anyway, I suggested they head for Mount Athol and the shallows there. If the worst comes to the worst, they can beach, plus I have a contingent of troops stranded there."

"It never rains…," muttered Nesvorny. "But much as I'd like to contemplate these astonishing events, I can't say I'm too sad about the storm at the moment. Tania – I need your reserve here, not floating on the ocean or battling some terror from the deep."

And suddenly, as if to emphasize how serious their situation was, all the lights went out.

The sounds of shouts and curses came from next door.

Nesvorny muttered an expletive. "I suppose it had to happen at some point. They've got control of the fusion reactors and the electricity distribution centres. They've cut us off from the grid."

"As you said, Eric, it never rains but it pours…"

Chapter 35

Kate's resolve to keep her group's new secret about the aliens lasted only a couple of hours.

"You did *what*?" she said to her mother – that evening – as she responded to a question about what she'd been doing that day.

"We went out to the site of the disaster," Marie repeated quietly. "In the *Fortunata*." She looked distinctly sheepish. Uncomfortable. Even guilty.

"Don't you think that was a bit risky? Stupid, even?"

"No, Kate. We had to go–"

"And risk leaving me an orphan? That's great. You should have warned me about these suicidal tendencies. Maybe I should have stayed on Earth with Dad." Kate was somewhere between annoyed and shocked.

"I'm sorry, Kate, but this is my job. We took precautions."

"So, you all made it back safely? Well done. Oh…" Kate saw it instantly – the change in her mother's expression; the way she broke eye contact; the way she brought a hand to the side of her face. "Something happened. What?"

"I shouldn't say – not before… before people have been informed. Just in case."

"Right, now you're scaring me. Tell me what happened *right now*. You know I'm not going to take to the ship-net to share with the class."

Her mother looked down and closed her eyes. "You remember Raul Garcia? He–"

"Was it *them*?"

"Yes."

"Okay, Mum. You're not off the hook. I want to hear everything. But first, I've got to talk to Tonio and Sara quickly. No, not about Raul. I *am* actually trustworthy. In fact, that's why I need a moment. Stay there. I'll talk in my room and be right back."

* * *

"I'm going to tell her," Kate said to Tonio and Sara via a three-way conversation on her tablet. "This is too big and important." She waited for the resistance, the comeback – but it never arrived.

"Of course you are," said Sara, smiling wanly. "Go ahead. I don't care about this – not as much as the Bowl. It's Tonio's sanctum anyway, not mine. The monsters stole the Bowl from us, and that's all I care about."

Tonio shrugged. "Yeah, I figured this would happen. It was kind of inevitable. In fact, I knew as soon as we left earlier today that you were going to rat on us." He smiled sardonically. "Thanks for at least checking this time." Then he sighed: "Que sera sera."

* * *

An hour later, Kate and Marie were in the old control room in one of the deepest levels below the waterline – in august company, for not only were Marie's most senior work colleagues present, but the Captain-Governor had come, too. They were waiting there when the main door opened and a sheepish Tonio entered.

"Ah, so you are the talented Tonio Janeiro," said a voice from behind Kate, which rose in volume as the speaker came forward, light from the strip in the ceiling glinting off the gold emblems on his immaculate uniform.

"Uh… yes, sir!"

"Well, come in. Dr Lockard's daughter says that you are the genius who found and upgraded this old place. You know, I do have vague recollections of this room from maybe thirty years ago, or even further back. You and young Ms Lockard discovered the other bowl, too, didn't you? As well as a certain Sara Velasquez? Can we expect her, too?"

"Uh, no, sir," said Tonio. "Sara has gone off this place because of the monsters."

"Monsters?" Nacimiento smiled grimly. "It seems these intelligent aliens are being renamed continuously – farmers, reapers, and now just plain monsters. Well, given what they did to our ships, I will not argue with that label." He came to a halt beside the chair in front of the main console – the others clustered to one side. "I believe, Mr Janeiro, the controls are yours. Please…" He smiled in an avuncular manner, stepped back, and motioned to the empty chair.

Kate caught Tonio's eye and smiled encouragement. "Go on, Tonio. Show them what you've got."

"Uh, okay. I guess Kate mentioned I've been able to, um, patch into the cameras at the Bowl and record events. I'll show you what we recorded earlier. Let me…" He tapped away; the large monitor in front of him lit up; and then the earlier recording played out. There was no accompanying sound with the moving images, but soon the audience provided its own soundtrack in the form of gasps, exclamations, and curses.

At last, Kalmik declared: "They're under the *Lisboa* right now. Right beneath us."

"It seems so," said Figueroa. "But why?"

"And what were they carrying?" said Teixeira. "The shapes… the larger shapes… they looked like…" Kate noticed her mother quickly reach out to grasp the woman's arm as she leant across to whisper in her ear. She thought she heard the word 'kids' mentioned.

"This is… *disturbing*," said Nacimiento. "I don't like the thought of these creatures under us. What are they doing – and why?"

"Could they damage the *Lisboa*?" asked Kalmik. "Maybe even sink us? They took out the harvesters without any problem, but surely we are far too big. They must realise this."

"I don't think it's possible," said Nacimiento cautiously. "But it's not a problem we ever considered. Certainly, there are some large creatures in the deep, and in the early days there was concern about them, but we've never had any serious attack. We are so big, it's been assumed that we scare away predators, and we're undoubtedly unappetising. I do not think these farmers… reapers… will see the *Lisboa* as food."

"Not the ship, no," said Kalmik, "but maybe what's in it."

"Come on, Katerina," said Marie. "You don't believe that. They seem to live an existence full of bounty from their forests, and presumably, from all the sea life around. You don't think they've developed some rapid addiction to human flesh…" Kate saw her pause and flick a quick glance at her, "in spite of recent events."

"Not really, no," Kalmik replied. "But their intent is suspicious, don't you think?"

"Maybe not," said Marie. "The number of them, and the way they were carrying… *supplies*… almost looked like a migration. Maybe they are using the *Lisboa* as a shelter from the sunlight to aid them to cross the open water."

"Ha! To where? They don't know where we're going. And as you said, they live a bountiful existence – they're hardly fleeing ecological ruin. So, what else is there? We stirred the hornet's nest. Maybe they are determined to sting us so we can't threaten them again?"

"Even if they have this vengeful character," said Figueroa, who had slumped into a seat at the console next to Tonio, "I cannot see how they could possibly hurt us."

"Would we know?" asked Kalmik. "They could be chipping away as we speak and we wouldn't have a clue."

"Ah…"

"Tonio?" said Kate, on seeing her friend twitch and half raise a hand. Many her age would not have dared speak in the presence of such high-status adults, but Kate wasn't like most. She assumed she inherited it from her mother, who never shied away from saying what she thought needed saying. "Please, everyone – Tonio's had a thought. What is it?"

Nacimiento's eyebrows arched, but he smiled and raised a hand himself. "Dr Kalmik, Dr Lockard – I suggest we pause this discussion. Young Mr Janeiro – you want to add something?"

"Uh, yes, sir. About these monsters and what they're doing. Maybe…" his fingers started to flash over the keyboard. The paused recording blinked off the screen, and was quickly replaced by a menu. A cursor moved up and down, then the menu was replaced by another, then another, and then the screen filled with some sort of schematic – clearly the turtle-like shape of the ship. "This is beneath the ship," he continued, tapping. "And here…" a net of points appeared, "are a set of sensors across the hull. They seem to record lots of things to do with the hull itself and the environment outside." The adults shifted to get better views of the central monitor, some moving to stand behind Tonio, while Figueroa and Nacimiento occupied the chairs to his side.

Sharp-eyed Luisa Teixeira spotted it first. "There. Just port of the mid-line, two-thirds down."

Tonio peered at the screen, then moved a cursor and selected a darkened point – one of several in a small cluster. A reading came up at the side of the schematic. "It's down," he said. "No output."

"But this could be old, couldn't it?" said Marie. "We shouldn't just jump to the conclusion that the farmers have anything to do with it."

"That is certainly true," said Nacimiento. "It could have ceased functioning years ago. The sensors – and this room – are a vestige from the early years, when we had less confidence in our mighty ships. But the super-strong, low-friction poly-carbon coating over city ship hulls has never caused any issues, so continued monitoring gradually ceased – here and everywhere else, I imagine. The coating doesn't oxidise, degrade, or in any other way react with the water and its elements. But the sensors are not likely to be anywhere near so robust. So, Dr Lockard, I suspect you are ri–"

"*Wrong!*" said Kalmik, excitedly. "Just there to the left."

"I saw it," said Tonio. The cursor moved to another darkened pinprick, and the details on this one now appeared to the right of the schematic.

"Did that just…" started Figueroa.

"I didn't see," said Nacimiento.

"It did," said Tonio, firmly. "Miss… er…" he glanced at Kalmik in embarrassment, not knowing her name. "Miss was right. It just went off."

"Among those details," said Kalmik, "does it indicate exactly when the sensor failed?"

"Um… I don't know. I'm not used to looking at this. Maybe if I–"

"Let me at it," said Kalmik, moving to place a hand on the boy's shoulder.

"Wait, Dr Kalmik," said Nacimiento. "Let Tonio continue. He is the expert here. Please continue, young man."

"Yes, sir." Tonio continued at the keys and controls. As he did so, Kate – and the others – strained to look at the image on the monitor, looking for other anomalies; waiting for something else to happen.

At last, Tonio hit a key and the schematic disappeared to be replaced by a table, which seemed to show the status of all of the sensors. Tonio must have memorised the code of the particular misbehaving sensor, for he scrolled the table onto a new a page, placed the cursor over a cell in a particular column and said. "Yes! The sensor stopped working… two minutes ago. And these others…" he scrolled up and down, looking at cells in the same column, "stopped over the last… day."

"There we have it," said Kalmik. "They're damaging the ship *right now.*"

"Some sensors," said Marie, "not the hull itself."

"So you say," said Kalmik. "But we don't know. Is there any way we can check?"

"Um… maybe," said Tonio. "I think…" the table disappeared and the hull schematic appeared again. This time, half-a-dozen spots started to wink green. "I think you could through these."

"Inspection hatches," nodded Nacimiento. "Again, from the distant past when our confidence in the ship was still shaky. Chambers in the hull – like airlocks – giving access beneath the ship. I can't recall the last time one of these was used, but I see no reason why they won't work."

"Good luck finding a volunteer to go through one of those into whatever waits on the other side," said Kalmik.

"Yes, I agree, it would require high courage, even insanity, to try." Nacimiento raised both hands. "A moment, everyone. Let me think."

Kate watched as their leader closed his eyes and interlinked his fingers in front of his face, almost as if praying. From the side of her eyes, she noticed everyone else watching, rapt.

After some seconds, Nascimento opened his eyes and dropped his hands. "I don't like this matter at all. I can see no benevolent reason for these intelligent creatures to take residence beneath my ship, and I want them gone – and gone now." He swivelled in his seat. "Miguel, my friend. Please consult your team and give me a plan for evicting these squatters before they damage the furniture, or even worse, raze the house. It's late now – I think we'll survive until tomorrow. But first thing, eh? Oh, and Mister Janeiro – I am deeply impressed. I will get someone from engineering here who has a greater familiarity with these matters, but I would hate to sideline you. I think tomorrow you need not go to school – I will have a word with them. You are now my consultant." He turned his chair slightly to look at Kate. "And you, Miss Lockard, we owe great thanks for alerting us to these matters. You seem to work well with Tonio – please continue to do so."

"And Sara?" Kate said. "We need her too."

"Of course."

Kate felt her mother squeeze her shoulder, and glanced up to see her smiling – in pride?

* * *

"So, how do we fend them off?" asked Teixeira. As one of the senior team, she sat at the small conference table with Figueroa, Kalmik, and Marie in Figueroa's office the next morning. The room's size had limited the number that could attend the brainstorming.

"Well, we know light works," said Marie. "They absolutely hate it. But they've adapted to it. They've made themselves *sunglasses*. I'm not sure how effective their seaweed wraps really are, but they seem to make things sufficiently bearable for them to approach our lights close enough to take them down."

"But *big* lights?" suggested Kalmik. "High power? Spotlights?"

"Yes, I'm sure those'll work," said Marie, cautiously. "We can but try. Still…"

"You have doubts?" asked Figueroa.

"I'm just wondering how many lights can we make, and how much area can we protect with them? What's the surface area of the *Lisboa's* hull, Professor? If we put lights under one critical part, maybe they'll just congregate beneath another. And how do we get them there anyway? Divers?"

"So, what are you suggesting?" said Kalmik. "That we don't bother?"

"No, we should, but…" Marie shook her head. "But we need to experiment more. Not put all our eggs in one basket. See what else they don't like. I mean, they've evolved to live in a very precise environment around the cenotes. I wonder how happy they are in the open ocean away from them. Can they tolerate it for long? If we draw them away from their 'hood, will they get fed up, even pained, and have to leave us to return home? Maybe *time* will win this for us?"

"And if it doesn't?" persisted Kalmik.

"Then as I said, we need to experiment. Compare and contrast the nature of the water in the broad ocean and in the cenotes. We've got plenty of samples, but we've put analysis of them on the backburner, as we've been focusing on the new lifeforms we've found, and on the farmers–"

"*Reapers*," corrected Kalmik.

"Er, yes. *Reapers*. What I'm saying is: maybe there is something in the nature of their water that they need, and if we can find out what it is, we can develop another weapon like… like dumping gasoline in the water. Sea life generally hates that."

"Oil wouldn't work," said Kalmik. "It will float to the surface and coat the top layer only, molecular thickness. In fact, it would probably help reduce sunlight below and make things even cosier for them. *Cosier?* My God, Lockard, that sounds like the sort of phrase you'd come up with."

"Thanks… I think. You're right about oil, but you get my drift."

Figueroa had been slowly nodding during the latter part of Marie's exposition. "Yes, Marie. *Experimentation*. Let's see how we can somehow *poison* the water around the *Lisboa*… or at least make it less tasty, and foul enough that they decide to give up on us." He rubbed his hands together. "A scientific challenge! This, I like."

"Yeah, but what we really need is to grab one of the creatures and stick it in a tank," said Kalmik. "It'd make our experimentation so much easier."

"You mean," said Marie, "catch one and try to torture it?"

"You can frame it how you like, Marie," said Kalmik, "but at the end of the day we need to find a way to drive these fucking things away – maybe causing *one* a bit of discomfort is better than dumping something into the ocean to see if it works, finding it's like kryptonite to them, and so in one go wiping them all out. Now, *I* wouldn't have a problem with this, but I guess you would. So, what's your preference?"

Marie frowned and shook her head slowly. Kalmik was right. There was no painless way to do this. "Okay," she admitted. "You have a point. But there is just the one problem: how do we catch one of these things?"

Kalmik smiled. "All the trawlers carry a harpoon. They never know when they might accidentally snare something big and nasty trying to shred its nets or trash the boat. We might have to take some pot shots. Might harm a few. Kill a few before we impale one in a non-fatal way. But it's the start of a plan. We can work out details later."

"Sure," said Teixeira, "and it might also show them we're not toothless – as Katerina suggested before – and that wouldn't be a bad thing right now. And if we kill it, we can dissect it and check its anatomy and biology. That will help us understand it and its weaknesses."

Marie saw hate in Teixeira's eyes. She had been particularly close to Raul Garcia. And the more people that died, the more widespread that vengeful attitude would become among the inhabitants of the *Lisboa* – and who could blame them? Could she? What if Kate had been taken instead? She had little doubt she'd feel the same. "I hate the idea," she said after a pause, "but if we can't think of anything better, I guess we have no choice."

* * *

"We can't go out in that," said Marie, peering through the wall of glass that separated them from the walkway along the top of the starboard wing of the *Lisboa*, which curved away like the giant flipper of a sea-turtle. The *Fortunata* was invisible in its drydock, obscured not only by the fishing vessels in the nearer docks, but by the curtain of rain that lashed the window.

"Actually, we don't have to," said Marco Grande, who stood immediately next to her. "There is an access corridor within the wing, effectively at Sublevel One. It's wide enough to walk two abreast, and has a conveyor for transporting heavy items safely."

"But how do you get from that onto the boats?"

"Well, yes, for that you may have to emerge from a hatch and take your chances."

Marie flashed the bestubbled man a quick smile, then spoke to Kalmik beyond. "So, what now?"

"Now we're fucked. I'd completely forgotten about the storm."

Marie knew what she meant. The central coliseum of the *Lisboa* was normally open to the elements, but it had a transparent roof that closed over during storms. In short, they were so well insulated from sound – and the ship was so robust that it didn't rock, no matter how severe conditions – that unless you were in an outwards facing cabin you wouldn't know what was going on in the wider world.

"Actually, maybe not," said Grande. They'd recruited him and Mike Resnos to help with their plan; Resnos stood to Marie's other side, silently watching the deluge. "There are hatches from the sublevel into the docking bays. Bays nine and ten are sealed to allow sensitive work. They can be raised above the water to allow access to the footwell to work underneath, or lowered to sea level or even sub-one to allow maintenance workers direct access to the deck. Nine is occupied by a trawler undergoing a refit of its electronics. We can get through and onto its deck under shelter and access its harpoon in safety."

"Yes, but how do we deploy it?" asked Marie. Their plan had involved taking the trawler out a short distance and hoping something would come near to investigate, then shooting it, using the automated mechanism in the harpoon, which could be programmed to fire on sonar-detected objects above a particular size. She shook her head. "Sorry, Katerina, but this is just stupid. I don't see how we ever thought this was going to work."

"Stupid?" Kalmik frowned. For a moment, Marie feared she'd put her foot in it. But then the other simply sighed. "Yeah, maybe you're right."

"No, there is a way," persisted Grande. "When boats come to dock, they line up in their bay, then an automated cradle settles under the bottom and raises the boat from the water. But the sonar sits in the centre of the hull and isn't touched by the cradle. If we get on the trawler in Nine, we can lower it to sea level and then partially lift the protecting bubble, so we're sheltered from the worst of the storm above, but the sonar is under water and can function. We can then turn on the feed to the harpoon, which is at the stern, and let it go to work."

Kalmik smirked. "I always thought you were fucking useless, Grande. Maybe I've been a bit harsh."

Marie tensed, but Grande was calm: he'd clearly heard worse from the woman. "Okay," she said, after a moment. "But still, even if one comes to investigate, we're likely to kill it with the harpoon. And if we catch it, what then? You've been quiet on the details, Katerina. Drag it aboard, thrashing and screaming into the air to suffocate? Oh!" That's when Marie realised. "You never intended to capture one alive."

"As you say, it's not likely. But we need to know our foe. If you're uncomfortable with this, Marie, maybe you should join Luisa and the B Team analysing the differences between the water in the main ocean and the cenotes and coming at the problem from the chemistry angle. We three can cope."

Marie scowled. "I think even with four, it's going to be difficult to do this. I'm in. At least if I'm here, the creature may have a chance to survive. I'll give the matter some thought as we set up."

But she didn't have long to think, and was soon busy with the others, taking the sublevel corridor to the bay, climbing into the enclosed space around the trawler, and then boarding. Resnos found the dry dock controls and lowered the boat to rest atop the restless ocean – though still secure in its cradle – and programmed the seal around them to peel back twenty-to-thirty degrees, at which point elemental noises rose in volume and sea spray began to fill the air. As Resnos dropped onto the trawler and headed for the harpoon at the stern to ready it, the others scrambled off the suddenly slick deck and entered the main wheelhouse, where Grande settled before the sonar and started switching on various computer systems. When the sonar image came on – before they'd activated the harpoon and linked it to the sonar data or set firing parameters – it produced a shocking revelation.

"They're *everywhere*," gasped Grande.

Marie and Kalmik stood next to each other behind the seated man. "Are you sure?" asked Marie. To her, the readout was incomprehensible – a screen full of moving blobs.

"Hell, yes," said Grande. "Either it's them, or there's a school of large fish performing a ballet under our starboard wing."

At that moment, the boat tilted slightly in its cradle. Marie grabbed Kalmik to steady herself, and felt the other's hand grab back.

"I fucking well hope that's the wind," said Kalmik.

Although the transparent dome of the dry dock still covered most of the trawler, the small gap at the stern where it had been partially raised formed a kind of tunnel, amplifying the wind's strength as well as its sound – which was loud enough that even in the cabin the three had to half shout to be heard.

"It must be," said Marie, though with less confidence than her bellow might have suggested. "Right, Marco?"

"I can't really tell if it's the wind or *them*. There's no lights under the boat to deter them yet. Maybe we should have dropped them in first?"

Resnos had a string of lights, but the plan had been to deploy them after the harpoon was readied, when they would be gently flickered on and off in a way they knew tended to attract the creatures. They'd not expected to have close company right at the outset.

"Thanks for that insight, Grande," shouted Kalmik. The boat shifted again – subtly, but noticeably – and groaned in protest.

As everything had been rushed, they'd not established any means of communication with Resnos at the stern. Marie glanced at Kalmik, then realised it was down to her to act. "I'll go tell him now," she said. "We need to light up and keep the farmers away until we're ready." She didn't await a response, letting go of Kalmik's arm and heading for the door to the deck. At the door, she struggled momentarily, as the gusting channel of wind outside seemed to suck the door tight, then she wrenched at it, the pressure gave way, and she nearly fell backwards.

On the deck, the wind continued to push her away from the stern. She thought she sensed the boat tremble again, but now exposed to the elements, she couldn't be sure whether it had actually moved or not: certainly, the wind seemed powerful enough to shift the boat on its cradle.

She pulled herself along a railing on the gunwale, and was soon in view of Resnos, who wrestled at the deck gun, which was nearly the same height as him. She noticed glowing green lights from a display at the side of the weapon, which Resnos' tapping hand occasionally obscured. She also noticed the string of lights on the deck at his feet, sliding back and forth with every gust.

With some effort, Marie pulled herself close. "Mike!"

Resnos couldn't hear. She shouted again, and when he still didn't respond, she gave one last pull on the railing and reached out to grab the man's shoulder. At that, he tensed, and his head snapped around.

Marie pulled herself so her mouth was next to his ear. "They're already here," she shouted. "Below."

His eyes narrowed. "So?"

"Lights! Drop the lights!"

He shook his head with effort. "No need. Nearly set. Mountain has…" he got a face full a spray, and shook his head again, "come to Muhammed." Then he turned back to the display.

But Marie didn't retreat. She had a bad feeling about things. Instead, she dropped to her knees and scrabbled for the light string. She found the end of the string and its adaptor, which she pushed along the deck. She found the protected socket low on the rear bulkhead, in roughly the same place as on the *Fortunata. Parallel design.* She inserted it, and the lights came on, glowing weakly. The control was a separate box on the cable – already set for low intensity. As the boat suddenly bucked upwards in its cradle, she instinctively twisted the control to full intensity and had to raise a hand to protect her eyes.

Then she heard a shout, and – looking over the top of her shielding forearm – saw the harpoon judder to life. A series of new lights flickered on, these in red. Then the barrel – with a wicked looking barbed spear emerging from its end – began to move of its own accord. It slid forwards, then tipped down and tracked from left to right. Resnos staggered back, nearly stepping on the string of lights. Marie grabbed a handful of coils, wincing at the brightness, and dragged then out of the other's way.

As the harpoon continued tracking, and rose up several centimetres more, Resnos turned, spotted the light string, and managed to avoid it. He dropped to the deck and scooched over towards Marie, until he got his back resting against the bulkhead next to her.

She saw him open his mouth to speak, but whatever he was saying was lost in a sudden loud report from the gun. The harpoon shot downwards, a thin, immensely strong synthetic cable uncoiling from a box mounted beneath the barrel. And then the entire boat rose several centimetres, then fell, leaving Marie's seat momentarily behind in the air, before dropping. An ear-piercing shriek eclipsed the sound of the wind, cut through it, overwhelmed it. The coil grew taut on the guide loops under the barrel, and the boat juddered again.

Marie grasped the coil of lights and threw herself towards the gunwale, dumping them unceremoniously over the side. A second scream now split the air; the harpoon gun seemed to actually flex forwards; but then the coil became less taut and the boat settled back.

She saw Resnos move. With the deck now stable, he reclaimed his feet and grabbed at the pillar of the gun. He slapped at a control, and the coil began to rewind.

Marie sat, gasping for breath, eyes wide, looking around, the wind still blowing, spray stippling her face… yet there was a sense of greater calm, too. She put a hand on her chest to feel her heart rate, blew out a couple of times, then climbed to her feet. Stepping over the end of the cable for the light string – itself bare of bulbs – she made it to Resnos' side.

Together, they watched as the harpoon rose level with the stern of the boat, and its target became clear – a long, black creature, horrifically humanoid, impaled diagonally through its torso, and clearly quite dead.

* * *

Before retrieving the creature, they activated the docking mechanism, raising the boat from the water and closing the protective envelope fully. The sound of the wind dramatically fell, so they could speak at normal volume. All four gathered on the deck to appraise their catch.

"Fuck, it's big," said Kalmik. "You've don't really appreciate size in the water. Over two metres? Two-thirty?"

Marie felt uncomfortable. "Let's not leave it dangling there. It's disrespectful."

"Yeah, and ripping off our people's heads and throwing them at us *isn't*?" sneered Kalmik.

Marie shook her head but didn't respond. Instead, she approached the dangling corpse and reached out gingerly to touch its torso. The skin was smooth and cold. Just out of reach, looming over her – now the harpoon gun had been cocked backwards to maximum extent – the ovoid head was the size and shape of a large watermelon, and perfectly black. "They must be virtually invisible in the cenote," she murmured. There was no sign of eyes, but now, this close, she was able to see a fold in the lower part of the apparently featureless head. "Is that the mouth?" she muttered, mostly to herself. They'd only got an impression of the creatures' mouths in infrared, when one of them had opened up to bite on the neck of a drowned trawlermen. The thought made her shy back.

"Well, let's get it down," said Kalmik, from behind. "Mike. *Grande.* Nature has unfairly given you more muscles than us. If you please."

Marie stepped back, and the two men cautiously approached, tentatively reached for the corpse, and then together pulled it over the stern, then Resnos played at the gun's controls, and got it to dip down, allowing the dead creature to spool onto the deck. He pressed some sort of release, which separated the harpoon from its cable, and after a moment he declared: "This isn't going to be easy, getting it to the lab. Maybe you two should go and prep a space for it, and we'll fetch a trolley. A *big* trolley…"

Marie and Kalmik muttered agreement, and together headed to the Research Centre, back down the sublevel corridor beneath the drydock wing. The corridors seemed crowded with restless people, on unknown but clearly important missions, moving quickly, laughing nervously.

At one point, Marie felt her tablet buzz an alert, but accessing it was difficult, so she ignored it. She noticed Kalmik twitch and half reach for her own – and assumed that she'd also been called and come to the same conclusion as Marie.

A couple of minutes later, they entered the suite of rooms that comprised the Research Centre, and almost bumped into an excitable Teixeira.

"Katerina… Marie… thank God. Come quick."

They followed Teixeira down the main corridor to Figueroa's office. The woman didn't knock, but entered immediately; Marie followed Kalmik after her. Inside, they found Figueroa and Nacimiento, whose heads snapped around to view the new arrivals.

"Ah… ladies," said Figueroa. "I hear you have had some success… although I am unsure of the cost."

"What is it, Professor?" asked Marie, beating her compatriot to the draw.

Figueroa quickly looked at the Captain-Governor, who gave a small nod for him to continue. "Ah, it seems your efforts have already provoked a response. Mister Bellarriva and young Tonio in the control room have just informed us that the sensors under the ship have been, ah, going down."

"Going down?" said Kalmik. "You mean *taken* down? By the reapers?"

"Yes."

"How many?" asked Marie.

"It seems pretty much *all* of them."

"All!"

Marie's tablet buzzed again, and this time – in the moment of silence as the others contemplated the meaning of the news – she brought it from her thigh pocket and saw that it was from Resnos. Figueroa spotted her distraction, and asked: "A problem, my dear?"

"It's Mike. Hang on." She accepted the call, and saw Resnos' face – slick with sea spray and sweat. It appeared he was still in the dry dock, given the pearlescent light that she recognised from earlier. Indeed, it seemed he was down on the closed floor of the dock, with the hull of the trawler behind him. "Mike? What's up?"

"It *was* them," he blurted. "I mean, on the boat. It *wasn't* the wind. Look!" His face disappeared as he turned the camera on the tablet to show the underside of the boat. What it revealed was a scratched and battered surface, with some significant dents.

"But… it started almost as soon as we entered the water," said Marie. She had shuffled around so she could show the picture on the tablet to the others in the room, or at least, to the two men: Teixeira and Kalmik had to scurry around to take position behind their superiors in order to see.

"Yeah, I know, right," said Resnos. "And just look at the damage. The hull is polycarbon. It takes a helluva force to make any sort of impression on it."

"I think this pretty much confirms that the reapers took down the harvesters," said Kalmik. "And it seems they've now decided that anything we launch in their domain is fair game. Trawlers. Harvesters. The *Fortunata*, if we are stupid enough to set sail again while they're still about."

"And the *Lisboa* itself," said Nacimiento, speaking for the first time. "My child. My ward. And they seem to be attacking it as we speak." All in the room turned silent eyes on him. "I thought the ship impregnable, but now I am not so confident."

"What are we going to do?" asked Figueroa.

Nacimiento's tanned face suddenly seemed pale, as though all blood had left it. "You must continue your research, my friend. Expedite it. And I? We are near *Hibernia* – just a few score kilometres away. They have more resources. I… will call them. Ask for help."

"A mayday?" said Figueroa.

Nacimiento nodded sombrely.

Chapter 36

Deux couldn't resist a visit to his new domain. *His?* Well, not entirely, but to those on the *Marseilles*, the news network was strenuously promoting his role as the inspirational head of the brave liberators – although he really needed to be shown in *Hibernia* to cherry-top the story.

He'd barely slept for three days, unable to drag himself from the command centre set up by Captain Boursis, where the frustratingly scant reports from *Hibernia* had been collated. The loss of the *St. Jean De Luz* in the crossing had been a blow, but he'd been grateful it'd been the only casualty from his impromptu fleet. Then, for hours, there had been confused reports of revised plans, units wandering aimlessly through endless sublevel corridors, and the occasional sharp gunfight. But around late morning of that first day, the news had become more frequent with the proper establishment of a dedicated comms person within the Stokers' HQ – more frequent, and *better*.

One-by-one, the combined Stoker-*Marseilles* force (with the aid of a couple dozen New Socialists from Earth) had achieved its critical targets: power, water, food, communications, the commercial East Docks, and then the central government offices in the Hibernian command centre itself. By late afternoon, the Stokers had started announcing a new regime – in spite of the absence of news on the ruling triumvirate itself.

Further progress had been made the following night, and by the dawn of the second day, the Hibernian forces had been bottled up around the military West Dock. Though seemingly impregnable, with fire control over every sublevel access to their area, they'd had no way to advance into the rest of the city and appeared to appreciate that the battle was lost.

As the rebels consolidated their hold on the third day, Deux had fretted, needing to be in the centre of things where decisions were being made without him. So as soon as the storm diminished to a Class Three, he demanded to be taken to *Hibernia* – now just a kilometre away and looming large off the starboard side of the encroaching *Marseilles.*

Kai Dures agreed to meet him at a spot to the south side of the city, at a destination he marked with a flashing red beacon. Deux felt mildly nauseous from the bumpy crossing, and got drenched during the transfer from his converted assault boat – *The Boulogne* – to the low platform where they were able to moor, and then up some stairs to 'ground' level and across an exposed street to the doors of a three-storey stone building that was part of a block lining the thoroughfare.

"Welcome, Citizen Deux," said the Stoker, rising from a bench against a wall to approach him. They were in the foyer of a public building of unclear function.

Deux pushed back his rain hood and gave himself a shake. He was uncomfortable and discomposed. He fought hard to set aside a scowl and manufacture a smile. He allowed the other to close the space between them, walking slowly. It was the first time Deux had seen the other in the flesh: Dures was somewhat taller than him, and considerably broader, with long blond hair as opposed to Deux's long black, and he had a number of indistinct tattoos on his neck and hands. "Citizen Dures – at last!" Deux accepted the other's outstretched hand, but winced at the power of his grip.

"My wife sends greetings too," said Dures. "She will meet you when she can."

"Wife? Karyn?"

"The state had her in custody, but now she is free and making them pay. She is directing operations while I'm here."

"Excellent. I… ah… here is Citizen Lavie." A woman entered the building, struggling to open the wide front door against a gust of wind. The Stoker guard at the entrance had to take hold of the handle to enable her to enter. "I wonder if – before we talk formally – she can take a few pictures for the people of the *Marseilles.*"

Dures cocked an amused smile. "A reporter? Well, that is the game we all play. My own gurus are broadcasting critical messages to the city as we speak. Why not?"

Deux's smile flickered in annoyance. "Yes, it is part of the game we play. Lavie – get us shaking hands. I know I look windswept, but it adds authenticity."

The woman quickly pulled out a tablet from a shoulder bag and started taking photos. Meanwhile, Deux suffered further pain to his squashed hand, while he couldn't help but notice the wry expression on the face of the Stoker. At last he released from the other's grip, and flexed his hand to start blood flowing back into it. "Thank you, Citizen Lavie. That will do for now." He turned. "Kai – if I may – what do you propose now? I would appreciate a full update and a chance to discuss our future plans."

"Plans? For the *Marseilles*? Oh, you mean for *Hibernia*." There was that wry smile again. "Of course. But first – is this a flying visit, or would you like to stay?"

"I was hoping for a tour and a chance to meet my brave revolutionaries."

"Photo ops. I understand."

"No!" Deux attempted to calm himself. "No, Kai. I think we have much to discuss. We are in some ways one people now. Not just comrades in arms, but also in peace. This is just the start. There are many more ships on this world where injustice rules, and the poor are oppressed."

Dures was silent a moment, his smile and eyes firming. "World-wide revolution? Why not. *I suppose*. But, Citizen Deux, you need to realise that my focus is *my* home, *my* people. We are grateful for your aid, and we will ensure you receive a reward for it – as well as deep and friendly relations – but do not expect us to easily go to war with anyone else."

Deux had made a mistake. He'd approached this meeting expecting an indebted people, and been thrown by the modest reception. He needed to reframe the relationship, and see Dures as just another competitor, like the members of the People's Committee. He nodded slowly and smiled, regaining his equanimity. "Of course, Kai. We have been happy to help you free yourselves – and seeing this is a reward in itself. But as you say, our wider ambitions are – for the moment – just ours. There has been a slight misunderstanding, perhaps. And that emphasises why we need to talk more deeply, and freely."

Dures' firm expression held, but he did slowly nod. "Yes. Sure. So… you wish to stay? You are welcome. Give me a few minutes. I will talk to my people and arrange a secure passage for you and your team to *Hibernia's* premier hotel, near our new seat of power. Okay?" He wandered off to the rear of the foyer, where a couple more Stokers in green jumpsuits waited for instruction. After some words, one pulled on waterproofs and headed for the door.

Dures returned. "It'll be a little while. Shall we begin negotiations… I mean, *discussions*… here? There's a conference room on this floor."

Deux gestured for the other to lead off, following with Lavie and the two armed Marseillaise guards who'd ferried him to the building. The second Stoker by the rear wall fell in behind the procession.

At the end of a carpeted corridor, Dures pushed open a set of double doors, invited Deux to enter, then held up a hand. "Just us, I think. Your escort can wait outside, or maybe in the lobby. Amadou – take care of them."

The Stoker guard smiled at the other visitors and spoke soft words, then ushered them away.

Deux took a seat at the oval conference table dominating the room and waited for his host to join him. Dures slumped into a chair, then leant back and put his feet up on the polished table, showing the soles of his rough boots. Deux frowned and looked around, but there was no sign of refreshments, and he decided he wasn't going to ask for them.

"Right," said Dures. "You want to know the current state of play? Let me tell you."

For five minutes, Dures related the course of the conflict. He soon swung his legs down from the table top, so he could lean forwards and thud the surface for emphasis with one thick, callused finger. His report focused on the activities of the Stokers themselves, though he did (grudgingly?) note some successes for the *Marseilles* contingent. At last he finished.

Deux watched the other through hooded eyes. "And they still hold out?"

"At the West Docks, yes. But they are in the dark and getting low on ammunition. We are preparing an overground assault for this afternoon. The weather is still bad, but if it gets any better they'll be able to escape using the ESU's boats. That's both good and bad. It will give us full control of *Hibernia*, but allow them to fortify Athol. We'd rather collect as many of their forces as we can while they are in reach."

"I understand. And what of O'Neill?"

"We assume she is at the Docks."

"Could that be a problem?" Deux had read Machiavelli's *The Prince*. He knew a ruler should eliminate their predecessor to prevent them returning. "Might she act as a germ of resistance for the, ah, *other* people of *Hibernia*? The Stokers are behind you – but what of the rest of the population?"

"Yes, you have a point." Dures leant back in his chair and softly drummed the fingers of one hand on the table. "As long as our policies are not too harsh or go too fast, I suspect the majority will remain meek and accepting. That is what Karyn advocates. But to aid a sense of transition not transformation, we have a surprise addition to our new ruling council – one of the triumvirate."

Deux couldn't hide his surprise. "Who?"

"Kerrie Sullivan."

"Really? How? Was she working for you all along?"

Dures smiled broadly. "Not at all. She's never expressed any positive sentiment towards us – although she's never said much against us either. She made this clear when we apprehended her, and my people checked. She's right. Most of the vitriol in the past has come from her partners in crime."

"A typical politician. But do you trust her? Why has she turned?"

"She turned because she had little choice. O'Neill and Traore deserted her – probably unintentionally. She seems to have been left her behind when they couldn't find her. And so now she's faced with making an accommodation with us or, well, we hadn't really thought about what to do with her."

"Still, I'm surprised. Why do we need her? Did you offer her anything?"

Dures shrugged. "I suggested that if she was compliant she might avoid a public trial, and hinted that we might allow her to keep some of her toys."

"Really?" Deux scowled. "I would strip her of everything. She is a fascist and oppressor. She has no cards to play… or does she?"

"It turns out she does. *Mount Ardol*."

"Ardol? Where the *Marseilles* is headed? What do you mean? Why is that important?"

"Ah – you haven't heard, have you?" Dures sat forwards again. "It always surprises me how insular we are. Apparently, the miners on the *Stavanger* found a deposit that contains rare earths. It seems it's a viable prospect, too. In fact, it's almost certainly the most important find on Tethys since humans arrived."

"Then it's *our* site now," said Deux, unthinkingly. "*Our* turn."

Dures tensed. "Actually, Citizen, it is *Hibernia's* site which *we* allow other city ships to mine."

Deux raised both hands in apology for his choice of words, though he felt a sudden excitement. Resources? Within reach? "Of course," he said. "Go on."

"The key point is that the triumvirate confiscated it – to the great displeasure of the Stavangerans – and now the site is under Hibernian control. There is a detachment of the ESU there, plus dozens of miners who just happen to work for Sullivan's mining company."

"I see. So you haven't yet secured this place for the people? I suppose an assault would be difficult?"

"*Very*. Their ESU still has its small fleet spread about the Range and at the West Docks. A seaborne landing would be perilous and success couldn't be guaranteed." Dures shook his head in resignation. "In any case, we need Sullivan's experienced miners to progress the dig as quickly as possible."

Deux eased back in his chair and looked up to the ceiling. Dures hadn't proven as accommodating as he'd hoped – or as malleable. He wondered whether he might have more luck with his wife. Or with Sullivan? And who else had a say in matters? The Earthers? Whether or not he was able to ultimately negotiate a seat at the table of power in *Hibernia*, a new horizon was suddenly open to him. He needed to find out much more about this find and what it held. The reward for the *Marseilles* hadn't been nailed down before the uprising, but it seemed prospects were brighter than he'd dared imagine. A broad smile settled on his face.

He managed to remain on best behaviour until a Stoker arrived with news of his arranged accommodation, by which time he'd managed to wheedle from Dures a more comprehensive story of the deposit on Ardol and the political fault-lines in *Hibernia.*

* * *

The last couple of days had been deeply unpleasant for Nesvorny. When the power had gone down, he'd briefly lost contact with the troops protecting the ISU HQ, as well as those protecting the route between there and the West Docks – their last bastion, where he was trapped. In the confusion, the enemy had managed to isolate and overwhelm several of his units: once their back-up generator had powered up and given them access to their battle systems once more, it had revealed disarray, surrender, and retreat. The HQ section had been conceded, and with it, much of their remaining ammunition plus the few armoured vehicles the ISU possessed – which had been useless since the advent of the storm, but which Nesvorny feared might soon prove more valuable to the foe as the weather cleared.

And then there had been the arrival of Major Fukuda with O'Neill and Traore. While Traore had been far less smug than usual, O'Neill had retained her combativeness: she'd been a horror in the confined and increasingly cluttered, unhygienic, and foetid sublevels of the West Dock, demanding the impossible and interfering with every military decision.

But now crunch time had come. It was day three since the start of the revolt, and reports from watchers on ground level were encouraging… from a certain perspective.

"The weather is improving," said Joseph. "We should leave." She, Fukuda, and Nesvorny stood, while O'Neill and Traore occupied the only chairs in Joseph's small office. "On Athol, I have more troops and resources. We have energy. We have food supplies. We could set up fishing lines, too. And when the rebels send out trawlers to fish, we have the force to capture them. Once we've got a couple, we'll be well fed and they'll have to send the rest further afield."

"But if we leave," wondered Traore, "will we ever be able to return? And what about the *Lisboa* and these aliens you told us about? Are they a threat?"

"Aliens?" scoffed O'Neill. "I still can't believe it. What are the Lisboetas doing about the situation now?"

Joseph shrugged. "You know as much as I do. I haven't been able to contact them since we started getting jammed."

"The *Lisboa* has boats, too," noted O'Neill. "And other resources. Maybe this is opportune. If we help them, they won't deny us reasonable requests. We'll allow them to moor off Athol, and you can shoot some of these aliens for them, Joseph. Then they'll be grateful and in our debt. *Quid pro quo.*" O'Neill looked away a moment, her mind working. More softly, she said: "Yes… I'd rather be on Athol than here. Okay. Retreat is the best option for now. As soon as it's safe, we'll go."

"All of us?" asked Nesvorny. "Joseph's boats can only carry so many, and you'll need a rear guard to let you get away. What of those left behind?"

"A reasonable sacrifice," said Traore. "They're doing their jobs. They've taken their pay all these years – it's about time they earned it."

"That's right," said O' Neill. "If they can get away afterwards – great. But they need to hold out as long as possible. Cause attrition to the enemy. Tie them down. Tell them we'll be back soon with reinforcements."

"Will we?" asked Nesvorny.

"Probably not. But they need to have some hope. Motivate them. For fuck's sake, Nesvorny, you should know all this."

Traore now smirked. "And what of you, Colonel? Do you plan to do the honourable thing and stay with your troops? Or do you want us to save space on a boat for you?"

Nesvorny felt an urge to get up and strike the sneering man. But he did have a point. What would he do? If he stayed, the Stokers might well hang him from the highest tower in *Hibernia*. But could he just walk away from his duty? And suddenly, all was clear to him. He felt the tension drain away. He smiled back. "Yes. I'll stay. Someone needs to show leadership. What will be, will be."

The look of shock on Traore's face – a man who would never have considered such a sacrifice, or envision it in others – was priceless. *But was it worth the risk of being executed?*

* * *

Nesvorny had various duties to perform before the departure of O'Neill and her party. One of these was to interrogate the prisoners captured over the last couple of days to get a sense of their intentions, numbers, and capabilities. He was somewhat surprised at the man now brought in to face him in the small office.

"I *know* you," said Nesvorny. "I remember our very first encounter, when you seemed to think it amusing to insult me, *Mr Mitsos*. We had our eyes on you, but it seems we should have paid closer attention to your New Socialist colleagues who joined you on the *Marseilles*. You were an annoyance to start, and then a distraction."

"But not an enemy," said Mitsos. "Never an enemy. I'm just a businessman trying to sell his wares. No one on *Hibernia* wanted them, but the *Marseilles* did. Well, they did at first."

"Not anymore?" Nesvorny smiled without humour. The man before him – in a set of grey overalls with a red armband – was rather less cocksure than he remembered. "I'm not surprised. Your machine didn't work?"

"Oh, it did, but not well enough. They took a gamble, but when it didn't pay off, rather than admitting their own fault, they decided to place all of the blame on me. Or at least, that bastard Deux did."

"The *Marseilles* leader? Sebastian Deux?"

"The First Citizen, yeah. A complete cunt."

The other's passion seemed genuine. Nesvorny frowned and looked over the man. His clothing was a surprise, bearing no resemblance to the 'uniforms' of either the Stokers or the Marseillaise. "So, now you're here – paying off your debt to him by attacking my people?"

"No! Absolutely not! When your troops captured me, I didn't have a gun or weapon of any sort. You need to check with them. They picked me up because I was in the corridors breaking curfew, and then they saw my armband – which was my mistake. I should have taken it off. In fact…" He grabbed his armband and stripped it roughly from his arm, dropping it on the desk between them. "Is that clear now?"

"It's a bit late, isn't it? You can't remove your allegiance so easily."

"I have no allegiance. This was a disguise to stop me getting shot. To be clear, I *didn't* volunteer to come here and murder people. I smuggled myself on one of the assault boats in order to get off the *Marseilles*, and was found when we docked. I figured they wouldn't immediately chuck me overboard, but it was a risk I was willing to take, and I was lucky to have a sympathetic person on board to watch out for me. A… *friend*."

"An interesting story." Nesvorny was unconvinced. "So you arrived in *Hibernia* and then your captors just let you go?"

"Not at all. They kept me under guard. But then we got ambushed from behind and everyone in the unit got killed. *Almost* everyone. I managed to slip away. Then I blundered into one of your patrols, and here I am. You know, I was almost relieved to be captured by you. I'd got away from *them*. But now it seems from the panic all around that this will soon be *Marseilles* too, and then I'm truly fucked." He shook his head angrily. "I need to get out of here before they find me. I wish you'd fought better."

Nesvorny stiffened. "We fought as well as we could against a surprise attack with superior numbers."

"Yes, well, I'm sorry for your losses. For *everyone's*." Mitsos broke contact with Nesvorny's glare, and looked away. "It's all just so… *stupid*. The woman shot in the face. My old crew. Abdul was okay. Marc could be an arsehole, but he didn't deserve to be killed." He looked back up. "I'm not a politician, Captain… ah, no, I remember. I did insult you last time, didn't I? I'm sorry. It's Colonel, isn't it? Well, Colonel, I'm not a politician. I don't know who is right or wrong here. In my experience, you're probably both to blame. But this killing? *Really?*" He shook his head again, slowly this time. "There are some real villains here, with a lot of blood on their hands. Sebastian Deux is one. He doesn't give a fuck about anyone but himself. Maybe there's some on your side the same. We should just put them in a room together and give them rusty knives and leave them to it." Now he gave a lopsided smile. "But I fear, if you leave me here and they win, then the rusty knives will be used on me." He held up a hand with two misshapen fingers. "Personal experience of their justice, you see."

For once, Nesvorny wasn't quite sure what to say. The other's speech seemed heartfelt, stripped of the mockery of their last encounter. And it was *what* he said, too. Traore and O'Neill and Deux and Fukuda and Dures… His brow furrowed. *Dures?* Kai or Karyn? He didn't know the man, but the woman was complex. Was she the same as the others? He couldn't decide. He looked back to the prisoner, who waited patiently for him to continue. "Mr Mitsos, I–"

"You're going to leave, aren't you? It makes sense. I've even heard your troops talking. *Athol.* They keep repeating, *Athol.* Take me with you."

"Mitsos – we're not running a ferry service. You're a prisoner."

"Yeah, but I can help."

"How can you possibly do that? You're not a fighter, as you admit. You're not a patriot to any side, let alone ours. We don't need your machine or your dubious skills. We don't–"

"*Knowledge,*" Mitsos blurted. "I have knowledge. Of the enemy. I came with them. I can tell you about the *Marseilles* contingent – its strengths and weaknesses. You want to know how many boats they have, and how they're armed? Their force, and weapons? How they were trained? Who trained them? I can tell you. I won't resist, or keep mum, or try to deceive. And while they've been dragging me about underground, I've seen more. I can tell you about the Stokers and the Socialists from Earth. I can even give you insights on their leaders and their psychology, especially Deux. I can't say for sure what is relevant, but there must be *something* that you'll be able to use. I've a lot to tell, and frankly, I'm surprised I haven't been grilled before."

"It's a bit late now," said Nesvorny, dryly. "And as you surmised, we're leaving." He paused, correcting himself: "*They're* leaving."

"It's not too late to learn what I know if I go too. Then there'll be plenty of time for me to talk. And you'll need all the intel you can get if you're going to try to return." He smiled weakly. "And if that isn't enough to get on your boat, what about simple human compassion? If you've got room, why would you leave me to Deux and Boursis and her fucking pliers?"

And that was it. Nesvorny wasn't entirely sure afterwards, on thinking back, which cue it was that turned him – intel? Compassion? *Pliers?* But it was something. Mitsos was genuinely afraid – *honestly* afraid. And here was a chance for him to do something right among all the wrong.

* * *

Nesvorny watched the loading of the ESU patrol boats from the harbourmaster's office, perched on the edge of the West Docks. There were a dozen berths below, protected by retractable transparent roofs that prevented any moored vessels from being inundated by Tethys' storms. Only six of the berths were occupied: he knew Joseph's other two boats had been in safe harbour at Mount Athol, and that these were already en route to *Hibernia* over the choppy seas. Now that the rain was merely very heavy as opposed to torrential, the boats would be making multiple crossings, carrying cargo as well as personnel, until either they succeeded in the full evacuation, or until the enemy got close enough to make further trips hazardous. Even now, he could hear gunshots away to his right. Their foe had also come onto the sodden streets, and in that direction they were attempting long-distance shots at the boats as they departed.

"You can still change your mind," said Joseph, standing at his shoulder. She'd been outside, so wore a heavy rain cape over her black uniform, which steamed gently as the warmth in the cabin and of her body caused some of the water to evaporate from her costume.

"No, I really can't."

"You mean *won't*."

"Don't quibble, Tania. If the situation were reversed, would you take leave of your command?"

She sighed. "No, of course not. But if you're staying, try not to do anything too incriminating. Remember, we may in the end have to serve different masters – if they'll have us. Unlikely, I know, but not impossible. Just don't burn all your bridges, especially not for the sake of those two."

Nesvorny didn't have to see her face to know where she was looking. Below, O'Neill was being helped aboard one boat by a couple of ESU marines, while Traore waited on the quay behind her, an expensive-looking suitcase in each hand. He chuckled: "Who'd have thought I'll soon be answering to others with whom I'm even *less* popular."

"I know. Big shits to the left of us, massive cunts to the right."

Nesvorny's smile broadened. "Never a truer word. But watch out for them – especially Fukuda and his Squad Five. He's now my replacement. He's not likely to ask you for things as nicely as I have, especially with Traore pulling his strings. And his force may still outnumber yours if we manage to complete the evacuation."

"How many are staying with you?"

"About eighty. That's the minimum we need to man our perimeter here and keep the enemy from us below. They're all volunteers – mostly with family they won't leave."

"Don't worry, Eric. They should be okay. They are *workers* after all."

"Maybe. I think the Stokers will be fine with them. They know who they want, and most of those are with Fukuda. I know nothing about the Marseillais, but speaking to Mitsos, I suspect they may not be so forgiving of the 'class traitors'. Painful re-education may be in order."

"Mitsos? The prisoner?"

"Yes. I've given him to you, not Fukuda. He says he'll tell all, and I believe him. So get what you can and don't let the Major have him. Fukuda's methods will be brutal, and completely unnecessary."

"Sure." Joseph was silent for a moment, then she asked quietly: "When we're gone… how long will you hold out?"

"Not long. I want to minimise deaths – on our side, but also on theirs. I'm a lawman, not a soldier. If this is war, then I suppose all this fighting is somehow legitimate, and neither they nor us are criminals. As soon as the last weapon is laid down, they'll hopefully all return to be law abiding citizens – but perhaps according to new laws."

There was another pause, then Nesvorny felt a hand upon his shoulder. "Time for me to go," said Joseph. "You look out for yourself, Eric."

He didn't respond. And a couple minutes later he watched Joseph appear on the quay below and head for her passage to temporary safety.

Chapter 37

In the end, they got an escort to the Science Institute, which De Voe attributed more to their 'captors' wanting to get rid of them safely than any real desire to help them in their quest.

The sublevel door had an electronic call pad. "I think you'd better let us in," said Heiko, speaking into the mic. "We are here to collect Dr Frost. The *Stavanger* Ambassador is here beside me, and on my other side is an armed man who has little love for you or your leadership. I suspect if you don't let us in, he might start shooting, first at the door, then at whoever is inside."

De Voe smiled at that. Heiko had such a nice way of making threats. She would have just battered at the door and kept cursing until they let her in. She peered at their escort – a bored-looking Stoker with red hair, toying with his rifle and constantly looking back the way they had come. He clearly wanted to get this over with so he could get back to the real action.

The door was quickly opened by a young woman. She smiled uncertainly and declared herself the live-in caretaker. De Voe followed Heiko and Solbakken inside.

Heiko turned to the escort. "I think we'll be okay. Perhaps you can wait here and guard the exit?"

The man shrugged. "Your call. But don't try to leave by another route. I've instructions to take you directly back to the embassy."

"Of course."

They followed the caretaker up some stairs and entered an ornate lobby, with rich wallpaper and a small chandelier that sparkled with lights. An elderly bearded man came towards them haltingly.

"Who are you? Becka – why did you let these people in?"

"We're here to collect Makka," said De Voe, determined not to be sidelined.

"Ah… Ms De Voe? Is that you?"

"Too damned right. I don't remember you, though."

"Dr Ravindra Singh. We met a few years ago."

"Right. I remember now. I hope you've been treating Makka well. He is here, isn't he?"

"Yes, yes. Upstairs. We have tried to make his stay as comfortable as possible. This is all very unfortunate. Please follow me."

The young, black-uniformed guard standing outside the room upstairs looked at them nervously as they approached – De Voe striding next to Singh, the others now behind. "You," she shouted from several metres away. "Unlock the door and piss off."

"I… who are… what…" The guard fumbled with his gun – a wide barrelled affair that looked more for crowd control than warfare.

"Point that at me, and I'll fucking shove it up your arse. The lock?"

"Uh…" The man seemed torn. He stepped back. "It's not locked, but…"

"You do know that *Hibernia* is under attack, don't you?" De Voe said, slowing as they came close to the guard. "And from what we've seen, you're losing. Don't make things hard for yourself."

"Okay. But what'll I do?"

"That's your problem."

Singh raised his hands in a calming gesture. "Martin – I suggest you let Dr Frost go, and then come downstairs with me. The curfew is still in effect and it's probably not safe outside. Let us raid the liquor cabinet, eh?"

The man seemed relieved. He retreated several steps back down the hallway, and set his weapon on the floor. "Go ahead."

"Wise choice," said De Voe. She opened the door to what appeared to be a storeroom – and inside found Frost lazing on a single mattress set on the floor. "Makka!"

"Melissa?" Frost scrabbled awkwardly to his feet, a broad smile on his stubbled face. "I don't know how you got here, but thank God!"

"Rennie and Magnus are here, too." She twitched her head towards her right shoulder. It was good to see the boss. She gave him a helping hand, which turned into a hug.

Frost appeared to catch a glimpse of the others behind her in the corridor: he nodded a greeting at them, then focused on De Voe. "But how?"

"What do you know of the revolt?"

"Revolt? Melissa, what have you started?"

She laughed. "Not us, boss. The Stokers. And it seems they've got all sorts of weird help. I'll explain later. Let's get back to the embassy. We've got an escort down below, but I still don't know how easy it's going to be."

Getting back to the embassy actually proved relatively straightforward. They heard gunfire echoing through the sublevel corridors, but took a route that kept a healthy distance from the noise. And so they accomplished the first aim of their trip to *Hibernia.* But their second – getting back their stolen supplies – proved an altogether more complex matter.

* * *

On the second day after the start of the revolt, the rebels lifted curfew in certain parts of the city for a limited time, but with conditions that were communicated through the suborned state alert system. Inhabitants were only allowed out singly or in pairs, initially within a two-hour slot – to enable them to gather food, medicine, or other necessities they might not have had at the outset of the affair. The *Stavanger* contingent got around the regulations by leaving the embassy in several pairs, taking different routes via the sublevels to the East Docks – which were now secured by the rebels and beyond the conflict zone. But these forays achieved little.

"No chance," said Sergeant Judd Stallings – dressed in civies. "We got to the warehouses on Sublevel One okay – the ones at sea level loaded directly from docked cargo ships – but everything is shut up and guarded by people with guns. Unless you actually get inside, there's no way to see what's stored where. They moved us on quickly."

Heiko, Solbakken, Frost, De Voe, Remillard, and Pedersen sat in chairs in a semi-circle, listening to the report from the standing segreant. Heiko slouched, his long legs spread out before him. "I don't think we expected otherwise. Direct assault is out – and we're not equipped for that anyway. Before recent events, we might have hoped for a light guard with non-lethal gear, but not now. That leaves subterfuge."

"You mean dressing up as dockworkers?" said De Voe.

"I guess so. But that would require gaining appropriate costumes and credentials, and not being ratted out by real employees. And we still don't know when people will be allowed to return to work."

"Any thoughts based on your martial experiences, Rennie?" asked Solbakken.

"I'm afraid not. There are many factors at play here. My guess is the rebels are already close to victory, so conditions will gradually ease over a number of days. But they'll want to keep tight control over critical facilities for considerably longer."

Solbakken pursed his lips. "Hmmm, the situation seems to have changed drastically, and so must our plans. A political solution was out – but maybe it's back on the table again. I really wish I could talk to Margarethe and Nila about this, but I suspect access to the satellite comms system will also be prohibited for some time."

Heiko brooded for a moment, then looked up: "Ah, sorry, Judd. You did well. Take a break."

"Yes, sir!" Stallings turned and left the room.

After the man had gone, Heiko sat up and took the arms of his chair, twisting about until he was looking at Solbakken directly. "Political, Magnus?"

"Yes. I am still ambassador – it's just the court that's changed. We met the crown prince yesterday – Kai Dures. He seemed sympathetic. There is hope. But we will have to wait until the new rulers are established, comfortable, and ready to receive petitions."

"So, what do we do in the meantime?" asked De Voe. "I don't fancy sitting about here for days – or maybe even weeks. It's too crowded and starting to smell."

Remillard coughed a laugh.

Solbakken smiled. "Yes, I had noticed. Additionally, you have already denuded my larder, and my embassy account is not particularly well endowed."

"Retrenchment," said Heiko. "I guess you are right. At least we have recovered Makka. I guess we should return to the *Stavanger* as soon as we can."

But that didn't prove easy, either.

* * *

"But it's *my* boat," said Cass Remillard, two days later, after victory had been declared and curfew had been lifted during daylight hours. "*My* private property."

"We can't let you leave," said the guard in grey with red armbands. "It belongs to the state now. We will decide what happens to your toy."

"But we're from the *Stavanger*, not *Hibernia*."

"So you say. In any case, you're still rich. You're from a rich ship built by rich Norwegians. It's time you learned to share with the poor of this world."

Remillard fumed. "I earned that boat."

De Voe looked askance at Heiko and arched an eyebrow, receiving a wry grin in return.

"I don't care what you claim," said the guard. A couple more armed people ambled over to see what the fuss was about – a man and a woman, both dressed in green. The trio looked miserable: although the worst of the storm had abated, there was still a persistent drizzle and they all looked very damp, presumably from spending hours outside.

"Problem?" asked the woman, pale-faced with black hair plastered over her scalp.

Solbakken stepped forwards. "I am the ambassador of *Stavanger*, and these are fellow citizens who have been stranded here since before the, ah, present difficulties. They merely wish to return home."

The woman quickly glanced at her male companion, then at the guard in grey. "Sounds reasonable. What's the problem?"

"The First Citizen made it clear that we need a full audit of goods and resources in *Hibernia* to decide on fair redistribution. No one leaves until then." He ignored Remillard and faced Solbakken. "You get signed authorisation from the Revolutionary Committee, fine. Until then, Citizen, you get nothing."

The woman wiped a hand across her damp forehead and flicked water onto the wet pavement. "Sorry, people. I'd let you go, but that's how it is for now."

De Voe looked around: their party numbered close to a dozen, and Remillard's boat was visible, ten metres away down at sea level.

She cursed under her breath – but loud enough for the woman to hear. She turned to De Voe, raised her eyebrows, nodded subtly at the guard in grey, and shook her head. De Voe flashed a smile in understanding.

"Hang on," said Remillard, "you can't–"

Heiko placed a firm hand on his arm. "*Cass.*"

Solbakken sighed. "Very well. It's back to the embassy then, and I'll redouble my efforts to gain an audience.".

As they left, De Voe took Heiko's arm. "What did you make of that?"

"There seem to be some fault lines among the conquerors. Could be an opportunity… but it could equally prove to be a nightmare."

"Given our luck," she replied, "I'm sleeping with the lights on."

* * *

Later that afternoon, while Solbakken continued his attempts to contact someone in authority in the new regime, and Pedersen led a supply run, Heiko, De Voe, and Remillard returned to the East Docks by a circuitous route to surreptitiously assess the lie of the land. By now, the city was coming back to life – albeit sporadically. There were some people on the still-damp streets, but these tended to walk quickly and look about nervously, trying to avoid eye contact with others – especially with the frequent two-person gun-toting patrols. Around half of the retail and service outlets were open, and half were still dark – their proprietors presumably taking a wait-and-see attitude.

They came to a large eatery opposite the docks set in a three-storey stone building, and found a table on the third floor that looked out over it. They would have gone to the roof terrace, but that was still closed on account of the weather. They were the only ones on this floor, and the second had been empty, too. Heiko could sense how torn the proprietor was: annoyed at the extra effort of schlepping up and down stairs, as well as at their small order of drinks and pastries, but also relieved to at least have someone spending money.

"Nothing's leaving," said Remillard, "not even the fishing fleet. That will need to change soon."

"Will it?" asked Heiko. "I heard there's a big hydroponics sector in *Hibernia*."

"Sure, but the curfew will have had some effect on production. Also, if this place is like the *Stavanger*, there will be storage for a few weeks' food at most."

"Why's that?"

"Limited space, a desire to ensure resources spent on freezing are minimal, plus an abundance of fresh stuff in the oceans and sea forests all around. Remember, Rennie – energy and food isn't a problem here, it's the rarer elements used in machinery that's the limiting factor on our society."

"I understand that all too well," said Heiko. "It drives everything on Tethys."

"Yep," said De Voe, "and it's probably the ultimate cause of whatever this is… revolt? Invasion? I'm not sure what to call it."

"So, when the fleet leaves," continued Remillard, hunching forwards and lowering his bushy brows, "that may be the time to move. The docks will be busy, and I doubt whether anyone will be watching for escapees."

Heiko looked between the pair sat opposite. They appeared to be eager for some action, but… "If we have to take illicit leave, then yes. Claude is still buried in the Hibernian systems, so he may get a sense of when things are going to open up. Maybe get a line into the harbourmaster's office. But I still worry about taking unnecessary action. I'd rather we leave with permission of the new overlords. I don't like burning bridges unnecessarily."

"Rennie – you've got to be the least bellicose military man in history," said De Voe.

"A military option should be the *last* option," Heiko emphasized. "Let's hope for the best – through Magnus' efforts – but, yes, let's also prepare for the worst. We can work up a plan back at the embassy."

They left the eatery soon after. As Remillard settled the bill, Heiko stepped outside into the drizzle with De Voe. As he turned to face her, he noticed something over her shoulder. "Ah, Melissa, it seems we have not gone unnoticed. There are a couple dressed in green loitering by the edge of the block."

"Are they armed?"

"One is."

"Hmmm, that's funny. A couple, you say?"

Heiko withdrew slightly so he could look directly into De Voe's face – and noticed that she was staring past his shoulder. "Your side, too?"

"Uh-huh. Same. Two in green, one armed, trying to look inconspicuous but making a shit job of it – probably like we are in trying to pretend that *we* haven't seen *them*."

Heiko laughed softly.

De Voe looked up. "What?"

"I suspect you're right. Our tradecraft is little better than theirs. Ah… Cass."

"You two look like you're going to have a snog," said Remillard. "Am I interrupting something?"

"Not between us. We just realised we have company. Don't look, but there are two left and two right."

"*And* two opposite," Remillard said. "They're over the road by the wall to the docks, pretending to read the electronic bulletin board there."

"Six?" said De Voe. "That's a bit overkill."

Heiko started at that. "*Overkill?* You're right. If they want to tail us, it's highly excessive. So, it's more than that. But they are the authority here now, so why be surreptitious? They can simply 'arrest' us if they want to. So they don't want to do that, either."

Remillard leant in to the pair. "I don't like where you're going with this, Rennie. That only leaves one option I can think of. We're outnumbered and literally outgunned. What now?"

"We get back to the embassy, but not, I think, the way we came." They'd taken Sublevel One from the basement and emerged at street level at some random spot half-way between the embassy and the docks. "This time I think we really *do* want to be seen. Come on."

Heiko turned to face the direction De Voe had been looking, carefully took her arm, and moved away from the front of the eatery, off the pavement and into the deserted road itself. He set off towards the couple De Voe had seen – who now jerked back around the corner of the block – taking it slow. Remillard fell-in on his other side.

"I hope you know what you're doing," said De Voe, sharply.

"I do. I just hope our followers understand the rules, too."

They ambled past the junction. Heiko caught sight of the pair in green standing several metres from the corner, beneath the fluttering flag of a bar. Ignoring them, he continued ahead.

The walk to the embassy took fifteen minutes. They moved along the widest throughfares, returning to the pavement when an electric cart headed towards them. Then Heiko started talking loudly to his colleagues – just small talk – initially startling them, until they appreciated his intent and responded in kind. And they made themselves a nuisance to other pedestrians, too, by hogging the pavement and causing them to step onto the road, sometimes with muttered curses.

When they turned into Consul Street, home to the embassies of the city ships, one of the pairs of followers was already there, waiting on the opposite side of the road. Heiko paused a second, then headed directly for them, gently tugging De Voe with him, knowing Remillard would follow.

"What the fuck!" hissed De Voe.

"Trust me," said Heiko, quietly.

One of the lurking pair looked away, while the second – a youngish man, maybe early thirties, with cropped hair and a fat nose – looked up angrily. His hand – which bore the smudge of a tattoo – tightly gripped the strap of a rifle slung over his shoulder.

"Can we help you?" asked Heiko, drawing to a halt opposite. "I mean, if you really want to talk, you just need to come and say hello."

The man stared at him – and Heiko noticed his eyes stray to the adaptor socket at the side of his left eye. "Me? No. I think you've mistaken me for someone else."

"Ah – I'm sorry. It's the uniforms. There are so many in green following us this afternoon. Are you sure you don't want to talk – out here in the open, where everyone can see?"

The man leant in. "Very funny, comrade. But take care, eh? You just need to make *one* mistake." He straightened, and addressed his partner. "Let's split."

Heiko watched them stalk away from Consul Street, heading towards the other pairs, who'd joined up to stand outside a utility store.

"Quick now," said Heiko. "Before they change their minds."

* * *

They let themselves into the embassy with a spare key, and slouched into chairs in the lounge. There was no sign of Solbakken or Pedersen, and De Voe assumed Vardem and the others were upstairs, continuing their efforts to hack into the Hibernian systems and improve their surveillance.

"The Stokers seemed less hostile to us than the grey fanatics," said De Voe. "What was that all about? What's changed?"

"Didn't you notice the tattoos, Melissa?"

"A lot of people have them on Tethys, Rennie, not just Stokers. Us too." She reached to caress the tattoo of an anchor near her brow. "What are you talking about? What did I miss?"

"One had a hammer and sickle on his neck, and another had an *AK-47* on the back of his hand. Those are typical motifs of New Socialists."

"You mean, our followers are from Earth?"

Heiko nodded slowly. "Yes. If two of them were NS, there's a good chance the other four were as well. I admit, I don't understand their distribution among the rebels." He rubbed a hand across his chin. "There was one NS in the leadership group we bumped into on the first day – and he was in green. Others were with the rebels from the *Marseilles* and have been wearing grey. It speaks of significant planning over quite a period of time – importing the expertise of these professional revolutionaries to help both the locals and their ideological kin on the other ship. Perhaps some have updated their wardrobes?"

"But why have they taken against us?"

Heiko gave a wry smile. "I'm afraid that could be me." He tapped the copper adaptor at the side of his eye. "On Earth, they've really got it in for anyone with augments. *Ubermensch*, they call us. It has historical connotations I won't go into."

"So you think their concern is about you specifically?" said Remillard. "Does that mean if you keep away from us, the rest of us should be okay?"

"Cass!" De Voe looked at the other harshly. "I don't like what you're implying."

Remillard raised his hands defensively. "I'm implying nothing, Melissa, just stating facts."

"He may be right," said Heiko. "I suspect if we leave the embassy and you go one way and I go another, they'll follow me."

"That's not going to happen," said De Voe, crossing her arms, "and not just because I kind of like you and you're not terrible in bed – stop smirking, Cass. We all know your preference for impressionable young things. It's to do with loyalty and all that shit. You're one of us now, Rennie."

Remillard was still smiling broadly. "Sure. I'm not arguing with you. I wouldn't dare."

"Thank you, Melissa – I think." Heiko actually seemed embarrassed – and De Voe was kind of touched by that. "But it's worth bearing in mind for the future. I'm responsible for the security of the *Stavanger* and the people on it, so I will act as necessary in order to do my job. I can handle myself. I'm a big boy."

De Voe laughed curtly, and was about to joke, when she noticed Heiko's pained expression: he seemed to know what she was about to say. She glanced at Remillard, whose smile had managed to broaden further, and decided to spare her part-time lover further grief. She closed her half-open mouth, and lifted herself from her chair. "I think that's enough about your manhood for now, Rennie. Coffee, everyone? Let's see if we can't find Magnus' secret stash."

Chapter 38

It had been a couple of days since Nacimiento sent a mayday to *Hibernia* and received a noncommittal response. During that time, the *Lisboa* had changed course to head for Mount Athol – as subsequently advised – but at reduced speed.

"I still don't understand how they can have damaged the screws," said Kalmik.

The new Crisis Team were meeting in the Captain-Governor's stateroom, which was usually used by the governing council to decide affairs of state. Although Nacimiento still consulted with the elected representatives of the people, these had – according to Nacimiento himself – recognised that the problem was scientific and technical rather than political, and been happy to cede control to the ship's leader and his hand-picked team of experts. This comprised Figueroa, Kalmik, and Marie herself, along with chief engineer Ernesto Blanco and Hector Bellarriva – a top systems analyst who'd taken over the hidden control room from young Tonio Janeiro.

"Nor do I," said Blanco, a balding man in his seventies who wore contact lenses that apparently no longer suited his changing vision, given how he constantly squinted. "You say they don't have tools, and the turbulence around the screws is great, so I don't understand how they can physically get close enough to inflict damage."

"Could they be putting things in the way?" asked Marie. "Things that are sucked into the propellors and somehow damaging them?"

"What, like fish?" said Kalmik, sarcastically. "How is that going to cause harm? Soft and squishy things?"

"Yes, it would need to be something hard to do that," agreed Blanco. "Rock. From the seabed?"

"But it's still deep here, isn't it," said Kalmik. "Can they really dive that far?"

"To be fair, we don't know," said Figueroa. "Perhaps we should find out – though I'm not entirely sure how we might do this."

"But we're approaching Athol, aren't we?" persisted Marie. "The water depth will soon be reducing. In any case, we really don't know what their limitations are. Underestimating them is dangerous."

"Whatever the cause, we can't do anything about it now," said Blanco. "None of my team are willing to go under the ship to check, and I'm afraid a fatal failure in one of the props would seriously damage the others, as well as the underside of our home."

Nacimiento had said little in the meeting so far. Now he shifted in his seat, drawing the eyes of all in the room. His peaked captain's cap rested on the table in front of him. "It is a dilemma," he said. "But I agree with Ernesto's suggestion. We will continue slow and steady. The Range is already visible, and with luck we will see Athol tomorrow, or the day after that. Much as I fear for our mighty sea turtle, it is the fate of our smaller vessels that currently worries me more. We have some supplies still, and our hydroponics work, but we have not harvested from a sea forest for some time, and our trawler fleet remains dock-bound – no, Miguel?"

Figueroa started at being suddenly identified. "Ah, sorry, my friend. I was still thinking… the trawlers? I am afraid that is still not resolved. Katerina?"

"We've tried a couple of launches," said Kalmik. "Even using high-powered lights to flood the area beneath a boat has had little success. The first boat was attacked as soon as its hull touched the water. When we ramped up the underwater lights further, we managed to gain enough respite to actually launch a second – but the boat didn't get clear of the wings before attacks started to get through, and the crew instantly reversed and returned to the dock. They just got out in time before the whole boat lifted up in the water and the last of the lights were ripped away. We have pictures of the reapers actually breaching the water and striking the underside as it was lifted into its cradle – turning somersaults and using their powerful legs."

"They literally kicked a hole in the hull," confirmed Marie. "That trawler will need major repairs before it launches again, but having seen the creatures breach, none of the dock workers want to go anywhere near the water to start repairs from the outside."

Nacimiento looked glum, his weathered face drooping like that of a beagle. "Is there no good news? What of other possible weapons?

What has been discovered from the corpse of the reaper that was caught?"

"Ah… can I?" asked Marie. When no one objected, she continued: "I think there is some progress there. We dissected the creature, and one thing we found is that it doesn't have any eyes as such, although its head is covered in all sorts of sensory cells, a lot of which are light sensitive. But it has other cells that are reminiscent of ampullae of Lorenzini."

"Ampu…?" started Nacimiento.

"They're cells that sense electricity, found in creatures like sharks back on Earth. They're used to detect bioelectric fields generated by animals from activity in nerves and muscles. We're not sure whether the farmers, er, *reapers*, use just passive electrolocation, or active processes, where they generate weak electric fields and detect distortions in them using their electroreceptor organs."

"So, this helps them 'see' in the dark?" said Nacimiento.

"Yes, sir," said Marie. "But I think the important thing is, it suggests another avenue of attack. Or perhaps *defence*. We know we can overwhelm them with light, but this suggests we might be able to do the same with electricity… or magnetism, which is really the same thing. Back on Earth, there are a number of devices used by surfers and divers to keep sharks away. One I've used before is a band that produces magnetic waves, and there are others that use batteries to produce an electric field. They tend to have limited effectiveness – just a few metres – but they do seem to work."

"That sounds positive," said Nacimiento, sitting a little straighter.

"Yes, it does," said Figueroa, "but we must be cautious and not raise our hopes too high. We don't know exactly how these creatures will respond to devices like these. Maybe they have defences that we're unaware of."

"And maybe it'll just piss them off even more," added Kalmik.

"Indeed, Katerina," continued Figueroa. "Nevertheless, we are considering a number of options to try out."

"Can I help?" asked Blanco.

"Thank you, Ernesto, yes. If we give you some rough designs, can you make them in your workshop?"

"Of course."

"Excellent!" declared Nacimiento, now fully alert.

Marie smiled at their leader's show of enthusiasm. But she knew that time was short, success uncertain, and that, ultimately, someone was going to have to get in the water to try out the new devices – and she was well aware of who that person was likely to be.

* * *

"I hate to say this, but I think I'm missing school," said Sara.

Kate knew exactly what she meant. Although she'd been honoured to become a special advisor to the Captain-Governor with her friends – they'd been set up in a small, hastily repurposed storeroom just along from the old control room they'd discovered – the truth of the matter was that it was Tonio who was really in demand… at least *initially*. Kate looked back from a scowling Sara to the screen on which she'd been reviewing details from the autopsy of the dead alien. She shook her head. "I never thought I'd agree with you, but…" She shrugged. The added responsibility meant she was actually working harder at acquiring new knowledge than she would have at school, and to her dismay, much of what she'd been learning was biology. She pushed the keyboard away, muttering: "Not my major."

Tonio sat next to Sara in the over-lit room, his feet up on the desk. "You two are mental. You should revel in the freedom. No irritating classmates. No bossy teachers. No boring assignments on boring stuff we have no interest in. Bliss!"

"I just feel like a fraud," said Sara. "I don't know why I'm here. It's you two they want, not me."

"You're here because we need you," said Kate, who instantly knew it wasn't actually true. "I mean, you keep us entertained."

"A motivator?" Sara pouted. "Yeah, right." She sighed. "Look, I'm glad you didn't leave me out, but I think I'm going back to school tomorrow. I need some light and air. This is like a prison cell."

"Well, we don't actually have to stay here," said Kate. "We can go somewhere else. We won't be missed. Well… us two. I suppose Tonio might be."

"Ha! Me neither."

"But Mr Bellariva *needs* you," said Sara. "Don't you like him?"

"Mr Bellarriva is okay. I mean, he tries to be kind, but it's clear he thinks I'm in the way."

"After all you've done!" said Sara.

"Yeah, well, he's acknowledged that. I really don't want to diss him. He's been kind, but now he's focused on the job, and having me around just means he has to stop and explain things when he wants to get on with it."

"Maybe we've already played our role," said Sara. "I mean – with the Bowl and the control room… we've done a lot. Maybe it's time to let the adults get on with things and we can get back to doing our stuff."

"School? Going to the Terrace?" Tonio smirked at that. "Hanging out? Really? You hate all that stuff. And Kate is too much of a nerd to like it either."

"Hey!" said Kate. "Take that back! I'm a well-rounded person. Intellectual *and* sociable. It's you guys who stop me partying and hitting on boys."

Tonio's smirk turned into a leer. "Well, there's a boy *here*."

"Yuk! It'd be like making out with my brother… if I had a brother."

"Well, the feeling's mutual," said Tonio, whose smile became an embarrassed one, as though suddenly uncomfortable at having said too much. Kate wondered if he'd have turned red had he been capable of blushing. "Still," Tonio continued quickly, "you can't deny you want to be involved with things."

"Of course I do, but I'm not sure *what*. Staring at screens isn't helping. The scientists are much better at deciphering the new information than we are. I think our worth is elsewhere – especially when I see my mum at work. She's pretty good at what she does, but I just think that sometimes she doesn't see the wood for the trees… ah, that's an Earth expression by the way. Trees are these tall spiky things with leaves and–"

"Ha-ha!" said Tonio, clearly relieved at the change of subject.

"Anyway, I think she could benefit from an alternative perspective sometimes, and I give her that. I mean, isn't it amazing that with all these adults in charge we're still in this terrible situation? Are they *really* the best people to be running things?"

"Queen Kate," sniggered Sara.

"Are you going to run for Captain-Governor next election?" said Tonio.

"Hmm, well," said Kate, grinning, "there's a thought! Next time? No. But maybe the time after."

"Kate – you're serious!" gasped Sara.

"No, I never really thought about it, but… well, maybe *not* no. What's wrong with ambition? If Mum forces me to stay here and we don't go back to Earth, I have to do something with my life."

"Serve the community?" said Sara, slyly.

"Ha – *boss* the community more like," said Tonio. "Okay then, Captain-Governor Kate Lockard… you're now in charge. Hypothetically. *Virtually*. What next? What is everyone else missing? How do we get out of this?"

Kate nodded once. "Fine. Challenge accepted. But let's get out of here and do our thinking somewhere more inspirational." As she rose from her seat, she caught Sara's face twist into a wicked smile. Laughing, she added: "By which I *don't* mean the Chilly Cow!"

* * *

"They'll be ready tomorrow," said Mike Resnos, slumping down at the table occupied by several members of the science team. "That's what I'm told. First thing. They're going to pull an all-nighter if needs be."

Marie slid a beer across to him, which she'd ordered in advance. At the table with her, in the Faro Bar on the deck above their offices, was Luisa Teixeira and Marco Grande. Early evening sunlight speared through the full-length glass walls, creating shadows from their glasses that seemed to Marie like daggers pointing symbolically at their hearts.

"What, exactly?" asked Teixeira.

"Two things," said Resnos, pulling his glass close, but not drinking. "Some bracelets that emit a strong magnetic field – for personal use – and a device they're calling the Electric Field Emitter, or EFE, which is larger, like a battery in a case, which can be worn as a backpack or fixed on the hull of a boat."

"That's good, isn't it?" Teixeira looked at Resnos, then at Marie, who sat opposite, with Grande in between them.

Resnos had been selected as their liaison with the engineering team, being the most technically minded of the research team, and to Marie, his clear lack of enthusiasm was not a good sign.

"Well, yes and no," continued Resnos. "Yes, in that it'll give us *something*, but no in that it won't give us *much*. They don't have a lot of gear in their stores – we all know that. So they've had to go on the scrounge, cannibalising all sorts of machinery to get the necessary parts. In the end, they reckon they'll have four bracelets and two of the EFEs ready for trial."

"There's still something you're not telling us," said Teixeira.

Resnos sighed. "It's not just quantity, but quality. There's a *range* issue." He looked directly at Marie. "Anything you'd like to add from your past experience?"

Marie suddenly felt uncomfortable. "Ah, well, if they're like the gear used on Earth… the magnetic field perhaps has a range of a couple of metres. And this EFE… double or triple that?"

"Yeah, that's quite close to the figures the engineers were estimating."

"That's not a lot of leeway," said Grande, rubbing a hand over the dark shadow of stubble on his chin. "Even if it does work."

Resnos responded by picking up his glass and taking several deep gulps.

"So, how are we going to test it?" asked Teixeira. "On the bottom of a trawler? You're not going in the water, are you?"

Marie sensed an edge of panic in Teixeira's voice. She'd been particularly close to Garcia and clearly feared losing another of her colleagues. Even Marie herself, in spite of the fact that it was she who had pushed for them to go search the site of the sunken harvesters in the first place, the expedition that cost Garcia his life. Indeed, no one had blamed her for that – not even Kalmik, who was always quick to note mistakes and call out stupidity. Marie still wondered whether she ought to feel *some* guilt, yet whenever she thought about the event, mentally patting herself down, she discovered sorrow but nothing more. Going to check on the scene of the disaster had been the right call: if she'd been asked a hundred times, she would have replied on every occasion that it was the correct thing to do. Hindsight – that tempting though treacherous mistress – didn't change that fact. Still, in her mind, she was clear on one thing: she was not going to put anyone else at risk in her place.

When Resnos maintained his silence, she answered instead. "Not initially, Luisa. We'll try the electric field device on another trawler first. But at some point, we're going to have to test the bracelet."

"But you don't have to do it personally," said Teixeira. "It's too dangerous, especially without the cage… ah, sorry, Marco." Grande waved the matter away: it was only Kalmik who truly blamed him for the cage's loss. "You could attach it to a pole or something."

"True," said Marie. "But I don't think that would tell the whole story. Maybe it would deter the farmers from approaching *if* they had no especial desire to investigate. But with a human in the water – food, an enemy, we still don't know how they see us – their motivation might overcome whatever discomfort the device might cause. So sometime – maybe not tomorrow, but soon – I'm afraid someone's going to have to try the bracelet out."

"I'll do it," said Resnos, "*if* I have to."

Marie nodded. "I think we'll be drawing straws."

"Well, I just hope you do get a chance to try this EFE tomorrow," said Grande.

Marie caught something in his voice. "You have doubts, Marco?"

The man frowned and composed his thoughts. "Maybe. These reapers… they are clever, aren't they? We're not sure where they are, but we are sure they're watching the dock area around the wings. When you tried to launch the trawlers, they attacked instantly." He tapped the table and made sure all were watching him. "*Instantly.* That means they are watching constantly. I don't know how this new device works, but if it's not very powerful, I fear the creatures will push through whatever deterrent it has and strike the boat as before, just as they ignored the lights."

"And who's going to install it?" wondered Teixeira. "The boats are all resting in cradles, but only a metre of so over the water. I wouldn't want to get that close – not after seeing the creatures breach."

"We could try a trawler on the opposite wing," suggested Marie. "We've been using those at the starboard wing, as that's where the *Fortunata* is docked. It makes sense to try the port wing."

"Maybe you should forget the idea of attaching it to a boat altogether and just drop the thing in the ocean on a cable," said Grande.

"But that might lead to the same problem as attaching one of the bracelets to a pole. We won't be sure it works unless we see the farmers in the water and watch them bolt from it. If nothing happens, again, it could just be because of a lack of interest. So, we need to use something – a boat, or a human – that we *know* will lure them close. Keeping them away from *us* will be the acid test."

But the conversation had given Marie plenty to think about, and she was still mulling over options when she got home later that evening.

Kate was sitting at the table in the small kitchenette, an empty plate and half-full glass of water before her, and her tablet flat on the surface.

"So, Special Advisor, how did it go today?"

"Are you mocking me, Mum?" said Kate, scowling.

Marie fought with a smile. She was proud of her daughter, but also slightly amused at her earnestness. "I'm sorry. I should show more respect. Seriously, what have you been up to?"

Kate brushed her hand against the tablet – its surface dark. "Reading. Looking at your autopsy videos. Talking about…" she shrugged, "this and that."

Marie nodded slowly. "Ah. I see. Well, don't worry. No one's expecting you to come up with any sort of breakthrough. We think of you as a resource. A sounding board. Has Tonio shown Hector the ropes?"

"He did that yesterday. He's surplus to requirements today. We all are, really."

Marie paused a moment, scanned her daughter's disgruntled face, and then pulled out the sole free chair and sat down. "Well, okay, sounding board, maybe you can help *me*."

"No need to take pity on me, Mum, really."

"I'm not. Do you want to hear what I've got? I'd really like to talk it through with someone. Please?"

Kate's frown lifted slightly, and she sighed. "Okay, then. Go on. What's the problem?"

"You saw the data on the electrosensors in the farmers, yes? Well, Ernesto in engineering has produced a couple of gadgets for us to try. Here's the problem. We're not sure they'll work well enough to protect us or the boats. We can drop them into the ocean to see if they deter the farmers, but I think there might be a difference between dissuading them from investigating a neutral object protected by the magnetic or electric fields, and protecting us or our boats – which they've taken a real dislike to."

"Yeah, I saw the videos – the way they were leaping out of the water to attack them. *Scary.*"

"Right. So, we want to try entering the water with these devices to give them a real test, but we're afraid the farmers won't let us. They're near the docks and will probably attack instantly. We'd rather not risk another life or trawler finding out."

"Then don't enter the water by the docks. Try somewhere else."

"Yes, we considered that. But there's no easy way to enter the water from the rest of the ship, or getting out again in a hurry. We don't have any cages, so the best option would be to lower someone on a rope over the side."

"Like bait? Ha! You'd have to be a suicidal idiot to try that."

"Er… *quite*. So, we've dismissed that idea."

Kate stared down at the table for a moment in contemplation. Then she looked up suddenly. "So… you want to enter the water in a controlled environment – where you can have a good look around, and get out quick if you need to? Right – so, go out *under* the ship. Use one of the old inspection hatches. I think there are six – Tonio found them when he was in the old control room – the same time he discovered the hull sensors. I think they're like air locks. You enter a chamber, close the door, flood the chamber, open an outer door and… there you go."

Marie nodded. "I'd forgotten about them… or to be fair, never processed their presence in the first place."

"Probably because you've been talking among yourselves – bio-nerds only." She grinned at that. "You didn't discuss this with Mr Bellariva, did you? I'm sure he'd have made the same suggestion. Anyway, he knows where these are now, because Tonio showed him. Tonio found a camera still working in one of the chambers and showed me and Sara once, but I couldn't really work out what I was looking at. Obviously, using the hatches wouldn't be risk free, but I think the outer hatch is small so you might be able to look out, attract the monsters, and then pull yourself back in if your kryptonite device doesn't work."

Marie gently clapped her hands and laughed. "You see, Kate – you're invaluable!"

She managed to rouse Bellariva from bed and explain the issue and potential solution to him. Bellariva then went to check on a few things, calling her back fifteen minutes later with instructions on where to meet the next morning. Marie then conducted a frantic round of calls to Figueroa and the rest of the team to update them and make further arrangements.

During all this, Kate maintained her place at the kitchenette table, most of the time looking quite smug.

* * *

Inspection Chamber C was at the very bottom of the ship, below even the hidden levels that held the hydroponics facilities and the fusion drive. They had chosen C because it was the only one with actively functioning cameras – as Tonio had discovered – although Bellariva assured everyone that he would eventually be able to make the cameras in the other five chambers functional if required.

In the old control room, Bellariva sat at the main console, with Tonio to his left. He had brought up the inspection chamber on the main screen, so all of the room's occupants could see what was going on. The audience comprised Nascimento, Figueroa, Kalmik, plus Kate and Sara – who stood together at the back.

Visible on the screen in the Inspection Chamber were four others: Marie, Mike Resnos, Luisa Teixeira, and Ernesto Blanco – the latter having brought along some of the kit his engineers had put together during the night. Marie and Resnos were both suited up in their diving gear.

Kate watched proceedings with some concern. When she'd suggested this option, she hadn't realised that her mother would be one of those volunteering to test out the new devices. She caught Sara's worried glance.

"I'm sure she'll be okay," Sara whispered. "She knows what she's doing."

"Does she?" muttered Kate.

Sara had no answer to that.

On the screen, they saw Marie and Resnos approach a wheel in the wall of the room, which opened the door to the airlock itself. Resnos twirled the wheel while Marie accepted an oblong box from Blanco, which she began to affix by straps to her chest. Kate could see that both of the divers – who presently were bare headed, their helmets unattached – had thick bracelets on their wrists. Teixeira was sitting at a console in the darkened room, which was lit by just a single flickering overhead light strip: her voice came over the speakers: "They're going to exit one at a time. Mike first, with just his bracelet, then Marie with hers. They'll wait to see if they draw any interest, then hit the EFE to see what effect that has."

Marie was now ready. She nodded at Blanco, then turned to enter the airlock behind Resnos. In the control room, the two screens to either side of main one came to life, showing views from the helmet cameras of the divers. The screen in front of Tonio showed that of Resnos; the one to the right that of Marie. The images then showed the two divers looking at each other, each giving a 'thumbs-up'. Resnos had a wicked looking spear gun in one hand.

"Switching channels," said Bellariva, then: "Marie… Mike… do you hear me?"

"Roger that," said Resnos through his helmet mic.

"Loud and clear," said Marie.

"Well, it's over to you now. Good luck."

In the central screen, Teixeira activated some control, then the air lock started to fill with water, entering through now-open holes in the hull. The chamber – which could have accommodated four suited divers – filled smoothly and remorselessly.

Nascimento spoke over Bellariva's shoulder into the open mic. "Luisa – how long should this take? And perhaps as importantly, how long will it take the pumps to clear the chamber of water when they return?"

"A couple of minutes, sir – I hope."

The water continued filling the small chamber and then, with both divers fully immersed, a light beside the exterior hatch – set in the floor – turned from red to green. In the control room, the party watched as Resnos grasped a wheel set in the floor beside the hatch and began turning it. The tension in the air was palpable. Kate noticed Nacimiento grasping his hands together behind his back, while Kalmik reached a surreptitious hand across to touch Figueroa's arm comfortingly.

"The bracelets *are* activated, aren't they?" whispered Sara – clearly only meant for Kate's ears, but Kalmik heard and looked at them sharply. The scientist's grim face flickered into a brief smile and she nodded once, then turned back to the screen.

Through Resnos' eyes, they saw the hatch slowly slide open – recessing into a groove in the hull. The water beyond was completely black. As the door fully opened – creating a space perhaps a metre-and-a-half-wide – Kate found herself holding her breath and squinting her eyes as she would at a scary scene in a horror movie, half expecting something to suddenly jump through the gap… but the darkness remained undisturbed.

They heard Resnos curse quietly. "Going to infrared," he said. As he did so, Kate noticed that Marie had already activated that function – judging by the strange, reddened blur that was Resnos' tank-obscured back. The quality of the picture through the man's camera changed subtly and became somewhat washed, yet the water directly beneath the hatch remained clear. "Okay," Resnos continued, now hefting his speargun in front, "here goes…"

The man slowly slid into the black, face first, though he didn't go far, and quickly jerked to the vertical, with the *Lisboa's* hull forming a ceiling above his head. He slowly turned three-sixty, keeping his weapon outstretched, though with frequent glances into the depths to ensure nothing was rising towards him. After four or five seconds, they heard him gasp: "Okay, Marie. Down you… *wait*!"

Kate nearly jumped as Sara suddenly grasped her arm. She wasn't the only one: Figueroa twitched, and something profane slipped through Kalmik's lips.

"Is that one?" asked Nacimiento, scarcely above a whisper.

"No," said Kalmik. "Not *one*."

Ahead of Resnos, a smudge of red resolved from the background, and then somehow split, until there were two, and then three distinct blobs. The shapes approached slowly, eventually allowing more features to be made out. Kate gasped at the sight: farmers... reapers... *monsters*.

"Mike?" said Marie, her voice coming through the intercom. "Can I come? What is it?"

"There are at least three. Wait..." he momentarily took his eyes from the shapes and looked down and around, in sharp movements that seemed panicked to Kate, then he refocused. "Yes... three. They're curious. They seemed to have stopped. Five metres maybe... now they're moving apart."

"I'm coming," said Marie. "You need more eyes."

Kate noticed the screen on the right jerk, turn black, then fill with colour to one side as Marie settled beside Resnos.

"Okay," said Marie, her voice strangely calm. "I'm right behind you. Don't panic..." she reached and touched the other for reassurance. Then Marie trod water, moving slightly to edge past Resnos so she could see the shapes. "Ah... I see."

Resnos moved again: one of the shapes in the middle stayed face on, looking at the divers, but those to either side were languidly moving apart. *Circling.*

"I don't like this," said Figueroa. "I don't like this at all. It's hunting behaviour." He raised his voice: "Mike... Marie... they're hunting."

"I know," said Marie, quietly. "But they *are* keeping their distance. They haven't rushed in. The bracelets must be having some effect. It's making them think twice." She shifted further around, tracking the creature that was circling to their right.

"Try the EFE," said Kalmik, suddenly.

"No... not yet," said Marie. "If the bracelets work then I'm confident the EFE will too. But we need to see how effective the bracelets are first."

The creature to the front of Resnos appeared to be almost standing up, treading water in a very human manner, though in an effortless way, it's ellipsoid head swaying as though it was looking about or – Kate thought – almost sniffing the water. And then it began to move closer – slowly, but definitely.

"I can't watch both," muttered Mike. On the left-hand control room screen, the image kept flicking between the creature dead ahead, and the one circling left – until that also came to a halt.

"One-twenty," hissed Marie, her head flicking around too. "The three of them have maximally dispersed. One-twenty degrees apart. If they're going to move…"

"Mine is," said Resnos. On the screen, all could see him extend his speargun in front, pointing at the creature, which was now perhaps four metres away, and still drifting.

"Uh… mine too," said Marie.

Then Kalmik strained forwards and shouted: "Watch their legs! Marie – watch their…"

Kate was watching Marie's camera… and then she saw it: the creature's legs tensed, whipping with sudden vigour, as though winding up, and then… she heard a shriek from Sara, but was too shocked to scream herself. The creature somehow *lunged*, and from being four metres away it was two and its wicked talons were reaching out… and then as if hitting an invisible plate of glass it twisted into a somersault and shot away as though burned.

In the control room, various adult voices let out exclamations, of which the loudest was from Nacimiento: "Oh, Dios!"

Resnos also shouted, and must have kicked back, for his picture tilted, and so did Marie's – presumably as she was nudged by the man from behind.

"What… what just happened?" stuttered Figueroa. "Marie?"

They heard a loud exhale of breath, then Marie's voice came through: "Thanks, Katarina. I saw it as you shouted. Miguel – the EFE works. I hit the button as they came for us. You saw their response?"

"Hell, yeah!" said Kalmik. "They did *not* like that."

"Uh, yeah, well save your celebrations," said Resnos. "They might not have liked it... but they're back, and this time, they're brought their friends."

In the control room, on both the left-hand and right-hand screens, the darkness had suddenly become speckled with red. Whatever was there was staying further away than before, but...

"Dozens," gasped Figueroa. "There are dozens. Mike, Marie... they're all around you."

"And beneath us, too," said Resnos. "Marie – how long do you want to stay out here?"

"Me? I wanted to leave thirty seconds ago, but we still need to see if the field will actually keep them away. When I turned it on, it was like a shock. Now they know."

Resnos' expletive was barely audible. Then he said: "Okay. One minute then. But if they start to come in again, we leave immediately."

The creatures did begin to edge closer – but after a minute, none had gotten nearer than about eight metres.

"We have a weapon," sighed Marie. "Or at least, a shield. I think this test is done."

"Great," said Resnos, "now let's get the fuck out of here."

Chapter 39

The ISU's last stand had come to an end about fifteen minutes after Joseph's patrol boats pulled away from the East Docks bearing the final complement of troops that had decided to continue resistance. In spite of having given O'Neill the impression that he would fight on as long as he was able – and cause the rebels to 'bleed' – Nesvorny had had no intention of overseeing unnecessary loss of life. Once the boats were well beyond shooting range, he'd raised white flags, and – while discussing terms with the rebel leaders – ensured his people surreptitiously dumped their arms into the ocean to prevent them being used on the survivors of their own side.

Nesvorny had surrendered after being assured that his troops would be looked after; he'd asked for no guarantees regarding his own welfare. But he'd not been mistreated – beyond the odd rough shove from an impatient guard – and he'd spent a couple of days locked in one of the few cells back at the main ISU complex.

When the interrogation came, he was collected and escorted through still-quiet (though not empty) streets to the main command centre complex, brought in a lift to the top floor to a conference room he'd last visited a few weeks previously for a meeting with the triumvirate. A smile crossed his face: that had been a useful prep for today, and indeed, he doubted the upcoming grilling would be as severe as he'd experienced then.

He was ushered into the room by one of his pair of escorts, who then stepped back and closed the door behind him. There were just two people waiting inside, both dressed in Stoker green: a woman sat opposite, while standing near her was a man he knew to be her husband. The woman looked up and smiled; the man – who'd been standing at one of the broad windows, turned to glare and folded his arms.

"Welcome, Colonel Nesvorny," said Karyn Dures. "It seems the tables are quite literally turned. Take a seat."

Nesvorny wordlessly did as asked, sitting up straight and arranging his uniform to reduce creases.

The woman spent a moment appraising him with her clear blue eyes. As on the last occasion they'd met, her fair hair was swept over one shoulder and shaved short on the opposite side, revealing the white welt of a scar, though this time she was cleaner, her hair softly sparkling under the strip light in the ceiling. "Nothing to say, Colonel?"

"What is there to say? You appear to have won. Congratulations."

"You think this is a *game*?" scowled Kai Dures, whose black hair was as long as his wife's, but cascaded over both of his broad shoulders. "Do you think you now just get to stand up and leave the table?"

"You can misinterpret my words all you like, Dures. I'm not trivialising the situation. What happens now is up to you. I will not apologise for my actions or my past. I will only say this: you now rule all of *Hibernia*, *not* just your own people. They are shocked now, and pliant. But that won't necessarily last. They are watching how you behave, and how you treat them, and maybe even how you treat me. They will remember, and they will judge."

"Is that some sort of threat? Is that–"

"Kai – please!" Karyn raised her voice sharply, at which her seething husband looked at her and clamped his mouth shut. Then she smiled at him affectionately and spoke more softly. "This is a tense moment. I *understand*. He has been the face of our enemy for so long, and now here he is, at our mercy. But what he says is worth considering."

"He lacks contrition," said Dures. "He isn't to be trusted. He is our scourge. Our people will want their revenge."

"Scourge?" Karyn turned a smile upon Nesvorny. "Are you?"

"A scourge of criminals – yes. I'm an agent of the law. I have arrested many of your people when they did wrong. I don't deny it. I don't regret it. I served the elected government and saw that the laws it created were followed."

"Elected?" Karyn looked bemused.

"Yes, elected. They may have jury-rigged the process over recent years, but the people allowed it. As you know, the triumvirate and their government are corrupt – but not egregiously so. At least, they *weren't*. What they might have become is open to debate."

"Oh, come on," said Karyn. "They were heading that way, and quickly. And if they got there, what then? Would you still have been a loyal little servant?"

Would he? Maybe in the past. But now – with age and an evolved cynicism? "I can't honestly say. Maybe not. But I'm not going to make claims of redemption in a bid for mercy. I am a hard man. A hard *law*man. But I'm not the devil you're trying to paint me to be."

"And what of the attacks on our people?" said Kai Dures, pushing from the wall, advancing half a step. "The deaths. That wasn't you?"

"No."

Karyn placed a hand on the corded forearm of her husband, who now stood close. "I believe him." She kept her focus on Nesvorny. "I remember our little discussion when you were interrogating me, Colonel. Your surprise. You had no need to feign that." Her smile slipped. "Your unwillingness to beg is commendable. I don't want you to beg. I just want you to tell the truth. Don't sacrifice yourself for something you're not guilty of. Don't shield the unworthy."

Nesvorny was surprised. The thought of speaking to the enemy, of collaborating, was anathema to him. But the woman seemed genuine. She wasn't offering him a way out, but maybe a chance of a certain redemption. The truth? He sighed. "The deaths… that was my deputy, Major Fukuda, working behind my back with Manfred Traore. It seems they were trying to provoke a response – and in that they succeeded."

"You might not have sanctioned what your deputy did," snarled Kai Dures, "but I bet in the end you approved."

"No!" Nesvorny slammed a palm down onto the table in sudden anger. "*Do not* compare me to those men. I told you, I upheld the law. That *was not* the law. So go ahead and hang me if you must, but don't you *dare* misrepresent me."

Dures eyes widened at the burst of passion, and he swayed forwards in anger. Again, his wife grasped his forearm forcibly. "Kai – maybe it is time to sit down. We are not children here. You accused him – he responded. That's his right."

"You really believe him?" said Dures, looking down.

After a brief pause, she admitted: "Yes, I do." Then she smiled gently at her husband. "Kai – I *do*."

"So what are we to do with him?" said Dures. "If you won't let me hang him, what then? Even if he is not be the worst of our enemies, he's not our friend."

"We keep him in detention – but safe." Karyn turned a calculating look upon Nesvorny. "Let's see what opportunities arise. Maybe détente is not totally out of the question, eh, Colonel? What do you think?"

"I think… I think you are a very clever woman, Karyn Dures. And… *not* bad. Nor your husband even. I will never accept your uprising. But maybe if there is a return to law – law that is fair to *all*, including your people – then I could see rapprochement. And I for one would be glad to see the criminals responsible for the violence against your people brought to justice."

"Well said, Colonel," Karyn nodded solemnly. "I think I need to talk to my husband now – and allow time for our passions to cool." She shouted: "Guards!"

* * *

They'd had to wait a couple of days for their audience, fretting at the embassy and completely cut off from any communication with the *Stavanger* due to continued restrictions on the use of the state's satellite communication system. When they got their summons, it was both a relief and a source of tension.

Now, Heiko and De Voe followed Magnus Solbakken into the small meeting room in the central tower of *Hibernia*, on the level where the bridge of the ship used to be before it had outgrown the possibility of ever moving again. Although all three were allowed to enter, the guardian at the door instructed Heiko and De Voe to stand by the back wall and forbade them to speak. They did as asked, allowing Solbakken to occupy the sole chair set up in the middle of the floor facing an oval table side-on, while the guardian – a man in green with a golden armband – stood at the back wall next to the ambassador's aides.

As they'd entered, those at the table had turned to look: directly opposite was a woman in green, flanked by a tall, broad-shouldered man, also in green, and a slightly shorter man wearing grey, both of whom had long hair. These were flanked by two more, sitting at the edge of the table, who had to turn their chairs slightly to face the newcomers: a woman in an expensive-looking suit, and another man in green, this one with cropped hair and notable tattoos. Heiko recognised the two men in green from their previous wandering in the underground when they'd been trying to rescue Frost, and the woman in the suit from a previous video conference: *Kerrie Sullivan*. He quickly glanced to De Voe at his side, who responded with a puzzled look.

"Ambassador Solbakken, hello," said the woman in the centre. "I don't think we've met – though my husband says he remembers you. I am Karyn Dures, the acting Chair of Hibernia's Revolutionary Committee. You have been persistent. How can we help?"

"I'm pleased to meet you, Ms Dures," said Solbakken. "I do recall your husband," he nodded his head, "Mr Dures. And… I recognise one other. Ms Sullivan?" Sullivan simply nodded, but chose not to speak. Heiko wondered at her position in this new administration. "I'm glad you agreed to see us in these difficult times. I am sure you must be busy. I'll therefore get straight to the point. In the embassy, I currently have a party of compatriots who are somewhat stranded. They came to collect a colleague – held by the previous administration – as well as a consignment of our resources that were illegally confiscated, and now we find themselves unable to reclaim what is ours, nor even to leave."

"Confiscated?" said Karyn Dures, turning to look at Sullivan.

"An exaggeration," said Sullivan. "I told you of the *Stavanger* find. They were attempting to keep quiet about it. The illegality was theirs. We took a few containers of resources as a bond for good behaviour, and this colleague Solbakken mentions was simply a guest who came of his own free will."

"Free will?" said Solbakken. "Would you like me to bring Makka Frost here so you can hear from his own mouth how much choice he was given?"

"It's not necessary," said Sullivan, waving a hand dismissively. "If he's changed his mind and wants to go back with you, so be it."

"Thank you, Ms Sullivan." Heiko watched the ambassador give a small bow from the waist, but there was mockery in his words. "And the resources?"

Sullivan gave her head a brief shake, opened her mouth to speak, then paused and looked to Karyn. "I… would not advise it. The *Stavanger* is still close to the mine. Still capable of obstruction and sabotage. Still culpable for their own dishonesty."

"I agree," said the man in grey, leaning around to look at Karyn. "I was shocked when told of the find on my arrival here. There is some deep dishonesty somewhere, and we need to get to the bottom of it. If these Stavangerans have attempted to cheat the people of *Hibernia*, and indeed, of the whole world, then there should be some consequence." He turned to look at Solbakken, his expression cool, languid. "And were you going to keep this find from us, too?"

"I'm sorry, but I don't know who you are."

Heiko watched the man in grey tense and his eyes widen.

"Me? I am Sebastian Deux, First Citizen of the *Marseilles*, which is due to shortly take up position off Athol. And before you think to dismiss me, you should know that I am here because it was *my* forces that came to the aid of the oppressed of *Hibernia*. We feel as one with the citizens here. As such, your possible treachery burns us twice."

"Mr Deux, this talk of treachery is nonsense, and nothing but a ruse by the previous administration to steal from us. When we were boarded by Hibernian forces we were in the process of completing a report on the find that we were about to submit to the rulers here. Surely you are not taking the side of the previous administration – the one you have just overthrown?"

"Ms Sullivan contests your explanation," said Deux with a sly smile. "I find her persuasive. Not everything done by her and her compatriots was wrong. It is important that we sift the good from the bad. Karyn…" he turned. "Isn't this why Sullivan is with us? For continuity? We must not dismiss *everything* she says out of hand."

Kai Dures now laughed. "You've changed your tune, First Citizen."

Deux's smile never wavered, but even from the back of the room, Heiko noticed his eyes harden. "I'm adaptable, Kai. But understand this: my first priority is the people. *Always*. And what do we have here?

The wealthy *Stavanger* – built with the immense Norwegian Sovereign Trust Fund on the basis of unethical oil drilling, then populated by privileged scions – attempting to hoard resources while our people suffer. These resources Sullivan mentions – we don't know what they comprise of, but I have little doubt that the *Stavanger* can spare them, and that they should share them with those of us who have little. Consider it a fine, then, and they should count themselves lucky if we let them have even a little back. But before making such a hasty decision, we need to conduct a full audit of the resources in *Hibernia*."

"That is… that is outrageous," said Solbakken. Heiko found himself clenching his own fists, but knew they could do nothing.

Karyn raised a hand for silence. "I do not like this idea of taking this material if it truly belong to the *Stavanger*, but it does make sense for us to fully review this matter – the location of the deception, the nature of the resources. I don't think we can rush this matter. Kai?"

Kai Dures shrugged his large shoulders. "As you say. I have no issue with the *Stavanger* and would trust their word more than others here but… yeah. We shouldn't rush a decision now."

"But Ms Dures–"

"Ambassador Solbakken, I have sympathy for your position, but please give us a little longer to consider this matter. As you noted, we are busy and have other priorities right now."

Heiko could see Solbakken's shoulders slump. But then the diplomat straightened himself. "Very well – Ms Dures. I trust *you* to see that the right thing is ultimately done. But what about our boat? When my colleagues tried to depart a couple of days ago, they were denied the chance. Will you at least allow my people to leave and return to the *Stavanger*?"

Heiko could already see how this was going to go. The First Citizen of *Marseilles* was clearly enjoying himself, and considered himself ahead in whatever game he was playing. He wanted to double down.

"I'm not comfortable with this," said Deux. "Again, I say let's not be hasty. Beyond *Hibernia*, the ocean is still largely ruled by the Hibernian rebels and the boats of their External Security Unit. If our friends here set out, they might be captured or sunk. And if they successfully make it to the *Stavanger*… what mischief might they cause? How might they brief against us? Perhaps they will try to take Athol, or even ally with the rebels to develop this find between them?" He shook his head slowly and attempted to look troubled. "No, we need to develop a policy towards the *Stavanger* and this broader issue. Once we have done that, they can leave with our blessing and take our message – and perhaps some small part of their bond – with them."

Sullivan struggled to hide her smile behind a hand; Kai Dures shook his head slowly, but seemed disinclined to make an issue the matter; and the fifth member of the council remained silent – though Heiko noticed he was staring directly at him, or rather, was it at the copper interface beside his eye?

Karyn sighed. "Again, there is some sense in what the First Citizen says. I'm sorry, Ambassador, but I must decline your request. Please bear with us a little longer."

There was little more they could do. Heiko and De Voe fell in behind Solbakken as he exited the room. As they left, Heiko was sure he could feel the eyes of the silent man on the back of his neck.

* * *

After the Stavangerans had departed, Kerrie Sullivan and Georges Hollande shifted their chairs around to face the centre of the table.

Deux struggled to keep the smile off his face.

"Well done, Deux," said Kai Dures, with more than a hint of sarcasm.

Deux chose to accept the compliment as genuine. "Thank you, Kai. We are surrounded by tricksters everywhere. We have to be on our guard for the sake of our people. But the *Stavanger* still worries me, as does the situation on Ardol. Perhaps it would make sense for the *Marseilles* to continue to its station?"

"And take your little fleet with you?" said Kai. "And your forces, too… to perhaps claim Ardol for yourself?"

Deux tensed. "Not at all. But if we are nearby we might deter any reinforcement of Ardol."

"And leave us to deal with the much greater force on Athol by ourselves?" said Kai, with just enough of a smile to hint at a joke, although Deux knew he was serious.

"This is a side issue," said Karyn, frowning. "You are squabbling about the prize before the game is even won. Our enemy is still out there, and strong." She looked at Sullivan and barked: "What will O'Neill do now?"

Deux almost winced at the woman's abruptness. It had been clear from the start that Sullivan was only here because of Karyn's realpolitik – but that didn't mean their Chair had anything but contempt for the former member of the triumvirate, and she didn't care letting it show. Deux certainly shared Karyn Dures' perspective, but he was at least able to moderate his demeanour towards the other woman.

Sullivan twitched and looked away from Karyn's fierce gaze. "She – Marissa – will… *endure.*" She composed herself, looked back up, accepted the challenge. "It's what she always does. She won't give in. She will be thinking about how to reclaim *Hibernia.* How to defeat you. How to regain what she thinks is hers. Manfred's the same… mostly. He'll back up Marissa until he thinks there is no hope, or until he gets a better offer."

"Like you did?" said Karyn.

"I'm a realist, not an ideologue. I never had any issue with you – with Stokers. You know that. You checked my public comments. Manfred is different. He sees you as lice…" She paused, and Deux could sense her thinking that she might have gone too far; certainly, Karyn tensed. "I'm sorry. That's a word he's used before. So, you can't trust him. If you make him an offer to come across, he might take it, but he'll stab you in the back as soon as you turn around."

"You're suggesting we have no option?" said Karyn. "We cannot leave them in place? Wait them out?"

Sullivan slowly shook her head. "I hate to say this, but Marissa is clever. She will be thinking about this continuously. And she still has the only purpose-built war craft on the planet – aside from a few in Taiwan. And more, she still has perhaps half of the troops of the ISU. If we wait, they'll fortify Athol. Fortify Ardol. Maybe she'll find a way to reach out to other ships like the *Stavanger* and make them an offer.

Others might be more inclined to deal with her rather than you.. or the *Marseilles*."

Deux scowled at that. "What are you implying, Sullivan?"

Sullivan's expression was neutral. "Just that you have a certain reputation. Not many other ships will likely agree to buy in to your… *culture*."

Deux calmed himself. Smiled. "Maybe you're right about their ruling elites, but their citizens might feel differently."

Sullivan shrugged. "If you want to hold a popularity contest – go ahead. Who can tell how it will pan out. I'm just suggesting that Marissa might have options. Whatever we can think of, she will too, and more."

"She's not omniscient," said Kai, rousing himself. "She didn't see *this* coming."

"No," agreed Sullivan. "She didn't. But now your cards are on the table. She's seen them. She won't be bluffed again."

"In other words, we have to end this now," concluded Karyn. "Before she has time. While they're still disorganised. And while we are all together." She turned to look at Deux. "They are still strong on Athol. If we are going to assault them, we will need everything – your new navy and troops in addition to our own."

Deux nodded slowly. "This will be costly. Maybe *very* costly."

"We couldn't have had our revolution without you, Sebastian." Beyond Karyn, Deux noticed Kai's face cloud over. "Come with us to the end. We will make it worth your while."

Deux knew how to play. He closed his eyes, but already had his answer: he didn't actually need the time to think. At last, he sighed. With seeming reluctance, he said: "And after Athol… *Ardol?*" The implication was left hanging.

Karyn looked grim. "Of course. Maybe you could oversee the new mining for us?"

It seemed as though he might get what he wanted after all. Deux smiled: "Death to *all* tyrants. Let us plan."

* * *

O'Brien's had been the meeting point for the New Socialists from the *Leviathan.* After the majority had left for the *Marseilles*, the remaining few – Georges Hollande, Jacques Danté and Babatunde Odile – had moved from the nearby Crown Hostel to the underworld of the Engine Quarter. Now that some of the *Marseilles* contingent had returned, and victory cancelled any need to hide, O'Brien's had regained its prominence. Georges Hollande looked at the etched mirrors and old Guinness posters with some fondness. The place reminded him of Earth.

"To Babatunde!" said Hollande, raising his glass of beer in a toast.

"To Baba," replied Danté and the eight others sat around the two pressed-together tables.

As they lowered their glasses, a woman named Lola, who bore an AK47 tattoo on her left forearm, asked: "What happened to him?"

"He wanted to fight," said Hollande. "He should have stuck to his gunpowder manufactory, but he missed the Paris revolt, and he wasn't going to miss this one. He joined one of the cadres from the *Marseilles*. They got ambushed. There was only one survivor."

"The *Dieppe*," said another woman, whose name Hollande didn't know. Like Danté and many of the others, her hair was shaved close to the scalp. Hollande had also adopted the style, having cut his long blond locks during his stay underground. "It's true: just one made it."

"That's bad shit," said a man with heavy eyebrows and a completely bald scalp. "Big loss of comrades."

"But the sacrifice was worthwhile," said Danté. "Look at where we are? The fascists are defeated. We've won." He raised his glass and shouted: "We've fucking won!"

Others raised their glasses and bellowed cries of victory, but not Hollande. Danté clearly noticed, and frowned. "Comrade – what's up?"

"Up?" Hollande shook his head slowly. "We haven't won. Not the war – only the battle. The enemy still hold the Range." He paused, and waited for the others to calm and turn to him. "I've been meeting with the Revolutionary Council, and it's been decided – we're going for Athol."

"What – an amphibious assault?" said the bald man.

"We did it before," said Lola. "We did it here… in much worse weather. Fucking *crazy* weather. This should be piss easy by comparison."

"Except they didn't know we were coming before," said the man. "And they have proper patrol boats with proper guns, not converted harpoons. It's gonna be hard. We go, then more of us are going to be joining Baba pretty damned soon."

Hollande raised both hands to quell the murmuring. "Calm! We're needed here to continue weapons supply and training. Only volunteers will go. The Stokers and the Marseillaise will make up the bulk of the assault force."

"Well, count me in," said Lola. "The job's not done until all those bastards are strung up."

Several more chimed in, echoing the woman's words, but others – Hollande noted – looked down, or exchanged glances with friends, and said nothing. He nodded: "But that's not the only thing. There is still revolutionary work to do in *Hibernia.* Unfinished business. Unfinished from Earth."

"What do you mean, brother?" asked Danté.

"The *Augmented.* There is at least one still here."

"The one from the *Stavanger*?" said Danté.

"Yeah… him. It turns out he's important over there, and the *Stavanger* has been holding out an important find from the rest of us."

"What find?" asked Lola.

Hollande waved the question away. "I'll tell you later. The important thing is, he's here, and no one's doing anything about it."

"You told the Council about him, yeah?" said Danté.

"I did. But they don't understand. Not many on Tethys have augments, and those that do tend to keep quiet about it. Dures… Deux… they don't appreciate how important this is to us from Earth."

"They're not going to do anything about him?" asked Danté.

"No. If we want to deal with the elitist, we have to do it ourselves."

"Well, you can count me in on *that* one," said the bald-headed man.

And this time, the enthusiasm within the group was universal.

Chapter 40

The *Lisboa* limped on at an ever-decreasing pace. Kate knew from her involvement with the Crisis Team the reason why, but she'd been sworn to secrecy along with her friends: the performance of a couple of the screw drives was becoming severely degraded, likely as a result of attacks by their unwanted underwater passengers. Consequently, the barren Range had grown in their vision painfully slowly over the last couple of days. Currently, Kate was flanked by Sara and Tonio, standing at the railing of a terrace of the Fado café on the sea-facing side of the central coliseum, six levels up. This had become a popular location recently, and so there was hardly any space along the sixty-metre curve of railing, with the many observers blocking the exterior view for the diners and drinkers sat at tables further back under an overhang of superstructure.

"Where's *Hibernia*?" asked Kate. "I thought we'd see it by now."

Tonio waved an arm to his left. "About thirty kilometres that way, I think," he said. "I guess we're steering well clear of it because of the sea-gremlin hitchhikers we're carrying."

Kate laughed. "We've really got to agree on a name for these things; it's getting too confusing. Aliens. Farmers. Reapers. Monsters. Sea Gremlins?"

"Don't forget Boogeymen," said Tonio.

"*Monsters*," said Sara, heatedly. "Just… monsters."

Kate glanced quickly at Tonio, who frowned and nodded. It was time to change the subject. "So – this is what Tethys calls land, eh? It just looks like a big lump of rock to me. No vegetation at all." They were maybe a couple of kilometres from the nearest land – brown-grey rock that rose in a number of steep-sided hills.

"Pretty much," said Tonio. "Apparently, they've tried to plant things at the Mount Athol settlement, but not a lot grows in the soil. That's maybe another ten kilometres to the north. There are some flatter slopes there, so they've built a small town."

"You mean *miners' camp*," said Sara. "I read it's just docks, miners' dormitories, and a few shops."

"And that's *it*?" said Kate. "On the whole of Tethys?"

"Yeah – apart from the old shipyard about another eight kilometres further north," said Tonio. "That's where they used to build all the ships in the early days. It's got a couple of spurs that jut out into the ocean. It's still got lots of platforms and cranes and stuff... oh, and a half-built Town Class ship. But it's a ghost town, apparently."

"It's been abandoned?" said Kate. "Why?"

"They started running out of resources from Earth to keep building – and immigrants with money wanting a new life. The main mining complexes were between the shipyard and where *Hibernia* chose for its permanent anchorage, so they decided it made more sense to set up the Mount Athol *camp*." he leered at Sara on the other side of Kate. "It's somewhere between the two locations, on a flatter piece of land. I think they stopped working on the last ship about ten years ago. There's lots of resources at the shipyard, but the Hibernians haven't been desperate enough to strip it out, maybe hoping the good times will someday return."

"That might change now," said Sara. "If Earth delivery doesn't come back, they'll have to salvage what they can."

"Agreed," said Tonio. "And that will be the end of expansion on Tethys. I doubt they'll revive the shipyard after that."

"So, we're heading for a ghost town," said Kate. "That's just great. First monsters, now ghosts."

"It makes sense, though," said Tonio. "There are four great quays there. We can tie up to one, and the equipment is there – theoretically – for us to inspect and carry out repairs under the ship – if we can get rid of the hitchhikers."

And that was the problem, as they all knew. They'd watched from the control room as the new repellent devices had been tested, and seen Kate's mum and her colleague face the monsters. They'd also got insight into the subsequent discussions of the Crisis Team through her mother. The bracelets did work, but clearly could be overcome by the monsters, though the EFE did have a more dramatic effect. But the problem was, to cover the entire underside of the ship, they'd need a very large number of the EFE devices, which they had no resources to build. A couple of trawlers had been fitted out with the devices and would soon be ready for trials, but even if they worked, that would just mean they could restart fishing. They still didn't know the state of the underside of the *Lisboa*, but they did know there was some damage to the screws at the very least. Various schemes were being devised to allow them to use the hatches under the ship to let divers get a look, which would rely on using a number of EFEs, but the devices were still being constructed. And finding out the nature of the damage was then just the first part of dealing with it. Carrying out the repairs was a whole other matter.

Kate's musing was disturbed by a shout from someone at the railing off to her left. She startled and looked about. Sara and Tonio were also straining to see what the fuss was about. There was an increase in noise, further shouting, and the arms of observers closer by started to extend, pointing.

"Ah, I see," said Tonio. He raised his own arm, roughly parallel to that of others at the railing. "There's something in the water. Between us and the land. Coming from the direction of Athol."

"You've better eyesight than me," muttered Kate.

Then Sara shouted. "Yes! I see it. A boat. Kate, it's… about fifteen degrees to starboard."

Kate shook her head. "What does that even *mean*? Remember, I'm from… oh, yes!" It was clearly a boat, and approaching rapidly. At first she felt a jolt of excitement. Other people were coming. And the *Hibernia* was much stronger than the *Lisboa*. If anyone could help, it would be them. She knew from her mother that the Captain-Governor had been in contact with them, and it had been the Hibernians' suggestion that the *Lisboa* head for the old shipyard. Now, it seemed that they were going to get an escort. But as the boat approached, Kate's excitement turned to something else. "No! What are they doing?"

Tonio and Sara turned, clearly unsettled by her tone of voice.

"Someone needs to warn them," said Kate. "Someone should have *already* warned them."

Tonio's eyes widened. "Shit. You're right. Maybe–"

He didn't get a chance to finish. The babble of excitement became punctuated by gasps, then shrieks. Kate and Tonio both looked back out to sea. The boat was now maybe four hundred metres away –

sleek, and mounted with a gun on the front deck – and it was in trouble. The line of its wake was clear in the calm, green-blue sea, until the last few metres, where it wriggled like someone attempting to draw a line with a pen while having their elbow jostled. The prow was actually jerking to-and-fro. The *Lisboa* steadily inched towards the scene as the patrol boat desperately tried to continue progress.

"*Dios!*" muttered Sara.

Tonio said something that would definitely have drawn a rebuke from their parents.

And then the craft seemed to buck, like a horse trying to get rid of its rider, and this had a similar effect: they saw one of the crew stagger and pitch over the side, to instantly disappear under the surface.

Some along the railing were now holding hands to mouths, and one or two were crying.

The boat gave one more abrupt twist to the side, and then it began to sink – rapidly.

The crew rushed onto the deck and then began to leap overboard.

"Oh, no!" said Sara, turning away from the railing.

But Kate couldn't. She watched in horrid fascination as the crew hit the water one-by-one, and then almost immediately sank from view in a halo of bubbles and spray. Within thirty seconds it was done, and not a trace of the boat or its crew remained on the calm sea.

* * *

Two hours later, Marie found herself in the *Lisboa's* shuttle, making a small hop to Mount Athol – a journey that would take a mere five minutes. The excursion had been arranged shortly after the sinking of the Hibernian patrol boat after two frantic conversations with those on the land – first with a Colonel Joseph, who was the head of what seemed to be the Hibernian navy, and then second between the Hibernian leader – a woman called Marissa O'Neill – and the Captain-Governor. The latter had been a private affair which had resulted in the invitation. But what Nacimiento then revealed to the Crisis Team (who'd been waiting in another room down the corridor) was almost as shocking as the loss of the patrol boat. There had apparently been a coup on *Hibernia*, with the elected leaders having been forced to flee to Athol – with much of what remained of the state's military. Their team had barely had time to consider what this meant for their own prospects of salvation before they were called to the flight deck.

"We'll just have to go and see," Nacimiento had said. And after a quick debate, he'd decided that it was the marine biologists who'd be most valuable to take with him to explain the nature of their own problem.

As promised, the flight was indeed short – essentially up-and-down – for they were close to the Mount Athol site. It almost seemed a waste of precious fuel to take the large shuttle, but they couldn't risk a boat, and after the loss of the patrol boat they had been instructed to make a broader detour around the settlement than they'd initially planned.

Three of the *Lisboa* party preceded Maria down the shuttle's short flight of steps. The reception committee – waiting some metres away on the apron of the dusty runway – comprised a woman with an odd haircut, as though a bowl had been placed on her head as a stencil for a hairdresser, with the aftermath puffed out so that it looked as though she was wearing a helmet; a handsome black man in an expensive suit; and two others dressed in black military uniforms – a pale woman and a man of East Asian appearance.

"Welcome to Athol," declared the woman with the extravagant hairstyle. "I am Marissa O'Neill, elected premier of *Hibernia*, and these are Manfred Traore, my second, Colonel Joseph of the ESU, and Major Fukuda of the ISU. Captain-Governor – we have met before."

"Yes indeed, Ms O'Neill," said Nacimiento, with a small bow. "Thank you for receiving us. With me are Professor Miguel Figueroa, Dr Katerina Kalmik, and Dr Marie Lockard."

"Scientists?" said O'Neill, with what seemed a hint of distaste.

"Naturally. This is our specialty on the *Lisboa*."

"Humph, well, that might explain your lack of resistance to the bizarre creatures attacking you."

"Perhaps so, Marissa – if I may. But I am sorry to say your force of arms did no better, though I am hoping that by combining our brains with your brawn this might yield a solution."

"Don't consider us brainless, Joao," snapped O'Neill.

"That wasn't my intention, Marissa. I was simply elaborating the difference between us."

O'Neill nodded brusquely and turned her attention to the other Lisboetas. Marie felt uncomfortable as the other's calculating gaze swept over her. After finishing her survey, O'Neill announced: "Maybe you do have more brains on your side. I certainly despair at the absence on mine. But I don't like the odds, here. I don't want to be bored with technical details or talked down to. So, let's split, and we'll limit the strategic meeting to the grown-ups. I want to hear what your problems are, and what broadly you hope from us… and what you plan to offer *us* in return. The kids can go and talk the grubby tactical details and minutiae. Joseph – be useful. While Manfred and I discuss matters with the Captain-Governor and the Professor, you entertain the others. Get a sense of the siltation from a military perspective. Fukuda – there's no point wasting your time here: go see to your troops."

* * *

"I'm not sure what I'm doing here," said Joseph. "I can't help any more militarily. I only had eight patrol boats, and now I have one fewer. And we don't have depth charges since we've never had to prepare for war against submarines, so I really don't see how we can help."

"Blunt military force might not be what we need anyway," said Marie. "We don't necessarily want to kill the creatures – just repel them."

"Like using shark repellent," said Kalmik. "But more powerful."

"Well, I can't help you there, either," said Joseph, now perched on a desk, swinging one leg back and forth. "No sharks, for a start – though plenty of things that could *eat* an Earth shark. Have these things got any weaknesses?"

"Light," said Marie. "Though we can't get enough lights of sufficient strength in the water to do more than nudge them around a bit, and they've found ways to reduce the effects anyway by putting a kind of wrap over their heads." She paused to consider how to best frame their latest findings. "But they seem to be sensitive in other ways. From looking at their anatomy, we found they have various electroreceptors that help them navigate around and detect prey – which kind of makes sense as they live in the dark and need other, er, *senses*. We have developed a couple of devices that use magnetic or electric fields to repel them and these do seem to work – to a limited extent. The problem is, we haven't got the material to produce enough of these to protect much of the ship."

"I saw an old Earth film in which someone got electrocuted by dropping an electric hairdryer in a bathtub," said Kalmik. Then she smirked: "I don't suppose you have several massive hairdryers lying around, do you?"

"Wouldn't the charge dissipate quickly?" asked Joseph.

Marie shook her head. "Katerina is joking. You're right, and that's why our own devices have little impact. We can't electrocute them, though something that produced a large charge might unsettle them. Blind them. Physically pain them."

Joseph scowled. "Still makes no difference – we've got no hairdryers at all. No, we've got nothing… ah, *except*…" She stopped midsentence and her brow furrowed. "I wonder…"

"What is it?" asked Marie.

"It's probably nothing, but I have a peculiar prisoner on my hands. He came with the assault squads from the *Marseilles*, apparently trying to escape. He says he invented a machine to try to extract rare elements from seawater. He claims it works, too, but nowhere near well enough to make up for resource costs. I don't get the science, but basically they were drawing a long net of fine filaments through the water between two converted trawlers – like jellyfish stingers – passing currents through them. The filaments are weighted, and something about their material composition and the charge seems to attract certain molecules to it. Anyway – could it prove an electricity delivery system with a broader field of effect?"

Marie noticed Kalmik staring at her, questioningly. She was certainly no longer laughing. "Ah, that sounds… interesting. Do you have more details?"

"Not on me. But, hell, I've got the man locked up in one of the cells we use to hold drunken miners. Want to speak to him?"

"It wouldn't hurt."

Joseph slipped off the desk. "Fine. I'll call… oh, fuck, it's easier if I just collect him myself. Fewer questions. Be back in five."

In fact, it was around eight minutes until Joseph returned, prodding a man before her – tanned, with short hair and a gold stud in one ear, wearing a dirty blue set of overalls. With a final shove, she commanded: "Sit!"

"I'm not a fucking dog," murmured the man, though he did as he was told.

"This is Eddard Mitsos, from someplace on Earth I've never heard of," said Joseph. "The inventor of the not-so-wonderful machine I mentioned."

Marie exchanged glances with Kalmik, and the other waved a hand for her to continue. "Ah, hello, Eddard. I'm Marie Lockard and this is Katerina Kalmik. We're natural scientists from the *Lisboa.* I don't know what you've heard, but we're having some, ah, problems."

"With aliens?" Mitsos' face creased into a smile. "Yeah, I've heard the rumours. My bijou hotel room has one wall made of an attractive set of bars, so I hear all the gossip from my hosts. And the chief jailer…" he twitched a thumb towards Joseph, "tried to update me on our way here. She said you might be interested in the REEN for some garbled reason."

"Yes, your invention. Well, we know the aliens are highly sensitive to all sorts of stimuli, such as electric currents in the water. The Colonel suggested your machine might somehow deliver this?"

"Yeah, it does, I suppose. But, look… Marie? To be honest, I'm not a scientist, I'm a businessman. I got hold of the spec on Earth and tried to interest buyers on Tethys, and the revolutionary bastards of the *Marseilles* decided to give it a go. But I only understand the basics. A significant current is passed into the micro net from a big generator on one of the boats… that's true. But how big, and whether it's of the right nature? Fuck, I hate to admit this, but you need to talk to Youssef Bennani. He's the real brains. He and his team took my design and made it work. I also no longer have the template – that shit Sebastian Deux has it. In any case, the problem is, it took the nerds the best part of two months to build the REEN, and they had to strip the *Marseilles* to get all the parts for it – which didn't make me too popular. From what snippets I've heard, you don't have that long."

"No, Eddard, I don't think we do. But... is your device whole and working?"

"Last I saw, yeah. But it's on the *Marseilles*, under the control of Bennani, who you can't talk to. It sucks, I know."

Marie turned to Joseph. "Is there any way we *could* talk to this man?"

Joseph found her old spot on the desk she'd occupied earlier and hitched herself onto it. "We've no access to the satellite link on *Hibernia*, but the *Marseilles* is nearby, so it's within range of our regular electromagnetic comms. If you could supply a contact number, I've got specialists who could probably connect you to the *Marseilles* network." She redirected her attention: "Do you, Mitsos?"

"Do I look like I'm carrying that detail with me?" he scoffed. "I've probably got calls registered on my tablet, which I brought with me, but who the fuck knows where that is now."

"Ha! I happen to know: Eric gave me your gear for our intel people to hack into. I suspect it's already naked before their eyes. Come on – let's all go see, shall we?"

Joseph led them from the room to another area of the building through corridors that hosted scurrying people in black uniforms. She had them wait in an annexe at one point – issuing Mitsos firm instructions to behave – then emerged with another officer in tow, and they all marched briskly to a larger office full of consoles and monitors showing various scenes from overhead drones, and then through another door to a small adjacent suite. Joseph barked an order, and the three people within vacated the area; even so, there was barely space for the five of them.

The officer they'd picked up started tapping at a keyboard, and then brought out a tablet from a shoulder bag. *Mitsos'?* After a minute or so, in which Marie and the others watched silently, the woman leant back and said. "That's it. Placing the call now."

"Thanks, Morton. Give us some room – but don't go far in case we need you. Mitsos – take the seat. If your colleague answers, I don't want them seeing an officer of the ESU facing them."

"Yeah, that wouldn't go down well, would it?"

For some seconds it seemed as though the call wasn't going to be answered, but then the blank monitor facing Mitsos cleared, and a dark man with jet-black hair appeared.

"Mitsos?" said the man, eyes widening. "What the fuck? Where are you? We heard you were in *Hibernia*. Gone AWOL. Dead, even."

"Missing me?" said Mitsos, wryly.

"Not a molecule. But the Apparatus would like to see you. They've got a lot of questions. They came to question *me*, too, you bastard! I couldn't tell them anything, but they forced me tell them that nothing a *lot* of times in a lot of different ways. The rest of the team, too. And… who's that with you?" Bennani paused his ranting. "I can see people at the side. Their clothes…"

"Look, Bennani, it's time to rein it in. I've got news. Important news. Something so big… well, if you can help, you could even end up a hero."

"Hero? What? I still don't know where you are, or who you're with."

"It's a long story and I haven't got time to tell you everything now. I went to *Hibernia* on the *Dieppe*, we got ambushed, I got caught, and now I'm a prisoner of the Hibernians on Athol."

"Athol!"

"Yeah. I get around. Anyway… have you heard about the *Lisboa*?"

Bennani looked even more confused. "*Lisboa?* What? Not the… the stupid rumours about being attacked by aliens?"

"Yes, that's the one. Well, listen: it just happens to be true. The *Lisboa* is crippled and listing in shallow water off Athol. But here's the thing – they think the REEN might be of use in driving these alien monsters away."

"The REEN? What–"

"This is pointless. Look, Bennani, I don't know much more than you – but I've got people here who do. They're nerds like you. White-coat types. They've got more evidence of what these things can do, and they want to talk science about the REEN. Forget about me now, eh? This is about something much bigger."

Mitsos looked around, and noticed that it was Marie directly to his right. He took her arm and started to rise from his chair – but in a crouch to remain in camera shot. "I want you to talk to them. Let me get out of the way and remove myself as a distraction. There's a Dr Kalmik, and this is Dr Marianne Locket, a marine biologist or something like that. They're from the *Lisboa*. Here… I'll hand over."

Marie smiled wryly as she slipped into the chair. "It's *Marie Lockard* – but thanks, Mr *Mindos*," she winked, then waited as Kalmik moved into view, standing behind her, while Joseph and Mitsos – after a sharp whispered exchange – exited the room.

"That's better," Marie continued. "Dr Bennani – it's great to meet you. I'm glad you're sitting down, as my colleague and I have some pictures that'll shock you. I hope after you've seen them, you'll be happier to talk about this machine of yours."

* * *

Mitsos looked up as the door opened and an ESU officer ushered the pair from the *Lisboa* into the conference room in which they'd originally met, Marie followed by Kalmik. He had been brought here by Joseph, and spent the last half-an-hour ignored, staring at the walls in boredom.

The ESU leader set aside her tablet, through which she had apparently been receiving constant updates from her subordinates, and asked: "What's the news?"

"Good and bad," said Marie. "The good is that Dr Bennani thinks it's entirely possible to adapt the REEN to deliver what we need, and it should be quick. More than that, he's prepared to do it and says he will start straight away. He says he can probably have it done in a couple of days with help from his team."

"I'm surprised," said Mitsos. "He was never so accommodating with my requests."

"Ah, well, he said, and I quote, 'the REEN is a useless piece of shit, so changing it into something useful would be a pleasure'."

Mitsos scowled. "He could have expressed that opinion much sooner and saved us all a lot of grief instead of concluding his analysis with cautious optimism and allowing Deux to give the go-ahead. *Bastard!*"

"That's the good news, is it?" said Joseph. "What's the bad?"

"The bad is that the craft are on the *Marseilles*, and obviously he isn't prepared to steal the two boats to bring them here, and nor is he prepared to put his neck on the line by approaching the authorities about the matter. He says that making the changes 'in case' is fine – he was somewhat spooked by our pictures of the aliens and what they've been doing, and I think his cooperation was driven by self-preservation – but we need to secure approval from the *Marseilles* authorities and sort out the rest ourselves."

Joseph folded her armed and looked at Mitsos. "How do we do that?"

Mitsos scowled and shook his head. "We don't. There is no way Deux will allow us to have the boats. First, he will think it's a plot to steal more *Marseilles* resources to bring them here to *Hibernia's* new HQ. Second, if he believes these aliens actually exist and are likely to cause us problems, he will sit back and watch us suffer, then maybe come in at the end to pick up the pieces."

"In that case, how do we get the boats?" asked Marie.

Kalmik filled the pause with a curse, which made Mitsos smile. He noticed the two Lisboeta women exchange glances then turn meaningful looks upon the Colonel, who well understood their non-verbal query.

"Oh, no," said Joseph. "You can forget that. My boats are needed here for defence. There's no way I'm going to risk some sort of raid on enemy territory."

"But the aliens are already *here*," observed Marie. "You've already lost one, and it's only a matter of time before the farmers migrate here from the *Lisboa* and then you could lose the rest. Ultimately it's in your own interest."

Joseph looked troubled. "Their presence here isn't certain. For now, they seem happy vandalising your ship."

"Care to wait it out and see?" said Kalmik, coming to Marie's aid. "Because once they're *here*, it'll probably be too late."

"I appreciate that. But just like this Bennani, I'm also liable to have trouble with my superiors. O'Neill would almost certainly forbid me from risking the fleet – it's all we have to stave off the rebels."

"What about one boat, then," said Marie. "And what if… what if *we* supply the personnel for the mission instead of you. I mean, the *Lisboa*."

"Fuck, Marie," said Kalmik, turning to face her. "What are you suggesting? We don't have an army. We don't even really have a police force – just a few part-time busybodies who keep the well-behaved citizens of our serene city on level tracks that most of us are happy to follow anyway."

"I don't mean soldiers. We can't fight, and I *won't* fight. I mean, people to crew these two REEN boats."

"That the *Marseillaise* are just going to let you take?" said Joseph.

"Ah, no," Marie clearly began to feel flustered with everyone's eyes now upon her. "I was just wondering whether we could, somehow, board quietly and then… well… *steal* them."

Kalmik threw back her head and laughed. "We're not thieves either, Marie, or specially trained saboteurs. *Come on*."

"Well, I'm trying…"

But Joseph wasn't laughing. She narrowed her eyes and began to tap on the table. "They won't be expecting something like this," she said, cautiously. Turning to Mitsos, she asked: "What's the security like around the dock? Could we get in?"

"I can't say whether the dock will be open or closed to the elements. It's closed during storms and when we're on the move, but I'm guessing the *Marseilles* is at now rest off *Hibernia*, so it'll probably be open to ease passage. But if you try to sail inside in one of your patrol craft, you'll definitely be spotted before you off-load your band of thieves."

"Even at night?"

Mitsos shrugged. "I don't know. Normally there's minimal security overnight – maybe a couple of members of the Apparatus at a station by the entrance to the port facilities. I know that for sure, as I had reason to try and get in myself." Now he grinned. "But I guess you might be able to get in if you swam in from outside. Otherwise…" he raised his hands and dropped them.

"Swim? Hmmmm."

"Marie – what the fuck are you thinking?" said Kalmik. "Stop it now!"

But Joseph was nodding too. Mitsos watched her catch and hold Marie's gaze. "With one boat, I could get you close at night and remain undetected. My boats aren't exactly stealthed, but they are from an old Earth military template and have a low radar profile. I also doubt the sophistication of the *Marseilles'* systems. At night, will they have a well-manned radar suite with some an automatic alert, or failing that, diligent staff fixated on their scanners? Even on *Hibernia*, nobody gives a fuck – why would they? Nobody alerted us when the *Marseilles* fleet arrived, because it was the first event of any interest since… well, since *ever*."

"So, you would do that?" asked Marie. "Let us have one boat?"

"A visit might serve multiple functions," mused Joseph. "A recce of the enemy, and even a warning shot: it'll let the bastards know we can get to them easily enough if we want. It might make them withdraw some forces from *Hibernia*. And if we did manage to extract some resources… yeah, I could sell that to Her Majesty. But it would have to be on the quiet. O'Neill *might* sanction one boat – but then again, she might not. And if she said 'no', then that would be it for me – I won't disobey a direct order. But she did tell me to liaise with you about this matter, and hasn't *expressly* told me what I can and can't offer. I think I can tolerate *not* burdening her with the fine details." She grinned. "After all, she has a lot on her plate at the moment."

Kalmik was still shaking her head, looking at Marie. "Swim? You're mad. Those *things* are in the water."

"Not near the *Marseilles*," said Marie.

"Not *yet*!" emphasized Kalmik. "In any case, they're not the only things in the water. Haven't you noticed since arriving from your lovely, placid planet Earth that no one goes swimming here? The sea forests – maybe. The open ocean? No way."

"But it wouldn't be far," insisted Marie. "And our drysuits are *robust*. I know people fall overboard and survive – they're not instantly attacked by predators from the deep."

"Not always, no," said Kalmik. "And who exactly would go on this ridiculous jaunt anyway? You?"

"Yes. And we can ask for volunteers. I'm sure there would be some. Mike would come."

Kalmik pushed back her chair and for a moment stared at her compatriot. Mitsos noticed her face warp through a range of emotions. At last she declared: "Well, if the Colonel is prepared to take a chance, and you are too, then... *fuck it.* I won't get in the water near *them*, but for a *short* swim?" She shook her head vigorously, apparently angry at herself as much as at the situation. "I must be fucking stupid."

Marie beamed. "Thanks, Katerina! If *you* come, others will follow your lead. So – Colonel," she turned, "we need to allow Mr Mitsos' colleagues a couple of days to do their work. Perhaps if we aim for tomorrow night?"

"Sure. What the hell."

But Mitsos was slowly shaking his head. Marie saw him, and asked: "You have a problem?"

"I think you're too blasé. Even if you swim through the entrance and get aboard unseen, as soon as you start up the engines and try to launch the boats, someone is going to see or hear you and come to investigate. The Apparatus aren't usually armed with guns – and I guess the weekend warriors now on *Hibernia* have got all of the recently manufactured ones – but they won't just let you go. Maybe it'll come down to whether you can get away before the night detail call enough reinforcements to stop you."

"You're right," said Marie. "There are a lot of unknowns. And that's why we need someone with us who knows the environment and can react appropriately."

"You mean *me*, don't you? You've got to be joking. There is no *fucking* way I am going anywhere near the *Marseilles* ever again."

Chapter 41

"So much for not courting trouble," said De Voe, but with a sparkle in her eye.

"Situations change," said Heiko. They were in Solbakken's lounge, along with Solbakken, Cass Remillard, and Makka Frost, seated in a circle of chairs. "It's important to react to new information. I'd still rather act with permission and keep under the radar until we get it, but that meeting…" he shook his head. De Voe knew what he meant; they'd talked about it on the walk back to the embassy with Solbakken, and Heiko had clearly been dwelling on matters overnight. "I've seen people like Deux before. Worked with them. He's an agent of chaos. A contrarian. Maybe even a psychopath. He'll make mischief for the sake of it – getting people to jump just because he can, just for fun. It's not worth trying to negotiate with such people. So, while he is part of this Revolutionary Council, we're stuck. That means we have no option now."

"Is that how you see it too, Magnus?" asked De Voe.

Solbakken pouted and nodded. "I'm afraid so. I wouldn't know how to even start going about diplomacy with him, and remember, I've had to deal with the triumvirate these past few years. I must admit, I was surprised by Karyn Dures, though. I suspect she might be someone we can work with in future… as long as we don't cross any red lines. So whatever your plans, Rennie, please try to avoid killing anyone, especially Stokers."

"Oh, I don't plan to," said Heiko. "I came to Tethys to avoid having to do that again." He noticed De Voe frowning at him, and his face flickered into a brief, wan smile. "I'm a soldier, Melissa. I was a soldier. Don't judge me on my past."

"Oh, I don't," she said. "Maybe you misunderstood my look. Frankly, if you want to kill some of these fuckers, go ahead. There are shit people on this world, too, and we'd be better off without them."

"Shit people *with families*," said Heiko.

De Voe winced. "Ouch! You're too good, Rennie. Really, too good. You're starting to come across as a pacifist. Nice ideals… but maybe not when you're swimming in an ocean of sharks."

Remillard cleared his throat noisily and deliberately. "That's a good point, Melissa. On the one hand, I'm somewhat relieved at Rennie's words. I had some concerns about recruiting a professional soldier as my replacement, and this dispels any last doubts. On the *Stavanger*, under my term, we didn't have to use lethal force once, and I only ever faced two homicides. But on the other hand, we never had to face angry, unreasonable people with real-life guns before. As Melissa wonders, will they be respectful of *our* temerity? I suspect not."

Heiko sighed. "Yes, Cass, Melissa, you're right. I'm not ruling out violence, just emphasizing that we should keep this to a minimum. My stalkers from Earth are particularly liable to need firm handling. But for others, as Magnus says, we mustn't cross red lines."

"Fine," grunted De Voe. Then she noticed Frost smiling at her from behind a hand. "Makka – something funny?"

"What? No. Sorry, Melissa. Just impressed by your elevation. You seem to have occupied the Chair."

De Voe smirked. "Well, you lot can't make a decision. It's time to be bold. You got a problem with that?"

"Far from it. If we get out of this in one piece, I think I'd rather return to the field – and I can't help thinking there are no better hands for the Department to be in than yours… *boss*."

De Voe arched an eyebrow and shook her head. "Lots of water has to pass under lots of bridges before then, Makka. I'm still not sure what we're doing *right now*. Rennie…" she swivelled in her chair to face the man. "Sometime overnight you decided we must act. I did too. But I doubt you spoke without having some sort of plan."

Heiko nodded gently. "I do – kind of." He smiled. "And the first step is to deal with my shadows. But rather than stripping them of their lives, I think just their *clothes* will suffice. Listen up…"

* * *

"Yep, they're still there," said Claude Vardem, nodding at the two screens on the desk at which he was seated. "There's at least two at either end of the street. And that's just above ground. I've no cameras down below, but Judd and Monique have been out twice in the last couple of hours, and each direction from the lower exit on Sublevel One had a pair of armed watchers at the closest junction."

"And below that?" asked Heiko.

"There isn't an accessible 'below that'. Under the embassy, all levels from Sublevel Two down are taken up with service tunnels, power conduits, and the like. I suspect maintenance engineers know how to get in, but these levels are blocked to us unless we do some major excavations in the basement."

"But they're blocked to the New Socialists, too," muttered De Voe.

"Yes, true," said Heiko. "Did Judd and Monique have any problems?"

"No," said Anders Pedersen. He had joined Heiko, De Voe, and Remillard in the small office on the top floor of the embassy, with Frost and Solbakken having been content to cede their space to the current team to allow it to finalise details. "They reported that they were carefully watched, but not interfered with or followed."

"I guess you're right, Rennie," said De Voe. "It's *you* they're after."

"Indeed, I'm relying on that for the plan. Anders – did they get what they were sent for?"

"Oh, yeah. Magnus' directions were sound, and the shop was open and stocked. Better yet, its printer was online and they had the template Claude found in their inventory. Funnily enough, they didn't have any other customers, so they were happy to do a rush print job, and then Judd paid an excess to get the product delivered – just in case they got stopped on the way back. The delivery cart turned up ten minutes ago. The rest of the team are now getting ready."

"Great," said Heiko. "Claude – can you show a map of the surrounds, please. Ground level on one screen, Sub-One on the other. Excellent. Now..." he leant over Vardem's shoulder, and started to point at the map. "Here's what I suggest..."

* * *

The embassy had been all but emptied over the last hour. Aside from Vardem, squirreled away in Solbakken's small office upstairs, the only ones remaining were the ambassador and Heiko. These two stood by the black front door.

"I hope you know what you're doing, Rennie," said Solbakken. "There are armed people outside, gunning for you."

"Maybe not *gunning*," said Heiko. "At least, not yet. They didn't shoot us on our recce to the docks a few days ago, nor on our visit to the Revolutionary Council."

"I assume our letter of safe passage had something to do with the last one, and maybe they hadn't decided what to do with you on the first occasion. They might have a clearer idea now."

"They might," admitted Heiko. "Though I still doubt they'll shoot me in broad daylight, especially on this street, under the eyes of representatives of the city states of this world."

"But down a darkened side street?"

Heiko nodded grimly. "Sure, but I'm almost counting on that. Anyway, it's got to be done."

"Well, good luck then." Solbakken held out his hand, which Heiko took. "I'll join Mr Vardem upstairs and follow proceedings there. You and he are in communication?"

Heiko released the other's hand and momentarily closed his eyes. In his head, he saw a menu from which he was able to choose various options, including a street plan and the view from the cameras mounted on the roof of the embassy. He tapped at a device in his ear. "Claude – you there?"

"Here, sir. I'm watching out for you."

"Roger that, and *out*." Heiko opened his eyes. "Thanks, Magnus. Time for me to go." He turned and grasped the door handle and exited the building.

Heiko sauntered slowly down Consul Street, past the three-storey buildings made of white-painted volcanic stone, with their black doors and Doric columns. Soon he spotted the first set of watchers at the eastern end: they had no place to hide, and weren't making any special effort to remain unseen. Given recent events, having a couple of armed people at an important intersection was hardly suspicious – though their reaction on seeing him certainly was: the pair – both men

– stiffened and turned towards him. One – in his late twenties or early thirties, with cropped hair and an ugly nose – made eye contact, and smiled. Still focused on Heiko, the man spoke to his dark-complexioned companion from the side of his mouth. Both hefted their rifles, the first man clasping and unclasping his hands around his, as though weighing up options for its use.

Heiko drew close, and nodded. "Good day," he said, then he carried on past without waiting for an answer. Feeling eyes on his back and an itch between his shoulder blades, he turned right, heading deeper into the Derry quarter.

"Both pairs are behind you," said a voice in Heiko's ear. "I'll update their position on the street plan. They'll be in red."

Heiko kept moving at a steady pace on the empty sidewalk. Momentarily closing his eyes, he selected the street plan from his augmented visual system, and sure enough, saw two pairs of moving red dots, one keeping an even distance behind him, the second moving more quickly along Consul Street, trying to catch up with the first.

Branigan Street held a mix of two- and three-storey buildings, built of similar material to the embassies. Some were residential, but others were service outlets. There were a few people about, and even a couple of carts moving along the narrow, one-way street, though it was undoubtedly less busy than it would have been before the revolt. Heiko's target wasn't far away. He crossed one junction and headed for a second, where a narrow alley led off to the right, forming a divide between the backs of two blocks. The exact purpose of the passageway was unclear, but its dimensions were just what Heiko needed: it was private, and better still, bisected half-way down by a similar passage, essentially quartering one large rectangle of masonry.

Heiko slowed now, allowing the second pair of dots to catch up to the first – now a mere five metres behind him – by pretending an interest in the menu posted on the restaurant on the corner. What he was about to do next would probably seem like a gift to his followers: he had to hope they would hold off firing – if that was their intent – until they were all deep down the alley. He closed his eyes to access the street view again, and smiled. The four red had dots coalesced. But what his stalkers were unaware of, was the half-dozen blue dots that now showed on the schematic in Heiko's head, having been put in place around an hour ago…

He started forwards again, taking the alley, now moving at a brisk pace. He needed to get to the cross-section before the others decided to act. As he expected, they allowed him something of a head start, undecided on their next step, as following him down the alley would mark the crossing of some Rubicon. He was twenty metres down before the others made a decision to follow him – all four. He now ensured his progress was somewhat inconstant, not just moving directly ahead, but edging to the left hand wall, then the right, just in case someone behind decided to line him up to shoot. He knew the revolutionaries weren't fully trained soldiers; they weren't marksmen who'd honed their skills over many hours of practice on the rifle range. Even at this distance, it was quite possible they'd miss, or maybe only clip him.

The cross section was another twenty metres away. *Not too fast, not too slow*, he thought to himself. Then he heard a clatter echo down the alley from behind and heard a deep voice speaking loudly – whether to him or its colleagues was unclear. Then – in his internal vision – saw two blue dots appear at the entrance to the alleyway behind, coming from different directions: these began to follow the red.

"Stop!"

This time it was clear that Heiko was being hailed. But he had a few more metres…

"Stop, or we'll shoot!"

The junction was just there. Ten metres. He started to slow, and raised his hands. Eight metres. He began to turn, but continued stepping backwards. He saw the party dressed in green approach in a cluster, in each-others' way in the narrow space, their rifles waving about as they advanced. Six metres… five… he shuffled backwards, and was maybe three metres from the entrance to the cross passage when the others pulled up, just out of bayonet-thrust reach. They were all breathing heavily: two men at the front, two women just behind.

"Can I help?" asked Heiko, arms still aloft.

The man with the fleshy nose grinned. Heiko could see the NS tattoo on the back of the hand resting on the trigger. "Yeah, comrade, I think you can."

"Shoot him," said one of the women behind. "Now we have the chance."

"Shoot me?" said Heiko. "Why would you do that? I'm not your enemy."

"You and your kind are," scowled the man. "Whether on Earth or here. You're supremacists. You think you're better than the common citizen. You have advantages from wealth, installed to guarantee your separation from us."

"I have advantages, yes, but not from wealth. I was a soldier. They came with the territory. Are you against all soldiers?"

"Only those like you."

"Sounds like envy to me," said a new voice – this from behind Heiko. *De Voe.* One of the blue dots that had been waiting out of sight at the intersection. He knew she was holding a weapon of sorts, which clearly registered with the man in front of him, whose smile slipped. "Sounds like you dickheads need to grow up," De Voe continued. "Focus on yourselves. Spend that frustrated energy more appropriately. Or maybe just have a wank and get all that tension out."

"And leave that crap back on Earth," said a second new voice from behind. *Remillard.* He'd been hiding on the opposite side to De Voe, and was also 'armed'. "Don't bring your hang-ups here."

The leader of the New Socialists clearly didn't know where to look. He had his weapon still, but now had the dilemma of who to point at. "What the fuck…"

Heiko slowly lowered his arms, then he lifted his head and directed his voice over the now-anxious cluster in front of him. "Are you there, Anders?"

"Yes, sir," said a voice from behind those in green. "With Stallings. The rest will be here soon."

"*Don't look back!*" barked Heiko suddenly, as several of those in front tensed and started turning their heads. "*Drop your weapons.* If anyone so much as twitches, you'll all die."

"What the fuck…" muttered the leader again, his hands gripping his rifle more tightly. But the other man and one of the women let go of their rifles, as if they had somehow been electrified.

But the second woman muttered. "Pistols? Where did they get…"

Heiko decided he couldn't allow the play to develop further: he took two steps toward the leader, slapped his left hand on the rising barrel to push it down, and with his right he delivered a closed-fist blow to the side of the other's neck. But as the man crumpled, falling back into his comrades, the woman at the back stepped away, swore, and lifted her own weapon… but couldn't fire without hitting her own side.

Then Heiko noticed a grey shape rise into the air behind the woman, hover, then descend upon her head. As the woman fell back, Heiko heard Remillard behind chortle. "See, Melissa. They *do* work… sort of."

They confiscated their opponents' weapons and then had the NS team strip out of their green coveralls. The leader – who one of the others referred to as Jacques – quickly came to his senses and followed instruction, but De Voe had to physically strip the felled woman, who remained concussed from the blow to her head and leaked blood from a scalp wound. They then secured the quartet by tying their hands behinds their backs and propping them next to each other along the alley, wearing nothing but their underclothes.

"What are you doing?" asked the man called Jacques. "You can't leave us here like this."

"It's more than you deserve, shithead," said De Voe, standing beside Heiko. "You would have left *him* dead, so just be grateful we're not like you…" she smiled, "and that the weather's not too cold."

"Pistols," muttered the woman at the end of the line, her head lolling, her voice slurred. "Where…?"

"What, you mean *this*?" said De Voe, taking a step and crouching down. She raised the pistol in her hand, pointed it at the other's head, and pulled the trigger, but there was nothing more than a gentle *click*. "Suckers! We got these from a toy store."

Remillard looked at his own weapon. "Extraordinary, Rennie. How did you know this would fool them?"

"They're not professionals, Cass. Few on Tethys would have held a real gun before recent events, although I was worried some of the NS might be more savvy." Heiko gestured at the woman De Voe had been teasing. "In fact, it nearly didn't work. *She* suspected."

"I'm glad you noticed and acted," said Remillard. "And Anders, too." He looked about and saw the other. "Good job, son."

"Well, it's different now," said De Voe, straightening up. "We've got four genuine pieces to replace the props."

"And hopefully we'll soon have four more," said Heiko. "But the clock is now ticking. We need to deal with those below, and get their clothes and weapons before this lot wriggle out of their bonds and raise the alarm."

"There is a solution to that problem," muttered De Voe. She fixed the leader of the others with a steely gaze. "You! Don't think you're out of this just yet. We'll leave a sniper at the end of the street until we get off *Hibernia*. You won't see him, but he'll see you. So stay put – *or else*."

Heiko exchanged glances with Remillard, who shrugged his shoulders. The problem with De Voe was that she was so convincing it was sometimes difficult to tell when she was being serious and when she was playing. But on this occasion, Heiko was very glad she was as she was.

* * *

The East Docks were a hive of activity – a far cry from the Stavangerans' last visit a few days ago, when their first attempt to leave had been thwarted. It was late afternoon, and the sun of Tethys was sliding towards the western horizon.

They pulled up across the road from the main gate into the Docks and formed a loose huddle. There was a round dozen of them: De Voe, Heiko, Remillard, Frost, Pedersen, and seven troopers. Eight now carried rifles and wore the green coveralls typical of Stokers; the rest were dressed in the casual clothes they'd worn on arriving at *Hibernia*. De Voe had insisted on bagging one of the disguises in spite of the fact that she wasn't a member of the Security team. "Point and pull the trigger," she'd said, on collecting her rifle. "No problem.

Anyway, Rennie, your team aren't much more experienced in using guns."

Now De Voe grimaced at the congregation surrounding the gate. "Something's going off," she said. "But what?"

"Not fishermen, that's for sure," said Remillard. "It's too late for that – unless they're being forced to fish at night to avoid the ESU's patrol boats."

"No, most of them are armed," said Heiko. "And quite a few are wearing grey. I think they're planning something military. An attack on Athol?"

"Well, that leaves us in a pickle," said Remillard. "How do we get to the *Cormorant*? And I will remind you, we really do need to leave *now*."

De Voe knew what he meant. The Earthers on the sub-level had been approached from behind and held up by members of the troop, their faces hidden. They might not know who had ambushed and stripped them, and might even now be reporting to superiors that some underground resistance movement was at work. But the one's they'd dealt with above ground had been following Heiko, and they knew exactly who their attackers were: once they got loose, the Stavangerans were liable to be on a wanted list, and the East Docks were liable to be one of the first places searched. They couldn't afford to return to the embassy and come back another day. They had to leave now… "Bluff," she muttered.

Heiko looked at her, with understanding. "I agree, Melissa. We've got to front this out. Everyone keep close. Let's go."

De Voe matched Heiko's stride as he led them over to the gate. They filed in behind what was clearly the crew of one of the *Marseilles*' converted trawlers, whose captain was negotiating with a flustered man by the gate. Words were exchanged, then the boat's captain – a shaven-headed woman – beckoned her crew to follow her through.

De Voe and Remillard flanked Heiko as he marched to the gate. Beside the green-uniformed man with a tablet in his hands were two armed guards, who lounged next to the farther gatepost, eyeing the newcomers suspiciously.

"Boat!" demanded the overseer.

Remillard nudged in front. "The *Cormorant*. Bay Eight."

The man frowned at his screen. "Not on my list."

"It's a new one," said Heiko. "Just assigned. We only heard we were going half-an-hour ago."

"Who said so?" The man looked between Remillard and Heiko.

"Patrick," blurted De Voe. She knew this game. Overwhelm and confuse.

"Patrick who? I don't know anyone by that name… unless you mean Patrick Collins, but he's a drunk with no authority."

"Look," said Heiko, "we don't know your chain of command. We just know we got told to come here and take this boat at Gate Eight. Anyone else been allocated it? You want us to go home? Fine. You explain."

"Wait! Let me…" The man scrolled on his tablet. Meanwhile, another crew of Marseillaise turned up, noisily assembling behind them. De Voe turned and called. "Forget it, comrades. This prick isn't letting anyone in."

"I said *wait*! The boat at Eight isn't allocated. It's not ours. Registered on the *Stavanger*?"

"That's right," said Remillard. "It's being *borrowed*." He grinned. "They don't know anything about this either."

The noise behind started to increase, the Marseillaise crew unsettled. Someone shouted an insult towards the gatekeeper. De Voe smirked as she recognised Pedersen's voice.

"Oh, I don't fucking know. Okay. Go on then. Set her up. But once you're in, you stay on site until the off."

"Of course," said Heiko. "And when's that?"

"Not up to me, but I'm told first light."

"Not a great time for an attack," said Heiko.

"You a soldier, buddy?" the man scowled. "I didn't think so. And nor are we. It's bad enough trying to do a raid in broad daylight when we can see where we're going, let alone at night in boats designed for fishing not as landing craft." He scanned the party. "I see you got guns. If you need extra ammo, see Janie by the harbourmaster's office. Red hair like a fucking explosion. But I'd steer clear of her unless you're desperate. She a real bitch. Move on."

De Voe was first through the gate; she led the way across the top level, until she spotted Remillard's boat and the steps down to the lower quays at which various trawlers, converted gunboats, and miscellaneous pleasure boats were moored.

They swiftly boarded and got out of sight of prying eyes.

Soon after, De Voe joined Remillard and Heiko in the wheelhouse, where Remillard slumped into his captain's seat and began to run his hand lovingly over the controls. "Miss me, my dear?" he muttered.

De Voe caught a smile ripple across Heiko's face, but for once decided to rein in her inclination to mock. Instead, she said: "Well, we made it, but I'm not sure whether that's good or bad. What next?"

Heiko folded his arms and leant against a bulkhead. "*Out of the frying pan.* It's not going to be easy to slip away during the night, but at least we're onboard."

"Yeah, that's an understatement," said De Voe. "And if we can't – what then? Join the armada?"

"Sure," said Heiko. But then his firm expression turned wry. "Initially. Until, alas, we develop engine trouble and are forced to leave the fleet and return home."

Remillard laughed. "I like your thinking, Rennie. We stick to the crowd like baitfish. Get protection from the fleet in case there are any ESU marauders out there, picking off lonely boats, and then we slip away west around the Range."

De Voe could see the sense in the plan. She only hoped their earlier misdeeds remained undiscovered until then. It was going to be an anxious night.

Chapter 42

Kate and her friends had spent the day moving from one part of the *Lisboa* to another in an attempt at escaping their classmates – for whom today was a rest day from school. They'd been driven from the Terrace to their favourite ice cream parlour, and from there to the Fado, where they'd been cornered by the charismatic Vita Fernandez and her doting retinue. On each occasion, their classmates – envious of their special status, yet also appreciating their greater knowledge of current affairs – had attempted to cajole information from them. The teenagers had been nervous, excited, and sometimes a little afraid. Tonio had been struck dumb by Vita's appearance at the Fado – *fortunately*. If he'd managed to get his tongue working, Kate suspected he would have happily told the temptress absolutely everything. But Kate was aware of their responsibilities and had taken the role of spokesperson for the group – a role Tonio and Sara were very happy to concede.

In the end, they fled to Sara's home on the fourth level – a place of similar size to Kate and Marie's apartment, even though it housed three rather than two. When Sara's mother returned at the end of a shift at the fusion power plant, the apartment became too crowded to talk, so Kate and Tonio had decided to call it a day and returned to their respective homes.

Marie was already back, the kitchen table covered in a mess of equipment; she looked up sharply and smiled anxiously on Kate's entrance. "Ah… Kate… there you are."

"Okay – what's up?" Kate waved a hand at the clutter. Her mum was usually well organised – the sort of person who cleaned up as she went along when cooking, and then placed all of the pots and utensils she'd used in the last stages of meal prep in the dishwasher before sitting down to eat. This chaos reminded Kate of the day she'd come home from school to learn that her parents were separating.

"Oh, I'm afraid I'm going to have to go shortly. It's… complicated."

"Go where? What happened at the meeting?" Kate knew her mother had accompanied several others on the shuttle to the mainland the previous day, but they'd not seen each other since then. She guessed it was to update the Hibernians on their problems and ask for help, although she was sceptical about what aid could be offered: news had leaked out to the *Lisboa's* general population about the coup on *Hibernia*.

"Ah, well, we may have had a bit of luck. Sit down, Kate. I've just got time to tell you…" Marie related the story of the coup, the role of the *Marseilles*, and the revelation about its special piece of kit that might be useful against the farmers.

Kate sat back at the end of the tale, eyeing her mother suspiciously. "That's not all, is it? What's the catch?"

"The problem is, it's unlikely the authorities on the *Marseilles* will let us have these boats. It seems their rulers are difficult people."

"Then how are we going to get them… *ah*! We're going to borrow them… without asking?" Kate watched Marie turn her face away to avoid her eyes. "Mum – what have you got yourself into?"

Marie at last looked up, almost shy. "This is important, Kate. Our experiments worked – at least partially – but we haven't got the resources to make sufficient devices to protect the ship."

"Mum!"

"Ah, well, the Hibernians are also in a difficult position. Thank God the leader of their navy understands the seriousness of the problem and is willing to help–"

"You're going to the *Marseilles*, on a Hibernian navy boat, to steal these special boats? That's it, isn't it?" Kate shook her head angrily. "You're not some sort of ninja, Mum. You'll get shot, or at least arrested, and then we'll make enemies of the *Marseilles*, too."

"I won't get shot. Kate – we have some inside information. They won't have many guards at the docks–"

"*Many*?"

"Uh, probably not." Marie looked away again, then scrunched her eyes and looked at Kate from the side. "The, ah, real issue is that we can't just sail into the docks without giving the game away, so we'll, well, some of us, will have to…" in a small voice, "*swim*."

"Swimming in this ocean? Are you *crazy*?"

"We won't be near the farmers," Marie held up her hands defensively. "The *Marseilles* is near *Hibernia*, and they haven't got there yet."

"You think."

"No, we're quite sure. It'd be clear if they had."

Kate could scarcely believe what she was hearing. "Still, there are other nasties in the water. *Nobody* goes swimming on Tethys."

"We have our protective drysuits, and it won't be far. We'll just have to be careful."

Kate didn't know what to say. One thing she did know was that her mum, like her, could be stubborn. This thing was going to happen, for good or ill, no matter what Kate said, and she wasn't going to plead – she had too much dignity for that. At last, the only thing she could think of saying was: "Don't you dare leave me here alone on this alien world. You come back, Mum! You bloody well come back!"

* * *

Joseph had been worried about the noise of a shuttle waking people at the main camp, so she'd suggested meeting the *Lisboa* party at the old shipyard several kilometres north of Athol instead. Just before 2a.m., the shuttle dropped onto a concrete landing pad, following a single flashing beacon and the programmed coordinates supplied to the pilot by the Hibernians earlier in the evening.

Outside the lights of the shuttle, all was dark. Marie took a moment to blink away the fuzzy images on her retinas and allow her night vision to acclimatise. She heard Kalmik cursing as she shambled past, weighed down by her breathing tanks and other gear.

"This way, Marie," said Mike Resnos, pausing beside her a moment. "I see lights down by the water. That must be it. Come on."

Marie muttered an indistinct acknowledgement, reached down to heft the bag at her feet, and followed the man. She was aware of others behind her: Marco Grande, Arantxa Perez and Bennie Zico – the other volunteers for the 'Crazy Marie Commando', as Kalmik had christened it. They'd decided on a team of six – three per each REEN trawler – and been fortunate that Bennie, Arantxa's understudy, had agreed to fill the complement. But the real surprise had been Grande.

"It's time I faced my fears," he'd told Marie earlier. "I truly hate this, but if it gets Katerina to shut up, it'll be worth every moment of terror."

There was a path from the pad through long-deserted buildings down the dusty slope to the waterside. Once away from the sharp lights of the shuttle, viewing became easier, aided by the soft light of a sky resplendent with stars. She startled at the sudden realisation that the mountain off to her left was actually unnatural. "Wow!"

Behind her, Grande was forced to pull up too. "Marie? What is it?"

"It's… look at the size of it."

Grande followed the direction of her gaze. "Yes, it's huge. I guess it's no surprise, though, given that ships like the *Lisboa* were built here."

The area to Marie's left – a couple of hundred metres down the slope and extending a considerable distance forwards, out into the water – was like the silhouette of a great Earth city under a power outage: tall, irregularly crenelated, with lines of warehouses, manufacturing bays, and giant, spindly cranes like winter trees. The volume of material was vast, perhaps equivalent to a deconstructed *Lisboa*, spread out over a huge area the size of a multitude of football pitches. She'd read that in its heyday, the shipyard had worked on two City Class ships at a time.

Grande didn't wait; as Marie continued to stare, he muttered something apologetic and moved around her. Zico and Perez also passed, leaving Marie at the back of the column. She shook her head, picked up her dropped bag, hitched the tank carried on a strap over her shoulder to a more comfortable position, and continued down the path.

The patrol boat blazed with light, clearly intended to provide guidance to the newcomers. It was situated off a small, quay to the south side of the complex. Joseph waited, standing at the rear of the boat next to one of her crew, dressed in her black uniform, but capless. "Quick. Leave your gear on the deck and then go into the main cabin."

Marie was last aboard, helped up by a crewman dressed in a black uniform like Joseph, though he wore a yellow uninflated life vest over this, like a plastic gilet. As soon as her feet touched the deck, the outboard motors began to thrum, the deck vibrated slightly, and the craft began to edge away from the quay.

Shucking her kit into the pile in the centre of the deck behind the main cabin, Marie followed Perez, stepping over a raised sill through a door to the interior. It was something of a squeeze inside, with fixed tables and bench seating. She saw her crewmates from the *Lisboa* – and one other.

"Ah, hello, Mr Mitsos. You decided to come after all?"

Mitsos sat on one bench, arms crossed, his features suffused with anger. "No, I didn't *decide* to come. I was pressganged into coming."

"Ah, I'm sorry."

The boat jolted and began to pick up speed. Marie swayed, then slumped onto a bench. And then one other entered the cabin, closing the door behind.

"So, you're coming with us?" said Kalmik, who'd settled on a bench opposite Marie. "That's a surprise. I thought you'd delegate."

Jospeh stood, legs apart, resting her back against the closed door, a wry smile on her face. "Normally, I would have," she said. "But if I lose this boat, I might as well go down with it. The alternative doesn't bear thinking about. O'Neill wouldn't just relieve me of command, she'd probably get her pet, Major Fukuda, to shoot me in the face as an example to others."

"My heart bleeds for you," muttered Mitsos. "At least you got a choice. I said 'no', so why the fuck am I here?"

"You're here because I'm here," said Joseph. "It means I can keep an eye on you. It also keeps you out of the clutches of the Major, who I suspect would be happy to torture you a little just to relieve boredom. But mainly, you're here because we're going to need you to get on the *Marseilles* and start-up your machine."

"I won't get in the water," scowled Mitsos. "I've heard about what's in there. *Seen* it. I was on a fishing boat for a while. I once saw someone fall overboard. Before we could get him out, he was grabbed by something – we never saw what. All that was left was a big pool of blood. So, fuck you if you think I'm going for a swim."

Joseph smiled, but without humour. "It's up to you if you swim or not, but you're going in. You can float about until something comes for you if that's your preference."

"You're as bad as Boursis. No – worse. She only broke my fingers – you're trying to get me killed."

"This Boursis sounds like a restrained person," said Joseph. "Maybe I'd like her."

"You're like evil twin sisters. One day you'll both burn in hell."

Marie looked between the two and gently shook her head. *Someone* needed to intervene. "Mr Mitsos – we really do appreciate your presence. We're all going in the water, too. We'll look after you, I promise."

"You promise some devil fish isn't going to rip me apart? Really?"

"Well, promise is a strong a word, but… yes. You'll be in a proper drysuit with protective inbuilt mesh and explosive reactive sensors. We'll put you in the middle, and we'll all have spearguns. Plus, we've found that the worst of the sea life tends to stick to the open water or follow trawlers. They seem to find the bigger ships a bit sterile. If we're quick, I'm confident we'll make it without difficulty."

"Sure, and even if we do, then there's just the guards to get past in the docks… and Boursis again, if captured. Fuck all that."

"We can deal with the first part," admitted Marie. "But we're relying on you for the second, once we're on the *Marseilles*."

Joseph crossed her arms. "Seems fair to me," she said. "I'm putting my ass on the line to get us close, our friends from the *Lisboa* are taking over in getting from my boat to the docks, and then it's your turn to shine, Mitsos. So, if you've got any more intel or secrets, now's the time to speak up."

Mitsos shook his head angrily and broke eye contact with Joseph, folding his arms even more tightly across his chest. Marie thought he was going to clam up completely, but then his shoulders sagged and he sighed. He closed his eyes, gave a smaller head shake, and looked up. "Okay. Maybe I've got *one* more card to play. But it's a risk. A *big* fucking risk. I'd need you to place another call for me."

"To this man Bennani?" said Joseph. "He's already said he won't help."

"No. To Noma. She's a friend."

Joseph choked out a laugh. "You – a friend? Well, why not. I've got your tablet on board. Our comms officer can connect you if you've got this woman's number stored. But if you do this, you do it in front of me. And if I hear you ratting us out, you're going in the drink immediately *without* any protective gear – do you understand?"

The anger reappeared in Mitsos' face. "If you want her to help us, I'll have to tell her *something*. She's not going to get up in the middle of the night and roam about the ship doing things that could get her arrested by the Apparatus without a good reason."

"Do you trust her?" asked Kalmik.

"Ah... trust? That's an interesting question. I don't think she'll betray me for the hell of it. And she kind of owes me. But this is all I have – my only inside source who might help. Take it or leave it."

The cabin fell silent for a moment, then Marie looked to Joseph. "We really could do with all the help we can get. We're *all* taking risks tonight. Maybe just one more?"

"Very well," sighed Joseph. "Mitsos, come forward with me to the wheelhouse. Lockard – Kalmik... it's tight. Maybe *one* of you can come, too?"

Kalmik gave a sardonic smile. "This is your mission, Crazy Marie. Off you go."

* * *

It *was* a risk. For a start, Mitsos didn't know where Noma was, or even if she was still alive. The last time he'd seen her was when they'd parted after the ambush on *Hibernia* in which the rest of the crew of the *Dieppe* had been wiped out. Given that he'd been picked up soon after by opposing forces, maybe she'd blundered into them too? In short, she might be dead, or a prisoner, or she might be recuperating in *Hibernia* – all three of which options were unhelpful to the mission. He was hoping she'd been evacuated back to the *Marseilles*, but even so, if she was in a hospital bed, this would likely put her out of touch or action.

The comms officer connected Mitsos' tablet to her system, feeding pictures through to her main monitor. Mitsos then took the officer's chair, while Colonel Joseph and Marie Lockard stood off to the side.

He was allowed to tap the appropriate application and send a call to Noma's private number. They were now some eight kilometres from *Hibernia* and seven from the nearby *Marseilles*, which meant they were in range for electromagnetic communication to both.

The picture on the screen remained blank, with a winking red icon, for thirty seconds. Mitsos was starting to fear the worst, when the red icon turned to green and the screen brightened to reveal a dark-skinned face, features barely distinguishable in low light.

"Who… what…?"

"Noma? It's me. It's good to see you. Thank fuck, I thought you might have been captured – or worse."

"Mitsos?" The face resolved slightly as the woman moved closer to the screen. "You're alive? Where are you?"

"First, where are you? And how are you? The side…?"

"Eh? I'm okay. A bit sore and stiff. But I've been sewn up and pumped full of drugs."

"I can't see where you are. Hospital?"

"No. We've got few beds, and they're occupied by others who really need them. I'm in my apartment."

"*Marseilles*," Mitsos muttered. "Thank God! It's great to see you made it."

The woman was clearly in bed. The tablet picture dropped and momentarily darkened as Noma wriggled more fully upright, then she focused on the screen again. "You're alive too, I see." She smiled awkwardly. "Well, I'm glad too. But where are you?"

"You're not going to believe this, Noma, but I'm close. Very close."

"On the *Marseilles*? How? Were you caught?"

"No. It's a long story. I'm near, but I'm coming now and I'll be there soon. Listen, this is important. Have you heard about these aliens attacking the *Lisboa*?"

Noma's face broke into a smile. "What is this, Mitsos? A joke? Children's stories?"

"No, Noma, listen. It's true. I got caught by the Hibernians and taken to Mount Athol when some of them escaped. The *Lisboa* is near – a few kilometres off shore. The rumours are true. These aliens are real, and they're fucking monsters."

Noma's smile began to fade. She must have seen the anxiety in Mitsos' face, perhaps highlighted by the harsh light of the cabin. "You have lots of stories, Mitsos. Lies–"

"What lies? Everything I've ever told you is true. Do you mean about the REEN? That works – just not well enough. When else have I lied to you or done anything to undermine your trust? Didn't I *help* you in *Hibernia*?"

Noma's expression firmed, but she nodded. "You did. You saved me. I won't forget it. Okay. Go on."

"Thank you, Noma. You're the only one on the entire ship I can turn to – the only one who ever gave me a chance."

Noma looked down on the screen. Embarrassed?

Mitsos continued: "These aliens are real, and they're close. If they transfer to *Hibernia* we're all going to be fucked. Severely fucked. But there might be something we can do about them: the REEN."

"REEN?" Noma looked back up. She seemed somewhere between incredulous and amused. "Still that?"

"No, listen, Noma, the REEN… what does it do? It passes current into the water, and because of the chemical composition of the fine filaments, it can attract certain elements from it. But the key thing is really the electrical output: it's powerful and widely dispersed. You never saw the size of the generator on REEN 1, did you? It's a monster. And it can help beat monsters. It seems the creatures don't like strong electromagnetic currents. It repels them. I'm telling the truth."

"Okay. Let's say I believe you. What do you want?"

"I said I'm close, and that's true. I'm in a boat with some Lisboetas. We've come to get the REEN boats. And to prove how serious we are, we're going to have to swim from our boat to the dock of the *Marseilles*."

"Swim? Take the boats?" Noma's eyes widened in shock. "Are you mad?"

"We're coming, Noma, no matter what. This is too important. Look – Deux thinks the REEN is a joke. Everyone on board thinks it's a joke. So no one wants it. But we can't ask because for it because, well, you *know* Deux. People are going to die, and we can prevent that, but Deux will play games and be deliberately awkward. Tell me you think that won't happen."

"The equipment on the REEN might be useless, but the materials in the generator, and the net, and the trawlers as well, they're ours. You can't just steal them."

"Noma – the Lisboetas aren't thieves. Apparently they have a good reputation – well, that's what they tell me. I don't know, I'm from Earth. They say they'll return everything. I'm sure they'll even be prepared to pay something later. A hire fee? I don't know. But we haven't got time to argue about this now, or to let Deux play a lengthy hardball session."

Noma shook her head and was silent a moment, then: "Why did you call me, Mitsos? What do you want?"

"We need help. It'll make our task a lot easier if the boats are ready to launch and our path is clear. If the guards at the dock are distracted somehow. I don't know how many there are, or where they'll be, or if they're armed – nothing. Some intel would be great, but it would be even better if you could do something about them."

"You want me to disable the guards?" The disbelief in Noma's voice was clear.

"No. We don't want you to hurt them. *We* don't want to hurt them. We don't want to hurt *anyone*. This whole exercise is to *save* bloodshed, not cause it. Please, Noma. Help us. In any way you can."

Noma was silent for a moment. But as she opened her mouth to speak the image cut out and the screen went blank.

"What the fuck just happened?" shouted Mitsos.

The comms officer squeezed past Marie and attended to the tablet linked to the main console.

"What it is, Corporal?" asked Joseph.

"It's unclear. Let me try to call again." The officer tapped the appropriate app, then turned to look at some diagnostics on a secondary monitor. On the tablet and the main screen, the red icon appeared, winking incessantly. "It's not at this end. Maybe… maybe a comms shadow? I don't know, ma'am."

"Fuck!" hissed Mitsos.

But the call went unanswered and the minutes passed.

At last, Joseph declared. "We're approaching the *Marseilles.* Dr Lockard – time for you and your team to get ready. You too, Mitsos."

"So where does this leave us?" asked Marie, waving a hand towards the darkened monitor.

"Possibly up shit creek," growled Joseph. "Mitsos – will she help?"

Mitsos pushed back in his chair, away from the screen. "I honestly don't know. She's a woman of principle, loyal to her cause. And her opinion of me is, uh, *complex.* I know she'll do the right thing in her own eyes, but the problem is, I'm just not sure in this case what that is." He shook his head bitterly. "She did put herself at risk for me once when she didn't have to – she got me on the *Dieppe*, and that got me to *Hibernia*, and I repaid her by helping her out when we were ambushed. So, are we even? Does she still feel some debt?"

"I guess we're going to find out shortly." Joseph looked at Marie. "Dr Lockard – this is it. I'm not going to risk my boat any further. I'll nudge us as close as possible, and once you're in the water I'll draw off a short distance, out of range of attack, and wait for an hour in case you decide to swim back. After that, I'll assume you're captured or dead – by one means or another. Then I have to get back to Athol before the camp rises and I'm missed. Understood?"

For a moment, Mitsos hoped Marie would get cold feet and have second thoughts. But instead the woman's expression firmed.

"Thank you, Colonel Joseph. You've done plenty. I have faith in Mr Mitsos and his friend. We'll see this out."

Mitsos groaned and closed his eyes.

* * *

Mitsos slipped into the black water off the side of the patrol boat, the last of the seven-person assault team. The six from the *Lisboa* trod water in a hemi-circle around him, several armed with spear guns. Three wore full diving gear with air tanks on their backs, while the rest were like him, in drysuits with masks, snorkels and flippers.

Mitsos was comfortable enough in his kit: he was used to swimming and snorkelling in the Mediterranean, so he'd earlier brushed off attempts at instruction. "I'm not a complete novice," he'd muttered irritably. "Let's just get on with it."

Off to one side was the bulk of the *Marseilles*, lights stippling the water from upper decks that were invisible from Mitsos' angle: all he could see was the hull, looming like a great wall across the horizon, though it was a wall with a breach, for off to his right light spilled into the night from some hidden interior. Their destination. Mitsos had cursed when they'd confirmed the entrance to the docks was indeed open to the ocean: had it been closed, they'd have had to abort the mission. *Just my luck…*

The water was cool through his suit, not cold, and yet still he shivered. Without allowing himself time to wonder what might be beneath him, he pulled on his mask, adjusted his snorkel, and instantly struck out towards the spilling light: he was a decent swimmer, and perhaps not the worst of the present team. He certainly had no desire to hang about: the others would have to adjust their formation as best they could to keep their protective circle.

He tried not to think. Stroke. Stroke. Stroke. Glance up. Stroke. Stroke…

Another glance to the side revealed one of the others languidly keeping pace with him. At his next breath, he looked to the other side, and saw a shape there, a body-length away. They were making progress. And then, as he looked down, his heart leapt on seeing a great eye of light slipping under him, which began a zigzag. He took in a mouthful of water, raising his head up to gasp and splutter – and then a dark shape glided up to him and a hand was on his arm. "Mitsos?" It was one of the men.

"Below… fuck!" He drew up his legs, saw the glowing eye… and then realised it wasn't an eye at all, but a helmet light from one of the divers, patrolling the water immediately beneath. Angrily he slapped the water. "Stupid fucking…" He thrust the snorkel back in his mouth and pushed forwards, thrashing out deep strokes, determined not to look down or think again… and suddenly he was at the hull, able to reach out and touch it, which he did for the sense of security. He paused to look about, and found the experienced divers had rotated to all be to one side of him, away from the hull, and beneath were now two lights. He put his head back in the water and continued his power crawl, following the hull for ten, fifteen metres, and then this dropped away, and he realised he'd crossed some threshold and was now within the docks, and suddenly there was more light from above and ahead.

He bobbed up once more, and now saw two of the Lisboetas in the water pulling ahead like seals, calmly and efficiently slicing through the water. They were headed for the end of a jetty, one of several that filled the vast interior space, with a number of moored vessels pointing at him with their bows or sterns. Now it was his turn to follow others, and he was more than happy to do so.

The whole team soon clustered at the end of the jetty, bobbing in the water, hidden by a single trawler from anyone further in the space. Mitsos itched to get out, but the logical part of his mind tried to calm him: the water here was no more than two metres deep, a thin layer above the steel floor over which some of the *Marseilles'* fleet floated, and into which other vessels held aloft in cradles could be gently launched. When the great ship was in transit, the water would be completely purged, but when at rest, as now, the docks were allowed to flood to enable easy passage. And though small, fish-like creatures could often be found darting about the jetties, it was rare for anything significant to venture over the threshold into such shallow water.

"What now, Eddard?" asked Marie, suddenly beside him, her mask pulled up onto her forehead and snorkel dangling. "Where are you boats?"

Mitsos tried to orientate himself while treading water. "Ah… we're in the inner dock. Wrong one."

"Inner?" said Kalmik. She had been one of the divers, so was burdened by extra tanks and a close-fitting helmet, which glowed from a light at the forehead. She was currently grasping a rung set in the jetty to keep herself steady. Her voice was muffled through the helmet. "Explain, Mitsos."

"There are two docks. The 'inner' isn't actually further inside the ship, it's just closer to the main entrance. It's the everyday dock, home to the trawler fleet." He pointed at a wall off to their right, beyond the parallel jetties. "The outer dock is beyond that bulkhead. It's where other types of craft are kept, and it's also used for maintenance and repair. It's where they turned fishing boats into the attack fleet. The REEN boats are there." He realised the implications of this.

"*Fuck*. We need to go there and then swim around to the outer dock's separate entrance."

"Well let's go," said Kalmik.

Mitsos held up one hand, causing him to sink into the water, until he slapped his hand back and continued with a steadying horizontal stroke. "*Fuck this*. Wait." He recovered his composure. "That means having to go outside again. Maybe not far, another ten metres, but I'd rather not. We can climb out here and walk through instead."

"What about the guards you mentioned?" said Marie.

Mitsos closed his eyes. He'd almost forgotten about them. He tried to think of the last time he'd visited the docks. "I think there might be one at the main entrance, ahead…" They were close to the left hand wall at the first jetty. "And then at a desk between the two docks. But that was when it was busy during the day. Maybe there's no point having anyone around now?" And then there were the cameras along the dock with face recognition software, but he decided not to mention them. Surely there'd be no one poring over these in some control room of the Apparatus?

"Well, we can't tell from here," said Kalmik. "Someone needs to get closer."

"I'll check," said Resnos. He was another of the divers. "I'll swim to the end. Perhaps it's best if it's only me – fewer waves."

Others muttered assent, and Resnos slipped beneath the surface.

As they waited, Mitsos struggled closer to the jetty and took a handhold next to Kalmik so he could pause his efforts to stay afloat, and others spread out to do the same. No one spoke: the only sounds were from the odd slap of water caused by the team, and a low hum that seemed to suffuse the space. To Mitsos, that was both a good sign and a bad one: it meant the place was truly asleep – with no all-hours repair work in progress – but it also meant they had to move especially carefully in the case there were guards.

After some minutes, Resnos returned, his head emerging from the water less than a metre in front of Mitsos, giving him another fright. "Shit, man!"

Resnos's voice was muffled, even though he was almost shouting to be heard through his helmet. "Sorry. I've been exploring. Do you want the good news or the bad?"

"As you want, Mike," said Marie.

"Right. The good news is that the desk between the docks Mitsos mentioned is empty. I even climbed out to confirm. But there does seem to be someone at the far end, guarding entry into the docks as a whole. I couldn't see how many. A couple, I think."

"Do you think we can get through without being seen?" said Marie.

"Maybe. I watched from behind a crate on the quay by the desk. The guards didn't seem especially interested in things on *this* side. Why would they be? There shouldn't be anyone here."

"Well, that's not so bad," ventured Mitsos.

"No," said Resnos. "But that's not the bad news. After I saw the guards, I thought it best to check the outer dock, and swam along the wall and outside. If we could get in from the open ocean then that would take the guards completely out of the equation. As Mr Mitsos said, it's just a few metres around the hull between the two openings. The problem is, there wasn't a second opening. The outer dock bulkhead door is closed."

"So we have to open it," said Marie.

"Can we?" asked Kalmik, her question directed at Mitsos.

"In theory, yeah. But I've no idea where from." He looked around. "So, does that mean we abort? Joseph should still be waiting for us."

"Do you really fancy another ocean swim, Mitsos?" smirked Kalmik. "We were lucky once. We might not be again." She looked beyond Mitsos. "What do you think, Marco, eh?"

"If needs be," said one of the swimmers – a man with a shadow of stubble. "But get me to some sort of control panel and, well, maybe I can figure something out."

"I think we have to try," said Marie. "Can we at least get to these special boats and see where we go from there?"

"Or *not go* from there," muttered Mitsos.

Kalmik nodded slowly. "While we're here, it would be a shame not to push on. Mike – can you take us to the best spot to get out of the water..."

Resnos led them directly across from the end of the first jetty to the end of the one nearest the far wall. There were no boats tied up along this, although there was a line of trawlers along the previous one, which provided good shelter from the view of anyone near the entrance to the complex, and in any case, they would be almost impossible to see in the water. They swam along this jetty to its end at the quay – passing under a couple of empty ship cradles and several cranes. Resnos then pulled himself up from the water, using a series of convenient handholds set into the side of the quay, and crouched at the top, moving his head this way and that, ensuring there was no one near. He beckoned the rest up, one at a time. When Mitsos clambered onto the quay, Resnos held him by the shoulder and pointed at those who'd preceded him, hunkered down by a large metal container. Mitsos grasped his flippers tightly in one hand, nodded, and scuttled across to join them.

At last, the full team were in the shadow of the container: they were about ten metres from the wide doorway to the outer dock, and maybe eighty to the main entrance in the opposite direction. Mitsos could see a checkpoint podium in the doorway, and it was unattended, though a quick glance up also revealed a camera above it, black and hemispherical, like a fish eye. Then he felt other eyes upon him, and half-turned to find a now-helmetless Kalmik coolly appraising him; she followed the direction of his gaze…

"Camera?"

"Looks like it," said Mitsos.

"Maybe it's turned off," said Marie.

Mitsos frowned. "I doubt it. But I'd be surprised if anyone's looking at it at this moment. The *Marseilles* has hundreds of cameras. Will a night shift be poring over the images in the main control room?" He shrugged.

"We should move quick anyway," said Marie. "Mike?"

Resnos was now at the edge of the container, peering towards the entrance. Like the other divers, he'd divested himself of helmet and flippers, which he held in his hands, but he was still somewhat burdened by the slim tanks on his back. "I can't see clearly. I think there are two. Are they talking? Shit, let's just…" He made a decision and dashed for the doorway as fast as he was able, given his encumbrances.

The rest of the team startled at this, then crabbed after him, drawing Mitsos with them. They reached the doorway, passed through it, and emerged into the outer dock area, following Resnos around the bulkhead wall, where they'd be out of sight of the guards.

"What the fuck was that!" gasped Mitsos.

"Sorry!" said Resnos. "It just seemed the right thing to do."

Marie laughed lightly. "My daughter did warn me that I wasn't a ninja."

"You can say that again," growled Kalmik. "Mike – next time, let's discuss, eh?"

Resnos had the decency to look sheepish. "Yeah, sure. But I think we got away with it."

"Don't get cocky – we're still under this camera," noted Mitsos. His heart was racing. He felt a sudden urgency: there'd been no shout of alarm from the guards, but who knew what was happening in the hidden control centre. "Follow me."

Mitsos strode off along the quay. The arrangement of the outer dock was similar to the inner: yellow lights glared down from the high ceiling; a series of jetties speared out from the quayside towards the closed front wall. There were fewer boats here – maybe a half-dozen in grand total – of various designs, including one trawler that seemed to be in the process of being converted to military use, with a renovated harpoon towards the bow. The REEN boats were at the far end, opposite each other at adjacent jetties. Mitsos was pleased to see the water hadn't been flushed, and the boats were afloat and moored rather than set in cradles. His pace quickened until he was at the end of the quay between the jetties. He looked up and saw a camera high up on the wall that seemed to give a wide view over the whole dock: there was no hiding from that.

"Okay, plans?" said Kalmik.

"I'll take REEN 1 – to the left. It's got the generator and main controls. Three of you need to come with me, and three go to the other."

"Arantxa – maybe you, me, and Katerina can take REEN 1," said Marie. "Mike, you take Marco, and Benny can pilot REEN 2."

"Gotcha," said Resnos.

"But there's still the problem of the bulkhead door. How do we open up?"

They were still discussing this option, when Mitsos heard a noise from the entrance, turned…

"Oh… *fuck*!"

* * *

Marie heard the noise a split second after Mitsos. She turned to see a small party heading towards them from the entrance to the inner dock: at the front strode a tall, grey-haired man in a peaked cap – dressed in a dark grey uniform with golden bands around the sleeves – and a black woman with short hair who was dressed in a grey uniform with a red armband. Behind and around these marched four others, also in grey, carrying rifles.

"Noma, what have you done," gasped Mitsos.

"Stay where you are!" shouted the man in the cap. Behind him, the armed party lowered their guns to point in their direction. "Drop your weapons."

"Weapons?" said Marie, in a soft voice. Then: "Oh!" She heard a clattering behind. *The spearguns.* She had a knife at her belt, but decided for the moment it was best to keep her hands raised and well away from it. At the corner of her eye, she noticed Grande and Kalmik also raising their arms – but just in front, Mitsos was looking about. He took a half step towards the water. *Surely he wasn't…*

But if the man were planning to dive, he waited too long, and the other party were quickly upon them.

"Fuck!" hissed Mitsos. Then he looked towards the black woman, and repeated more loudly: "Noma – what have you done?"

The woman looked stern but didn't answer. Instead, the man in the cap said: "She did her duty, that's what. And in the end, you may end up grateful for it. Who's in charge?"

Marie flicked a glance to one side and saw Kalmik looking pale. She slowly lowered her arms and took a small step forwards. "I… I suppose I am. My name is Dr Marie Lockard. I'm from the *Lisboa*." Now that he was close, Marie noticed that the man had a fine grey goatee beard and a heavily weathered face. She guessed he was in his late fifties, and maybe even older.

"Dr Lockard – I am Marcel Louvain, ship's captain. We do things differently on the *Marseilles*: I am the captain of the ship, responsible for its operation, but not the ruler, unlike Joao Nacimiento – who I've had the pleasure of meeting on a couple of occasions." He reached up and took the cap from his head with one hand, and scratched his scalp with the other before returning his cap. "I say not the ruler, but actually, by default, I currently am, given that the First Citizen is in *Hibernia* and the People's Committee are not well placed to make immediate decisions." He looked over at Mitsos. "And lucky for you, Captain Boursis also recently transferred to *Hibernia* to take command of the new internal security apparatus there, or else she would be here instead of me."

Marie saw Mitsos' shoulders sag and his head droop; he muttered: "*Thank fuck.*"

Louvain quickly returned his eyes to Marie. "So, I hear you've come to steal our ships. Citizen Obuya told me everything."

Marie opened her mouth to respond; to deny it; but closed it quickly and gave her head a sharp shake. Denying the reality would be absurd. She gave a sigh. "Yes, Captain Louvain, I'm afraid it's true, although I'd prefer to phrase it as 'borrow', as we certainly have no plans to keep your property. I'm sorry, but we're kind of desperate, and there didn't seem much else we could have done."

"You could have asked."

"Well, yes, but we were assured that your leader, Mr Deux, would probably have said no."

Louvain was silent a moment, observing her, mulling his response. At last, he said: "You're right. He *undoubtedly* would have said no. But I am not Sebastian Deux, and perhaps that is why Citizen Obuya came to me after speaking to Citizen Mitsos."

Marie noticed the other's severe expression *twitch*, and she felt sudden hope. He was trying not to smile! "Ah… and what… what would *you* have said if we'd asked?"

"*Are* you asking?"

Marie noticed Mitsos half turn to look at her from the corner of his eye; and glancing to her side, she saw Kalmik wearing a puzzled expression. "Uh… yes, sir. Now that we are here, I wonder if, uh, for the sake of the people of the *Lisboa*, and possibly for the people of all Tethys, you would allow us to borrow these REEN boats."

Louvain looked at Mitsos. "What do you think, Citizen Mitsos? What do you think the Frist Citizen would make of this?"

"He'd hate it."

"Yes, he would. Yet I have command here and now, and a gesture that leads to enhanced friendship with another state of citizens is likely to be a difficult one for him frame as treason. And so he will seethe, and no doubt he will try to get me another time, another way, but I have been waiting at that door for some time anyway. Dr Lockard..." he was back addressing Marie. "Please take the boats, with my blessing, and send my regards to Joao. But please take them quickly, before someone else finds out and alerts the First Citizen on *Hibernia*."

"Thank you, Captain! Of course! If you could open the doors, we will leave immediately!"

* * *

"Thank you, Noma. I shouldn't have doubted you."

"Oh, you should have. I didn't know what to do. But in the end, Citizen Louvain was right. I went to him because it *was* him. But there was no guarantee he wouldn't have arrested you. I thought it was fifty-fifty."

"If offered those odds of surviving when I was forced on this stupid mission, I would have happily taken them. I'll look you up some time, but now I need to get the fuck out of here before Deux or Boursis fly back to sabotage all this."

"Good luck, Eddard. Stay safe."

Mitsos turned to go, paused, turned back, leant forwards, and gave Noma a swift kiss on the cheek. But he avoided eye contact, and hurried off to the REEN 1 boat, while the exterior bulkhead doors began to part in the mid-distance.

Chapter 43

O'Neill was woken around dawn after a fitful sleep on an uncomfortable single bed in the officers' quarters of the ESU. "Apologies, ma'am," said the black-uniformed woman assigned to her service, peering through the half-open door. "Major Fukuda has important news. He requests that you come to the command centre urgently."

O'Neill reached around the floor, found the nearest object, and threw it at the woman: an expensive shoe smacked into the door a few centimetres away from her head. As the other ducked back out of the room and closed the door, O'Neill screeched: "Fuck Fukuda!" She dropped back onto her pillow and began to massage her tired eyes. But after a few seconds she sat up again, threw off the covers, and dragged herself from bed.

* * *

"So, what is it, Major?" O'Neill swept through the door, held open by her orderly. Her ill mood had not been helped by the fact that she'd not had time to properly bathe and had been forced to wear the same suit she'd worn yesterday, which was now crumpled and somewhat dusty.

Fukuda looked up from a table on which he'd spread a map of the Athol area, having been indicating something to Manfred Traore – the only other present. "Ah, Premier…" He rapidly stood to straight-backed attention. "Apologies for–"

"Yes, yes, I know, you're fucking sorry… Manfred, how the fuck do you always manage to look so sharp? Never mind." O'Neill slumped into the nearest chair. "Sit down, Fukuda." She turned to look to her orderly. "Coffee. *Now*." Then back to Fukuda: "Tell me."

Fukuda sat back down. "Premier, I received some worrying news from a contact in *Hibernia*. Throughout the evening and night, there has been much activity at the East Docks. Lots of armed personnel have been assembling – Stokers and their allies. This is where the converted *Marseilles* trawlers have been docked, but it seems they've been loading up a large part of the Hibernian fishing fleet too."

"An invasion fleet?" said O'Neill, sourly. "Well, it's clear where they're going."

"I have posted lookouts on high ground between here and the land nearest to *Hibernia*. My contact will alert me when their fleet leaves."

O'Neill looked at the two across from her. "So, where the fuck is Joseph? Why isn't she here? Is she already at sea?"

"She's been difficult to get hold of," said Traore, with an enigmatic smile.

"That's true, ma'am," said Fukuda. "None of her staff knew where she was… but her boat docked ten minutes ago. She's been informed and is on her way."

Just as Fukuda finished speaking, the door swung open and Joseph entered, her uniform blotchy with smudges of dirt and her cap in her hand.

"Speak of the devil," said O'Neill. "Where the fuck have you been, Joseph?"

The woman straightened to attention. "Out on patrol, ma'am."

"Shouldn't you leave that to your underlings?"

Joseph's expression was firm. "Some of us like to get our hands dirty."

O'Neill scanned the other's uniform. "And not just their hands. But I can hardly talk, eh? We look like a couple of tramps." She sighed. "Sit down, Joseph. Have you heard the news?"

"The Major's messenger filled me in en route."

The door opened again, and O'Neill's orderly entered, bearing a steaming cup. She gingerly approached, laid it down on the map table by her charge, then backed out without a word. O'Neill raised a warning finger to still the others, then lifted the cup, frowned, blew gently, took a sip, grimaced, and replaced the cup on the table. "Of all the crimes recently committed, *that* has to be among the worst. *Fuck*. Okay – Fukuda: plans."

"I still have over two hundred troops. I have placed most of them in strong points protecting the settlement. Here… here… and here." He indicated the map. "The land of the Range is barren with little cover, and steeply sloping apart from here and over at the shipyard away to the north. They'll not find it easy to land while under fire."

"Could they land somewhere else and then trek here?" asked Joseph, now pulling out a chair, but leaning over the map rather than sitting.

"That's an option. There are a couple of flatter slopes here… and here." He indicated places on the map. "But it wouldn't be easy, and then they'd have to march several kilometres without cover. Just in case, I have a couple of squads as a mobile reserve. If it looks like they are going to drop off short, I'll send them to their landing zone to make things difficult."

O'Neill nodded slowly. "It seems we have some chances still. Do we know how many boats and soldiers the enemy have?"

"My contact's initial assessment is about ten of the converted Marseilles trawlers with their front deck canons, and perhaps thirty trawlers holding the Stokers' force. So, maybe forty craft, with maybe twenty-to-thirty on board each. There could be close to a thousand."

"A thousand?" said Traore. "They can arm that many?"

"We don't really know, sir. They must have been secretly manufacturing weapons for some time – in both the Engine Quarter and on the *Marseilles.* They've been helped by Earthers from the *Leviathan.*"

"Can we beat them?" asked O'Neill. "Five to one aren't good odds, even if we have the terrain."

"It's better than that, ma'am," said Fukuda. "We have the Colonel's ESU. About another two hundred?"

"My troops aren't armed like yours, Major," said Joseph. "I only have a few guns, and most of them are non-lethal. They're sailors not soldiers."

"But you have your boats too, Joseph," said O'Neill. "And they have guns. Fucking big ones for this planet. You can intercept this rag-tag fleet at sea and sink them."

"I think you over-estimate my capabilities, ma'am. I only had eight patrol boats to begin with, then we lost one to the sea monsters when it approached the *Lisboa.* You also had me send one to cover Ardol yesterday, so I've only got six available."

"But yours are proper boats with proper weapons and experienced sailors, Joseph," said O'Neill. "So – intercept them. You can surely defeat this rabble."

"I can damage them, yes," conceded Joseph. "Defeat them entirely? No. And at what cost? It would be better to keep my boats safe and let the rebels try to land. That's when they will be weakest."

"Are you disobeying an order?" said O'Neill.

"No, just making an observation."

Traore leant across. "Ah, Marissa. I wonder if we shouldn't retain at least one of the Colonel's boats for a getaway in case all else is lost. While we two are still at liberty, *Hibernia* lives as a free state."

"And where would we go? Ardol?"

"The source of wealth, yes."

"But if they take Athol," said O'Neill, "Ardol will pose no problem."

"Maybe," said Traore. "But that depends upon how badly mauled they are here – on how good a fight Joseph and Fukuda put up. They might think twice about attacking again so quickly. Maybe we could even, I don't know, sabotage the deposit in some way and threaten to destroy it if they come on."

O'Neill frowned severely. "I doubt whether that would be feasible… still, the threat could have some deterrent effect. Uncertainty plus desperation. Maybe they would deal." She appraised Joseph through hooded eyes. "Leave one boat, fully fuelled and armed. Your best crew. Take the rest and destroy, or at least, delay this flotilla."

"You mean, repel them with my *five* boats?" Joseph's scorn was evident to all.

O'Neill's eyes widened at the impertinence, but before she could lay into the other, the door opened once more and a trooper leant in. "Ah… apologies. Major Fukuda – there's news from the contact in *Hibernia*."

"Yes, Corporal," said Fukuda. "What's the message?"

"*They're on their way*."

Fukuda stood rapidly. "Ma'am… Mr Traore… please excuse me. I need to see to my forces."

"Go, Major," said O'Neill. Then she turned in her seat: "And you too, Colonel. And let me be clear – unless you put up a good fucking fight, don't think of coming back at all."

Joseph stood with stony face, nodded, and followed Fukuda out the door.

* * *

"*Cormorant* – you're falling behind. Keep up."

"We're trying, *Admiral*," Remillard managed to choke off a laugh. He shook his head and grinned at Heiko and De Voe, who stood together at one side of his captain's chair. "But we've got some engine trouble. Battery, I think. We're doing our best. Over."

"Well get it sorted! I don't want to have to tow you. Out."

"Admiral?" said Heiko, with the arch of an eyebrow.

"Well, I can't remember the guy's name," said Remillard. "I don't even know what boat he's on. The pompous fool probably thinks he's the next Nelson."

Heiko shrugged. The little armada was being run with hardly any military discipline or order. They'd been given a radio frequency and told to listen in to commands – but after a waffling pep talk from someone called Falcome (he did remember the name) reminding them of their purpose of smashing the elitists on Athol, they'd receive scant information on intended strategy or tactics. The only commands they'd received were to stick together within the encircling embrace of the Marseillais converted gunboats and to keep listening for further instructions. It was a highly amateurish display.

De Voe patted him on the arm and smirked. "This whole adventure is a joke. Cheer up. Or does this rankle with your professionalism?"

"Sure it does. I'm also worried about the competence of our opponents. They won't have fought any proper military engagements, but I would expect them to at least have some theoretical knowledge on how to play this. We saw the ESU on the *Stavanger*. On board, they were somewhat inept, but I got the sense that they were far happier in their patrol boats on the water. If they've got the ammunition, I expect they'll have the range on the jerry-rigged canons on the

Marseilles boats. They could stay at a distance and pound us. I want to get away before that happens."

"Chill out, Rennie," said Remillard. "It's all going to plan so far."

"That's what I'm worried about, Cass. In war, nothing ever goes to plan. At some point, something unexpected will happen, and things will get dark."

Remillard was right so far: they'd hunkered down on the *Cormorant* through the early hours and remained undisturbed – which meant the NS members they'd tied up had not risked freeing themselves and raising the alarm, while the ones they'd merely robbed had failed to identify them – and then they'd begun to lag behind after setting sail with the armada, slipping from somewhere in the middle to the very rear. They were now level with the two *Marseilles* gunboats at the back of the formation and had allowed a small gap to develop. It was just a question of time as to when they decided to feign engine failure and head off to the *Stavanger*. Heiko didn't take their commander's threat to have them towed seriously.

"So, when are we going to break away?" said De Voe.

"Cass – what do you think?" said Heiko. The Range loomed large ahead – perhaps a kilometre distant.

"That's the south-east corner directly ahead," said Remillard. "You can see Mount Athol now in the distance. The armada will be heading starboard, passing the eastern edge. We want to head to port, and skirt the southern edge and follow the length of the Range to Ardol and the *Stavanger* beyond. So, in terms of breaking off, I'd say any time in the next five minutes. I'll slow her further."

Heiko took no delight in his prediction rapidly coming true.

They'd slipped about a hundred metres off the rear of the armada, when one of the rear guard swung towards them. "*Cormorant*, we're coming alongside," came a voice on the radio. "Prepare to receive. Over."

"What the fuck?" said De Voe.

"Just stay calm," said Heiko. "Look grateful for the help we are about to receive."

The converted gunboat negotiated itself to their starboard side, and its crew tossed a couple of ropes over to *Cormorant's* disguised Stavangeran crew, who tied them off on cleats on the gunwale. After some pulling and gentle coaxing of respective motors, the craft drew close, and a man with a full black beard wearing a grey uniform with a red armband leapt down from the slightly higher deck of the old trawler.

Heiko and De Voe met the man while Remillard stayed at the wheel.

"Citizens, I'm here to help." The man looked at the *Cormorant* crew – forward then aft – and made a circular motion with one hand. "Release us!" Then he turned and shouted back to a couple members of his own crew watching from the deck of the converted gunboat. "Allez allez! To victory, my friends!"

With the ropes cast off, the gunboat edged away and then, with an increased thrashing of motor blades in the blue-green water, began to churn away, back to its original position in the formation.

The man turned back to Heiko and De Voe. "I'm Matthieu. Engineer. Show me your problem."

"I think it best if you come see the captain, Matthieu," said Heiko. He noticed De Voe scowl, but managed to find a cheerful smile. "He'll explain."

Shortly after, Heiko and De Voe left their guest in the company of Remillard and moved to the front of the boat. Looking back, Heiko saw their captain waving his arms about through the window: he'd been talking about an intermittent problem and sudden power drops.

"Let's chuck him overboard," muttered De Voe, giving the engineer the evil eye through the wheelhouse window. Fortunately, the man was too engaged in his conversation to notice.

"Now that *would* give the game away," said Heiko. "This is just one of those things. We'll have to finesse our plan."

"I'm not sure what you mean by that. With this shithead on Cass' shoulder, we're going to be joining the crazies for their own version of D-Day... *unless* we slip down to the engine room and do a bit of sabotage."

Heiko frowned. That was certainly one option, but… "If he's capable, he'll spot anything unsophisticated, and I'm not sure any of us have the competence to do anything clever. And before you suggest just taking a wrench to the motor, Melissa, I don't think we want to properly cripple the *Cormorant* and be stuck out here, adrift, ultimately waiting for rescue."

De Voe gave a roguish smile. "Aw, you read my mind. So, what other option is there?"

"The only one I can see is we cautiously follow the fleet until the firing starts. At that point, when all eyes are elsewhere, we may have a chance to peel away from the back."

"And *then* we chuck the dickhead in the drink?"

With De Voe, it was often difficult to tell, but Heiko thought she was probably joking.

* * *

Colonel Tania Joseph sat in the wheelhouse of her flagship – the patrol boat *Swiftsure* – with the craft's captain sat opposite: they had swivelled their seats to face each other, away from the comms and navigation equipment of their respective stations. The pilot's seat further forward of them was occupied; looking past this, Joseph could see that the heavy machine gun through the front window was manned, too.

The *Swiftsure*, like the rest of Joseph's fleet, was twenty-two metres long, and had a normal complement of eight – though it could carry more than twice that many when necessary, as in their visit to the *Stavanger* several months previously. Today, the ESU marines had remained ashore, as their firepower was limited and Joseph had absolutely no intention of risking their lives in trying to board anyone.

"The gunner looks keen," noted Joseph. "Maybe too keen."

Captain Rahul Singh rasped his neatly trimmed beard. "What do you expect, ma'am? He has a toy and wants to play with it. Aside from target practice, I can't recall the last time it was fired."

"Yeah, and that's the problem. We're not tested in war – personnel or equipment. That's not our job. I never thought war would ever come to Tethys."

"But it has, ma'am, so we must do our best. Do our duty."

"By shooting fishermen?"

"They're not fishermen any more. They have guns. They rose in revolt. They started killing people. And now it seems they're coming to kill the rest of us."

Joseph scowled. "Are you a drinking buddy of Major Fukuda?"

Singh looked surprised. "No, ma'am. I'm sorry, I don't understand–"

Joseph waved a hand to cut the other off. "It doesn't matter." She sighed. "Rahul – to be honest, I really don't know what we're doing. Or what they're doing. Trying to do an amphibious landing on Athol is going to get a lot of them killed, and a lot of our people, too. To what end?"

"Final victory?" mused Singh. "It's in all the manuals, ma'am. Gotta keep pushing until the enemy's unconditional surrender. Gotta plant your flag in the capital. Gotta kill or capture the leaders."

"Perhaps it would be best for everyone if our leaders just surrendered," mused Joseph. "Or we trussed them up and surrendered them ourselves."

Singh rasped his beard some more, him hand covering his mouth. At last he said: "That might be considered treasonous, ma'am."

Joseph laughed. "Fuck you, Rahul. I can see that smile. You know what I mean, *Captain*."

There was a twinkle in the other's eye. "Perhaps. It would save a lot of unnecessary bloodshed. But Her Majesty is stubborn, and we're out here while the ISU is more loyal."

"Some of them, Rahul. Not all."

Singh nodded. "I get your meaning, ma'am, but there's enough that are loyal."

Joseph swivelled her seat so that she was looking forwards, past the shoulder of the pilot. She stretched her legs out before her and crossed her arms over her chest. After a moment, she said: "The gunner… does he have an understudy?"

"Ah, you mean, someone less skilled, and perhaps less *eager*?"

Joseph laughed again. "You read my mind." She turned back and fixed the other with a solemn stare. "But seriously – whatever happens, I don't want anyone on our side to get hurt. *No one*. I'll be damned if any of mine are going to be zipped in a bag to receive an honorary burial at sea. If the crazies in this armada want to fight

O'Neill's crazies ashore, there's nothing I can do about it. But I'll not have the blood of our people on my hands… and I'd rather not have any of theirs on mine either. Understand?"

Singh nodded slowly. "Fire from a distance – maximum range. And aim for the stern – take out their motors?"

"Good man." Joseph leapt to her feet. "All ahead slow, Captain. Give me a couple of minutes to compose a suitable message for the comms officer to relay to the fleet."

"Needs to be quick, ma'am. We'll be in range in five minutes. Perhaps I might suggest: *Hibernia* expects that every man… *won't* do their duty?"

Joseph laughed once more. "Every anti-Nelson needs their anti-Hardy. Two minutes."

* * *

"Was that gunfire?" asked De Voe.

"Sounds like it," said Heiko. "Heavy calibre machine gun. But at some distance." He leapt to his feet: he and De Voe were in the main cabin of the *Cormorant* with most of the party of Stavangerans. "I'd advise everyone to stay inside. I'm going to have a look… *Melissa*?"

"You're not brushing me off, Rennie." De Voe rose. "Let's go. Pedersen – keep this lot inside, yeah?"

Pedersen looked bemused. He turned to Heiko. "Sir?"

Heiko laughed. "Do as Melissa asks, Anders. It'll be easier for all of us."

"Damn straight," said De Voe. "Now go, Rennie. I want to see what's happening."

They emerged onto the deck on the starboard side and walked in line forward to the wheelhouse. Through the side of the large wraparound window, Heiko could see Remillard and the engineer, along with Claude Vardem – who sat at a navigational array. He noticed all three were staring forwards, craning necks. He pulled open the door and peered in. "Cass – news?" Just then, a second, longer rattle of machinegun fire came to him, to be followed a moment later by a hollow *boom* from a cannon.

Remillard started, and looked at him – as did the engineer. "Here… or out there? In here, my friend insists on stressing the engine more than I would like. Out there… who the hell knows?"

"Our escort's off," said De Voe, from Heiko's shoulder. "Look!"

Heiko turned, and saw De Voe was right. The *Marseilles* gunboat to their starboard side, which had been tailing the small armada, was heading off at speed – or relative speed, for the trawlers were not rapid vessels – to the back edge of the formation, in the rough direction of the gunfire. Heiko couldn't see the other rearguard vessel to the port side, as it was obscured by the superstructure. The noise of gunfire was growing, rising and falling with the gusts of the modest wind. A second cannon sounded, and then a third.

"It seems the battle has begun," said Heiko. He turned to look at Remillard again. "How far are we from Athol?"

Vardem turned in his seat, just beyond the pilot's chair. "A little under four kilometres, sir."

Heiko noticed Remillard gurning strangely and twitching his head towards the engineer at his side. He gave a quick shake of the head in return. *Not yet.* Then he felt something pressed into his back from behind.

"Rennie… take it. Let's be safe."

De Voe held a lifejacket in her hand. He noticed she'd already put one on. The Tethyn jackets were an improvement to those of Earth – like a gilet, they would explosively inflate when a certain surface area came into contact with salt water. In the cabin, no one wore them; but now there was no excuse. He smiled thanks, took the jacket, and wriggled into it as he moved further forwards onto the foredeck, where he sat on the raised gunwale and clasped the safety rail that came just above his waist. De Voe settled beside him. Now Heiko could twist and look to port, where he saw the second gunboat maintaining station between them and the edge of the Range, which rose maybe half-a-kilometre beyond. They would have to slip past that one to get away.

"There!" said De Voe, suddenly. "I see something. North-east. A flash."

Heiko focused, and with a blink and mental command, activated his visual augment. His vision zoomed, and a tiny smudge resolved into the form of a motor launch with significantly sleeker lines than the repurposed trawlers of the rebel fleet. Then he saw sparkling at the front, which was accompanied by the rattle of machinegun fire. The enemy boat's target, however, was invisible to Heiko, obscured by the loose pack of the armada. Between him and the distant boat, the *Marseilles* gunboat passed the edge of the 'troop carriers' and headed in that direction, though it was not yet close enough to fire its own weapon.

The next ten minutes proved frustrating viewing for Heiko. He provided commentary for De Voe when he could, but all of the action was taking place forward of them. The bulk of the armada slowed and – like a school of fish – condensed into a tighter formation, as though each boat was trying to lose itself from the external view of the circling predators. But then they came across the first result of the battle: sixty metres to their starboard side, they came upon one of the *Marseilles* gunboats, sitting dead in the water. *No… not dead.*

"Rennie? I can't see. I wish Cass would nudge over a bit."

"In one way, I agree, but he's doing the right thing." Remillard had begun steering slightly to port, and so they'd slipped from being behind the middle of the armada to approaching its left edge, decreasing their distance from the second gunboat stationed at the rear, which had kept its original position. "The boat to starboard is out of action, but stable. *Interesting.*"

"Rennie?"

"It's been shot through the stern. The back is chewed up. And the cannon at the front seems to have been strafed. But that's all."

"That's all? Sounds enough to me."

"Yes, Melissa. That's the point. It *is* enough. Once disarmed and disabled, its assailant could have pumped the main cabin and sunk her – but it didn't. It shows restraint. But that's not just a magnanimous gesture – see, forward of it."

The *Cormorant* came level to the stationary boat, and then passed it, revealing a second boat close by with a flurry of figures at its stern.

"Ah… I can't see what they're doing," said De Voe.

"It's one of the troop carriers. Its crew at the stern are throwing ropes to the crippled boat so they can tow it. And so the attackers have reduced the fleet by two instead of one." Heiko nodded in appreciation. "In battles, the wounded are a bigger burden to their own side than the dead are. They need taking care of. Evacuation. The dead can just be bypassed."

As they slipped by the pair of vessels, the sounds of gunfire continued. Three minutes later, the armada parted slightly, some boats curving to port, others to starboard, negotiating around the obstacle of another stricken boat – this time one of the Hibernian trawlers. As before, its rear was torn up, disabling its props and rudder, and again, a second boat was in attendance, attempting to connect up tow ropes.

"There's no way these can take part in the battle, can they, Rennie?"

"Not in the early assault, no. At best, they might be towed to Athol to disgorge troops at the end, once the battle is over. But it won't take many more disabled boats to reduce the attack force to something the defenders can probably fend off from shore. Ah… and there's another." Heiko pointed. "Way out there. I think it's the starboard rearguard boat. It's drifting well off the pack. If the rebels send another boat to retrieve it, that'll probably get taken out too."

De Voe shook her head and frowned. "I've gotta get me some eyes like yours. No wonder the socialists are pissed off at you. I'm feeling a bit envious myself. Whoa… what was *that*."

Heiko looked around at De Voe and saw her pointing at the water, which here was a pale blue colour with a green tinge, and calm like a bath, the gentle wind doing little to stir its surface. "What did you see?"

"Something in the water. Dark. Fast. Came from the side and went under the boat."

"There are lots of things in the Tethys ocean, no?"

"Yeah, but…" she frowned. "Never mind. What else can you see?"

"Smoke ahead," said Heiko, pointing. "But even you can see that with your inferior eyes."

"Ha-ha!" said De Voe. And then the boat rocked slightly, as though struck off centre. "Fuck!"

Heiko instinctively grabbed the rail, and tensed. But the boat settled, and after a few seconds, he wondered: "Debris in the water?"

"Or we just hit something that got too close," posited De Voe. "If so, it'll have a sore head and think again about getting too close."

Then a faint cry carried to Heiko from somewhere at the edge of hearing. He scanned the armada – the nearest boats now about sixty metres distant. Nothing drew his attention. The boats they'd passed were some way behind, obscured from view by the wheelhouse, so he turned to focus on the boat adrift to starboard. He winked his augment to maximum magnification – and saw that there were figures on the deck, swaying as though drunk. No. *They* weren't swaying – the boat was. And then, as that trawler began to tip, the *Cormorant* juddered a second time…

* * *

In the end, Joseph had agreed with Singh to leave the enthusiastic gunner at their post – as Singh noted, they were the best shot onboard, and accuracy was required for the new plan Joseph had radioed to her small fleet. But she had gone to perch beside him to ensure he fully understood his orders.

The *Swiftsure* raced towards the armada and targeted the nearest converted gunboat. They started shooting at farthest range, but after three or four cannon shots impacted the water some distance away – almost as close to the firing 'warships' as to their target – Joseph had laughed and returned to the wheelhouse. She got on the radio to her fleet. "Joseph here. Ignore their gunboats. They'd miss even if you pulled alongside them. Their cannons are only good for shore fire. Direct approach, disable, disengage, repeat. Over and out."

"We could probably sink the whole convoy," noted Singh.

Joseph nodded sombrely. "Probably. If we had enough ammunition and the full fleet. But selective targeting takes more ammo. We'll give them a bloody nose and something to think about and let them limp home. No one dies today who doesn't have to."

"Very good, ma'am."

Soon, Joseph was receiving reports of success. When the *Swiftsure* took out a gunboat that had been aggressively approaching from the rear of the armada, she added it to the tally: "That's now nine."

The comms operator announced. "Colonel – the *Dart* reports their front line has dropped to dead slow. Their captain thinks they've got the message."

"Victory, ma'am?"

Joseph couldn't restrain a smile. "If only we had flags to hoist – what Nelsonian message would we send to base?"

Then there was a shout from the foredeck. Joseph looked through the window and saw the gunner pointing off to one side. She shrugged at Singh and went to look for herself.

"Ma'am – the boat we hit… it's in trouble. They're…"

The cannon of the gunboat went off again. They were only a couple of hundred metres away, but even so had no fear of being hit. Joseph raised a hand over her eyes to shield it from the glare of the early morning sun, which was barely fifteen degrees over the horizon. She couldn't work out what she was seeing to begin with. It looked like the gun was pointing down at the water.

She turned to look in the wheelhouse window and motioned with her hand to direct the pilot to take them towards the enemy vessel. At about a hundred metres distance she started to notice shadows in the water, which seemed suddenly choppy, the *Swiftsure's* smooth progress becoming bumpy. And ahead, she noticed that the deck of the other boat was now full – the crew having all come outside. Then the cannon fired again, and she saw clearly that it was pointing down. A short distance from the boat there was a sudden fountain of water… water tinged with an unnatural colour. *Reddish.* Then the boat began to swivel, this way and that, as though resting on a flat piece of paper being jostled by a giant, and then it flexed up. They were closing fast when she saw the boat violently tip one way, sending the crew staggering across the decks, tipping a couple into the water. The sounds of fear and panic rose in volume, and then there was a piercing scream. Members of the *Swiftsure's* crew were also scrambling on deck – perhaps on the instruction of Singh inside. One of these shouted and pointed at the water: there were black shadows everywhere.

* * *

Even after the bulkhead door had been opened to allow their exit, it had taken well over an hour for the two REEN boats to be made ready to depart. Sailing the boats wasn't the problem: Arantxa Perez took the pilot's chair in REEN 1 and Benny Zico in REEN 2, and both found the controls to be standard and familiar. What took time was establishing how to control the REEN mechanism itself, and for this Mitsos had proven of little help. The large generator occupied much of the hold of REEN 1, but the extremely fine filament net was spooled in the hold of REEN 2. They realised that the two boats would have to cast off separately, then rendezvous outside the docks in open ocean, navigate to be adjacent, then make a series of connections between the net and sockets in REEN 1 through which the power would be delivered. Only then could the boats set off, gently parting as they progressed in choreographed symmetry, with the net gently spooling out between them while being pulled roughly vertical by weights on the lowest strand. At one point they feared they might need to send for Bennani and his team to help out.

"Come on, *come on*," Mitsos had fretted.

"We're going as fast as we can," Kalmik had replied. "It's a good job your colleague decided to rouse the boss, otherwise we'd never have had the time and space to sort this out. And we really need twice as many to crew the boats as we have. So, respectfully, *shut the fuck up*!"

Marie had appreciated her colleague's frustration – but also Mitsos' concern. As dawn approached, and with it, the prospect of the early shift of fishermen taking to their boats, the chance of someone alerting the *Marseilles'* leaders on *Hibernia* grew. Even Captain Louvain became restless. "I can only do so much," he said. "Whether ready or not, you need to leave."

And so, without being certain they would be able to operate the mechanism, they had. They sailed for a position about two kilometres from the *Marseilles*, and then the boats closed up and Marie, Kalmik, Grande and Resnos put into practice what they had learnt.

"If this fails, I'm not sure what we can do," said Marie. "We can't risk approaching the *Lisboa* – we'll be an easy target for the farmers."

"Jesus, Marie, it's *reapers*," snarled Kalmik. "Words have power. No one's scared of farmers, and we need to be scared of these things."

Marie grimaced. "Point taken." Resnos stood up: he'd crossed the gap from REEN 2 to REEN 1 to fix the final connection, which needed more than a little effort, and which he supplied with his thick, powerful fingers. "Ready?" she asked.

"Let's see, eh?" said Resnos. He took a long step back onto his own boat. "Over to the pilots – and you at the generator."

Marie stepped out of the way, retreating to where Mitsos watched warily at the bow. Kalmik went forwards, and shortly after, Marie heard her yell a command to Perez. The noise of the engine rose and the boat began to vibrate slightly. Marie noticed the other boat start to pull away – and out the net came, the bottom weights sliding from REEN 2 into the calm water, the net itself so fine it was barely visible. She held her breath as the slithering continued and the distance between the boats increased… but the connections held, and then the net tightened at the optimal distance, the top strand hovering a few centimetres above the water.

"How much give is in the net?" Marie asked Mitsos, though with little expectation of a useful reply.

Mitsos didn't disappoint. "Frankly, I don't know. But the net being pulled apart hasn't been a problem, and we've done dozens of trials. I suspect if you drift too far apart, the strength in the net itself will pull the boats back in line."

Kalmik wandered back to join them. "Shall we try the generator now?"

Marie again looked to Mitsos. "How much power does it have? How long have we got?"

Mitsos smirked and raised his hands.

"Fuck, you're useless," said Kalmik. "At least tell us about any limits you've encountered."

"Again, none that I'm aware of. This baby has the mother of all batteries. It's not failed during a trial yet. But it's up to you whether you want to go for an extended cruise with it on. Still, if you're afraid of it not starting when you want it to, I wouldn't worry: it'll start when you press the big red button. Bennani and his engineers knew what they were doing."

"Thank you, Mr Mitsos," said Marie. "That is something. I think maybe we should hold off. There are no farmers… reapers… nearby.

We might not know if it works, so let's save it until we're close to the *Lisboa* and we can see for certain."

"But not too close, eh?" said Kalmik. "I want to have a chance to escape if it looks like a flop."

They continued towards the *Lisboa*, skirting past *Hibernia* and heading towards the Range in the mid-distance. Perez alerted them to other boats in the water – showing on the low-quality radar displaying by the wheel – a short time before the others saw them. And *heard* them.

Marie joined Kalmik at the front of the boat; she was aware of Mitsos following, though he stayed by the door to the wheelhouse.

"Lot of boats," said Kalmik. "Hibernian fishing fleet? But what's that noise?"

Marie could just make out a line of dots on the horizon, with the grey-brown peaks of the Range ahead and off to the port side. "I don't like the sound of that. Explosions? And why would they be fishing out here? They've got three-sixty degrees of ocean to fish around *Hibernia*, and they head towards… ah."

"An invasion fleet? Might make sense of the sound." Kalmik's brow furrowed. "Mount Athol is dead ahead. The shipyard is a few kilometres further on. And the *Lisboa* is slowly approaching the shipyard, having kept a wide berth from Athol. I doubt whether this lot have come to visit us."

"Should we detour around?" said Marie. She looked down at the deck, then up again. "But we're in a converted *Marseilles* trawler. I don't see why they would threaten us."

"Unless they've heard we've stolen the REEN boats," said a voice from behind.

"Jeez, Mitsos, you're paranoid," said Kalmik. "Do you think really they've sent everyone out to find us? And told them to sail close together for protection?"

Marie's frown deepened. "Why are they getting bigger? We're gaining on them. How is that possible in *these*?" She waved a hand to indicate their slow-moving vessels.

"I don't know," said Kalmik. "Trouble? The noise suggests a sea battle… *whoa* – that was definitely a big gun of some sort. And… that buzzing? Machine guns? Fighting the ESU?" She made an independent decision, and headed to where Mitsos stood by the cockpit door. "Arantxa – steer to starboard. Give them a bit of room. We don't want to approach Athol too close anyway."

"Roger that," said Perez. She was quickly on the radio, agreeing a new course with Zico, and then the boat began to head in a more north-easterly direction.

But still the boats grew in Marie's vision – and then almost directly ahead she spotted two more that seemed to have strayed from the pack. Kalmik noticed them too, opened her mouth to speak, but then raised a hand to shield her eyes from Tethys' star, glimmering low above the eastern horizon. "Something's going on," she muttered.

A cold feeling began to creep up Marie's spine. "Katerina… I think now might be a good time to see if the generator works."

"Uh… yeah. I think you might be right."

There was indeed a 'big red button', wired up in the cockpit. Marie turned to peer in the front wheelhouse window. "Arantxa – generator please." Then she sat down on the gunwale to the starboard side, where she could view the other REEN boat and the net below – invisible in the water save for the top strand, along which a line of red LED lights was strung, currently unlit. They were heading roughly towards the pair of boats, which on present course would slide past their port side. The booming of some sort of gun increased in volume, and as they neared Marie started to make out the sound of the machine gun, and on top of this, human voices – shouting, screaming. The nearer boat was listing badly, and then Marie noticed the water being ripped up into a hundred fountains by the machine gun.

"Three… two…" counted Perez loudly, "… one… *go*."

The red lights along the top of the net winked on… and the water about fifty metres ahead exploded.

"Holy…" Marie started, and behind her, Kalmik used much rougher language.

For an arc from roughly thirty degree to port of REEN 1 to fifty degrees starboard, it was as though a line of depth charges had been set off just below the surface of the water. Something beneath was clearly distressed – immensely distressed – and was using every ounce of energy to propel itself, or likely, themselves, away from the REEN boats.

Behind Marie, Kalmik began to laugh manically. "Well, I think you can say that's a fucking positive test. Mitsos, you're useless, but maybe not *fucking* useless."

For a moment, Marie could not speak: she stared at the water, trying to process what was going on. The thrashing line was diminishing, like a receding wave, sweeping up towards and past the two troubled boats. She stood suddenly and looked back. "Arantxa – twenty degrees to port. Straight at the boats."

"But not into them," added Kalmik.

Marie heard a mutter as Perez got on the radio, then they began to turn. The nearest boat was still perhaps two-hundred metres ahead; the second – a much more streamlined affair, which was making dramatic turns in the water – another fifty metres on. As they neared, the wave swept past the two boats and then petered out in the distance. The machine gun stopped firing, and the patrol boat straightened and came up besides the sinking vessel. Nearer still, and Marie – now on her feet, at the bow – was able to see pools of red splotches around the trawler, and people floating within these.

"Dead slow!" Marie heard from behind. *Kalmik.* But she didn't turn – too horrified at the sight of bodies in the water. Partial bodies. She saw one woman – wearing an inflated Tethyn lifejacket – bob up and roll over, revealing that she had been dissected just below the waist. There were more screams, moans, and shouts, and then she thought she heard her name called. *Her* name? She looked up: on the deck of the approaching patrol boat was Colonel Tania Joseph – smiling grimly.

* * *

After Joseph leapt aboard the now-still REEN trawler, her patrol boat edged away and went to aid the remaining living crew of the trawler, which was somehow still afloat in spite of an unseen battering below the water line.

"Thanks for waiting," said Kalmik.

"When you didn't come out, I thought you'd been captured," said Joseph. "I got you to the *Marseilles* and left when I said I would."

"You did," said Marie quickly. "Thank you, Colonel."

"Yes, thanks," said Kalmik, breaking into a smile. "I was just teasing you."

Joseph nodded. "I know. But I'm truly glad you made it. That is some machine you have. I think we can safely say it works. The question is – what are you going to do with it now?"

"We're heading for the *Lisboa*," said Kalmik, eyes narrowing. "That's what was planned all along."

"Sure. But plans change. I'd hoped for a relaxing day sunbathing, then got back to Athol and was told to meet this invasion force and kill everyone in it. That was O'Neill's plan. I changed that, too. You might want to reconsider your plans now."

"Why?" asked Marie. "What's happened?" But she knew what had happened. She turned to face the mass of boats several hundred metres away, the Range rising in the background. During pauses in conversation, she thought she heard more gunfire.

"Shit!" muttered Kalmik.

"Uh-huh," said Joseph. "On the radio, it sounds like chaos. Three of my four other boats have been bumped. The *Dart* was getting trashed until it lay down suppressing fire and got out of there. I hope to fuck it managed to get to Athol, but we lost comms with it a short while ago. But my guys at least have a chance. The reports I'm getting is that the foe are faring worse."

"That's good, isn't it?" said Mitsos, who'd been waiting in the shadow of the wheelhouse door, listening to the conversation on deck.

"Good for your prospects, you mean, Mitsos?" said Joseph. "Maybe good for Melissa O'Neill and Manfred Traore. Probably not actually that good for anyone else. I think Eric's mid-life mellowing has got to me, curse him."

"Eric?" asked Marie.

Joseph waved this away. "The point is, while we're jabbering here, people are getting killed."

"We have to save them," said Marie.

Joseph looked surprised. "That was easy."

"Fucking go-gooders," muttered Kalmik. "Okay. Of course. We'll head for the armada."

"Thank you. But first…" Joseph turned to face her craft, which had finished picking up the survivors from the *Marseilles* gunboat, and waved. Someone on deck rushed to report to the pilot, and the patrol boat made a sharp circle and expertly came alongside.

Joseph scoured the deck, where a dozen survivors in lifejackets were spread. "Who's in command?"

A bearded man with short, black hair slowly got to his feet. Joseph beckoned him to step across, which he wearily did. She caught his arm as it appeared he might stumble and fall into the water. He muttered thanks.

"I'm Colonel Joseph, commander of the ESU. Who are you?"

"Bernard Gascaux, captain of the *St. Malo*."

"Captain Gascaux – we're in trouble, as you've seen, and we're running out of time. What happened to you is happening to the rest of your fleet. We can stop this, but you need to cooperate."

"Oui. I understand. What do you want?"

"I need the radio frequency for your boats. Or better still, I need you to speak to them – and then I'll speak to mine. A truce. No shooting. Your boats need to make way for this pair of boats and then they'll need to settle in close to them. Agreed."

His eyes were wild. "If you can drive off these sea devils – anything!"

* * *

Joseph returned to her boat with Gascaux, while the rest of the rescued crew were transferred to the REEN 2 boat. Two radio messages were duly sent, and the REEN craft headed as fast as they could to the centre of the fleet. As they got close, the water erupted as before, the thrashing, foaming wave rippling through the armada and then continuing through the farthest side where it dissipated. A lot of the boats had been severely damaged below the water line; over the course of the next half-hour, five were abandoned, their crews transferring to other boats of the fleet. It was reported that three more had been sunk before they arrived, and it was presumed that the ESU's *Dart* had perished too. The other three boats of Joseph's command duly cruised around the edges of the armada and took position by the *Swiftsure* – their machine guns pointing warily at the opposing force surrounding it.

Shortly after that, with crews being settled and temporary repairs being made, Joseph returned to REEN 1, and soon after the boat received two more guests. The first was a Captain Luc Falcome, the head of the *Marseilles* fleet, and the second…

"Kai Dures," said Joseph, in a whisper. "Well, well, well…"

Marie had not seen the leader of the Stokers before, though she had heard about him. He was tall, broad shouldered and handsome in a rugged way. "Mr Dures," said Joseph, "this is a surprise."

"Not just for you," he growled. "But for my dear wife, also. Or it will be, when she finds out. But I thought it apt to lead my people. I'll not hide in the depths of the Engine Quarter again." He considered the others gathered there: Falcome – who nodded and gave a half-salute – Kalmik, Mitsos in the background, and Marie herself. He looked between Marie and Kalmik. "I suppose I owe you thanks for saving us from these creatures, though I don't understand how you did it, or who you are."

"Ah, I'm Marie Lockard and this is Dr Katerina Kalmik. We're from the *Lisboa*."

"Now I understand how you know how to beat off these things – it was you who brought them here in the first place."

"Fuck that," said Kalmik, angrily, before Marie could continue. "You make it sound like it was intentional."

"I didn't say that," said Dures, his expression neutral. "It was an observation. A correct one, no?"

"Yes, I suppose," said Marie quickly. "But we didn't realise they would come so far from the *Lisboa*. We must be nine or ten kilometres from it. We deliberately kept away from *Hibernia* and Athol. It seems they're more inquisitive than we thought."

"Probably drawn by the sounds of you killing each other," said Kalmik.

Dures shrugged. "You're the experts. So – what now?" He looked at Joseph. "We are in something of a stand-off."

"You can't carry on to Athol, that's for sure," said Joseph. "Once you're outside whatever protective radius their special machine has, you'll be torn apart if the creatures are still out there. In any case, I doubt you've got the numbers to force a landing now."

Dures looked quickly at Falcome – and Marie noticed the other give a barely perceptible shake of the head. "Maybe, maybe not. So… what else? Assuming we give up this attempt, will you ferry us back to *Hibernia*?"

"I don't think that would be wise," said Marie. "If the reapers follow us – which I suspect they will – it will reveal *Hibernia's* location to them. They like the dark, and living beneath *Hibernia* would suit them fine. Once settled, I don't know how you'll get rid of them."

"Well we can't go to Athol," said Dures. "Even if the Colonel gives her word that we won't be fired upon, I doubt whether O'Neill would stick to it."

Joseph gave a wry smile. "I suspect you're right. What about the *Lisboa* then, which is where this lot are heading?"

"No way!" said Kalmik. "First, it's the centre of their nest. You really do not want to go anywhere near it. And second, there is no way we want all you combatants aboard, bringing your war to our peaceful ship."

"In that case, we need somewhere neutral, with a dock where we can disembark," said Dures.

Joseph nodded. "The shipyard. It'll be a temporary solution only. But once we're ashore, we can think further. I admit, I want to get some solid ground beneath my feet as quickly as possible."

Marie looked at Kalmik, and was about to speak when she saw Mitsos behind her, resting against a railing, legs stretched out before him, a big smile on his face.

Kalmik caught Marie's bemused expression and turned too. "What the fuck are you smiling about, Mitsos? Are you okay?"

"Me? More than okay. My machine – well, not really my machine, but you know what I mean – it's not useless after all. There are people now alive because of it. Fuck you, Tethys!"

Marie couldn't suppress a grin. "It's a shame you only built one."

"Some people are never satisfied. Anyway, let's please go. Just like Colonel Bitch Queen, I'm getting sick of the water."

Once Joseph calmed down, they agreed to head to the shipyard.

Chapter 44

The attack by the creatures from below seemed to have started at the north-east corner of the armada and swept across from there. This meant the *Cormorant* had been relatively fortunate and subject to only desultory assaults. For De Voe, these had still been terrifying. They were often preceded by a dark shape moving through the green-blue water, which sometimes approached and then turned away, sometimes slipped under the boat and then re-emerged on the other side without touching them, but which occasionally resulted in a number of powerful strikes that reverberated through the hull. It was almost as if the unseen creatures were toying with them. They'd soon lined the decks, where those with rifles took ineffectual pot shots into the water. *Largely* ineffectual. Judd Stallings unleashed a full clip at one point, and must have hit something, for the water had darkened where he'd shot and they'd cheered at that. But the next time they saw a shape, its attack had been strident and the bottom had been hammered half-a-dozen times… but then the creature had ceased its efforts, and they'd been left alone for some minutes.

Remillard had been keen to try to escape then, but the presence of Matthieu the engineer had dissuaded him from stating this openly. When De Voe joined him and Heiko for a huddle at one point – with their guest distracted – Heiko had urged patience: "Their other gunboat is near and twitchy," he'd said. "In any case, these creatures – whatever they are – seem distracted by all the targets. If we're caught by them in isolation, they might press their attack."

And then, astonishingly, something had happened, with the water erupting into a thrashing wavefront that had gone from east to west across the formation in front of them while leaving the *Cormorant* untouched.

"The creatures are fleeing," said Heiko. "But there are none near us at the moment, which is why we're in a pool of calm."

They'd then spotted the two trawlers heading towards them from the starboard side, with one of the ESU patrol boats in attendance, and almost simultaneously received a message on the radio declaring a truce and instructing all boats to coalesce around the trawlers. At that point, they'd had no option but to nestle up to the remains of the armada and follow where it went.

It took around two hours for the fleet to reach the shipyard, heading in a loop that took them away from the Mount Athol settlement – to deeper ocean – before curving back north-west. De Voe had never been to the shipyard – few had over the last twenty years – and was impressed by the scale of the place. The abandoned settlement was bigger than that at Athol, and the two giant docks, with cranes, gantries, and construction sheds, could each have accommodated the *Stavanger*. As the two protector boats took station some three or four hundred metres from the smaller jetties for visiting craft, De Voe caught sight at one of the main docks of the shell of a giant ship, which had been started years ago but never finished. She pointed it out to Heiko.

"Rennie – see that? It's known as the Last Ship to some, and the Lost Ship to others."

Heiko took some time to consider the scale of the craft as they inched past it, being near the end of the queue of vessels trying to find space at the jetties. "It's huge, but not as big as the *Stavanger*."

"That's right. *Hibernia* and *Taiwan* are Nation Class ships, or basically states – many don't refer to them as ships anymore. The *Stavanger* and the others are City Class. There are a few Town Class ships too – like this one. It was meant to be for *Hibernia* to off-load some of its growing population, but Earth lost interest in pumping more resources into Tethys, and when the number of liners was reduced from one a month to about two a year, the plan was shelved."

"All this material," Heiko waved a hand. "I'm surprised it hasn't been scavenged."

"Believe me, that's been a persistent temptation. And criminals have occasionally snuck here to load up. Deterring them is part of the role of *Hibernia's* 'navy'. But I guess officially stripping the site would mark a kind of defeat that no one on the planet wants to admit. It's also the only place where a City Class ship can be repaired, so no one wants to remove that possibility, even though none of the big ships has ever experienced a significant disaster."

"A matter of time?"

De Voe nodded slowly. "Yeah. And you can be sure that as soon as this place is reduced there'll immediately be some sort of crisis. Sod's law."

"Perhaps the disaster is with us now. These creatures – what are they? They're like nothing I've read about."

"That's because what happened to us hasn't happened before. It seems the rumours of underwater aliens is actually true. What a cluster fuck."

"It's lucky these strange boats were on hand to save us all." Heiko shifted his gaze back towards the two trawlers, anchored offshore several hundred metres apart. "All trawlers look the same to me – so I've no idea where they came from. But they were escorted by one of the ESU patrol boats. Hibernian? Then why not let the creatures completely destroy the fleet? The rebels? Then why weren't they attached to the fleet to begin with?"

"Maybe they didn't know these sea aliens were going to attack?"

"Hmmm. But they arrived soon after the attack started, and wouldn't have been able to reach us from *Hibernia* if they'd only got the nod on the first encounter. Also, they escorted us here rather than back to *Hibernia* or on to Athol to continue the invasion."

"Yeah, it's a mystery," agreed De Voe. "Let's get ashore and try to find out what the fuck is going on."

The *Cormorant* was duly allocated a space on one of the jetties. As Remillard made final adjustments to settle them into place, the radio repeated a message that all crew should remain onboard for the moment.

"Fuck that," said De Voe. "I'm going to stretch my legs and see what's going on. Anyone coming? Rennie?"

Heiko gave a lop-sided grin. "Is there anything I could say that would dissuade you?"

"No, nothing." She looked around the party in the wheelhouse: Remillard was there, of course, though their *Marseillaise* engineer had gone to have a look at the engines and his place in the cramped space had been taken by Makka Frost. "And nor can you, boss. Sorry."

Frost also smiled and shook his head. "Melissa, I've long given up trying to order you around. But don't get shot, eh?"

De Voe nodded curtly. "Cass? What about you?"

"No. You go on. I'm not leaving that engineer alone." He seemed distracted. "In fact, excuse me, I'm going to go see what he's doing to my baby's innards."

"I'll have a quick word with Anders," said Heiko. "Please, Melissa, wait by the gangplank. We'll disobey orders together."

A couple of minutes later, De Voe and Heiko stepped onto the stone jetty. There were no guards enforcing orders; even so, the crew of the various trawlers and converted gunboats were surprisingly compliant for what De Voe had mentally classed as rough seafarers and rabble: the jetties were clear, though the decks of the boats were awash with curious crew holding excited discussions. All eyes turned on the pair as they walked boldly past the line of moored craft towards a cluster of low buildings set back from the quayside, but no one shouted at them.

Heiko leant in to whisper to De Voe. "Walk with confidence, and they'll just assume we've had special instructions that they haven't."

Where the perpendicular jetty met the quay, De Voe spotted activity around one small building a hundred metres further down. Several people were clustered by a door: they entered. And then she spotted a familiar face striding towards the door: "Rennie – there. Isn't that Colonel Joseph? The bitch who invaded our space and kidnapped Makka?"

"It is. I wonder if she was aboard the patrol boat with the trawlers?"

"Let's find out."

They arrived at the building to find two guards at the door – each eyeing the other warily: one wore the black of the ESU, another wore the green of the Stokers.

"Are we late?" asked Heiko, beating De Voe to the punch.

"Late?" said the ESU guard, rifle wavering uncertainly. "I… Who are you?"

"*Stavanger* contingent," said De Voe. "Colonel Joseph called us. She *must* have told you we were coming?"

The man looked confused. He glanced at the Stoker, who merely shrugged. "No, but… I guess it's alright. You're not armed?"

"Want to search me?" said De Voe, stretching out her arms, a wide smile on her face. "I guess you have to get your cheap thrills where you can."

The guard edged back and looked De Voe and Heiko up and down, likely noticing that they were wearing Stoker green overalls. "No. I guess you're clear."

"Thanks," said De Voe. "Rennie, as he's not going to open the door, will you do the honours?"

Heiko grinned and gave a small bow. "Of course, my lady."

De Voe bustled through the held-open door into an office, the function of which was unclear: it had three chairs, which were turned to face into the centre of the room, a small table pushed against a wall, and a console at one side, with monitors that were dark. The chairs were occupied by two women and a man, all dressed in drysuits – which must have been uncomfortable – while Colonel Joseph was propped on the table, one leg swinging languidly. Aside from these, there were two men standing with their backs to them, one wearing Stoker green and one wearing *Marseilles* grey. At their entry, those seated turned to face them, then the men – seeing the others' distraction, turned to look too.

"Ah, Colonel, here we are," said De Voe. "I hope we haven't missed anything."

Joseph's face scrunched uncertainly as she looked between the two. She crossed her arms. "Who the hell are you, and how did you get here?"

De Voe was emboldened by Heiko's presence at her shoulder. "You've forgotten us already? Here's a little clue. You boarded the *Stavanger* a few weeks ago and stole various things belonging to us. To save you foundering, this is Rennie Heiko, Head of *Stavanger* Security, and I am Melissa De Voe, Deputy Head of Material Resources–"

"And official representative of the *Stavanger*," added Heiko, nudging her gently in the back. De Voe smiled at that, but didn't turn around.

"Oh, yeah, I remember," said Joseph. "The troublemakers. I don't know how you got *here*, or why the guards let you in, but maybe it's time for you to fuck off. This is a private meeting."

Then the tall man in green chuckled. "You're persistent, I'll give you that."

De Voe frowned, then realisation dawned. "We spoke recently. You're Kai Dures. Rebel in chief. Or one of them."

The man nodded, a thoughtful expression on his face. "Speak? No, *we* didn't. I remember you were accompanying your ambassador and stood quietly behind him. I also remember we denied you permission to leave *Hibernia* – yet here you are."

"Yeah, well, we're an independent nation. We don't like people telling us what to do or stealing from us. Are you going to arrest us… or *try* to?"

Heiko cleared his throat. "Melissa… may I?"

De Voe was fuming. She took a couple of slow breaths and glanced at Heiko in annoyance, though she managed to calm herself quickly, and appreciated what the man was trying to do. "Okay. Yeah. Go for it."

Heiko turned to look at Dures, then pointedly ran his gaze over the others in the room. "As Ms De Voe says, we are a sovereign nation, caught up in recent affairs, and now very much a part of everything that is going on here." He made a small sweeping gesture with one hand. "I see representatives from the old and new Hibernian regimes, from the *Marseilles*, and…"

"The *Lisboa*," said one of the seated women, when his gaze settled on her.

"Ah, the owners of the trawlers with the protective device?"

The seated man barked a laugh. "I think who owns them is a matter of debate. In some ways, they're mine."

"Yeah, right," muttered the second seated woman. "You couldn't even start the fucking thing up, Mitsos."

Heiko raised his hands slowly. "I don't want to get into the middle of a dispute. But if the *Lisboa* is here too, then it seems there is representation from every interested party in local affairs – the Hibernian revolt, the Ardol find, and now these creatures. I'd say the *Stavanger* has a clear stake in whatever it is you're discussing here, no?"

De Voe saw Joseph glance towards Dures, but the man was still looking at them. At last, Dures gave a slow nod. "Maybe you're right."

He edged to one side. "Come join us, then. But you'll have to stand with the rest of us *supplicants*."

Joseph laughed. "Proper respect. I like it. Okay, you two can stay. But don't make a fuss – your role in current events is unclear to me."

De Voe and Heiko sauntered up to complete the circle.

* * *

Joseph had been distracted by the new arrivals – but not especially concerned. How the Stavangeran pair had ended up with the fleet attacking Athol was an insignificant mystery. What did concern her was the presence of Kai Dures. Something had been nagging at her since they'd met on one of the REEN boats: now she needed to get it off her chest.

"You have Eric?" she said to Dures, stilling her swinging leg and scrunching forwards to the edge of the table.

"Eric?"

"Nesvorny. Colonel Eric Nesvorny."

"Yes."

"Is he safe?"

"You mean, did I hang him?" Dures looked amused. "In truth, I wanted to, but my wife suggested it might not be the best idea; that he might be useful. So, yes, he's alive. But safe? We'll see."

Joseph scowled. "That is fortunate. If you'd harmed him, there'd be no discussion between us. *None*."

"More than just a colleague? A personal friend?"

"We have a long and complicated history."

Dures nodded slowly. "I understand. It seems my wife was right after all. But though we're talking, I'm still unclear what exactly we are talking about. Your surrender?"

"Or yours," bridled Joseph. "That seems more apt right here and now. If our colleagues sail off on their special boats, you're stuck here, miles from home with no way to safely return. Oh, and no food or other supplies."

"We can always trek to Athol," said Dures. "It's not an easy route along the slopes of the Range, and it might take some time. A day? Two? But it can be done."

"Your advantage in numbers has been reduced," said Joseph matter-of-factly. "And Fukuda will have Athol well defended. I don't rate your chances of defeating him. But go ahead." She folded her arms. "O'Neill ordered me to sink your flotilla and kill as many of you as I could. I decided I'd rather not have your blood on my hands, although it seems my efforts were wasted, as you're determined to get yourselves killed anyway."

"You were trying to disable the boats?" Dures looked surprised… and the man beside him let out a hiss. Dures turned: "Comrade Falcome?"

"Yes, it's true," the man said. "I see it now."

Dures pouted. "A mistake – but I'm glad you made it, Joseph. Perhaps I should thank you."

"Perhaps you should stop being an arsehole."

Dures tensed, but then let the insult slide. "So," he said after a moment, "where does this leave us?"

At that moment, the *Stavanger* Security Chief cleared his throat. Like the others in the room, Joseph found herself compelled to look at him. "If I may," said Heiko. "Perhaps the current situation is an opportunity – a chance for sane people to try to resolve these larger matters." His gaze alternated between Joseph and Dures. "I have seen the leaders of both your sides, and I've not been impressed. O'Neill was responsible for kidnapping our chief geologist and stealing our resources," he smiled at Joseph briefly but didn't press the matter, "while Deux ensured *Hibernia* kept them."

"Deux isn't the leader of *Hibernia*," said Dures. Almost amused, he asked: "And what about me and my wife?"

"You seemed more moderate," said Heiko. "We left that meeting with the impression that we might have been able to deal had the rest of the 'Revolutionary Committee' not been in the room."

"Moderate?" chuckled Dures. "Not fanatics? I'll take that."

Joseph quickly glanced at Falcome – but the captain of the fleet seemed content at the moment to just listen.

"That's right," said Heiko. "But consider this: between you, in this room, you have significance force and therefore significant influence. On the one hand, you have most of the Stoker army, and most of the *Marseilles* navy. And Colonel Joseph ultimately has command of the

Hibernian navy. Our friends from the *Lisboa* also seem to have the only means to fend off these creatures. In short, right here, you have command of most of the world's power. You can kill each other if you like. Or maybe our saviours can just withdraw and let these creatures kill the lot of you. Frankly, I'm not sure where the greater peril lies – in the water out there, or in the boardrooms of Athol, *Hibernia* and *Marseilles*. Do you want to carry on fighting?" A sparkle seemed to enter the man's eye. "Or maybe you lack confidence to make decisions and would prefer to contact your superiors?"

"Fuck, no," said Joseph suddenly. "O'Neill and Traore are poison. Fukuda too. The ESU are loyal to me… or what's left of it. The ISU…" she frowned and looked at Dures. "To Eric. They'll follow him – or most of them will. Fukuda's Squad Five will stick with him."

"Again, my wife shames me in her astuteness," said Dures. "I must admit, when I met Nesvorny he wasn't the devil I expected. If he was sincere in what he said at the time, then *maybe* he would fight for the light."

"Then why not bring them both here," said De Voe suddenly. "The adults. Your wife. This guy, Eric. Do it secretly, without the others knowing. Then you'd have two speaking for the new regime and two for the old."

"So… not Deux?" said Dures, looking askance at Falcome.

"No. I saw that cunt at work in our meeting," continued De Voe. "Would you trust him to do what was right, or would he do what was best for himself? Maybe the admiral here is more reasonable."

Falcome at last stirred. "I do not like this discussion. You insult the First Citizen." He looked at De Voe, then Heiko, then Joseph, and finally at Dures. "We are meant to be allies. We are here to free the people. To destroy the enemy. This is not what we agreed to. I must contact the First Citizen." He turned to leave, but Heiko moved quickly and was suddenly between the man and the door, arms raised in a sign of peace, but using his body as a barrier. Falcome didn't have a rifle, but he did have a knife in a scabbard at his belt. "Get out of my way."

"I think you should stay," said Heiko. "I'm asking nicely."

"Fuck off!" Falcome dropped one hand to the hilt of the knife and tried to push past Heiko, who refused to give way. The *Marseillais* started to draw his knife, but didn't get far: Heiko's hand shot forward, gripped the other's wrist, and twisted. Falcome groaned and struggled to disengage, but Heiko twisted more, forcing the other onto his knees.

Heiko looked up at Dures. "Your call. He's your ally."

"Is he?" mused Dures. He shook his head unhappily. "No. *He is*. More or less. We owe the *Marseilles* and I won't see them cheated for their efforts. But the comrade and his master are two men, not the whole ship. And I *would* like to continue this discussion, so… give me his knife."

Heiko retrieved the weapon and handed it over, all the while controlling Falcome with pressure on his elbow joint.

Dures stepped close, took the weapon, and held it before Falcome's eyes. "Comrade – you will stand in that corner and say nothing. I will bind you if I have to, but that would be undignified. And if you try to call for aid or rush out, I will cut you. Do you understand?"

Falcome winced as Heiko twisted his arm once more, then sharply cried: "Oui-oui!"

Heiko led the other to the inner corner indicated by Dures, released his hold, and left the man rubbing his wrist and elbow and muttering dark curses.

"Well, that was fun," said De Voe, once Heiko was back at her side. "Anyway, if you're going to fetch these others to have a proper peace conference – or whatever it is you're planning – you should bring Magnus Solbakken, too."

Heiko's brows rose. "Melissa? That is extending the brief."

"Yeah, well, maybe it needs extending. Look, Magnus represents the *Stavanger*, and we have a stake in this, too. Not just our stolen resources, but the Ardol find. We're nearby, so potentially at risk from these sea monsters. And we're not exactly weak – or won't be once you whip us into shape, Rennie. We have skin in the game. We might be able to help out. Allies or enemies…" she turned to the others. "It's your choice."

Joseph laughed. "I'm not sure how far I trust you, after you tried to hide your find from us. *You* were the authors of your own misfortune."

"Yes, that's what we heard," said Dures.

De Voe looked between Joseph and Dures. "Look, it's true we weren't totally up front in revealing our find to *Hibernia*, but that's because of O'Neill and her crowd. We thought they'd take the find away from us and leave us with little… and that's what's happened. And now this little shit, Deux, seems to have his eyes on the site. Would you two rather leave Ardol in his hands? With Sullivan? Or in ours? We're not hoarders. If we get our fair share, I'm sure we'll be more than happy to contribute our expertise and help develop the mine for all of us. In spite of what Rennie said, I don't really represent the *Stavanger*, and we can't contact our leaders, but Magnus can."

"So, let me get this straight," said Joseph. "You're proposing we have a secret conference with adults only? Use the shuttle? Bring Karyn Dures, Eric Nesvorny, and this Stavangeran guy–"

"Ambassador," nodded De Voe.

"Right." Joseph turned her attention to the seated trio. "And someone from the *Lisboa*, since you know the most about these creatures and have the only weapon capable of fending them off."

"Ah, yes, that's true," said Marie Lockard. "I mean, 'yes' to knowledge, but in truth the weapon – these REEN boats – they belong to the *Marseilles*… and to Mr Mitsos to some degree."

Dures scowled. "Which means we definitely need the *Marseilles* represented. I do not know how to square this circle."

"I have an idea," said Marie. "What about the captain of the *Marseilles*? We met him when we tried to, um, *borrow* the REEN boats. He caught us, but let us go. Eddard – tell them."

"Louvain?" said Mitsos. "I don't know much about him, but he's captain of the ship. With Deux and Boursis in *Hibernia* he seems to be in command. He's clearly not a fan of the little Napoleon, so he's good in my books."

Joseph looked between the seated trio and Dures – who suddenly smiled. "I like this plan," the man said. "Joseph?"

She shrugged. "It beats shooting each other. But there are still people out there who need to be dealt with. Meantime, sure, let's see if your wife is up for joining us and bringing Eric and this ambassador, and see if Louvain will come too. Where will we meet? Here?"

Marie raised a hand tentatively. “I would suggest the *Lisboa* as neutral territory – if you’re okay with that, Katerina.” She glanced at the woman at her side, who shrugged and waved a hand for her to continue. “Yes. And maybe the Captain-Governor can represent us, or at least, act as moderator. I can’t imagine anyone better.”

Messages were soon sent from the *Swiftsure.*

Chapter 45

Colonel Eric Nesvorny had been kept in solitary confinement since his capture, isolated from all others and from any information about what had been going on in *Hibernia* and the wider world. Aside from his meeting with Kai and Karyn Dures, he'd only been let out of his small cell twice – each time for the purpose of a rather desultory interrogation. Given the lack of urgency in these, he'd assumed that resistance on *Hibernia* was almost non-existent and that the rebels' victory was complete. In short, his captors didn't really know what to do with him. It was therefore a surprise when his door was unlocked one late afternoon several days after his surrender. A man in green overalls entered the cell.

"Up, prisoner. You're going on a journey. Don't make a fuss, or we'll shoot you."

Nesvorny stood up from his cot. "A journey?" A euphemism for a final trip to the scaffold? After his encounter with Karyn Dures, he didn't believe it. "Where? Do I need my things?"

The man smirked at him: Nesvorny knew he looked dishevelled, his only outer garment being the black uniform he'd been wearing on capture, the jacket of which hung over the chair by a small desk – the only furniture in his room bar the bed. He'd been given several changes of underwear, but apart from that, his only possessions were a toothbrush, comb, a pad of paper, and a couple of pens. Perhaps they thought he'd use the latter to write a confession? "No. Just your jacket. You should smarten up, but you can do that later. Come now."

The man hadn't been armed, but his two colleagues outside the door held rifles. One was keen to use the butt of his to give Nesvorny a small shove in the back, which he bore without complaint.

The trio led him – two behind, one in front – down to a sub level. It quickly became apparent that they were taking him by rarely used corridors. They dropped to Sublevel Two, then Sublevel Three. Given his cell was in the control complex in the centre of *Hibernia*, a route that lacked people was a carefully chosen one indeed. It was clear that this was intentional – but why? If some other faction was smuggling him out from under the Dures' jurisdiction, that had ominous implications. Someone wanting revenge? A rescue by his side was out of the question, so what else this could be? After some minutes he began to contemplate taking action to escape. His guards hadn't cuffed him, likely because he wasn't seen as a threat… or was it to encourage him to make a break, justifying shooting him in the process? He wasn't as fit as he'd once been, and age had slowed him, but he was still a strong man and could fight. He kept an eye out for opportunities, and yet he was curious. This was something unexpected, and therefore likely to be significant. He suspected that his life story was about to advance in one way or another, good or bad, and whatever resolution awaited him, it at least meant freedom from his claustrophobic cell.

North.

They were heading north – that was clear from the occasional marker painted in bright yellow at head height on the junctions they were passing. *Spaceport?* Was he being flown to exile? That would make sense: it would remove him as a threat forever – in one way humane, yet also inhumane, for he'd spent his entire life on *Hibernia* and had no desire to relocate to any of the other city ships. Nevertheless, he began to think about exile options. Where was close? He knew the *Stavanger* was off Ardol, and the *Lisboa* was near. He recalled from a discussion with Joseph that the latter claimed to have some improbable infestation. *Aliens?* Laughable. And then there was the *Marseilles*, which would definitely have been the worst option… but also the most likely? They'd be able to keep an eye on him there. But if so, where were the grey shirts? He would have expected a joint escort. Maybe they were waiting to receive him on the runway?

They at last took stairs up to the second and then the first sublevel. The group's leader called a halt in an undistinguished corridor, hissed a command to the others, then yanked open a small bulkhead door set in the grey wall; he disappeared, leaving Nesvorny behind with the armed guards. The man didn't reappear for several minutes, and when he did, it was only to poke his head through the door and silently beckon them forwards. He heard the man mutter to his men: "… been cleared."

They were in a service corridor normally used by automated carts, which again suggested they were near to the spaceport. Soon after, Nesvorny saw the spaceport logo – a stylised 'S' – on a closed set of double doors. He was right. At the end of the corridor was a lift: they entered, rose to Level Zero, and the door opened to reveal the admin section of the spaceport, with various offices behind glass walls and doors – all dark. At the end of the corridor, a door opened onto the outside, and a comforting breeze caressed Nesvorny's face. It was twilight.

The first man suddenly had a blanket in his hands. "Cover your head," he told Nesvorny. "Do not look up or I'll be forced to get rough. Got it?"

This might be his last chance to act, but Nesvorny's curiosity was greater than his fear. He allowed the blanket to be draped over his head. All he could see now was the concrete edge of the landing pad. He was bustled forwards until they came to a small cart, just big enough to take all four of them. He allowed himself to be manipulated onto it. And then the cart was off, on a journey that took barely thirty seconds. After they stopped, he was brusquely told to get down, and almost instantly, from under the blanket, saw the bottom step of a shuttle. The prod from a gun barrel got him moving up. He entered a dimly lit cabin, finding himself in an aisle with seats to each side.

"Thanks, Seumus," said a woman's voice, smooth and deep. Then: "Colonel – you can come out now. Take a seat."

Nesvorny felt the blanket tugged off from behind, and saw he was indeed in a shuttle cabin, next to an open section where pairs of seats faced each other across small tables. In one of these sat Karyn Dures, hair long on one side and short on the other, revealing a small, upraised white line of scar tissue. He straightened, quickly glanced around to confirm that – with his guards moving to the back of the cabin – they were otherwise alone, and slid into a seat opposite the woman.

"Ms Dures – this is a surprise."

"For both of us." The woman's blue eyes weren't unfriendly. Amused? "It's funny how circumstance can radically disrupt intentions. A month ago, I had plans to display your severed head atop the highest point in *Hibernia*. Yet here we are."

"Together in a shuttle? I take it you're not planning on having me thrown out from twenty thousand feet, so can I ask where we're going? I wondered about exile, but that wouldn't account for your presence here."

Karyn settled back in her seat and interlinked her fingers on the table in front of her. "I received a strange invitation several hours ago. I have spent the time since wondering whether to accept. In the end – here we are. I decided it would do no harm to hear what other players in this great game have to say."

"A meeting somewhere with other 'players'?" Nesvorny frowned. "You mean opponents?"

"Some yes. Some… probably no."

"And why am I here?"

She smiled. "You were invited, too. You see, I quickly decided that *I* would certainly go to this meeting – what I've spent most of the afternoon doing is pondering whether to bring you as well. In your little cell, you're no threat, but outside?" She momentarily unclasped her fingers and waved one hand airily. "You might pose a problem. But you might also provide an opportunity. I wondered whether *this* was actually the moment I've been subconsciously waiting for."

"Intriguing. Can you tell me more?"

Karyn paused a moment to consider him. *Calculating.* "It seems I must, for though it pains me to confide in you, you'll know soon enough anyway. In a nutshell, these are the facts. This morning, our revolutionary alliance set out to attack the remnants of the old Hibernian state on Mount Athol. En route, we were attacked by the ESU. We expected that. What we didn't expect was to then be attacked by a horde of underwater creatures that the *Lisboa* seems to have ferried with it from some cenote down south. *Vicious* creatures. They sank some of our fleet, but also attacked the ESU boats."

"Ah… would these be the aliens I heard about?"

"You knew?"

"Not really. Colonel Joseph told me a week or two ago, saying the *Lisboa* had called for help. Neither of us really believed what they were saying, but it seems they weren't exaggerating."

"No, they weren't." Karyn unclasped her hands again and leant forwards slightly. "In fact, these creatures might well have sunk the entire fleet – and claimed over a thousand lives – had it not been for an astonishing intervention. It appears that the *Marseilles* was actually in possession a device that is able to fend off the creatures. A party from the *Lisboa* found out about it, and they somehow managed to persuade the *Marseilles* to lend them a pair of trawlers on which it is stowed. They arrived in the nick of time, and ferried the combined fleet – ours, and the remaining boats of the ESU – to neutral ground at the old shipyard. And there they are all stuck, unable to move without the shield provided by these converted trawlers." She sat back again.

Nesvorny shook his head. An assault? Aliens? But the biggest puzzle was: "The *Marseilles*? If they countenanced this, why the neutral ground? I thought they were your allies."

"Very astute, Colonel." Another pause. Thinking what she could tell him? "The people of the *Marseilles* are our allies, as are their leaders… *mostly*. Their First Citizen seems to have wider ambitions. He is currently ensconced in the command centre behaving like a conquering hero. And he's been ferrying more of his armed cadres across, including a Captain Boursis, whose Apparatus has kindly taken over internal security – having the experience in these matters that my people lack."

Nesvorny smiled. "And replacing the people you sent to Athol?" The woman's expression turned severe; she didn't answer. "And I'm guessing most of your guns are on the stranded fleet, too? But that still doesn't explain this device you're talking about, or why… ah!"

"You're perhaps more attuned to matters of security, espionage, and politics than I am. Tell me what you see."

"The device on the boats came from the *Marseilles*, but the ship's leader is in *Hibernia*, therefore their donation wasn't necessarily authorised by him… or even known about by him?" Nesvorny looked down, thinking. He nodded and looked back up, holding the other's sharp blue eyes. "And this surreptitious departure with not a grey uniform in sight tells me that he doesn't know about this meeting either, and therefore hasn't been invited. And yet I have."

"Yes. There may be a role for you."

"The ISU. I sent half to Athol, and they're still a threat. They're probably under Fukuda's command, but if I reappear, their loyalty will revert to me. Ah – and the rest of my people are on *Hibernia*. Disarmed? Imprisoned? But they could still be reformed. A counterbalance?"

"Too quick," muttered Karyn. "Maybe you should go for a dive from twenty thousand feet after all."

"I'm not on your side, Ms Dures. But if I can help restore the law – and return the peace – and you can consider an accommodation for *all* the people of *Hibernia*, then I might not be your implacable enemy either."

Karyn held his gaze. "Yes, and that is why I decided to bring you. But be aware of this, Colonel: you are still my prisoner. We are going to the *Lisboa*, where you have no allies to rescue you. Do not play games or try to escape. Listen. Say your peace. And we shall see what develops. If I'm unhappy, the diving option is still open for the return flight. Understand?"

Nesvorny folded his arms. "I understand. Though what I don't understand is why we're still sitting here on the ground. The longer we wait, surely the greater the chance of this flight being discovered."

"True. We're waiting for one other." Karyn looked past Nesvorny at the sound of the exterior door opening. "And hopefully, this is him." She stood, and Nesvorny watched her face break into a smile. "Ambassador Solbakken. Thank you for coming…"

* * *

Kate was angry when her mother came through the door to their apartment. "You're alive! Well, thanks for telling me!"

Marie's face fell instantly. "Oh, Kate, I'm sorry. Really. It's been a hectic few hours."

"You could have called. I've been waiting here all this *bloody* time for news, expecting to get a call to say that you weren't coming back." tears sparkled at the edges of her eyes, which she vigorously brushed away.

"Oh, Kate…" Marie dropped the kit bag she'd been carrying in one arm and awkwardly approached her daughter – mere metres away in the kitchen section – raising her arms to embrace her. They'd always had a mature relationship, rather than an affectionate one. It was her ex-husband who had always seemed to have a better emotional connection with their child. Kate stiffened, but then sagged, let her head briefly rest on Marie's shoulder, but then raised her arms to gently disengage and stepped back. She raised another forearm to swipe at her eyes.

"*Fuck*, Mum…" Kate quickly raised a finger, "and don't say anything about swearing. I've been inventing new phrases the last couple of hours that would make adults turn white. What the *hell* has been going on?"

Marie looked down shyly. "I'm glad to see you too, Kate. I'm exhausted and need some sleep before this evening… but let's sit and I'll tell you everything. I know I've been bad, but I could really do with a coffee."

"Do you want to sleep *or* have coffee, Mum?" snapped Kate. "You can't do both. Oh… *hell*." She turned away to the kettle, which at least gave her the chance to hide her face.

"Thanks, Kate. Let me go change…" Marie was still in her drysuit, "and I'll explain all."

When Marie returned from her bedroom, now casually dressed, she found her daughter sat at the kitchen table, arms crossed, trying to maintain an angry expression. Marie had to quickly disguise a smile with one hand. There was a cup of coffee set on the small table where she was expected to sit. She removed her hand, nodded thanks, flashed a smile, then sat and picked up the cup; blew; sipped.

"Well?" said Kate impatiently.

Marie lowered her cup. "It's been an interesting few hours…" She related how she had taken the shuttle to the shipyard, then been ferried to the *Marseilles* on Colonel Joseph's patrol boat. She told of the unproblematic swim to the internal dock, and the surprising denouement to their attempt to steal the so-called REEN trawlers…

"REEN?"

"Apparently it stands for 'Rare Earth Extraction Net'. It's a nice idea, but doesn't really work. Anyway…" Marie continued to describe the return journey and their happening upon the invasion fleet as it was being attacked.

"The monsters! I thought they just hung around here, vandalising the ship."

"It was a surprise to us, too," said Marie. "But maybe it shouldn't have been. They're an intelligent species. Inquisitive. Maybe they have been sending the equivalent of search parties out all the time, perhaps to find another cenote or sea forest."

"And instead they found more food."

Marie frowned. "Well, I'm not sure why they keep attacking us. Food is one possibility, but I don't really buy it. They're apex predators in a rich world. I'm sure their environment provides them with plenty enough to eat."

"I might almost forgive them if they *did* see us as food," said Kate. "That's *Nature*. Otherwise, they just seem like a species of murdering psychopaths, and that makes Sara right: they are monsters. Anyway, go on."

Marie concluded her tale about how they had convoyed the battered fleet back to the shipyard, and the meeting they'd had there with the principals of it. They'd then left the REEN boats behind, and flown back to the *Lisboa* on its shuttle.

"Who's on the boats if you're here?"

"Mike, Marco, Arantxa, and Benny. They're at anchor, so the boats just need to be kept in place – they don't need a full crew. Katerina came back with me, as did Eddard Mitsos and a few others."

"Who exactly?"

"Colonel Joseph of the Hibernian's ESU, a man called Kai Dures – one of the rebel leaders – and a couple of others from the *Stavanger* who were with the fleet for some reason that's still unclear to me."

Kate thought a moment. "You said something about this evening. What's happening then? Is it something to do with these others?"

Marie smiled over the top of her raised cup. "Yes, that's right. There's going to be some sort of conference – about the aliens, the Hibernian rebellion, and other things. Apparently, there's been an important geological find at the opposite side of the Range that might provide important resources to us all. Anyway, it's a big thing. Invites have been sent to other important people. There's been one acceptance already, and Joao Nacimiento will be there too, of course."

"And you're going as well – as an expert on the monsters?"

Marie nodded. "And Katerina. And probably this man, Mitsos."

Kate's anger had now well-and-truly dissipated. She looked thoughtful. "This sounds like a chance to make history, Mum, and you're involved. Wow."

Marie's tablet flashed an alert. She'd left it on the table before heading to change. She pushed her cup aside and brought the tablet towards her, tilting it up so only she could see. "I'd better take this – it's from the Captain-Governor."

Joao Nacimiento appeared on the screen. "Dr Lockard," the other smiled through his heavily lined face. As usual, he was in his uniform. "I am glad to catch you. I suspected you might be asleep after your long night."

"That's where I'm going shortly, sir. How can I help?"

"Ah, well, it is just a logistical issue. Professor Figueroa has agreed to moderate the meeting. As a participant, I can't do it myself. He suggested that he could use a hand – a notetaker, rapporteur, that sort of thing. A thought occurred to me. Why not have someone young, enthusiastic, competent, and with intimate knowledge of what has been going on with these reapers."

"Uh, yes, that sounds like a good idea. One of the junior scientists, maybe?"

"Oh, I was thinking about someone much more involved than that – someone who has proven remarkably astute in current affairs." Nacimiento's smile broadened. "What about your daughter, Dr Lockard? Young Kate. Do you think she would be interested?"

Across the table, Marie heard a gasp. She glanced up to see Kate with a wide smile on her face and her hands clasped together in a pleading gesture. She fought her own smile, then looked back at the screen, and declared: "I think that's a good idea, sir. I think I can guarantee her positive response."

"Excellent! Well, enjoy your nap, doctor. Then brief dear Kate, and bring her with you. Miguel is making arrangements, and he'll inform us of the exact time and place beforehand."

The picture turned to black, and Marie lowered the tablet to the table. She looked up: "Want to join me at an historic event, Kate?"

For once, her daughter was lost for words.

* * *

Shuttles from *Hibernia* and the *Marseilles* now crowded next to that of the *Lisboa* on the great ship's landing deck. Some of their occupants had been met and escorted to the conference room in the science centre where the meeting was due to take place, but not all: several armed people wearing green had been asked to remain behind on the Hibernian shuttle – much to the annoyance of Karyn Dures. For a tense few minutes it looked as though the rebel leader might fly home, but in the end she agreed to attend the meeting, though only on the understanding that one of the other passengers – a Colonel Eric Nesvorny – would not be allowed asylum, and would be compelled to return to the shuttle with her at the end of the event. Apparently – Kate was told by her mother, in a whisper – the military man had also been made to promise the woman on his honour that he would abide by this agreement.

Kate currently sat at a small table next to Miguel Figueroa, who was to chair the event. This table had been a segment of a bigger, hollow, oval table, until it had been pulled slightly away from the rest to create separation between the administrative and the active meeting participants. As Figueroa made introductions and set out the meeting's purpose, Kate momentarily looked away from the tablet on which she had already tapped some notes to consider the others present.

To her immediate left was the rebel contingent – Kai and Karyn Dures – who had arrived in separate shuttles. Next to these were a trio from the *Stavanger*, who she'd recorded as Ambassador Magnus Solbakken, Deputy Head of Material Resources Melissa De Voe, and Head of Security Rennie Heiko. She recognised the latter, with the copper interface by the side of one eye, as the man who'd sat next to them on the *Leviathan's* shuttle – a fact that her mother had missed. She remembered he had been kind, and she was pleased when he'd recognised her too – his eyebrows rising and his face contorting into a smile as he'd winked at her. Next – and almost opposite to them – was the Earther, Eddard Mitsos, whose status was unclear. He'd made a fuss about his seat, refusing to sit near either the Hibernian or rebel representatives, attaching himself to the *Lisboa* contingent – perhaps unsurprisingly, as he'd spent his recent time with them. Her mother had told Kate beforehand that she suspected Mitsos wanted to stay on the *Lisboa* afterwards, and that he had no intention of going to either *Hibernia* or the *Marseilles* again.

The *Lisboa* contingent sat to the other side of Mitsos: her mother and Katerina Kalmik flanking Captain-Governor Joao Nacimiento. Beside Kalmik was a grey-uniformed individual with a peaked cap and a small black beard who was apparently the actual captain of the *Marseilles*. Though not its ruler, Marcel Louvain had informally acquired that role because of the First Citizen's absence in *Hibernia*.

And finally, there were two people in black uniforms (both somewhat stained and crumpled): Colonel Eric Nesvorny and Colonel Tania Joseph. Nesvorny was the figure of contention, and where he sat had been the source of some debate, though in the end it had been decided that he belonged next to the other Hibernian representative. Kate had watched the pair's faces light up at the sight of each other: the woman's with open pleasure, the man's slipping from a severe expression and then back again once he managed to re-exert control.

Kate startled at the mention of her own name: Figueroa had just concluded introductions, ending with: "… who in spite of her relatively young years, has already played an important role in helping to identify and understand the creatures we refer to as *reapers*. Kate will ensure all agreements and critical points are recorded." Kate noticed the eyes of those around the table now upon her, and found herself blushing. She caught another smile from Heiko and dropped her head to attend to her tablet.

"Now," said Figueroa, "let us begin. If I may be presumptuous, it seems to me that a critical matter we should attend to first is the reapers. Indeed, it is their presence that has forced the various parties here into juxtaposition. If there are no objections, perhaps I can ask one of my colleagues from the *Lisboa* to relate the state of play here."

Nacimiento nodded. "Just so, Miguel. Katerina, would you like to go first?"

Kalmik slouched back in her chair and waved a hand. "To hell with seniority. Marie – you've always seemed to have a better handle on them than the rest of us… you and your daughter." Kate winced at that. "Go ahead."

"Ah, yes," said Marie, "thanks, Katerina. I'm not sure how much detail to go into. We are preparing a lay report on the creatures, which we can send to you all shortly. In brief, they live in and around the black cenotes and seem to be responsible for cultivating the fringe forests. In our research, we found that these forests have slightly different characteristics to the ones in the open ocean – notably, better nutrient profiles – but it's their ordered nature that first gave us a hint that there was intelligence behind them."

"Ordered?" said Karyn Dures.

"They are planted in rows, like crops on Earth. Completely artificial. Anyway, I guess we thought their planters must be herbivorous, so we initially named them *farmers*. However, it seems that they – like us – are omnivorous. We have found very clear and visual evidence of this."

"They're quite partial to *human tartare*," said Kalmik.

"Yes," continued Marie, "but – as I was saying to Kate not long ago – I don't think they regard us as an important food source, as opposed to opportune nutrients. Another theory is that their aggressive response to us is a reaction to a perceived threat. Our initial interactions with them were cagey until a couple of boats attempted to harvest from their forest. That's when they *really* turned."

"They didn't attack you until then?" asked Karyn, her expression intent.

"That's a matter of dispute," said Kalmik. "To me, they've seemed quite aggressive all along, but…" she shrugged, "it was Marie who had the first interactions, so I guess I have to defer to her."

"They were certainly curious," said Marie. "But no, the incident with the threshing boats was a critical moment. They sank the boats, and ever since, they have been hyper-aggressive towards us. They even followed us beneath the *Lisboa*."

"That seems odd," said Karyn, who had taken the role of chief interrogator. "Surely that's out of their comfort zone. The environment must be completely different to their home."

"Ah, yes, it is a puzzle. I do have a thought, though – one I mentioned briefly, but which we haven't really discussed yet. I wonder if they are using us as an opportunity for a migration event."

Kalmik sat forwards and peered at Marie around the intervening bulk of Nacimiento. "Migration?"

"Yes. We know they are sensitive to the light, and we know they are territorial and aggressive. Maybe the population at their cenote is reaching its limit, and rather than migrating through the open ocean to find another cenote, they opportunistically decided to accompany us. Under the *Lisboa* they have a full twenty-two hours of darkness, a place to anchor, and – as we've found out – a source of food if necessary. And that might explain why they were so far away from the *Lisboa* when they encountered the fleet – they have been ranging out every day in search of a new, more permanent home."

"Yes, Marie, my dear, that makes a kind of sense," said Figueroa. Then his look turned sheepish. "Ah, as moderator, I perhaps exceed my remit, but that is a hypothesis worth considering."

"Yeah, but what I want to know," said Joseph, "is why you decided to bring these things here. Why didn't you get rid of them at the outset instead of ferrying them to the most important human hotspot on the planet?"

Kalmik tensed. "We didn't know they were with us at the start!"

"That's true," said Marie. "It was only a few days after we left their cenote that we found them… or the kids did… I mean, Kate and her friends. But then we were in trouble and worried about damage to the ship, and this seemed the only place on the planet where we might be able to beach if necessary, or find a dock to conduct repairs."

"Exactly, Dr Lockard," said Nacimiento. "We certainly had no intention of bringing these creatures here, but we were left with little choice. And I am still unclear as to the extent of damage being done to our beloved sea turtle. These reapers might be doing anything under our ship."

"We're not going to sink, are we?" said Mitsos, jerking forwards in his chair. "*Fuck!* Is nowhere safe on this damned planet?"

"Calm down, Mitsos," said Kalmik. "We're still upright, and we haven't seen any debris from beneath the ship floating in our wake." But then she frowned. "Though they took out all our sensors, so who knows?"

"The main problem at the moment," continued Marie, "is that our fishing and harvesting fleets are confined to docks. The reapers seem more than happy to attack them if they try to leave. But if this is a migration event, then I wouldn't expect them to damage their shelter. That wouldn't be… *intelligent.*"

"*If?*" said Mitsos. "Why don't you go and check?" He raised a hand to his forehead. "Because they'll eat you, of course. Idiot!"

"Is there no way you can check?" asked Karyn. "No defence against them? You said they don't like light. And then there is this weapon you found on the *Marseilles*, no? I'm not in your inner circle. Please explain."

"You're right," said Marie. "They don't like light. And they seem to use electromagnetic detection – a bit like sharks on Earth – which can be overwhelmed by high levels of electricity. We developed a couple of devices that give a small amount of protection, but only over a short range because charge dissipates rapidly over distance in water. Also, we don't have the resources to build many of these devices. But then we heard about the *Marseilles* device."

Mitsos scoffed. "You mean, the REEN. Or, if you want to give appropriate credit, call it 'the Mitsos Miracle Machine'."

Marie gave the other a quick smile. "Sorry. I'll stick with REEN – it's less of a mouthful. Anyway, this device is an ultrafine net suspended between two trawlers that passes high current through the water. After we acquired–"

"Stole," Kalmik coughed into her hand.

"*Borrowed*… with permission…" Marie nodded towards Louvain. "We found that it does work to deter the reapers and has a much bigger area of effect than our devices."

"Lucky for us," said Joseph. "It saved the fleet – and as the Chair said – brought us together here today."

Karyn made an odd gesture, reaching up to caress the scar at the side of her temple visible through her part-shaven hair. "I understand a little more now. These creatures seem an existential threat. It seems that this device is all that is holding them off from destroying the fleets of *Hibernia* and *Marseilles.* We sent the largest part of our fishing fleet to Athol. If this is destroyed, it's doubtful we have the resources to replace it."

"And that would be a tragedy for *all* Hibernians," said Nesvorny, looking intently at the woman. "Not just Stokers."

"And for the *Marseilles* too," said Louvain. "I was always against this stupid venture – and I do not just mean this armada. Losing a dozen boats will undermine our viability."

Figueroa cleared his throat. "In summary, it seems that we sit in a sea full of monsters, who now know about humans and, for whatever reason, have taken a great dislike to us. Your fleets are at risk, while the *Lisboa* is essentially stranded and, of course, we are cut off from Earth and may be for a very long time. So, what are we to do?"

De Voe spoke for the first time. "For a start, we should stop being arseholes. If we can avoid killing each other and being killed by these sea devils, there may be plenty of resources at Ardol from the *Stavanger* find. But it's difficult to suggest a solution when we all have different aims. For example, the Hibernians have appropriated our find and are trying to freeze us out from benefitting."

"Don't look at us," said Kai Dures, catching the direction of the woman's glare. "It was the previous regime that did that, not us."

"Well, it's you and the *Marseilles* tossers who decided to keep our stolen resources and impound our ship, stranding us in *Hibernia*."

"Citizen, this is news to me," said Louvain. "But it does not surprise me: we follow the orders of the First Citizen and he can be a bit… *intense*. I assume this is why I was invited, and not him?"

Kai looked at his wife for approval, then continued. "It is. We learned that you showed surprising grace in allowing the Lisboetas to take your boats, and they suggested you might be a reasonable man. But I now wonder at your authority."

Louvain shrugged. "The First Citizen is meant to be accountable to the People's Committee, but he rapidly outgrew them. Now he wields total power, backed by Captain Boursis and her security apparatus. They have gone to *Hibernia* with all of their most dedicated followers. The Committee look to me now to lead the *Marseilles* in his absence." Louvain smiled. "And I have control over our only working shuttle, and the remnants of our fishing and harvesting fleet: all the boats Deux took to *Hibernia* are now bottled up at the shipyard. Should he return, my prospects may not be good. Should he not, then the Committee is likely to allow me leeway in this time of crisis."

"So we mustn't let the fucker return," laughed Kai Dures.

But Karyn was less happy. "He certainly seems to have taken a liking to *Hibernia.* I suspect he sees himself as part of our future – and though we appreciate the help we received, we didn't do so to share our prize. The sooner we have paid our debt and he leaves, the better. I am beginning to suspect he may need to be moved on firmly. He has outstayed his welcome."

"Feed him to the monsters," said Mitsos. "Then everyone will be happy."

"Agreed," said De Voe. "He's a fucking arsehole from what I saw. In fact, I don't know who's worse – O'Neill and her lackeys…" she gestured towards Joseph, "or Deux and you rebels."

Joseph baulked at this. "You're quick with the insults–"

"Please, people, let us be calm," said Figueroa. "We on the *Lisboa* have enough problems without you bringing more strife here."

De Voe waved a dismissive hand, but subsided.

"So, what now?" asked Joseph.

"This is an existential crisis for us all on Tethys," said Nacimiento, "and all these disputes are part of it and need to be solved. Maybe there is an opportunity to do that now, or at least, head in that direction. After all, we here represent significant factions from the *Lisboa*, *Stavanger*, *Hibernia*, and the *Marseilles* – all in trouble, all trying to find our individual ways out. It seems to me that the simple answer – which ultimately solves little – is that my people escort the various parties stranded at the shipyard back to their respective bases using the REEN ships. That would leave the *Lisboa* at continued risk while the REEN boats are away, and what would follow anyway? A renewed attack by the rebel and *Marseilles* contingent on Athol, and the good Colonel here having to fight them."

"And don't forget us," said De Voe. "We're also stranded at the shipyard and we don't want to go to either of these places."

"Indeed, I haven't forgotten you," said Nacimiento. "It seems to me that in this crisis, the *Stavanger* has a critical role. You found a gold mine–"

"More like a cerium and lanthanum mine," said De Voe. "But go on."

"Yes, you found this and understand it. If carefully and efficiently developed, you could help us all: to repair the *Lisboa*, provide the

Marseilles with enough resources to meet their needs and obviate any claim from *Hibernia*, enrich the Hibernians – and maybe even," Nacimiento turned to the Karyn and Kai Dures, "complete the Town Class vessel languishing in the shipyard a short distance away. So you and your colleagues, Ms De Voe, are not the least of us. How do we all benefit, then, and defeat the evils that menace us?"

"You mean the reapers?" said Kalmik.

"Yes, but not only," said Nascimiento.

"Sebastian Deux," spat Mitsos, "*the bastard*."

"And the fascists on Athol," said Kai Dures.

"Who stole our find," added De Voe, mischievously.

"Of course," smiled Nascimiento.

"And the rebels on *Hibernia*," said Joseph, tensely.

"We are here," said Karyn. "Show some respect." But she didn't speak with anger. She half-raised a hand to retain the attention of all. "But if we can truly benefit as the Captain-Governor says – if this find does have that potential – then we ultimately have no desire to lord it over *Hibernia* and a partially unwilling population."

"Karyn?" said Kai.

"No, my husband. This revolt was meant to free one set of people – *our* people – not to enslave another." Kate noticed the woman look across the table at Nesvorny, who nodded slowly.

"I think I can speak for the *Stavanger*," said Solbakken, "that we would be happy to develop the find on Ardol for all – including the *Marseilles* and the *Lisboa*. We never wanted to hoard everything; we merely wished to ensure our fair share."

"I still don't get it," said Joseph. "Are we talking about some sort of alliance? The rebels of *Hibernia*; the moderate faction of *Marseilles*; and… *us*?"

Nesvorny reached a hand and rested it on Joseph's arm. "I said to you once before, Tania, that we are servants of the people of *Hibernia*. Maybe in the past there were some in *Hibernia* we didn't serve. If Karyn and Kai give appropriate assurances, then by continuing to fight, who would we be fighting for?"

"O'Neill and Traore? Fuck them. But I haven't heard what they…" she waved at the pair across the table, "are offering."

"A caretaker government," said Karyn suddenly. "Under us. For now. With representation from the people of *Hibernia* – but not from the old regime. In the end, it was a mistake to involve Sullivan. She must go. And O'Neill and Traore. And once my people are fully enfranchised, proper elections. In five years."

"Three," said Nesvorny.

Karyn smiled. "Let's split the difference. Four."

"Eric – you don't trust them, do you?" said Joseph, looking at the man beside her.

Nesvorny stared into Karyn Dures' eyes. "No. Not entirely. But Ms Dures is clever. I think she truly does want what is best for her people. Can we say the same about O'Neill? This might be our best chance of achieving some sort of peace."

Kate watched as Kai Dures looked between his wife and the pair in black sat opposite. At last he blurted: "Nesvorny is to return?"

"No – he is to retire," said Karyn, looking grim. "But before then, he is to do the people of *Hibernia* one last service… along with Colonel Joseph, if she agrees."

Joseph shook her head. "This is crazy but… what the fuck. It seems I have been infected by Eric's insanity. I guess this means we are offering you the forces of *Hibernia*."

Karyn started to speak, but then paused and reached down to her thigh, below the level of the table top. She brought out her comms tablet, on which a red light was winking insistently. "Apologies. I said only to interrupt in the case of an emergency." She produced an earpiece, which she inserted in her right ear, and then – under the gaze of all – accepted the call. "Go ahead," she muttered to the hidden screen.

Kate watched as the woman's eyes widened, and then her face took on an enraged expression. "Bastard!" she hissed. After a few more seconds, she concluded: "I'll get back to you." Then she looked around the table. "It seems our elegant solution is already being undermined." She looked at her husband. "The admiral of the *Marseilles* fleet managed to get a message back to his master. Deux has conducted his own coup with the support of the New Socialists from Earth, Sullivan, and the O'Hares…" she looked at Nesvorny to explain: "one of whom was murdered by the ISU, perhaps by your deputy." She threw the earpiece onto the table. "It seems we are now *all* exiles."

Kate ended her transcription with a number of exclamation marks.

Chapter 46

Luc Falcome's message had come as a shock to Sebastian Deux – with details on the alien attack and the rescue of the combined fleet being the least of the matter. Indeed, as Falcome's report unfolded, Deux's shock had rapidly segued into anger, and then fury. It seemed that the REEN boats *he* had sanctioned had proven valuable after all – and Louvain had allowed others to take them without consulting him. Worse, the survivors from the invasion debacle had then arranged a high-powered meeting without him, inviting Louvain instead, with the ship's captain refraining from communicating with Deux about this. It was clear that the snake was attempting to usurp power. Well, he would make him pay. He'd let Boursis unleash her investigators on him for a month, and then, after allowing Louvain to think the torment was over, unleash them again…

But it wasn't just Louvain. The captain of the *Marseilles* hadn't initiated anything, merely responded to requests and offers. It was others who'd seen the man as a viable replacement for Deux. In particular, it was the Dures couple who he'd help attain power, and yet who'd never shown him the respect he was owed. Apparently, it was Kai who'd convinced the assembled powers at the shipyard to exclude him, and Karyn had proven a ready accomplice. But Falcome's intel had come too late for Deux to intercept her: as soon as he'd broken the comms link with his admiral, he'd tried to contact Karyn to establish the truth, but she'd been unavailable; it hadn't taken him long to find that *Hibernia's* smallest shuttle had left some minutes previously.

He had left Boursis with orders to shoot down the shuttle on its return, with the intention of framing this as a tragic accident – firing on an unresponsive craft suspected of bringing saboteurs. And in place of the much-feted power couple, was there anyone else with the authority or power to challenge him as ruler of *Hibernia*?

Deux looked at the others in the conference room on the top floor of the command centre. They seemed loyal, but did he really trust them? After all, he hadn't thought the Dures pair would betray him.

"What now?" asked Georges Hollande. The Earther had been more than happy to transfer allegiance once he'd learned of the secret conference taking place aboard the *Lisboa*. He was still smarting from an embarrassing attempt to liquidate some Earther from the *Stavanger* contingent – an obsession that had been belittled by the Dures couple, but with which Deux had shown sympathy.

"The traitors won't be allowed to return, although I am concerned that they have not yet come. Their meeting should have ended hours ago."

"They must have been tipped off," said Magdalen O'Hare. She was a woman in her fifties, with greying hair cut raggedly to frame a pinched face with severe eyes. The matriarch of a large family, she'd apparently once been the most important Stoker until the Dures couple came along, and she was keen to regain her pre-eminence. "They have a loyal following, though many of their best took to the boats for the Athol adventure."

"And yours remained?" said Sullivan, the final member of their clique.

O'Hare gave a wicked smile. "They preferred to collect their weapons and hang back, yes. I suspected the raid would be costly; our supporters are now more evenly matched in number in *Hibernia*. The Dures supporters won't be happy, but without their leaders they have no deputies with suitable heft or charisma. They'll mutter, but do as I say."

"As *we* say?" said Deux, with an arched eyebrow.

O'Hare frowned. "Of course. I am aware of the important role played by the Marseillais and the socialists from Earth." She eyed Sullivan but chose not to comment. "This is a victory for all the oppressed peoples of *Hibernia* and Tethys. There is plenty of oppressors' wealth to go around."

"Yes, and now that my diligent Head of Security is here, the reckoning with them will be able to start."

"But what about the others?" insisted Hollande. "The plotters on the *Lisboa* and the *Marseilles*?"

"There is only one plotter on the *Marseilles*," scowled Deux, "and once I am able to return to my ship, he will be rapidly dealt with." He still seethed at his efforts to contact the *Marseilles* over the last few hours having come to naught: there was a convenient 'comms blackout' on his ship. "But first, I need to retrieve my gunboats from the shipyard. I have instructed Falcome to act. I hope for news soon. Until then, we still control *Hibernia* – the most important ship on Tethys – and there is no force that can wrest it from us."

* * *

After Karyn Dures' announcement of the apparent coup in *Hibernia*, the meeting had been paused so that different actors could contact their respective people at the shipyard to find out what exactly was going on there, while Marcel Louvain had got in touch with the *Marseilles* to ensure that his parting command for 'radio silence' was maintained, thus preventing Deux from sending orders from afar.

When they reconvened, Kai Dures spoke first. "It *was* Falcome who alerted Deux."

"How?" asked Joseph. "He was left in your care when we broke up."

"Tania – what is this?" asked Nesvorny. "I don't understand."

"When we met to discuss events, obviously we had to include the leader of the *Marseilles* gunboats. Naturally, he didn't like the drift of our discussion and the idea of inviting Captain Louvain as their representative, and we had to restrain him. At the end, Dures sent for a couple of his men to take him somewhere where he couldn't cause a problem. I couldn't do it with mine – that would have caused uproar in the rebel fleet. I guess the *Marseilles* contingent took exception to this."

Kai scowled: "Yes, they did. It took a while, but eventually his crew demanded to see him, and my guards ended up exchanging position with him in the temporary cell. They've just been found and released."

"So where is Falcome now?" asked Nesvorny. "And what is he doing?"

"At the moment, not a lot. He's on his 'flagship', lying low. What he's planning, though, is what worries me."

"What can he do?" asked Joseph. "His boats are ranged over several jetties, surrounded by our boats. He can't leave by himself or else he risks being sunk by these creatures. We don't know if they're still coasting off the shipyard, or whether they've come back here to the *Lisboa*. Do you have any idea?" She looked towards the *Lisboa* contingent.

"Not, really," said Marie. "Sorry, but their behaviour is still a bit of a mystery to us, as are their numbers. Even if we could conduct some sort of census, we wouldn't have a baseline to compare."

"So, if he's not willing to risk it, he needs to use the REEN boats," said Kai. "But if he sets off now, he'll be seen and the crew of the other boats will respond."

Heiko suddenly looked up. "The sun sets in an hour. We need to get back to the shipyard before then."

"Mr Heiko?" Kai frowned. "What is it? What have you deduced?"

"The obvious move is to wait until darkness and then make a play for the REEN boats. Once they have them under their control, they can lead – or drag – the fleet anywhere they want, whether to *Hibernia* or the *Marseilles*. Activity on the boats would alert the rest of the fleet, but they could swim out to the REEN boats in the dark unnoticed."

"Swim?" laughed Joseph. "You're betraying your origins, Mr Heiko."

But Marie didn't laugh. "Why not? We swam to the *Marseilles* from your boat."

"A very short swim," said Joseph. "Even then, you were lucky not to get investigated by something with a lot of teeth."

"Well, how much further would they have to swim than we did?" continued Marie.

Joseph sat back in her chair and considered. Then she sobered. "Yeah, okay. You got a point. If they swam from the end of the jetty nearest to the boats, it probably wouldn't be more than a couple hundred metres. And maybe this electromagnetic effect will have an impact on other creatures, not just these reapers."

"And you've got to remember, these guys are fanatics," said Mitsos. "If you managed to get *me* in the water, I promise you, the comrades won't baulk at it."

"Makes sense," muttered Joseph. "Captain Singh is still at sea as chaperone. I'll alert him. Our patrol boats have spotlights. I'll make sure he keeps an eye on the waters around. Dr Lockard – you should warn your friends, too. But I agree with Heiko – I suddenly feel a need to get back to the shipyard, even if we haven't decided on the next move in our game yet. If we lose these REEN boats and this guy Deux gets his gunboats back, that's not going to help anyone."

"Agreed," said Kai Dures. "I'll come too. We need to neutralise those boats."

"Softly," said Louvain, leaning forwards in his chair. "*Please.* These are my people, and our boats, which we cannot afford to lose."

"Understood, Captain," said Dures. "But if there is a fight we may need to be robust."

Louvain folded his arms and looked severe, but, after a moment, he nodded.

"Yes, you go, Kai," said Karyn. "You can take the Hibernian shuttle. I will remain here. With Deux in charge, I do not want to rush back into his custody."

"Custody?" Heiko gave the woman a wry smile. "Ms Dures, I'd be highly surprised if he let you even land."

"All the more reason for me to remain." Karyn looked around the table. "With Kai and Colonel Joseph gone, we still have representatives of the different… allies? Perhaps we can have a break, then discuss options for the future."

Kai Dures and Joseph both stood to leave… then so did Heiko. "If you don't mind," said the latter, "I have a boat full of armed and competent security personnel. We may be of assistance. Mr Solbakken and Ms De Voe speak better for *Stavanger* than I can."

"Sure, Heiko," said Joseph. "Welcome aboard."

De Voe looked as though she was about to object, then announced: "Okay, Rennie – but don't do anything I wouldn't do."

Heiko smiled and bowed to her. "No backward step will be taken."

* * *

They weren't in time.

As *Hibernia's* small shuttle was descending to land at the murky, ill-lit landing pad set back from the waterline amid deserted low-storey buildings, Joseph and Dures received messages via their tablets almost simultaneously.

"It's Singh," said Joseph, reporting first. "He's under attack."

"From swimmers?" asked Heiko.

"No. The gunboats. It seems you were half-right. They waited until dark when their activity onboard would be less visible, then started their engines while those on the rest of the fleet were kicking back."

"Not on *all* of the other boats," said Heiko. He held a hand to a receiver in one ear. "Cass has cast off."

The shuttle settled, and its engines cycled down in volume. Dures was first up, with Joseph and Heiko right behind him: he activated the exit hatch, and they started down the telescoping stairs before the door was fully open. On the night breeze, the crack of canon fire was soon audible.

The three hurried from the small landing field, between dark buildings, down the gentle slope towards the quay, which was sporadically lit by lights from the mass of boats crowded up against the jetties. During the journey, Heiko received updates through his earpiece and then more: Vardem patched him into a portable camera networked to his tablet, and by closing an eye and blinking in the right manner, Heiko was able to see what it saw in his mind's eye. Initially, this was little and indistinct: a fuzz of light to one side, and darkness in front, and then a number of blotches of light coming from the cabins of different boats. Vardem related that they had set out parallel to the departing gunboats and perpendicular to the REEN boats, ensuring they stayed out of the way on the flank.

As they jogged down a small road and emerged onto the broad stone quay – with the main shipyard an indistinct blur of colossal machinery away to their left – Heiko held out an arm to draw the others' attention.

"What is it, Heiko?" asked Joseph.

"At least four of the gunboats got clear of the jetties unhindered. Most are firing on your boat, Joseph, but one has reached one of the REENs and boarded it."

"We need to get out there," said Dures. "My people are confused and sitting tight, watching the show."

"That's just as well," said Joseph, who'd also been in comms link as they moved. "There's already too much confusion here and too little room to manoeuvre. Follow me: the *Slipstream* is at the end of Jetty Three, fired up and waiting."

They jogged along the quay under the eyes of the curious crew of a number of the Stokers' trawlers. Dures shouted commands as they passed. At the appropriate jetty, Joseph turned and headed towards its end, ignoring the low-lit Stoker boats moored to either side of it. The sound of high calibre machinegun now filled the space between cannon shots and overbore the excited voices of crew members from the surrounding boats.

At the stern of the end boat, two of the crew, in black uniforms with un-inflated life vests, waited to receive the newcomers. The three were helped aboard, and then Joseph led them forwards, shouting orders to cast off. Heiko was directly behind her, attempting to make sense of the data coming to his left eye from Vardem's wireless connection on the *Cormorant* while retaining sufficient peripheral sight to not fall overboard. They entered the wheelhouse and almost instantly were jolted by the surge of electric motors.

The Captain of the craft looked to the new arrivals and declared: "Ma'am – the *Swiftsure* has been hit."

"Go to her, Captain," said Joseph. And then: "Report!"

The grey-haired man in a peaked cap announced: "With us included, it's two against six. Our other boats are hemmed in, and the Stokers aren't letting them leave…" he quickly noticed Dures and Heiko, both wearing the Stokers' customary green overalls; frowned; gestured. "Ma'am?"

"We're on the same side now, Captain Bellamy," said Joseph. "The message just hasn't got through yet. We'll have won or lost before everything is disentangled." Then, from just out the window at the front of the craft, the machinegun roared into life, tracer bullets zipping through the darkness. "How bad is the *Swiftsure*?"

"Still afloat and giving better than it's getting, but everything is tight to these REEN boats. As they tried to get away, they got bumped and had to swing back."

"Bumped?" said Joseph.

"It seems the reapers are still around," said Heiko.

"They are," said Bellamy, looking between Heiko and Joseph. "In fact, they seem to have crippled one of the *Marseilles* gunboats."

The comms operator behind Bellamy declared: "Gone, sir. The gunboat. The monsters got it."

"Five to two now," said Heiko. "Or make that… three." He held up a hand; his eyes went vacant; and the occupants of the cabin heard him announce. "Cass – lights out. Take the one at the REEN."

And suddenly, so small was the theatre of operations, they blazed through the space between two of the gunboats, their machinegun raking the side of the boat to port.

"Focus on the cannon!" shouted Joseph. "Disable only. Minimal causalities!"

Bellamy took to a handheld mic and relayed the instruction to the gunner.

As they surged ahead, Heiko noticed a stationary boat a couple of hundred metres away to starboard. One of the REENs. Alone. The action was taking place at its twin, a couple hundred metres further away in that direction.

"Cannon disabled," declared Bellamy. "Gunboat disengaging. The second…"

And then an explosion from a cannon shell somewhere to the rear of the control cabin sent a concussive wave through them. The roof at the rear of the cabin tore off in flames, revealing stars beyond. Heiko was thrown into Dures, who himself stumbled and dropped to the floor. Joseph had also been stunned, and Bellamy lolled in his captain's chair, a piece of shrapnel embedded through his cap and into his skull. The *Slipstream* began to turn, the pilot slumped over the wheel. Heiko had been lucky: the shrapnel from the hit had flown over his head and peppered those in front. He staggered past Dures, who was on hands and knees, and placed a hand on the pilot's shoulder. The woman sat back groggily.

"Are you okay?"

"Uh… yes. Yes, sir…" She righted the wheel and peered through the front window. "Where… where…"

"Starboard," Heiko yelled. "Swing past the nearer REEN boat. Use it as cover."

The pilot did as asked. There was another boom of cannon fire, but they'd put some distance between the gunboat that had hit them, and the accuracy of the Marseillais gunners didn't appear to be great.

"Fuck," said Joseph, behind him. "Sorry, Bellamy…"

Heiko turned to see that Joseph had tipped the dead captain from his chair and taken control. The comms operator beside her was shaking his head, but seemed uninjured. He adjusted the headphones he was wearing, then reported. "*Swiftsure* reports it's gun's been disabled. It's trying to avoid two gunboats. Captain Singh says one is the *Marseilles* flagship."

"Do we know where? Bearing?" Joseph looked at the radar display to the side of the wheel. To Heiko, it seemed an incomprehensible field of dots, but Joseph clearly understood it. She identified a likely target and instructed the pilot to head for it. "Lop off the head, and maybe the rest will listen to you, Dures." She looked across to Dures, who'd regained his feet. "You okay?"

"I'll live."

Heiko closed his eyes – and suddenly he was on the *Cormorant*. A new message in the menu revealed that Vardem had patched in the personal camera worn by Anders Pedersen. Heiko selected this, and he was suddenly on the deck, in the dark, the boat's lights having been switched off, though light glared on the near horizon from a pair of boats – a *Marseilles* gunboat tied alongside one of the REEN boats. The nearest, starboard side of the gunboat was clear of crew – presumably all of whom were occupied with their captured vessel. Heiko could also hear through his earpiece: the *Cormorant's* electric motors were quiet; then a voice made him jump: "Ready to board," said Pedersen to the half-dozen armed others arrayed beside him on the deck. "Only shoot if you have to. Ready… ready…"

The distance shrank, and then the *Cormorant* slowly swung around so that it was abreast the gunboat and its prey: they'd approached from towards the stern, so the cannon was only visible at the last moment as they came fully alongside.

"Now!" said Pedersen.

On the *Slipstream*, Heiko declared: "My people are boarding."

The image behind Heiko's closed eyelids became momentarily confused as Pedersen bound onto the gunboat. There was a confusion of images, and then shouting. Gunfire erupted… from Pedersen? Then there was more shouting. Through Pedersen's eyes, Heiko saw Judd Stallings point his rifle at the boat's gunner, who raised his hands and stepped away. Then Pedersen was in the cabin, gun elevated, another trooper at his side, a shocked set of crewmen twitching and shying away; and as Pedersen moved his eyes, Heiko noticed several more from his team moving around the cabin and bellowing as they moved onto the adjacent REEN boat…

"That's it," said Joseph. "He's not seen us – too busy with Singh."

"Second boat to port," announced the pilot. "And the one behind hasn't given up."

"Fuck it," said Joseph. "Ignore the others. Focus on the flagship. Strafe it's decks. And someone get me a gun. We're going to board."

"Me too," snarled Dures. He produced a knife from somewhere: it seemed he was content with that.

Heiko blinked off the image coming from Pedersen's camera: he trusted his team, though there was no way he could help them now anyway. He followed Dures onto the starboard deck – his only weapon his hands, but in close combat, they might be enough. Ahead, there was a gunboat, curving in front of them, following Singh's boat, which itself was curving around, unable to escape directly ahead for fear of exiting the protective sphere of the REEN boats. Then the machinegun at the front of the *Slipstream* opened up. It raked the side of the gunboat, chewing through the starboard side and then slicing upwards towards the forward cannon as it came into view.

They closed quickly, cutting a hypotenuse and moving faster than the converted trawler. A couple of cannon shots struck the water to either side, but then firing ceased: the following boats could not shoot without risking hitting their commander. As they came alongside their foe's flagship, their gunner swept the deck, and a number of the gunboat's crew – crouching on the starboard side with rifles raised – fell back in a bloody heap. Heiko and Dures swept past their gunner and leapt onto the deck of the other boat, with Joseph and one of the *Slipstream* crew – both armed with short-barrelled guns – emerging from the port door to the wheelhouse just behind them.

Heiko felt energy surge through his muscles. He was literally built for this; adapted for it. He was through the cabin door first, and saw Falcome there, a rifle held loosely in his hands, confusion on his face. There was another man by the door, but Heiko was too close for him to use his weapon: he used his fist as a hammer to fell him, and in two strides was at Falcome while the other's rifle was still rising. Heiko thumped the heel of his palm into the other's sternum, then when his adversary wheezed and lowered his head, he continued with his palm into the other's jaw, smashing it: the admiral of the fleet crumpled to the floor.

Then Dures was behind him. "You know who I am!" he bellowed at the woman on comms. "Send an order for the boats to stand down, or I'll have the fucking lot of you thrown to the monsters. Do it now!" His knife was suddenly close to the operator's now-pale face. In a tremulous voice, the command was delivered.

Heiko slumped down, sitting atop the fallen admiral. He closed his eyes and was back with Pedersen. "Anders, it's me. Do you receive?"

"Yes, sir. All under control here. The REEN boat is safe. No one's been harmed. Couple of bumps and a non-fatal gunshot wound to the team, otherwise we're good too."

"Well done, Anders. Make sure the comms officer is receiving and relaying the commands from the flagship, then accompany their boat back to dock."

"You got it. *Out*."

* * *

"The fleet is loyal as long as I'm here," said Kai Dures. He was with Heiko and Joseph in an old office near the landing pad that had clearly once served as some sort of communication centre. They'd managed to repower the equipment with a portable generator from one of the boats: the wall screen in front of which they were seated showed the meeting room in the science centre on the *Lisboa*, the active participants having moved to one side of the table so that all appeared in shot. "I dare not risk leaving here. If I do, the *Marseilles* contingent might rise up again, and I cannot tell what would happen to the ESU boats. Our people are somewhat ambivalent about the supposed alliance."

"Yeah, and I can't leave either," said Joseph. "It seems every time I do, I return to a smaller fleet. I've only four functional patrol boats left. In the light of this, what have you decided in your discussions?"

Karyn Dures was in the centre of the table and took the lead. "Our first step must be to reclaim *Hibernia* before Deux and his allies consolidate control. The problem is, I can't fly back – as Mr Heiko noted earlier, I might not be allowed to land. That means the only option seems to be the fleet. *Hibernia* has a big shoreline and no defences as such, so they couldn't stop us returning that way. But it seems the reapers are still lurking outside the protective radius of the REEN boats, and we definitely do not want to have them follow us to *Hibernia*. That would be a disaster. So… we're stuck."

"Not quite." Heiko had been silent as his colleagues had delivered their report about the battle, the capture of Falcome, and the aftermath. But he had quickly turned his thoughts to this very matter. "There is a third option that combines the two elements you mentioned, Ms Dures."

"Go on, Mr Heiko."

"The key seems to be to get certain people from our new alliance to *Hibernia*. I assume that were you to arrive, you could quickly muster your supporters and contest rule?"

"Contest? Yes." Karyn looked at another sat a short distance to her left. "But victory would not be certain. I do not know who has thrown in with Deux. Our source mentions Magdalen O'Hare. But would she fight fellow Stokers, or is this opportunistic? I don't know. But I could tip the balance with Nesvorny's ISU – the ones that remained and surrendered. They were disarmed, but only the officers held for lack of prison space. If he could gather them up, and I could arm them, our chances would be much better."

"Yes," said Nesvorny. "I would do this, trusting the agreement about governance we made earlier."

"In other words, we just need to get the two of you there," said Heiko. "You don't need the fleet for that. A single boat will do."

Karyn frowned. "A trawler from the *Lisboa*? Wouldn't that look suspicious?"

"Perhaps. It might be better to have one of your own deliver you from over here. One of your fleet with a crew appropriately dressed in green."

Karyn stared out from the screen. "If I take your meaning, I appreciate the offer, but the problem of the reapers remains – in fact, increases. You can't leave without the protection of the REEN boats."

"Can't we?" Heiko smiled gently at the camera above the screen back at the shipyard. "Is that true, Dr Lockard? I remember you telling us that you do have other protective devices, though these have a much smaller range. Are they big enough to protect one boat?"

"You mean the Electric Field Emitters," said Marie. "Yes, in our field experiment the device seemed to work, and would protect a single boat."

"Even so," said Karyn, "there's still the problem of being followed by reapers to *Hibernia*."

"Hmm, yes, but would the reapers leave the fleet to follow a single boat?" asked Heiko. "Dr Lockard?"

"I can't really say. They might, or might not. But probably not *en masse*. I suspect most would continue to shadow the fleet… that is, the rest of those that aren't presently below the *Lisboa*."

"And maybe if there were just one or two, we could deal with them in the open water, well away from *Hibernia*," said Heiko.

Marie was clearly thinking hard. Heiko watched her face scrunch as she turned away from the camera, looking down at the table. Then she nodded slowly and looked back up. "Okay. It's worth a shot. I think it could work. We can send an EFE to you, but you'll need someone to operate it… and someone to go in the water to check that all is clear and to do what needs to be done. I'm familiar with the kit. I've dived amongst the reapers more than anyone else." She looked to the woman at her side. "I'm happy to go, unless…"

Kalmik laughed. "Marie, believe me, if you think I'm going to argue with you over this, you are *loca*. I wish you luck."

Marie smiled sheepishly at the other, then back at the camera. "I guess I'm in."

"Good," said Heiko. "So, if you agree with this plan for an insertion, Ms Dures, we need to get you over here with this device. My crew are competent and armed, and though Cass may not be happy about this excursion, it'll at least get the *Cormorant* away from the fleet, which has been our goal all along."

"You're going nowhere without me," said De Voe, suddenly.

Heiko's smile returned. "Of course not. You can take Makka's place. I think the excitement of earlier has been more than enough for him. He can take your place back on the *Lisboa* to keep Magnus company."

So they had a plan, and soon a second: Kai Dures and Joseph would lead an overland trek with the majority of their force to Mount Athol, leaving just a skeleton crew for the boats. It would likely take them a couple of days over rough terrain to reach their destination, though on arrival, there was no immediate plan to launch a bloody assault: as Heiko noted, it was more a case of moving pieces into position to be ready for the end game, once they decided what that might look like. Meanwhile, Falcome was coached into reading a prepared message to *Hibernia*, announcing a delay in his attempts to seize the REEN boats: it was agreed that he would be brought to Athol with the main force to keep him out of trouble, while the remaining Marseillaise – from their five remaining gunboats – were disarmed and held in an old warehouse under guard.

* * *

It took a couple of hours for the contingent from the *Lisboa* to assemble with their gear. As Marie waited in the lounge outside the shuttle landing pad, she saw her daughter enter.

"Mum – you're doing it again."

"I'm sorry, Kate. But compared with the swim to the *Marseilles*, this should be a walk in the park."

Kate shook her head. "You mean, going into the open ocean again? And if there are reapers, are you going to have to fight them? And even if there aren't, there are other things. *Stupid*, Mum, real stupid. Are you determined to make me an orphan?"

"This has got to be done. You were in the room, Kate. Was there a better option? And going with this plan, who better than me?"

"Mike Resnos, that's who."

Marie smiled sadly and shook her head. "If the situation were reversed, would you let one of your friends – Sara or Tonio – go in your place? Mike's good, but I'm better."

Kate closed her eyes and bowed her head. "Just… stay safe." She looked up and held Marie's gaze – and suddenly it occurred to Marie how adult her daughter now looked. "I suppose I should let you get on with it then. The Professor needs my help drafting the words of the treaty document. Each to their own." She nodded, turned, and left.

* * *

It was about midnight before the *Cormorant* was loaded, the EFE installed, and the insertion party was ready for the off.

Chapter 47

The lights from the REEN boats fell astern and gradually faded from view. But no attack came.

"It seems your device is working," said Heiko to Marie.

"Famous last words," muttered Nesvorny, standing at Marie's other side.

The three stood at the bow of the *Cormorant*, close to where the weighted line of the EFE entered the water. The lead was attached by a connector socket to a large, heavy battery that had been hefted into the centre of the deck; the controls to the machine were a simple 'on-off' switch, which was Marie's responsibility, but which could have been operated by any child. But a more difficult task would soon be upon her, for which she had already donned her orange Tethyn drysuit, having laid out her dive gear and spear gun on the other side of the battery. "I hope not," she said. "I admit I was worried at the outset, because we trialled the EFE directly beneath the *Lisboa*, not in a moving boat that makes the wire trail out from the vertical. It's pulling the zone of protection towards the rear, but…" she shrugged.

"I see what you mean," said Heiko. "You're worried the bow may now be unprotected."

"Yes. Possibly. But as you said, we haven't been attacked yet. If we are, I suggest we come to a dead halt and allow the lead to return to its original orientation."

"That makes sense," said Nesvorny. "But do they know about this in the wheelhouse?" He pushed off a railing and turned. "Excuse me. I'll pass this intel on to the pilot."

Marie was left alone with Heiko. They stood in silence for some seconds, looking out over the dark ocean, caressed by a cool breeze, beneath a glorious sky full of stars and whisps of nebulae.

"At times like this, it really does feel like we're on another world," said Heiko.

Marie glanced at the man beside her and saw light from the cabin behind glint off the copper-coloured adaptor at his temple. "Yes, Earth seems far away." She paused, then said: "Sorry I didn't recognise you before – unlike my daughter. She clocked you as soon as you entered the meeting room on the *Lisboa*." She smiled. "I've no excuse really: you're quite distinctive."

A half-smile formed on Heiko's lips, but he continued to stare out over the water. "I forgive you. I'm sure you had a lot on your mind at the shipyard, and we all had other matters to focus on during the escape from the *Leviathan*. Unfortunately, there are others in *Hibernia* I wish to avoid who recognised me all too well on my recent visit there."

"Are you talking about the New Socialists?"

"Yep. We had an encounter with them when trying to leave. I made sure they weren't harmed, but at the time I wasn't expecting to return so quickly. Old colleagues of mine would say I've gone soft. I hope my error doesn't come back to bite us."

"So, I'm not the only one worried about bumping into old friends?"

Heiko turned, saw Marie's smile, and returned it. "Indeed. But your acquaintances may be nearer." Then his smile dissipated. "Marie… there's one thing troubling me. Perhaps you can help me out. I didn't want to speak earlier on the conference call: your daughter wasn't in shot, but I suspected she was there with the Professor, out of the picture."

"Ah. Go on."

"You're going into the water to check whether we've been followed, right? But with the EFE fully functioning…" He didn't finish.

Marie nodded. "Thanks for keeping your thoughts to yourself. Kate would have worried even more. Yes, when I'm down below, you'll have to turn the machine off to allow whatever is out there to get close enough so I can see whether we are being followed or not."

"And switch it back on again if something does emerge?"

"I'll yell on my internal mic."

"Will you really?"

Marie opened her mouth to say 'yes', but was unsettled by the other's penetrating gaze. "Uh… maybe. Believe me, if there are several of them, I'll shout. But if there's just one? It sounds as though we desperately need to get these people to *Hibernia*, but we can't risk letting the reapers know about the place. I'll have my spear gun."

"And you'll use it, Marie? *I* wouldn't hesitate. It's my metier. But would *you* kill an intelligent being in cold blood?"

"I can't say I love the idea, but after what these things did to Raul… a friend… I think I have it in me."

Heiko held her stare, then nodded slowly. "Okay, Dr Lockard, maybe it's time to find out?"

"Yes – now is as good a time as any. Let's do this."

Ten minutes later, Marie sat with her legs over the side of the boat, her helmet on, with a speargun in her left hand. Behind her, the deck was crowded: Heiko, Nesvorny, Karyn Dures, and De Voe were there; Pedersen had joined them briefly, but decided there wasn't enough space and returned to the main cabin, where most of the Stavangeran security crew waited. Cass Remillard remained at the wheel of the now-stationary vessel, aided by Claude Vardem.

"I'll wait for your command," said Heiko. He stood by the control of the EFE machine, the lead from which trailed over the opposite side of the boat.

"You sure you can hear me?" asked Marie.

"Not only hear, but also see. Claude is an electronics wizard. I've got feed from your helmet directly into my brain through the adaptor, and I'm tuned into your mic's frequency." He quickly scanned the others around: "If you please, once Marie enters the water, can I have total silence."

"Sure thing, Rennie," said De Voe. The others simply nodded.

"Okay," confirmed Marie. "I hope to be quick about this. I want to be in the water as little time as possible. I don't want to tempt anything else to come and investigate." She turned and slipped off the side into the black water.

Marie experienced the usual brief disorientation on passing through the barrier to the submarine world. She dropped a couple of metres beneath the hull, stabilised, and said: "Now."

"Roger that," came Heiko's voice. "Now… *off*."

Marie gently wafted her arms to stay in position, her left hand holding the speargun. She could see very little: her helmet light illuminated a limited sphere around her, and was of insufficient intensity to ward off the light-sensitive reapers… though it might well attract other things. She breathed deeply and felt her heart beating fast. She was surrounded by gloom. An itch started somewhere between her shoulder blades: she tried not to panic, but the feeling immediately came that there was something behind her. She slowed her breathing and began to rotate in the water, ever expecting to see something just over her right shoulder.

After a few seconds, she heard Heiko: "I see nothing, Marie. Do you *sense* anything?"

The man's voice was calm, low, comforting. "Not yet. Still looking." She managed to make a complete three-sixty turn, scanning left, right, down. How long had she been here? She completed a second turn, raised her legs, looked down, dropped them again to be vertical in the water. "Still nothing," she said.

"Confirmed," said Heiko. "I see nothing either."

But the feeling that she wasn't alone didn't go away. Time was passing and she felt exposed: there could be almost anything just beyond the shadow line. *Once more…*

On her third turn, as she moved her head to the right, she shuddered and jerked, drawing around her speargun. "Oh… *fuck*!"

"Marie?"

About four metres away, at the edge of the light, also floating vertically, was a reaper.

"Fuck!" gasped Marie. "Yes. There is one."

"Ah, I see it now. Only one? What's it doing?"

"It's just watching me."

The creature gently drifted in the water, its eyeless head – or arguably, *eye*, since it was covered in light-sensitive cells – remained motionless, clearly focused on her. Marie brought the gun around so that her right hand was by the trigger: but it still didn't move. What was it doing? Thinking? Trying to work out what she was doing? Deciding whether to attack, and how?

"Can you get a clear shot?" came Heiko's voice.

"Uh, maybe, but I need to be sure first… sure it's *alone*."

Her speargun wavered, pointing roughly towards the reaper, but not directly at it; she didn't want to make the threat obvious and induce a response. She continued to scan the water, left, right, below…

And then the creature seemed to decide. Its arms – with their wicked, taloned fingers – clawed vigorously at the water; its legs kicked back to the horizontal; its head came forwards and down.

Marie jerked the gun around, but in the process her finger touched the trigger: the spear jetted through the water just to the left of the creature's head.

She didn't have time to reload, with the reaper suddenly halving the distance between them. She pushed the weapon in front of her as a barrier and would have screamed if her throat wasn't tight.

It reared close and then…

There was a blur, and the water was suddenly full of bubbles. Marie felt a pressure wave ripple through the water, the light from the headlamp dimmed, occluded, glinted off the dark flesh of something large, something larger than the reaper… and suddenly the reaper was gone, borne off, leaving a slick of blood as a wide patch of roiling shadow within lamplight. She kicked furiously backwards, and surged to the surface, the voice of Heiko in her ears indistinct…

Marie broke the surface and slapped the water. Two pairs of arms reached down to grab her, belonging to Nesvorny and De Voe. Somehow she'd lost the speargun, which was just as well: she reached up and kicked violently, jetting upwards.

And then she was over the side and on the deck, on her face, where she sprawled, let her limbs go limp… and then began to laugh.

They righted her and helped her removed her tanks and helmet. Looking up, she noticed Heiko directly before her – his arms crossed and a wry expression on his face. "Something amusing, Marie?"

She shook her head and blew out her cheeks. "Sometimes being small and weak has its advantages."

"Really?"

"Uh-huh. I just made a less-appetising meal than the reaper did for something else that was hungry."

They paused twice more before they got to *Hibernia* to test for the presence of reapers, but on these occasions, they simply switched off the EFE for five minutes to see whether anything decided to start tapping on the *Cormorant's* hull, and after the latter, they turned off the device altogether. Marie did offer to dive once more, but was relieved when her comrades suggested that doing so would be an unnecessary risk.

* * *

It was somewhere between three and four o'clock in the morning Tethys Adjusted Time when the *Cormorant* nudged into the West Docks. The place was deserted, given that much of the fishing fleet had been purloined for the Athol raid. Remillard had to try several frequencies on his radio to eventually get a response from the harbourmaster, who'd clearly been asleep. They were grudgingly told to dock wherever they wanted and to stop bothering the man.

"Very lax," said Remillard, "but not a surprise. Everything about this revolution is amateurish."

Heiko gave a shy smile at Karyn Dures' scowl; surprisingly, it was Nesvorny who came to the rebels' defence: "Yet still they beat us," he muttered. "So what does that make us?"

There were intermittent lights along the main quay, and more near the harbourmaster office, but not a single person was in sight as the group left the *Cormorant*. Remillard and Marie Lockard stayed behind, along with one of the Stavanger security men who'd taken a flesh wound from a bullet during the fight at the REEN boat. Once on the top level, they were let out of the dock entrance gate by a pair of surprised guards who saw no reason to question a party of armed compatriots dressed in Stoker green overalls.

Outside, they hurried along the ground level to a sub-level access stairwell, then descended two flights, finding themselves in a deserted corridor with large, shuttered warehouse doors to either side, and a single yellow strip light in the ceiling.

They clustered around Karyn Dures, who removed the cap she'd used to aid her low-key appearance on passing the gatehouse. "You're clear on the plan?" she asked.

"We are," said Heiko. En route, they'd plotted their insertion. "Claude has a full map of *Hibernia* from his research beforehand – which means I do too." He tapped the adaptor at the side of his temple. "Take care. We'll rendezvous in three hours."

Karyn nodded and turned to head off; Pedersen gave Heiko a desultory salute, and fell in behind the woman with two more of the *Stavanger* security contingent. Heiko watched them head to a nearby junction and disappear off to the right. That left Heiko, De Voe, Nesvorny, Vardem, and two troopers from the *Stavanger.* They had four rifles between them: the three held by the security team, and Heiko's – which he duly handed to De Voe, causing her to smile. "Thanks, Rennie. I'll try not to shoot you in the back."

"Appreciate it." Heiko turned to look at Nesvorny. "I can navigate from my internal map, but I guess you can do it from memory. For show, I'll lead off and you follow behind, surrounded by our escort. By all means, give me instructions."

Nesvorny nodded curtly. "Sounds reasonable. Okay. We need to head south-east." He pointed…

It took them twenty minutes to get to the old ISU central base, keeping to deserted sub-levels. They'd dropped down to Sublevel Four, where the lighting was barely adequate to see by, when Nesvorny called on them to halt. "We're directly underneath. There's only one functioning entrance from this level – a vestige from the early days of the *Hibernia.* Others have been blocked off or simply forgotten from lack of use."

"A real backdoor," said De Voe.

"Indeed," said Heiko. "Does anyone else know about it?"

"Oh, sure," said Nesvorny. "It's not exactly a secret. Why would it be? No one has ever had a reason to lock it, for who'd want to pay the ISU a surreptitious visit? But the number who know is small – simply because it's an extraneous piece of information. "

"Will it be protected above?" asked Heiko.

Nesvorny shrugged. "I don't see why. During the rebellion, we placed a trooper there just in case, but the Stokers never came, so I guess they don't know about it, and even if someone has told them now – why place a guard? Who would they be expecting to attack?"

"Okay. Let's take it easy, and hope the security here is as lax and limited as at the docks, and any guards are at the front desk, as it were. Do you know where to go once we breach?"

"You just need a computer with access to our secure mainframe, yes?" asked Nesvorny. "I think I can deliver that. The level above has storerooms with an inventory office. I can't see why anyone would be about on that level, or in the office, at this time."

Nesvorny was right.

Aside from the guard they left on Sublevel Four, and a second they left at the door to where they emerged on Sub Three, the rest crowded into the small inventory office, and Vardem got to work at a computer. Nesvorny's passwords still allowed access.

"Again, careless," said Heiko.

"Yeah, but you said it, Rennie," said De Voe, somewhat defensively, "we don't have armies or wars or spies. On Tethys, we just have policemen, and apart from this place – and a few other paranoid places like the *Marseilles* – they're few in number or part-time. No one here has a book on how to carry out a revolt. No one has your experience."

"Some of us do," snarled Nesvorny. "But time and complacency has undermined that."

Shortly, Vardem found what he was looking for: a list of contact numbers for every member of the ISU from personnel files. "Over to you, Colonel," he said. "Do you want to place voice calls or leave priority messages?"

"A mixture of both, I think," said Nesvorny. "The problem is, some are dead or injured, and many are on Athol. I am assuming the personnel officer hasn't been in a position to update matters, so it'll be pot luck, although I'm confident some will respond."

"Perhaps if Claude passes over his tablet and the list," said Heiko, "you can make a start while he searches for your imprisoned officers."

Vardem soon had more intel. "There's no specific list – in the chaos, no one has been keeping files. But I can see that all of your cells on Sublevel Two are locked, implying they're occupied. It makes sense that they'll be filled with ISU." And a little later: "Aha! Into the security cameras. It seems you only have four in the entire complex."

"Again, why would we need more?" grunted Nesvorny, turning from the borrowed tablet.

"Patch me in, Claude," said Heiko. Soon after, he declared: "Okay. It's pretty lifeless up there. I can see down a corridor with cells to either side. And I can also see into an annexe with a security station. It has two people, one asleep on a cot. *Interesting*. They both seem to be wearing a proper uniform – a *grey-and-black* one. Ms Dures talked of the Marseilles Security Apparatus being shipped over en masse: this seems to support her claim."

"And this would be the place for them to stay and operate," said Nesvorny. "That implies the barracks on Sublevel One and on the ground level may be packed with them."

"Heiko – do you have any idea how many members of the Apparatus came over?" asked De Voe.

"Ms Dures hinted at over a hundred." Heiko closed his eyes. "Checking the camera at the front desk, Level Zero. Okay. Two more in uniforms there. It seems the Apparatus have taken over the ISU compound. We're in the middle of enemy territory. This is going to make breaking out your officers more difficult."

"We'll have to do it at the last minute, once we've assembled a force."

"*If* we assemble a force," said De Voe. "Your people have to turn up, and Karyn has to deliver the weapons and some force of her own."

"Oh, we'll definitely have some of mine," said Nesvorny.

Heiko exchanged frowns with De Voe. In half-an-hour, Nesvorny had only managed to speak to two others face-to-face, although he'd sent a blanket invitation to his entire list. There was nothing for it: they settled down to watch Nesvorny's recruitment attempts and await news from the leader of the Stokers.

* * *

Less than an hour had passed when the sentry in the fourth sub-level called in.

"Yes, Judd?" asked Heiko.

"I've got company. A man in a black uniform just rolled up. Oh… wait… and there's a couple more coming. A man and a woman."

"Hopeful," said De Voe, in the small office. She'd felt like a spare part during the operation so far.

Nesvorny grunted and returned to the next name on his list.

Further reports of arrivals came in increasing frequency, until Heiko called a halt: "Thanks, Judd. We've got the message. No need for further updates, unless it's about our other allies."

"Understood, sir. Out."

"Well, we've got the basis of an army," said De Voe. "Or at least, an assault group."

"Basis only," said Heiko. "But without weapons, they might as well go home. Plus, we also need the validation of having a joint force. Having no Stokers involved would make it seem like the old regime was fighting back and would likely unite all of those wearing green and grey."

"Patience," said De Voe. "I'm confident Karyn will come good." She'd been rather impressed by the Stoker leader, who she saw as firm, determined, and yet also rational. The main problem was whether she'd be captured by the new ruling group before she could succeed, though Vardem had now hacked into the comms of the Apparatus, which had been piggybacking existing systems, and he'd recorded no alerts so far.

And then, at last, after nearly two-hours…

"They're here, sir!" said Stallings, over the comms. "Stokers. Ten, twenty of them, and they've brought a cart full of guns."

De Voe smiled at Heiko, who she could see was struggling to maintain his own equanimity.

"That's excellent, Judd," said Heiko. "How's the interaction?"

"Well, the two groups are wary of each other. Frankly, some of the Stokers look like they want to start shooting, though their leader has had some sharp words with them. But you should get here quick. They need an authority figure."

"Will do, Judd. Be there in less than five." Heiko turned to De Voe and Nesvorny – who had slumped back in his seat and cast the tablet he'd been using onto the desk. "I'll soothe things out, ensure all are armed, and then quietly bring them up to this level. Claude… any news from Karyn?"

"No, sir, not yet. But the new arrivals show she's been successful, doesn't it?"

"*Partially*," said Heiko.

"What about the enemy above us?" asked De Voe. It was approaching seven o' clock ATT: their tight schedule was meant to ensure they struck while their foes slept. She noticed Heiko and Vardem exchange sharp glances. "Come on, Rennie. The Colonel and I need to know."

"The camera on Level Zero shows heightened activity. The one in the area of the cells shows the sleeper has woken and is drinking coffee with their companion. Lack of cameras limit what else we can see around the barracks."

"In other words," said De Voe, "they're starting to rouse and we have to strike now."

Nesvorny suddenly stood. "We do. I need to see my troops. I'm coming with you, Heiko."

"As long as you're sure the twitchy Stokers won't forget their restraint on seeing you, then fine."

De Voe picked up her rifle. She hated asking, but: "What about me?"

Heiko thought a moment. "Claude should be okay in here. Come with us. Join Monique at the stairwell: she could do with some company. We'll be bringing the attack force up that way once they're organised."

De Voe did as asked. Soon after, she watched the men descend to the lower level and joined trooper Monique McGregor at the stairwell entrance.

"Anything happening?" she asked.

"Dead quiet," said McGregor. "I can't believe this will go on much longer. Why has no one come down to this level?"

"From what I can gather, there are fewer members of the Apparatus than the full complement of the ISU, so there's plenty of space in the habitable levels. They're probably a bit disorganised, too. They don't know what they've got here, and they're probably not inclined to poke around at night."

McGregor nodded. She was red haired, like some of the Stokers, with freckles across her thin, pale face. "But it's not night now."

Suddenly, the door along the corridor opened, and Vardem hurried out – his rifle on a strap across his shoulders, a tablet in one hand. He trotted towards them. It was clear that something was up.

De Voe looked quickly askance at McGregor, then she moved forwards, her rifle in both hands. Before she reached him, Vardem hissed: "Activity. This is only one of four ways between the levels, and the only one that gives access to the one below. But someone's just come down the lift from the main connecting shaft." He waved his tablet, implying he'd recorded activity on a systems site.

Then McGregor was with them. "Quiet!" she said sharply. "I thought I heard voices!"

The three were towards the end of one wide corridor, with the inventory office part-way down to the left and closed storerooms to either side of them. Another corridor bisected theirs just past the office, and there was another stairwell at the far end, which only allowed access upwards. If they'd had a bigger force, they would have left a sentry there and at the other two entranceways, which presumably lay to either end of the cross corridor, down which the voices – which De Voe now also heard – were coming.

De Voe cast about, and quickly came to a conclusion: "Let's all head to the junction," she whispered. "There's no need of a guard here – the only ones coming from below will be our team. Then we'll play it by ear… literally."

She had no official command, but she knew she had *presence*, and the others silently obeyed. They crept to the edge of the cross corridor, passing the inventory office, the voices rising all the time. It was difficult to tell how many there were, but De Voe didn't think there were more than two. They paused at the corner, waiting. But the voices ceased rising in volume: whoever they belonged to had come to whatever room they'd been aiming for. De Voe vacillated: maybe the others would collect something and leave? A minute passed, and then there were new voices – from behind. She looked back: "Fuck!" It was the assault group. They were speaking low, having clearly been briefed, but it might not be low enough to go unheard by the enemy around the corner. "Okay. Claude – stay here so our friends can see we haven't been abducted. Monique – with me."

De Voe turned the corner and confidently marched in the direction of the main elevator, which she could see some way in the distance at the end of the corridor. There were more storerooms here, and along the ceiling of was a metal rail for a movable hoist, which could be seen further along, currently inactive. Part-way down on the left, a broad door had been raised up into a socket, and extra light spilled into the corridor from out of the room. An electric cart was parked outside, sitting on wide rubber tyres, filling most of the width of the space. Such carts were quiet – perhaps its gentle hum had been overlain by the voices?

Hitching the rifle from where it hung off her right shoulder, she marched to the wide portal and turned to face inside. Within, she noticed all sorts of boxes and crates, some broken open, which seemed to hold packets of food and bottles of drink. Rummaging amongst these were not the two she expected, but *four*. She faltered, but quickly recovered. As one woman in a grey-and-black uniform with a closely shaved scalp looked up, De Voe said: "What are you doing here? Do you have permission to take these things?"

The woman's eyes widened, and she glanced to McGregor at De Voe's side. Like the others – who ceased what they were doing, turned, looked around – the woman was only armed with a baton dangling from the belt at her waist. Then De Voe heard McGregor click her tongue and mutter: "Right wall." A single rifle was propped there.

A man in the depth of the storeroom slowly walked forwards – clearly the leader of the group. He was also shaven-headed, and had a haughty, confident expression. "We need to eat, don't you think?" He was now just one metre away, where he came to a halt. "The question is, what are *you* doing here, citizen? We agreed that this would be the HQ of the new security division. *Our* HQ. How did *you* get here? A secret way? Come to help yourselves, perhaps?" Behind the man, the others were also moving slowly forwards.

De Voe moved her rifle ever-so-slightly, directing it to one side of the man. "I think you should tell you friends to stop moving, *comrade*." Without taking her eyes from the man, she said: "Monique – shoot the first person to lay hands on that gun."

The man's smirk evaporated. "What is this? Are we not allies? If you wish to…" He lunged forwards, his hand instantly on his baton. He clearly knew what he was doing, for he moved inside the swinging arc of her rifle, but De Voe managed to get a shot off anyway, which ricocheted off the floor and punched through the side of a crate. But then he was on her, and they stumbled back into the corridor, just missing the cart. Then there was a shout, and another shot: McGregor?

De Voe managed to keep on her feet, back-peddling until she slammed into the far wall, and the man, overbalancing, slipped onto his face. He started to rise, baton in one hand, but he didn't get a chance to use it: with a vicious swing, De Voe clubbed him on the side of the head, sending him to the ground. Then there was another shout, and she turned: at the junction, Heiko was there, unarmed but moving quickly, and then there were others streaming behind, mostly wearing black. She glanced back at McGregor, to see the woman standing firm, rifle levelled, but none near her, and when she looked back into the room, she noticed the three Marseillais standing still, arms aloft in surrender.

The man at her feet wasn't getting up. She blew out a deep breath, and turned to face the slowing Heiko. "Rennie – glad you could make it."

Heiko drew up, looked down, and smiled. "The Melissa De Voe approach to negotiations?" Then he chuckled. "Well, I doubt the Makka Frost one would have been quite as effective."

"Nah, we'd still be negotiating come nightfall. You wanted speed? You got it."

* * *

Heiko stood to one side of the assault group near the junction at the centre of the complex on Sublevel Three, with De Voe, Nesvorny, and a Stoker called Seumus. Around forty members of the ISU had answered their old leader's call, while around a dozen armed Stokers had been sent by Karyn Dures along with a cart bearing weapons. But the cart only held another ten rifles with limited ammunition, meaning most of Nesvorny's force had nothing but their bare hands – or now, some batons plus the one extra rifle that had been retrieved from the storeroom pillagers. With the guns held by the Stavangerans, they had fewer than thirty rifles and no grenades or heavier weapons. Still, they had just concluded a plan…

Nesvorny scowled. "I hate dividing forces, but we've no choice. There are four entrances from this level to the one above and we need to cover all of them to prevent any escapes *down*. Unfortunately, there are five ways up from Sub Two to Sub One. There's a central atrium directly above our heads with a stairwell and a bank of elevators. If they're awake and competent, they can hold us off and get out that way, then hold all five routes against us on Sub One, and we'll never shift them."

"I see what you're saying," said Heiko. "We'll just have to hit them hard and move fast. Claude is in their systems now: as soon as we breach, he'll cut all the elevators including the central one, and we'll just have to hope the shock leaves them disorientated. But I agree, we must rush the centre from four sides, leaving pairs of armed guards at the stairwells."

Heiko led the Stavangaran party to the most northerly stairwell, while Nesvorny led a second group, a sergeant of the ISU called Taylor led a third, and Seumus led the Stokers in a fourth. They synchronised their ascent: the four parties emerged onto Sublevel Two simultaneously, at which point Vardem shut down all the lifts.

But in spite of their fears, the level was quickly taken: there were only eleven members of the *Marseilles* Apparatus on that level: two were on the wing with the jail cells; two more were in an office; and seven were making use of a large training and exercise hall that took up one quadrant of the level. There was only one rifle on the entire floor, emphasizing the scarcity of arms amongst all the combatants in *Hibernia*. Seven imprisoned officers were released, and one of these – a Lieutenant Worsley – took charge of Sergeant Taylor's squad. The freed cells were then used to hold the new prisoners, as well as the four from below, who were temporarily squeezed several to a cell.

"Sub One will be harder," said Nesvorny. "Bunk rooms and more offices. But if we're quick…"

They were quick, but not quick enough. Maybe it was because the elevators had all stopped working; maybe it was because one of the new prisoners had managed to send an alert, or caused concern by not responding to a call; but when they stormed from the central stairway into the plaza above, they found people in uniform milling around, some by the lift, several of whom were properly armed. All it took was a single shot to cause panic; in the plaza, too close to shoot, a mass brawl erupted, with more force being fed into each side like wood onto a bonfire: the raiders rushing up from below, the Marseillaise being fed from the bunk rooms on this level. And this time, they could not prevent some of the enemy ascending to the ground level to alert their colleagues, or in the case of two of the corridors, set up barricades behind which even one or two riflemen could hold off an assault.

After ten minutes, it was stalemate: there were eight dead – six of the foe, one ISU, one Stoker – and around a dozen injured from bullets or with broken limbs or concussion from baton strikes.

"What now?" asked De Voe. She'd stuck close to Heiko – much to his relief, for though she was a force of nature, she clearly appreciated that she wasn't a soldier and had allowed those who were to engage in the fighting.

Heiko looked at Nesvorny, who squatted beside him in the plaza, away from the entrance to the corridors down which bullets were occasionally being fired to ensure the invaders kept back. "Where's Seumus? Ah…" He spotted the Stoker and beckoned him over. The man hesitated a moment, then came over in a crouch.

"Okay – so, options?" Heiko asked.

"We could try to come up behind them," said Nesvorny. "We control the stairwells from below. But, I am sure they are wise to this and they'll be watching. They might even try to do the same to us."

Heiko held up a hand and closed his eyes. A moment later, he opened them again. "Claude's got a tactical warfare system running. They've just tried. South-east stairwell. But they were put off by a couple of volleys from our guys."

"Without explosive, we're going nowhere," said Seumus. He seemed willing to speak to Heiko, but struggled to even make eye contact with Nesvorny. "The Earthers made some for us, but now their production line has come under the control of the traitors. Fuck O' Hare!"

"If they can get hold of some grenades, we'd be in the shit," said Nesvorny, "even if we had an advantage in numbers, which I doubt."

Heiko nodded slowly. "I was expecting this. *Nil desperandum.* We have done our part. The rest is now up to Ms Dures. Seumus – has she sent you any news?"

"If she has, I've been too jacked up to see it." He flipped a comms device from a thigh pocket of his overalls. His eyes flickered over the screen. "No. Not yet."

"In that case, we just wait," said Heiko. "We've taken out a lot of their force and have focused the attention of the rest." He slumped back, folded his arms, and closed his eyes.

"Don't pretend you're accessing your internal vision, Rennie," said De Voe. "I've not slept this night either, so I know exactly how you feel."

Heiko smiled gently but kept his eyes closed.

Though it would have been unprofessional to sleep, age was catching up with him. Whether he actually did or not, he couldn't tell, but it seemed an instant after he closed his eyes that an internal alert from Vardem caused him to open them: De Voe was slumped beside him, most definitely asleep, snoring softly, but Nesvorny was stood over him, a wry smile on his face.

"She's here. Apparently, she just walked into the complex on ground level, saying she'd heard the ISU were back in business – then her lot levelled their guns and the Marseillaise had no choice but to drop their weapons."

Still reclining, Heiko asked: "And the holdouts on this level?"

"I suspect the message is just being relayed to them. Seumus is shouting at them to surrender, and by all the gods he's got a pair of lungs on him. Enough to wake the dead… yet somehow not the sleeping."

Heiko smiled gently, then glanced at De Voe. "Indeed. But let's keep that between you and I."

A short time later, with the members of the Apparatus disarmed, Heiko and the assault team met Karyn Dures on the ground level.

* * *

Deux had been woken and told of trouble at the ISU compound. By the time he'd dressed and left his luxury flat in the Boston Quarter –

confiscated from an industrialist, who'd been thrown onto the street – and journeyed to the command centre in the central tower of *Hibernia*, the fight had resolved. A report from a member of the Apparatus who'd been on patrol outside at the time, reported that an unusual force of Stokers and others in black uniforms had taken over.

Hollande had already been in the building; O'Hare and Sullivan arrived shortly after. They assembled in the office that had once been O'Neill's. It was here that a message reached them – displayed on the main comms terminal by a technician, who accepted the call and then hurried from the room.

Karyn Dures peered out at the committee. "The rulers of *Hibernia*?" she said sarcastically. "President Deux and his lackeys? The Earther, the turncoat and… *Magdalen*." An eyebrow arched at the last word. Deux suspected the woman wanted to say something rather insulting, yet somehow managed to hold her tongue.

"Karyn," said O'Hare, leaning in. "It's good to see you in one piece, though I'm not sure how you got here. And you seem to have acquired some new allies. The ISU? Really? Is this what we fought for?"

Deux looked at O'Hare and scowled: she was stealing his thunder, yet asking the questions he wanted to ask, so he closed his mouth and let the women talk.

"Some of the ISU, yes," said Karyn. "But my allies go beyond these, and have significant material and intellectual resources to add to our partnership. They also appear to have scruples that you and your clique don't. Will you fight me, Magdalen? Stokers against Stokers?"

O'Hare seemed unperturbed. "I was informed of treachery. There was an opening. I took it."

"I ask again: will you fight me?"

Deux swore under his breath: he knew the response before the other gave it.

O'Hare placed her hands on her chair's armrests and levered herself to her feet. "Now that you are back, whole, and in control… you are the leader of our people." She turned a smile on Deux. "First Citizen… it has been an amusing-if-brief tenure. Thanks for your offer, but I must resign."

"Bitch, I'll…"

O'Hare's face turned serious and she raised a finger. "I am leaving, and those of my people in this building with me. Dare try to harm or detain any of us, and the whole community will rise up and rip you apart." Then she smiled, though with little sincerity. "But in recognition of our past relationship, I and mine will sit out this little dispute." She laughed, turned to nod at the image of Dures on the screen, and strode from the room.

Deux looked from the closing door back to the screen, where Karyn Dures struggled to restrain a smile. "One down… three to go," she said.

"It was you who brought this on, Dures, not I," said Deux. "It was you who betrayed the revolution. It was you who slunk to the *Lisboa* to plot behind my back with that snake, Louvain, and it seems with the old regime too. Is O'Neill with you?"

"Her? Oh, no. She still squats on Mount Athol. Her turn is coming. The ISU units I have with me serve the people of *Hibernia* more widely – *not* her; not any longer. There are some reasonable voices among them. An accommodation has been made. Stokers will no longer be disrespected or disenfranchised, but I'll not replace one corrupt system with another, or one oppressed people with a second. And your system, Deux, would set you and your bigots up as first among equals, lording it over the majority of *Hibernia* – just like O'Neill."

"That's a lie! I serve the citizens."

"Serve?" Karyn almost seemed affronted. "You serve no one but yourself. *Enough.* It is time for you and your Apparatus to go. Most are already under guard at the ISU complex. I want you to come to the foyer on the ground floor – unarmed. At present, no harm has been done, so we'll escort you to the docks, where you'll remain until the *Marseilles* sends boats to pick you up. The Earthers can remain or go, whatever they wish, but they must also surrender their weapons."

"And me?" said Sullivan, speaking quickly while Deux tried to get his emotions under control.

"Your power ends here and now. Cooperate, and I see no reason to harm or imprison you." Karyn looked grim. "I give you the same option as Colonel Nesvorny, who is currently behaving himself: retirement at the end of this affair, or exile."

"Retirement!" blurted Sullivan.

"Two down," said Karyn. "Hollande?"

"Georges!" snapped Deux. "The people will never forgive treachery."

Hollande nodded. "I am with the revolution. The First Citizen is the purest embodiment of it. Whatever he decides for himself, he decides for us."

Deux laughed. Sullivan was inconsequential – he didn't need her. But the New Socialists, though few in number, had skills and weapons. Better still, most were in the building, as was Captain Boursis and her best people, who'd been formed into his presidential guard. He knew Falcome was loyal and still had his gunboats. And he also knew that, once back on the *Marseilles*, no matter what that fool Louvain, or Dures, thought, he would soon have the People's Committee twisted around his finger as before, and the ship would return to him. As such, there was still a game to play; still prizes to be won – not least this new find on Ardol. And if he held that with his new fleet and new weapons, then all would have to deal with him for the resources needed to survive – even Karyn Dures. "I only wish the citizens of *Hibernia* well, but if my regime is not wanted, I am certainly no tyrant. I accept your offer – but with a proviso: the arms we bear were made with our resources, and borne by our citizens, some of whom paid in blood for the aid they gave you. They come with us. If you wish, we'll unload them and carry them empty, but carry them we will." His eyes steeled. "Say no, and you will have to take them from us. I will not negotiate on this."

Karyn was quiet a moment; he could almost see the thoughts forming in her head. He knew he had judged the matter well. At last, she said: "Very well. But you and yours must exit one at a time, have all ammunition ready to hand over. All will be searched. Please do not try to smuggle bullets out – that will only delay matters and cause us to increase the thoroughness of subsequent searches."

"Very well." Deux cut the connection. At least he'd had the last word.

* * *

"So, we're going to the *Marseilles*?" said Jacques Danté. The New Socialists formed a scrum around Georges Hollande, totalling thirteen in number. Several of their party from the *Leviathan* had been killed during the insurrection, including Babatunde Odile, and several more were currently with the fleet stranded at the shipyard, whether on Hibernian trawlers or the *Marseilles'* converted gunboats – though who still lived and who had died was unknown. A couple more still laboured in the weapons manufactories set up in the Engine Quarter and would presumably be brought to join them at some point.

"It seems we are not as welcome here as we once were," said Hollande. "The Stokers have instead decided to make peace with the bourgeoisie."

"You mean, sell out," said Danté, his voice rising above the unhappy murmurs.

"Ingrates," hissed one woman, who bore an NS tattoo on her neck.

"Yes," said Hollande. "But this isn't the end of the revolution. The First Citizen will keep the flame alight. We'll join him. Recuperate. Make more arms. We knew achieving utopia wouldn't be easy – but unlike Earth, if we stay true and continue the struggle, it is still possible here on Tethys." He looked over to the second group that occupied the large foyer on the ground floor of the command centre building. Deux was there, with Captain Boursis at his side, surrounded by nearly a dozen of the most committed members of the Apparatus. They had started to break up as, one by one, they headed towards the third group present – a mishmash of Stokers and members of the ISU in their cursed black uniforms, most of whom stood with rifles low and pointed directly at them – in contrast to Hollande and his colleagues, whose weapons were, by order, kept on straps across shoulders.

The group quietened and turned to watch with him. The first member of the Apparatus held a magazine of bullets out in one hand and their rifle in the other. The bullets were confiscated and the rifle was taken and checked – while one of the ISU patted the man down – and then, satisfied that it was unloaded, the rifle was handed back.

The grey-uniformed man was then escorted through wide front doors, presumably to some vehicle that would take them to their new accommodation near the docks.

Just off to one side of this activity stood their captors' leaders. Hollande saw Karyn Dures in conversation with a man in a black uniform with short silver hair – Colonel Nesvorny. He felt a surge of anger at the sight and formed a fist with one hand. But then he recognised another, standing just back from these, resting against the glass wall, arms folded and weaponless. "*Him!*"

Danté must have been following the direction of Hollande's gaze, for he swore. "I thought he'd gone – but here he is again. We should have known."

"He should be made to pay," said the woman with the neck tattoo. She was one of the group that had been humiliated by the Earther soldier and the people from the *Stavanger*: fooled, assaulted, stripped, and left overnight until discovered by a search party the day after.

"I have a bullet," said another, leaning forwards, speaking quietly. "In the breech." The man had a fleshy nose and various tattoos on the backs of his hands. Another of the failed hit squad.

"Give it to me," said the woman. "I'll do it."

"No," said Danté, "I will."

"Is this wise?" asked another woman. "They'll kill us all."

Hollande shook his head and quickly looked around. "No, they won't. They're weak. If Boursis were in charge of them, we'd all end up in the sea, but this lot haven't got the strength to do what is necessary. They made a point of not harming you, didn't they?" he spoke directly to the first woman. "But whoever does this is taking a risk."

"I said I'll do it," said Danté. "I'll drop the gun straight after. Claim it was an accident. If they shoot me first, I'm happy to die for the cause – as long as I take that fascist with me."

Hollande nodded. "This time, Jacques, don't miss."

The group shuffled together: surreptitiously, Danté exchanged weapons with the man who had a loaded gun.

"We'll go last," said Hollande to Danté. "After they've inspected all the others and found no problems, their guard will be down. You go before me: I want to see that bastard die."

"Me too," said the first woman.

Hollande admired her ardour. After a moment, he nodded: the pair of them would watch.

In due course, the foyer emptied. Deux was the last of the Marseillaise to be inspected and passed. Hollande watched him exchange words with Karyn Dures, although the pair spoke softly and he couldn't make out what they were saying. The New Socialist contingent was then processed. Finally, there were just the three of them left.

"Next," shouted one of the ISU screeners.

"Long live the revolution," hissed Danté. He stepped forwards as the others had done, but only held the rifle, having passed all his ammunition to a previous man, leaving his extra hand free.

Hollande and the woman had shuffled forwards so that they were no more than four metres away from the search party and the watching leaders off to their side. He saw their target – the man called Heiko – suddenly become alert. And then he noticed the woman to his side, who leant in to speak to Heiko while keeping an eye on Danté. One of the Stavangerans?

Danté started to lower his rifle in his right hand, clasping the stock near the trigger. He advanced another step and allowed the gun to swing further right so that it was pointing towards the leader group. Hollande could only see the back of his head, but something in Danté's face must have revealed his malign intent, for he saw Heiko's eyes widen and the man started to move…

Danté's shot rang loud and was immediately followed by breaking glass as the bullet shattered the window of the foyer… after passing through its intended target? There was blood, and a shriek from Danté, as the recoiling rifle, held just by a hand, snapped back, perhaps breaking the man's thumb or finger, causing him to let it drop. But while most of their watchers had been lulled into complacency, the woman beside Heiko had already been raising her own rifle. A split-second later, she pulled the trigger – holding the gun at waist level, but in both hands. Her aim was poor: there were several shots, then Danté crumpled, blood fountaining from his head… and then Hollande also jerked back. Someone had punched him. Punched? He looked down: his green Stoker's overalls had turned red just below his sternum. *Red?*

Chapter 48

The news from *Hibernia* had been mainly positive, but not entirely so.

Colonel Tania Joseph joined Kai Dures at the impromptu observation post – a gulley in the side of the dusty, red-grey slope of the Range. They'd arrived the previous evening after two days of scrambling across steep slopes by the ocean, without shade, under a hot sun. This position gave a reasonable view over the Mount Athol settlement and the bulk of their force arrayed on the flatter slopes below, which was now rousing itself after an uncomfortable night sleeping in the open. They were also able to glimpse a couple of manned positions held by Fukuda's ISU – just out of rifle range. "News from Karyn?"

"She's going to send her message in about ten minutes," said Dures. "We will be patched in when needed. And we should be formed up by then, looking like we mean business."

"Only *looking like*? Are we going to do this, or not?"

"Hopefully not – it depends on how persuasive my wife is. She can be *very* persuasive. But if not…" Dures gestured at the enemy positions on the outskirts of Athol. "You tell me. You're the military person. I'm just a street thug. They're dug in with fire control over the land between us. Do you think we can assault them and win?"

"With determination, possibly. We have the numerical advantage. But we'd lose many. Maybe hundreds."

"And *without* determination?" growled Dures.

"Let's not think about that. For one, I don't want to have to trudge all the way back to the shipyard in defeat, carrying wounded. And we barely had enough supplies to get here, so we'd be on water rations only." She paused a moment and frowned. "What about our colleague? What news of him?"

"Heiko's hanging on, but the shot through his pelvis was messy. Still, the odds are improving with each passing hour."

Joseph nodded. "Good. I liked him. He knew what he was doing. I hate to say it, but we could have used him here."

Dures grunted and looked away, back down the slope.

A moment later, Joseph asked: "What about the other one? The leader of these New Socialists?"

Dures shook his head. "The news is *worse* there." He looked up and smiled grimly. "Seems like he *is* going to live… at least for a while. But he's going to do so without a spleen and part of his liver."

Joseph returned the grim smile. Without a spleen, he'd need to be on antibiotics for the rest of his life, and antibiotics production was limited on Tethys. And then she laughed. "I hear that on Earth they make artificial spleens that work better than our natural ones. I wonder if he'd let them put one in?"

"He bored me with that obsession," said Dures, his smile becoming more genuine. "If he did and became *augmented*, he'd have to declare himself public enemy number one and kill himself. An interesting dilemma."

"Somehow, I think he'd find a way to rationalise things so that he didn't have to. It's always the way with these fanatics." She looked back at the nearest enemy outpost, which was at about the same altitude as their own. There was a sparkle of reflected sunlight. Binoculars? "It seems they're watching and waiting, too. Come on Karyn, deliver your bombshell."

* * *

O'Neill took the call in the ESU's command centre with Traore. The first thing she noticed on her screen was that Karyn Dures was sat in O'Neill's old office in *Hibernia*, as if to rub in her victory.

"Hello, Ms Dures. Are you calling to announce your surrender?"

The woman with the unusual hairstyle – long on one side, shaved on the other, with a raised scar visible through the stubble – narrowed her eyes. "I'm glad to see you've retained your sense of humour."

"What is funny, Dures, is what happened to your invasion fleet. How long ago did it set out? Three days? I heard it had some difficulties. Something absurd about sea monsters. Anyway, without it, you seem to have nothing to dislodge me."

"I have more information on the fleet than you have. In any case, does not the loss of your own naval contingent bother you?"

"Oh, yes, of course. Colonel Joseph was an adequate officer, and I rue the loss of her boats. But our losses seem to be dwarfed by yours. And I was prescient enough to have her leave two aside, so both Ardol and Athol are protected from whatever old fishing boats you may still be able to throw at us."

On the screen, Dures was unable to contain a smile. "You seem to be labouring under a number of misconceptions. Now I see why you are so cheerful. I'm sorry I'm going to have correct that. This may be difficult for you."

O'Neill managed to retain her smile, though she suddenly felt less confident. "Really? Well, do go on, Dures. I'm interested to hear your fabrications."

"Okay. First, the fleet was damaged, I agree, but with some exterior help I won't go into, was largely saved. I admit it wasn't in a fit state to continue a seaborne assault, but it was escorted to the shipyard to your north. You must have noticed the sizeable force on your doorstep."

"Survivors of the shipwrecks," muttered Traore. "That's all."

O'Neill frowned at the man but didn't speak.

"Perhaps you should ask your Major Fukuda," said Karyn. "He must have been counting. How many survivors – *armed* survivors – does he report?"

O'Neill held up one hand to stay Traore. "A reasonable number, true. But my forces are dug in. You are welcome to throw your unhorsed riders at us. Let's see if they fight better than they sail."

Karyn nodded slowly. "I said 'first'. Now 'second'. You seem to think that Colonel Joseph expired. I'm sure you'll be happy to learn that she actually lives."

"Yes, ecstatic," said O'Neill, sarcastically.

"I'm going to patch in another feed. You will need to accept it."

O'Neill nodded at Traore, who hit the appropriate control, and the image on the screen split. To the left of Karyn Dures another image appeared, this from somewhere outside – the two new figures in it having sky and steep greyish terrain as a backdrop. One was Kai Dures, the handsome, brooding husband of Karyn, the other… "Joseph?"

"Ma'am."

"What the fuck is going on?" said O'Neill. "Why haven't you reported in? You let them catch you?"

"Not exactly, ma'am." Joseph had looked neutral; now a wicked smile stole across her face. "The sea creature attack put life into new perspective. It seemed stupid for us to be killing each other when these other things were trying to do so as well, and showing no favouritism. At the shipyard, we talked and came to an understanding."

"You've betrayed me," said O'Neill, her anger barely under control. "You've betrayed your people. Your state."

"Betrayed *you*? Oh, yes. Absolutely. But you are not the people or the state. You're a parasite."

"Fuck you, Joseph!"

On the screen the other raised a hand. "Oh… and I heard you mention the two boats I left you. I'm sorry to say that you overestimate your resources. Their captains and crew still answer to me. If you want to check, you'll find that the one at Athol has just set sail and will sit off the coast a safe distance until it receives further orders from me."

"That's our escape route," muttered Traore.

"Shut the fuck up, Manfred. It makes no difference. We don't need to escape. We're safe here. They still can't oust us."

"Oh, really?" said Karyn Dures. "And that is your plan? You are stranded there. You have no hope of fleeing without Colonel Joseph's boats, and I wouldn't recommend swimming. Without a fleet of your own, your food supplies will start to dwindle. You cannot return to *Hibernia* without transport, and you don't have the strength to assault it anyway. You have nothing."

"While I have my freedom, there is always hope."

"While you have it," said Karyn. Her smile had evaporated. "Where did I get to? Second? You'll like 'third'. Colonel?" She called off screen, then moved aside slightly so that a new arrival could slip into a chair beside her."

"Nesvorny!" hissed O'Neill. "Not you too? I thought they would have hung you by now."

Nesvorny didn't smile: he didn't have the face for it. "I'm surprised, too, but Ms Dures is a surprising person, and a magnanimous one. She only wants equality for her people, not superiority. Not revenge."

"What the Colonel hasn't mentioned," continued Karyn, "is that, while we were speaking, he was sending an open communication to all of the ISU at Athol, telling them an agreement has been reached; that there will be peace if they lay down their weapons; that they can come home; that they will be free and most will retain their jobs under new management."

"Sneaky," said O'Neill. "You keep me talking while the Colonel is busy stabbing me in the back? However, I doubt he'll be believed. There will be a degree of confusion at best. But Fukuda is in charge now. They'll follow him."

"Perhaps, perhaps not," said Karyn. "But how hard will they fight for him, and for you? Do you want to bet your life on it? Because I swear, if my people have to come, and there is further bloodshed, then that is the price you will pay."

"So what's in it for us if we surrender now?" blurted Traore. "Amnesty?"

O'Neill saw genuine fear in the man's eyes. She faced the screen. "Amnesty… and a return with status to *Hibernia*."

"Do you really think, in your present circumstances, you can demand a return to the way matters were before?" said Karyn. "As though nothing has happened?"

O'Neill held Karyn's stare from the screen for a moment; broke and looked away; then looked back with a sharp smile. "I had to try. But as Manfred said – *amnesty*. No less. We'll not return just to be put on trial."

"Return? Not to *Hibernia*. Anywhere else you please, but not here."

"That's not amnesty," said O'Neill. "That's banishment."

"That's the best offer you're going to get," said Karyn. "You'll be free, but not in a position to plot and scheme and undermine your way back to power."

O'Neill sighed. She was a chess player, but one used to a vast board with many pieces. She was cornered; her pieces steadily removed or even turned. This game was over. "Very well. It's what I would have done in your position. I'll go. But what's mine is mine. I'm not going to be cast out in penury."

"What's in your immediate bank account can go with you – which is generous enough, given what you've inflicted. Everything else goes to the state."

Traore started to object, but O'Neill cut him off. "*Fine*. But where do we go?"

"Not the *Stavanger* or *Lisboa*," said Karyn. "These have suffered in their own ways, and will not harbour you." She smiled. "The *Marseilles* might accept you, though you might have to adjust your expectations and lifestyle."

"But…"

"Shut up, Manfred," said O' Neill. "We're not going to do better. I've always liked the *Rotterdam* when it visited. They are due at Ardol after the *Lisboa* and *Marseilles*. They cannot be too far away." And she thought to herself: *And their rulers are weak.*

"Very well," said Karyn. "I will contact them, though they may need some remunerations."

"If so, you can pay that," said O'Neill, suddenly feeling a weight lifted and – curiously – rather than depression, excitement and a sense of possibility.

Karyn nodded. "That just leaves you to surrender. Your forces must throw down their weapons."

From the second screen, Kai Dures growled. "I'd like to receive the surrender of Major Fukuda personally."

O'Neill nodded in understanding. "I suspect the Major is excluded from the current bargain, yes?" When neither of the Dures couple spoke, she continued. "So sad – but there's always a fall guy. Manfred – you are formally his superior. I'll leave it to you to tell him."

* * *

Nesvorny knew he was a pawn – or to be fair, maybe a knight or rook – now being moved about a chessboard by Karyn Dures' skilled hand. She'd moved him to *Hibernia*, where he'd managed to act as the seed around which the defeated element of the ISU had coalesced. After victory was achieved over the *Marseillaise* and their allies, his services were no longer required on *Hibernia* – but they were at Athol, and so he'd been put on the shuttle that was currently heading to that dusty site on the eastern edge of the Range. But before leaving, he'd ensured his old unit was well treated: though the re-formed ISU had had its recently provided firearms reclaimed, it had been retained in uniform and tasked with resuming its well-worn law-and-order brief over the city state. Of course, he'd had to accept Karyn's word that his people would be safe and respected on his departure, but he'd decided to do just that: he'd been exhausted by the last few years dealing with the fickle and malign influence of Traore and his superior; it had been time to try another approach: *trust.*

His new task was to reclaim control of the ISU element on Athol – something that no one else on Tethys could do, perhaps not even Joseph, given the fraternal rivalry that existed between the ISU and ESU. Before he'd boarded the shuttle for the short flight, Joseph had confirmed that the units facing the invaders had indeed surrendered, allowing the combined force of Stokers and ESU to warily march from its camp into the settlement, but she'd also noted a great deal of wariness and tension. He was the emollient that would soothe the situation.

But the shuttle had only just lifted off, when Joseph called again.

"Eric? Problem."

"Fukuda?" he said, into the tablet-sized comms device he held between his hands.

"Yeah, that fucker. He's disappeared, and so has his unit, Squad Five. Traore insists he told the man to stand down, and says Fukuda agreed, but I don't know what to believe from that arsehole."

"Has he left Athol?"

"We don't really know. It's confusion here. The Stokers and ESU are wandering about among the ISU, who seem to be complying and handing in weapons. And then there are the miners and regular citizens, too, who are frankly getting in the way, mostly trying to get some food. What's your ETA?"

"Twelve minutes."

"It's not going to be resolved by then. Maybe you should abort. Maybe he's just itching to take you out as you come in to land."

Nesvorny shook his head. "The longer he's free and I'm absent, the more chance he has to set himself up as a credible resistance leader. He won't know I'm coming on this shuttle, and if he starts firing he'll give his location away. In any case, the only weapons that could bring the shuttle down are on your patrol boats – the light rifles he has won't cut it, unless someone gets off a very lucky shot."

"Okay, Eric. Just thought I'd tell you. I'll make sure there's a good perimeter around the landing site so no one takes a shot at you when you emerge."

"Thanks, Tania."

The small Hibernian shuttle duly arrived and settled onto its landing pad. Nesvorny was unstrapped and moving before the engine noise died out. He descended the retractable steps to find Joseph in a cloud of dust, holding a cloth to her mouth. He squinted to keep the dust out of his eyes and followed the woman a short distance to a nearby building; he was relieved when the door slammed shut, the noise level dropped, and he was able to wipe tears from his eyes and see clearly. He instantly noticed one other in the room, standing on the far side.

"Nesvorny," said Kai Dures, brusquely, by way of greeting.

"Dures," he replied. "I hear you've lost Fukuda."

"Hey, you two, play nice!" said Joseph, shaking some of the sand from the cloth she'd used to protect her mouth. "We're meant to be on the same side now."

"Are we?" said Dures.

"Your wife seems to think so," said Nesvorny. "I trust her. Don't you?"

Dures tensed, but after a couple of seconds, his shoulders sagged. "It's difficult. For years, Nesvorny, you've been the bogeyman. But now we're meant to work together." He shook his head softly. "But you've done what you've said you would do – so far."

"I understand, Dures. It's tough for me, too. But I've never been the enemy of your people, and maybe, you've never really been the enemy of mine. I can't say most Hibernians have a good opinion of Stokers – you've not given them a good reason for that." He raised a hand to stall the other. "But maybe you've had a good excuse. I admit that."

Dures closed his eyes momentarily. "Fine," he said. Then he looked at Nesvorny intently. "*You*… I can just about accept.

Especially now I know who was behind the worst of the excesses against my people. But I'm struggling with others."

"O'Neill and Traore?" said Nesvorny.

"My wife gave them a deal. It tears me up to see them so smug, escaping justice."

"And maybe still toying with us," said Joseph. "Especially Traore."

"Sure," said Nesvorny. "I need to see my troops and let them see me to calm the situation. But perhaps we should first have a quick chat with your prisoners."

"Both?" asked Joseph.

"No. Divide and conquer. If Traore is the main issue here, let's bring him in alone."

Joseph looked to Dures, who shrugged, so she left the office. An uncomfortable couple of minutes of silence followed after the woman left, but, fortunately, the ex-leaders of *Hibernia* were being held nearby. She soon returned, trailed by Traore, who was gently shoved inside by a Stoker guard, who then left to stand outside the building.

Traore still looked sharp in an expensive suit. He gave a disarming smile and took a chair without being asked. "Ah, Colonel Nesvorny, have you come to join the party? How may I help?"

Nesvorny, Joseph, and Dures formed a semi-circle around the prisoner: Nesvorny sat facing him, while the others stood off to Traore's side.

"Fukuda," said Nesvorny. "What *exactly* did you say to him, and what did he say to you?"

"Him? Oh, I simply told him the truth. A deal had been made, and we decided – for the good of the people of *Hibernia*, and in order to save lives – to allow your force to enter unmolested. I asked him to convey this to his troops, and he seems to have done that. No one fired on you, right?"

"So where is he now?"

Traore shrugged and grinned. "Perhaps he is having a moment to himself? Baking a 'welcome back Colonel Nesvorny' cake?"

"You're not taking this very seriously," snarled Dures.

"I really don't know what you're worried about. You're in control, aren't you? So what if one man has momentarily disappeared from view? I'm sure you'll find him eventually. Our deal didn't involve anything more specific. If you wanted him trussed up and delivered in a sack, you should have said so. We can't be held accountable for your poor negotiation skills." He leant back and smiled broadly. But as he turned to look at Dures, the Stoker's fist flashed down into his face, knocking him from his chair.

Nesvorny watched as a shocked Traore held up an open hand to ward off further blows. "Wait... stop…"

But Dures hadn't finished: he grabbed the intervening chair in one muscular hand and tossed it aside, and then dropped a knee onto the other and started raining down blows.

"Eric!" said Joseph sharply, looking at him as she pushed herself from the wall against which she'd been leaning. But even though she was close, she didn't try to intervene.

Nesvorny watched through hard eyes, and only after a punch that was so hard it slammed Traore's head into the floor, did he slowly rise. "Okay, Dures. I think that's enough."

Dures still had a fist raised: for a moment it hovered, ready to descend again, but then he dropped his arm, straightened from his semi-crouch, and stepped back. He breathed heavily as he glared at the prone man on the blood-splattered floor.

"Happy now?" asked Nesvorny.

Dures turned to look at him and smiled fiercely. "No. But happier… *thanks*."

Nesvorny manoeuvred around the table to stand next to Joseph on the other side of the felled man, whose handsome face was swollen and bloody.

"Please… no…" said Traore weakly, through broken lips. "No more."

Nesvorny crouched beside him. "I am sorry for the slippery floor, Mr Traore. Now, you were telling me about the Major. Do you have anything more to add, or would you like to return to your cell? Mr Dures would be happy to take you there personally."

"No!" Traore's voice strengthened and he held up a hand. "Please… no. I didn't… I just… I just told Fukuda that he might be at risk. That it might be best for him to be elsewhere. That's all. He understood. But he didn't tell me what he would do or where he would go. I swear!"

Nesvorny ran his eyes over the other's face; he nodded and stood. "You had better hope that Fukuda causes no mischief, Traore. The floors in this place seem incredibly slippery. I would hate for you to have any more accidents."

The guard was called; he looked at the scene with ill-disguised amusement. Joseph had to help him drag Traore back to his place of confinement.

When they were alone, Dures nodded at Nesvorny. "Appreciated, Colonel."

"In my younger days, I might not have been able to resist doing the same myself. But as others have noted, I've mellowed. So, Mr Dures, shall we go hunting? Tania's drones will pick him and his troop up if they've left the settlement. But before we go, I suggest you bring at least a dozen of your very best. Fukuda and his thugs won't come quietly."

"Sure. It'll be a pleasure hunting with you."

* * *

While Dures assembled a squad, Nesvorny visited the members of the ISU who'd been rounded up, and who now sat in small groups in the open – under light guard – scattered in the area around the landing pad and the ESU's command post. His words appeared to reassure, and grim moods quickly lifted. Before long, there was some laughter, and even some banter with the Stoker guards, who'd already been conditioned to the new situation during their march from the shipyard in the company of the ESU.

He then visited Joseph's command centre, where she had installed four of her team, each controlling a drone, the views from which – via monitors – showed different aspects of the Mount Athol mines and settlement. Dures joined them, leaving his squad outside, and for some minutes the three watched the coverage.

At last, Joseph concluded: "The area beyond Stonetown is clear. He can't have headed north, as we came from that direction; if he headed inland, he'd be easily visible and won't have gotten far without climbing gear; and the coastline south is also clear. It means he's holed up somewhere close."

"Where might he go that's out of the way and has space to hide?" asked Dures.

"The mines on the outskirts," said Nesvorny. "They've clearly been left unworked since O'Neill came here with the remnant of the ISU."

"Yeah, I agree," said Joseph. "It's either that or the miners' dorms. They might be able to change clothes and mingle in, but Fukuda would stand out. And a lot of the miners are Stokers, so they'd grass him up straightaway."

"Then let's go to the mines," said Dures. "I'm keen to make acquaintance with the servant, much as I did with the master."

Joseph handed an earpiece to Nesvorny. "Take this. I'll stay here and keep you updated. I'll redirect two of the drones to follow you close."

Nesvorny, Dures, and their squad, piled into four electric carts and took the road to the mine works several kilometres from the command centre. There was no fence around the mines, or even a control gate – for no one would want to visit the place apart from to work, and there was nothing to steal except rock. There was, however, a cluster of low buildings around a large tarmac square at the end of the road. All of the buildings were dust covered with grimy windows, the older and nearer ones dilapidated, the newer, more-solid ones built a little further away. There was also a transport depot to one side of the square – a vast, open-fronted garage that held various electric trucks, carts, and excavation machinery. Indeed, the depot only had two walls and a roof, with the rear side open too, allowing specialist equipment for drilling, scooping, and material collection easy access to the open cast mine itself.

They pulled up in front of the transport shed. As he stepped down from his cart, Nesvorny noticed one of the drones hovering overhead, and a voice came to his ear: "I'm afraid you'll have to check out the shed manually, Eric. I don't want to risk crashing a drone into the roof or ceiling. But I can say no one has entered or left the shed since you started moving."

"Thanks, Tania. That'll be our first target."

Dures directed his team of Stokers to fan out and enter the huge building, making their way between lines of vehicles. But the anomaly was easy to see.

"They've been here," said Nesvorny to Dures. He clambered aboard a small cart like those they'd taken from the command centre. "This one… and the two beside. Less dusty. Haphazardly parked. *Sloppy.*"

"They were clearly in a rush," said Dures. "How long have they had since they were warned by Traore?"

"Two hours?" mused Nesvorny. "No more than three." He looked into the depths of the depot. Some of the machinery towards the back was large, but it would be difficult to hide inside a driving cabin or cargo compartment – and pointless, too. He turned to look back at the buildings around the square.

"What are you thinking?" asked Dures.

"I'm wondering about their end game – what they're hoping to achieve."

"Staying alive," grunted Dures.

"Sure – but then what?"

"Maybe they've not thought that far ahead. Flee first, worry about the future afterwards."

Nesvorny nodded slowly. "That's my thought, too. But after they'd arrived here and got out of sight, they'd have to decide." He turned again to look through the shed, beyond which the first signs of excavations were just visible. "It's called a mine, but it's really a quarry. The rock has simply been stripped back into the mountainside. There are exploratory mine shafts – not just here, but at other points beyond, kilometres away. But unless Fukuda was organised, they'd have little to no food with them. Sitting down a mineshaft would just lead to slow starvation. They'd have to come out sooner or later to find sustenance."

"Somewhere in the site offices, then?" suggested Dures. "Canteen? Stores?"

Nesvorny looked back towards the other buildings, and suddenly felt exposed. Anyone hiding in the nearer ones might be able to shoot at them through the windows: they'd reveal themselves, but maybe think making a statement would be worth it. He slowly got down from the cart and moved a bit further into the shadow of the depot; in three steps he was out of direct line of sight of the nearest buildings; Dures clearly sensed his unease, for he followed. Nesvorny touched his earpiece and his eyes lost focus. "Tania? They're at the site – they've left their carts. We're scouring the transport shed, but I don't think they're here. Can you leave one drone flying over the quarry and works, and use the second to watch out for movement in the site buildings. I'm pretty sure they're holed up in the latter."

"Sure thing, Eric," came Joseph's voice. "Any idea where?"

"Not yet. Some intel would be useful, like how many buildings are on site."

"Hang on." After a pause, in which Nesvorny noticed Dures peering at him expectantly, Joseph's voice returned. "Large and small, there are a total of fifteen aside from the depot, and various shelters, shacks, and lean-tos ranged away along the edge of the quarry – but these would be too small to hold Fukuda's entire squad."

"That's what I figured. They must have lookouts watching us now from the nearer buildings, and be holed up further back in one they might fortify. Thanks, Tania. Out."

"So, what now?" asked Dures.

"There's the sensible option, the semi-sensible option, and the stupid option. The sensible one is that we withdraw and starve them out. They'll show themselves before long, and a drone will pick them up. They will likely need to come to us at some point for supplies, and they'll be easy targets if they try some sort of raid. Waiting it out allows time for sanity to prevail and for them to realise they've no choice but to surrender. That option probably leads to fewest deaths – as long as they don't decide to go out in a blaze of glory. With Fukuda, I just don't know. It's not impossible."

"That option also takes longer and is less… *satisfying*," said Dures.

"Yeah, true."

"Option two?"

"We hold tight here. We've at least got control over the transport pool, so they won't be able to go anywhere unless they try to displace us. Then we wait for reinforcements. Bring up a hundred troops from the settlement. Surround the site. Move in slowly, clearing everywhere. But urban warfare can be costly, especially if done wrong."

Dures scowled. "We need to fly Heiko in. It sounds like his area of expertise."

"It does, but he's in no fit state to help."

"And option three? The stupid one?"

Nesvorny smiled grimly. "We try to flush them out ourselves. It gives them less time to fortify and for Fukuda to work them into a state of martyrdom. It also means there are fewer targets for them to shoot at. But of course, it means the odds are levelled and it's our own lives on the line."

"Me and mine are ready for this," said Dures, his look severe. "So don't worry about us. Tell us what to do. Taking the stupid option is exactly what my wife would expect me to do anyway."

"Sure. I also feel some personal responsibility. Fukuda was working for Traore behind my back. I never realised. His sins are my responsibility to a degree. If anyone is going to put themself in the firing line, it'll be me."

"Well said. But, Colonel, perhaps you ought to at least arm yourself before we move. Here… take my rifle. I'll claim another from one of my troops."

Nesvorny took the gift and arched an eyebrow. At last, he had his old adversary within reach… He noticed Dures smiling at him and felt a moment of embarrassment. "Am I that transparent?"

Dures actually laughed, leant forwards, and slapped him on the shoulder. "I'll be back." He headed into the depth of the depot, where his force had dispersed. Nesvorny checked over his weapon, contacted Joseph for an update, then sat in the nearest cart to think and wait.

When Dures returned with half-a-dozen armed followers, Nesvorny related his plan.

Ten minutes later, the first decoy cart – holding four of the Stokers – left from the square outside the transport depot.

Shortly after, four more took the second cart and followed the first.

They waited twenty minutes more, then Nesvorny made a great show of talking to Dures in the open before they took their final two carts with the last of their team – or at least, troopers that totalled the full twelve they had arrived with, and which Nesvorny was sure would have been accurately counted by a spotter in one of the nearer buildings. "That two-storey admin building," said Nesvorny to Dures, more quietly – but without pointing. "The upper floor. That's where the spotter will be."

They duly departed in convoy, but didn't go far. Just around the curve of the mountain, perhaps three-hundred metres from the square, they came across the first two carts, parked in a line at the side of the tarmac road. They dismounted and came together. The path their predecessors had taken was obvious: they followed it, slithering down the slope on which the road was set, and made their way back from whence they had come, keeping beneath the road level, sweeping further downslope. They were shortly able to discern the top of the roof of the tall depot building. They slowed, and headed not for the square and the front of the depot, but to the open rear, at all times keeping beneath the road and sight of anyone in the mine buildings.

At the back corner of the depot, they found the previous eight Stokers, sitting quietly in the shadows.

"Any movement, Tania?" said Nesvorny.

"No, you're good," came Joseph's reply to his earpiece. "They're staying hidden. I've pulled the drones back a bit to be less obvious. I don't reckon they'll be able to see them without climbing onto a roof."

"Now what?" asked Dures.

Nesvorny broke comms with Joseph. "We should be out of view here, and they think we're gone. They'll remain where they are until nightfall. If they move, it won't be until then, although I still don't see their endgame." He looked towards the large machines parked nearby and asked a woman who seemed to be the most senior of the early decoy team. "Any luck?"

"Oh, yeah," she smiled, revealing a couple of missing teeth. "Most of them are still charged. I've picked a couple that should do the trick. The motors will be quiet, but once they're moving they'll make some noise – how much, I can't tell."

"Show us."

The woman took Nesvorny and Dures to two of the largest pieces of equipment. The first was an excavator with a single arm and bucket scoop, the second, a tall dump truck with high tyres. "Good," said Nesvorny. "Now we strike – front and back – to cause confusion. With luck, they'll cave in."

"And if they start shooting?" said Dures.

"Simple. Shoot back."

Dures decided to go with the digger, riding alongside a driver with past mining experience. The woman took the dump truck, with two riflemen riding in the back who were able to provide cover over the rim of its container. The others came with Nesvorny to the front of the building. He kept in the shadows, peered out, and calculated the best route along the side of the square to allow minimal exposure to anyone looking out from the two-storey admin building.

At the appointed time, Nesvorny heard the vehicles behind him begin moving – the crunch of wheels on gravel and clank of swaying metal. He waited until the sound first decreased and then, suddenly, increased, with the noise of heavy metal contacting the plastic and stone of one of the mine buildings.

"Move," he said to his team, and in a crouch he exited from under the depot's high roof and sprinted along the edge of the square. He sensed his team following, heard some cursing, and then the louder sound of collapsing walls. At the first building he slammed the door open and peered inside a small office; others from his team did the same at a second. These were empty, so the team moved on. There were more sounds of destruction as the digger moved on to another target. Now Nesvorny was at the wall of the two-storey building, which was larger than any other along the square. He shouldered through open a ground-floor door and his team piled in, shouting warnings.

A man in a black uniform was at the far end of the first room: he'd been relaxing on a cot, and had clearly just risen. There was a rifle nearby, but he had no chance to reach it.

"Who else is in here?" demanded Nesvorny, striding rapidly towards the man through a gap left by his escort, who now stood to either side with guns levelled at the startled trooper.

"Ah, there is… uh… one…" he pointed upwards.

"Call to them. They have ten seconds to throw their gun down the stairs or they die. One and only chance."

The man stood, arms held high, and edged to the stairwell at the back of the room. He called up as he'd been told, and a moment later a rifle clattered down the stairs. Nesvorny gestured for two of the Stokers to ascend and clear the top floor.

"You know who I am," said Nesvorny, tapping the double golden shamrocks on his shoulder.

"Uh, yes, sir."

"You were told to lay down your arms, and yet you're here."

"Sir – Major Fukuda is my immediate officer. I had to obey him."

"Now I am here. You will be court-martialled, but you can make matters easier for yourself. How many more does he have, and where is he?"

The man dropped his arms slowly to his side and stood to attention. "The Major has six more, sir. They are in the refectory building."

"Show me."

With three of the Stokers, he followed the man out of the front door and along a path between a couple more prefab buildings. It was then that he heard the first shots fired from ahead. At about the same time, Joseph's voice came to him: "Two just made a run for it. In the open. Heading your way, Eric."

A pair in black rushed across a scrubby space in front, between two buildings. Before Nesvorny could call out, one of the Stokers began to shoot. One of the figures jerked as they were hit; the second looked around in confusion, saw them, and dropped to a crouch…

"Cease fire!" roared Nesvorny. "Trooper – drop you weapon. Now!"

As though stung by electricity, the woman in black threw the rifle in front of her and raised her arms. Nesvorny shoved his prisoner to continue on, and motioned with one finger for his followers to take control of the wounded man and crouching woman. He moved on, with the final member of his team just behind him.

Ahead, the sound of firing increased.

"Eric, the big building just ahead. That's where the shooting is coming from."

"The refectory," muttered Nesvorny. "Thanks, Tania."

The prisoner paused at the corner of the next building. "There, sir."

Nesvorny peered around the corner. Most of the buildings on the site were tightly clustered, but this one had a ring of empty ground around it, perhaps three-metres wide. It seemed a central meeting place, and had a number of entrances. He couldn't see the two vehicles from the depot, but heard them off to his left, where it seemed they were using their mass to smash through another building on that side.

He told the last Stoker: "Stay here and watch the doors. If they plan to get away, this is the closest side to the transport depot. And Keep an eye on *him*." He hefted his rifle, jogged across the space to the refectory wall, then turned right to edge away from the shooting and noise of demolition. He reached the corner and continued up the perpendicular side of the building. Set in the middle of that wall, at the end of a dirt path, was another entrance. He approached it cautiously. Like the other doors here, this was manual – no electronics. He leant on it, and it moved inwards slightly.

Nesvorny took a deep breath. Although he'd had many years' experience of policing, he wasn't a proper soldier, and wasn't used to wielding firearms. He looked down at the rifle in his hands: he'd not fired it yet. It had come from Dures; was it even loaded? He shook his head angrily, looked up, and barged through the door.

What he found inside was a large canteen, full of tables and chairs, with a serving counter along the wall to his right, and kitchens and storerooms beyond. At the far end, were two people in black, pointing their rifles through a broken window. They were too engaged to hear him, so Nesvorny moved stealthily towards them. He'd halved the distance, however, when two more figures appeared behind the long counter, presumably coming from the kitchen – one of whom was Fukuda.

Nesvorny stood tall and set the rifle to his shoulder. "Major! Stop there!"

The two men at the window turned on hearing his voice: one stared dumbly for a moment, then dropped his weapon, but his colleague, after a brief pause, raised his rifle and fired… at which Fukuda and his colleague dropped behind the counter.

The bullet missed, but made Nesvorny duck, using the nearest long table as some sort of cover. A second bullet ricocheted off the plastic table top and sizzled past his left ear. Then the surrendering man had second thoughts and dropped to pick up his own weapon. Nesvorny swivelled back to the pair by the window and pulled the trigger. The rifle bucked against his shoulder, but the bullet flew into the ceiling. He now caught shouting from ahead, but the words were indistinct. Fukuda didn't reappear, but the other man behind the counter and raised his weapon and started to fire too.

Nesvorny couldn't move forwards, but the waist-high furniture between him and the others gave plenty of protection. "This is Colonel Nesvorny," he yelled. "I order you to drop your weapons."

The firing paused – whether because the shooters were considering his order, or because they realised they had no clear shot at him, he couldn't tell. He rolled quickly to the next row of tables, closer to the serving counter.

A moment later, one of the others responded: "We follow the Major."

"You'll follow him to death," shouted Nesvorny. "Is that what you want? Is that what your families will want?"

"Wait!" came a voice. Then it dropped in volume; two were talking, but Nesvorny couldn't hear what they were saying.

The first voice came again: "Okay. Show yourself. Prove it's you."

Nesvorny moved a little further to his right. Could they tell exactly where he was? He didn't think so. He quickly looked over a table top: "Here I…"

A bullet slammed into the table, sending sharp splinters at him, one of which sliced his cheek. He ducked again, and heard cursing from in front: "Fucking idiot! What are you doing…"

But the answer that came in the direction of the men by the window didn't come from a human voice, rather, there was a loud crash and then a scream of pain. Nesvorny looked up again, and saw that the ceiling of the building had collapsed, with a large steel bucket – like the front leg of a praying mantis – now occupying that space. The bucket rose up, and he could see a smear of blood on its underside. He leapt up and advanced between two rows of tables, switching his view between the counter and the breached wall: one of the men had his arms up, but the main shooter was down and sprawled in a pile of debris, blood pooling around the remains of his head. The area by the counter was silent. At that moment, Dures entered through the hole in the wall – a wild look in his eyes.

Nesvorny ran up to him, half an eye still directed at the counter. "There's two more. Fukuda and one other. They've gone back through the kitchen."

The driver of the excavator now picked through the debris. Nesvorny pointed to the surrendering man. "Guard him – come, Dures." He led the way past the man in black, beyond the counter, and then they were through into the kitchen area. It was deserted. With Dures behind, he raced through the kitchen, and then quickly peered into one storeroom, then a second. And then he heard more gunshots. There was a fire exit at one end of the kitchen: he moved to it and flung the door open.

Several metres away was the dump truck, sitting at an angle on the rubble of a flimsy prefab. And then he noticed the truck jerk forwards, pause, reverse… and he saw a body below the step to its high door. Wearing green. A woman. He raised his rifle and fired at the door. His first shot ricocheted; his second went through the passenger side window and shattered it. There was a shriek, but then the truck was clear of the obstruction, and put in forward gear once more.

"Fuck!" shouted Dures. He lifted his own weapon and fired, but the bullets pinged off the metal cabin. Then other shots came – from the two Stokers who'd originally been riding in the back, but had dismounted for action.

Nesvorny placed a hand on Dures' shoulder. "They can't get far. To the depot."

The pair ran back towards the transport depot, and climbed into one of the three carts that had been driven by Fukuda's rogue squad. As he started the car up, he received an update from Joseph. "Eric? Big truck on the move. It's heading for the road back to Stonetown. I'm going to sort out a roadblock, but… fuck, that's a beast."

Nesvorny threw his weapon in the back, and pressed the accelerator. He gunned the cart through the square and back onto the road to the settlement. The cart wasn't fast, but it was considerably quicker than the stolen truck. They rapidly came up to its rear.

"What now?" shouted Dures, the barrel of his rifle waving in front of him.

"We should stay on him. Where can he go? When he stops, we can get him. I think I hit the passenger – so Fukuda might already be down."

"You want to bet on it?"

"No. I also worry what carnage he might cause in town with the truck – and who he might take with him."

Jospeh's voice came to him. "Eric? I can hear you. You're right. He'll drive through any roadblock. Oh, *fuck*. I've few enough drones as it is, but… Eric, don't get too close. *Banzai!*"

Nesvorny tamped on the breaks and spoke to Dures from the side of his mouth. "Joseph is about to introduce him to a little friend of hers. Watch."

As if from nowhere, there came a loud buzzing noise and then ahead they saw a small dark shape in the air, which rapidly grew in size and descended…

The drone disappeared behind the truck: there was a loud *crash*, and the vehicle swerved violently, first left, then right, and then it tipped over the edge of the road and hit the slope to the side. It picked up speed and headed towards the water's edge perhaps eighty metres distant. Nesvorny slammed on the breaks and controlled a fishtail. He leapt out of the cart at the same time as Dures, and the pair started to slide down the slope. They hadn't got far, when the truck hit the steep shelving and entered the water with a monstrous *splash*, before continuing forwards more slowly.

Nesvorny slipped onto his butt and slid most of the way to the water's edge; Dures managed to retain his footing, but it meant he arrived second.

For a moment, it looked as though the truck would sink completely, with all who were aboard. But then an arm appeared, followed by a head and another arm, and the driver managed to heave himself out of his seat and onto the cabin's roof. The figure was in a torn uniform and bloodied, yet still Fukuda's features were evident. The man balanced on the roof on all fours, looking back at them. Dures lifted his rifle to aim…

"Are you sure you want to do that?" said Nesvorny.

"Want? Oh, yes, I want."

"Very well. At least it will be quick."

Dures paused at that and slowly lowered his rifle. "Quick?" The truck continued to sink. The water was now less than a metre below the roofline.

Fukuda struggled onto two feet and looked at them. His face twisted into a sneer, but he had no words. Instead, he lifted one hand to salute Nesvorny.

Suddenly there was a dark shape in the water by the submerging truck. It drew Nesvorny's attention. "Ah… it was only a matter of time. The shipyard is close. They've made it here."

"I hope the Lisboeta have an idea how to get rid of them," said Dures. "Or we may all end up the same as the major." He folded the rifle across his chest and watched.

The water reached the cabin roof, then continued to rise. Fukuda was suddenly consternated. His head whipped around. He staggered back in the calf-high water. A black, long-fingered hand reached up, grabbed his leg, and tugged him off his feet, onto his back, and then – in spite of the man's thrashing arms – below the surface.

Chapter 49

"Well, they're still there," said Marie, clambering out of the access hatch to the airlock at the bottom of the *Lisboa* and casting aside the high-powered torch she'd taken on her dive.

"Yeah, we saw through your head cam," said Kalmik. Apart from Figueroa, she was the only other in the cramped chamber. "Thank God the EFE works. But I still don't know how you do it. Antifreeze in your veins?"

Marie laughed lightly. "I just try not to think about it. Anyway, I've also got my bracelets for extra protection." She twisted one wrist, drawing attention to the heavy device encircling it.

Figueroa cleared his throat. "Yes, Marie, my dear, but still we fear for you every time you dive."

This had been Marie's fifth dive in the last six hours. They'd moved their remaining EFE device to each of the four underwater airlocks in turn to enable her to access the underneath of the ship, plus she'd made a dive from the stern. The result of each dive was the same: "Anyway, as you saw, the scenario was identical. They're lurking everywhere, and come to inspect me from three or four metres away. But what they're *not* doing is vandalising the bottom of the ship. Again, there were no signs of scratches or indentations."

"Yes, and the stern inspection showed no further damage to the propellors," said Figueroa.

"Right, just a hell of a lot of tangled kelp vines."

"While this sounds promising," said Kalmik, looking between the other two, "I'm not sure I like the direction this is heading."

"Ah, and where is that, Katerina?" said Figueroa.

"That the prop damage was somehow accidental."

"I don't see why you fear that conclusion," said Marie.

"Because it changes perceptions," said Kalmik. "You two *want* these things to be benign… or *relatively* benign. That means we don't need to do anything harsh to them. I just hope it doesn't cloud your judgment and you begin to see them as basically decent but misunderstood beings. Because if you try to hug one of them, I guarantee it'll rip your face off. In any case, you seem to be forgetting about the sensors and cameras. They destroyed those."

"I've been thinking about that," said Marie. She'd taken off her helmet and now dropped it to the steel floor by the torch. "That might have been because of the light they emitted when they were activated. We know they don't like light at all: the level of illumination wouldn't have been enough to drive them off, but it may have irked them, so they put them out."

Kalmik raised and dropped her hands. "There you go again: violence and destruction explained away, just like that. All an accident. Nothing to see here. Except we're still harbouring these creatures, and they're ranging further and further from us, their base. They're not just at the shipyard now – they've reached Athol."

Marie frowned at that. The creatures had indeed turned up at Athol, forcing Colonel Joseph's one patrol boat there to flee after a brief attack. It had decided to go to the Mount Ardol site, rather than try to get through the picket line of reapers around the REEN boats at the shipyard. The reapers had also attacked two transport barges moored at Athol, but in a desultory manner only, perhaps finding them too hefty to sink easily. "I know we need to get rid of them, Katerina. I'm seriously *not* considering trying to keep them as pets. And actually, I *do* have an idea. It came to me earlier talking with… well, anyway, I don't want to say it here. I'd rather change and get a coffee first."

"Of course, dear Marie!" said Figueroa. "You have certainly earned one."

* * *

They assembled in Nacimiento's state office. Aside from Nacimiento, Figueroa, Kalmik, Teixera, and Marie, also present were Eddard Mitsos and the Stavangerans, Magnus Solbakken and Makka Frost. All others from the previous conference had departed to Athol, the shipyard, or *Hibernia*. Marcel Louvain had returned by shuttle to the *Marseilles*, where he still held precarious command. Mitsos had refused to join Louvain or take part in any of the other operations, while the

Stavangerans had been left behind and were at a loose end until they could somehow find a way back to their home ship or to *Hibernia.*

"Thank you for keeping us in the loop," said Solbakken.

"You are welcome," said Nacimiento. "But I do not see you as redundant. The threat we are facing on the *Lisboa* is one that reverberates across our world. Even if you cannot directly contribute to solving our problem, I think it is still valuable for you to act as observers as to what goes on here, able to record and translate our efforts for the other peoples involved in this drama." He accepted the nod of recognition from the Stavangeran ambassador, then turned to face the four Lisboetan scientists. "So, Miguel, my friend, what have you got to report?"

"Alas, the creatures are still below the ship in considerable numbers," said Figueroa. "But on the plus side, they do not seem to have caused any further damage."

"They are not trying to tunnel through the hull?" Nacimiento was clearly relieved. "But they did damage at least one of the propellors."

"Marie believes that may have been accidental," said Figueroa. "The creatures have with them a large supply of kelp, perhaps as food, and somehow a quantity became entangled."

"*Marie* believes," emphasized Kalmik, sardonically. "I am yet to be convinced."

"Ah!" said Nacimiento. "Discord! Miguel – what about you?"

"I think, on balance, I agree with Marie. These reapers do not see the ship itself as some sort of enemy to attack, rather they are using the *Lisboa* as a floating shelter."

"Yes," said Marie, "and why would you trash your own shelter? It'd leave you exposed."

"Precisely," said Figueroa. "And as such, maybe Marie's hypothesis that this is essentially a migration event has some substance."

Nacimiento nodded slowly. "Okay. If so, what does this mean for us? How do we test this hypothesis? And how do we rid ourselves of these unwelcome and ungracious hitchhikers?"

"Excuse me," said Frost. "But what about these REEN boats that Mr Mitsos developed? Can we not use them in some way?"

doesn't. The Courland Line is a relatively short stretch of cenote, perhaps seventy kilometres long and not part of the interconnected network."

"Great," said Marie. "If it's unoccupied, it'll be free for the reapers to plant their own forest."

"That's a long way to travel to test out a hypothesis," scowled Kalmik. "The Meridien system is closer. If it's already occupied, so what? If its occupants are as psycho as our lot, then maybe it'll cause some sort of war between them. Let them fight it out. If our lot win, they leave and take new territory, if they don't, they die. It's win-win for us."

"You don't really wish that, Katrina, my dear?" said Figueroa.

"You know, Miguel, I'm just not sure. Scientifically, I get the importance of all this. But now we've found one set of reapers, logically there are many more sets around the fringe forests. Our lot are not unique, and if they are wiped out, the universe won't be worse off. I just can't get the image of Raul out of my head, or the poor crews of the harvesters. I know emotion is trumping my scientific dispassion, but… " she shrugged. "That's how I feel. But if we can get rid of them without having to kill them or see them killed… okay, I can live with that, even if I don't like it."

"So shall we try?" asked Marie. "Given the state of the ship, can we make it there and back?"

Nascimiento had been listening intently. He shuffled in his seat. "Dr Lockard, we can make it, I think. Our beloved sea turtle is a robust beast. But at half speed it will take us about a week. So, I am happy to pilot us to the Courland Line – but no further. We cannot ferry these creatures endlessly across the ocean as they cherry pick the perfect home. And after that jaunt, we really will need a proper and prolonged visit to the shipyard."

"What about these REEN boats?" asked Frost. "I admit I am nervous about these creatures getting to Ardol and even to the *Stavanger*. What will happen to them?"

"If we are right," said Marie, "once we move away, the farmers will break off their attacks as they won't want to get separated from their main host."

"Unless they decide they like it better here," said Kalmik.

"True," said Marie. "I guess this is then the first test of the migration hypothesis. I don't think they regard this area as a suitable home, or else they would have all left from under the ship. They're hanging on, hoping for better. But if we are going to go, we should go now and go quickly in order to bring relief to the besieged areas around the Range. At that point, the REEN boats should become redundant and they can join us. As Katrina noted earlier, we will need them to chaperone our own fishing fleet."

"And what of us?" asked Solbakken.

"You can always swim," smirked Mitsos. "It's easy. Even I've done it."

"I will contact *Hibernia*," said Nacimiento. "I will ask them to send a shuttle. I am sure you would like to rejoin your colleagues, Ms De Voe and poor Mr Heiko. I suspect Ms Dures will be accommodating, now that she is back in control. You can relate our thinking to them. But what of you, Mr Mitsos?"

The man sat back in his chair and absently stroked the gold stud in his ear. "Now there's a dilemma. Continue on a boat infested with murderous sea aliens, or return to *Hibernia* and hope that Karyn Dures really has got Deux and Boursis under control?" He frowned deeply. "On balance, I think I'll join the Stavangerans… but I'd rather not make an obvious entrance and draw attention to myself."

"Perhaps we can rustle up some sort of disguise?" said Nacimiento, his lined face creased in humour. "As you wish." Turning to face the others, he announced: "Thank you, everybody. I think we now have a plan."

* * *

Kate had been nervous on first being asked to sit in on the peace conference involving the powers of the region, but she had never considered saying 'no'. And once involved as 'notetaker', she had enjoyed it very much. Watching the interplay between the different people, with their different motives and interests, had provided a fascinating insight into the psychology of important people and the workings of power. But after the second meeting, with the different parties splitting up and going their separate ways, her services had no longer been required. Ever since, she'd had to rely on her mother to update her on the key decisions being made, and she felt somewhat resentful at having to ask. She knew that her mother wasn't intentionally holding back information, but she tended to become distracted by whatever was her key task at any moment, which meant she often forgot that Kate was around. Thus, Marie had readily told Kate about the plan to sail to the Courland Line, but had then omitted to tell her when news had come in that the reapers had indeed abandoned their picketing of the shipyard and Athol: Kate had only found our two days later, when Marie inadvertently mentioned the arrival of the REEN boats.

"What – they're here?" Kate had said in astonishment.

"Yes, that's right," her mother had replied cautiously, the expression on her face clearly indicating that she realised she'd somehow blundered. "They pulled into position behind the *Lisboa.* But they have to keep the device switched on to be safe, and we're a bit worried about how long their generators can keep going."

Kate had waved this away in annoyance. "What I mean is, what happened at the shipyard? Has the fleet been attacked now that their protection is here?"

"Oh… ah… *no.* The farmers seem to have all returned to the *Lisboa.*"

Kate had kept a lid on her anger, and afterwards been proud of this. Something she'd picked up from watching Karyn Dures? At the first meeting, Dures' eyes had suggested that she'd been on the verge of volcanic eruptions on a number of occasions, and yet she'd somehow resisted, maintaining an iron self-control. Similarly, Kate had limited her response to her mother's delayed revelation to sarcasm, but Marie had taken the message, and made an effort in the three days since to tell Kate absolutely everything that was going on… even if only to say that *nothing* was going on.

Not only had Kate and her friends been gradually eased out of the key meetings, but they'd also found themselves quietly disinvited from both the Bowl and the forgotten control room they'd found. It was clear that they'd served their purpose, and that the 'adults' thought they'd sufficiently pandered to their sensitivities by now: *thank you and goodbye.*

And that was why they were now in the public bowl, which sat beneath the base of the coliseum in the centre of the ship. Normally, this was covered by a floor that was used for sporting events or the occasional concert, but at other times – usually on Tuesdays – this was retracted to allow the Lisboetas to observe and wonder at the submarine world passing under the ship's hull. For the last three weeks, given the current crisis, the bowl had remained closed, but with the return of a kind of calm over the last few days – after a couple of successful fishing expeditions by the trawlers, and rumours that the alien creatures weren't actually attacking the ship, but simply sheltering under it – a decision had been made to allow its opening.

"Lot of people today," said Sara as they descended the stepped aisle from the uppermost tier, situated just below where the sea-level floor had been recessed. The two girls were slightly behind Tonio, who seemed to have an objective.

"I wouldn't know," said Kate. "I've never been before. I've usually been busy with you guys."

"Well, you haven't missed much. It's bigger than our bowl, but you don't get so close. You can't lie in the bottom, and the stepped seating means the angles through the glass are all funny."

"I get you," said Kate. Physics wasn't her strong point, though she vaguely knew about light distortion. The creatures seen through the toughened glass would likely appear unnaturally elongated or shortened, depending upon your viewing angle. She came to a halt as Tonio abruptly stopped in the aisle. Kate saw that they were five rows from the bottom, with the space below largely occupied. She heard Tonio curse.

Sara leant in and laughed softly. "Poor Tonio. Look. She's over there. It's as close as he can get."

"She? Oh!" In the dim light coming through the already-closing 'roof', and from LEDs set in the floor along the aisle, she made out the winsome Vita Fernandez, two rows down and some distance to their left. "I thought he'd got over that."

"No, he's just done a good job of hiding it."

Tonio started along the row in the direction of where Vita sat with a clutch of friends. Their progress was halted by people coming towards them from the next aisle. The boy turned and smiled uncertainly at Kate. "Er, I think here will do. It's as close as we can get."

"To where?" came Sara's voice just behind Kate's shoulder.

Kate grinned. "Fine, Tonio. Let's sit."

The auditorium continued to fill. There were perhaps twenty rows, steeply banked, which had the capacity of over a thousand, though by the time the roof above fully closed, sealing them into this space in the hull below the waterline, the place was perhaps half-full, with the upper rows only sparsely populated. A low hum of conversation slowly faded in parallel with the dimming of the aisle lights.

Seeing that Tonio's attention was elsewhere, Kate turned to Sara. "What now?"

"They usually switch off all the lights and remove the cover from the inside of the bowl. Normally there will be some 'luminescents'. After that, they'll turn on a few lights so that we can see things that aren't self-lighting. Anyway, this is usually the best part."

The last of the lights flickered out, and the murmur of a working mechanism could be heard. The sunken arena below seemed to subtly change in hue, from a faint grey to a deeper black. The people around ceased conversation, causing Kate to abort her latest question to avoid breaching the unspoken protocol.

And so they sat there – for one minute, two, five…

Soon, the blanket of silence was perforated, and an increasing number of whispers could be heard like a wind blowing through a reed bed.

"It's *them*, isn't it," said Sara – bitterly – into Kate's right ear. "We should have known. They've driven the luminescents away. Or eaten them."

It was so dark Kate couldn't see the expression on her friend's face, even though she was immediately next to her. "Yeah, you're right. We're not going to see much, except for…" She didn't want to say it, and suddenly felt uncomfortable. Really, what had those in charge of the arena expected people to be able to see? And suddenly, she wondered who was in charge of the ship's entertainments, and what were their freedoms and liabilities. Had they gotten permission from the Captain-Governor? Had the scientists been consulted? Or had someone with independent authority sanctioned this – perhaps wanting to see the hidden monsters for themselves, to make this a kind of haunted house experience?

Kate looked about, but could see nothing – whether in the dark bowl, or of the people around. "I don't like this," she whispered to Sara. "Why the hell are we here?"

"Not my obsession this time," said Sara. "It's *his*. Tonio suggested it. Hmm, I wonder why?"

Kate sat back and turned to her left, where Tonio was utterly silent, though what he was looking at… *trying* to see… she couldn't tell."

After a couple more minutes, a low announcement came from hidden speakers, which made Kate startle. "Ladies and gentlemen, the lumos don't seem to want to play tonight. Let's see what else is out there."

Around the black hole below, a ring of gentle lights slowly increased in luminosity, casting their glow downwards into the water, bringing it up to a grey mist of a different consistency to when the bowl had been covered.

Again, the voices around – which had been rising – began to subside. And more. This time, it seemed to Kate as though the entire audience was holding its breath. She could now pick out people in the rows below, backlit, and noticed that Tonio was fixated on the small group two rows closer to the bowl and a little over to their left. Normally she would have smiled at this, but she quickly refocused on the bowl. Still there was no sign of life.

"They don't like the light," Sara muttered. "I think everyone's going to be disappointed."

"No, they don't," said Kate. But there were two responses to something unliked, and avoidance was only one. "They came to investigate when we first started lighting the bowl," she said, almost to herself. "But they know enough now not to bother."

"So they won't come to investigate," said Sara. "What a shame."

But Kate thought about the other response – the one the reapers had taken to the cameras and sensors on the bottom of the ship; to anything that emitted any light at all in the visible spectrum. She leant forwards in her seat until her chin was over the head of the woman sitting in the row below. The grey mist – swirling as the ship's motion churned microscopic creatures, adding texture to the vista – suddenly darkened here and there. Shadows in the water. And others noticed, too, as evidenced by excited exclamations and the pointing arm from someone in the bottom row.

The thump against the glass caused some of those closest to jump, shriek, laugh.

"So they *have* decided to come and play," said Sara.

Kate frowned at the other, whose face she could now see – pale patches and dark lines. The lights in the ring brightened further, and the lines on Sara's cheek bones and above her eyes sharpened. Sara looked back at her. "What?" she said.

"You're not worried?"

"Why? I'm here and they're down there. I've been much closer to them than this."

There were more bumps and startled yelps, followed by embarrassed laughter.

"But what–?"

"Chill, Kate," said Sara. "I know what you're thinking. But they couldn't get through the glass of the Bowl, and this is thicker. Let them knock themselves out."

Some of the boys were now catcalling and yelling insults. Here were the monsters, and they weren't so tough after all. As far as they could see, the emergency was over. The creatures couldn't get at them, were sensitive to a growing number of weapons developed by the clever scientists, and would hopefully soon be gone. Even Sara seemed relaxed, and clapped when one of the creatures appeared from the gloom and slammed into the glass with no apparent effect.

But then there was an especially loud *thud*.

Kate had seen the cause. A larger blob of black had risen up and struck the glass below at the rim, directly beneath a recessed spotlight.

"Wow," said Tonio. "That was a big one."

"That wasn't *one*," said Kate. "That was two… maybe three. Acting in concert. Swimming up, doing their somersault thing, and striking with their legs."

"So what?" said Sara, though suddenly she sounded less confident.

"We mustn't forget, they're *intelligent*," said Kate. "They're problem solvers. If something doesn't work, they try something else until it does."

"Yeah, but that doesn't mean they can solve every problem," said Tonio, his attention now fully on Kate. "The glass is too strong here, no matter what they do."

"I hope you're right." Kate began to look around, to look up. Then she saw the control booth where the announcer sat and where a technician controlled the arena's lights, just under where the floor of the coliseum became the roof of the arena. It was obvious, being the only place within the arena that had light aside from the ring around the bowl below. Top level… and not too far around. Maybe thirty degrees. Kate suddenly stood.

"Kate!" hissed Sara. "What are you doing?"

"I think… I think we should stop this. Just in case. There's no point tempting fate. I'm going up to the control booth."

"Party pooper!" said Tonio, though there was an edge to his voice.

There was an even bigger *thud* from below, and the laughter of those nearest cut off as though guillotined.

Kate squirmed past Sara and headed for the aisle, past a number of muttering people who had to twist their legs to the side to let her out… her *and* Sara.

In the aisle, Kate turned and arched an eyebrow at her friend.

"Well," said Sara, "if *you're* worried, then I'm shit-scared. Go on."

"Tonio?"

Sara turned to look, then turned back. "Still has his eyes on the prize. Keep going."

Kate continued up the steps. In spite of increasing her distance from the bowl, the thudding of reapers on glass increased in volume and frequency, until it sounded like someone insistently rapping on a front door with their knuckles. She noticed those scattered around the upper rows leaning forwards, whispering, pointing; then one or two rose in their seats and started for the aisle. She caught the face of a young mother with a child, who made eye contact – eyes wide and fearful. Kate reached the top row, where there was a broad aisle ringing the top of the arena, with the control booth visible, forming a wall ahead of her, with a facing door. She had only taken a couple of steps towards it, however, when a high-pitched scream came from below, closely followed by several more as well as some harsher shouts.

"Oh, fuck!" cried Sara, from behind. "How–?"

Kate looked down, and at first struggled to work out what she was seeing. The bowl was no longer circular, or at least, one edge seemed to have buckled, blown-out, the ring of lights somehow incomplete, partly occluded…

Water had somehow burst through a gap, and the people in the lower rows were turning, scrambling, not for the nearest aisles, but directly upwards, climbing over seats and the people in them. There was a real sense of fear now, and the whole arena was on its feet and turning. Kate had the advantage of being out of the direct line to an exit and having fewer people near her in the upper rows. She heard Sara cry: "Tonio!" But she knew her best chance of saving him lay ahead, not behind. She upped her pace towards the door – still dim from the absence of any light save the low glow from the booth's front. Suddenly, a man vaulted over a seatback into the aisle and turned to face her: the panic in his face suggested he barely saw her; she threw her back against a wall as he raced past, catching her a glancing blow to the stomach from a pumping elbow.

From this position, Kate could better see the chaos below. Black water was pouring in from some fissure in the bowl; it was already up to the second row and rising rapidly. A wall of people were heading up, ascending like mountaineers, though some were still at the lower level, now waterline, perhaps confused, stunned, unable to pull themselves up. And then directly below, she saw a woman who'd been trying to climb suddenly throw her arms in the air and somersault backwards into the water, whatever scream she issued lost in the noise and bedlam. Grabbed from behind. *They've got in!*

It was five more paces to the door, which suddenly opened in front of her, revealing a neatly dressed woman wearing a head mic. The announcer?

"Run!" the woman cried. "Get out of here!" Then she was shoved from behind as another – the technician? – abandoned his post. The woman stumbled and Kate once more avoided being bulldozed by flattening against the wall. The man was past but then, perhaps ashamed, turned and helped the woman up.

Suddenly, Sara was against the wall beside Kate. "Dios… Dios…"

Kate waited a moment for the pair from the booth to get out of the way, and then she pushed through the flapping door and felt Sara's hand on her back, following her in. The first thing Kate saw was a flashing red light – an alarm – indicating a breach in the seal of the dome.

"They must know," said Kate, looking at a bank of controls under the window of the booth which provided a view over the arena and down onto the bowl. The space was even darker now: water – several metres deep – had reduced the illumination from the spotlights, several of which seemed to have been taken out by the reapers, given that the indistinct ring was no longer complete.

"What do you mean, *know*? Who–"

"What?" Kate quickly glanced at Sara. "Ah, the alarm. They must know in the main control room. But what do you do when there's a hull breach? Oh, shit!"

"Kate? What is it?"

"You shut the bulkhead doors. You seal the breach."

"But *we're* inside. With *them*."

Kate glanced once more through the window. The water was now at the level of the fourth row, the fifth. Where was Tonio? Most of the people had now made it to the upper reaches, but there was a scattering of others below – lolling insensibly, perhaps broken in the stampede. And then she saw him: Tonio's dark form, just above the rising water, dragging something, someone…

"We have to go," said Sara suddenly. "People are getting out. The exits aren't locked yet. Kate!"

"No. Not yet. There are still people below. *Tonio.* They need a chance…" She frantically looked over the console. There were all sorts of switches and dials, and various digital displays. First things first: "Lights? Where are the lights?" She started hitting switches until suddenly a constellation of dim lights flashed on along the floor aisles. It wasn't much, but it was something. Out the window, down and to her left, Tonio came into clearer view, and so did the person he was painfully manipulating up the next wall of seats – the dark lustrous hair of Vita Fernandez, seemingly hurt and abandoned by her desperate coterie. The lights also revealed more clearly that there were shapes in the water, breaking the surface. But the aisle lights now acted as something of a deterrent, and the creatures that had made it through the breach were tending away from the aisles, towards the unlit middle sections… such as where Tonio laboured.

The water was rising more rapidly now: Kate saw that it was just below Tonio's feet. A shape came towards him… but then veered away towards another figure, an elderly man a short distance away, who was standing on a seat back, his calves immersed, trying to pull himself up to the next row.

Sara clearly saw what Kate saw, for she shrieked and pressed her face to the glass.

The old man was grasped and violently ripped backwards into the black water.

Kate returned to the controls. She saw where the aisle lights were, and started attacking the cluster of switches around it. She hit the main lighting – a master switch – and in the ceiling, a blaze of powerful lights speared down into the arena. In the water below, there was a fountain of activity, an explosion, water jetting into the air. And Tonio and Vita…

Kate saw, as if in slow motion, a long black limb with wicked fingers reaching up, reaching for Tonio's trailing foot… hesitating…

And then whipping away as though burned.

"Take that you bastards!" screamed Sara, pounding at the glass. "Monsters! Fuck you, monsters! Fuck you!"

Kate pushed from the console and grabbed Sara's arm. "Quick! We need to help him! Help them all! Before the bulkheads…"

She didn't have to finish. Sara followed her and they hurried to the nearest aisle. And suddenly, others near the closest exit turned and saw them heading down. Shamed? Needing a cue? Kate and Sara took the closest aisle and raced along the row directly above the struggling Tonio. Together they pulled up Vita, and between them were able to drag her to an aisle from where they were able to make a quicker getaway to the nearest exit. Others were with them now, tense but measured, hauling some of those who'd been left behind. They didn't save everyone, but they saved some.

Kate and Sara got Tonio and Vita up the ramp to Level Zero – sea level – to the floor of the coliseum, which seemed to be serving as the evacuation point from the arena. Less than a minute after they slumped down, exhausted and still shaking, the arena was sealed air-tight, leaving the space to the reapers and the last of their victims.

* * *

The *Lisboa* reached the Courland Line cenote three days after the incident at the public bowl. The tension aboard – which had been dissipating since their departure from the Range – had grown steadily again since the thirteen deaths in the bowl, and the clear demonstration that the reapers were not to be taken lightly. The importance of the success of this next stage was clear to the entire population, many of whom now clustered on outwards-facing balconies wherever space on these could be found, or else followed events via reports over the public news channel: little work was going to be done this day.

The bridge of the *Lisboa* was situated in the upraised nub to the bow of the ship that rose in front of the out-swept wings behind which the ship's fleet of smaller vessels sheltered, which were themselves forward of the rounded bulk of the main vessel with its central coliseum. The bridge was on level four of the head-like structure of the 'sea turtle' – its uppermost level. But atop this, open to the elements, was a viewing platform, often used by the ship's officers on breaks, containing not only easy chairs and a few tables, but meteorological equipment and a number of fixed telescopes. It was here that the Crisis Team assembled as the ship coasted slowly the last few kilometres to the cenote.

Marie stood with her daughter and her friends off to one side of Joao Nacimiento – as ever in his pristine uniform and cap. Just to the other side stood Figueroa, Kalmik, Grande, the engineer Hector Bellarriva, and a couple of senior ship's officers whose names Marie had forgotten. Directly behind Nacimiento, Luisa Teixeira stood at a table on which various pieces of electronic equipment were arrayed.

"What now?" asked Nacimiento, who'd posed the same question in a number of different ways several times over the last hour. The dark line of the cenote was not visible from this height or distance, though Marie knew it was less than half-a-kilometre away.

"Now we see if they like the new home we've brought them to," said Marie. "How long it takes them to decide is anyone's guess, though I suspect it'll be quick."

"Surely the cenote is more amenable to them than the underside of my ship?" said Nacimiento.

"I would have thought so," said Marie. "And the absence of a fringe forest suggests it's pristine and untenanted."

"Indeed, a blank canvas," said Figueroa, nodding slowly. "Ready for occupation."

Suddenly, there was a shout from a spotter somewhere over to their left, presumably stationed along the front side of that 'flipper'. Marie couldn't make out the words, or even see the person from this angle, but an officer standing at the starboard edge turned and relayed the hidden person's message. "They say there's movement in the water."

A moment later, another shout came from the port side, and an officer there, peering over the edge, looking slightly backwards, turned and shouted excitedly: "Here too."

Teixera behind them momentarily took out an earpiece. "Similar reports from the tips of the wings. There's a lot of activity." She replaced her earpiece and bowed her head to look at information coming in to various monitor screens, which showed camera shots and radar images.

For five minutes, reports from all the forward spotters on the bow indicated black shapes in the water, streaming away from the ship towards the cenote, and then… *nothing.*

"Is this it?" wondered Nacimiento at last. "Have they gone?"

"There's only one way to find out," said Marie.

"Yeah, but in the meantime, sir," said Kalmik, "I suggest we get the fuck away from here – just in case they've gone but have second thoughts and try to come back."

"Good idea, Dr Kalmik," said Nacimiento. He gave orders for the ship to turn due east and proceed as fast as it was able with its damaged propellors.

They put over twenty kilometres between the *Lisboa* and the cenote. After around an hour, Nacimiento called for the ship to come to a dead stop. Then the Crisis Team clustered together – and Marie noticed all eyes turn to her.

"Ah, is it that time?" said Marie, smiling wistfully.

"Mum!" said Kate, sharply. "Not again."

"It's alright, Kate. I'll take care–"

But Marco Grande placed a hand gently on Marie's shoulder. "I think you've done enough, Marie. Let someone else go check."

"Who… you, Marco? Are you sure?"

Grande smiled, flashing white teeth through his dark stubble. "The swim we did to the *Marseilles* was… *exciting*. If I could manage that, I think I can do this. I'll never be as comfortable below the waves as you, but I can dive again – in many ways, thanks to you."

Marie felt her daughter suddenly at her side, a hand grasping her elbow.

"You've done enough, Mum. We both have. It's time to let someone else take a risk."

"Yeah, Marie," said Kalmik. "In any case, you're too important. If they're still there and they decide to snack on Grande, it'll be no loss." But she smiled at Grande's furrowed brows and actually winked.

Grande blew out his cheeks, nodded, and went to suit up. Over the course of a couple of hours, he made several dives through the airlocks, and his report was the same each time: "They're gone."

"Fuck, Marie," said Kalmik, as the team stood about in the failing light, now clustered around a table on which hot drinks had been delivered. "It seems you were right after all."

"To the shipyard, then," declared Nacimiento, happily. "Let's spread the good news."

Chapter 50

Rennie Heiko limped into the sitting room of the Stavangeran embassy, having been admitted through the front door by a surprised member of the security team. He used a walking stick and was accompanied by a fretful Melissa De Voe. As they entered the room, several faces turned their way, and two people instantly rose from their seats and started towards them.

"Rennie – thank God!" said Magnus Solbakken, who reached him first. "Let me give you a hand."

"Thanks, Magnus, but I think I can cope. A chair would be nice, though."

Makka Frost was right behind Solbakken, and suddenly at Heiko's other side. "Here, take mine."

The two shepherded Heiko over to one of the now-vacant blue-fabric chairs. As Heiko slumped down and De Voe took the seat next to him, Cass Remillard and Anders Pedersen slowly lowered themselves into their own chairs – having stood at the pair's entrance and muttered their own welcomes.

"Let me get you a coffee," said Frost, heading for a sideboard. "I think I remember your taste, and I know Melissa's like the geological strata of Ardol."

Solbakken pulled another chair around, completing a broad circle, with light pouring through broad windows forming a spotlight on the newly arrived pair. "While I'm delighted to see you, Rennie, I heard you would be bed-bound for at least a couple more days."

"He should be," said De Voe. "But short of putting him completely under, there was no way he was going to wait any longer." She looked askance at Heiko. "But if you start leaking red fluid, Rennie, you're going back, even if I have to carry you."

"I have a fearsome nursemaid," chuckled Heiko. "But as I keep telling anyone who will listen, I have a surprisingly robust constitution, not all of it natural."

"Cass told me the bullet went through your pelvis," said Solbakken.

"Right through," confirmed Heiko. "But it missed all of my arteries and deflected off bone."

De Voe smirked. "The bullet came out of his ass, broadly speaking. Fortunately, it missed all the key bits when entering on the other side – which would have made him useless to me."

"It's nice to know the extent of your compassion," said Heiko, looking pained – and not from his injury. "In any case, as they say, you should have seen the other guy. Melissa riddled him good."

"One of the New Socialists from Earth?" said Solbakken.

"Yes. One of those whose clothes we borrowed. He clearly took that theft very personally."

Frost came over, carrying two cups of coffee. As he handed them to Heiko and De Voe, he asked: "What about their leader, comrade Hollande?"

De Voe's smile broadened. "Oh, I got him, too. He's alive, but apparently shitting through a bag – as well as being unable to make insulin and reliant on antibiotics for the rest of his life, poor thing."

Heiko took a sip and smiled at the strong, bitter taste. In *Hibernia's* main hospital, they'd limited him to water and small, bland meals of unidentifiable protein plus a few vegetables from the hydroponics plant. Worse than the food, though, was his embarrassment at having been caught out at the surrender ceremony: he was meant to be the professional in the room, yet both the New Socialist who'd shot him and De Voe had made him look amateur in comparison. A momentary lapse? Age catching up with him? Perhaps he had done the right thing in taking a desk job, even though Tethys had turned out to be somewhat more challenging than he'd expected. Maybe next time he'd leave the action to Pedersen.

Heiko sat quietly for the next few minutes, nursing his coffee, as the others exchanged news about events in *Hibernia* and back on the *Stavanger*. Frost reported that their home ship had returned to its station close to Mount Ardol and that Sven Ibsen had resumed foremanship of the site. There was currently little work being done, however, as the crew from Sullivan's mining company had downed tools – worrying about events back in *Hibernia* and wanting repatriation (or at least, according to Frost, a bonus to continue). Boats were now plying the waters around the Range, though with some nervousness, and the invasion fleet had returned to *Hibernia*. The fleet's converted gunboats had returned to the *Marseilles*, though there were rumours that Captain Louvain had ensured they did so singly, to allow him to disarm the returnees and vet their crew for fanaticism, with a number being held in solitary confinement until the First Citizen's fate was finally resolved.

At last, Heiko roused himself: in a pause in the conversation, he cleared his throat. "It's interesting to hear about these matters – but we really came because we'd heard a rumour about the aliens, and that a shuttle arrived this morning from the *Lisboa*. We were hoping to find out what was going on with them."

"The rumours are true," said Solbakken. "In fact, Makka and I have invites to attend a big meeting with the Hibernians and the Lisboetas shortly."

Remillard huffed. "Okay for some. Others of us have been left off the invite list." He twitched a thumb towards Pedersen, who merely shrugged.

"You retired too soon, my friend," said Solbakken. "And maybe they haven't given due credit to the important role played by the *Cormorant* and its crew. I wouldn't take it to heart, though: this meeting is clearly intended for, ah, a select few representatives."

"What about us?" asked De Voe.

"If you weren't informed, I guess it's because Rennie was in his sick bed and you were at his bedside. I suppose if you joined us, there would be no big issue. Your importance in recent events is clear to all. But to be on the safe side, I will put in a call to Karyn's secretary if you want."

"Damn right," said De Voe.

Solbakken rose. "Very well."

"When is this meeting?" asked Heiko.

"In about an hour – so your timing is impeccable. We'll be collected and chauffeured to the government building. Let's have another coffee while I make that call, and we can take it from there. Makka – since you're a natural barista, perhaps you'd do the honours?"

"Yes, Ambassador!"

When Solbakken returned five minutes later, he was all smiles. "All fine. I even got invites for Cass and Anders – if they want to tag along. But the plan has now changed. We're to meet at the spaceport. It's a nice enough day, and not too far, so rather than asking for an extra cart I suggested we walk. Oh, Rennie, I'm sorry. I forgot…"

Heiko gently shook his head, but he was smiling. "No problem, Magnus. I need the exercise. And if it gets too much, I'm sure Melissa won't mind carrying me on her back."

The woman swore, but in an affectionate way.

* * *

Eddard Mitsos had returned to *Hibernia* from the *Lisboa* just over a week ago in the company of Solbakken and Frost. He'd initially been uncertain what to do and where to go, though for once in his life he'd found himself craving anonymity – at least, until he was sure that he was safe from the vengeful Marseillais and their allies. But his wider prospects clearly depended upon him taking advantage of his… fame? Notoriety? He'd appreciated this rapidly, for while the Stavangeran pair headed to their embassy, he'd been left adrift with little money, a problem he failed to resolve on visiting the bank nearest the spaceport, where he discovered that the account he'd set up on first arriving in *Hibernia* had been frozen. Apparently, he'd been deemed a foreigner of suspicious status, and no amount of shouting or pleading made them budge. And so he'd gone to the main government building – the old command centre of the ship – and asked to see someone in authority, refusing to leave until that happened. At last, after several hours, someone had recognised his association with the magical boats that had saved the invasion fleet, alerted their superiors, and Karyn Dures had deigned to see him.

Mitsos usually prided himself on being able to read people, but he'd gained nothing from Karyn's stern demeanour as he described his plight. At the end, he'd half expected her to throw him out; instead, she not only put him up in a modest suite meant for visiting dignitaries, but provided him with an armed watcher to assuage his concerns at being assassinated by some New Socialist fanatic or Marseillais loyalist.

And so to today, and his invitation to 'a special occasion that might amuse' according to Kai Dures, who'd spoken to him via the comms device in his room. Dures had seemed amused himself, so Mitsos thought *why not?* And that was why he was here, following his escort through the corridors of the spaceport building and onto the edge of the runway itself, emerging under a clear sky on this warm day.

"It's Mr Mitsos," he heard a woman say. He recognised her from the *Lisboa*: *Dr Lockard*. She was standing amid a small group of her colleagues. With them were Colonels Joseph and Nesvorny, dressed in their black uniforms, and Karyn and Kai Dures, attired in their traditional green. All turned to look his way as he approached; his guard pulled up a couple of metres away, allowing him to complete the journey alone.

"Ah, hello," he said. "Am I late?"

Karyn Dures frowned. "Not at all, though the Stavangerans are. Perhaps Mr Heiko is finding the walk from the embassy a greater strain than he expected?"

"Here they come now," said Kai, looking past Mitsos. "And Heiko is definitely hobbling. He's using a new-but-crude augment also known as a stick."

Mitsos turned to watch the *Stavanger* party of six emerge through the door, moving slowly at the pace of Heiko and the woman at his side.

"And now we're all here," announced Karyn, as the new group came to a halt and spread out. "I'm glad to see you up, Mr Heiko. I think you'll find the discomfort of your walk well worth it." She reached a hand to the shaved side of her head with its scar, an instinctive gesture perhaps, though Mitsos noticed it allowed her to partially hide a smile. Perhaps to help mask her emotions further, she abruptly turned and waved at a shuttle that was parked a dozen metres away. "The *Rotterdam's* chariot. It's ready to receive some special guests."

Kai Dures chortled at this and Mitsos noticed a variety of smiles spread through the party – gentle, almost bemused ones from the Lisboetas, to something steely in the case of Nesvorny and downright wicked in the case of Joseph.

Karyn looked back towards the spaceport building and a second door a little to the side of the one Mitsos and the Stavangerans had used; she raised a hand over her head to catch some unseen person's attention. The door instantly opened, and out came Marissa O'Neill and Manfred Traore, goaded on by a couple of guards with rifles. O'Neill – with her peculiar haircut – looked furious at the treatment, while Traore was in a sorry state, his face badly bruised, his expensive suit crumpled, his white shirt open at the neck and stained pink in places.

O'Neill came to a halt a short distance away, Traore standing at her shoulder with head bowed. "You said we could take the money in our accounts. Two thousand Tethyn dollars? Are you taking the piss?"

Karyn's smile matched Joseph's for devilry. "That is what was present in your account. *One* of your accounts. You should have been more specific. In any case, the *Rotterdammers* proved hard negotiators, particularly when we changed the package. It seemed only right for you to contribute to your future upkeep."

O'Neill bared her teeth but managed to keep herself under control. "You also said I'd get a chance to say my farewells on return, but you've kept me locked up since then with no company but *his*." She twitched her head towards the shoulder behind which Traore lurked.

"*Hibernia* is here," Karyn opened a hand and spread one arm. "You can say your farewells now. And as for your acquaintances, we did ask them if they'd like to speak with you…" – Mitsos instantly wondered whether she meant *join* – "… but most demurred, and others said they'd contact you once you're settled on the *Rotterdam*." Karyn was clearly enjoying this. "I've heard of fair-weather friends, but fair-weather family?"

"You threatened them!" hissed O'Neill.

"Trust me, I didn't."

O'Neill seethed a moment longer, but then a peculiar expression crossed her face. "Wait! You said 'changed the package'. What are you talking about?"

Kai Dures couldn't contain his laughter, while Joseph clapped a hand over her mouth. Karyn smiled affectionately at her husband before returning her attention to O'Neill. "Ah, well, I have a surprise for you. We thought you might get lonely on the flight, and in your exile, and so we've provided you with some company. Perhaps you'll be allocated adjacent cabins on the *Rotterdam*? Maybe you'll become friends?" She again took a step to one side so that others in the spaceport building could see her from around the intervening party. Another wave, and this time the door Mitsos had previously used was opened.

A larger party exited the door and shambled across the runway apron, again escorted by armed Stokers. At the front was a man with long, dark hair and an aquiline nose, and a middle-aged woman in a grey uniform with a peaked cap. And behind these, two men in grey carried a stretcher on which lay an injured man, with bits of medical equipment dumped on his chest and clasped between his arms. Several more men and women – wearing grey, with cropped hair – followed.

Mitsos' instinct was to shy away and merge into the crowd. It was *him*. And *her*. But then the meaning of their appearance struck home: Karyn Dures wasn't taking any chances, and that meant his own prospects were drastically improved. He set his shoulders and edged away from those nearest, allowing him a better view of the approaching party and giving them the opportunity to see him.

If O'Neill looked furious, Sebastian Deux looked volcanic: his eyes were wide and his mouth clamped so tightly Mitsos feared his teeth might explode through his closed lips. He started to hurry forward, making Boursis jerk in an ungainly way in order to keep in step.

"What the fuck!" shouted Deux. "What the… where is… what…?" He came to a halt next to O'Neill and Traore – O'Neill for once speechless.

Karyn folded her arms across her chest, while Kai moved to stand close to her and the rest of the party peeled back as though afraid of the wrath of the First Citizen of the *Marseilles*. "You seem confused, Deux."

Deux pointed at the waiting shuttle. "That isn't mine! What the fuck are you playing at, you bitch? What is going on?"

Kai's smile took on a dangerous edge. "Calm yourself, Deux." He took a half pace forward to be in arm's reach of the other. Deux wasn't exactly short, but Kai towered over him and oozed an animal strength. "Swear at my wife again and I'll rip your fucking tongue out."

Deux was trembling with rage, but also now with a little fear. He swayed back, and Boursis reached out a hand as though to support him. "I… what…?"

"Do you think we're idiots, Deux?" said Karyn. "Did you really think we'd just let you return to the *Marseilles*, with your weapons, your Apparatus, and your ambitions? To cause more mischief? To re-arm, replenish, and to try again? You truly underestimate us."

"Him?" said O'Neill, at last. "You're sending us to the *Rotterdam* with *him*?" She gestured at the others. "With *them*? Is this a sick joke?"

And suddenly, with the pressure released, Mitsos couldn't help himself. He exploded in laughter, drawing the confused and outraged looks of the combined party of exiles. "A joke!" he gasped.

Kai Dures turned to him, and though his eyes remained hard, one corner of his mouth twitched. "I said it might amuse you, Mitsos."

"Oh, yes, oh yes! It's… *hilarious*."

"Mitsos!" scowled Deux, perhaps relieved to have some weaker target on whom to focus. "What are you doing here? I'll teach you not to laugh–"

"Oh, fuck off, Deux, you and your Nazi whore. You're gone. Done. *Finished*. Go preach your brand of slavery and tyranny to others."

"Mr Mitsos is right," said Karyn. "You are done. The Rotterdammers wanted a fair bit of money to take you and your allies. Fortunately, ex-Premier O'Neill and her battered sidekick have picked up that tab." She drew herself up and looked between Deux and O'Neill. "As of this moment, you are barred from *Hibernia*, and Captain Louvain – acting First Citizen – has barred you from the *Marseilles*. Should any of you attempt re-entry in the future, you will be arrested and dropped in the ocean to fight it out with the other predators there." She leant forwards and addressed Deux in particular. "And I suggest you are especially careful in your new home, Deux. Trust me, they will be watching you for the slightest mischief. I have been asked to tell you that they will happily cast any one of you overboard if your behaviour is less than perfect. Understood?"

Deux opened and closed his mouth, but no words came out, while O'Neill simply stared. There was really nothing more to say.

"Get them out of here," scowled Kai, motioning to the guards.

One of the Stokers cheerily prodded Deux in the back. "Move."

The combined group were shepherded towards the waiting shuttle.

But Mitsos couldn't resist a last farewell: as the exiles approached the lowered ramp at the back, he called out. "Oi! Deux! Boursis!" When the pair looked around, he extended the middle finger of his once-broken hand. "It still works, you cunts."

The final look on Deux's face was priceless.

Once the shuttle was loaded and the doors closed, Karyn turned to the assembled group. "Now that we've taken out the trash, I invite you all back to mine. We Stokers have always been good at throwing a party – even on illicit moonshine and heavily dosed havelik. Today, however, our larder is somewhat better stocked."

Even Nesvorny laughed.

* * *

It wasn't really a party, though the range of food and drink on offer was certainly wider than any Marie had encountered on the *Lisboa* – especially the array of Earth-made spirits that Karyn Dures claimed had been found in the offices of the old triumvirate.

"Liberated for the people?" said Nesvorny mischievously, raising a glass filled with a golden liquid. He stood next to Joseph and Kai Dures; Marie was at a long table next to the group, trying to decide on her own poison.

"We *are* the people," growled Kai. "But fuck that Marseillais language. *The people?* Ha!"

"You don't believe in equality, then?" said Nesvorny.

"Equality of Stokers with the rest of you, yes. Imposing poverty on normal people in order to level down, just so that the elite – like Deux – can live in secret luxury? No. We were never socialists like the Marseillais. We believe in the right to advance through hard work – it was just that *you* never gave us the chance."

"I think Mr Mitsos will be happy to hear that," said Marie, joining them, a glass of red wine in her hand – the first she'd come across since arriving on Tethys. "He's the ultimate capitalist, I think."

"I'm not sure he's a good example to follow, though," said Nesvorny. "He stole the design for his REEN boats, and came to Tethys to flog it because he thought it would be safe."

Kai laughed. "Safe? I bet he regrets that choice now."

"A lot of us regret things we have done in life."

"Don't get maudlin on us, Eric," said Joseph. "I know what you're thinking, but we were following orders. We're not politicians. The fault lay there… and with a few bad apples, like Fukuda."

"Maybe, maybe not." Nesvorny peered at Kai from under heavy brows. "But power corrupts – if too much is held, without balances. A gentle word there, Dures. Be careful."

"We're meant to be enjoying our victory, and you are trying to dampen it." Kai sighed and shook his head. "Look, Nesvorny, I know what you think. What you fear. But Karyn is honest, ah…" he gave a wry smile. "*Mostly*. O'Neill and Deux got what they deserved… *better* than they deserved. I mean, she's honourable. Once the Stokers are emancipated, she'll do as she says. There will be elections. Democracy will return. Everyone in *Hibernia* will get a vote."

Nesvorny held the other's look for some moments, then gently nodded, as though having come to a conclusion.

Marie looked around the now-sombre group. "Ah, well, that sounds promising. But what are everyone's plans for the future?"

"That's an interesting question," said Nesvorny, "but I think only Mr Dures can answer that – for all of us."

"Me?" Kai seemed surprised. "Ah, well, I suppose my wife will listen to my advice. But I'm not a politician. A security role for me, perhaps." He eyed the two in black uniforms. "Colonel Joseph, I guess, might retain her post, if she wants."

Joseph raised her glass. "Oh, yeah, I want. Messing about in boats is my thing."

"And Nesvorny…" said Kai.

"I was offered the chance to ride off into the sunset," said Nesvorny. "And if Karyn is truly as you say, and holds to this, that is exactly what I plan to do. I've served my time. Done my duty. Made some mistakes, perhaps, but mostly kept order. That means there's a vacancy for you, Dures. But if you take it, I advise you to listen to some of my senior staff and not dismiss them. They know what they're doing."

"Yes, I've seen that since we joined forces. Even you, Nesvorny, I hate to say, might be worth consulting from time to time."

Nesvorny suddenly smiled and raised his glass again. "You know what? Lay on hospitality like this, and I'll be happy to stop by on occasion to allow you to pick my brains."

Dures laughed and raised his own glass, and then so did Joseph.

Soon after, Marie made her excuses and returned to the side of the room where she'd originally been seated. She passed several knots of people milling around, holding small plates of food and glasses of drink – Stavangerans, Lisboetas, Stokers, and even Marcel Louvain, who'd been enticed to leave his ship and fly to *Hibernia* for discussions with the new rulers. She passed Karyn Dures in deep conversation with a pair of women from the *Stavanger* – one elderly and white-haired, the other younger and dark-haired: she'd heard the names 'Olson' and 'Moroni' uttered.

At her table were Rennie Heiko, Melissa De Voe, Eddard Mitsos, Katerina Kalmik, Miguel Figueroa, and Joao Nacimiento – the latter having joined since Marie's foray to the drinks table.

Nacimiento looked up and waved a hand to suggest Marie come sit in the vacant chair beside him. "Dr Lockard! Please!"

"Thank you, sir." She noticed Nacimiento had loosened his top button and tie, and his cap was nowhere to be seen. Her smile twitched. "You seem relaxed, sir. I noticed you talking to Ms Dures earlier."

"Indeed I did. Now, that is an intense lady. I feel quite frazzled – so please excuse me if I sit here silently and enjoy this superb port from the Douro valley. Ms Dures said she found a crate in Mr Traore's suite, and she'll allow me to take a few bottles back to the *Lisboa*. I think I like her."

Figueroa had acquired a glass of the tawny fluid too; he raised it. "Hear hear, old friend!"

Once Marie was settled, De Voe turned to her. "We were just talking about the creatures. You seem to have been shy about your role in events. The Prof. said this migration hypothesis was yours. What made you think of it?"

"Ah, I'm not entirely sure, but I think it was seeing Mr Heiko when he came aboard the *Lisboa* with the others from the shipyard, and being reminded by my daughter that we'd sat next to him on the shuttle from the *Leviathan*."

"Rennie? Please don't give him any credit in this. I don't want him to get a saint complex." De Voe smiled at Heiko next to her and reached out a hand to rest on his forearm.

Heiko smiled back. "Don't worry – I'm really not inclined to delusions of grandeur."

"I know," said De Voe. "It's part of your appeal."

"Thank you," said Heiko. "But.... Marie, I'm not sure I understand."

"Oh, well, it's because it made me think about what you, I, and Kate are. We're *migrants*. We hitched a ride on the *Leviathan* with a lot of others. And migrations aren't always smooth affairs – as we saw. And for every migrant bringing something positive–"

"Like you?" smirked Kalmik, arching an eyebrow.

Marie felt herself blush, something she'd not done in years. "No! I was thinking of Mr Heiko, and even Mr Mitsos – in his own way." Mitsos started at this, grinned, but didn't respond. "But for every one of these, there are others that have negative impacts. These New Socialists, for example – they brought weapon-making abilities and a desire to upset the current order. But that's beside the point. Post hoc rationalisations. I really just wondered about migration, and it seemed an obvious omission. I never bought the 'food' explanation. And while the reapers' aggression towards us might have been a consequence of their territoriality, their behaviour seemed a bit extreme, almost vindictive, and that's not really a trait Mother Nature goes for in a big way: it just brings renewed risk of harm for no benefit, so it's not a trait readily selected for in a population."

"True enough," said Figueroa. "I'm not aware of any creatures on Earth or Tethys that have that characteristic. I suppose the way cats toy with their prey might almost seem like wanton cruelty, but the behaviour is more a case of practising the capture than sadism, which is what 'play' is really all about."

"Right, Professor," said Marie. "And so that left migration as an explanation. But we were too confused and afraid to think coherently at the start, and so we thought the damage to the propellor was part of some vengeful behaviour to try to get at us and kill us."

"It's difficult to dispel powerful ideas once they have taken hold," said Heiko. "And that's why I've been rather impressed by Ms Dures and Colonel Nesvorny. They both had firm views about each other and their respective sides, but they were able to adapt to the situation and shift perspective. Hopefully, this will lead to peace, and ultimately, a more just *Hibernia*."

"And Tethys as a whole," said De Voe. "Without *Hibernia's* bully boy behaviour the whole planet will be a better place. But I'm still to be convinced that this trend is over. We'll have to see if the new rulers' actions match their words, or whether Karyn transforms into another O'Neill."

"That's certainly possible," said Heiko. "But until she starts to show such signs, maybe we should give her the benefit of the doubt?"

"I was just with the Colonels and Karyn's husband," said Marie. "I think they – Joseph and Nesvorny – are of the same opinion."

"I see Margarethe and Nila are talking to her now," said De Voe. She smirked. "If anyone can outwit Karyn, it'll be Nila. Still, we've got the management of Ardol back as head contractor, so I'm happy, and Makka is ecstatic. Let's leave the bigwigs to argue about who gets what cut of the resources we dig up."

"So, it's back to the dig for you then, Melissa," said Marie, "and to the *Stavanger* for you, Rennie?"

"Oh, yes. I found the place does have some endearing features." Heiko winked at De Voe. "I'm not sure there are many other options anyway – none that Melissa would allow."

"Damned straight," said De Voe.

Marie noticed Mitsos sitting on the other side of Heiko. He'd said little since joining them. "And what about you, Mr Mitsos? What are your plans?"

"Me? The refugee from Atlantis?"

"Plato's mythical island that sank in the Atlantic," said Figueroa, perking up. "Now, do you mean *Hibernia*, or do you mean Tethys as a whole, since we might *all* metaphorically perish beneath the waves if we cannot come together to resolve our resource issues?"

"Both. And maybe neither. Maybe I mean Earth itself." Mitsos shook his head. "Everywhere I go seems to burn, sending me on and on." He lapsed into silence and stared at the glass of whisky resting on the table between his hands.

Marie exchanged frowns with Figueroa. "So… Eddard… do you think you'll go back to Earth?"

"Is there anything to go back to? There's been no ship from Earth since the *Leviathan*. Until there is…" Mitsos shrugged. "I'm going nowhere near the *Marseilles*, that's for sure. Even though this Louvain guy seems reasonable, it's still a ship of fanatics. And *Hibernia*? I tried that once. Got rousted by Nesvorny on arrival, then rubbished by its industrialists, then stitched up by the Stokers." He sat back in his seat, then looked up almost shyly. "The *Lisboa*, though, seemed nice in the short time I was there. No one tried to torture me for a start. Maybe…" he looked at Nacimiento, "maybe I could come and stay for a while?"

Nacimiento seemed surprised at the request. "I don't see why not, Mr Mitsos. This REEN is at least partly your device, which gains you some credit, although Captain Louvain has been clear he wants everything back, given the resources used in its development. The reapers are gone for now, but we know they exist and where they live, so we may need to be prepared for further encounters."

Mitsos sat up straight and his expression changed. "As you say, I do have some claim there. I am owed. And I have contacts on the *Marseilles*. Bennani. Noma. I know how to negotiate. I'm happy to help if I can."

"In that case, Mr Mitsos, I am sure we can find a use for you. Welcome aboard."

De Voe laughed. "Thank God – I thought you might make a play for the *Stavanger*! Only joking, Mitsos. But what about you, Marie? You've quizzed us all, but said nothing about your plans. I presume you'll remain on the *Lisboa* to continue studying the reapers?"

"I have to, Melissa, not least to protect them from Katerina's wrath." Kalmik mock-scowled and poked out her tongue. "But seriously, it's not just my decision. Before I commit this time, I think I need to talk to my daughter."

"A teenage girl?" said De Voe, raising an eyebrow and making her anchor tattoo bob, as though being drawn from the seabed. "God, you're fucked."

The others around the table laughed.

* * *

The *Lisboa* was lit up like an old-style Christmas tree – lights strung along the deck edges and open-air plazas in white, yellow, green, red, blue. On calm, warm nights like this, with a gentle breeze over the ocean, and the sky full of stars and whisps of nebulae, it was a magical place to be.

Kate met her mother at the Café Braga on the ninth level, on the outer side of the colossal central torus, facing to starboard of the bow. The canvas roof had been fully retracted and settees and comfortable chairs circled low tables, littering the terrace like an archipelago of small islands, with the most sought-after being those on the edge with a clear view over the starboard flipper of the great sea turtle. Along that wing, a line of small boats and trawlers could be seen, resting in cradles just above the ocean surface, some brightly lit as crews worked on them in preparation for the next morning's expeditions. Kate had managed to grab one of these prime nests – after all, she had been lurking on the terrace for the past two hours.

Her mother looked slightly flustered – and flushed – as she hurried up to her. "Oh, Kate, I'm sorry. I really didn't think the event would go on so long. The shuttle just got back."

"I know. I watched it land. Don't worry, Mum. Beyond your control. You're off the hook for that. And you did hurry."

"Ah, that's a relief." Marie gave a pained smile. "I did fear the worst."

"Because I'm a teenager?"

"Ah, well, we all were once."

"So… raging hormones? Rampant bitchiness? *Really*, Mum?"

Marie winced. "You see… you are going off on one." Her smile suggested a tentative gambit. "QED?"

Kate was tempted to string her mother along. And she had been annoyed for some time, but then she'd thought: *how would Karyn Dures act?* The mature thing to do was to let it go, although there was *one thing* she couldn't just let lie – but she would bide her time. She smiled and rolled her eyes. "I was only teasing." Then she reached down to the display on the low table into which she'd already programmed her mother's expected order. She sent it. "Small beer on its way." She herself was drinking a lime-flavoured concoction and was currently on her third and getting rather sick of its sweetness. "Go on, sit then."

Marie did so, collapsing into soft cushions on a small, two-person settee upholstered in a red-and-orange-patterned material. She still seemed flushed.

"How much did you have to drink, Mum? Should I cancel the beer?"

"No-no. I'm fine. But the hospitality was great. Joao and Miguel were duetting some old Portuguese love song by the time we left – and the Prof. was wearing Joao's cap. I think they'll be late to their posts tomorrow."

Kate nodded and smirked. "You're fine? Hmmm. I suspect I have an advantage. *Excellent.*"

"We'll see," said Marie. She looked around. "You haven't been waiting alone, have you? I thought your friends would be with you."

"They were initially. *Hours* ago." Kate winked. "But Tonio left for a date, and Sara went home."

Marie nodded absently, then looked up sharply. "Tonio – on a date?"

"Oh, yes. And he didn't even have to ask. Vita came around and dragged him off."

"A *real* date?"

Kate laughed. "I know, it's unbelievable, isn't it? I mean, just because he saved Vita's life in the public bowl. Some girls are cheap, eh?" She winked again, but then her smile dissipated. "It probably won't last, but I really hope it does. He deserves it."

"Yes, he does. You all do. Everyone was impressed by your behaviour at the bowl – you were calm, when everyone else panicked."

"Impressed?" Kate felt the tension creeping back. "But maybe not impressed enough, eh?"

"Uh-oh. You've got that look. What have I done to annoy you?"

"You – nothing, I guess." Here was *the thing*. "No, I'm just annoyed at not being able to go to *Hibernia* with you and the others for the celebration, or whatever it was. Haven't we done enough? I guess the whole science department went, and most of them did very little to help in this crisis," she waved a hand airily, "you know, with the reapers and everything. But they are adults and we are just *teenagers*." She had to bite down on a swear word.

"I know, Kate. I didn't think, and we got the call at short notice. But if it's any consolation, it was just a few of us – Joao, Miguel, Katerina, Luisa, Mike, and me."

Kate wasn't mollified, but she managed to retain her equanimity. "So, what happened then?"

"Ah, well, it wasn't really a celebration as such. We witnessed an exiling. A *multiple* exiling…" Marie related the events at the spaceport, before giving a brief reprise of the social event that followed.

At the end, as Marie sat back to drink from her now-delivered beer, Kate quietly said: "I would have liked to see that. The villains getting their marching orders. And the meeting. I bet it wasn't as trivial as you're making out. There were important people there, discussing important things. I guarantee it."

Marie sighed. "Yes, I guess you're right. I'm just a simple marine biologist – the politics are over my head."

"But not mine." Kate's voice firmed. "And next time there's an event like it, I *will* be there."

Marie seemed amused and tried to hide it. Kate saw this, tensed, then once more thought about Karyn Dures. She breathed out deeply. Calmy, she said: "You don't believe me?"

"No, Kate, actually, I do. Well, maybe not for the next meeting, but for others in the future. You're so focused. Ah, but… next time." She tailed off and looked down, away from Kate's eyes.

"Mum? Now there's *your* look. What is it?"

This time Marie sighed; she looked back up. "Next time. That's what I need to talk to you about. Last time I dragged you away from Earth, from home, from… your father. And look where I've brought you? We're stranded here. We barely escaped an exploding star liner. We've faced revolts and monsters. And things aren't likely to get better soon. There'll be belt tightening until another ship comes, or this mine on Ardol starts producing key elements, or Mr Mitsos can get his machine to do what it was originally intended to do. I can't help feeling a little guilty that I've brought you here."

"Are you kidding?" Kate's eyes went wide. "It's been… it's been… *fantastic*!" She saw confusion settle on her mother's face. "I really mean it. Everything that's happened has been so, I don't know how to put it, *life affirming*. I wouldn't have missed it – any of it – for the world. For *any* world. Certainly not for Earth."

"Ah… right. So, next time a ship arrives from Earth…"

"You can take it, Mum, but I won't be on it – and I hope you won't be, either. I'm a Lisboetan now. A Tethyn. This is my home, for better or worse. I mean, for better. I'll make it better – not just for me and you, but for Sara and Tonio and everyone else. You can laugh, Mum, but I mean it. I'll show you."

And from the expression in Marie's eyes, it was clear she believed her.

Epilogue: Eight Years Later

The message from orbit identified the space liner as the *Eroica* – a name unfamiliar to all on Tethys. From what could be seen on ground-based instruments, recorded by technicians on the *Lagos* and transmitted around the world, the design was novel too. But the message was in standard universal English, if strangely accented, and it was polite, almost apologetic. The ship belonged to a multinational company from the New European Alliance, although it brought greetings on behalf of all Earth – as well as supplies.

Hibernia became a magnet for ships in the Northern Hemisphere as did *Taiwan* for those in the South – as the only two places big enough to receive shuttles from the orbiting liner. The City Class ships that were near enough to one or the other Nation Class vessel started sending their representatives straightaway; those too far away rapidly changed course and moved closer until they were also in shuttle range.

The Premier of *Hibernia* graciously received all who came, holding a reception at the spaceport that began a couple of hours before the first shuttle was due from the *Eroica.* There was a cordon of tape keeping the milling guests from the runway edge, but most seemed happy to stick close to the long table set along one wall of the spaceport, which currently dispensed what was reputedly the last of *Hibernia's* Earth-origin stock of booze. Clearly, the hope was that more might be on its way in the hold of the liner.

Rennie Heiko had arrived with the *Stavanger* contingent a short time before – their shuttle being the last to the party on account of their ship being among those closest. Although still Head of Security, he allowed a younger officer to accompany the Premier as she headed off to greet her equals, leaving him and Melissa De Voe to circulate without any particular duties. They soon acquired drinks, but hadn't moved far when they bumped into a familiar face in a black uniform bearing two golden shamrocks on each shoulder. The woman's hair was longer than when he'd last seen it, and greyer too, and her face was lined and darkly tanned from the sun – much like De Voe's.

"Melissa and Rennie – still together, I see," said Colonel Tania Joseph, smiling broadly.

"You tried to part us once, I remember," said De Voe. "We're only staying together as a kind of middle finger to you and yours."

"Is that the only reason?" said Heiko, grinning.

"That, and your augmented body, although I still think they augmented the wrong parts." De Voe gently elbowed him, jostling the liquid in her glass so that it nearly overflowed. She turned her attention back to Joseph. "He's a bit worn, but I've still got my lawman. What about yours?"

"Mine? You mean Eric?" Joseph shook her head slowly. "Apart from a brief fling when we were considerably younger – and I do mean both *brief* and *considerably* – we were never an item. But, yeah, he's always been a friend and confidante."

"So let's just call him your partner in crime," continued De Voe. "He's not here, no?"

"I suppose that was how we were seen in earlier days, especially by our Stoker friends." Joseph sobered. "He's so-so. In spite of saying he's happy with retirement, I think he's bored. Kai Dures has occasionally brought him in as a kind of consultant to pick his brains on a couple of criminal gangs that weren't from the Stoker community…" she shook her head sadly, "… but he's yesterday's man. I suspect he'll be on his fishing boat, perhaps keeping a watch on the spaceport from just beyond the horizon." She shook her head once more, as though to clear it of some unwanted image, then said: "But you seem short of your usual complement, too. What of Dr Frost?"

"He wouldn't leave his precious dig, even for this," said De Voe.

"A man of true dedication."

"More like a man with OCD and questionable social skills," said De Voe.

"Makka?" said Heiko, turning a surprised look on his partner.

De Voe laughed. "I'm joking. He always was a better, more diplomatic communicator than I was."

"And yet *you* replaced him as Head of Resources," said Joseph.

"A position forced on me by Makka and Premier Moroni."

"I'd hardly say forced," said Heiko. "I remember all those years ago your delight at getting hold of Makka's 'plush' office and working cafetiere. Then the power went straight to your head."

"Rennie!"

Heiko smiled gently. "Okay, now *I'm* joking. But talking of power, there's a fair whiff of it about." He scanned the area. "I understand the leaders of the *Alexandria* and the *Mumbai* are here. Of course, Nila is around too. And then there's Her Majesty of over there." He indicated a woman with an unusual hairstyle – long and straight on one side, and shaven close around one ear. She wore a well-made suit in green. "What's this – her third term? Fourth?"

"Third," said Joseph. "But it does seem like she's become a fixture: *the Great Tyrant.*"

They laughed at that. It was Karyn Dures' nickname – but an ironic one. In fact, she was far from a tyrant. As she'd promised, she'd allowed free elections after a couple of years in charge, during which time she'd brought her people out from the shadows and somehow managed to increase their rights without impinging (too much) on the rights of other Hibernians. And then, to great surprise, she won the subsequent election, securing almost as high a percentage amongst the Hibernians as the Stokers. And then she'd easily won a third term.

Joseph nodded and looked at De Voe. "As much as she is a great operator, her job has been made easy by you lot from the *Stavanger* – in large part thanks to your find, and the wealth of the… seam? Pitch? I'm not a geologist so I don't know the right words."

"Try 'treasure trove'," said De Voe. "It's a term we use now."

Joseph smiled. "I haven't been to Ardol for a couple of years – I made the mistake of putting Captain Singh in charge of a small contingent there, and for some reason he doesn't like the boss visiting his turf. It's quite a significant site now, isn't it?"

"Yup. It's bigger than Athol," said De Voe. "There was no point transporting all that material to the *Stavanger* for refining and processing, so we set up a number of plants around the mining site. And that's led to a permanent settlement with close to a thousand bodies, with workers from every ship in the hemisphere. It's still a dusty, soulless place though, so I'm happy to let Makka preside over it while I put my feet up on his mahogany desk and drink his excellent coffee."

Heiko continued to scan the other attendees, who moved in and out of shadows and bright sunshine – a consequence of the intermittent, fast-moving, rather dark clouds above. The forecast was for the rain to hold off another three hours, although Heiko wasn't convinced. Then he spotted another luminary and nudged De Voe, using an elbow that was attached to a hand that held something with an aniseed flavour that, in truth, he didn't especially like. "And there's another. The First Citizen of the *Marseilles*. I wondered if she'd come." With a nod of the head, he indicated a small group off to one side, dominated by a dark-skinned woman with thick, black hair that was silvering at the edges.

Joseph turned to look too.

"Why wouldn't she come?" said De Voe. "They also have a stake. I hear *Hibernia* is still paying them for their contribution to the rebellion all those years ago, and for the loan of the REEN boats."

"Sure. But I heard relations aren't as smooth now as they were when Louvain was in charge."

Joseph looked around. "Oh, they're not. Obuya is a hardcore socialist, while Louvain was more tolerant – at least of people who weren't actually citizens of his ship. But it's minor stuff. They're not building an invasion fleet, if that's what you mean." She looked back: "Oh, *hello*… what's this?"

Heiko couldn't help chuckling. A man approached the small and insular *Marseilles* contingent, which opened up to give him access to their leader – who suddenly broke into a wide, white smile. "*Mitsos.*"

"*Citizen* Mitsos," smirked De Voe. "About as un-socialist as it is possible to get."

Joseph looked around again. "You've been keeping an eye on the newsfeeds then?"

"Oh, yeah," said De Voe. "The world would be a lesser place without the string of controversies surrounding him. Failed businesses. Law suits. And how many wives does he have?"

"You mean now?" asked Heiko. In the near distance, Mitsos and the First Citizen embraced like long-lost friends. First Citizen Noma Obuya still seemed to be smiling, though he couldn't see Mitsos' face.

"Only one, I think. But she's at least his third since he arrived on Tethys."

"I bet you're glad he's still on the *Lisboa*," said De Voe. "He might tax your investigative resources if he were on the *Stavanger*."

"Frankly, a bit of excitement wouldn't go amiss," said Heiko. "But the media will miss him if he goes."

"You think he's going to return to Earth?" said Joseph.

Heiko shrugged. "Who knows. But I suspect he's started to wear his welcome on the *Lisboa* thin. *Very* thin. What then? Back to *Hibernia*? But is even this place big enough for him?"

"I'll tell you who might know his plans," said De Voe, leaning in between her two colleagues. "*They* will." She pointed with her glass of brandy. One of the pair of women she indicated seemed to catch the motion, half-turned, raised eyebrows in surprise, spoke to her younger partner, and then the pair sauntered over.

"Ah… hello," said the older woman. "It's been some time, hasn't it. Hello, Mr Heiko… Ms De Voe... and Colonel."

"Why so formal suddenly, Marie?" said De Voe. "I think you can cut that crap." Then she smiled and bowed slightly to the other woman. "But maybe first names aren't appropriate in your case, Captain-Governor."

Kate Lockard smiled broadly. She had grown into a handsome young woman and wore her well-brushed hair in a ponytail. Though she wore a suit rather than a uniform, it still had gold symbols of authority stitched into the sleeves – an understated, yet still evident, mark of power. "I don't think we ever actually spoke, back in the days of crisis, did we?" she said. "But of course, I know who you all are. Maybe by the end of today we'll be on first name terms…" and now her smile turned wry, "but we'll see." Then she spotted something behind Heiko's shoulder. "Ah… and there's someone I really need to talk to. Please excuse me – Mother, if you bump into that chief advisor of mine and her incorrigible husband, let them know I'd like to see them before the shuttle arrives." She broadcast a smile at the other three in turn – oozing charm – then hurried off to continue networking.

"Who'd have thought your daughter would rise so high, so quickly," said De Voe. "Isn't she the youngest leader of a city ship ever?"

"Yes, she is." The pride in Marie's eyes was clear to Heiko. "The only surprising thing is that at the elections last May, there was ever any doubt who would win. From the oldest leader ever to the youngest."

"Remarkable," said Heiko. "But what of Mr Nacimiento – is he here?"

"No, Joao is a bit frail now. I suspect he and Miguel are sitting on an upper deck of the *Lisboa*, in the sun, playing cards, reminiscing, and praying that this new ship has brought a stock of fortified wines from the old country. If it has, I guarantee Kate will find a way to get hold of it first. She knows how to keep people happy and onside."

"Sounds a bit like our Tyrant there," said Joseph.

Marie's cheeks dimpled – age had made them plumper – and said: "I think the comparison is not accidental."

"If you're going to learn, learn from the best," said Heiko. "But we were just musing about faces from the past. We noticed Mr Mitsos somehow got an invite."

"Yes, how he got onboard the shuttle yesterday, no one really knows," said Marie. "We suspect the pilot was bribed."

Heiko chuckled. "Indeed! But what we were wondering, though, is whether this might be a one-way trip. Do you know what his plans are?"

"Well, he didn't bring his wife," said Marie, "and I think they are still… *okay*." Heiko noticed Joseph mouth 'number four'. "So… maybe not. Or maybe he'll see how the land lies and send for her. To be honest, he is an enigma. I'm not sure even he knows what he's going to do next."

"And what about you, Marie?" asked De Voe. "Got fed up with studying the reapers? A hankering for Earth?"

Marie paused perhaps just a bit too long. "I can't say I haven't thought about it. The work is rewarding – they're going to be shocked on Earth when they hear about these creatures, and the team and I have a score of articles ready to submit to Earth journals – and the environment is pleasant, if maybe a bit quiet. And I'm not sure I could leave Kate, while Marco–"

"Marco?" said De Voe, suddenly alert.

"Ah… my husband. I got married three years ago. Didn't you know? Ah, well, I suppose there's no reason why you should. Anyway, Marco has really grown over the last few years. At the time of the crisis, he probably would have killed to get back to Earth, but now… probably not. But maybe if this is the start of a regular service resuming…"

"You could just go for a visit," said De Voe. "We *all* could. What do you think, Rennie? Would you introduce me to your family? Your kids?"

And suddenly Heiko felt a knot in his stomach. *Home. Kids.* It had been eight years. Nine, actually. What crisis had afflicted Earth? Had there been a nuclear war? Was his family still alive? Maybe he had grandchildren? And then he felt a twinge in his thigh – a reminder of the bullet he'd taken. And though his enhancements had aided his recovery, it was well past time they were serviced. And then he realised that he'd frozen, and the others were looking at him with concern. De Voe surreptitiously took his free hand resting at his side. "Ah, I'm sorry. Melissa – I'd be honoured to introduce you. I think my kids…" his voice faltered, "they would like you." He straightened his back and said more firmly. "Yes, they would. And perhaps you could do a tour of some proper geology while there."

"A busman's holiday?" said De Voe, her eyes kind, her voice soft. "Do you think I'm Makka?"

"Ah, no–"

"Tonio!" Marie suddenly called out. Then she looked back, embarrassed. "Oh, I'm sorry, it's just… orders. I must just… but don't go away just yet."

"From this spot," said Heiko, "or do you mean from Tethys?"

Marie's eyes twinkled. "Neither. We arrived on the same shuttle, so if we leave – for a break, of course: this is home now – then we might as well go back together." And then she was off, calling: "Tonio… Vita… wait up."

A sonic boom sounded. Heiko turned to look skywards. It seemed that once more the shuttle was early.

Acknowledgements

I owe many thanks to a number of wise readers of my early drafts, in alphabetical order, Paul Beacon, Adam Carpenter, Adrian Deasley, Alexander Mo, Natalia Perez, and Gary Wortley. As ever, any errors are entirely down to me.

About the Author

Gene Rowe was born in Bedford in 1966 (the glorious year!), although he didn't stay there long, having to move around a lot as a child thanks to his father's job in the United States Air Force (his father is a Mainer). He read psychology at Bristol University and subsequently completed a PhD at the Bristol Business School. Years of toil as an academic followed before he transitioned into a self-employed consultant. He now seems to spend almost all of his time scribbling stories in Norwich, where he lives with his partner and two increasingly large children.

Atlantis Afire is his sixth solo novel. His others include *The Greater Game*, *The Price of Freedom Part 1: Ghuraj to Arkon*, *The Price of Freedom Part 2: Velasia*, and the books of the Norwich Chronicles: *Of Yellow Shirts and Little Green Men* and *Of Spilt Ale and Alien Revenge*. He is also co-editor of the British Science Fiction Association's (BSFA) *Fission* anthologies.

Printed in Dunstable, United Kingdom

75189472R00428